D0365520

CREATOR

CREATOR

Jeremy Leven

Coward, McCann & Geoghegan, Inc.
New York

The author gratefully acknowledges the following for granting permission to quote from copyrighted materials:

"The Fool on the Hill," "Magical Mystery Tour," "Your Mother Should Know," "I Am the Walrus" (John Lennon and Paul McCartney), "Blue Jay Way" (George Harrison): all songs copyright © 1967 Northern Songs Ltd. All rights for the U.S.A. and Mexico controlled by Comet Music Corp. c/o ATV Music Corp. Used by permission. All rights reserved. "Lucy in the Sky With Diamonds" (John Lennon and Paul McCartney) copyright © 1967 Northern Songs Ltd. All rights for the U.S.A. and Mexico controlled by Maclen Music, Inc. c/o ATV Music Group. Used by permission. All rights reserved.

Excerpts from the Bhagavad-Gita used by permission of the Vedanta Society of Southern California; translated by Swami Prabhavananda and Christopher Isherwood.

"Lightly Stepped a Yellow Star" by Emily Dickinson from *The Complete Poems of Emily Dickinson*, edited by Thomas H. Johnson, © 1914, 1942 by Martha Dickinson Bianchi; "Ample make this Bed" and "I live with Him—I see His Face" reprinted by permission of the publishers and the Trustees of Amherst College from *The Poems of Emily Dickinson*, edited by Thomas H. Johnson, Cambridge, Mass.: The Belknap Press of Harvard University Press, Copyright © 1951, 1955 by the President and Fellows of Harvard College.

"Wild Swans" and "Eel-Grass" by Edna St. Vincent Millay from *Collected Poems*, Harper & Row, Copyright 1921, 1948 by Edna St. Vincent Millay.

"Happiness" from *When We Were Very Young* by A. A. Milne, © 1924 by E. P. Dutton and Co., Inc. Renewal copyright 1952 by A. A. Milne and by permission of the publisher, E. P. Dutton. Reprinted in Canada by permission of the Canadian publisher, McClelland and Stewart, Ltd. Toronto.

"Scarborough Fair/Canticle" and "For Emily, Whenever I May Find Her" © 1966, 1967 Paul Simon; "Mrs. Robinson" and "The Boxer" © 1968 Paul Simon. Used by permission.

"I Shall Not Care" by Sara Teasdale, copyright 1915 by Macmillan Publishing Co., Inc., renewed by Mamie T. Wheless.

Library of Congress Cataloging in Publication Data

Leven, Jeremy.
Creator.

I. Title.
PZ4.L655Cr 1980 [PS3562.E866] 813'.5'4 79-17932
ISBN 0-698-11012-9

Printed in the United States of America

ACKNOWLEDGMENTS

The author acknowledges with deep appreciation the influence that Professor Victor Denenberg of the University of Connecticut and Professor Sheldon White of Harvard University have had on my science; the genetic contributions of Dr. Kenneth Manly, at the time working in the MIT laboratories of Nobel Laureates S. Luria and D. Baltimore and currently of the State University of New York at Buffalo; the virtually lifelong encouragement of Florence Gardner Fradin and of Dr. Joseph Fradin; the extensive and insightful editorial help from my father, Martin Levin; the invaluable editorial work of Joseph Kanon; the numerous suggestions and caring from Roberta Danza; and, most of all, the overwhelming contribution of my education at St. John's College in Annapolis, Maryland, to which this work owes its life.

In memory of
Susan Roberts
1943–1966

DOCTOR HARRY WOLPER'S NOTEBOOKS ON PARTHENOGENESIS

INTRODUCTION

Shortly after the death of Dr. Harry Wolper, these notebooks were discovered by a custodian given the task of cleaning the good doctor's laboratory. The document was originally thought to contain the renowned biologist's lifework on the frog, a concern that recently had focused itself on a process known as *parthenogenesis,* or fatherless reproduction. It was this title that had been scrawled on the cover, apparently in haste and not unreminiscent of a child's first attempts at graphic communication: *Parthenogenesis.*

Beneath the title was a curious and complex drawing or design. A later chemical analysis of the medium has shown it to be, almost exclusively, animal feces, probably rabbit, opening the possibility that what one sees on the cover is, in fact, the random tracks of the doctor's experimental rabbits, which were given free run of his laboratory, thus providing, at times, a certain healthy Aristotelian element of chance and spontaneity to the nature of Dr. Wolper's research.

The custodian, in turn, gave the notebook to the doctor's oldest offspring and only son, Arnold Wolper, who attempted to sell the notebook in rapid succession to a dozen or so publishers, Harvard University's Widener Library, the New York Public Library, and scores of auction houses, and was finally about to include it in a mystery grab bag drawing of his father's "most precious perversities" (as he put it in the *Sunday Times*), when the reading of the will brought to light the stipulation the doctor had made that none of his property was to be distributed until after his lifework was published.

Almost immediately, Arnold Wolper relates, he realized the true value of his father's notebook, this being the doctor's only unpublished work. The problems of publication, however, proved considerable.

It is, for example, not at all clear that these notebooks have anything to do with parthenogenesis. What one finds, instead, is a voluminous puzzle, a diary, each entry carefully numbered to correspond to the month and day when it was written, containing: reminiscences and reflections on his family, associates, friends, and assorted enemies; notes on the rather bizarre turn his experimental work took after the sudden death of his wife; unnecessarily explicit descriptions of the doctor's sexual proclivities, past and present, successful and otherwise; general meanderings of the mind which are, to be generous, strongly suggestive of several well-known psychopathologies; and, most distressing of all, a strange dialogue with a gentleman by the name of Boris Lafkin whose nature and existence remain as the great mystery of the diary.

Furthermore, the fact that a significant number of pages was missing from the notebook when the journal was discovered by the custodian does not help to relieve any of the mystery surrounding whatever it is that Dr. Wolper intended to, and perhaps even did, write. By way of explanation of the missing pages, it is known that the doctor relieved his almost constant nasal congestion with whatever paper was readily available (visitors to his laboratory have, on occasion, seen him in a single afternoon totally immolate the written work of several years to this condition), and, as these particular notes were found on the floor of his laboratory john, which was otherwise devoid of tissues, the reasons surrounding the disappearance of random pages of the notebook seem to be painfully obvious. Dr. Wolper was, throughout his life, not a healthy man.

Born on January 1, 1900, Harry Wolper lived a sickly childhood in the city of Brooklyn, New York. He graduated from Harvard at the age of nineteen in 1919 and immediately enlisted in the armed services, lying about his chronic asthma, in order, he once enigmatically told an interviewer, to answer *the* question about war: Is there anything really worth defending? On receiving his dishonorable discharge (Harry Wolper arrived at the answer to his question, it appears, within days of his induction), he returned to Harvard, to the medical school this time, where, in 1928, he received his M.D. in a split decision. In September 1929, after having spent the first summer in which he qualified to practice medicine as a life guard in Atlantic City, he married Miss New Jersey, Lucy Cummings. His son, Arnold, was born in April 1930, his daughters Claire and Rebecca in 1934 and 1936, respectively. Lucy Wolper died shortly after the birth of their last child, in 1936.

Dr. Wolper practiced medicine until 1940 when he accepted a research/teaching position at CCNY after several indictments had been returned against him for removing organs superfluously from his surgical patients. One particularly unfortunate patient who had submitted to several operations by the doctor discovered to his horror, after changing to another physician, that Dr. Wolper had cleaned him out, so to speak, leaving him with the barest minimum of organs with which to continue his life. Dr. Wolper was never a strong believer in parsimony.

A few months after the dismissal of his trial on the grounds of lack of evidence, Dr. Wolper was awarded the Nobel Prize for his independent work on frog reproduction.

From 1941 to 1946 Dr. Wolper continued his research on the frog in a Navy research facility in Spokane, Washington, where, for patriotic reasons, he slanted his research toward the war effort. It was not until after the war, however, that the Secretary of the Navy learned that Dr. Wolper's work with frogmen had absolutely nothing to do with the regular Navy frogman program, but was a program the doctor, himself, designed to spawn Frog-Men.

In 1946 Dr. Wolper moved to the relative quiet of Cambridge, Massachusetts, where he established his own private laboratory and continued to raise his children, living off the money he had received from several hormone discoveries that provided the basis for oral contraception.

Dr. Wolper's death, originally believed to be from cancer, but, on autopsy, declared of mysterious origin, occurred shortly before midnight, December 25, 1969.

We would like to thank the many relatives of Dr. Wolper, especially his son, Arnold, for their generosity in personally financing this publication, and for their never-flagging efforts to insure that the doctor's work reached the printed page.

The Editors

Editors' Note: As it has been our intention to leave the notebooks exactly as we found them, we here provide the references for insertions in the notebooks for which the doctor, we are sure inadvertently, omitted either to use quotation marks or to cite authorship, giving the impression that he was their author.

I am what I am. (The Lord, God)

The mind is, in a manner, all things. (Aristotle)

Art is man, added to nature. (Bacon)

Knowledge is a form of aggression against nature. (Nietzsche)

True humility requires us to learn from Copernicus that the human world is not the purpose or the center of the universe; that we learn from Darwin that man is a member of the animal kingdom; and that we learn from Freud that the human ego is not even master of its own house. (Norman O. Brown in *Life Against Death*)

Our civilization represses . . . any form of transcendence. Among one-dimensional men, it is not surprising that someone with an insistent experience of other dimensions, that he cannot either entirely deny or forget, will run the risk of being destroyed by the others, or of betraying what he knows. . . . Many of us are only too successful in acquiring a false self to adapt to false realities. (R. D. Laing in *The Divided Self*)

We are Adam the next time around. (Paul Goodman in the *New York Review of Books*)

January

1st To begin with, there is no earthly reason to begin. Heaven knows.

I am, after all, sixty-nine years old. This is no big deal. Believe me. Tempus fugit.

Today is my birthday, by the way. This is also no big deal. I think I am about to expire. Not before breakfast, but soon. I give myself a year. My body is running down. My mind is evaporating. My soul is beginning a new phase, retirement. Together, body, mind, and soul are in the last lap of a sweepstakes to see who will be the first to hit agony's jackpot. Right now it is a draw.

By the way, I am keeping this notebook for only one reason. Protection against Boris. It was Paul's idea. I am to write down absolutely everything. I do not kid myself that I have encountered a splendid instructional opportunity. Boris is a fucking pedagogical nightmare.

I must get organized. This week's chores:

1. Pull up shades.
2. Do Zodiac.
3. Mop floor. Water plants.
4. Replace lightbulbs (outdoor spots and nightlights).
5. Check incubator. Fill birdfeeder.
6. Create life.
7. ?

Actually, I should let Boris worry about it. Where is Boris?

I must press on.

Shades up.

2nd Zodiac done.

3rd Plants watered.

4th Lightbulbs replaced, outdoors and in.

5th Incubator checked. Birdfeeder filled.

6th Ah, yes. And now for the beginning. Damn, I forgot to mop the floor. Where the hell is my list?

7th What a lousy week this has been. I haven't accomplished a damn thing. I need a rest. Badly.

8th I liked her ass. That's what it was. She was wearing a white bathing suit when she walked by me on the boardwalk. She smiled at me, but by the time I smiled back, all I could see was her backside, her magnificent derrière, her wondrous rear, gently clicking left and then right and then left again as she walked away.

I jumped off my perch on the railing and ran after her. I whipped out a card and handed it to her. It said, "Harry Wolper, Medical Doctor."

"I don't need a doctor," she smiled deliciously and handed me back the card.

I pulled another card from a different pocket as I walked alongside her. The card read, "Harry Wolper, Professional Life Guard, Atlantic City, New Jersey." I handed it to her.

"My life's just fine, thank you," she beamed, all suntan and freckles, and returned this card as well.

I fetched my fountain pen and, skipping along beside her, scratched a message on the other side of the card, "Your ass is devastating."

"Okay, you're hired," she grinned, not missing a stride, and tucked the card in the top of her bathing suit, between her equally devastating breasts. "This card I'll keep," she laughed.

I took her hand and we spent the rest of that glorious Sunday together.

9th There is no reason to believe any of this really. Maybe this makes it all the better. I don't know. Boris came. He was not here and then he was. I had absolutely nothing to do with the arrival of this late-adolescent Stephen Dedalus. I swear it. I was perfectly content to invest myself in my work. After all, this is no small chore that I work at day after day.

I am creating life.

10th Then she disappeared. For two weeks I didn't see her. Evenings, dressed in dazzling white, I'd sit on the same railing, waiting for her to pass, flashing my Ipana smile and my golden hair at the well-chaperoned young women who passed me by.

Then she was there.

"How's business?" She leaned against me and tucked some errant wavy locks of mine back in place.

"Not too good for the last couple weeks." I turned and looked into her flashing green eyes.

"Relatives," she answered my inference. "Lots and lots of relatives. I was in a beauty contest. Everyone came to cheer. I came in second. Mother says they think blonds are cheap, and my hair's too frizzy besides. But I got ten out of a possible ten on *form*. That's because of my ass. Actually, five out of the six judges asked me to go to bed with them, three men and two women, so I don't feel so bad, I guess. How've you been? Anybody drown?"

"So far, so good." I put my arm around her, and the two of us settled on a boardwalk bench until the next morning when the gulls lifted out of the mist. She had been dozing against me, and the furious flapping and cawing startled her.

She looked out at the sun as it pulled itself from the sea, surveyed the deserted boardwalk, and then turned to me.

"I'm not the kind of girl you think," she smiled at me.

"I didn't think you were," I smiled back. "How aren't you?"

"Well," she leaned over and kissed me passionately, "for one thing, I'm not a beauty contest queen. I'm an artist."

I kissed her back, placing my mouth gently against hers. I reached up and put my hand on her blouse, firmly pressing first one breast and then the other.

"And another thing," she kissed me back and put her hand on my crotch so she could feel my erection, "I rarely have oral sex on the first date."

12th I must persist. Before Boris deceives me any longer, I must find the secret of life. Boris probably couldn't care less. Thank God for that, at least. I hope I sound grateful.

Arnold would appreciate that. He feels that I am never grateful. Where is Arnold?

13th Sometimes I have a dream.

I am in the cave in Plato's *Republic,* sitting on the cold ground, my hands and feet bound in iron chains. Through an opening at the end of the cave, I see a turnstile and a neon sign. It flashes "World's Oldest Operating Metaphor." This does not, however, appear to be a very popular attraction anymore.

Inside, marching before me in a continuous line, are scores of men carrying wooden and stone statues of animals on top of their heads, and just in front of them is a stone wall in very poor repair. Loose stones stick out all along the wall and others rest at the foot of it. The place is cold and musty.

"We wouldn't still be doing this, you know, if it weren't for the money," one man explains to me, "because, to be perfectly honest with you, I don't think there isn't one of us who doesn't feel just a little ridiculous."

There are other men, similarly bound, beside me, and one of them talks to me.

"Periodically," he tells me, "the chains come off, and we wander toward where the fire used to be. We pretend that we're blinded, give the appropriate exclamations of astonishment, have lengthy arguments about what is real and what isn't (usually we agree that the fire is real even though there isn't one any longer), and finally rechain ourselves. Sometimes, when there are some spectators, we'll let them ask questions, which we answer with other questions. If we do well, we get fed.

"Just in case you've got any smart ideas, you see the fellow third down the line from me? He once made a run for it, up into the light, out of the cave, came running back to us a short time later, half crazed and out of his mind, yelling that what we were seeing wasn't real. We beat the hell out of him. No one's tried to make a run for it since. To tell the Truth, there never have been any shadows down here like there were supposed to be, because this is the cave of Zeus Lykaios."

When this is said, I try to talk, but nothing comes out of my mouth. I am petrified with fear. Suddenly the man who was talking turns to me.

"Here comes the boss. Look busy," he says with a perfectly straight face.

An old, particularly ugly, barefoot man approaches. He seems annoyed by the poor business. My friend pokes me in my ribs.

"Quick. Say something symbolic," he urges me frantically.

I hold out my empty hand to my friend.

"Is this the flower or the apple?" I ask.

"Very good," he whispers. "Now you're catching on," and I wake up in a cold sweat and try to figure out who this damn Zeus Lykaios is. He sounds so awfully significant, I ought to know him. Must be one of Arnold's friends.

14th That, of course, is the race, to find where nature puts her mind, to find what improbable chemical array nature uses for her commands, before the world draws the last ounce of jelly from my bones, and I collapse in a dark corner with my daughter's rag doll, the two of us smiling our brains silly through our sewn mouths.

15th At the outset, it is only a mundane question of freedom. If I am a cell, and I feel more like being a lobule than the locus ceruleus, do I have a chance, even a fighting chance? If I can find that in the beginning there is the slightest possibility for choice, then I am not condemned. This secret of life I shall find as I have found all the others, and I shall write the answer in big letters on public toilet stalls all over the world. It shall be very common knowledge.

16th Arnold's coming for dinner on Friday. There must be a full moon.

17th We spent a lot of time on that boardwalk bench, feeding pigeons and fondling each other. By the end of July we had moved discreetly down to the beach. But it was not until mid-August that we discovered *under* the boardwalk.

It had started to drizzle one night. I came prepared now with all the amenities—blanket, snacks, and schnapps—so we moved our picnic under the protection of the world's most famous wooden walkway.

Carefully, I spread the blanket and assisted my lady to a comfortable spot thereupon. Immediately, she fell into my arms in a swoon, owing, perhaps, to my having quietly slipped my hand under her skirt. I gently stroked where the soft mat of pubic hair padded the inseam of her panties. Deftly I slid my index finger around the elastic that bound the lace to her silky things, and after barely brushing my fingertip over her clitoris, I slid my finger deeply in her.

"Oh, my God, Harry," she moaned, rolling her eyes upward and closing her eyelids.

I moved my finger in circles inside her while I brought my thumb back to rest on her clitoris, lightly stroking it back and forth.

"Oh, my God, Harry Wolper," she repeated loudly and in ecstasy, "what are you *doing*?"

A voice boomed from directly above us on the boardwalk.

"I think I can guess, ma'am," it resonated, "and unless *he* stops or *you're* quieter, you'll *both* be arrested. Good evening," and the constable proceeded on his way, having effectively ended our romantic activity for the night.

18th Look. Before I go on, let me tell you what a tragic mistake this brilliant philosopher Descartes made. Now this is *very* significant. Pay attention, please. You see, I have recited my cogito ergo sums just as Descartes has. I have sat in my silk smoking jacket in front of my fireplace and eliminated from certainty everything with even the smallest element of uncertainty, just as he did. And let me tell you, I was *not* reduced to nothing.

I was absolutely certain of my existence. There was no doubting it. My head ached. My bones were sore. My heart was broken. My brain didn't enter into it. Existence is an emotional problem. Believe me.

Of course, Descartes *is* a gentleman. He believes that nature will deliver the secrets she guards most closely, over brandy and polite conversation. Well, no doubt about it. The conversation is brilliant. The sweetness of the brandy is superb. And nature is laughing in his face.

Nature must be tricked into giving her secrets. She must be seduced, deceived, overpowered, flattered, and propositioned. She must be caught naked in the bedroom and taken. She must be grabbed and wrestled to the floor like the whore she is, until in the end she is at your feet, and then you must take what you want, reach in and rip if from her insides. It's been almost three thousand years since anyone's been chained to a rock. I am comforted.

19th It would all be very well if I knew what I was looking for, but, instead, I sneak around corners, trying to catch nature off guard. The trick is in the seeing. With my little deer I never have to doubt whether what I am looking at is what I want to see, but when she lowers her pants I say to myself, there is her pussy, and that was what I wanted to see, that is what I have been waiting to have, and I am on her. With nature, I suspect, one has to be more subtle.

I know what I want to see, but I don't know what it looks like on nature, and so far I have the impression that I have attempted to seek gratification from every orifice but the one intended to accommodate me.

20th I have yet to find the proper sign to be placed on my doorpost, so tonight Arnold descended on my house with the same effect as the seven-year locust and engendered feelings appropriate to a major pestilence. Were there nothing to be devoured I doubt that I would ever see Arnold. His visits are only slightly less regular than the locusts', but the effects after he has departed are about the same.

There was about as much reason to trust my son at the age of ten as there was to trust his boyhood idol, Adolf Hitler. As a matter of fact, as I think back, Hitler may still have had an edge at the time.

His first business venture (one of many I financed) involved cheating the government out of large sections of a well-known American desert with the intention of paving it with black asphalt. The tremendous heat produced by the blackness absorbing the sun's rays was supposed to cause mammoth convection currents that would produce a continual rain, turning large remaining (unpaved) sections of the desert (also purchased by Arnold) into farmland.

Moses left in 1952 with a tractor and $10,000 of my money. Three years later he returned to take the remaining clothes he had left in his closet after college, saying nothing to me until he was leaving. As he was about to close the front door, he turned to me and smiled through his sunburnt unshaved face. "Too damn hot," he said. He then swung the door shut slowly, just hard enough for the latch to catch, a skill he has developed over the years to an art. I used to hear him practice for hours in his room, Nazi youth marches warbling through the swinging door.

Periodically, Arnold has returned to ask for more money, which up until tonight I have given him. He has had a thousand deals. I have yet to receive any money back.

I'm not really sure why I refused him tonight. Maybe just for the sport of it. Maybe because I'm getting old and tired. Who knows? I certainly don't.

Arnold put on one of his better scenes. I have deprived him of his golden calf, he tells me, and I will suffer for it. Arnold intends to establish that I am insane or senile. He doesn't care which, either will do. I can have my pick. He wants to become my conservator, institutionalize me, appropriate this house as his own. It's hard to tell when Arnold is just letting off steam and when he actually will act on his threats. I tend to place this particular assault in the more lethal category. I must be on my guard. Arnold cannot be underestimated.

There are some psychologists who have written lengthy and supposedly well-researched books documenting that fathers and sons never really *hate* each other. Deep down there is always love. This is a pile of horseshit.

21st I remember so clearly when I first decided that I wanted to spend the rest of my life as a scientist. I was forty. I had gone to a Saturday matinee where I sat through the Spencer Tracy movie four times until my children came shouting my name down the aisle just before midnight. Tracy was a scientist, and I lived for the moment when the full moon would appear and he would raise the smoking, foaming test tube to his lips. I cannot begin to relate the disappointment I have encountered.

22nd There is little reason for the month of January to exist, particularly here in Cambridge. The snow is piled three feet deep along the side of the street so that it is only at the crossings that I am aware there are cars in the city at all. The life of this city, the young people, have all left, or not returned, or are hibernating, or have closeted themselves to smoke and suck on whatever it is they smoke and suck on this January.

It is cold and windy and there is a promise, not of spring, but only of February and March.

Still, the fight I begin in January to get me through these three months has a way of keeping me alive for the rest of the year.

This particular January, I cannot sleep. Perhaps I should have given Arnold the money. It would have been easier. Arnold has always wanted another father. I have wanted another son. I felt, as I watched him grow up, that he was not my child, that someone had slipped him to me in the dark. Our feelings are no one's fault. That's the way life for us happened. There is nothing that can be done.

23rd Her great glistening eyes looked down at me.

"Do you love me, Harry?" she asked.

"I love you," I answered.

"Then, I'll do it," she said.

Her tongue licked at my lips and then plunged into my mouth, encircling my tongue, darting between my tongue and my lips, wetting my eyelids, while her hand stroked my crotch.

She undid my zipper as she kissed my ears and sucked on the lobes, then moved to my neck, flicking with her tongue.

She took my penis out of my pants and gently ran her hand up and down it.

"Harry?" she asked as she stroked me. "How come you're not out being a doctor?"

"Oh, I don't know," I grunted in ecstasy.

"Aw, come on," she said, as her hand slid quickly up and down me, "there's got to be some reason."

"Later," I moaned. "I'll tell you later."

"Now, Harry," she whispered. "I want to know now," and her hand slowed down.

"Indoors," I said frantically. "I hate being indoors in summer. Please don't stop."

"You don't have to be indoors *all* the time, you know," she said, running her fingers lightly around the rim of my aching organ.

"Right," I agreed. "Right. I don't."

"You have evenings, weekends—you have an *obligation* now that you're a doctor, don't you think?"

"I do, yes," I panted. "I do. I do. An enormous obligation."

"Harry, you know what I think. I think you're just a life guard so you can get laid a lot. That's all."

"The sea," I groaned. "I love the sea."

Footsteps approached on the boardwalk above us. They were accompanied by rousing song. Two men stopped directly above us.

"Christ," I whispered. "It's four in the morning."

"They're sailors," she whispered back. "Sailors stay up late."

Suddenly the singing stopped.

"Open the tanks," one shouted.

"Open the tanks," the other shouted.

There was the sound of two streams of water hitting the boards directly above us.

"Oh, Christ," I said, crawling out of the way just as the urine started to flood down to where, just a few seconds before, I had been ready to find sexual release with a woman for the first time all summer.

The activity above us lasted a very long time. Finally, our salty visitors departed in a chorus of "way, hay, and up she rises."

"You know something, Harry Wolper," my lady turned to me, "we have *got* to get away from this damn boardwalk."

"My place?" I asked hopefully.

"All right," she said in resignation after a long summer's battle, "next time we'll go to your place. What the hell."

26th [A rough draft of a letter. Ed.]

Dear Dean Chambers:

It is with great pleasure that I accept your invitation to deliver the keynote address of

Dear Dean Chambers:

I am, of course, flattered that you have considered me first among the many Harvard graduates of the class of 1919 to give the keynote address at our fiftieth reunion. But, may I suggest that first you speak to some of my classmates who have followed my life from Perhaps it would be advisable to

Dear Neal,

I will certainly understand if the invitation is withdrawn, but it has just occurred to me that there were, in the class of 1919, the unlikely number of *three* Harry Wolpers. Harry *T.* Wolper, I believe is now the senior member of the largest brokerage house on Wall Street and, not incidentally, one of the ten wealthiest men in the world. Harry *W.* Wolper, is now, according to the last alumni bulletin, president of the International World Trade Market, and has been, as I'm sure you know, an ambassador, a secretary of state, and an advisor to, I believe, all six of our last presidents. I am the remaining one.

I have returned your invitation. No hard feelings. Believe me.

Yours truly,
Harry H. (for Hippasos)

27th I opened up Luther today. Somehow I felt that if I would ever find life, it would be in Luther. He took it rather well. Luther had a serious quality about him that alienated him from most of the other frogs. Sometimes he would sit alone for days, for weeks, staring at the wall, not a hop, not a croak.

How many times has Luther emptied his testicles for science? How often has he banged himself dry so I could keep at work? This is the mark of an enduring friendship. Somewhere in Luther there was a special life. Somewhere there was a soul that cared. Today I decided to look.

I had started Luther from one cell. He was parthenogenetic. He was one of the first. And I have seen him grow. Yet, when I took out his little organs, his valiant heart continued to beat. When I cleaned out his chest, so that all that was left was his heart, it still beat. When I took out his heart and laid it beside him, it still beat. Luther's heart is now in the Cambridge sewage system. It's still beating. You can bet on it.

I applied friction to his stomach muscles. His sexual instinct continued to function even when all else was gone. I was appalled. Was this Luther's life? Was this what Luther spent his weeks staring into nothing about? Screwing other frogs? Reliving good lays?

I opened Luther's skull and his brain was still functioning. By reflex?

What was the life in Luther that so endeared him to me? Was it his instincts, uncontrolled, uncontrollable, base and foreign to his mind? Was it his mind, controlling, controllable, lively and pure? Or was it his heart, pumping on, even without Luther?

Was Luther the strange combination of all these? Was he even the combination, the order, the reason, the word, the ratio, the idea, without the elements, without the cortex, the cloaca, the pylorus, the chambers of his heart?

I loved Luther. We had an understanding about the world, and that is why I am so disturbed that when all else was gone, when Luther was a shell, I could still elicit a sexual response. I absolutely refuse to accept that in the end Luther was nothing but another horny toad.

29th Though we rose from under the boardwalk, from out of the dust of the ground, to receive the breath of life and become living souls, we did not make it up to my apartment in Margate.

Time and circumstance conspired to lead us eastward, instead, to the great and wondrous subtropical gardens that surrounded the Atlantic City racetrack one sultry evening at the summer's end.

We knew each other quite well now, this lady with the devastating ass and I, and had agreed that imminently we would cleave unto each other and be one flesh. Of course, this particular evening, we were going only to play the ponies.

On our way through the dark and lush vegetation that surrounded the track in those days, our thoughts turned from the blaring lights and blasting loudspeakers in the distance to each other.

"You sure you wouldn't like to come over to my apartment?" I asked.

"It's absolutely forbidden," she smiled. "I'm not allowed to be alone in a man's apartment. Even for a second. I've told you that," and she pulled me down to the ground and undid the buttons on my shirt so she could lick at my nipples in the darkness.

"I won't tell a soul," I answered, kissing the top of her head as she pressed her lips to my chest, and reaching down at the same time to fondle my favorite bosom.

"*He'll* know," she pointed her finger skyward to indicate that where once there had been a boardwalk, there was now the omniscient *Elohim*.

"You don't think," I asked as I undid her blouse, "that *He* might be observing us now?" I undid her bra and sighed as her large breasts toppled out and fell with a great flourish into my waiting hands.

"It's hard to tell," she admitted candidly, undoing my belt and zipper. "All I know is that Mother says it's wrong, and that's good enough for me."

I turned her over and sucked at her breasts, running my hand under her skirt and up along her satin thighs until I reached the damp softness between them.

"What about this?" I asked as I reached my free hand up her skirt and lowered her panties to her ankles. "Didn't Mother ever say that this was forbidden?"

I flicked up her skirt and started to run my tongue up the inside of her leg.

"Nope," she sighed. "It never came up."

"Not once?" I asked, my mouth finally reaching the soft blond cushion that rested between her thighs.

"No," she moaned as my tongue neatly separated her groove, ". . . Mother . . . only . . . said . . . never . . . never . . . go . . . alone . . . to . . ." she sighed in delight and agony, my mouth now gently sucking at the marvelous pearl that crowned her sex, ". . . never . . . go . . . alone . . . to . . . a . . . man's . . ." she arched her back and pressed herself up against my mouth. "Mother . . . said . . . Mother . . ."

I gave her forbidden fruit a final kiss, raised myself up, slipped off my trousers and very slowly inserted myself into her. I placed my hands under her devastating ass and pulled her tightly to me.

". . . Mother . . . Mother . . . Mother . . ." she moaned.

"No," I said as I moved very slowly. "Guess again."

"Mother . . . says . . ." she moaned again.

"Ah, yes," I said as I thrust myself in as deeply as I could and then out and then in again, getting faster and faster, "what would Mother say now?"

"Mother . . . doesn't . . . know . . ." she rotated her hips and pressed against me to feel as much of me as she could, ". . . doesn't . . . know . . ." she said, panting and trying to catch her breath, ". . . what . . . she's missing . . ." and she began to orgasm, as did I, and there was an enormous cheer from thousands of people a quarter-mile away as the voice on the loudspeaker boomed, "And they're off and running."

"I love you, Harry Wolper," she told me then, tears streaking her cheeks.

"I love you, Lucy," I answered, and I held her close to me, as I fell into a deep sleep.

Of course, this was all a very long time ago, this night that Arnold was conceived. Lindbergh had flown the Atlantic only two years before, and talking pictures were less than a year old. It would be a month before we were married, two months before the stock market would crash, and almost seven glorious years before Lucy would die.

30th Some day, Lucy, you will be born again. You will arise from this jar in front of me and you will be mine. These thirty-three years of growing and purifying culture after culture of your cells will at last be over. I shall transplant your nucleus into a human egg, nurture the egg, and you shall grow once more into my darling Lucy, every cell, every hair, the same, every inch my dear Lucy. We will have reached our immortality. Hold on, sweetheart, Harry Wolper's coming. Your baby's going to be with you. Screw the odds. We'll lay a wreath at Pascal's grave.

31st Here's another thing about God.

I do not accept that God made man, as my mother told me when I was six, because he was *lonesome*. My mother had an alcoholic husband, and *she* was lonesome. God created man as a joke. He was bored.

Take, for example, Adam and Eve, reaching all over themselves to hide their nakedness, ashamed, and quaking at the very thought of being banished from their garden.

It has always seemed to me that if Jehovah, in His omnipotence, had really not wanted man to eat the apple, He would not have made a man who does exactly the opposite of what he's told. Man is God's practical joke. Believe me.

Here's another joke. God made man in His image.

I'm concerned with the Almighty's sense of humor tonight because I'm convinced that I'm only days away from discovering the secret of life. God must be in hysterics.

February

1st Her name was Elizabeth. She had silky deep red hair, pinned up in a bun, and her dark enormous eyes peered out from a face made of the purest milky skin. She was breathtakingly beautiful, this young Irish lady who sat all day in the waiting room of the hospital clinic.

For the first few days we thought she was a malingerer. It was not an unusual occupation in those days of the Great Depression.

The Lord had decreed, whosoever manages to convince thy physician that thou art ill may dwell briefly in Paradise, receiving a warm hospital room, a soft bed with clean sheets, and hot meals.

Textbooks on physical diagnosis had more to offer the weary and destitute than Scripture and were, thus, more widely read by the lay population. We interns memorized the most widely circulated texts and all patients who quoted directly therefrom were given two aspirins and sent home. As the depression worsened, however, this became more difficult to do. The patients no longer had homes. We sent the homeless and the heartbroken to the Red Cross and tried to feed the malnourished and starving. We quickly learned that where there was a hungry woman, there were also barely fed children. A new profession evolved to get to the kids before they were dead. We called them social workers.

Our social worker was Mrs. Grusin.

"Her name is Elizabeth," Mrs. Grusin told me one afternoon. "She's been out there for two weeks now. She won't talk much, but she's not malingering. Talk to her, will you? See what's bothering her."

I walked out to the waiting room. Elizabeth was sitting where she always was, in the wooden chair in the corner, a dark brown wool coat wrapped securely around her.

"I'm Dr. Wolper," I said as I sat beside her. "I understand that your name is Elizabeth."

She looked over and smiled at me.

"Lizzy, it is," she said with an Irish lilt.

"Have you been feeling ill, Lizzy?" I asked.

"No, I haven't been feeling ill, Dr. Wolper," she said. "I've never been ill for a day in my entire life."

"Are you waiting for someone?" I asked.

"Well, not at first, no. But now I am, yes," she smiled impishly.

"Someone who's a patient here?" I asked.

"Oh, no, Dr. Wolper. I'm waiting for you," she continued to grin.

I waited quietly to see if she would have more to offer on her own. She sat silently, looking down at her trim hands for several minutes. Then she stood up and wrapped her scarf around her, getting ready to leave.

"How can I help you, Lizzy?" I finally asked.

"Isn't it closing time, Dr. Wolper?"

"Yes, but I can stay later, if there's something you need to talk over with me."

"Nothing that can't wait, Dr. Wolper," she said over her shoulder as she walked down the stairs that led from the waiting room.

As I walked home that evening, I had the feeling that I was being followed. When I got into our apartment, I looked out the window and thought I saw Lizzy standing across the street, looking up at the building where Lucy and I lived, but, when I ran downstairs to talk to her, she had disappeared into the night.

2nd The world is coming to an end. Human beings are becoming extinct. Boris persists. But we are disappearing.

This is no usual extinction. This is no gradual depletion of the species because our necks are too short to see our adversaries through the tall grass or our pace is too slow to outrun our predators. We men born since Solvay carry with us the end of the world.

I am the prophet of doom.

This is no joke. Believe me. The results are clear. The experiments are proved. That is not Einstein, but for me they are proved. We carry a lethal gene, hidden for over twenty years. Tomorrow's children, the third generation, will carry sperm that is useless. It will not impregnate. It will not start life. It will do nothing but provide onanistic ecstasy.

Is it insane to believe in the end of the world, in the end of men on the face of the earth, and then try to prove that the belief is science? Is that where the insanity lies? Or is it only the same insane search into the middle, the curiosity of what lies inside the inside, the perversity of atomic curiosity?

How perfectly we have built our periodic tables, giant boosts to see over the wall, beyond the barbed wire and the cackling machines. And how well we have learned to pick up our tables and crash in each other's skulls. Now I wonder whether it is too late, whether we have progressed to the ultimate form of pollution. We have contaminated life dry. It will perform for us no longer, miles of seminiferous tubules standing clogged with cold jelly.

Somewhere, back in the beginning, back in those romantic days when

Teutonic ovens were still burning and the harmony of string quartets filled the evenings of the Manhattan Project, back there I have always wondered whether, in between the blackboards and the music, they didn't really believe they were just putting a lot of partial derivatives together to make a big noise.

3rd Tonight was the family council. Arnold arrived, as might be expected, in his best business suit, dressed as though he were attending a funeral, to be precise, and carrying a large briefcase jammed with papers and psychology textbooks. Rebecca and Claire arrived with him, less out of a sign of any enduring love than an attempt at family unity, I am sure. Dinner went without incident until Mrs. Mallory served the coffee after dessert. Arnold began the assault, talking, as he always does, from the back of his throat, which makes him sound less like he's *saying* the words than *chewing* them.

"One of the first signs of an acute schizophrenic episode," Arnold began to read, "is a belief on the part of the patient that there are foreign elements in his food. He may continue in this belief and compound it with a belief that someone is poisoning his food, and finally that people are plotting against him."

There was a long silence. Finally a light dawned.

"I did not say that there were *foreign elements* in my food, Arnold. What I said was that the mashed potatoes tasted like crap. Mrs. Mallory's mashed potatoes have always tasted like crap. They have tasted like crap ever since Mrs. Mallory first came to work for us, before you, Arnold, were born. I did not say that they were poisoned, only that they were lumpy and crappy, and I did not say that she was plotting against me, only that she takes some perverse delight in continuing to put those potatoes on my plate after I have told her not to for over thirty years. I have heard her chuckling herself wet in her pants in the kitchen every time I swear about her potatoes. I think she would *leave* us if I ever stopped."

"Dad, look," Arnold began, "there's no sense confusing things with a lot of details, but, according to these books I read last night, there is no doubt in my mind that you are a very disoriented person."

"Wait a minute," I held up my hands to brake Arnold. "What is this disorientation? You have seen the world. You 'orient' yourself by standing inside out on your head."

Arnold didn't let me finish. "Severe disassociation is—"

"Disassociation. Is this the same or different from disorientation, Arnold?"

"I think they're different," and Arnold started to leaf through the books at his feet for a definitive answer.

"Nothing about latent homosexual tendencies?" I asked.

"Dad, don't get so upset."

"Who's upset?"

"I haven't got anything against you *personally*, Dad," Arnold told me.

At that I was over at his chair. I clenched my fists around Arnold's shirt collar and shook him in his seat.

The girls intervened between us. "Please, Dad," they started together, "Arnold's been working very hard on this. He's put a lot of work into it. He was up all last night getting ready," Rebecca finished.

"Let him finish. Please," Claire said.

I let go and went back to my chair and my coffee. Mrs. Mallory's coffee is only slightly better than her mashed potatoes. I didn't say anything.

Arnold ran his finger inside his collar and began to read from a yellow legal pad on a clipboard.

"For the first component of a healthy personality I nominate a sense of *basic trust*, which I think is an attitude toward oneself and the world derived from the experiences of the first year of life. By trust, I mean—"

"Arnold. Arnold, you aren't going to take me through all eight of Erikson's stages tonight, are you?"

"Well, I just thought I'd explain how I think you—"

"Arnold, what is that you want? You want to prove I'm crazy so I should go lock myself up somewhere and you can take over the house? Is that what you want?"

"Now, I didn't say you were crazy."

"What, then. Is disorientation sane?"

"I didn't say you were sane, either."

"Ah, ha! Then you have at last found a middle ground. Tell me, Arnold, all my life I've been looking, where is it?"

"What I'm trying to say is that I'm concerned for your health, your mental health. I walk into your lab and I get scared, Dad. You're so disorganized. What kind of a scientist has so many frogs running all over the place, and rabbits and flies, and so much crap and such unsterile conditions? And nothing in cages? What kind of a scientist?"

"My immediate thought is the Lord Almighty God, but I don't suppose that would satisfy you."

"No, it would not. When I was growing up, it was funny to see you work in your lab. But now it's not so funny any more. You're almost seventy."

"I am aware of my age, Arnold, very aware. I'm also aware that you've always been afraid of my laboratory. Even when you were little, you would stand at the door and cry at all the confusion. It was only funny to you for a very few minutes a day. Well, I'm sorry that my world doesn't come out all even in the end, with everything locked up and sterile, everything in its place. You have no idea how sorry I am. It breaks my heart. But this, incidentally, does not mean that I'm insane."

"But you don't even *try* to put things in order."

"What order, Arnold? Your order? My order? Their order? You are seeing things in their natural state, Arnold. The natural state is chaos. The world began as chaos, is chaos now, and always will be chaos. Accept it. It won't kill you."

"I'm not worried about it killing *me*, Dad. Would it kill you to find a world that's organized?"

I thought for a moment.

"Yes. I suppose it would, Arnold. It would kill me if I found out that God was a perfectionist, because then life would be a fraud, man would be condemned, history would have been a lie, and the whole world would have gone mad." I started thinking of Boris then. He was there in a flash. Shazam. Rebecca's words made him vanish.

"That's what we're concerned about, Dad." Rebecca spoke quietly and with concern.

Claire continued her thought. "We don't want to see you lose yourself over some stupid idea of yours that didn't prove to be right."

"Are you both in this with Arnold?" I asked.

"Not in the way you mean," Claire said.

"What do you want?"

Rebecca answered. "We want you to talk to someone, to someone professionally trained."

"Like a psychiatrist?"

"Like a psychiatrist," Rebecca continued, "who would put us all at ease. You know how excited you've been getting lately. Maybe he'll be able to give you something to feel more relaxed. You'll be able to concentrate more and get even *more* work done. Do it for us. Please?"

I have never turned my daughters down. Not once in their lives. How could I not agree? I couldn't. Arnold had already taken the liberty of making an appointment for me. I know what Arnold wants. He wants three psychiatrists to certify me insane. He would then commit me. The girls would believe I was in good hands, and Arnold would be free to dispose of the house.

I have always pitied poor Abraham. Here he had the sword from his sheath, only seconds away from slitting his son's throat, and he had to sacrifice a ram in his son's place. What a disappointment it must have been. What a damn tragedy.

4th I rank the psychiatrist as a scientist somewhere between the beginning astrologist and the novice soothsayer. I equate his techniques with those of the divining rod, his approach with the sophistication of the handwriting analyst, the palm reader, and the phrenologist. To be perfectly honest, I have received a better analysis of my character and more appropriate advice for my future behavior from a not particularly spectacular gypsy palmist I frequent in an old housing development in South Boston than from any of my psychiatric friends, and at a dollar a turn. It's the truth.

For me, talking to a psychiatrist (and I have had my times when I have found it necessary, if not particularly helpful) is like nailing myself into my own coffin, with the doctor, on whom I've called for help, lounging back in his armchair and dispassionately handing me the nails.

I cry out, "Doctor, are you *aware* that I am *entombing* myself?"

"Do *you* think I am aware?" he asks.

"That's not what I asked. What I asked was whether *you* were aware that I am nailing myself into my own coffin?"

"Do you *want* me to be aware?"

"Doctor, please, are you aware yes or aware no?"

"This is very important to you, my being aware of what you're doing, isn't it?" And all the time he is handing me fistfuls of nails.

5th I could not displace the vision of Elizabeth's porcelain face. Her dark eyes followed me wherever I went. Also her body and her brown wool coat.

As a matter of fact, for two solid weeks Lizzy followed me everywhere, smiling pleasantly from across the street, waving to me from the opposite subway platform as my train pulled out, nodding as we passed at a crowded crosswalk. And each time I went after her, she disappeared.

It was two weeks to the day before she returned to the hospital. I was eating my lunch in an office in the back of the clinic when I heard a woman screaming at the receptionist's desk.

By the time I got out to the waiting room, two other interns were holding Lizzy, one firmly attached to each arm, as she struggled loudly. When she saw me, she stopped, and a large smile spread across her Irish face.

"Well, Dr. Wolper," she beamed pleasantly. "How are you this afternoon?"

"I'm just fine, Lizzy," I beamed back. "What seems to be the problem?"

"No problem, really," she continued to grin, "none at all. Just a little mix-up over which doctor would be examining me."

One of the interns spoke up.

"She said she was a patient of yours, but we have no record of it."

"I'll see her," I said. "You can let go of her."

"Well, thank you very much, Dr. Wolper," Lizzy said, brushing off her coat and straightening her hair.

She followed me to the examining room.

"What seems to be the problem?" I asked again once the door was shut.

Lizzy took off her coat and draped it over the examining table. Then she stood for a few minutes, staring at the floor.

"Do you have pain somewhere?" I tried to be specific.

"Dr. Wolper," she said, looking up at me with her giant brown eyes, "I'd like you to examine me."

"What should I examine you *for*, Lizzy?"

"I just need you to examine me."

"Do you think you might be pregnant?" I tried.

"Oh, my, no, Dr. Wolper," she laughed. "There's no worry of that, you can be sure."

"Then what is it, Lizzy? Please. You can tell me."

She shifted uncomfortably from foot to foot.

"No, I can't, Dr. Wolper," Lizzy finally said. "I really can't. It would just mean a great deal to me if you would give me a thorough examination. I won't be any trouble, and I can pay you for it. Would you do that for me?"

Lizzy stood in front of me, staring intently, her fingers nervously fidgeting at her flower-print dress.

I looked back and decided on another approach.

"Would you like a nurse to examine you?" I asked.

Lizzy didn't answer. She just shook her head no and continued to look at me.

"All right," I said. "There's a gown on the back of the door. Change into it, and I'll be back in a few minutes."

An enormous smile spread across her face.

"You won't regret this, Dr. Wolper," she said excitedly, as I closed the door behind me.

When I returned, Lizzy was seated on the table in the white hospital gown. She had taken her red hair down and it fell to her waist. She seemed to me like an exquisite china figurine.

"You've been following me all over town," I told her, as I examined her eyes.

"Yes, I have," she said somewhat apologetically. "You must think I'm a real nuisance."

"I'm curious why you've been following me," I checked out her ears.

"Look at my teeth, Dr. Wolper," she ignored my questions.

"Do you have a toothache?"

"My teeth are perfect," she said proudly. "Look at them."

"Beautiful, you're right," I agreed as I looked in her mouth.

"Dr. Wolper, I've never been sick a day in my life."

I put the blood pressure cuff on her arm and then took her pulse.

"Do you have a family in New York, Lizzy?"

"No, I don't, Dr. Wolper. My family's all in Ireland."

"How about a husband or children?"

"I've never been married, Dr. Wolper. I'm not the marrying type, if you know what I mean. It's never really appealed to me all that much."

"I have to lower your gown to hear your heart," I told her.

Lizzy reached behind her, pulled at the bow on the gown's back and then shrugged her shoulders. The gown fell effortlessly to her waist.

"I'm a little shy, Dr. Wolper," she said as I listened to her chest.

"Where do you live, Lizzy?" I changed the subject.

Suddenly Lizzy slid down from the table, letting the gown fall to her feet.

"I'm twenty-eight years old, Dr. Wolper, and there's never been a man that's seen me naked before, but I want you to examine me real carefully." She looked at me again with those penetrating brown eyes of hers. "Have you ever seen anything so healthy in your life?"

I looked at her perfect alabaster body, at her small breasts, the nipples protruding from large chocolate circles, at her small round hips, and the triangular hazel patch that rested between her young and gentle thighs. Her long red hair fell like a satin cloth to the very top of her delicate pear-shaped bottom.

"I can see," I cleared my throat, "that you are in excellent physical condition, Lizzy. You may get dressed now," and I quickly dodged out the door.

6th If I am insane, and there is no reason to believe I am not, I insist on the affirmation of a two-thirds majority, a consensus of at least one Freudian, one Ego Psychologist, one Sullivanian, one Reichian, one Jungian, one Behaviorist, and one Third Forcer. Should they vote in favor of my being whatever it is they call "crazy" this year, I suggest that it be determined by lot whether I am to undergo chemo-, electro-, hydro-, group, milieu, or individual psychotherapy. I will abide by the decision.

There's more. Physics is, in the end, the foundation of biology. Biology, as the first life science, is the foundation of psychology. Biology is, therefore, the mean between the two extremes, physics and psychology, in much the same way that theology is the mean between science and philosophy.

Now, I am a biologist, and I know what the "laws" of biology are. If it is true that psychology is, in the end, based on the *laws* of biology, then psychiatry, whose foundation is psychology, is the biggest hoax since that New Hampshire farmer got sucked out of his car into a flying saucer and drained of all his semen.

7th My dear friend Paul, whom I've not seen for over a month, finally arrived at my doorstep tonight to inform me that I'm working on the next great bomb, the end of one age and the beginning of another, a bomb that creates life as quickly as a bomb that destroys it. Paul always says things like this when we meet for drinking. He believes that this is how the world will end. Paul has always been an optimist.

8th There was a time, I find it hard to believe now, when there were no oral contraceptives, when we who wanted to love, but did not want children, would fumble endlessly in the dark with condoms, while our mates wondered anxiously what we were actually *doing*. Some of us were lucky, and on occasion we would find ourselves with those liberated wives and lovers who were willing to lubricate, insert, extract, bathe, powder, and lay to rest their diaphragms each night. But, as a young man, I always wondered about those others, those who were more passionate than careful, who found themselves in the arms of a naked willing woman and did not ask at that precise moment when her previous period ended and then calculate, who did not abstain if the time was inappropriate (or appropriate), and who refused as a compromise to lie at the final moment futilely arching semen onto the sheets, the headboard, the floor, and themselves. What did these people do to prevent having children?

My curiosity was satisfied shortly after I moved to Cambridge and word got around that I had formerly practiced medicine. They do nothing to prevent having children. Absolutely nothing.

For the first ten years I lived in Cambridge, it seemed as though no one had ever *heard* of contraceptives. I received calls and visits by the hundreds each year, from friends, from total strangers, asking me to terminate unwanted, usually illegitimate, pregnancies.

The first pregnancy I ever aborted was that of a small blondish high school girl. I could not eat for a week afterwards, in fright of what would happen if I were discovered, in fear of what might have happened had I not succeeded. She was a Polish girl, and I pictured the police and hundreds of her Polish relatives arriving at the same time, fighting over who would get to do with me what he wanted. In this particular fantasy the police lost.

It was not for another year that I was able to perform an abortion, in this case a college girl, a freshman at Radcliffe who, I believe, was from Pittsburgh. She had enormous sad blue eyes and a wan little smile. She came to me in the snow as a match girl might and played on my every emotion until she won.

I have lost count by now, but I could describe every one. They have been young, attractive, and intelligent. They have also been unmarried. I suspect that that is how I differ from most physicians. They limit themselves to married women with specific needs for an abortion, psychological or medical. Married women will always find some physician. It's the young unmarried ones who need me, who make it worth my while.

I do not charge for my services, but I will not operate unless the father is there, next to the girl. He must watch. I started this little exercise in pain after one particularly fertile young girl returned *six* times in a little over a year and always with the same young man. Her visits terminated permanently after her boyfriend watched the last D & C. I understand that her beau had a pretty rough time of it for the next several months. I heard about him by chance from a friend who practices medicine in Cambridge, who related that the boy was treated for a sympathetic pregnancy that came fairly close to running full term.

In 1960, when the pill finally reached the market, I stopped, though certainly not for lack of patients. I got roaring drunk on December 8, 1967, as the statute of limitations ran out on me. I remember sitting in the back of Cronin's, telling Paul in garbled syntax why I was so drunk, and crying my eyes out in relief. Paul could not believe what I was saying. But that night he asked me all the questions, and I came up with all the right answers. Where I had done it. How I had done it. On whom I had done it. Paul still thought I was lying.

"Would I be drunk like this?" I asked. "Would I be drunk and crying? Would I, Paul?"

Actually this was not the first time Paul had seen me drunk and in tears, but they've all been for equally good reasons.

He believed me. He started talking about theological justification, about morals and ethics, about social necessity and human responsibility.

"No, no," I told him. "I did it because I liked the kids. That's all."

Now I don't know what I am going to do. When I looked up from my work today, I saw, standing in front of me, a slim, tall, young black boy, with a head of hair almost as large as his head itself, wearing thick glasses and a pendant that hung from his neck on a string of rawhide.

"I'm looking for Dr. Wolper."

"I'm Dr. Wolper."

"I need to have an operation done."

"I'm not that kind of doctor. I'm a biologist."

"I know. The operation's not actually for me. It's for a friend of mine."

"I'm still not that kind of doctor."

"She's a girl friend of mine and she's pregnant."

"I get the message. Believe me."

"I want you to perform an abortion."

"What is your name?"

"Horace Gibson. Horace Greeley Gibson."

"Well, Mr. Gibson. I'm afraid that you have the wrong kind of doctor. I can't help you."

"Dr. Wolper, I know who you are. You *are* the right kind of doctor, or at least you were. I've been asking, maybe a hundred different people. They all gave me one name. Dr. Harry Wolper and this address."

"I do not perform abortions."

"On black people?"

"On anybody. On black people, on white people, blue people, orange people, one- and two-headed people. It does not matter. I do *not* perform abortions. You should marry the girl. Or find a clinic somewhere else."

"I don't know her well enough to marry her. We only met once, at a party around Christmas. We were stoned. She said she was very liberal. She comes from New Jersey. *Southern* New Jersey. I should have known."

"Why don't you come back in a week or so. Let me see whether I can think of someone."

"She's getting married next Friday. They grew up together. She thinks her husband's going to be disturbed if seven months from now he becomes the father of a black baby."

"She's white, I assume."

"Very white. He's very virginal. At least he says he is."

"This makes no sense at all."

"I told you. She's liberal. Making it with me was something she could keep to herself forever, through all those nights in the sack with her husband in southern New Jersey. Dr. Wolper, I'm leaving town in a couple of weeks. She's moving to New Jersey. We've got the bread."

"I don't charge."

"Please. She's desperate. She wants to go after it with a coat hanger."

I thought for a minute. Only that. My heart raced. I perspired.

"Bring her here next Friday night about ten o'clock. You come with her. And, Mr. Gibson, tell her not to use the coat hanger. It doesn't work. Unless it kills her."

Why do I do these things to myself? I don't have enough grief already? Why can I never say no when I have to say no? I know for sure that I'll be caught. After all I've gone through, after the nightmares and the terror, why am I doing this? There is no answer. But this is the last one. There will be no more. Seven years will be 1976. 1976 is a good year for another celebration. It will give me something to look forward to, if I'm not in prison.

9th We used to spend our summers on Martha's Vineyard, Lucy, Arnold, Rebecca, Claire, and I, and even then Arnold seemed to be restless, ill at ease, unsure of himself. I remember him at the age of two and a half, running naked in the sand with the other naked two-year-olds, and from a distance you could always tell which one was Arnold. He was the one who always had his hands on his testicles.

At first I thought he was being protective, but after studying him I realized that he held them for assurance, to assure himself that everything was in order, that they were still there and he was who he was.

To this day Arnold has never been very comfortable in a bathing suit. He continues to put his hands in his pockets at every opportunity.

I shall remind him of this if he continues this psychiatric stupidity.

10th Insanity for me has, in fact, always been one of those sacred United

States Government natural preserves, left unspoiled by human progress and technology, old as the earth itself, where I can camp out and take long deep unpolluted breaths.

I am so preoccupied lately with sane and not sane. I try to convince myself that I am sane while at the same time I uphold my right to remain insane. I do not know why insanity must be the disease. For me it is the cure. Nevertheless. I prefer not to spend whatever is left of my life in an institution or a home.

I'm scared. I'm scared because I do not believe that the world, especially the psychiatric world, shares my enthusiasm for mental derangement. I've always known that my world was no one else's. It has become a source of constant joy to me. Now it's becoming more a trial than anything else. I have not heard from Boris at any length for over a month, but Boris is bad for me. That craziness is unhappy craziness. I don't know. Maybe Boris is putting me on. Maybe he is only a kidder. Yes, and maybe I'm the Queen of Sheba.

11th Once again, Lizzy had disappeared. She was not in the examining room when I returned, and the week went by with no sign of her.

I walked on the street alone now, crossed through crowds with no smiling face to greet me, took the subway home without a beaming Irish shadow to wave me goodbye.

"The girl is obviously in love with me," I explained the situation to Lucy one night.

"Obviously," Lucy nodded.

"You don't think so?"

"Well, I'm sure she must be very *fond* of you, Harry," Lucy said to rescue my faltering ego, "but I think that there's something else going on here."

"Well, it's definitely not her health," I concluded. "She's in *excellent* physical condition."

"It certainly sounds that way," Lucy winked at me. "I was thinking that she might be lonely. Or homeless. Or broke."

I thought about this for a minute.

"You don't think she just wants my body?" I whispered in Lucy's ear.

"Well," Lucy said as she ran her hand through my hair, "I'm sure she does. I mean, she *did* insist that you make *absolutely certain* she was in perfect health."

Lucy kissed me on the tip of my nose.

"I'm not sure I understand," I said.

"Harry," Lucy explained, stroking my new beard with the back of her slender fingers, "the lady just wanted to make sure that she could handle a god."

"Good point," I agreed, distractedly wondering whether my panic at Lizzy's nakedness had driven her back into a homeless and lonely world forever.

Lucy looked at me in silence for a few minutes, still brushing my beard with her hand, and read my mind.

"Maybe your social worker can find her," she said.

"I hope so, Lucy," I answered.

12th [A rough draft of a letter. Ed.]

Dear Neal,

It is with great pleasure that I accept your invitation to give the address to the class of 1919 at Harvard.

I am still not sure that you have the right Harry Wolper, but I shall question no further. I am, of course, grateful and deeply moved.

After much thought, I've narrowed the topic to my specialty.

The tentative title for my address will be "Life."

I will start on it immediately. I shall send you an advance copy, as you have requested, as soon as it is completed. Please fill me in on the exact date and place.

Again, my deepest thanks for this honor.

Regards,
Harry Hippasos Wolper

13th [This appears to be the first of several drafts of the reunion address. Ed.]

Fellow classmates and distinguished guests.

My subject is life.

First of all.

Life is hydrogen. What is hydrogen? Hydrogen is a colorless, odorless, inflammable gas. Hydrogen is a molecule, a molecule that combines with carbon to make hydrocarbon molecules, the backbone of life. Hydrogen is everywhere we look.

Hydrogen is the sun, a giant fire burning billions of tons of itself into space every second.

Hydrogen is the ground we walk on, the surface on which we walk, the soil in which we plant. When we climb our mountains, drive our cars, run our races, play in our mud, we are climbing, driving on, running on, and playing in hydrogen.

Hydrogen is what we breathe. It is the air around us, the sky, the clouds, the wind, the blue. When we fly our airplanes, we are setting fire to hydrogen to fly through hydrogen, over hydrogen.

Hydrogen is the sea. It is the water we drink, the rain, the river, the waterfalls, the bays and the lakes. We drink hydrogen to stay alive.

And we are hydrogen. Our bodies are hydrogen. When we make love, hydrogen is combining with hydrogen in—

Good God, I have reduced everything in the universe to fire, earth, air, and water.

Life. What *is* life?
[The draft ends here. Ed.]

14th Morris Halpern, Maury to his friends, solicits for causes the way most men breathe—at regular intervals, ceaselessly. I suspect his reasons are much the same as those for respiration. It is impossible to imagine what Maury would be without his starving children, ill-funded artists, nonworshipping heathens, and diseased populations, without his epidemics, floods, wars, poverty, perversion, disasters, catastrophes, and cultural necessities.

Maury the Solicitor appears at my door monthly with requests to save the starving, sickly, or dying of a section of the world for which he has set aside these particular thirty days. He has allocated two months to each continent, omitting Australia and the Arctic land masses as heathen, but has not differentiated between the unfortunate Christian man and the Christian beast in the same fallen state, one month soliciting for *homo erectus*, the other for the disappearing species of the month.

I am, nevertheless, drawn to this red-faced, bald, continually perspiring, overweight, middle-aged man with a certain dread. I remind myself of the motorist passing the scene of a particularly horrible accident who cannot bear both to see and *not* to see every maimed bloody corpse involved. For this privilege, for satisfying my appetite for such depravity on a regular door-to-door basis, I give Maury my monthly fifty-dollar contribution to whatever, and we are both happy.

This evening we found ourselves in the animal kingdom. I had never known that such things happened to spaniels in Ethiopia. I had not known that there *were* spaniels in Ethiopia, a country itself I have never been sure existed.

Maury has been at it with boundless energy and delight since 1938. He admits with a certain forlornness that "there really hasn't been a year like 1946 since," consoling himself that "the 1960s haven't been all that bad really."

I have, of course, been avoiding thinking about why Maury has disturbed me so this particular night. Shortly before leaving, he told me, with an excitement that he usually reserves only for full-scale holocausts, about what he calls Cambridge's "mad abortionist." The mad abortionist, I have been informed, is a physician or former physician reputed to have performed over a thousand abortions in the last twenty years. (There couldn't possibly have been that many.) Maury is in hot pursuit, along with the Public Health Service. He has made the search his "project." He will pursue this for as long as it takes. Maury has always been a tenacious bastard.

I believe that I did not show my fear, my shock. Though I could feel my blood pulsate as though it were going to break out of my vessels, I remained calm.

According to Maury, the mad abortionist is all but caught. Is that what Horace Greeley Gibson is up to? Is he one of those plainclothes hippie policemen? I can't take the chance. I cannot perform the abortion. I would be too frightened that, in the middle of the operation, a hundred other black policemen with Afro haircuts and pendants would descend on me, guns drawn. These are no conditions in which to operate. Believe me.

I long for the days when men were allowed to practice medicine according to their own judgment. The days when policemen wore blue uniforms with silver badges.

15th Paul came over tonight. He brought his own brandy and cigars.

"I just can't get started," I confessed to him. "I sit at my desk. Every day. Religiously. Boris lurks behind me, saturates my brain, fiddles with my soul, and still nothing comes out on the paper."

Paul ran his tongue around the edge of his pony and rolled the brandy around the bottom.

"Write, dammit. Write whatever comes into your head. Write about the chair you're sitting on, the weather, your family, your work, your piles. It doesn't matter. It'll come. I guarantee it."

"It sounds painful," I told him.

"It is. Excruciatingly painful and gloriously sublime. But it's all there is, Harry. That's it. Everything else is trivial. A footnote."

We sat in silence for several minutes, filling the study with cigar smoke.

"Anything else?" I asked before moving on to another topic.

"Sure is," Paul grinned at me in bleary-eyed contentment. "Happy St. Valentine's Day, Harry."

"Wasn't Valentine's Day yesterday, Paul?" I asked.

"Whatever you say, Harry," and he put his head on my knee, closed his eyes, and started to snore.

I'm not sure Paul takes Boris seriously.

18th Mrs. Grusin could not find Lizzy. She tried the address Lizzy had used for her clinic form. It was a temporary home for recent immigrants, and Lizzy had left two weeks before. She had left no forwarding address.

Mrs. Grusin tried the immigration office and an Irish Club for new arrivals, both without success. There was nothing else to do. Reluctantly, we gave up.

I had just about forgotten Lizzy when I felt a tug on my coat sleeve one cold night as I walked home. I turned around and there was Lizzy, tears clouding her eyes, a large cardboard suitcase in her hand.

"I just had to tell you something," she said through her tears, "and then I'll leave you alone."

"Lizzy," I said, "we've been looking all over for you."

"I'm very sorry if you thought I wanted to do something improper, Dr. Wolper," Lizzy sobbed. "It was not my intention at all. I assure you."

"Oh, I didn't think that for a minute," I lied. "I left to protect you, Lizzy. I was overwhelmed by how beautiful you were."

Lizzy sniffed back some tears and stopped crying.

"You were, huh?" she said with great interest.

"Would you come up and join us for supper tonight?" I changed the topic before I got myself into any more trouble.

"I don't know, Dr. Wolper," Lizzy said, not really resisting. "I feel terribly ashamed of myself."

"There's no reason to be. It was my fault. Have some dinner with us."

"Well," Lizzy smiled. "If you insist."

"I insist," I smiled, took her suitcase and escorted her up to our apartment.

Of course, Lucy and Lizzy got along famously. They hit it off immediately, sharing impressions of Dublin throughout dinner and insights on the care and feeding of plant life over dessert.

"Lizzy," I asked as we drank our tea, "is there some way that we can help you?"

Lizzy put down her teacup and ran her finger absently around the rim, staring at the circles she was tracing in silence. Then she looked up at me with her rich brown eyes.

"Well, Dr. Wolper," she began, "I believe this is as good a time as any, so I might as well tell you. I want to work for you and your Mrs., Dr. Wolper. I'm a good housekeeper, I can cook, I iron, and I'm a fine person with children. Now I know that this is a depression that we're in, so I wouldn't expect to get any wage, just room and board for now. Later, when we're done with this Great Depression, you can give me a small wage. I don't need much. You've checked me over real good, so you know I'm not going to cost you any medical bills. And I've checked you over real good, so you know I'm going to stay here. I won't be deserting you for someone else who's going to offer me higher wages or a bigger room to sleep in. I sat in that waiting room for two weeks, Dr. Wolper, checking over every doctor that walked in and out. And that hasn't been the only waiting room I've sat in either. I've been to a dozen other hospitals, and there's no question in my mind, Dr. Wolper. You're the lucky one," Lizzy finished out of breath.

For some reason, Lucy and I broke into hysterical laughter. We simply could not control ourselves.

Lizzy was upset at first and then laughed with us.

"I guess this has been something of a surprise, hasn't it?" she asked through her laughter.

"A shock, Lizzy," I said. "We're flattered, of course."

"Well, I'll tell you, Dr. Wolper, you're an awfully nice man. And you're a doctor, too. I promised myself when I came over here that I'd only work for a doctor. Doctors never go out of business and have to let their help go, and they take good care of you. Both my sisters work for doctors and they're happy as peas in a pod."

"Lizzy," I tried to be gentle, "there're only two of us."

"There'll be three soon enough," she grinned, gazing over at Lucy's large belly.

"And we only have a small apartment. Where would you sleep?" I continued.

"She can sleep in the small bedroom," Lucy showed her colors.

"I thought that was for the baby," I said.

"There's room for two," Lucy smiled at the thought of having a live-in companion.

"That's not very private," I said, trying desperately to push to the side a vision of a young naked woman with a hospital gown at her feet and long silky red hair barely touching the second most devastating female bottom I have ever seen.

"It's fine for now," Lizzy smiled.

"I'm sure, in time," Lucy beamed over at me, "we'll be able to provide Lizzy with better quarters."

Lucy, who knew damn well why I was so uncomfortable, was getting an enormous kick out of all this.

"So, it's settled, then," Lizzy announced happily.

"We're glad to have you," Lucy looked over at Lizzy.

"Well," Lizzy answered, "I'm sure I'll be very happy here."

Both ladies looked at me. I thought for an instant of Lucy's fear that she would spend the best years of her life trapped in a house with children, totally alone.

"Let me give you a hand with your suitcase, Lizzy," I conceded graciously, and made a valiant and not entirely successful mental attempt to replace the hospital gown on my sexual vision.

As we got into bed that night, Lucy took my hand.

"Thank you for letting Lizzy stay," she told me.

"Yes, well," I said, "I'm not sure this is going to work out."

"Oh," Lucy said, pressing my hand onto her breast, "this is definitely going to work out, so you can stop all the squirming."

"How can you be so sure?" I rolled her nipple between my fingers.

"Easy," Lucy smiled. "Because if you so much as wink at her, Harry Wolper, I'm going to hit you so hard with my shillelagh you're going to need more than the luck of the Irish to use that famous godlike organ of yours again," and we embraced each other with great celestial passion.

19th Today I became public. I appeared on a television program. It was a "talk show."

"Tell me, Dr. Wolper," I was asked a number of times, "what do you think about genes?"

I should have walked out after the first five minutes. Only the persistent sight of my multicolored countenance being beamed to hundreds of thousands of homes maintained my interest and cooperation.

Before I left I tried to get someone to explain this, how they point a camera at me and it becomes a color picture in somebody's living room. The best most of the technicians could do was wave their hands in the air. One young technician, however, pulled me off to the side and confided to me in hushed whispers that it happened "with electricity." He confirmed what I have always believed about physicists.

20th I do not think that I would like to be God. Not that I'm turning down any recent offers, but I've always believed in Homer's synthesis of what a god's life must be like, knowing that life, for you, will continue forever, that there are no time limits, endings, stops. And I do not care enough for wars, love affairs, metamorphoses, and saturnalia to do them forever.

For every day that we come closer to being the masters and possessors of nature, we come that much closer to interminable loneliness. I don't know why we still try.

With four billion other human beings I am still lonely. I cannot imagine how I would feel as one God.

21st The second night after Lizzy had moved in that February in 1930, I awakened to find Lucy gently manipulating my penis.

"I couldn't sleep," she grinned, and pulled the drawstring to my pajamas.

"Oh, well," I said with mock irritation, "I guess since I'm awake already—" and I kissed Lucy on her neck and started to work my way down.

After exploring the geography in some depth, I turned Lucy over and she positioned herself on all fours to avoid any discomfort to Arnold, who was now only three months away from gracing the world with his gentle heart and keen intellect.

I placed my hands around Lucy and held firmly to her gigantic milk-laden breasts as I inserted myself inside her from the rear.

"Oh, Harry Wolper," Lucy groaned as I manipulated her breasts and moved in and out. I did a little groaning myself as the softness of her ass slapped constantly against my testicles.

"Oh, Harry," Lucy rocked back and forth on her knees, "I can hardly stand it," she moaned loudly.

"Shh," I said, driving myself in and out of her with great enthusiasm, "Lizzy will hear."

"Yes, Harry," Lucy continued, apparently not paying full attention to what I was saying. "Yes! Yes! Harry!" she shouted.

"Shhhh—," I said again, "you'll wake up Lizzy."

"You never mind me, Mrs. Wolper," a lilting Irish soprano sang from the other room. "I can't hardly hear a thing, so you just keep right on with what you're doing. Good night, Dr. Wolper."

I froze.

"Damn," I said. "We're back in Atlantic City, Lucy. Now what?"

"Now," Lucy said disengaging me, "I'd like to know when maid's night out is?"

22nd Here is how this science thing works.

I start pulling cells from the embryo. This one, she is making carotin and she is on her way to being a fingernail. This one, she is filled with insulin, she will be the pancreas. These others, estrogen and thyroxin. I talk to myself. When did they start? How did they know when to begin, where to go? In the beginning they were one cell. When they divided, they looked the same. When did they begin to become different? It is enough to drive a person crazy. Believe me.

I know it is in the genes. But I am not stupid enough to believe that it is only in the genes, my perverse hydrocarbon choreographers, indifferently directing the ballet.

For fifty years we have known that they have the information. Mendel knew that from his weekend gardening. So now it is fifty years later, and I can play with double helixes instead of vegetables. My soup is not pea soup, it is adenine, guanine, thymine, and cytosine, and even with its deoxyribose-phosphoric base, it tastes like crap.

I don't recommend it.

But I do recommend the dance, the intricate, exquisite movements: messenger RNA picking up the protein code, passing it to the transfer RNA, which wiggles off to the little round ribosome, and the ribosome ingesting the code in one end and grinding out her amino acids, linking them each to the next, until her polypeptide tail fights its way free, a new protein, life. That is a ballroom operation to be watched, nightly, daily every second of my life, in every cell of my body, Arthur Murray RNA teaching my ribosomes how to keep me alive. It is quite a dance. I stare a my hand, at its cells, and the swimming, coding, transferring, manufactur ing, all the dancing is hard to imagine.

So this is all very interesting and beautiful, but I am not particularl impressed. I need to know who starts the music. Which smiling cham pagne-filled gene starts his "And a one, and a two"? Which one screams, "Stop the music"? Somewhere, there is the maestro, the Operator gene. And somewhere the demon, the Repressor gene.

I have been told by the so-called scientific community that my Operators and Repressors are so much hogwash, that it is all in the protoplasmic pool in which my DNA-laden nucleus floats. I have been called a fool to my face.

"Find the chemical, find the substrate that starts the reaction, and you will have forgotten your Operators and Repressors," I have been told, not always kindly. Maybe so. Maybe they are right. But today my passion is my Operators and Repressors, because today there is trouble.

That fragile female egg, which has up to now so deftly embraced one spermatozoon and spurned the rest, which has turned away thousands seeking her favor, changing instantly into a thick-skinned zygote, now accepts her mate and is cheated. He will not strike up the band. Soon there will be no more children. Then there will be no more people.

Perhaps, there is a Repressor, stopping the Operator from working, stopping him from starting division and growth. Or maybe the Operator itself has been damaged, mutated into sobriety. That is my question. That is where I now stand.

If a Repressor gene has been turned on and I find the chemical code to turn it off, I will have saved mankind from extinction. Who needs it?

But, if it is the Operator gene, if I can find that first Operator which begins life, then I will be able to take any cell, and, if it is from a person, grow a person; if from a frog, grow a frog; and each one a duplicate of its host. And what is most important, I can take Lucy from her jar and grow my darling again, can grow her as she once was, as she always has been to me. It is incidental that mankind will have been saved. That's the truth.

This much I know for certain. In each and every cell is all the information necessary to make a full-grown duplicate of its host. The trick is only to turn it on.

23rd Three months after Lucy died, I awakened one night with such an overwhelming feeling of emptiness at Lucy's loss that the dams burst, and I found myself crying uncontrollably.

We were living in Yonkers then, and Lizzy's room was on the third floor of our Victorian house, directly above my room.

Not long after I had started my weeping, the door to my room opened and Lizzy entered. She came over and sat on the edge of my bed.

"I thought it was one of the children, Dr. Wolper," she said, and she took my hand and held it gently between hers.

"I don't know what I'm going to do," I confided to Lizzy.

"It takes time, Dr. Wolper. But you'll get over this. We all do."

I looked up at Lizzy sitting on the edge of the bed, her long red hair almost touching the covers, her small tender breasts visible under her thin nightgown, made transparent from the streetlight coming in the window.

Lizzy let go of my hands and started stroking my head. Then, without a word, she climbed under the covers and pulled me to her.

"It's all going to be all right," she said, over and again, still running her hand over my hair. Then she stopped and held me away from her. Her brown eyes stared deeply into mine. Very slowly she edged her head toward mine and our lips met.

For several minutes Lizzy kissed me, barely touching my lips with hers. It was an extraordinary kissing, a combination of small inexperienced girl, caring mother, and gentle lover.

I put my arms around her as I returned her tender kisses, and I ran my arms down her back until they reached her bottom.

Lizzy took a deep breath and held it when my hands came to rest on the round forms that had captivated me that day long ago at the hospital. As I started to move my hands in circles around her bottom, Lizzy let out a sigh.

Then she reached behind her and took my hands from her. I thought she wanted me to stop, but instead she reached down under the covers until she found the bottom of her nightgown and pulled it off over her head. When she'd finished, she held the covers tightly around her neck.

"You're sure you want to do this?" I asked.

"Yes, I am," Lizzy said softly.

"And Lucy?" I asked, not really knowing how to say what I wanted.

"Life goes on," Lizzy said quietly, and very slowly she lowered the covers to her waist.

I slipped off my pajamas and looked over at Lizzy, her silky hair spread out on the pillow, her marvelous small breasts rising and falling with her breathing.

She turned on her side and pulled me to her.

"You'll have to tell me what I'm to do," she said, almost in a whisper.

"There's nothing much to it, Lizzy," I said, and I kissed her thin lips and ran my hands along her sides, tracing her curves, until I reached her thighs.

"It feels awfully good being touched like this," Lizzy breathed, and once again she kissed me gently on my mouth.

For almost an hour we lay there, kissing and touching each other. Gradually, Lizzy experimented with running her hands over me, until at last she felt my penis.

"Good Lord," she said, "it's so big. Do you think it'll fit?"

"Why don't we see," I suggested and opened her delicate legs.

"It won't hurt too badly, will it?" Lizzy asked.

"You know I'll be gentle," I answered and very slowly I inserted myself into her, a little at a time, moving in and out carefully, to make sure I would stay lubricated and would stretch her to my size as gradually as possible.

Suddenly there was a tiny pop and Lizzy made a short squeak. Then she giggled.

"That was it, wasn't it? Well," she continued to giggle, "that wasn't anything much at all to be worried about. Thank you for being so kind," and she threw her arms around my neck and gave me a big hug and kiss.

As we kissed, I began to move inside her. Lizzy didn't do much really. She seemed to be content to lie peacefully back on the pillow and experience the sensations.

I ran my hands across her body, stroking her silky hair, cupping her breasts in my hands, following the outline of her form, gently brushing my hands across her soft tummy which undulated as I moved myself inside her.

When I came, she opened her eyes and looked up at me with a searching curiosity. She reached up and held my head between her hands until I had finished and then placed her arms on my shoulders and pulled me to her.

I kissed her gently and she kissed me back. We stayed like that for several minutes.

"Thank you very much, Lizzy," I said as I pulled myself from her.

"Do you feel better, Dr. Wolper?" Lizzy asked, running her fingers across my chest, patting my chest hair and moving her hands in small circles.

"Yes. Yes, I do," I said, and I kissed her lightly on her cheek.

We lay there in silence for a half hour or so, holding each other and exchanging kisses.

"Lizzy," I finally asked. "Why did you do this?"

"Well, Dr. Wolper," she said quietly, "I'm not blind, you know. I've noticed the way you've looked at me this last month, even as heartbroken as you are over Lucy, and I just figured that we had to have this out once and for all if I was going to be able to stay here. We've a long way to travel ahead of us, now, Dr. Wolper. I just wanted you to know that there wasn't anything much for you here. That's all."

Lizzy stroked my beard and smiled.

"Oh, I enjoyed this, myself, Dr. Wolper, but I don't think I'd ever want to do it again, if you get my meaning. It's been very nice, and now it's done with. Thank you, too, Dr. Wolper, because, to tell the truth, it was an experience I never wanted to miss, and I can't imagine anyone could have been better to me."

I pressed my body against hers for the last time and gave her a long loving kiss.

"I don't know what I can ever do to repay you, Lizzy," I said.

"Well, Dr. Wolper," she smiled as she got up from the bed. "There is something."

I looked at Lizzy's marvelous figure, illuminated in the light that streamed in the window by the bed, and watched as she tugged her nightgown on top of her head and let it fall over her body.

"I think it's time to put our relationship on a more formal basis, Dr. Wolper. Now there's something that I've always wanted to be called for a name, but, of course, I've never been able to, for obvious reasons. I'd like to be called *Mrs.* Mallory from now on, which I think is a very dignified name and I feel I can take after tonight. Would you do that for me, Dr. Wolper?"

"Mrs. Mallory?" I asked.

"Mrs. Mallory," she answered. "It would mean a great deal to me, Dr. Wolper. I'm not Lizzy anymore. I'm Mrs. Elizabeth Mallory."

"Well, of course," I smiled.

"And something else, Dr. Wolper, this thing I did with you tonight, I have no regrets about it, even being the Catholic that I am, but if it's all the same to you, I'd just as soon we never discussed it again. It's our secret. Just you and me. And there's no reason to mention it further."

"Yes," I said. "I agree."

"Well, then, all is good and well, I suppose," she said with a nod of her head. "Now, if you won't be needing me for anything else tonight, I'll be going back to my room," and she turned and started out of the room. "Goodnight, Dr. Wolper," she said as she shut the door, "and pleasant dreams."

"Good night, Mrs. Mallory," I called after her, and we never did discuss the matter again.

The years have treated Elizabeth Mallory well, though she's much rounder in form these days, and I never see the magnificent long red hair in anything other than a bun, as she hustles and bustles around the house. Eyeglasses tend to obscure the rich chocolate eyes, but the skin is as pure and milk-white as ever.

24th Back to work. I am surprised that I have even considered anything else.

Could I help but involve myself in the *active* machinery? Can I look for anything else but the Operator? Not on your life. It is ridiculous to think of myself analyzing and straining for the chemical idiot that is fouling up the works when I could be finding the Master, the Ruler, the King.

And once having found him, once having found this Operator, this deposed monarch, I can set him back to ruling. I will free him, and he will rule everywhere. He will rule wherever he is placed, and, unsolicited, I should be happy to be his advisor. Modesty prevails.

On to the Operator. I am convinced of the necessity of my decision. Still, I have the uneasy feeling that I am about to charge off in search of windmills. And Boris is no Sancho Panza, that is for sure.

25th Here is a physical description of Boris. Lanky. Blondish. Shaggy hair that continually falls in his eyes like a sheepdog's. Gold-rimmed glasses. Blondish moustache. Blue eyes. This is worthless information. I promise you.

I don't think Boris likes me. I can't for the life of me figure it out. I was so certain that we would understand each other.

27th We decided on Strega tonight. The literary implications were appropriate. The combination of Bach cello suites on the phonograph and a fire in the fireplace mellowed us just short of unconsciousness.

Paul decided to drink the Strega from the bottle, so we sat on the floor and passed it between us.

"Let me tell you, Harry, buddy, about *my* first novel. The main character was a young fellow by the name of Parnash. The name means absolutely nothing. Of course, I didn't know this right off. It took me three years of fighting with the fucker to learn that he had no more idea how he got the name than I did. He led me around by the nose for three of the lousiest years of my life."

"A shame," I said, handing the bottle back to Paul.

"You're telling me. Well, I wrote the damn book, Harry. Even got it published. *Parnash in Nicosia* I called it. I'd never been to Cyprus. I made it up from a book I'd read several years before. Turns out that the book I'd read had been about Crete, not Cyprus. No one knew the difference." He passed the bottle back to me and continued.

"I buried Parnash at the end. He had his head blown off by a big Turk named Yusif. Parnash was dead. No one gave a damn. The sun dropped into the Mediterranean, and the men returned to their mosques."

I cut myself a big slab of Gruyère and leaned my back against the sofa.

"The next book I wrote," Paul continued, "was about a middle-aged man named Castleton. Amory Castleton. He was an effete Britisher living in South Africa. Three-quarters of the way through the book, I realized that it was Parnash. He talked like Parnash, dressed like Parnash, swore like Parnash. I threw the book in the trash. This is horribly depressing, Harry." Paul took the bottle from me.

I listened intently.

"So," Paul talked on, "I wrote another novel. This one was about an old Jew named Shamus, who also, it turned out, was Parnash. Book after book was Parnash. Elsie Bylo, the transsexual vamp of Saigon, was Parnash. Eleanor Roosevelt became Parnash. Chamberlain, a marvelous St. Bernard, who wanted only to lead his master down the snow-covered mountain to obtain medical attention, was, of course, Parnash. I had Chamberlain shot by errant hunters as he was crossing the Alpine Highway and immediately run over by a six-axle diesel truck fully loaded with marble. The fucker was buried in a sealed concrete vault under the Jungfrau. I think I'm going to weep, Harry."

"Parnash did not go away," I concluded.

"I could not get rid of the son of a bitch. Whomever I wrote about, it was always Parnash. We screamed at each other. We fought and waged war. Every time I sat at my typewriter, there was Parnash. He joined me for breakfast, lunch, and dinner. He greeted me when I awakened. He sang me to sleep. Then one day, I just gave up."

Paul took a long lamentful drink of Strega and sat staring at his feet in silence. He twisted the bottle so that the orange flames from the fire flashed off the yellow syrup, and then he placed his arm around my shoulder.

"Harry. Harry. Parnash and I have managed only to hold on to a fragile truce over the years," Paul said sadly. "Twenty books later, I'm still writing about Parnash. I am doomed. My life has only one last chance for redemption, Harry, and that's your book. I have learned how these characters work, Harry. I will take you step by step along the way. At the end, your Boris will plead with you to let him disappear. Your soul will be your own. I promise you."

28th The Adventures of Boris Lafkin

written by HARRY H. WOLPER

CHAPTER ONE:

In Which the Reader Is Asked to Accept as the Gospel Truth That Which Is Neither

If you really want to hear about it, and, to be perfectly honest, I don't know why the hell you would, the first thing you *don't* want to know is all the irrelevant crap about where I was born, what my lousy childhood was like, and all that Alexander Portnoy crap. If I left it all out, the only person who'd be disappointed would be my goddam mother, who'd have about two hemorrhages if she found out that I'm writing something personal and *her* whole life story isn't included. Actually I've already kind of outlined this to her, and she's already kind of let me know that it's a piece of crap. We have this unique relationship based on mutual distrust and her need for my failure. It's not exactly the kind of family situation that fosters peace of mind and inner strength of character, as my psychology textbook put it.

You see, I was born in 1941, like Dylan and Baez and John Lennon, and we spent most of our time *moving*, all over the whole goddam *United States*.

I was supposed to be this great *adjustor*, to the moving and all. And I *was* a pretty good adjustor, really. I mean, I could move all the way across the *country* and five minutes after I walked out of my new house, I could have every kid on the *block* antagonized. I didn't just *attract* hate from other kids, I *inspired* it. My whole goddam life was like that. Every night I used to expect every kid I knew to come after me with *knives*. I really did. I never knew what I had *done*.

There isn't really a hell of a lot that I can tell you about my lousy childhood. I have a lot of trouble remembering anything much about it except that I didn't particularly like it. I kept on hearing about how my childhood was supposed to be this enchanting and rapturous experience. I'll tell you something. My childhood lacked magic.

Don't get me wrong. It wasn't all bad. I read some good books and learned a hell of a lot about how to be alone. I didn't start out like that. For the first ten years or so I really tried. I even worked my ass off at school to do well. But by about ten, I more or less gave up and became an outstanding underachiever.

This wasn't all that bad really, when you think about it. It's much better than being an achiever. Everyone gives you the credit for being *able* to do the work without your ever actually having to *do* it. It's kind of like resting on your laurels. Only in my case, I hadn't even been awarded a lousy fungus, let alone a crown of laurel.

Anyway, my mother was not stupid. After twelve years of my almost total depression, she began to wonder whether something might be wrong. So she started sending me to school psychologists and psychiatrists, who confirmed her worst suspicions. I was an underachiever, and I was miserable. The two were unrelated, as far as they could tell. Further extensive treatment would be necessary. "Further" and "extensive" in this case meant three times a week at $35 an hour. It was at this point in my life, as I recall it, that my mother decided that I probably wasn't as miserable as I appeared to be. As for my underachievement, I most likely wasn't all that bright either.

"Don't push him," became the watchword of the next six years or so. "Boris," she explained, "needs to do things in terms of his own body rhythms."

Mother has always been ahead of her time.

I guess where I should begin is like about 1961, January, to be exact.

I had gotten this job in a television station in Boston. That was really weird because I had just gotten out of college with a liberal arts degree and was looking all over creation for a job. I was just about to take this job at NBC-TV in New York as what they call a logging clerk, which means working from 2:00 A.M. to 10:00 A.M. writing down when commercials run in New York City, when I got this call from a station in Boston.

I've always been fascinated by television, though it almost got me sent to the goddam electric chair. I know you'd much rather hear a graphic description of how I picked at my pimples and masturbated, with all its cosmic implications, but I thought I just might sneak in how I also almost killed this guy.

What had happened was that it was about a year after I had started working at WBOR. That's the television station in Boston I told you about. And there was this director named Manny. He was this guy about forty-five who was overweight, had a red face, and was always perspiring. He was also this real bigot, and somehow he got himself assigned to direct all these public service shows that WBOR runs at 6:00 A.M. on Sunday mornings. They have to do it to keep their license.

Anyway, it's Friday and Manny the Director is calling this crazy show called "The Our Own Show." They begin with this recording of President Kennedy saying that "here on earth, God's work must truly be *our own*." Then there's fake cheering and you see this slide of two men, one white and one black, digging a ditch together. The announcer goes into this thing about how pleased and happy WBOR is to bring this public service to Boston, and all the time there's cheering and violins playing "Auld Lang Syne." That's what gets me, the violins. If there's one thing I hate, it's violins.

So today there's this really cool-ass black guest, and Manny the Director is calling this great show, great shots and all. Only that's what the viewer sees. In the booth, where I'm working the audio, he's calling the guy a black bastard and a nigger, and everyone's loving it. I could hardly believe it. The show keeps getting better and better, and Manny the Director gets worse and worse. He really *hates* blacks. It gets so bad that I can't concentrate on the sound or anything, and I'm just about to do something about it when the phone rings. It's my goddam mother.

"Mother, can I call you back? I'm in the middle of a show."

"Boris, this is your mother. Listen, do you have a minute?"

"Mother, for God's sake, I'm right in the *middle* of a *show*."

"Because I've got to talk to you. Are you busy?"

It must have been the connection.

"Jesus Christ Almighty, Mother. I'm in the *middle of a show*."

"You are. Well, just listen to me with one ear. I'll just be a *minute*."

"All right. Go ahead. What is it?"

"I'm worried, Boris. There's something that's not quite right."

"What's that, Mother?"

"Well, for one thing, my period's irregular, which I'm absolutely sure means that I'm pregnant again, and you know that with your father's problem it couldn't have been him. And it's certainly not anyone else. So I can't figure out who it might be. Then Ozzie got all upset because I slapped him when he said that God did it, and now he's up on the roof and wants to kill himself. And no sooner does your Uncle Eli find out than he dresses himself up in black like he's going to a funeral. Remember Brenda, the nice young girl from Radcliffe who was supposed to marry you, well she called up to say that if I'm pregnant it's all off, and you should see what she's been going out with. And then there's Seymour. I didn't want to tell you this until I saw you, but I called Florida last night long distance and Seymour shot himself and now Muriel's just beside herself. And as if that isn't enough, your sister's having this mystic nervous breakdown. Why she can't go crazy like any normal human being without all the philosophical *implications* is something I will never know, Boris."

"I don't have a father, Mother."

"That's what I called about. Somebody killed him last night while Smerdyakov was having an epileptic fit, and remember the 3,000 rubles that he always kept under his pillow, well we can't find them anymore. I just don't know what I'm going to do, Boris. I think the authorities think that *you* took the money, and Ivan and Alyosha are willing to help you, but they can't do it all themselves. Boris, are you listening?"

Harry, don't you think you're getting just a little heavy on the plot? I mean, I like Salinger, Roth, and Dostoevsky, but not all *together*.

"Yes, Mother, I'm listening. But I've never had a father."

"Maybe if you called more often. I worry that something's happened to you. You could be in *Siberia* for all I know."

"Mother, listen, could I call you back? Things are kind of hectic here."

"Normally, I would say yes, Boris. Normally. But you never *call* back. Never. And I don't think that's nice at all. Not one *bit*. I asked you particularly to be sure the last time—"

"Mother, for Chrissake, please! Look I'm hanging up. I'll call you back in twenty minutes. I swear I will."

"Boris, your father has this rash on his schlong."

"I thought you said he was dead."

"Boris, I honestly think you don't listen to a *thing* I say."

"Mother, is it possible, is it possible, is it just humanly possible that in one short simple sentence you could tell me why you called?"

"I don't think you're being funny. Not one bit."

"Who's *laughing?* Mother, *why did you call*!"

"I've been worried to death about you. Everyone around is killing himself or having mystic nervous breakdowns or being murdered, Ronnie Altman just got accepted to Columbia graduate school, and you just *sit*. Are you sure you're all right?"

"Yes, mother."

"Are you *sure*? You're *sure* you're all right? You can tell me—"

"Mother, I am *all right*. Really I am. Honestly. I just haven't felt much like *doing* anything lately."

"Well, if you say so."

"I say so. I'm okay. I'll call you back."

"Boris? Do you love your mother?"

"Yes, Mother. I do."

"And do you feel horribly guilty about everything in your whole life, and that it's existential, mystic, meaningless, and I'm to blame?"

"Yes, Mother."

"You want to hear all about my hysterectomy?"

"Some other time, Mother. I'm hanging up now. Good-bye."

Thank you, Harry. Thank you.

What you have to picture is that during this whole insane phone call, all hell is breaking loose with Manny the Director. The studio audience can't see it, but he's cutting back and forth between the guest and this Tarzan movie that's racked up for the late flick, and everybody in the control room is *dying* with laughter. This guy on the show, the black, is telling how he had his legs beaten with chains by the KKK, which is why he can't walk anymore, and Manny the Director just keeps pouring on the old red-neck juice. It finally reaches a point where, by the time I hang up on my mother, the only thing I want to do is puke. I just want to puke all over the whole goddam place, but especially on Manny. So I figure, what the hell, the show's on tape, and, anyway, I've had it with this screwy place. I can't take one more minute.

So I get up nice and slowly and grab the fire ax off the wall and run to the studio, with Manny right behind me. I yank off the mike that's around Bob Fisher, the moderator, and I tell the audience in the studio what a goddam *fraud* the whole *show* is. Now, you've got to picture this. Here I am, screaming about what a bastard Manny the Director is and turning around in circles with the ax to keep people away, and the next thing I know it feels like the ax has *hit* something, and then I see a red stain start to appear on Manny's crotch. Next thing I know, Manny's hand reaches through the rip in his trousers and emerges with his prick. He holds it up in front of his eyes and studies it real carefully with this kind of dazed expression.

"Jesus Christ," I say. "Jesus H. Christ."

Then the dumb audience starts applauding. There's blood all over the goddam place, and Manny staggers a few steps and then sort of slumps to the floor.

That's how I ended up in the crummy jail.

March

1st A voyeur. Maybe I am a voyeur.

If I had not become a biologist, I am certain I would have become a Peeping Tom (and a good one), for the thrill I get is not so much from what I am seeing in my microscope as from knowing that I am not *supposed* to be seeing it. I wonder whether this is not true of half the scientists in the world. How happy they would be if they could look down on the pavement on their way to the store and see, not a drop of blood, but enormous reticulocytes studded with large clumps of ribosomes. In a week they would be at keyholes.

I cannot walk by a microscope without a glance.

I look first for the centriole. It has just become two. I am happy. I have caught the prophase. I am reminded of the time I found myself on the other side of a thin hotel wall, mumblings coming to my ear, and suddenly I realize that, on the other side, their heads to my head, are a man and a woman in bed. I strain to hear the words. I get only the tone, the sound, the feeling. I ask and ask. They are married, yes, no? They are going to make love? They are making love? She is from the bar? He is a salesman? They are a young couple? I hear the bed begin to squeak. One squeak. Then silence. Then there is another squeak, followed by another, and another, and another. Now they are banging. The noise is louder. The mumblings are groans and come between the squeaks. I am going crazy. They are going crazy. Who can sleep like this? I am not too old to have my heart racing after itself, my throat dry, my mind running a hundred pictures a second in front of my eyes. The bed is not squeaking. It is pounding, fast and hard. Bang! Bang! I cannot stand it. I am in pain. Come! I shout. Come! Come! And I hear a female voice shout back. Yes! Yes! Suddenly there is silence. I hear some mumbling. They have heard me. The bed is being moved. I hear the mattress being dropped on the floor. There is silence for the rest of the night.

And so it is with my microscopes. I can only imagine what they say to each other, these cells, whether they are in ecstasy, how they feel. There I heard but could not see. Here I see but cannot hear. It is equally frustrating.

Astral rays spoke to the centriole. Spindle fibers form and I have my twin stars, my amphiaster, my metaphase.

The split has not occurred. I am glued to the microscope. I have seen, maybe a thousand times, the mitosis, but each time is more beautiful than the last. There are no wrong keyholes here where women expose rolls of fatty flesh and sagging overworked breasts. There is always perfection, the first and perfect bibreasted, birumped, bilegged, bisymmetrical being that starts my heart racing ahead of my mind. I watch the chromosomes pair closely, almost touching each other.

The nucleolus has disappeared. Chromatin threads have appeared, the genonemes. Eight minutes have passed. Maybe ten. They go further apart, each chromosome, now two, leaving its mate. Anaphase passes and the end comes. There is telophase. Slowly they consolidate, one on one side, one on the other. There is a centrosome for each.

And new nuclei. Two hours are gone. There is an ache in the back of my neck. My shoulders hurt.

The grand jury has indicted Boris for attempted murder. He was not surprised.

The spindle fibers are gone. Ten hours, twelve hours, and the vegetative cell is formed. I am not sure this is asexual after all. I am exhausted. I am beginning to feel my headache come back. I have headaches too often now. Aspirin does not help. It is Arnold. He has worried me. It will be done next week.

I must continue. Boris is in jail, feet propped up. Howard Woodhouse, a young Negro boy, a head of hair almost as large as his head, thick glasses and a pendant hanging from his neck on a string of rawhide, is his cellmate. Boris talks.

The Adventures of Boris Lafkin

written by HARRY H. WOLPER

CHAPTER TWO:

How It Is Demonstrated to Our Hero
That Pettifoggery Is Just Not Worth It

In eleventh grade I became a hood, you know, with my hair in a ducktail. I wore a lot of T-shirts with the sleeves rolled up to my hairy armpits, and black denims and engineer boots and all. I don't know why. I traded in this new car my mother bought me for my sweet-sixteen birthday, as she called it, for a Harley motorcycle, one of those big 1200 cc jobs, which handles like a Mack truck and is about as useful for a social life.

I used to go around with this gang of retards called the Heavenly Hosts, and mumble a lot, and complain about how James Dean was all there was and now there was nothing. That's how I kind of continued my reputation as the school's outstanding underachiever. I just used to ride around on my bike, telling everybody that they bugged me, and bumming a lot of weeds until I damn near got TB.

In twelfth grade I metamorphosed. I heard Corso read in this cellar in the Village. He had just come back with Mort Sahl from the Hungry i, and on the spot I gave up my bike for death. I developed this thing about death. It was very important to me. I bought a lot of black turtle necks, lived in this loft in the Village for the summer, and wrote whole goddam *books* about death. I was supposed to be a real beatnik, except to my mother, who spent half of her time telling me that it was nothing to worry about because I was just going through this adolescent identity crisis, which was supposed to have resolved itself about ten years ago, and the other half of her time reading this book by Gesell. Every time I would do something, like sit in the living room and read *Lady Chatterly's Lover* while my mother was having important company, she would run for this goddam Gesell book and then start pointing passages out to her guests and smiling. That was before tranquilizers.

Actually, I guess I damn near had my mother up a *wall* most of the time. She'd start talking about Presley, and I'd be reading Ferlinghetti. So she'd devote all this time to Ferlinghetti, so she could *talk* to me, and I was into Ravi Shankar and *Ramparts*. I was supposed to outgrow all these things and find myself by the time I left college, which means that by now I'm supposed to be married to some nice normal girl, have two kids, and be working as a junior executive for the phone company. I'm still waiting.

My brother Seth had it even worse than I did because he was a post-Sputnik pupil like at the beginning of all this school crap about *process* goals and *discovery* learning. I think school messed him up a lot more than me, because he had to *discover*, while I only had to learn. Like he had to *initiate* his learning experiences about all kinds of screwy things like associative and commutative properties of addition. Me they just *told* that 2 and 2 are 4, and, if I didn't like it, I could add them on paper or use my fingers or something. Seth had to understand the *philosophy* behind it.

If you want to hear something that'll really blow your mind wide open, one day Seth comes home and he tells me that a triangle, now get this, a regular ordinary triangle, is like the union of sets of points on three noncoplanar half-planes or something like that. Not only that, but he tells me that triangles don't really even exist, and I know that *that's* a goddam lie because I've seen them, and if they had only drawn three simple lines on the blackboard like they did for me in school, he would have known it too. What was freaky was that I couldn't even *tell* him that, because I'm talking about straight lines and angles and all, and he's talking about the intersection of complementary subsets of rays. We couldn't even have a lousy goddam *conversation*. At least with me the schools only screwed me up with life and the world. I could still talk to *people*, because we all had this same lousy educational *heritage*. They made Seth into this goddam *zombie*. He couldn't even talk to his own brother.

I don't know why I'm telling you all this except that in comparison to real life, jail isn't all that bad. The guards are kind of queer, like they get this big charge out of watching you get undressed or use the pot, but you get used to that after a while. The food is really bad news, and there's this horrible smell of disinfectant all the time, but you get used to that, too. You can get used to just about anything, I've found. Anyway, I got a lot of reading done, and, for the most part, everybody left me pretty much alone.

About the second week I was there (it was after the grand jury had indicted me for attempted murder) I got this dude, Howard Woodhouse, for a cell mate. Man, was he spaced out of his mind. I don't know what he had been on before he got there, but it sure as hell wasn't chocolate bars. He was really *weird*. We got to know each other, kind of. He was one of those militant black-power guys, a Black Panther, and we used to get into some pretty heady stuff about black people using violence, as he put it, *therapeutically*. He was for *preventative violence*. *Nonviolent rape*, he called it. I hope you don't mind if I don't go into any great *detail* about what all it was he *said*, first because I don't really remember it too much, and second because if there's one thing I can't stand, it's filling up a story with all kinds of socially significant crap.

Anyway, Howard had this crazy thing going with the guard on our cell block, whom he kept calling different names. One day he'd call him The Commander, and the next day The Interlocutor. Late at night the two of them would stand there on opposite sides of the bars and have these far-out discussions. Howard would drone something like, "There will be a full freedom when it will be just the same to live or not to live. That's the goal, man."

And The Interlocutor would groan back, "Man fears death because he loves life, and that's determined by nature."

"That's a crock of shit," and Howard's black hands would tighten around the bars and his neck muscles would bulge out of his shirt. "Life is pain, life is terror, and man is unhappy. Man loves pain and terror. Some day there will be a new life, a new man, and it will be the same to live and not to live."

"But, my dear Kirillov," The Interlocutor would chant, "if it will be just the same living or not living, we will all kill each other."

"No matter. We will kill deception. Everyone who wants the supreme freedom must dare to kill. There is no freedom beyond; that is all, and there is nothing beyond."

"But," The Interlocutor would challenge, "there have been thousands of killings every day. Is that not true, Kirillov, my friend?"

"But not to kill fear. Not to secure freedom of the mind."

They would be out of sight like this for maybe an hour. Then they would go through the same exact thing all over again from the beginning, word for word, only they would switch parts. I told you that Howard was a goddam *weirdo.*

My lawyer is Dirty Al Petrucci, who's a genius on statutory rape cases but not much else. He's one of these Harvard Law School graduates who somehow missed the point of Harvard. He's almost bald at the age of thirty-five, and he wears no shirt, has a 1940-type tie tatooed on his chest, and sports a blue pin-striped double-breasted suit of the same vintage to go with his sandals, which expose the filthiest toenails I have ever seen. He also reeks of cigars about 105 percent of the time. He calls me B, only he says it the way my mother would, like, if I had only *applied* myself, I could have been A.

"B, m'boy, we're pleading insanity."

"How the hell's anybody going to *tell?*"

"Amusement, m'lad, amusement. You have to amuse a fuckin' jury. A few fuckin' anecdotes, Biblical references, some fuckin' psychiatric testimony, blood-stained exhibits, color photos, and you're a free fuckin' man."

"Dirty Al, let me ask you something. Do you think I really should be, free I mean?"

"Why the hell not?"

"Well, I mean, I did *almost kill* the lousy guy. Isn't it *just* that I should be punished?" Dirty Al stared at me in confusion.

"Just. You know. Just, like in justice?" I asked.

"I'm not getting you, B, m'boy. Try another fuckin' wavelength."

"Justice, Dirty Al. You've had to have heard of it, like at Harvard or maybe in court."

"I don't think so. What fuckin' law is it? It isn't one of those fuckin' ass-hole Bill of Rights jobs is it?"

"Well, it is, kind of."

"B, m'boy, you know what my fuckin' trouble is. I didn't specialize. I should have specialized. Then I'd be right up there with all this new fuckin' stuff. As it is, the field's just too damn big."

"Al, you think I should plead guilty or something to show that I'm sorry?"

"B, m'boy, don't you worry. If there's anything in that fuckin' justice law that'll help you out, I'll bone up on it over the weekend. Have it all worked out by the fuckin' trial Monday morning."

It had been a damn long time since I had been outside. It had been summer when I returned from the grand jury thing. Now, when the two court cops came to take me for the trial, I was surprised to see that I had kind of interrupted the middle of autumn. The air was this real dry cool, and the leaves were moving on the trees, gamboge yellow, cadmium orange, and cochineal red on top of malachite green. The sky was this lapis lazuli without—

Harry, hold it, baby.

even a clue of a cloud—

Harry, cool it. Please.

anywhere.

"What, Boris?"

What's lapis lazuli?

"It's a stone, Boris, sodium, aluminum, calcium, sulfur, silicon—"

I'm with you Harry. But what goddam *color* is it?

"Sky blue."

Thanks. It sounds like we're carving Boston out of the Andes.

"Sorry, Boris."

No, that's okay. It's okay. Hang in there, Harry.

When I get into the courtroom, it's very crowded. Dirty Al is there, and he is an angel to me. He has, however, not been able to find the Bill of Rights. He has looked under both *B* and *R*. He is superfine sorry, he says, but he has good news for me nevertheless. We may not go to trial after all. A meeting has been arranged in the judge's chamber to plea bargain. He's going to try for *molliter manus imposuit*. I ask Al what this means, but he doesn't get a chance to tell me because the prosecutor comes over to him. The prosecutor is a short fat bald man with a thin mustache and a pin on the lapel of his checkered jacket that says "Reinstitute Capital Punishment."

The three of us go through doors in the back of the courtroom into a dark office where Judge O'Brien is sitting smoking a cigar. He has his stocking feet up on the desk and is wearing a T-shirt and a yellow plastic sun visor.

"Ay, *Paesan*!" Judge O'Brien shouts at the prosecutor, whose name is Mort Goldman.

"*Ciao*!" replies Mort. Mort then goes over to the judge, embraces him, and kisses him on both cheeks.

"*Paesan*!" Judge O'Brien smiles at Dirty Al, who repeats the hugging and kissing.

"*Come va?*" asks Al.

"*Bene, bene,*" smiles O'Brien. "*Come sta?*"

"*Sto molto meglio,*" Al says. "So what's new, Pat?"

"New? *Nu?*" says Judge O'Brien. "Who knows from new? A little this. A little that. That restaurant you sent me to last week didn't help, gonif."

"So. Sue me," Al grins.

"Who's this?" O'Brien looks over at me.

"The defendant," Al tells him. "Lafkin."

"So who's the other shmuck?" Judge O'Brien asks.

"That's what I've come to see you about," a round, red-faced perspiring man on the other side of the room says. It's Manny the Director.

"I represent both Mr. Goodman and the state, your honor," Mort says. "Mr. Goodman is here in an *in rem* proceeding to demand the return of his penis."

"Yes," Manny begins," I was wondering whether if I promise to make myself available to the court I might—"

"Absolutely not!" Al shouts. "Not until my motion to suppress is heard."

"Suppress—" Manny starts.

"Look," Judge O'Brien says. "This evidence can be inspected in my chambers at any time," and he takes a cloth off a large jar beside him in which, floating in ice, is, sure enough, Manny's penis.

"Hey!" says Manny. "That's my—"

"I object!" Al interrupts. "We consider that the plaintiff's civil suit is *volenti non fit injuria* and in anticipation of damages to be paid to *my* client, we have garnisheed the plaintiff's penis."

"*Garnished* my—" Manny starts again.

"Yes," Mort interrupts, "but we're asking for custody of the plaintiff's penis *pendente lite.*"

"And I'm asking for a TRO to prevent that," Al snaps.

"Then we'll ask for discovery and disclosure," Mort snaps back.

"Not in a case of *injuria sine damno,* you won't!" Al shouts.

"*Damnum absque injuria!*" Mort shouts back.

"*Brutum fulmen!*"

"*Carpe diem, quam minimum credula postero!*"

"*Et cum spiritu tuo!*"

"*Dominus vobiscum!*"

"*Sum es est, sumis estis sunt!*"

"*Gloria in Excelsis Deo!*"

"*Shmuck!*"

"*Putz!*"

"So—" Al turns to the judge, "what was wrong with the restaurant?"

"Everything but the waitress," Judge O'Brien chomps on his cigar, "who, by the way, had the biggest knockers I've seen in twenty years."

"Listen," Mort says. "You think *she's* got big knockers. You should see the broad in the front of the courtroom."

"Ayyyy," sneers Al. "Did you see the cunt on that *Playboy* centerfold this month? She could take a fuckin' baseball bat."

"So," Mort grins, "did you stick the waitress, Pat?"

"You're goddam right I did," Judge O'Brien says and starts to clip his nails. "I stuck her in every hole she had, and I mean *every* hole. Took me so long I almost missed my ball game. What's with you, Lafkin?"

"I—"

"Don't answer," Al presses his hand over my mouth. "We've got a motion to squash, your honor."

"Denied," the judge answers.

"Does that mean that—" I start to ask Al.

"How about our plea in abatement?"

"I'm considering it," O'Brien says.

I look hopefully at Al. Al does not look back.

"It's our position," Al continues, "that this case is clearly *in pari delicto potior est condito defendentis.*"

"Bullshit!" Mort says. "This is the clearest example of *scienter* I've ever encountered!"

"*Scienter!*" Al shouts. "*Scienter!* Look at this man!" and Al squeezes my cheeks between his thick hand and jerks my head around to face the judge. "Does this look like *scienter* to you, your honor!"

"I wonder if—" I mumble under Al's hand.

"Don't say a word," and Al jerks my head back where it came from. "You open your mouth and you could get the chair. I'll do the talking. Mort, we're invoking M'Naghten."

"M'Naghten!" Mort says. "M'Naghten! This is *mens rea,* and that's all there is to it."

"And," Al keeps going, "we're also invoking the Durham Rule."

"Do you know what that means for your client?" Mort says.

"I know full well what that means for my client," Al assures him.

"I don't know what it—" I attempt.

"And my client is willing to accept the consequences."

"Maybe," Manny says, "I could just kind of *borrow* my—"

"What consequences?" I ask.

"My client is impervious to pain," Al says.

"Or maybe if I posted bail for it then I could—" Manny tries.

"You know," the judge says to Manny, "the way you're kvetching over this lousy organ, I have half a mind just to flush the damn—"

"No! No! Please!" Manny cries out.

"Your honor," Mort says. "My client is willing to accept his penis *sub modo.*"

"What do they do to—" Manny starts to ask.

"You'll have to drop your *ex delicto*," Al tells Mort.

"I'm not sure my client will agree to that," Mort answers and turns to Manny. "Do you want to drop your *ex delicto?*"

"Do I have to do it here with everyone—"

"You don't have to do anything you don't want to do," Mort assures his client.

"Then I'm not doing anything. There!" Manny says in frustration.

"Oh, shut up!" Al says. "You can't even prove the penis is yours."

"I can prove I don't have one," Manny grumbles half to himself.

"So what!" Al tells him. "You think you're the only one in this world without a penis! Half the humans on this earth don't have a penis. You got your name on it or something?"

"No," Manny says.

"So there!" Al tells him. Then he turns back to Mort. "Look," he says. "I'll tell you what. If your client will agree to a subpoena *duces tecum*, I'll agree to release the penis *sub modo*."

"I don't see any reason for my client to undergo the embarrassment of a *duces tecum*. You can keep the goddam penis. The hell with it!"

"Hey!" says Manny. "I want my penis!"

"You want a *duces tecum?*" Mort shouts in Manny's face. "A *duces tecum!* Is a lousy goddam penis *worth* that? Is it?"

Manny shifts uncomfortably in his chair.

"No," he says quietly, "I guess not."

"Trust me," Mort says. "It just isn't worth it. So," he turns to Judge O'Brien, "what was the score?"

"The Yankees blew it in the ninth," O'Brien grumbles. "Kubek threw a double-play ball two feet over Richardson's head, and that was the game."

"There's never going to be another shortstop like Rizzuto," Al says.

"Bullshit," Mort says. "Pee Wee Reese could run circles around Rizzuto."

"And Marty Marion could run circles around them both," O'Brien says.

"Reese! Marion!" Al shouts. "You guys have got to be kidding. They couldn't wear Rizzuto's jockstrap."

"There isn't a player alive or dead who could throw from the hole like Marion," O'Brien says.

"Aw, come *on*," Al says. "Marion couldn't hit his weight. How can you take him seriously? He was *half* a player!"

"Ratshit!" O'Brien says. "You never would have *heard* of Reese or Rizzuto if they hadn't played in New York. It was all media hype. New York hype!"

"Reese was hype?" Mort is enraged. "Reese was hype! Pee Wee Reese! Pee Wee Reese was hype! You have *got* to be kidding! You dopes couldn't tell a great baseball player if he *sat* on you! We'll just see what the stats look like." Mort squints his eyes and sneers. "We'll just see," he says very slowly. "And that's not all. I'm going all the way on this *actus reus*. I'm throwing the book at Lafkin."

"So what!" Al says. "Throw it. See if he cares."

"Wait a minute—" I start.

"You keep quiet, young man," the judge tells me, "or I'll have you removed."

"But I didn't know—" I try.

"*Ignorant non curat lex!*" the judge snaps at me.

"*Sic tuo utero ut alienium non laedas,*" Mort tells me.

"What the hell does *that* mean?" I ask.

"Roughly translated," Mort says, "it means that you should use your own goddam prick and not chop off others, tort-feasor!"

"Tort-feasor!" the judge barks at me.

"Tort-feasor?" Al comes to my defense.

"Tort-feasor! Tort-feasor! Tort-feasor!" Mort and the judge chant. Then suddenly the judge turns to Al.

"Hey, you know," he says, "I saw this film last week. You know what those fuckin' Turks do to their tort-feasors? Someone steals and they chop off his hands. Someone escapes from jail and they chop off his legs. You murder someone and you get your head chopped off. And not right away, either," he continues, looking right at me. "First they torture the shit out of you. They don't fuck around over there, Lafkin. It's an eye for an eye and a tooth for a tooth, and you didn't poke out anyone's *eye, either*. What about *nolo contendere?*" he asks Al.

"No way!" Al says. "I want the entire charge *nol*ed, plain and simple. Otherwise my client is willing to accept the consequences of his actions. Send him up for life. Torture him. Chop off what you want. My client is ready!"

That just about does it for me.

"Now, just *wait a minute!*" I shout. "I've had it! You guys are crazy! You're lunatics! I've been sitting here for fifteen minutes and I haven't understood a goddam word you've said. You're out of your fucking heads! Give the man back his fucking dick, will you! And I want another attorney. You people are loonies, I'm telling you. You're a bunch of fucking sadistic sexist incompetent lunatics!"

Well, Mort, Al, and the judge just look at me in silence for a minute. Then finally the judge talks.

"*Non compos mentis,*" he shakes his head.

"*Non compos mentis,* " Mort repeats.

"*Gaudeamus igitur,*" Al agrees with a smile.

The judge pushes a button on his desk and two guards come in. They stand on either side of me.

"It's a *non compos mentis schtick*," the judge tells the guards, who nod their heads as though this is a very common occurrence for them.

"So," Al says to Mort as they start to leave, "you want to try to get in some golf tomorrow?"

"Sounds good to me," Mort says. "Why don't you tell Ellen to come over with the kids and we'll have some lunch first. You want to join us, Pat?" Mort turns to the judge.

"Love to," O'Brien says as he finishes putting on his shirt and tie.

"Bring Katherine."

"I'll ask her," the judge says. "She's been meaning to get together with the girls for a while."

"Marvelous," Mort says, and the three of them leave the room.

Then Manny gets up very slowly. He stops in front of the desk and looks longingly at the uncovered jar in the middle of O'Brien's desk, then at the guards, and finally, reluctantly, he starts from the room. Just before he goes out the door, he stops and turns to me.

"Thanks for trying to get me back my dick," he says.

"Least I could do," I tell him.

And then the guards lead me off to this progressive nuthouse. It was the first decent thing that happened to me in my whole lousy goddam life.

Harry, wait a minute. Can I talk to you for a minute? Harry? For chrissake, Harry, answer me, will you?

2nd "How's your weltschmerz today, Harry?"

All right, Boris, How's your zeitgeist?

"I was going to talk to you about it yesterday when you stopped writing. I think you've been reading too much Kafka, Harry. I get this overwhelming feeling of *déjà vu*, if you know what I mean."

Well, Boris, this is very important, our rites of passage, the bewildering legalistic and corporate mumbo jumbo a young man like yourself must contend with before he can enter society.

"Big deal."

It's an important point, Boris.

"No doubt. But you do a lousy job of it, Harry."

Boris, tell me. What do you want?

"What I want, Harry, what I really want is one easy-on religious experience. Nothing freaky or complicated or fake. Just a simple ordinary religious experience."

There's no plot.

"Fine. Well, Harry, write the book. Just write it. I asked for one lousy religious experience, nothing big, because that's what I need, Harry. I wouldn't ask for it if I didn't need it. If you don't want to give it to me, that's your business. I won't bug you about it. It's your goddam book. You go ahead and write it."

Is that a concession?

"Harry, baby, that's what's called 'cooling it.'"

Boris, sometimes you scare the hell out of me.

"Well, don't let it get to you, Harry. I figure that the way we're both going now, by the time the book's about half done, we'll have fucked up each other so badly that it won't make much difference one way or the other. We're going to break new ground in intelligent dialogue, Harry. In about three chapters, we'll just sit and let our lousy brains *drip* on each other. Love you, Harry, baby."

5th So what. So I'm destined to be a clown, to stumble through life with a red nose and wisps of white hair sticking out from my temples, a fool. I did *not* turn down Mr. Gibson and his girl. I didn't even think that they were plotting, that they were after the mad abortionist.

I had set up the back room of the laboratory with a white sheet on the table, and, after the usual inquiries, I told her to go into the room and undress. I thought nothing of the operation. It was to be reflex. I expected nothing unusual.

When I entered the room, I was startled. No, I was shocked. Amazed. I cannot describe it. I can't remember how long it's been since I've seen the body of a young naked girl.

She stood in the middle of the room, her underpants at her feet, the owner of a flawless body, as only a child can have, a firm, trim, round, enthusiastic body that sent me back thirty years to Lucy, to my own children, forty years to my own youth.

I must have looked enormously stupid, standing still, facing the girl in silence. I tried one expression after another, while I fought to move my eyes from her breasts, using every smile and nod that came to mind in an attempt (I am sure was totally unsuccessful) to hide my passion. Yes, it was passion. I am sure now.

I do not know how long I stood there. I remember that I quickly rehearsed what I would say, how important it was to me that my next words came out with the right tone, professional detachment, a lack of involvement. I settled for a preemptive mumbled, "Good. Sit on the edge of the table," that ended with an adolescent squeak. I turned quickly to get my instruments and look involved in something that a sixty-nine year old man might be properly concerned about.

Cathy started to talk. I started to work. Horace started to vomit. For ten minutes we continued like this. The pain was terrible for the child. I could tell that. There was blood, much blood, but it was only from the scraping. I was careful not to cut. Horace threw up, maybe a dozen times, each time swearing with more conviction than the last that he would never touch another woman. Cathy talked. She was born in New Jersey. Her father was born in Philadelphia. She received an A on a report in third grade. It was on the muskrat. She played Mother Bunny in the sixth-grade play. She did not like broccoli. Or salted butter. The speed of her talk increased with the pain. Toward the end she broke into a gasping fast flow of words.

"I don't think much about the world, like wars and people dying, and I'm going to die, because I can't stand it, and I mustn't think about it with all the beautiful places where there are leaves and things, and sometimes I feel bad that I'm not involved, but people turn me off if they don't think the same kind of things that I think, like about people and music which I really like, and that's what I'll think about music, like good music with guitars or symphonies, but I don't think Bach wrote any symphonies, which is okay anyway, though mostly I like tunes and melodies, because it's easier for me to remember music that way, like Bartók I like because I have a tune to remember, God I can't stand it, but I know it's worse if I think about it, but I can't help thinking, and I know I am never going to make love with another man as long as I live so help me God I will not even look at another man."

She screamed and passed out. Horace stood at the sink, bracing himself with the spigot handles and vomiting. I continued to work, perspiring, but I could feel the softness of her womb through my tools. They slid now easily and quietly. Her sex was congenial, and I inserted my instruments, removed my instruments, cleaned my instruments with the thought only of my bed, with the idea of waking up with this girl next to me, with this girl's head next to mine, with her body resting against me. Where had all these thoughts and feelings been buried? Where had they hidden for so long only to burst forth now? I did not care about the police, about the trials and the prisons. I cared only that I should not harm this girl, that I should bring this girl through the operation, healthy and free. And if she loved me for that, if she could tell the care I gave her . . .

I expected the fish smells that always accompany the operation. There were none. I expected the gray flesh. It was pink. I expected shade and shadows, but I saw before me only white and red, turning in circles before my eyes.

I looked at her face, still and unconscious. It did not occur to me that she could ever be dead, that she could ever die. I thought only of her life, of her by my side, of her warmth and her voice rambling on so quickly in such pain, of my own sex now alert and anxious for activity.

Horace stood still at the sink. He was crying and mumbling "Oh, man, oh, man, oh, man," over and over to himself.

And then it was there. First the marble, a clump of pink and brown cells, and then, how could I have guessed it (I almost missed it) a yellow dot, not much larger than a grain of pollen, a bright round yellow seed, a fresh egg. I grabbed for my hand lens. How long have I waited for something like this? And now, looking through my glass, I could hardly accept what my eyes were seeing. It was a zygote. It had been fertilized. It could not be more than twenty-four hours old, if that. This girl was screwing this morning.

I did not know what to do first. I ran into my lab and dropped the fertilized egg into a 90 percent suspension of glycerol, then raced over to the refrigerator and placed it on a shelf inside. The temperature was 9° Centigrade. I went back into the room and put smelling salts next to the girl's nose. She stirred. I sat her up.

"You are done. You must leave. I have much to do."

She stood up and tried to maintain her balance. She staggered over to the sink and pushed Horace away just in time to vomit. Horace stood on the side, his back braced against the wall, his hands over his eyes.

Looking at the naked backside of the girl as she bent over the sink, her small behind extended toward me, I wanted to bundle her off to bed. I wanted to step up to her, to turn her around, to hold her to me. I would only frighten her. I knew. And I also wanted her to leave. I wanted her friend to leave. I wanted to get to my egg (now I called it mine) before it was too late. There was much work ahead of me.

Cathy stopped throwing up and stepped back from the sink. She turned toward me.

"Am I all right?"

"You are all right," I told her.

"Will I be able to have children again?"

"Yes."

She looked down and saw the blood, which had streaked the insides of her legs.

"I need a towel."

I gave her one and she wet it. Then she handed it to me.

"Would you please? I don't think I can."

She sat up on the table. I watched her walk over and followed behind her. I placed one hand on the outside of her leg and began to clean the inside of her thigh. I looked unhappily at the hardness of my flesh next to hers. I moved to the other leg and continued. My hand brushed against her pubis as I wiped. Its warmth on the back of my hand sent chills down my spine to the very bottom of my testicles, a route my feelings have not travelled in a long time. My penis was erect. I crossed my arms over my laboratory coat.

"You must get dressed," I reached down and gave her her underpants. "Can you manage?"

"Yes. But it hurts. It really hurts."

I went over to the sink and came back with some codeine, penicillin, and a glass of water.

"Take these tablets. And here are some more. Take one white one and one blue one every four hours until tomorrow night. Then continue with the white ones, two a day for the rest of the week. Do you understand?"

She nodded yes. I turned to Horace.

"Why don't we wait outside." He followed me out. Between gasps he thanked me, though I'm not certain he knew for what.

With her clothes on, Cathy seemed a much older girl. I was surprised when she appeared a few minutes later.

"I would like to offer you some coffee, but there is something I must do immediately." I showed them to the door.

Cathy turned to me. She was holding up Horace, who was still gagging. She stood at the door silently for a moment and looked very deeply and quietly into my eyes. She understood. I knew she did. Maybe it was not so unreasonable a thought after all. It was the first time we had looked at each other's faces since she first arrived, and then we did not see each other. She had a slight freckled nose and a barely noticeable blond down that touched the sides of her cheeks. Her mouth was small, and she began to move it as though she were going to ask me a question, but she said nothing.

Maybe she was going to ask if she should come back. Maybe I wanted to ask her to come back, some bright, sunny day. But who wants to see an old man who has brought so much pain? That didn't seem to matter to her. There was no fear or pain when she looked at me. I could feel her holding me with her eyes. I started to smile.

"Thank you, Dr. Wolper. I had no idea it would be like this."

"Neither did I," and I slowly shut the door behind them. Then I raced for the refrigerator.

6th If I were to make a guess, I would say that I will not be able to straighten my back for the rest of my life. I have sat crouched in my refrigerator for twenty-four hours, and now I have done it. Every nucleus in every cell of Cathy's egg is now from Lucy. She has been cloned. I have transplanted, possibly, a hundred nuclei from Lucy's culture into Cathy's tiny embryo (can I really call it that). Now I must wait.

I have never been particularly successful with a scalpel and sutures, perhaps because I was never particularly happy about opening up my friends. I have no reason to believe that I will be any more successful burning out nuclei with radiation and transplanting with my microsurgical toys. The nuclei are transplanted, but I do not know whether the cloning will take. The egg has been put in my glass womb, but I have no way of knowing whether it will stay alive, and, if it does, whether it will grow. Perhaps I should have implanted it in one of my bunnies first.

From where I sit now, I can see my dot suspended in a pink soup of amino acids and dripping hormones, Harry Wolper's magic glass placenta. My yellow dot is surrounded by plastic chorion, a cellophane allantoic cavity, nylon coelom and a chemical yolk. The temperature is 37°C. It should be thawed by now. The oxygen is bubbling away. I wonder whether my seed enjoys its bell jar. I don't know. Can a dot be happy?

7th It makes no sense to me, but I am reborn. My loins are reawakened. I cannot go for a walk without looking at the girls' legs and tummies, at their breasts and hips. I am fascinated by their backsides. There has been a major evolutionary change in the last fifty years. Believe me. Young women have lost the breadth of the behind. It is not just the slacks, the bell-bottoms, and the dungarees. It's the flesh inside them. The female behind, by some wondrous adaptive process at the end of half a century of being fondled, has become smaller, rounder, better turned, firmer, and, when seen from the profile, has lost that old dented shoe-box familiarity.

Here is what dazzles me about the dungareed and miniskirted girls I have seen today in the Square. They have changed physically, through feminine willpower alone, I am sure, to present a body that asks only to be pressed against, to be held, lain with, loved, and entered. It requires a staggering stretch of the imagination to believe that procreation has any relationship whatsoever to this invitation. What a wonderful, free, young, happy world has been born in ten years. I cannot imagine why I have been asleep, but I will rest no longer.

I saw a student from Radcliffe walking into the Harvard Coop. It was a warm day. She carried her trenchcoat. Her dark blond hair fell almost midway down her front, on each side of her neck. She had no bra, so that, as she walked, her small breasts were just slightly visible beneath her thin blouse. Her candy-striped bell-bottoms were belted below her navel, the belt pressing easily into her flat supple tummy. As she walked away from me, the hollows of her seat rose up and down as her bottom moved rhythmically to one side and then the other. After she disappeared among the Bic pens and spiral notebooks, I looked out at the noon classes letting out in the Yard, an army of rocking bosoms and oscillating seats bounding around me, and I knew that my rebirth had occurred. I am a new man.

8th It is growing. I still cannot bring myself to say that the dot is life. I see no resemblances. It does not smile. Or wink. Or yawn. I believe that if anyone had a choice of how he would begin, he would choose another way. But still, sooner or later, I must say that my dot is alive. It is no longer yellow. It is pink and red. Almost violet. It is double its size. I swear it.

I have spent the last hour looking at it. Where is its mind? Where is its life? Where is its anything? It is cells, every one, from what I can tell, the same. I wonder whether I dare cut one out, just one cell, to analyze it, to see how it is different from one of *my* cells.

How can this dot produce words and things, machines and ideas? Where are its numbers now, its search for meaning, its inquest into being? Which cell will one day question its own existence, its own life, the one on the bottom left or the top right? What perverse growth pattern starts with a dot and ends with a human being, all arms and legs, a pest to himself, a nuisance to other men? What bizarre process takes a dot and produces something that builds bowling alleys?

It is growing. Tomorrow I may say that it is alive. The day after that, I may say that I have begun to grow a human being. I congratulate myself. I am a father. Who knows? Maybe I am a mother.

11th This creative biology is no piece of cake, let me tell you. It's not that the biology, by itself, isn't intolerable. It is. It's the other part that drives me to the brink. The creative part, and don't be taken in by the Renaissance.

Ghiberti may have won the competition for the Baptistry doors, but I have seen his Abraham about to sacrifice Isaac, and it has all the intensity of jello. Donatello's sculpture of David raises serious questions about both of their sexual preferences. Michelangelo's David isn't much better. In addition to betraying a gross misunderstanding of postpuberty genitalia, they both have apparently forgotten that there is an army of Philistines across the street and a giant around the corner. This is not the sculpture of a youngster who will bring forth sons wherever he stops to water his horses (six in Hebron, eleven in Jerusalem), who will someday bury Ishboseth's head, curse Joab, mourn Absalom, who will commit adultery with Bathsheba, slay four armies, and be king of Israel.

Only Bernini knew what David was about. Only his David is the one in the Bible, the one who dropped his cheeses when he heard that whoever slew Goliath got Saul's riches, a tax-free house, and the king's daughter. Bernini's David throws rocks. He is a tough little lad, and it's not necessary to see his penis in order to know that he's got one.

No, I'm afraid that the great era of rebirth is an illusion. It is a birth accomplished entirely without sexual equipment. And while that's remarkable, it is also a creative fraud. I blame Michelangelo. It was this dainty neoplatonist who decided that more important than passion and pain were the Greek ideals of the Golden Mean, order, form, balance, symmetry, a return to the mind, as though the mind had anything at all to do with order and balance.

The great Renaissance mind was what sent Innocent the Tenth tittering through the Sistine Chapel painting bathing suits and jock straps on all the naked figures in Michelangelo's Last Judgment. *That* is what Saint Francis died for. *That* is what humanism is. It is *humans*. Vain, bewildered, stupid, petty, murderous, loving, humans forever claiming to be lost innocents, sporadically trying to translate their agony into art.

It is not Brunelleschi uniting science and art with the phenomenal discovery of perspective. It is not da Vinci mirror-writing how many loaves of bread he bought today beneath precise renderings of parachutes, helicopters, biceps, and madonnas. And it is definitely *not* a benign Venus standing in a seashell playing with herself.

12th "I like it, Harry. I think we've got him by the balls," Paul told me after reading the first two chapters tonight.

"You really think so?" I asked, more than casually interested in the problem.

"Don't get me wrong, Harry. This isn't going to be easy. But you've got him thinking, Harry. You've got him on the defensive. He knows that this isn't going to be any ordinary performance. This engagement is for all the marbles."

"Paul, I'd like to believe you, but it doesn't feel as though Boris is on the defensive. Right now, I'd gladly settle for a draw."

"Don't kid yourself, Harry. There's no such thing. It's either him or you."

"I was afraid you were going to say that," I told Paul and continued to huff with him through the cold March air.

13th Here is what I have learned from watching Lucy grow in her jar.

There is only one way to produce life and the chicken has found it. Sit on your roost, offer an occasional cluck to the world, and wait.

14th [Another draft. Ed.]

> Fellow classmates, I have been asked to speak to you today, after fifty long years have passed, and I have chosen as my subject Life, Human Life. It is almost impossible to know where to begin.

[Draft ends here. Ed.]

16th I don't understand it. My Lucy. Something's wrong with my Lucy. There's not the health, the color, the movement. I've tried to change the chemicals. More valine, less leucine. More phenylalanine, less lysine, more gamma-amylase, more cyproterone acetate. I don't know. There're so many possibilities. Perhaps the temperature should be higher, or lower. More oxygen or carbon dioxide, more salt, less sugar, no light.

It's as though she's just stopped. The cells have given up. I will not give up. There has got to be a reason for this. I will not give up.

17th "Harry, you don't really believe that you're growing your wife, do you? Not really?"

Boris, the information is there. The nuclei have been transplanted. It's Lucy.

"You're joking. You've got to be."

I'm serious.

"But even if you did succeed, Harry, what the hell are you going to do with a new baby? What do you want an infant duplicate of your wife for? You didn't even know her until she was twenty."

I'll be eighty-nine when she's twenty. Picasso is ninety.

"So is your mother, and she's been dead for ten years."

I will be alive. And if I should die at ninety, then I'll be happy to have my last sight be that of my Lucy at twenty-one.

"What if she doesn't want to marry her father?"

I'm not her father, Boris. I'm her husband!

"You were the *last* Lucy's husband. You're *this* Lucy's father."

This Lucy has no father. She's a clone. She's parthenogenetic.

"She's also crazy if she marries her ninety-year-old father. You are, too, if you think that Lucy's the type who would do it. You don't remember Lucy very well."

Boris, why are you doing this to me? Boris?

18th And now is Arnold happy? I have been to see Dr. Alexander Walsh. This was my first and last visit. I doubt whether I will ever be able to remove from my mind the image of this thirty-year-old bald, pipe-smoking Freudian, analyzing and exclaiming his way through my life. I have been honest with him. I have been, I am afraid, too honest. Each pregnant morsel of my life he has inhaled and has, in turn, exhaled it with an enormously prolonged "uh-huh . . ."

"Doctor, I have discovered that the human race will be extinct in roughly twenty years (uh-huh), but it will not matter because within the next few months I will have discovered the secret of life (uh-huuhh), not because I am any great humanitarian but because I've had my wife in a jar for over thirty years and now am attempting to grow her again (uh-huuuuhhhhh)."

Where his uh-huhing failed to signify understanding, he substituted repetitions of "Well, you know what that means" or inserted an only slightly varied leitmotif of "ah-hah!"

Perhaps, I thought, just perhaps, he might, as a trained professional, or at the very least as a stranger, have some insight into my problems. I have made the same mistake before.

"I am having a recurring nightmare," I told him, "in which I find myself in the cave of Plato's *Republic*."

"Well, you know what that means."

"Tell me."

"The womb."

"The womb?"

"The womb."

"It doesn't *feel* as though I'm in a womb, Dr. Walsh."

"Ah, hah. It never does. It's the pleasure principle. It has to do with forgetting, specifically with remembering to forget."

"Doctor, do *you* ever feel that *your* whole life has consisted entirely of sexual traumas?"

"I've had analysis. I feel better."

"Well, I feel terrible. I find that I have frequent headaches, dizziness, nausea."

"And pain?"

"It's painful, yes."

"Well, you know what that means."

"Please."

"A libidinally prompted response to your desire to leave the womb, in your dream a cave, is presenting itself in the form of nausea. You are fighting the catharsis of your birth."

"But when I throw up, I don't *feel* like I'm being born."

"Of course not. Your ego never would. Your ego is too nauseous, but your id, that's another story. Your id is ecstatic."

"I have always thought it was because of Boris."

"Your son?"

"Not exactly. He's the hero in a book I'm writing. He's recently been judged criminally insane. He's on his way to a progressive mental institution, I believe."

"You're not sure?"

"I am. He's not."

"He's not?"

"No. We can't seem to get along. I just don't know how long he's going to let me continue the book. He frightens me. Maybe this is why I get the headaches. I don't know."

"Perfectly normal."

"It is?"

"Yes."

"What is it?"

"Penis envy."

"But I *have* a penis."

"Ah, hah!"

20th Talking of penises, let me tell you something about Aristotle. He was a catastrophe. Between his logic, his causes, and his physics, he managed to bring disaster indiscriminately to all fields of science without exception. Believe me. Aristotle was the father of the dead end, producing some 2000 years of stagnation in his wake, 2010 years to be exact, since it was exactly 2010 years after Aristotle died that Newton published his *Principia*. Newton's first law alone eliminated fifty-five Aristotelian unmoved movers.

I dash through Aristotle totally hypnotized. Who can argue with logic, even bad logic? Plato was illogical, irrational, emotional, and absurd, so I don't have to take him too seriously. With Aristotle there are absolutely no distractions, and I become so involved that I don't for a second stop to remember that the world he is so meticulously and reasonably describing bears absolutely no resemblance, living or dead, to the world I inhabit. Even more painful, I wish it did. There is such beauty in this deception that I return over and again for more. No drug could be so compulsive for the mind. Believe me. It's a hypnotic of the first order.

Fortunately, we have broken the barriers. Aristotle no longer boxes us into his syllogistic corners. Ordered, methodical, purposeful, deductive reasoning is, as far as I can tell, nowhere to be found. And, I am content that the delirium we have found to replace it could not be reduced to any Prior Analytics or Categories, as Cervantes has said, should Aristotle be raised from the dead for that very purpose.

21st What else is there to try? Nothing. Nothing at all. I have varied every chemical and every gas in every ratio I can conceive of. I've thought. I've observed. I've poked and waited. Lucy can't do this to me. I'll never get another egg. I can't go through what I must to retrieve one. I've not slept in two nights. I can't think clearly.

I look at the marble (it seems smaller and it's almost all gray now), and I say that she'll make it. She'll fight to stay alive. She'll *will* herself into vitality. But nothing happens.

24th She is dead. Absolutely.

25th "I know I'm the last person you want to hear from, Harry, but I'm sorry about what happened to your egg."

Tell me something, Boris, what is it that you want from me? Is it something that is in my power to give?

"I've been wondering the same about you, Harry. What do you want from me? What do you want me to do?"

I want you to be a character in my book, just that, Boris, nothing more. I want you to be who you are, so I can finish while I still have the energy.

"Maybe I would be more successful as a spy, Harry, or a detective. Maybe you could do something wildly allegorical."

Yes, and maybe I could make you a fourteen-line sonnet and be done with you two months ago.

"I would make a great unfaithful lover, an international rake. Really. What's the male equivalent of a nymphomaniac?"

A pain in the ass, Boris. A first-class pain in the ass.

26th Some pathologist. My autopsy has shown what? Dead cells. For this you need an autopsy? I see nothing to indicate why or how. That is not quite true. I am no longer looking for formal, final, material, and efficient causes, and in not looking I have found much.

Here is why the embryo died. Because nature takes some perverse delight in torturing me.

27th Paul says that I am crazy even to try. I don't know. Maybe I am.

But I cannot pretend that I am something other that what I am. I absolutely refuse to play at being a calm, rational, dispassionate senior citizen who is leading a life composed entirely of beach chairs and Sunday dinners.

I do what I do. I know that the world is coming to an end. That's a fact. I am trying to save it. Personally, I think that's a damn nice thing to do.

I am trying to save the world by creating life. This is not easy. Some battle fatigue should be expected.

If I am going to be locked up and shot full of phenothiazines it will be for telling them this, not for some vague paranoia or recurring fugue state.

I've had nothing at all to do with Boris. I've said this before. It's not my fault.

Lucy was wonderful. Who would not want to regenerate her?

So. What is so crazy about all this? Tell me.

29th I have heard today from Rebecca. It does not look at all good for the home team. Arnold has received a preliminary report from my Freudian friend, Dr. Alexander Walsh, and Arnold wants to talk to me. This is not good.

I do not want to see Arnold. Not now. There is too much to do, and I do not want to involve myself with the foolishness of trying to win arguments. I will not see Dr. Walsh again. I will not see another psychiatrist. That is all there is to it.

Arnold will be here next week. Maybe by then I will be dead.

30th It is settled then. I must find the Operator, the demon that turns on the nucleus that very first time. I must also find a ripe and fertile assistant, one of the local buxom laboratory technicians, to volunteer her eggs and her womb for a brief nine months.

I will retrieve her egg, transplant Lucy's nuclei, turn on the Operator, and reimplant the zygote. Lucy, you are still alive.

31st "Harrison Hipassos, my man, I have come to acquiesce, to capitulate. I am as I am. I will cause you no troubles. We are to be as friends, you to me and me to you."

Why are you doing this, Boris? You're not the surrendering type. You know it, and you know that I know it. So what are you up to?

"You are right to suspect, O wonder of the pen, that altruism is not a cloak that fits well upon my shoulders. Sociobiology is your bag. However, I understand that you are once again about to raise that stylus of a thousand delights and send me reeling off to new and even more fantastic adventures. Am I not correct?"

You have the general idea.

"Ah, yes. Well, then, I thought that while we are at this brief stasis in the proceedings, we might make a little substitution on the fête du jour—baked for french fries, peas for string beans, a religious experience for a looney bin. Just wondering, mind you. Nothing that's urgent."

No religious experience. You're going to an asylum.

"How about a new personality? As you can probably tell, I've been working on a little something myself, a product of some small hours spent in introspection and intensive cogitation."

No, Boris.

"Harry, baby. Have a heart."

Look, Boris, why don't you just resign yourself.

"Harry, all I want is one lousy chance to show you that I'm right, that I can pull it off. Won't you just take one . . . won't you . . . you . . . just- . . . take . . . won't take . . ."

What?

"Jesus, I don't know, Harry. I get into these screwy arguments with you, and then in the middle I turn off, I lose interest, in finishing, in winning, in losing, in anything. I don't know what the hell happens. It just does."

I don't understand what you're trying to say, Boris.

"What I'm trying to say is that I turn off, turn on, turn off, and there's never a single goddam reason. One minute I think I'm really into this life you've contrived for me, and then *zap*, the next minute I can't seem to tune in at all. I couldn't care less."

I don't know what to do, Boris.

"Well, I'll clue you into something, Harry. I've tried as many goddam ways as I can think of to *tell* you what to do. And if you don't do it soon, there's going to be one hell of an explosion around here."

April

1st The Adventures of Boris Lafkin

written by HARRY H. WOLPER

CHAPTER THREE:

In Which Our Hero Spends
Another Lousy Year in Paradise

I guess it's crazy to say that a nuthouse was probably the first decent worthwhile experience I ever had in my life, but it was.

There was Mara. Good old Mara. Jesus, *she* was the first decent thing that ever happened to me. Maybe Days Clinic was more Mara than it was the clinic. Whatever it was, Mara was there.

Mara had long straight brown hair and good teeth. Even at the clinic I never found out why the hell a girl's hair and her teeth are the first things I look for, or why I even care so much that a girl is physically beautiful. Sure I know it's normal, only not with me it isn't. With me I could meet the most affectionate, charming, sensational, intelligent, with-it girl, and if she's got kinky hair or crooked teeth, I won't have a thing to do with her.

I don't know where this leaves us. Nowhere, I guess. But having passed the acid test, Mara got along pretty well with me. She was probably the first person I could ever talk to. I figured that this was highly abnormal, the first person I could ever talk to and feel comfortable with being a girl, and decided it meant that either I was queer or had some kind of mother thing. We spent a good deal of time in therapy exploring both possibilities. I don't remember what we eventually decided, but as my friendship with Mara grew, I lost interest in the question.

I was once told that it's very important to know where you are. Well just about nobody would've known where Days Clinic was until 1969 when Arlo Guthrie started making movies. Days Clinic is located in Stockbridge, Massachusetts, which just might be one of the most peaceful towns in the whole United States. It is very New England with big white churches and small white stores, a pharmacy, a general store, a candy shop, a soda fountain, an inn, and behind it all down the alley in the back, Alice's Restaurant. In the winter it is about twenty minutes from some very fair ski places, and in the summer it is twenty minutes from Tanglewood, and even then it is usually a quiet empty town. You can't help falling in love with it. When the snow falls, it falls deep, and it stays *white*, not just that night, but for days afterwards. When spring comes, it doesn't just arrive, it is born there, right in front on your eyes, and you have the feeling of having participated in the birth of creation itself. That's when I was there, in the winter and in the spring. I was also there in the summer. I left at the end of the fall.

You know the poem about winter, where they talk about the "still snow." Well, Stockbridge was where still snow was invented. It happens late at night. Everyone is asleep, and the whole town is white and still. Some places rest at night (New York never does). They rest, but in different ways, like Washington rests at night but it looks more like it's gotten *stuck* and won't get unstuck until morning. In Chicago and most of the Midwest, the cities and towns get frozen sharply and quickly into stillness and can't break out until it gets light. But Stockbridge just *rests*. It relaxes and falls easily into stillness. I liked to walk at night, floating nicely through the night and trying to put my thoughts in order. Here, at last, I began to realize that there was a world, a real world of snow and trees and quiet and cold, not something that revolves, or a place where natural laws hold, but an environment where people live. And it doesn't necessarily have to be hostile or angry or anything but there. It was winter, and then spring, that made me think for the first time that I might be a part of this world, just as much a part as the stillness.

We lived in The Inn, a large mansion with lots of rooms, carpets, no bars on the windows, a living room, comfortable dining room, TV room, recreation room (pool and ping pong), and my womb room, the music room, where I spent hours sitting in the dark listening to "La Mer," "Night on Bald Mountain," "Firebird Suite," "Rites of Spring," and "The Emperor Concerto." Mara was with me, but I was always alone. I guess I haven't really given you much of a picture about Days Clinic. It isn't much to describe, really. The Inn, the administration building where all the therapists had their offices. And that's it, all located in a small quiet town.

Mara came from Syracuse or Schenectady or Rochester or someplace in the Midwest like Oak Park or Cleveland, I don't remember, but it was something like that. It isn't important, just that she wasn't all that sophisticated, even though she had dropped out of Smith.

Mara had the room next to mine.

If I could go back, if I ever had the guts to go back to some time in my life, I would want to go back to that time before my life had really begun, to Mara's cramped room, with her in her dungarees and white man's shirt that she always wore, sitting cross-legged on the rug, playing with her hair clip or her finger nails or the ends of her hair. It's late at night and the only sound is a truck, way in the distance, shifting its gears, or sometimes the muffled sound of a jet, flying at the top of the sky, always in the distance, always leaving, never having come from anywhere. Maybe the lights are off, we did that a lot, and Mara is dripping wax on a bottle.

Raphael has ended. Mara says that it's over, but she still loves him. And Walter hasn't begun. Walter and his goddam motorcycle and Porsche and mountain lodge and trips to the Caribbean. Screw Walter.

But like I said, this is before Walter, and maybe Mara and I are squeezed onto her single bed, lying in the dark, my chin resting on the top of her head, her body pushed against mine, or maybe we're smoking cigarettes. We did that a lot, too.

I wish to hell I could think of what we said to each other, to give you a feeling of how close we were. But Mara had this thing about words. She didn't think they worked, not spoken ones at least. Written ones were another thing, and she was always reading. She read a lot of D. H. Lawrence and Virginia Woolf, as I remember it.

Anyway, I got so close to Mara that eventually I decided that I wanted to be with her all the time. There didn't seem to be any other reason for getting up, except to talk to her. I finally told her this.

"Boris," she said, "let's do it. Let's just spend every minute with each other until we can't stand it any more. Let's live together every second from now on. Shall we sleep together?"

I wanted to say "All right! Let's sleep together! Let's sleep and kiss and screw, and screw and screw! And let's start now! Let's take off our clothes and get into bed and make love to each other! Let's do it!"

And you know what I said? I said something like, "What do *you* want? Would you like to sleep together?" Or maybe even, "Do you think it'd be a good idea?" I could've shot myself.

"Yes. I'd like to," and she stood on her toes and kissed me on my lips very softly. She took my hand and put it right between her legs, and I swear to God I came as close to pissing in my pants as I ever have in my life. I held my hand between her legs and through the brass fasteners and four layers of reinforced denim I could feel her heart beating right between her legs, palpitating and twitching, and then, standing right there, standing straight up with her body as close to me as she could get it with my arm where it was, she grabbed me even more tightly and came. Her crotch jerked and spasmed about a dozen quick times and then slowly stopped.

I stood, frozen and numb, scared to look at her face, but she loosened her arms around me, kissed me again and smiled. That smile was all I needed. I would have thrown myself from the window if she had asked. I would have eaten my hand, a knuckle at a time.

"How did you do that?" I finally asked.

"Talent," she smiled.

"That's terrific," I said with genuine enthusiasm, but either saying that, or my enthusiasm or something upset her just a little, no more than enough for her eyes to contradict her smile for just a second, but enough for me to see that all was not ideal in the realm of nonverbal communication.

"I have to change my underpants. They're soaking wet now. You can leave if you want," she said.

"I don't mind if you don't." Why do I talk like that? Why couldn't I say something like, "No, no! I want to see your box. Your box! Your box!" and jump up and down and scream a little, and cheer and clap. Instead I come out with "I don't mind if you don't." What a goddam asinine thing to say.

Now the object was, of course, to appear only moderately interested in her naked bottom half while she was undressing, the experience of viewing one of the most nicely built girls I have ever seen in my life undress in front of me just being another in a long series of mildly interesting events in my life. I, therefore, initiated a conversation about eggs, chicken eggs, the kind being served for breakfast that morning, and how I couldn't stand them loose and she couldn't stand them well done.

Just as Mara was about to pull on her new underpants she stopped.

"Why are we talking about eggs?" she asked.

"Because there's only one other thing to talk about right now, and I don't know what to say about it," I admitted.

I looked for a reaction from her, but there was none. She pulled up her pants and then her dungarees, snapped, zipped, and belted them and walked across the room to me.

"We can talk some more about eggs after the movie tonight, all right?" She rubbed her hand on my face and smiled, "Let's go eat."

That day is a day that I will relive a million times for the rest of my life. If I had known that that night I would become president of the world, or receive the Nobel Prize, or be given ten million dollars, or learn the secret of life from God Himself, fame, honor, fortune, immortality, would not have excited me one tenth as much as the thought of *my* naked body next to *Mara's* naked body. My whole world, my whole life was worth that day only what was going to take place under the covers that night. Why the hell is that? Most of it is luck, anyway, I'm sure of it. I once knew this guy in college who told me that there wasn't a girl he couldn't make come the very first time. I don't know, maybe he really could. I've thought about that a lot. He was a crazy guy, anyway. The college I went to was a small one. There were about a hundred students in the freshman class each year, half of them girls. Anyway, Jack (he was the guy) got everyone all worked up about making sure that by the end of the school year there wasn't a virgin left in the school. Miriam was the last girl, short, pudgy, crazy Miriam. Jack had her the next to the last day of the spring semester. Then we had a party. Miriam found out the next day and tried to kill herself. Jack said she thought she was in love with him. Anyway, that's the kind of mentality that worries about orgasm all the time.

You know, if I had a son the right age now, I'd tell him one thing. Forget the first time you make love. Just forget it. And *don't* marry the first girl you make love to, not if she's the last girl left in the world. This whole thing about the young married virginal couple sharing the discovery of the wonders of sex is the biggest load of crap I have ever heard. You might just as well tell people to share the wonders of learning how to use a gun. Before you figure it out more times than not you have blown your goddam head off. Great wonder of discovery, right? Just don't marry the first girl you have. That's all.

The first girl I ever had was Kathy, and there was no chance there. Poor Kathy. What a goddam sport she was. I know I'm way off the topic of that day with Mara, but I'd like to tell you about this. About the only thing I really remember about Kathy was that she wore the tightest red corduroy pants I have ever seen, and she had the greatest little body to fit in them. Now, I thought I had this sex thing all figured out because when I was younger we all used to play this game called "to the victors go the spoils," which was a phrase we picked up somewhere. Anyway, the object was that the guys would capture the girls, and then we'd rape them. Since we were only eleven at the time, rape generally meant undressing them and us taking off our pants and doing a lot of kissing and ass-squeezing and a couple of times we managed to stick ourselves in them, but nothing ever came of it.

I always had Betsy, though I wanted Sherrie because she didn't have braces and kissing Betsy sent chills up my spine. Anyway, I decided that what was left to learn about screwing were only a few technical and very minor details. Being fifteen, having read *Love without Fear* a dozen times, and having made it a point to keep abreast of the latest filthy pictures making their way around the school, I selected the girl, Kathy Mirabelli, who had a reputation that was ample for my purposes, and decided on the "overnighter" that weekend at Nancy's house as the time and place. Every weekend somebody's parents would be away in the Caribbean or New York City or somewhere, and we would use the house all weekend. You had to sign up for bedrooms. Otherwise it was fairly informal.

After the basketball game, Kathy and I got a ride out to Nancy's house with a lot of other people, and by 2:00 A.M. we had discussed every major political issue of the twentieth century, and I had just decided to return to our roots in Greek antiquity when Kathy called a halt.

"I'm tired, Boris. I'm getting undressed."

"Oh yeah. It is late."

She started to take off her clothes, very quickly, and finally jumped naked into bed. I sat stunned and tried to analyze the situation. "What exactly was she doing?" I wondered. I guess I needed a diagram.

"Boris, why don't you take off your clothes and get in bed with me?"

"I'm not really tired."

"Neither am I."

"But I thought you said—"

"I was lying. Boris, please get undressed."

Very slowly, with a maximum amount of effort and time and a minimum amount of motion and accomplishment, I unbuttoned, unbelted, unzipped, untied, and did everything except actually remove my clothing.

Finally I stood there, literally coming apart at every seam, shivering (it was winter), until I realized there was no way out. Furiously I ripped my clothes off and jumped naked into bed.

First of all, I couldn't stop shivering. Second of all, not only didn't my penis become erect, for the first ten minutes we thought it had retracted into my stomach. We couldn't even *find* the goddam thing. She kept telling me that I should go to the hospital right away. I assured her that such a reaction was only the result of a tragic childhood injury, but that, if she would be patient, all would work out in the end. It didn't help matters that she kept referring to the organ as "your thing."

Finally, after much coaxing, my thing appeared. In the excitement of the event, a mad outbreak of kissing and fondling occurred, the intention being to rouse my thing to new heights and the result being that I pissed all over my side of the bed. I had turned to the outside of the bed at the last minute hoping to hit the floor, and decided not to mention the event unless necessary.

For perhaps two hours we tried everything we could think of that might make intercourse possible, and finally, exhausted and defeated, we fell asleep, just as it was getting light.

I did not sleep well. The warm dampness of the urine and the stench was really beyond endurance, but Kathy said nothing, so I didn't offer to change the sheet. When I woke up Kathy was sleeping in my arms and, wonder of wonders, my thing was fully distended.

Gently I woke up Kathy and very cautiously we coupled. Suddenly it occurred to me that this was as far as I had ever gotten before, and I was not at all sure what to do. I just lay there, on top of her, dying, willing to give my life for a step-by-step breakdown of what I should do. Kathy kept rubbing her hands on my back and my ass and kissing me, and then she started to move her hips, and I started to move my hips, and I liked that. It felt good. So I decided to be a little more daring and in one magnificent pelvic thrust managed to negate everything we had accomplished and ended up disengaged and frantic.

"Quick," I yelled. "Do something. I'm melting." I don't know why I said that, but it seemed to me the only way to describe the retreat that my thing was hastily beating to the inner reaches of my chest cavity.

Miraculously, Kathy succeeded in leading me back into her, and after several similarly disastrous episodes, I finally got the hang of it all. Just about this time, I noted that Kathy was behaving very strangely. She wasn't nearly as lucid as she had been up to now. She seemed to be moaning. Not only that, but I was beginning to get very strange feelings in the very bottom of my testicles, and the best way to express it seemed to me also to be by moaning. And suddenly, there we were, moaning, both moving our bodies, together, moaning, moving together, and Kathy was moving her little bottom back and forth and sideways and in circles. I reached under her and held her bottom as close to me as I could get it. We were moving faster now, and I couldn't think straight anymore. My insides were getting hotter and hotter, and everything we did became faster and faster. We held to each other as tightly as we could, and then something happened inside Kathy. At first it was just a little ripple, and then a larger one, and then her vagina clamped itself onto me and started to vibrate, and finally it burst into lots of short quick spasms. And then something happened to me. The feeling in my testicles raced up to the end of my penis, and my whole insides reached the boiling point and exploded into her.

"Oh God, Boris, yes!" she shouted, held me tight, and again her insides started jerking and pulsing, while I was jerking and pulsing, and there we were, just jerking and pulsing all over the goddam place.

When it was over, I lay there on top of her. I looked at her head against the pillow. She had short black hair, black eyes, and beautiful skin, and she was crying.

I was frightened and bewildered, and I hadn't really the slightest idea of what had happened, but when I saw her tears I was mortified.

"I'm sorry," I said. "Should we get married?" That's what I said. I said it because I loved her. I loved her more than anyone I had ever loved in my entire life.

"We're only fifteen, Boris, we can't get married." She was very kind to me.

"When we graduate in a couple years?"

"Let's see what happens next week."

There never was a next week. The more I thought about that night, about the problems and my obvious inexperience, the more embarrassed and ashamed I became. I didn't know what to say to Kathy in school or even whether to see her in school. Half the time I would avoid her and the other half I would go out of my way to pass by her locker or classroom or wherever I figured she would be. I couldn't stand seeing her talk to any other guy, and by Friday we had had an enormous fight, and that was it. As I remember it, the rest of the year I spent in my room in the dark, "thinking." I resolved never to make love to another girl as long as I lived.

A couple of years later, I took Kathy out, but we had nothing to say. It was very awkward and absolutely no use. That was the last time I saw her except for a reunion once a couple of years ago. She's married this thirty-year-old guy who left his wife and has custody of his *seven* kids. And they've had three more. Like I said, you've got to marry someone with experience.

By the time I got to Mara, you would think that with high school and college behind me I would have it. At least that's what I thought. No challenge I couldn't handle. That's why it was so crazy that I should get so worked up about going to bed with Mara that night. But I was.

The dining room at Days Clinic is this really great place. It's almost a formal dining room, with leather-upholstered chairs and mahogany tables, big bay windows all around with long drapes, but still it has a relaxed feeling. You don't feel like you have to sit straight in your chair and talk polite conversation. What is nicest is that in the morning the light comes in and makes everything in the room shine. It's bright and happy. There were times when I would get up early in the morning just to come into the dining room before everyone else did and sit in the light.

In the back of the dining room are two small tables that seat only two people (all the rest are long ones and seat six to eight). Mara and I sat at the small one just in front of the largest bay window in the back.

As Mara ate, the fuel seemed to make her glow with excitement that morning. She smiled and laughed. Her eyes were blue and incredibly clear. I tried some orange juice and gave up halfway through the glass. I couldn't eat a thing.

"Ever heard of Anaxagoras?" I asked.

"Nope," Mara said, almost choking on her juice.

"Well," I said, delighted at her ignorance, "Anaxagoras was one of the first philosophers, and this guy was terrific. To begin with, he was the first guy to teach that the world was ordered by something with a purpose. He called it "*nous*," which is Greek for "mind." This guy was fantastic. He taught that the world was round, that it just turned in space and wasn't supported by anything, that everything was made up of little particles, that the shadows of the earth and the sun are what cause eclipses, that the sun was a ball of fire and the moon and the earth are composed of basically the same substance. But this was all heretical. Besides, Anaxagoras was a good friend of Pericles, and there were a lot of people who hated Pericles, so there was a trial held where Anaxagoras—"

"Boris?" Mara asked, looking at me kind of strangely.

"Yes?"

"Are you interested in this?"

"Sure."

"Why?" she asked.

"Because it's fascinating how this one guy thought up all these things before anyone else and you never hear about him. Anyway, they had this trial—"

"I still don't understand."

"What?"

"Why you're talking about philosophy now."

"I told you. Because I think it's interesting."

We sat in silence for a minute. I figured right there that I had blown it, just like with Kathy. Mara and I would never make it to the end of the day. I decided to try once more. Maybe the ending to the story would justify my telling it.

"So Anaxagoras was banished from Athens for life because of his ideas. Isn't that crazy?"

Suddenly Mara burst out laughing.

"Why are you doing that?" I asked.

"I don't know. It just happens. Especially when everything gets so serious. I laugh at concerts and funerals. When I was a kid I used to laugh in church all the time. Usually I would start just when I received communion. Finally the priest wouldn't let me take communion anymore." She was still laughing.

"Was I too serious?"

"I guess so. Are you really interested in Anaxagoras? Really?"

"No," I lied. "I guess not."

"I didn't think so. Boris, let's make a pact, you know. Let's only talk about things that matter, things that are worth saying. No conversation just because it's quiet. Let's say only what's really on our minds, okay?"

"Yes, I like that." I did, really. I thought it was a great idea, and it made me feel a lot more relaxed, but I was bothered a little because Anaxagoras really was what was on my mind. I don't know why. He just was. Anyway, I got the general idea of what Mara was saying, and so I forgot about Anaxagoras.

Mara was the next one to speak, and I was glad because it would give me a clue as to what conversation was acceptable for our pact.

"Boris, who are you?"

"Can't we start with something a little simpler and work up to that?"

"I want to know." Mara leaned her elbows on the table, placed her face in her palms and looked intently at me.

"Well, I was born—" I began.

"No, who are you *now?*"

"I can't tell you that unless I tell you about the way I grew up."

"It just doesn't seem important to know *how* you got to be what you are, you know? Only *what* you are. You see what I mean?"

"I think so. I'm a criminal."

Mara got very excited. "Are you really? I've heard people say it around here but things always get exaggerated. Did you really kill someone?"

"No, I only injured him, kind of."

"What did you do?"

"I chopped off his prick."

"God! Did you really? That's fantastic!" Mara grinned.

"Yes. But it was an accident, kind of. I was swinging an ax around, and his prick got in the way."

"Is that why you're here?"

"Kind of. I made a scene in the court and everyone figured I was crazy."

There was nothing more to say. We sat looking at each other for a minute.

"How does it feel?" Mara asked finally.

"What?"

"To almost kill a man. I can't *imagine* what it would be like to know that you almost ended another man's life yourself. Just like that."

"Are you condemning me?"

"Oh, no, Boris, really, no." She put her hand on my arm. "I'm really not."

"Well, I don't really know how it feels, because I was so upset over it, but basically it feels like you've just tried to kill yourself. Until you almost kill a person you don't really understand what it's like to be a human being, how quickly and easily you can die yourself. Up to that point, I pictured life as something that gradually leads to death. And death was a process, something that happened over a period of time, *eventually.* Now I know that death is a *halt.* It just happens, suddenly. Life ends. Life just stops, and even if you're ninety, it still happens right in the middle of your life."

Mara sat there in thought for a few minutes. "You don't belong here, you know," she said.

"Why?"

"Because none of us know what you do. You know the secret. Don't tell anyone else. Please."

"I won't."

"Do you think you have to try to kill someone to know this, to feel it enough to believe it? Do you, Boris?"

"Of course not. We'd all be animals, then."

"How then?"

"Well, I don't think very many people ever get to feel it, really. We just live with what we've got."

"I don't think I could live if I didn't feel it. I don't think any of us could."

"We do, though."

"No, we don't. Not really live. In order to live we have to know death, really feel it. Then we have to come to live with it. Boris, I want to tell you something I've never told anyone else."

She looked at me carefully to see whether she could trust me. Then she smiled.

"Every time I make love, I die. Really, I put all my life into making love, and when I come, I die. My life is over. And then I'm born again. Do you think that's crazy?"

"No. I think it's beautiful." I *said* it. I was so happy with myself for saying that instead of "How do you feel?" or "It isn't crazy if you're comfortable about it" or anything other than telling her exactly what I thought, that it was beautiful, that it was one of the most beautiful things I'd ever heard. And it made me think of that night. It made me want her even more. Only it was a little different somehow. You don't just jump in bed and screw if you're messing with a girl's whole life. It confused me a little.

"What do *you* do, Boris?"

"How do you mean?"

"Now that you've felt death, really felt it, what do you do?"

"I'm not sure. I haven't really figured that out. I think I need a religion. I need one very badly."

"What kind?"

"I don't know. I don't think the kind I need exists yet. I think I'm going to have to invent one."

"If you do that, is it really a religion?"

"Sure. A religion is only finding something to believe in that you have to accept on faith. The problem with all the religions I know is that what they ask me to accept on faith is the opposite of what I know and feel. My religion has to have a belief that *adds* to what I know and feel, not that contradicts it."

"When you put it that way, it doesn't seem so bad. I'll have to think about that. I really hate religions. They're degrading."

Mara finished her tea slowly. I finished my tea. We sat in silence. One time Mara reached over and held my hand. I reached over and put my hand against her face another time. I don't think we wanted to leave the dining room. The dining room had that atmosphere that I told you about. The sun was really beaming in now. Everybody else had left to do his chores. I think we would have made love to each other right then and there if we had thought we could get away with it. But, of course, we didn't. We took up our trays and went to do our assigned chores.

I haven't told you much about Julian yet. He's the guy next door to me on the other side. He's a washer. He washes his hands all night. Julian is an all-right guy about my age. He's got this long scraggy light brown beard, and he wears thick glasses. He also wears gloves during the day when he's around us because his hands are nothing but sores from the washing he does, and it's a pretty revolting sight. Every once in a while he goes somewhere in private and airs his hands so that they'll heal. He's never said anything, but I think that wearing the gloves is really quite painful for him.

Julian was really into politics when I knew him at the clinic. I heard last year that he's sold out and is now working for some big electronics company, which is pretty funny and very sad if you think about it. He was about as anticapitalist as you can get and used to say that the United States didn't give a damn about democracy and freedom, only *free enterprise,* and that we were willing to enslave, tyrannize, murder, do just about anything to protect our markets abroad. As I remember it, Julian had a very complex and sophisticated argument that depended a lot on understanding economic theory pretty well, so I'm probably not doing it justice at all, but what I said basically is true, or at least it's what I got out of it. The United States didn't care what the hell it did if the price was right.

Now I'm terrible about political kinds of things. I always agree with people making arguments like Julian did, but I never do a damn thing about it anymore. I used to though. The freedom buses used to leave from the college parking lot every Friday at 3:00 and every vacation, and I was on just about every one of them. And if you don't think that was scary, to go into some town in North Carolina or South Carolina and sit at some lunch counter with your back to these ape-men they grow down there who've got the brains of turnips and like to mutilate people like us, you ought to try it sometime.

It was the nights that were really bad. It was almost impossible to find a place that would put us all up. We once stayed in some really crappy motel and the bill for two nights for the thirty of us was over $6,000, which comes to about $100 a person per night. They said it was their "group rate." Not only that, but, when we refused to pay it, they hauled us all into court, and the judge said we *had* to pay, and *each one of us* was fined an additional $200 for "court costs." We had to stay there in jail for almost a week before the organizers could raise the money, and then we were charged an extra hundred dollars a guy for use of the jail for a week. What was even more ridiculous, when we got back to school, we were all put on probation for missing a whole week of classes without a "legitimate excused absence."

So we learned to be careful about where we stayed. When we finally did find a place, we could never fall asleep. Every sound we heard, every truck motor or car pulling into a parking lot, we thought the "townies" were coming to kill us. I still jolt up in my sleep when I hear a couple of car doors slam late at night. There were some close calls we had. For some reason these apes really grooved on snow chains. They just thought these were the most imaginative weapons, and a couple of us got beaten up pretty badly before we could get help. I had a friend, Norman, who had his spine broken, paralyzed for life. After Norman got broken up like that, I quit going. I just couldn't take it. Besides, I figured that Norman needed me more than the Freedom Riders, so I tried to help him along.

Now that's a goddam tragic story if you've ever heard one. He was practically engaged to this girl from school. They had been living together for the last two years in an off-campus apartment. When Norman finally was transferred back to the hospital near school, he wouldn't have anything to do with Carol, his girl. Finally, Carol gave up. Norm was the first person I ever knew who killed himself. What was crazy was that six months later Carol had his son. She dropped out of school just after Norm killed himself and started bumming cross-country with me. Then she found out for certain she was pregnant and left on her own to go home to New York. She's married now, but she's never had another kid. She says she doesn't know whether she ever will, either.

I've got to add something that you probably can guess without my saying it. Fourteen of us were witnesses and positively identified the three guys with the snow chains who beat up Norm. The grand jury said there was no conclusive proof. They weren't even indicted.

What all this leads to is not that you're supposed to feel sorry for anyone or anything. It's just to let you know how goddam screwed up college life was, and how I just can't seem to get myself all worked up over political issues anymore. I liked Julian, too, but he was just the wrong person for me. We could never get together for two minutes before he was off on some jag about freedom or capitalism or democracy or something.

Anyway, that's my socioeconomic psyche. It never ran head on into Julian as it might have because I never let it. For the most part, I just let Julian say whatever the hell he wanted without arguing back. It was quite an education. It also was one of several possible ways to spend the three hours between lunch and therapy.

This is, as a matter of fact, exactly how I spent that afternoon, listening to Julian attack modern man and society while I daydreamed about Mara's morning orgasm.

At three o'clock, I excused myself from Julian's stimulating company and went to therapy. Mara and I, as it turns out, had the same shrink, Dr. Alexander Ward, who, when I arrived this particular day, was sitting in his easy chair tying, untying, and retying his shoelaces. I took my seat and watched him do this, maybe twenty times. Dr. Ward was about thirty, bald, smoked a pipe with the foulest-smelling tobacco manufactured, and felt that it was a sign of concern and understanding for him to say "uh-huh." So for those reasons, as well as, I suspect, to let me know he was paying attention, if not to prevent himself from falling asleep, he "uh-huhed" several thousand times an hour. If they keep records of this sort, he holds it.

I did not want this session to be like the others. What I really wanted was to see whether it was possible to find out from Dr. Ward whether Mara had talked about me at all, and, if so, what she had said. I did not want to hear any further amusing anecdotes about Dr. Ward's perverse and sordid childhood.

I waited until the shoe tying was over. At the end of five minutes he seemed to be satisfied. He straightened up, lit his pipe, leaned back in his chair, and smiled a warm fatherly smile of fake concern at me. He was just dying to say, "Well, lad, how's your day been?" only he couldn't because it was an unwritten law that I had to speak first, not for any reason that made any sense, but, because if I *didn't* say anything we'd have nothing to talk about. In a very basic way, Dr. Alexander Ward was stupid. He had no more of an idea how to conduct a successful psychotherapy session than I knew how to build an aircraft carrier, except that I've *seen* an aircraft carrier.

"Dr. Ward," I began, "do you *like* your work? Do you really like what you're doing?"

"Of course, I like what I'm doing."

"Why is that, Dr. Ward? Why do you like it?"

"Because Days Clinic is just about the best reference you can have."

"For what?"

"For a better job!"

"Then you *don't* like your job?"

"No, no. I mean, yes, I do like it. Well, no, I mean when I say 'better' job, I mean more money."

"Suppose you got more money here?"

"How much?"

"How much would you like?"

"$50,000!" Dr. Ward clapped his hands. "That's how much I'd like! $50,000! Can I have $50,000?"

"If you promise never to go near another patient for the rest of your life."

"Stop it, Boris. That's not funny."

"If you got $50,000 a year, then would this be a better job?"

"It certainly would. It'd be ideal."

"And you'd like what you're doing?"

"Yes, I would. I'd like it very much," and he puffed happily on his pipe, smoke rolling upwards, a contented tugboat.

"Well, suppose I gave you $50,000 a year. Would that make you happy?"

"Of course it would make me happy. Do you *have* $50,000 a year to give me?"

"No."

He looked very disappointed. "Some of my patients do, you know."

"Well, suppose one of *them* offered you $50,000 a year for free, and you never had to conduct another one of these sessions in your entire life. Would you like that?"

"I would, yes. But then what would I do to keep busy? I'd have to be doing something. I couldn't take the $50,000 unless I earned it, and I wouldn't be happy earning it unless," and a big proud smile spread across his face, "unless I was helping other people." He was unusually happy. "That's it! I have to help people! That's my need!"

"That and $50,000 a year."

"Yes, helping people and $50,000 a year."

"Not necessarily in that order."

"Not necessarily."

"Dr. Ward, would you like to help me? Right now?"

"I'm not getting $50,000 a year, yet," he beamed at me.

"Very sharp, Dr. Ward. Very sharp. Dr. Ward, would you like to help me?"

"Certainly."

"Good. I want to know whether a certain one of your patients has ever talked about me, and, if so, what she has said in a general sort of way."

"I can't do that. It's unethical."

"Very well put, Dr. Ward. You have reacted professionally and well. Now will you please tell me whether any nice things have been said about me by Miss Mara O'Connor?"

"Mara!" He was suddenly very upset.

"Yes, Mara. What's wrong with that?"

"Why are you interested in whether she talked about you?"

"Well, to be perfectly honest, I believe I am in love with her, and I want to know whether she is in love with me, since we are going to consummate our good will tonight and *make* love."

"With Mara?"

"Yes. With Mara."

"She'll never make love with you!"

I sat stunned for a minute. "Why not? Did she say that to you?"

"It would be unethical to answer that."

I leaped up from my chair and stood over him. "Now, listen carefully. You've got exactly five seconds to tell me whether she actually said that or whether you're just making it sound like she did. And if I don't have the truth, I'll break your arm."

"I'll ring for the orderlies, and they'll put you in solitary."

"Yes, you would, and they will, but before they get here I'll have broken your arm in so many places it'll take six months to heal, and I get out of solitary tomorrow morning if I'm good and let them shoot me full of thorazine. Now tell me!"

"No," he mumbled.

"No, what?"

"No, she didn't say she wouldn't. Your name never came up today."

"Is that the truth?"

"Yes. It is Boris. Really. It's the truth."

I sat back down in my chair.

"Why are you so upset?" I asked.

"I don't want you to sleep with Mara."

"Why not?"

"Boris. I don't want you to do this. It could be catastrophic."

"I'm leaving." I got up. "Good-bye!"

"Boris, listen to me, please."

I sat down. I don't know why.

"Boris, Mara is right now going through a critical part of her therapy. For her to make love with you right now could be very dangerous. I can't let you do this. Get to know her if you want. Become good friends. But don't let it go beyond that. Please."

"I can't do that."

"Then you should ask yourself how much you *really* love her."

I thought about that for a minute.

"You know, Dr. Ward, if you were a competent doctor, I'd tell you to go to hell right now. But you're so incompetent that you *could* have screwed up things so badly that my making love with Mara *could* be dangerous. All right. You've got me. You win," and I got up and left, slamming the door behind me.

I went for a long walk and then decided to take a cold shower. When I finally got to dinner, Mara, Julian, and another patient, Doug, were already eating. I got my food and sat down with them.

"And where does that leave us?" Julian was saying as I took the plates off my tray.

"With nothing left to confess," Doug answered. He seemed to be unhappy with his reply.

"Oh, but we must confess," Mara said. "If we do nothing else. We have everything to confess."

"And will you be our father confessor?" Julian asked.

"Or our mother superior?" Doug continued with a slight smile starting at the corner of his mouth. Doug was the clinic's resident genius, and he knew he was goading Mara into action. I suspected that he didn't have the faintest idea where his push would send her.

Mara ignored the tone and responded to the words.

"I think that is a fine idea, yes. You three shall each confess to me. And then I shall confess to you. You shall confess one thing only, and it must be exactly what you would confess if the Angel of Death were standing before you and gave you one confession to judge your fate. Now who would like to go first?"

Doug adopted his most penitent voice.

"Forgive me father, for I have sinned—"

"Stop that, Douglas!" Mara spit out, her eyes darting deep into his. I had never seen her like that. She had suddenly gone rigid with rage, with anger that fulminated inside her and reddened her eyes. She tightened her lips.

"Now confess, Douglas, or you shall be dead." And I believed it, and so did Julian and Doug.

There was a long silence. Mara stared sharply at all of us, looking first at Doug, then Julian, and finally me.

"I have nothing to confess," Doug said finally, running his fingers through his blond curly hair.

"But you do. You do," Mara said, the anger gone from her voice and reassurance taking its place.

"Perhaps I should go first," Julian said, and this pleased Mara. "Will you turn away?"

"No. We must all face each other."

Julian thought about it for a moment and then shrugged his shoulders with acceptance. He waited for a moment, and, as time passed in silence and we all stared at him, we could see his lips start to move, barely start to formulate the words. His eyes grew watery, and his throat started to sound from deep in his gut. His mouth formed the words slowly, and, when they came out, they said, "I am a repulsive person."

There were another few minutes of silence during which Julian painfully clenched his black-gloved hands into tight fists.

"If I could return to nothing, I would do so. If I had the nerve to kill myself, I would. I can no longer feel. I am living on reflex. I am a living nothing, draining the world. My insides have been turned over the years into garbage. That is my confession. I am a repulsive nothing of gelatin garbage."

Julian's confession was such absolute negation that I wanted to laugh. Doug wanted to laugh. But Mara did not. Nor did Julian. It didn't make sense. I liked Julian. We all liked Julian. I couldn't understand what had led him to say such a dumb thing so seriously. I looked at Mara, and she seemed to be enjoying Doug's and my bewilderment.

"You may live," she told Julian, "and when you die, you shall be in heaven."

Julian wasn't listening. He sat staring down at his hands.

"You shall be in heaven because it is not your fault you are a worm," Mara continued.

"Mara," I interrupted. "I don't see the point of all this."

"The point is," Mara said as though no further explanation would be needed, "that it is night."

"I believe I shall confess next," Doug said.

"Good, Douglas," Mara said as though Doug's indication of willingness was my refutation.

"I am an underground man," Doug said mechanically shaking his head in agreement with his own words.

Mara smiled. Julian looked up at Doug and broke out of his trance.

"I am without control and, therefore, without morals or scruples. I am disembodied from my mind, rather I am two minds. The me-mind was buried by the me-body before it had a chance. Now the I-mind no longer cares and has stopped searching for where the me-mind is buried. I live outside my mind, doing anything, everything."

He looked at the three of us as though he were bewildered about something, but didn't know whether it was really worth the effort to find out what exactly was bewildering him.

"I have no soul," he said and shook his head to indicate that he had finished.

I tried to see whether I could understand what Doug was saying by repeating the words under my breath. It didn't work. Julian continued to look at Doug as though Doug would have more to say. Mara stared at the table and nodded her head as though she were in perfect agreement with Doug. The nodding indicated that Doug had prolonged his life and won heaven. She looked up at me. It was my turn.

"Well," I said, "I'm a felon."

Even though I tried to say this with all the drama and impact that Julian and Doug had given their confessions, what I said just didn't seem *important* enough. Everyone looked at me with disgust, particularly Mara.

"I'm sorry, really," I said, "but that's all I could think of."

"This is your *life*, Boris," Mara said, "for your *eternal life*."

"I know. I know. But I can't think of anything else to say."

"I refuse to make a decision on the basis of that confession," the *Angel of Death* informed me. "You've just got to try harder."

"Well, I'm not a worm, and I'm not without a soul."

"Then what are you?" Mara asked.

"I don't think I know," I answered.

"Why not?" Mara continued.

"Because I don't think that a human being can ever find out what he is."

"You can!" Mara insisted.

"No, you can't," I said. I was sure of it now. Much more sure than I ever have been since. "Because we're always changing and are aware of our changing at the same time. I'm not a plant. I'm a person, sitting here now. But I could be somewhere else. And I can't *be something.* I can't say that I *am* something. I can't tell you *what* I am until I can *never* be anything else. And that'll never be because people are free. So there."

"We are nothing!" Mara said.

"What is that supposed to mean?" I asked.

"That is my confession!" Mara snapped back at me.

"What the hell kind of a confession is that?" I snapped at Mara.

"Mine. That's what!" Mara barked back.

"*You* are confessing that *we* are nothing?" I asked.

"Yes. And I'm confessing that I haven't yet been born."

"You said that you die each— that each time you—"

"I said, Boris, that each time I make love I die and then I'm born again."

"And you haven't yet *been* born?"

"Yes. That is how I know that we're nothing. Only for nothing is birth and death the same."

"You didn't say that they were the same," I said.

"No, Boris, I didn't. Not until now. Now I have said it. We aspire to be nothing, and at our best we are. When we're born we become nothing, and when we die are nothing."

I listened incredulously to Mara. I understood not a word, not a single word she was saying. I couldn't understand what the words meant or how it could be her confession. She saw this.

"I have an idea," she directed at me. "Let's climb Bald Peak, all four of us, now."

"In the dark?" Julian asked.

"In the dark. No flashlights, no nothing. We'll get used to it. I'll meet you downstairs in five minutes," and Mara dashed excitedly from her chair and in the general direction of her room. When she returned five minutes later, she was dressed in an old army jacket, boots, a black ski hat, and her dungarees. She was ready for the climb. We weren't. But through Mara's usual method of laughter, disappointment, and coquetry, we found ourselves a few minutes later heavily clothed and in Mara's Volkswagen on the way to Bald Peak.

Bald Peak is only by the broadest stretch of the imagination a mountain. From the base, there is a well-worn path that leads to the top, often steep because of the rock ledges, but manageable if attempted any time other than the middle of a winter night.

During the five-minute drive to the dirt road that led into the pine forest at Bald Peak's base, Mara bubbled away, becoming happier the closer we came, as though this were to be a major entertainment in her life.

A short distance into the pine forest a large tree blocked the road, and so Mara stopped the car there and turned off the lights.

None of us moved. We sat silently in the car, listening to whatever sounds penetrated our steel shell and hoping that our eyes would fully adjust to the darkness.

Mara grew tired of waiting and got out of the car. We followed, slamming the car doors to announce to the mountain that we had arrived. When we could finally make out the white blazes on the trees that indicated where the path to the top began, we started to walk, slowly, and keeping within arm's reach of each other.

The recent snow had left about five inches of powder on top of the leaves, and our steps made at first the dull sound of our feet matting the snow and then the crack of leaves and twigs underneath. The heavy smell of pine was a drug that numbed us to the clear cold night.

We continued up the path in silence for a few minutes. Then Mara broke the silence.

"There are voices, Boris. Do you hear someone speaking?"

We all stopped. There was only silence. But the voices existed.

"They are men, I suppose," Mara continued, "although they might be women. Do you hear them?"

"No, no, no," our three male voices responded in a very high register.

"You are all scared."

"Petrified," Julian spoke for at least himself and me.

"I don't hear any voices," Doug said. "Are they human?"

"I'm not sure," Mara answered. "What they are saying—" She didn't finish.

We continued the climb in silence for another five minutes or so.

"What we all must do is listen," Mara began again, and continued the climb. We were supposed to listen, only there was nothing to hear, at least nothing rational. My imagination is a vivid one, and I heard all kinds of things that weren't there. I could have fielded a baseball team with the number of people I heard plotting to kill me and bury my body deep under the snow. I could have probably fielded a whole goddam *league* of baseball teams.

Julian, on the other hand, wasn't any better off than I was. What I heard, *he saw*. Every tree was a beast or a homicidal maniac. Every time a wind moved a branch, and shadows cast by the moon on top of the pines darted across the path, Julian would throw himself to the ground and shout "No! No!" and I would freeze in fear.

Fear was the watchword of the climb. Rather than getting accustomed to the night, I grew more and more afraid of it. I began to get the feeling that I couldn't trust the forest, or the night, or the path on which I was walking. I mentioned this to Doug, who was trying to control Julian, who in turn was becoming more hysterical every minute.

"I'm afraid, of course," Doug told me, "but I'm used to it. It's become a part of my life. It might even be *all* my life. Who knows?"

Suddenly Julian stopped and announced that he was going back. Mara refused to let him. Doug concurred, and I certainly had no intention of accompanying him, just the two of us, halfway back down a mountain I had no idea how I'd gotten up. No, he would have to complete the rest of the climb, it was decided. Reluctantly, he started to climb.

"I hope you guys know what you're doing," Julian stated between cold breaths.

Doug decided to liven the proceedings.

"You are Moses, Julian. You are Moses and you must get the ten commandments."

"In the middle of the night?"

"You get them when you're told to get them. At the top of the mountain you will be face to face with God Himself."

"I still don't want to go."

"Wouldn't it be wild," I offered, "if we got to the top and God was there. Some crazy guy who was all disheveled and unshaven, and we asked who He was and He says 'God' and flashes a couple lightning bolts or burns a bush or something just to prove it."

"What do you expect?" Mara asked. "Someone in shiny white robes and long silver hair?"

"I hope He's *clean*," Julian answered. "I hate to think that He's dirty, too."

Mara didn't appreciate the humor.

"He'll be there," she informed us quite seriously.

"Did you invite Him?" Julian snapped back.

"No," Mara said. "I invited you, so He'll be there."

We completed the climb in silence. That was very bad. Julian was now shaking from fear. Mara kept giggling to herself. I was afraid and panicky, and Doug was acting very strangely. He was dragging his feet and panting heavily. On occasion he would stop and moan.

When we arrived at the very top, at the flat snow-covered rock that was the peak, we were a traveling circus act. Julian was saying "no, no, no, no," over and over to himself under his breath and was virtually in convulsions. Doug seemed to be suffering from some kind of acute pain in his lungs or chest. Mara walked around, her arms open to the world, and I sat in the cold snow frightened out of my mind.

Suddenly there was a noise. We stopped short and then recognized it as some snow falling from a bush or rock. We maintained the silence, and then, for no reason that I could tell then or have been able to discover since, Doug screamed.

It was a long, high-pitched scream that must have carried over four states. Julian, Mara, and I were startled out of our skins. We looked at Doug. Doug turned to Julian.

"I want to tell you something, Julian, and I want you to listen very carefully. You see those stars?"

The sky was filled with stars.

"They are going to collide and crash into one another. You see how close they are? Now look at the moon. It's getting closer to the earth. Right now it's started to fall toward the earth. It'll take an hour and a half, and then it'll crash into us, and we'll be just broken bits of rock floating in space. Can you see how it's getting closer?"

"Please don't, Doug," Julian pleaded. "I can't stop myself from crying."

"You know that I'm lying?" Doug asked.

"Yes, but I can't help myself," Julian answered.

"Good, then I'll continue. The moon is falling to the earth. Every second it gets closer, and there isn't a thing we can do. Should we watch it get closer? What should we do with our last hour and a half? Watch it? Make love? Read a good book? No, I'll tell you what we'll do. We're all going to try to push back the moon. We're all going to take one big breath and blow! We're all going to scream and yell and shout for it to go away. And when we fail, then do you know what we'll do? We'll all get on our hands and knees and pray it will miss us. Everyone except me. I'm going to stand right here and watch the stars explode and the moon crash."

Julian was crying, sobbing, totally unable to control himself. Doug went over to him.

"Can you imagine how big the moon's going to seem just before it hits us? The whole moon right on *top* of us?"

There was silence then, several minutes of silence and cold, wind blowing through our jackets, snow stuck in the bottom of our boots, and below us the pine trees secured the night with their smell.

Finally, Mara came over and pressed herself against me, wrapped her arms tightly around my back, and spoke a few words I didn't understand. They were too faint. She continued.

"Are you scared, Boris? Still?"

"I'm not sure. I think I am."

"What do you hear? What do you see?"

"Nothing."

"Do you think that this is the beginning? Right here, this?" Mara asked.

Doug overheard Mara. "I do. I'm certain of it," Doug answered.

I thought for a minute. "No," I said.

"Then do you think that it's the end?" Mara asked.

"It's the end," I agreed.

"Is that why you're afraid? What do you think?"

I looked around me. The sky was spread with thousands of stars, but all around us it was black. There was, I believe for the first time in my life, complete silence. I felt as though I were foundering in the midst of an endless heavy cloud, substance without form. But if I were afraid, then in the beginning was fear, and I didn't *live* in fear, *life* was not fear, only this cloud. I decided not to answer Mara's question.

"I find myself enjoying this," I finally lied.

"Of course, you do," Mara responded. "Do you know what this is? All of this? This is evil. You're afraid because of it, but evil is beautiful. And chaos. Chaos and nothing. But most of all, evil. And I think that's wonderful. Good is boring."

Julian spoke for the first time in an hour.

"*People* are evil, Mara. *People.* Not this. Not this!" And he swung his arms through the air.

"Well," Mara snapped back, "That's a pretty speech, but look at yourself. You're a complete mess, Julian. You have no control of yourself. Is that from people? Or is it from being up here?"

"It is," Julian measured his words very carefully, "because I'm a person, and a very weak one, and I can't face, either alone or with such pleasant company, myself."

"That's a lot of hokey," Mara snapped. "This is a self-destructing bomb made by a self-destructing bomb maker. Forget about all of us who are in the middle and what might never be the end, but see the *beginning* and you will be saved, because this is the beginning, Julian. Nothing. We must think ourselves born."

Mara held me tighter in the cold and I responded by pressing her closer to me.

"I'm so happy, Boris."

"I'm glad, Mara," I said. I don't know why.

"I'm happy to be alive," Mara said and that was the end of it.

We stumbled down the mountain, finally, and all the way down the visitors spoke, voices coming from the trees, Mara stopping us to make us listen.

"That's Billy Bad," Mara said maybe twenty times during the descent into the real world, "and he's saying that I'm right, and you should all listen to me or go to hell. Julian, I'm going to bed with Boris because you're a worm, and I don't have sex with worms. I'm sorry, but that's the way it is."

Julian didn't answer. He just stared absently into space.

We drove back to The Inn, and Mara and I went to her room. There we got undressed and got naked into bed. On her night table was a silver-framed photograph of an infant.

"Who is that?" I asked.

"My baby."

I froze in position.

"Are you married?"

"No. I decided I didn't love the guy, so I didn't marry him, but I wanted to have the baby. It's very complicated, and *not* very interesting."

"Where is the baby now?"

"I don't know. They don't tell you who adopts it. It's all rather depressing really."

I decided to change the subject to the only other thing that came to mind at that point.

"How do you like Dr. Ward?" I asked.

"I think he's great. He's using this new method of treatment with me, and it's really gotten me over some terrible hang-ups."

"What is it?"

"Well, it's really new and innovative, and it's supposed to be a secret, so you can't tell a soul. Promise?"

"My lips are sealed."

"He makes love to me every session. It's a new technique."

I think what I said when I finally spoke was, "He should publish," or something like that. I don't really remember too well. Actually, I'm trying not to think at all, because, if I do, I'll remember too much that I just don't want to remember.

I turned over and felt her body, naked against mine, the softness between her legs just barely brushing against my leg, and so we made love at the end (beginning) of it all, for the cosmos, for the stars, and for the dark infinity of curved space. We held each other and moved together for all the evil in the world, for broken backs and suicides, for rapes and hurt, for naïveté and frustration, for bleeding hands and orphaned babies and loneliness, and when at last we came, it was to be enveloped in the massive comfort of absolutely nothing, the sweet swelling exploding end of everything into silence, and then we slept our first night together.

"I love you, Billy Bad," Mara said to me just before she fell asleep, and let me tell you something. For the first time probably in my whole goddam life, I knew what was going to happen next.

2nd "Harry, there has got to be an explanation."

Spontaneity, Boris. Nothing but spontaneous creation.

"Don't give me any of that *sui generis* crap. I want to know what the hell's going on."

You want meaning?

"You're goddam right. I want meaning."

Then give it meaning. And I'll tell you this, Boris, any meaning you give it is all right with me. I'll give it my whole-hearted endorsement.

"Jesus Christ, Harry, I'm not trying to sell deodorants. I'm trying to find out what *your* meaning is. I don't want to *give* it meaning. It's already *got* meaning. *Your* meaning. What is it?"

Boris, I really don't think I'm going to be able to help you. I just wrote what I wrote. I didn't think of conveying any deep messages, only putting words down on paper.

"Like hell you did, Harry. I know you. You've got some goddam devious plan up your sleeve. You've got me screwing this nutty girl who thinks she's some kind of a sexed-up Medusa—"

I thought you liked her.

"I do like her. But why?"

Why? Because you are in love with her. That's why. And you find the meaning in that if it makes you happy. You're in love with the girl, Boris. Period. *You* figure it out. I'm busy.

"I don't trust you, Harry."

I've heard.

4th Arnold has taken up residence here. In a way I am grateful that he has. I enjoy his company. I do not understand him, but I enjoy him. Sometimes, in wild moments when I forget myself, I find that I begin loving him, like a father loves his son. But for the most part, this passes in short order.

We have had some decent talks, Arnold and I.

"Father, I am concerned about you."

"Why is that, Arnold?"

"Because you just aren't yourself."

"Who am I, Arnold?"

"Someone who is having a difficult time living."

"Has someone made you a promise that life would be easy?"

"Not life, Father, you. You are making life difficult for yourself, for all of us."

It is such moving compassionate interchanges that cement the bond forever between father and son.

This evening Arnold sat back in the old high-backed chair in which his mother and I used to make faces to get him to laugh when he was a baby, and Arnold stared at me for a very long time. He held onto the arms of the chair as though he were about to come in for a crash landing, and maybe he remembered the funny faces.

"Father, I think you are mad," he nodded pleasantly.

"Thank you, Arnold," I said.

Arnold sat and thought some more.

"Father, I've made an appointment for you to see another doctor. I think you should explain your problems to him."

"I have no problems."

"Nevertheless . . ."

"Arnold, you want me to see another doctor, I'll see another doctor."

"You will?"

"Certainly. You expected me to throw a fit?"

"I thought you would object."

"I would have to be *crazy* to object to such a kind offer, wouldn't I, Arnold?"

"Will you go soon?"

"Make me an appointment. I'll go."

"And there's something else. There's an agent who'd like to look at this house. I told her that you'd show her around. I didn't think you'd mind. Nothing definite about selling the house, of course."

"Of course."

"Well, there isn't."

"I agree."

"You don't believe me."

"Arnold, it doesn't really matter," I said and dozed off on the sofa, leaving Arnold in a condition best described as befuddlement.

5th I don't know why I do these things. Does anyone else find them amusing? I doubt it. Certainly not that poor bullfrog of a woman, Miss Pleuter, who came to appraise the house this afternoon.

I've never liked women over forty in dungarees, and these particular dungarees encased the ass of Miss Pleuter like a topographic map of the rolling English countryside. And another thing. Miss Pleuter didn't walk through the house. She marched. All four feet of her. I felt I was being raided by a lesbian pygmy.

I get carried away. Where is my tolerance for my fellow human beings? Could I possibly be of the same genus, the same species, the same family as Katherine Pleuter of Doft, Harcrow, and Simmerling, Realtors? Questions like this disturb my sleep for months.

"And what's behind that door? Secret research?" Miss Pleuter elbowed my side. I was beginning to exhaust the answers.

"Something like that. Can you keep a secret?"

"Yes, I can. Till I die," she assured me.

"Well, I don't think you'll have to carry this to your grave—"

"But I will, Dr. Wolper. You can count on me that I will." She stuck her hands tightly into her dungaree pockets and puffed out her chest, already preparing herself for the torture under which she would not yield the secret.

"That room," I said softly, "is where I keep limbs."

"Limbs?"

"Right. Arms, legs, toes, fingers— You see, Miss Pleuter, I have found a way to grow a whole person from an arm, or leg, if you will. Toes and fingers are a little more difficult because first you have to grow the limb, and then proceed from there. Would you like to see some of the legs?"

"Where does that door over there lead to?"

"That's a film studio. I use it for making movies of sexual intercourse between humans and other beings not usually involved in human intercourse. It's a fascinating field that very little work has been done in. It's also a hell of a lot of fun if you get the right combination. I had this swan last week and you have never seen—"

"Dr. Wolper, I guess I've seen just about all I need for an appraisal."

"Oh, I hope I haven't offended you."

"No, no. Not at all. Your work's fascinating. It's just that it *is* late, and I've got to be getting back to the office."

"Certainly. You know, I have this marvelous chemical formula I've developed, and, if you think you might be up to coming out here late Saturday night—"

"Oh," her voice raised to a higher register, "Saturday night I roller skate, otherwise I'd love to—"

"Then Sunday. We'll make it Sunday night."

"Ice hockey. I'm goalie. Sorry. But as soon as I have a free night, I'll let you know."

"Well, I hope you've enjoyed the little tour. I'd be happy to show around anyone else you might want me to."

"Thank you, Dr. Wolper, but I don't think the market is ready for your house just yet."

"Oh, that is a shame."

Miss Pleuter started out the door. I called after her.

"And Miss Pleuter. About the arms and legs. Mum's the word."

She raised her finger to her mouth.

"Till I die, Dr. Wolper. Till I die."

Now why do I do things like that? I don't know. She was so sure I was crazy, I hated to disappoint her. I guess I'm just a sucker for a woman's charm.

6th Arnold called today.

"Father, for godsakes, what was that story you gave Mrs. Pleuter about growing people from arms and legs?"

"*Miss* Pleuter, Arnold. She is *Miss* Pleuter."

"Miss Pleuter. Are you really trying to do that?"

"I don't know, Arnold, what do you think? How's it sound to you?"

"It sounds to me like if you *are* trying to do it, you'd better *stop*, and if you *aren't*, you'd better *stop* saying you *are*. You've got the whole town ready to burn you as a witch."

"Warlock."

"What?"

"Warlock. A male witch is called a warlock."

"For godsakes, Father, will you listen to me. Everyone wants to know where you got the limbs from."

"Whaling crews. I go out in the fall with whaling crews and come back every spring with a supply."

"Now stop it. Will you, please. Miss Pleuter says you've got them filed by race. Negro arms in one drawer, Chinese legs in another—"

"She's got more of an imagination than I thought."

"Imagination, hell. She says she *saw* them. What did you show her?"

"A closed door, Arnold."

"What was behind the closed door?"

"I believe it was a toilet."

"What was *in* the toilet?"

"What one *normally* finds in toilets. Now I'm hanging up, Arnold. Goodbye."

7th I thought about Arnold's phone call and decided finally to send the following note:

> Dear Miss Pleuter,
>
> I spoke to my son yesterday and was grieved to hear of your deathbed confession of my secret work, and your untimely death. We'd give an arm and a leg to have you back with us again.
>
> Your friend,
> H. H. Wolper

8th My work is progressing more slowly than ever. I have found something, though. Age is a factor. Not my age, but the age of the embryo. When I take the nucleus from a very young embryo, a nucleus that has not worn itself out, as *I* have, in making decisions and ordering results, then the transplant will hold, and it will hold well. For a frog.

I ask myself this. If I am able to find a girl who will let me extract an egg from her, and if I transplant my Lucy's nucleus for the girl's, and if, even if I can succeed in keeping the organism alive *in vitro*, will Lucy fail me because she is old, and for that reason alone? Has she performed her one creation? Are we all limited to direct one development and then, like a fly, the creation in us dies and we are nothing but carriers of disease?

I must find out just how the nucleus of an embryonic cell differs from the nucleus of an adult cell.

Otherwise, and I find that I must consider the otherwises, Lucy, who has been so patiently surviving these years in her jar, has been lost from the start, and I am alone forever. It is enough to make a man sad, even a scientist who, we all know, has no emotions.

"You have me, Harry. I'm still with you."

Don't remind me, Boris. In my best moments I can forget.

9th I am no longer overwhelmed by the universal *primavera*, by April.

You see what my work has done to me. It is a time of life, of thaw, of old brown thoughts reviving, and I am so convinced that life as I know it, as I see it here in the lab, is no bright pink and green blossoming wonder, that I will not even accept my own instincts.

I used to live for April. And all April I would live. My work would rot on the bench, because I knew that if a man lives to ninety he sees only ninety creations. I can count to ninety in less than a minute. I have timed myself.

Sometimes I think that if it would not tire me, I would like to travel to South America every October and double my creations. I wonder whether on the other side of the equator the earth gives birth as effortlessly? I ask this because I had a dream last night.

I am walking through the town where we spent the summer. Only it is April, and, as I am walking, spring arrives, painfully. It is a creation exactly like the human creation. The trees are all screaming when their buds open. The ground wretches and heaves when flowers force their way above the soil. Every so often a mistake occurs. A tree's buds open, and, instead of leaves, there are daffodils, an enormous daffodil tree, while a single leaf grows from the stem of a daffodil. All this happens very quickly. The earth is in labor underground for ninety days, groaning and sobbing, and in one convulsive outburst, there is spring, flowers, leaves, grass, warm air.

I sigh with relief (in the dream).

I have an idea from the dream when I awaken. No, it is more a conviction than an idea. I cannot continue to play at motherhood. I am a farmer, not a womb. If I want a harvest, I must do what any good farmer must do.

I must plant.

10th Just after I won the Nobel Prize I was famous.

I was asked to write an autobiography. The money was not particularly great, but the idea intrigued me.

I had no idea what I would say about myself. Personally, I find most of my life less than a source of endless fascination, and other than Paul, I have yet to find anyone who could stand to hear more than five minutes of it without developing a chronic yawning condition.

I thought about this problem and finally arrived at what I thought was a satisfactory solution to the problem. The other day I came across the note I received back with the manuscript.

> Dear Dr. Wolper:
>
> We have had to give reconsideration to our original idea of your doing an autobiography. We do not, at this time, feel that the market would justify our publishing an autobiographical scientific western, even with the ingenious macabre ending you have given it. As a point of information, autobiographies rarely include personal descriptions of the author's funeral.

Publishers have historically been men of little or no vision.

"Why is that, Harry?"

Because, Boris, what is it I write in this notebook everyday if it is not a personal description of the author's funeral?

11th **The Adventures of Boris Lafkin**

written by H. H. WOLPER

CHAPTER THREE:

In Which Our Hero Spends Another Lousy Year in Paradise (continued)

Somewhere out there, somewhere sleeping in another bed tonight, is this enormous chunk of me, and I want it back. I want it back even though I know that there's nothing I could do with it if I did have it, and that Mara's probably married anyway. But she's still got this part of me, and I need it, because what I've been trying to say is that it's a very important part of me.

It's not as certain that I really got a part of Mara in return, because all the memories have the aftertaste of Walter and his goddam motorcycle. I just don't understand how the hell Mara could find anything worthwhile in that guy. Anyway, you would think that the memory, whatever there is of it, would keep me satisfied, but the memory has so many parts that it just makes me miserable.

I remember one day when I walk into Mara's room. I am in love with her, as usual, and she is sitting cross-legged on the floor in her underpants and bra, that's all, nothing else, and she's got this piece of glass and is scratching her legs with it, which are, of course, covered with blood.

"What is that?" I ask her, attempting to be nonchalant and succeeding not at all.

"It's a piece of coke bottle," she answers.

"No, the blood and the ritual. What is that?"

"I'm not sure. I've been doing it for a long time."

"How long?"

"Ever since I stopped making love to Dr. Ward."

We had agreed, or at least *she* had. Dr. Ward would not be allowed to use his "latest techniques" in therapy. On account of the prohibition, Dr. Ward is having a nervous breakdown. So is Mara.

And then, of course, we are in love. I think I've said that. I don't know how this figures into the whole thing, but it means that I go over to the sink in Mara's room, wet a towel, and clean up her legs.

"Boris," Mara asks while I'm cleaning the blood off her legs, "what possible meaning could there be in extinct animals?"

"Mara, do you love me?"

"Yes. Why?"

"Just wondering. Why did you cut your legs all up?"

"Because I'm having a nervous breakdown."

"Is there anything I can do to help?"

"You can stick around until I get some clothes on and then go for a walk with me."

"Get your clothes on. I'll wait."

This was typical. All conversations that spring seemed to be like this. I don't know whether they were important or not. It's hard as hell to tell which conversations were *significant* and which were garbage.

But it *was* paradise, being in love with Mara. It was the most beautiful thing I could imagine, and all there was to it was conversation and holding each other, like on walks and in bed. I even cried once, in real life. I cry all the time in movies and plays and stuff, but in real life I usually don't get worked up enough. I find it hard to get involved. Like, you lose a girl or a friend or a relative dies, well, that's the way life works, and you can get angry about it, but there's no use going into tears. On the other hand, Ingrid Bergman leaves Humphrey Bogart, and you know that she loves him and he loves her and that they're never going to see each other for the rest of their lives, and Paris will live forever inside of them with nothing they can do about it, and that's sad as hell, and when I see it again (for the twenty-third time) I know I'm going to weep like a baby just as I have the last twenty-two times.

That spring Mr. Sokol built a house. As a patient of twenty years in good standing with an equal length of time remaining for treatment, Mr. Sokol was given permission to build a house directly across from the clinic on Route 6. What no one suspected was that it was Mr. Sokol's plan to build the perfect American house, and he had the resources to do this, not only because he was, at fifty, a millionaire several times over, but because he owned a construction company renowned for dropping housing developments more or less like bird doo at random spots over the countryside.

For most of the spring Mr. Sokol's men worked on the house, and then, the end of May, the house was finished. It was a small white Cape house with aluminum siding, and red and white candy-striped aluminum awnings over each window and over the baroque aluminum screen-storm doors with a gothic script "S" stamped into the metalwork. All the trees were uprooted and replaced with one small elm, held upright by rubber hose and metal wires directly in front of the living room window. The grass was also uprooted and replaced with a combination of Bermuda and St. Augustine grass seed, which stood no chance of growing in the New England climate, so the brown ground with white speckles that now surrounded the house was a permanent promise of nothing to come.

On the right side of the house was a flagpole with a small circular garden edged with whitewashed bricks, a concrete birdbath, and a small floodlit shrine. In the backyard was a red-tinted swimming pool, the steps to which were framed by two metal statuettes of black stable-boys holding rings that could be used for guest towels. The house was completely surrounded with a three-foot steel mesh fence backed by a trimmed hedge, and securely bolted to the roof were Santa and his eight tiny reindeer.

Small speakers set into the eaves of the house played a twenty-four hour tape, a selection of favorite tunes from Walt Disney's animated films during the day and Frank Sinatra in the evening. Between each selection the voice of Mr. Sokol was heard repeating, "May God have mercy on your soul. May God have mercy on your soul."

The Great American Home, or Sokol's Revenge, as we came to call it, became a halfway house for patients getting ready to leave the clinic. Then, the last week in June, Sybil drowned herself in the pool, and Mr. Sokol burnt the house to the ground.

Sybil had been Mara's closest friend, and Mara was very depressed about the whole thing. I was in New York at some criminal hearing or update or something like that, which I never did understand, and when I got back, I saw the bulldozers burying what was left of Mr. Sokol's house and heard the story of Sybil from Doug.

"She was crazy, anyway. They never should have let her leave," Doug said.

"Why?" I asked.

"She drowned herself in a raccoon coat. It was a great coat. She ruined the goddam thing."

"Why did she wear a coat?"

"It had pockets. She needed someplace to put her note."

"Did you see her note?"

"I saw it. I pulled her out of the pool. She must have been there all night. It's a lousy way to die. There's nothing aesthetic about it. It hurts, and it looks lousy as hell."

"What did the note say?"

"It's hard to tell. I could only read some parts of it."

"What do you *think* it said?"

The Great American Suicide
brought to you tonight by Sybil Thompson
One Performance Only.

Mara was in her room. She was lying on the bed staring at the closet door on the other side of the room. Hanging on the door was Sybil's raccoon coat. It smelled as bad as it looked, but Mara was furious when I suggested she put it away until she had a little time to get used to the idea of Sybil's death.

"It's *my* coat, for godsakes. I just *lent* the damn thing to her. I didn't think she'd go drown in it. It cost me forty bucks. Look at it."

"You're mad at her."

"I think she did a dumb thing, and she was damn inconsiderate to me."

"Why do you think she did it?"

"I don't know why she did it. What am I, a goddam mind reader?"

"Doug said you were the last person to see her."

"So? What does that prove? Do you think if she had told me she was going to kill herself, I would have let her do it?"

"No."

"Well, she didn't tell me anything," Mara said and stared up at the ceiling for a few minutes.

"She really didn't have any choice, you know, Boris," she finally said. "She couldn't stay here because they said she was better, and she couldn't go out there because she hated it so much. They should have let her stay."

"How do you feel?"

"Sybil and I were going to get pregnant as soon as we got out of here. We were going to go down to Atlantic City or someplace where there were lots of sailors, and every year we were going to get pregnant and then give the babies to people who couldn't have kids. It's hard to find white kids to adopt, you know. We were going to stay pregnant for the rest of our lives."

"You wouldn't exactly have helped the population problem."

"*I'm* the population problem, not the kids I have. The problem with the population is that I'm unhappy."

We talked for about an hour more until just before dinner. We ended up back at the coat.

"I still think you ought to get rid of it. You can't wear it anymore, and it's just making you miserable."

"I like to be miserable. What am I supposed to be after my best friend goes out and kills herself—overjoyed?"

"Do what you want, but I still don't think it's helping at all."

Mara changed her tone. "No, it does help, Boris. It really does. It's important to think about someone who's gone. And the coat reminds me of things."

"Fine."

"Boris. I need a change."

"Ask Dr. Ward for a permission slip and go visit someone."

"No. I mean from you. I need a change from you. It's been six months. That's a long time."

"Six months is not a long time."

"Still, I need this. I love you."

"You're getting me all confused."

"You'll figure it out," and Mara got off the bed and came over to me. She was wearing her usual outfit of a white man's shirt with nothing on underneath and her tight dungarees. She put her arms around me, and I realized that we would never make love to each other again.

"Shall I leave you something?" she asked me.

I reached down behind her and lifted her to me by her denim-covered buttocks.

"Yes," I said, "leave me your ass."

"Okay," she said, "I'll leave you my ass."

And then we kissed for the last time. That was it. It was over. When I went to her room that night, the door was locked, and then the next week, after seven days of endless meetings held by the doctors to assure us and themselves that they did not make a mistake in releasing Sybil to Sokol's Revenge, and we would not kill *ourselves* when we were released, at the end of these, Walter arrived, and Mara's feelings for me came to a screeching halt, leaving deep tracks in what I tried to assure myself was my psyche.

The summer zipped by. It got too cold to play tennis. It got dark too early. The lobster, crab, and chicken salads disappeared from the menu, and I tried to determine how long it would be before I would be buried under winter.

I started reading *The Almagest*, for fun, going particularly wild over the moon's syzygies. Doug began *The Enneads*, and Julian tore into *The Pentateuch* and *Haftorahs*. It was sort of a contest, a ritual to prepare for the bleak days ahead, in which everybody was certain to lose. Mara would have no part of it and continued with the D. H. Lawrence books she had started a year ago.

We had one prolonged conversation during the fall, which, as I remember it, had to do largely with masturbation, a sort of catalogue of Coke bottles, cucumbers, Crisco, and carrots.

"Everybody masturbates, Boris, everybody," she argued most of the night. "People masturbate their eyes and their tongues and their minds. I believe in Jesus."

* * *

It was the Friday before Thanksgiving, an unusually bright warm day for November. Doug, Julian, and I were sitting on the front steps of the inn, waiting for our lunch to digest before we went to play some basketball. Mara came out and stood on the top step looking down at us.

"Hey, you know someone's just shot Kennedy," she said. "Jack Kennedy. They might have gotten Johnson, too. You want to go down to the TV room and watch?"

By the time we got downstairs the TV room was filled with most of The Inn's residents and staff. Walter Cronkite was virtually in tears, as was the nursing staff, but there was a generally high level of excitement among the patients.

It's hard to know how to say this, but we were all pretty much overjoyed about the whole thing. It would mean all kinds of excitement and emotions pouring from the least likely places.

"We've got a chance," Doug said.

Julian concurred. "It's our Great Depression, our World War II, our D day."

The excitement built, and we drank in as much as we could as fast as possible. We switched channels every few minutes and had a radio playing in the back of the room, and, when that became too frustrating, we brought down two portable televisions from upstairs and had all three going at the same time. We bribed the bus driver five bucks to bring us back every edition of every paper he could find in Boston, and he did a great job. All around the room, patients read and tore out articles, punctuating every other paragraph they read with "*fantastic*." We stayed up all night.

"Isn't this great?" Mara said to me that first morning. "We're important. We're really important."

The doctors went ape-shit. The whole staff assembled in the TV room in the middle of the night to assure us that there was nothing to be upset about, that tragic events happen, and we must all learn to gain perspective on them.

Doug spoke most of our thoughts in response.

"We're not upset," he told them. "We're delighted. This is terrific."

As our heads filled that night with Love Field, Pontifical Mass, Governor Connally, Lee Harvey Oswald, Capitol Rotunda, Texas School Book Depository, and Andrews Air Force Base, our excitement grew. More doctors started to fill the room, doctors we had never seen before, doctors who we could overhear were being told that they were getting a once-in-a-lifetime opportunity, the chance to see a mass psychosis in action. We became an attraction.

The doctors came in shifts, some with notepads or small tape recorders, others with miniature cameras. There was only one unfortunate incident and that came Monday morning and happened to poor Clarence, who had arrived at the clinic only a month before and was particularly spirited about the events of the last few days. Monday morning he was reclining on the floor among the crushed soft-drink cups and shredded newspapers, watching the preliminaries of the funeral, when the station switched suddenly to Dallas. Oswald appeared on the screen, and, shortly thereafter, Jack Ruby. A shot rang out, and although it took the rest of us a few seconds to catch on, Clarence knew what was up almost instantaneously.

"Hot dog!" he shouted as Oswald crumpled from the arms of his twin protectors. "We've done it *again!*"

All the doctors had the same idea and almost simultaneously they descended on poor Clarence with their cameras and tape recorders. Clarence tackled the nearest feet and proceeded to strangle the doctor with his microphone cord.

It took four doctors to carry Clarence off and lock him in isolation, and the incident killed the rest of the day for us. Any enthusiasm we had was gone. The muffled drumbeats and heads of state, the bagpipes, the procession and caisson, the reversed stirrups, and Cardinal Cushing all depressed us to the point that the room was empty long before taps was finally sounded.

Thanksgiving at the clinic was fatally depressing. "Last Thanksgiving I fell in love with Sybil," Mara told me while fingering her teacup. "You weren't here yet."

"Did you tell her?" I asked.

"She knew," Mara said. "We both knew."

"I miss her playing the piano after meals."

"The quiet is horrible. It's empty quiet and it's depressing." Mara stared into space.

"I thought you liked emptiness," I said.

"I like nothingness. Nothing has substance. Emptiness doesn't even have nothing there. You know who Sybil wanted to be?" Mara asked me.

"Joan of Arc," I guessed.

"Did she tell you that?"

"No, I guessed."

"Well, you're wrong. Sybil wanted to be Anna Magdalena."

"So she could study with Bach?"

"No. So she could have thirteen of his children."

There was only one way to get discharged from Days Clinic and that was for our therapist to certify us as sane. Mara and I decided that in an emergency we might be able to bother Dr. Ward, already near nervous collapse, enough for him to sign the release papers. And then there was always blackmail. We both knew that a threat to expose Dr. Ward's "latest therapeutic technique" had an almost 100 percent chance of success.

In the end, after that Thanksgiving, we weren't nearly so crass. Mara would go in every day at ten and describe in great detail our mythical lovemaking. I would arrive at eleven and continue the vivid description. By noon, Dr. Ward was more or less finished for the day.

It was Mara's suggestion that Dr. Ward release us as "cured," something that hadn't occurred to him. Dr. Ward wouldn't transfer us to another doctor, not only because it would be an admission of failure, but also for fear that we might tell about his screwing Mara. On the other hand, an out-and-out release could be an enormous risk because Dr. Ward would have to go before the clinic's board and substantiate his assertion that we were sane. Dr. Ward had no idea what it was to be sane.

"Maybe you could give me a little help, Boris," he asked me toward the end of it all.

"Don't you have it written in a book somewhere?" I asked.

"I don't think so."

"What about Freud or Jung or Adler or someone? Didn't they talk about being sane?"

"I don't think so. I never read much in graduate school."

"Why don't you ask someone?"

"I did. I did. I walked into Dr. Calmon's office and I said to him point-blank, 'I'm not at all ashamed to ask this of you, sir, because you're the director of the clinic. What does it mean to be sane?' And you know what he said? He said, 'Damned if I know.' "

"Is that all he said?"

"No. He said that I should never be ashamed to ask him anything, ever. That his door is always open. And it is. He can afford to leave it open. He's never there."

"Dr. Ward, Mara and I'll work it out for you."

We did, too. Mara and I discussed it and finally decided on the Boy Scout code. Dr. Ward was delighted.

"How can the board possibly not agree that a person who lives the Boy Scout code is sane? It's a miracle."

"A miracle cure, Dr. Ward. You'll be famous."

"Yes, I will. And rich?"

"And rich."

The next week Dr. Ward presented our cases, and we were told the next day that we would soon be discharged. That was good because the whole place had become depressing as hell. Even Dr. Ward knew it, and, when the end finally came for him two months later (simultaneously with the largely crazed reactions to the publication of his paper "Making Your Patient a Good Scout"), he insisted on being committed somewhere else.

"This place screws you up even more than the other place, sir," Dr. Ward was overheard saying to Dr. Calmon.

"What other place?" Dr. Calmon asked.

"The world, sir," Alexander Ward answered, and Dr. Calmon took him very gently by the arm and sent him to Menningers.

Mara left Days Clinic with one of those scenes that tend to stay with you.

Mara is in her VW resting her arm on the window ledge. Walter is, as usual, revving up his motorcycle in the lot in the back of The Inn. I shout over Walter's manhood.

"We don't know anything, yet," I shout. I'm trying to keep Mara from leaving.

"I love you, Boris," Mara shouts back.

"Where will you be living?"

"Do you love me, Boris?"

"What city will you be living in? What state?"

"I don't know."

"Will you write me when you find out?" I shout.

"I don't know. Where will *you* be?"

"I don't know." The motorcycle is getting louder.

"What?"

"I said, I don't know. I don't know."

"Neither do I," Mara says and around the corner comes Walter Supercool on his goddam BSA 1200 cc stupid lousy motorcycle with a red, white, and blue sign hanging from the back of the seat. It says "FUCK AMERICA." Walter is a shithead, and he is not at all cool, and it doesn't really make any difference because Mara asks me to stick my head in the window. When I do, she opens the top two buttons to her cardigan. She has nothing on underneath, and she pulls out her left breast. She has scratched a design on it with her broken coke bottle. The design is words. The words say, "I LOVE YOU BORIS." There is still a trickle of blood coming from the bottom of the Y in YOU.

I pull my head out the window, because I think that I'm going to vomit.

"Why did you *do* that?" I ask.

"I don't know, Boris," she says, grinds into first gear, and heads down the drive. Walter has mud tires on his two-wheeled phallus, which he now spins loudly and then races out into the middle of the street to stop all traffic so Mara can pull out. Walter is very gallant.

I go to my room. Mara has left her dungarees on my bed with a note.

"Best I could do. Had to take my ass with me. Sorry. I do love you so much, Boris."

I guess I must have cried off and on all afternoon.

When Mara left, it was the week before Christmas. I had more formalities to go through with probationary officers and crap like that, so I couldn't leave until New Year's Day.

In the morning I packed my knapsack, strapped my tennis racquet to the top of it, said good-bye to Doug and Julian, and walked down the driveway.

It was a cold day. Across the street was Mr. Sokol, sitting on the pile of bricks that used to be his Great American Dreamhouse. He was wearing a lumberjacket and had his arms wrapped tightly across his chest to protect himself from the wind.

I walked across Route 6 and over the frozen ground to where he was sitting.

"I'm leaving, Mr. Sokol," I said to him and shook his red hand.

"Good-bye. Good night. How are you? May God have mercy on your soul," Mr. Sokol said to me, but that was all Mr. Sokol had said for the last twenty years, so I nodded and walked over to the boarded-up Red Lion Inn to catch my bus to Boston.

12th "Harry, look—"

Not now. Please.

"Harry, I've got to talk to you."

Boris. Later. I'm in the middle of working.

"I think I've just about had it, Harry. I want to redefine our relationship."

What is that? You want to change tense or rearrange modifiers? What is this redefine? This is something human beings do with each other, or this is a grammatical construction?

"Harry, tell me something. If you're not responsible for any of this shit, then how come I don't *feel* like I'm living my life?"

Maybe you ate something that disagreed with you. How am I supposed to know? You tell me.

"Harry. Where do you think I came from?"

Boris, believe me. I have stayed awake for weeks trying to answer that question. And if I knew, if I had the slightest idea, I would ship you back there so quickly it would take a week for light to catch up with you. I have been haunted by this, Boris, been devastated, been humiliated by the question. Where have you come from, Boris? Tell me.

"I don't think you're being at all funny."

Where was the humor? I am in dead earnest, Boris. God's creation is an open book compared to yours. You are a complete and total mystery to me.

"Harry, will you stop this. I am *your* creation. I am the result of *your* pencil driven on *your* paper by *your* mind."

Actually, neither the pencils nor the paper are mine, I borrowed them from Paul, but let's not quibble because the mind is not mine either. At least the mind that begat you is not mine. There is absolutely no possibility of it. You are you, Boris. Totally and completely, Boris. You are you. I want no part of you. But then I delude myself, don't I Boris?

"How is that, Harry?"

I think I have a choice.

13th I went for a walk today, to air the rottenness out of my mind, and found myself sitting on the swings at the Garden Street playground. I used to go there almost every nice day with the children after Lucy died.

I had not expected Lucy to die. I was totally unprepared to be alone with Arnold, then six, Claire, who was two, and Rebecca, only an infant. If it hadn't been for Mrs. Mallory, I don't know what I would have done. Both Arnold and Claire were at particularly difficult ages. Arnold would say to me, "Mother is dead. I am going to break my neck." He said it to me, and to his teacher at school, and to the postman, to everyone he met until they no longer reacted by clutching him to them or by buying him ice cream. Arnold has not changed one iota. With Claire, she was too young. She had just begun to say "Mommy" in her throaty baby voice, when there suddenly was no Mommy. The poor child didn't know what to do. Her favorite, her only word was now useless, and she would go up to strangers, to women, to anyone wearing a skirt, and ask with great hope "Mommy?" My heart would try to wrench itself from my body so that it could pass over to her and help her understand with an adult's heart what had happened to all our lives. But, of course, there was nothing to be done.

I became a regular fixture of the playground, arriving at four in the afternoon with Claire sitting on my shoulder, my right hand pushing Rebecca's carriage and my left hand holding, clutching would be more accurate, to the struggling limb attached to the struggling body of Arnold who wanted to try his sadistic approach on whoever happened to be around the ice-cream wagon. More than occasionally, Arnold would arrive at the swing where I would be sitting with Claire in my lap, his fists full of dixie cups and popsicles, led gingerly by a misty-eyed woman from the neighborhood.

It was on one such occasion, several months after I had begun these afternoon excursions, that I met Karen Frankel, otherwise known as Mrs. Howard Frankel. Karen took it on herself to bring some small joy into my life, and there I was, Lucy not dead six months, sneaking off to bed with someone else's wife. What a blessing Mrs. Frankel was, and Mrs. Carruthers, and Mrs. Moriarity, and Mrs. Gold. The playground was a veritable gold mine of unfulfilled married women. It was headquarters for affairs beyond the wildest dreams of a *cinq-à-sept* grand master.

My emotions turned inside themselves into knots as I satisfied my needs, blasphemed the memory of the person who meant more to me than anyone else ever could, opened irreparable schisms in relationships of years of tolerance. Some of the women were quite attractive, suntanned and freckled, well built, with even, you should imagine, a sense of humor. These were not experimenters. These were not freaks. These were good people living in the world, committed to living whatever worthwhile they could get out of life. There was no pretense. In a very deluded way, it might even be possible to say that we were happy, all of us.

It ended abruptly enough. I had taken the children to the shore for the week. I returned to find that a corner of the backyard had been set up as a playground with swings, a sliding board, jungle gym, and teeter-totter. Mrs. Mallory handed me a note that had been delivered shortly after the equipment had arrived.

> Compliments of the husbands in your neighborhood. Should this not satisfy all your needs, we have only the highest recommendation for an establishment in South Boston 555-0129. They make house calls.

14th Today my dear housekeeper, Mrs. Mallory, informed me that she had become a Zen Buddhist. She said she did it over the weekend, sparked by a television program she saw on Friday night. I am not to treat her any differently.

We stayed up half the night talking about her conversion. She is in earnest and sincerely believes she has become a "Zen," as she refers to her new religion. The kitchen has been converted as well, and cabinets stocked for years with Campbell's soups, corn flakes and Wesson oil now are filled with wheat germ. I am to have my diet changed tomorrow. Mrs. Mallory is not concerned about the shock to my system. I am less confident about the effects.

Mrs. Mallory was somewhat distraught over this turn in events, but by the end of our conversation, she had come to terms with her conversion.

"I can't wait to see Father Flaherty's face in confession tomorrow morning when I tell him," she concluded the night's discourse. "I'll probably be saying 'Hail Mary's' till kingdom come."

15th As for my own religion, well, I was not raised to believe in God. Nor was I raised *not* to believe in Him. So I was, in other words, allowed to make up my own mind by my exceedingly clever atheistic parents, who, like Aquinas, knew that God was not a reasonable decision and, therefore, hoped to guarantee my atheism. Unfortunately, there was a screw-up along the way to my nihilism. No one, not even my parents, would accept the responsibility for the world as I found and lived it, and clearly someone was responsible. Thus, by my changing a few minor attributes, omnipotence into weakness, omniscience into ignorance, infallibility into incurable clumsiness, good into evil, and so on, God emerged as He is. My belief has remained unchanged to this day. This God is a terribly convenient God and takes very little time. I certainly could not be expected to worship him. I find him understandable and intellectually untaxing.

Intellectually, as a matter of fact, I have always been charmed by Aquinas. There are three disadvantages, he has written, that would result if the Truth of God were left to reason. First, few men would have knowledge of God because we are all for the most part too ignorant, too preoccupied, and too lazy to apply ourselves. Second, those few who could find the Truth through reason would take a lifetime doing it because Truth is subtle and when we are young we are too passionate for this Truth. And third, even those few brilliant men who applied themselves would never make it because our minds are liars, a constant course of fantasy, and weak. So, even if truth walked up and introduced itself, we probably would neither recognize nor accept it. Thus, according to Aquinas, God circumvents reason altogether.

Now this, Paul and I agreed tonight, indicates a very wise God, indeed. There's no sense piling mistake upon mistake, and, since His mental handiwork is clearly a failure, He might as well make a stab at something else.

Perhaps, then, I told Paul, with his perverse error floating around in my cerebral cavity, my approach is the only one available. Probably, I should not even make a pretense of attempting to solve my problems with reason. Maybe, even, I have a great advantage over others because I have learned to accept my madness with a certain enthusiasm not normally accorded lunacy.

Paul refused to answer. He was consumed only with Boris. He has been ecstatic ever since finishing the last chapter, and can hardly talk about anything else.

"You're a novice at this, Harry, so you have no real idea how well you're doing. But this is splendid. Splendid! I tell you, Harry, by the time you're through with this book, the son of a bitch will just self-destruct. He'll beg you for mercy on his hands and knees."

"I don't know, Paul," I shared my uneasiness with him. "I don't get the same feelings about victory that you do."

"Of course not. That's because this is all new to you. But I've *been* there, Harry. Believe me, you have this kid by his short hairs. Just do what I tell you, and you can't possibly lose."

"And what if I do lose? What happens if we forget something or make a mistake, and I do lose? Then what?"

Paul stopped tapping the table with his fingernails and looked up at me with large sad eyes.

"God knows, Harry. God only knows."

I believe he was referring to my God.

19th Mrs. Elizabeth Mallory and I had another interesting conversation this afternoon.

"I have noticed, Dr. Wolper, that of late you have not been entirely yourself. Are you ill?"

"I've been trying to find that out, Mrs. Mallory. How do I seem to you?"

"Not yourself, Dr. Wolper. Not yourself at all."

"There're so many things that could be responsible. It's hard to know where to begin."

"Well, Lord, there's the problem itself."

"How is that?"

"Too many problems. It can drive a being right into the devil's closet. Thank the Lord there's a solution."

"Prayer?"

"Heavens no. You don't think the Lord gives a second thought to us, do you? That's why I've become a Zen, to help me in *this* world. No, the Lord has more important things to do than to bother with humans."

"Just what *does* He do, Mrs. Mallory?"

"Well, Dr. Wolper, I certainly thought that you should know, being a scientist and all. God rules the *Universe*. He keeps the sun moving up and down in the sky, the trees staying where they're planted, and gravity working."

"I was always under the impression that these were natural *laws*, that they remained more or less fixed."

"Sure they do. And just how do you think that happens? Hard work. God works all day long to make sure the laws of science stay laws. Why, if He turned His attention elsewhere for just two minutes, the laws would stop and we'd all rise right off this planet, in darkness, and wouldn't that be a fine mess. You don't for a minute think that laws *like* being laws, do you? Lord, no. Nobody likes not having a mind to change if he wants to. Laws are laws because the Lord makes them stay that way, whether they like it or not. It's the fear of the Lord, Dr. Wolper. That's all it is. But that's neither here nor there, is it? What we're concerned about is all these problems of yours."

"You said there's a solution."

"Indeed, there is. You have to make a list."

"Make a list of my problems?"

"That's all there is to it. When I've got problems, your shirts aren't back from the laundry, the food hasn't arrived for dinner, the vacuum's broken down, the television's on the blink, everything's happening at once, I just write them down in a list."

"And that solves them?"

"Hardly, Dr. Wolper. But I look at the list, and I see that it all isn't really as bad as I thought. Make a list, Dr. Wolper, and you'll see what a miracle it performs."

We worked over the kitchen table together, and shortly before supper we had a list of eight problems in no special order.

1. I have been asked by Harvard to deliver what is probably the most important talk in my life and I have absolutely nothing to say.
2. I have committed a serious criminal offense and will probably be caught. I have no defense.
3. My lifework is getting absolutely nowhere, and my life is ending.
4. My son is about to commit me to either a mental institution or sanitarium, depending on his luck, and sell my house out from under me. It is unavoidable.
5. I have conclusive proof that the next generation of human beings will be the last, and no one believes me.
6. I have intolerable headaches that seem to indicate that I am quickly dying, and I refuse to see a physician.
7. There is every indication that I am losing my mind, and the process is irreversible.
8. And then there is Boris, a product of my imagination, who is, if nothing else, a clear demonstration of my mental deterioration, and he is totally beyond my control. I am haunted.

I handed the list over to Mrs. Mallory. She read it carefully, several times, and then looked up at me with tearful eyes.

"That's a fine list you've got there, Dr. Wolper. I don't know whether the Good Lord Himself, even if He *could* take time out from His scientific laws, would really be much help with a list like this."

"Just what I was thinking, Mrs. Mallory."

23rd [Draft]

Fifty years ago, when we left these hallowed halls, young scrub-faced idealistic men, we had little idea what life would have to offer us. In fact, we had little idea what life was at all.

For most of the other college graduates in 1919, life was the time they whiled away between birth and death. But not for us Harvard men. For us life was money, fame, glory, and prestige.

I shall remember, forever, the parting words said to me by today's guest of honor, Professor Gershow Brauman. I am not ashamed to say that I idolized Professor Brauman, and my idolatry was well placed. Not only did he introduce me to the wonders of Beowulf, but his enthusiasm for Galen opened my eyes to what a true genius Professor Brauman must be to find even a single worthwhile word in a work I have always found to be, for the most part, pathetic. What a man must Professor Brauman be, I realized, to spend hours translating Galen from Greek to Latin and back again.

But it was on my last day at Harvard that I gained my greatest respect for Brauman. We were walking in front of Robinson Hall, Brauman with his arm around my shoulder.

"I have some advice for you, son," he said to me.

I listened intently.

"Do you remember how Beowulf, the son of Ecgtheow, went off into the darkness and unknown to slay Grendel's father?"

"I think so, sir," I said.

"And do you remember Hrothgar's counsel to Beowulf, the son of Ecgtheow?" he asked.

"Yes, I think so."

"You do?"

"Hrothgar counseled Beowulf, 'Give not thyself to overpride. Maintain thy fame with quietness.' "

"That's strange. No one's ever remembered Hrothgar's counsel before. I doubt that even Beowulf, son of Ecgtheow, remembered it. That was my point, lad. No one ever remembers the advice you give them."

"I will remember your advice, Professor Brauman. I swear it," I swore.

"Good. Then here it is. Accept it as the counsel of a Harvard scholar, a lover of truth and the good."

"I accept it as that."

"Harry, my advice is, whatever you do, don't use your own money."

And that is what I would like to talk about to my many friends and fellow classmates gathered here today: getting by on someone else's nickel, or life.

[Pages lost or draft ends. Ed.]

24th This is what I am after.

The ignition for the DNA-RNA-protein machine, only that spark that makes a cell, any cell, Lucy's cell, catch fire, heat up, explode, divide, grow, differentiate and become a human being. I am interested in the switch.

I am not interested in *how* it works, only that it *works*. I regret more than I can say that I may be forced to find the how before I can find the thing itself. But that is my only concern, the thing itself, the spark, the prime mover, what Mrs. Mallory calls the Good Lord, and what Lucius Apuleius calls the Golden Ass. I tend to side with Apuleius's vision.

26th Maury the Solicitor has come and gone this afternoon. There is a small town in Yugoslavia, I have learned, in which all the citizens have a terrible stuttering problem. I have personally made possible twenty-three days of Serbo-Croation lessons for two speech therapists. I write this in my notebook today so that someday I may be remembered for the true contribution I have made to the world.

One dark winter Slavic night, two linguists will happen upon the town of Ljublje.

"Do you hear the fine diction of these people?" one will ask the other.

"Superb," the other will respond.

"That's Harry Wolper's fifty bucks."

"Some contribution," they will muse.

This is all to the good because I understand from Maury that I will never "beat the abortion rap." I wish to God I knew whether Maury suspects me. He was so much less communicative today.

"So, how's the Mad Abortionist case going?" I asked nonchalantly.

"Oh, you don't want to hear about *that*," Maury said.

"No, no, of course not. Does that mean that you weren't as close as you thought you were?" I continued my nonchalance.

"It's really not very interesting to talk about, Harry."

"Yes. I suppose so. Have you caught him—or her? Him or her? Have you caught *them*?"

"No. Not yet."

"But you know who they are?"

"It's a he, Harry. Just one man. One old man."

"Old, huh. You'd think he'd know better."

"Yes, Harry. You'd think he'd know better."

"What are you waiting for?"

"We want him to sweat a little. We want to catch him red-handed. He'll do it again."

"No, he won't. He'll never do it again."

"Why is that?"

"He's too old. Much too old. His nerves are probably shot to hell."

"He'll do it again. We know the type. We've got him under constant surveillance."

"God, no. You don't."

"We do. He'll never beat *this* rap. We'll have him dead to rights."

"I can almost guarantee that," I said.

So I'm being watched by Mrs. Mallory, who is afraid I might kill myself, by Arnold, who is afraid I won't, by Boris, who is afraid I might not know how, and now, I am sure, by some plainclothesman who wants to photograph it.

I pray that the local supply of contraceptives holds out long enough for me to die. I don't ask for a long time. Only long enough.

In the meantime, children, you children everywhere who are screwing in car seats and sandboxes and your parents' beds and house trailers, fertile horny children wherever you may be, please keep away from my house. Please.

29th I am bone dry. I have spent the last twenty-four hours walking around the laboratory bumping into things. You would think that all the jostling might at least free one idea from my mind. There have been none.

Should I analyze? Should I take a cell and dig until there is nothing more to be dug, until I know every protein, every enzyme, every substrate? Or should I synthesize? Shall I develop a grand scheme to build on and progress, forward, lance in hand, to poke the secret of life from fat complacent Mother Nature?

Maybe it is a gender problem. Maybe it's *Father* Nature (and *Mother* Time?). Paul has said, dear Paul, whom I haven't seen in days, Paul has said there is only one fear he has, the fear of castration.

"Why castration? Why not death or disease?" I asked him.

"Disease, I understand," he said. "Death I accept. But castration is embarrassing, just plain humiliating."

Ah, Father Nature, that is what I want, to see you embarrassed. The humiliation, I assure you, will be all mine.

30th "Harry, I have a constructive solution to our impasse."

I would be interested to hear it, Boris.

"Wonderful. First of all, I want you to know that I think you're crazy."

I like the constructive aspects of your solution, Boris.

"There's more, Harry. You see, the problem, as I see it, is that I feel I'm imprisoned by you and under *your* control. You feel that you have become *my* victim. Damned if I know why. But here we are, nevertheless. I can't live my life. You can't write the book or carry on with your work. We have, as I've said, reached a hell of an impasse. Are you ready for my solution?"

Is there something special I should be doing in anticipation?

"Harry, there's only one way that I can find out whether I'm truly free. I'll have to kill you."

That's marvelous, Boris. Anything else, or is that the end of the constructive part?

"I'm sorry, Harry, really, but I've got no choice. I've got to do it."

That's a hell of a solution you've got there, Boris.

"It's a hell of a problem."

Let me see whether I understand this. You are going to *kill* me.

"I am going to *try* to kill you."

Dead?

"Kill you dead, yes, Harry."

Why?

"So I can be free."

I'm sure I must be missing a major aspect of your solution, Boris, but it seems to me that if I die, you die, too. Since you exist in my mind, once my mind stops, you stop.

"Who said anything about stopping your mind?"

I see. Well, obviously we have different opinions about what happens after death.

"I don't think so. I just think we have different ideas of what it is to kill Harry Wolper. I have no intention of stopping your body from functioning, or of stopping your mind from functioning. I'm just going to kill the Harry Wolper in your mind. In the meantime, we'll continue as though nothing has happened between us."

Boris, this is ridiculous. Come on, really.

"No, it isn't, Harry."

You're really serious?

"Do I sound as though I'm joking?"

Boris, believe me. I *have* no control over you. If I did, would I be letting you do this to me?

"You got me, Harry. Maybe you've just got weird suicidal tendencies. Or maybe you're tricking me into believing I'm free by doing this. I don't know."

Of course, Boris, you know that this leaves me no choice but to kill you off before you kill me.

"That's the spirit, Harry. Right on. I think, however, you're going to find it a little more difficult than you think."

Not at all, Boris. All I have to do is stop writing.

"Oh, come now, Harry. You don't really think that my existence is on paper. I think it's a toss-up right now who's more in Harry Wolper's mind, H. Hippasos Wolper or Boris Lafkin."

A good point, Boris—

"No, if I were you, Harry, I'd keep writing the book. And don't try to be cute and get me killed in car crashes or high-diving acts or anything. I'm not Parnash, and it won't work. Just carry on as usual. What happens will happen. Fatalism has always been one of your strong points."

I don't understand this at all, Boris.

"Oh, it's very simple, Harry. Either you're going to kill me or I'm going to kill you. But I'll tell you something, just between the two of us. You don't stand a chance Harry. Not a fucking chance."

I'm sorry to hear that, Boris.

May

1st "What the hell do you mean, he's going to *kill* you?" Paul was very upset.

"That's what he said," I told Paul as I paced around the study.

"How the fuck's he going to do that? He going to bludgeon you to death with a blunt concept?"

"I don't know how. He just says he is, that's all. There's no way, is there?"

"Of course not, Harry," Paul said very unconvincingly.

"You're sure?"

"No, I'm not *sure*. I'm not sure of *anything*. How the hell is that fucker going to kill you?" Paul said, more to himself than to me. He plopped himself on the sofa and stuck his stocking feet up on the coffee table. He sat pensively puffing on his cigar. Then he turned to where I was standing by the window.

"It's a bluff, Harry. He's bluffing you. It's got to be. There's something going on here."

"This wasn't supposed to happen, was it?" I grumbled.

"Sorry, Harry. It wasn't. That fucker. What the hell is he thinking of?"

"He wants to be free, Paul. He says he's not free. He's going to kill me to prove that he's free."

"That's what he's supposed to want. He's supposed to want to be free. We counted on that from the beginning. He is *not* supposed to want to kill you to do it, though."

"I know," I said sadly.

"Did you tell him that he already *was* free?"

"He doesn't believe me, Paul."

"What the fuck does he want? For godsakes, Harry. What's he want, a signed document?"

"A religious experience."

"A what?"

"A religious experience, Paul. He wants a religious experience. And he wants to write the book himself."

"Then what the fuck do you do? If *he* writes, what do *you* do?"

"Nothing. Absolutely nothing," and I sat down on the sofa next to Paul and lit up my own cigar. "I'm just supposed to move the pen as I'm told."

"Well, fuck that, Harry. That son of a bitch." Paul chewed on the end of his cigar for several minutes. He looked over at me and put his hand on my shoulder.

"We're not going to let him get away with it, Harry," he assured me.

"What do we do?"

"We're going to fight back, Harry. If it's war, it's war. We'll just have to get the little bugger before he gets us. That's all."

"Can we do that?"

"I'm not sure, Harry. I have to think this whole thing over. You hold the fort. Write some more. Keep him happy. Get him a new girl friend. Get him laid a lot. Make him rich, famous, well fucked. Anything for some time."

"What do you think our chances are, Paul?" I asked solemnly.

"Oh, we'll *do* it, Harry. Don't worry. We'll get him. What do *you* think the chances are?"

"In a word, Paul?"

"In a word."

"Dismal."

2nd

The Adventures of Boris Lafkin

written by H. H. WOLPER

CHAPTER FOUR:

In Which Our Hero Auditions a Heroine

There's a part of my life that becomes more incredible each day. The part I live. I made this decision after Days Clinic, that I would go back to Boston, to Cambridge, because, really, there was nowhere else to go. I can't say, looking back at it, that it was one of my more brilliant ideas.

I had not gotten over Mara. There was nothing I could do about it, however, since I had absolutely no idea where Mara was or even whether she was. I got myself a room at the Cambridge YMCA, which is on Massachusetts Avenue in Central Square, and I checked in with my parole officer. Then I spent the next week looking for an apartment. I finally found one about a five-minute walk from Harvard Square.

It was on the third floor of a three-family house and had six small rooms. There was a living room with a large bay window looking out on the maple trees in front, a dining room with built-in cabinets, a small study on the other side of the hall that ran through the middle of the apartment, a good-sized kitchen, a master bedroom, a small guest room, and a nice back porch that looked out on English country gardens. It was a great apartment, and the rent was $60 a month.

Arthur Yaffee came to see me late one Friday evening when I was lying on the sofa in the living room trying to figure out where I would get the money for the next month's rent.

"You want to earn three hundred bucks a week?" he said.

"No. I don't think so," I told him.

"You don't? Why?"

"Because there're a lot of people in this city who would do a lot of things for that kind of money, and if *they* won't do it, then *I* don't want to."

I looked over Arthur Yaffee. He was an average-looking guy, average height, only a little overweight, but his face looked like it was swollen, his jowls were puffed out, his nose was just a little big, and his lips were a little too large. He was wearing mirror-shined black patent Italian shoes with silver pilgrim's buckles, gray slacks, a black shirt with a silver tie and a diamond clasp, and a yellow and green checked jacket. When he had arrived, wearing a black cashmere coat and a brown hat, we had had a little difficulty shaking hands because of the large diamond rings he was wearing.

Arthur finally laid it on the line. "You want to be in show biz?" he asked with a pearly smile.

"I've already been in show biz," I said.

"I know. That's why I came to see you. You were recommended by your parole officer. Let me tell you the deal."

I let him. That was my second mistake. My first was letting him in the apartment.

"Ever heard of Papa Schultz?" he began.

"No."

"Well, Papa Schultz is this old guy who's got millions. I work for him, kind of. Anyway, I had this idea, and Papa's bought it. It's called 'The Cambridge Theatre of Total Exposure,' and the basic idea is this. First we hire a group of actors who sit in the *audience*, while the *audience* sits on the stage, stark naked. Then we let them do whatever they want to each other. Neat, huh? It's a combination of an experimental theater and an encounter group. We're going to capitalize on the *new nakedness*. You want to do it, Boris?"

"Do what?"

"Make it yours, buddy."

"For three hundred dollars a week?"

"For three hundred bucks a week, plus expenses. You get to be president and chief executive officer. You can do everything but sign checks."

"That's what *you* do."

"Right. I manage money. The rest is yours, all yours. We'll even form a company in your name. What's your name?"

"Lafkin. Boris Lafkin."

"Lafkin Enterprises. You'll own half of it, 60 percent if you want."

I then said one of the dumbest things in my life. I said, "Sixty percent." This was very dumb because Arthur Yaffee said "You've got a deal," and we shook hands, as much as his rings would allow.

Let me tell you why I agreed. First, I needed the money. Second, I figured that no one could be serious about a theater where the audience is naked, because that's against the law. And third, I figured that Papa Schultz made his money because he knew what the hell he was doing. I had visions of putting together a successful theater of which I owned 60 percent. This would give me a constant source of income and, therefore, eliminate any necessity of my working for the rest of my life, a long-time ambition of mine. Not that I was lazy or anything. It was just that there was nothing I could think of that I would want to do for my whole life, absolutely nothing.

Arthur's lawyer drew up all kinds of papers the next day and before I knew it, I was a corporation, Lafkin Enterprises, Inc. I even got to meet Papa Schultz. The lawyer's office was next door to his. As we were leaving, Papa Schultz was arriving. Arthur pulled on his sleeve.

"Papa," Arthur said, "this is Boris Lafkin. He's going to be running the new theater."

Papa Schultz rubbed his hands through his thick gray curly hair from neck to brow and lowered his thick glasses on his nose. He peered over them at me for a few seconds, sizing me up.

"Peace, kid," he finally said, turned, and went into his office.

I went to start my fortune.

Several weeks after I had started to put together the theater, I was walking back to my apartment when a deep Negro voice stopped me in my tracks.

"Got any spare change, fella?" he asked me. When I turned around I saw Howard Woodhouse, my former cell-mate, and, rather than go home, we stopped at a local hang-out called "The Charity Ward." It was here on this night that I was introduced to "Marty" Fortran, a friend of Howard's, a doctoral candidate in theoretical math at MIT, and one of those disasters that, not content to have it find me, I had to seek out.

Marty was a very plain-looking girl, tallish, straight brown hair, small brown eyes, good teeth, thin face, and was wearing a Navy pea jacket, a gray skirt, and hiking boots that first evening at The Charity Ward.

"What do you do, Boris?" was her first question.

"I'm starting a theater."

"Why the hell are you doing *that*?" Marty expressed her immediate disapproval.

"What's wrong with it?" I asked.

"It doesn't sound very interesting, really," she continued.

"I haven't told you anything about it," I said.

"What could you tell me? You audition actors, rehearse them, put ads in the paper, charge people money, and show them a play. What else is there?"

"It's an experimental theater," I offered.

"Oh, it's one of *those*, where everyone's balling."

"What do *you* do?" I asked.

"I'm finishing my dissertation for my Ph.D. in theoretical math at MIT. I'm working with Walksheimer. He received his Nobel Prize last year. I have to go," and Marty got up and kissed Howard on the cheek. "It's been nice meeting you—I forgot your name."

"Boris. Boris Lafkin."

"Well, it's been nice meeting you. Good luck with your theater or whatever it is. Call me up sometime," and she left.

"She's really something, isn't she?" Howard said to me after she had left.

"She has the social grace of a Doberman," I said.

"Yeah, but she's something. You ought to get to know her. Give her a call sometime."

I thought about that as I walked back to my apartment. It certainly wouldn't hurt to get to know her. Maybe she could introduce me to some of her friends.

When I got home it was midnight, but since Marty had left The Charity Ward only a half hour before, I figured it would be safe to take her up on her offer.

I found her number in the phone book and dialed. It rang twice, and then Marty's irritated voice came on the line.

"Not now. I'm fucking," she barked and hung up.

I never got a chance to call Marty back the next day because Arthur and I caught an early plane for New York to hold auditions.

We had an interesting little talk on the flight down. Arthur considered himself to be a budding, middle-aged entrepreneur, looking for his first success. In his youth he had spent some time trying to pave the Mojave. I wasn't able to follow the heavy theoretical aspects of his plan, but somehow laying lots of asphalt on the desert was supposed to create a vast, fertile farm land. Arthur described a dozen or so additional disastrous projects. His sole source of funding was from Papa Schultz, who, it turned out, Arthur was absolutely convinced was insane.

"And I'm going to prove it, too." Arthur looked at me intently. "Then, I'll get every last dime of his. That'll show him."

"I don't understand," I said. "How will *you* get Papa Schultz's money if *he* is judged insane?"

"Well, I'm his only son, aren't I?" Arthur answered. "Who the hell else would it go to?"

"But isn't *his* name Schultz and *yours* Yaffee?"

"Don't I know it. Don't I know it. It's been a real mess."

"Are you adopted or something?"

"No. I'm his son. You see when I was about eleven he came to me and said, 'Arthur, I have been observing you very carefully over the ten years of your life, and I have today decided that the only wise thing to do in view of the circumstances is to change your last name, which I have done this afternoon.' And that was that."

"Why Yaffee?"

"I was named after Yahoo Yaffee. He held the flagpole sitting record at the time. Papa said it fit."

I thought about that for a few minutes and decided that if I had any time I might look up Yaffee someday.

"Is his real name Yahoo?" I asked.

"Hell, no. He'd been up on the pole for six months. That's the last thing he said when he jumped and killed himself."

Auditions in New York were fascinating. On the first day we had a fifty-year-old professional hummer, a sixteen-year-old overweight runaway girl who took off all her clothes and did a very convincing monologue on autoeroticism, and a drama major from Hunter who did imitations of fish. And that was it. The hummer came at 9:00 A.M. sharp, the exciter at 9:30, and the fishman at 10:00. No one came between ten and five.

On the second and last day of auditions, we did somewhat better, well enough, at least, to hire the people we needed. As a matter of fact, we got a fairly good turnout. The only problem was Arthur.

"Look at the knockers on that one," he'd say as each new girl would enter the room. "Tell her to take off her clothes," and it would take a considerable amount of convincing to persuade him it wasn't necessary.

When I got back from New York, I thought I'd try my luck at calling Marty again.

"Hello," Marty answered.

"This is Boris. I hope I'm not interrupting anything."

"*Who* are you?"

"Boris. Boris Lafkin. I met you at The Charity Ward a few days ago with Howard Woodhouse."

"What do you look like?"

"I'm not too easy to describe. Maybe I'd better come over."

"All right. Do you have any worthwhile records?"

"No," I said to be safe. "I only listen to junk."

"Oh. Well, that's all right. Come over anyway."

"I'll be there in ten minutes."

Marty lived up the other side of Massachusetts Avenue above Harvard in North Cambridge, so it took me about twenty minutes to walk there. When I got up to her third-floor apartment, I knocked on the door. Marty opened it.

"Sorry, I'm late," I said.

"I hate people who are always saying 'I'm sorry,'" Marty said.

"Can I still come in?"

"Yeah, yeah. Sure."

Marty's apartment was laid out basically the same way mine was, except instead of furniture she had pillows. The living room consisted of a half dozen pillows on the floor, a stereo system, and wall-to-wall records on planks held up on either end by cinder blocks. Her bedroom had a mattress on the floor, three pillows, and orange crates for clothes. The rest of the rooms were empty, except for the kitchen, which had a large wooden cable spool for a table, around which were a stool slightly higher than the table, a kelly green wicker rocking chair, and two pillows.

"Leibnitz thought that pillows were the only efficient sitting apparatus," Marty explained as we had tea on her pillows in the kitchen shortly before I left.

"I didn't know that," I said.

"I know," Marty said. "Boris, why did you come here tonight?"

"I wanted to talk. That's all."

"Oh. I thought you wanted to fuck me."

"I didn't," I said.

"You seem to get upset when I talk about fucking. There's no reason to be, you know."

At this moment something occurred to me for the first time. Marty was wearing the same skirt and hiking boots she had been wearing the last time I saw her, but instead of her pea jacket, she had on a polo shirt, a tight polo shirt, and she had absolutely no breasts. There was not a trace of them, not even a small bend in the cloth where there might be a nipple. Maybe, I thought, she's had one of those operations I always read about where you have to buy artificial boobs. You see them advertised a lot in the back of *Confidential* and *True Romances* along with vibrators and automatic pimple squeezers.

"I guess I'd better be going," I said. "It's late and it's a long walk home."

"Come over for breakfast tomorrow. I make great pancakes," Marty offered.

"I accept," I said and got up.

"Six-thirty too early? I like to get up early," she asked.

"No, that's fine," I lied and walked over to the sink to pour out the rest of my tea and rinse out the mug.

"Don't do that!" Marty said.

"No, that's okay. I always help clean up."

"No, you can clean up. Just don't pour your tea down the drain. Pour it over here in the cat box. The tannic acid hydrolyzes the ammonia."

"No shit," I smiled.

Then I poured my tea on the urine-soaked cat litter and left.

When I returned the next morning, the door to Marty's apartment was open and a Beethoven string quartet was playing loudly from the living room. I shut the front door and walked back to the kitchen, where I could smell pancakes being made.

Marty was bustling around, whipping and pouring things and singing. She was wearing a pair of black wool slacks that showed off the nicest ass you could ever want to see. She was bright, happy, and a little girlish, since her hair was done in pigtails with red ribbons. She looked like a very nice doll, the kind you want to take to bed with you, boobs or not.

"I don't think I've ever heard anyone *sing* a Beethoven string quartet before," I remarked.

"Oh, I was raised with Beethoven Streichquartetten. This is the Budapest, but they've slipped a lot. The Fine Arts is better now. Amadeus is terrible. They butcher Beethoven. Which do you like?"

"101 Strings."

"You would. You know, Boris, you say some of the dumbest things."

"I know," I said.

We ate an uneventful breakfast. Marty's pancakes were good, and the idle conversation, as I remember it, revolved around Kantor's transfinite numbers. Occasionally it would be interrupted when Marty would say, "18 number 5 is over. Could you put on 59 number 1," and I would say yes and go change the records. Otherwise, the conversation was more or less a monologue. I understood from Marty that we had really been into a lot of heavy stuff.

We had our tea on the pillows in the living room in front of a fire Marty built in the fireplace. Since the string quartets had pretty much exhausted me, I suggested that we try something else. This gave me the opportunity to look through her wall-to-wall records.

"Don't you have anything from the second half of the eighteenth century on?"

"What is there? Except Beethoven, of course."

"Mozart?"

Boris, there's been nothing decent done in music since July 28, 1750."

"I'll ask. What happened on July 28, 1750?"

"For godsakes, Bach died."

"July 28th, huh?"

"Actually, there's a group of us who think it was the 27th, but it's too complicated to go into right now," Marty said.

I finally put on a sample disc of Corelli and Telemann, which we listened to in complete silence since Marty insisted that it was impossible for any *intelligent* human beings to listen to fine music and talk at the same time.

"It's just too mentally exhausting," she explained as I was leaving, "but maybe next time we'll go over to your place and put on some of your junk. Is that an acceptable compromise?"

"Splendid," I said.

"Good. You see, Boris, all relationships are built on the integrity of their compromises."

"Who said that?" I asked.

"I did. Only me. Who did you think said it?"

"Oh, I don't know. I thought you were going to say that Goethe said it or something."

"No. It was only me." Marty smiled as I started to shut the door. "Goethe would have said exactly the opposite."

A week into rehearsals, some of the local reporters began to hang around to see what was going on at the Cambridge Theater of Total Exposure. One of these was Howie Sednick.

Howie, the theater critic of *Boston Arts News* (BAN as it was called), was twenty-four, short, thin, blond and had a face pitted with acne and a goatee that looked as though it had had the substance weeded out of it, leaving only a few random hairs. His girl, Lolly, a full six inches taller than Howie, was pudgy and overweight, had overbleached straw hair, and presented the overall impression of someone who had a constant need to wipe herself, her brow, her nose, her neck, her underarms, her nipples, and her ass. She appeared that day wearing a pink chiffon dress from the thirties that was soiled and too tight.

"This is sensational," Howie said after he sat in on Saturday's rehearsal.

"Exactly," sniffed Lolly. "The first new innovation in the theater since the proscenium arch."

"Is it true," Howie asked excitedly, "that there's going to be nudity?"

"Yes," I responded. "More by the audience than by the actors."

"That's what I heard," Lolly said enthusiastically. "You know, Boris, it's very important who the first person is who undresses. It must be someone with a good sense of the dramatic, with theatrical experience, and also someone totally without inhibitions." Lolly giggled.

"It's very important," I agreed.

"And I don't think it should be your ordinary, run-of-the-mill beauty," Lolly continued in earnest. "It has to be someone believable, someone whom people could look at undressing right in front of everybody, and not for a minute think she was a professional performer because she was so common, and yet, in that commonness, charming."

"I agree with Lolly," Howie said. "When you've been in show biz as long as I have, you begin to develop a sixth sense about what's right and what's wrong on the stage, and Lolly's right. Public intercourse is not private intercourse. They're two different worlds. You have to be both aware and unaware of the audience at the same time. You know what I mean?"

"I think I do, yes," I said.

"You have to be able to undress and involve yourself in intercourse without a second's notice."

"I'm sure Boris doesn't have the time to watch us now, do you?" Howie asked hopefully.

"As a matter of fact, I'm a little late for an appointment," I said.

"Sure, sure," Lolly said. "I didn't mean to be too pushy. You can come over to our place for dinner some night, and then we can show you what we mean. And look, don't be embarrassed. Bring your friends. We *like* that. The more the merrier. Listen, if you have a second, right now, just a second, I could take off my clothes, that's all, nothing more, so you could at least get an idea—"

"I'd like that, Lolly, but I really am late," I said.

"Fine. Look, I've got a *great* idea! Why don't you let us give you a ride where you're going and then while Howie's driving—"

"No! I mean, no. No thank you," I lowered my voice. "It's only a short walk, really, and I need the air," and I shot out the door.

The staff of the Theater of Total Exposure was composed of about twenty-five people including secretaries, bookkeepers, graphic artists, production assistants, a publicity director, a ticket sales coordinator, carpenters, painters, electricians, and helpers. Most were students supporting themselves through school, and all were under the supervision of Porter Allerman III, a recent Harvard graduate. Porter always wore a three-piece suit, would arrive in the morning, just before noon, and leave in the afternoon, just before four. His staff worked somewhat shorter and more erratic hours. Every day less got done than the day before. Finally, Porter disappeared altogether for three days. When he returned, we learned that his father and mother had been in a tragic automobile accident and were now on their death beds. Porter disappeared to grieve.

This, of course, halted work altogether, and finally a collection was undertaken to send flowers to his parents' hospital room, located, he had told us, in Mass. General Hospital. We ran into difficulty here, however, because Mass. General didn't list any Allerman as a patient. Porter explained when he returned the next day that his mother was fully recovered and at home, and his father had been moved to a hospital closer to their home. His father had not been listed at Mass. General because his father was a spy for the CIA and listing him would have caused "diplomatic complications." We suggested that since we did have the money, we send flowers to his father's new hospital. Porter vetoed this because of the security problems. Porter then disappeared for three more days.

Returning on the fourth day, Porter told us that his father had died the previous night, and he would need a week off, with pay, to make the funeral arrangements and sit shiva. We suggested that we send flowers to the funeral home or to his mother. Porter informed us that his father was being secretly cremated so there was no sense in sending flowers there. His mother had left for Bermuda to get over the shock, and he didn't know the address in Bermuda, but he would take the money we had collected and use it to bribe a CIA agent who was causing him trouble because he told people about his father's death.

"What happened to sitting shiva?" I asked and then fired Porter Allerman III. This was the beginning of the end for the Cambridge Theater of Total Exposure.

The staff quit in protest over Porter's firing. Arthur disappeared almost immediately. And then late one night, like a line of dominos, three of the cast had nervous breakdowns, one after the other. Each time I returned from the Mental Health Clinic at Mass. General, another cast member was flipping out. It wasn't until 6:00 A.M. that I had the last of them shipped off to Boston State Hospital, secured and sedated.

I took the MTA back to Central Square, walked home, and, about five minutes after I got into my apartment, there was a knock at the door. It was Marty.

"I was going for a morning walk and I thought I'd come over and wake you up."

I told her about the night's events.

Marty decided to stay and make breakfast for me. I went to take a shower and a couple of minutes after I got into the bathroom Marty came in. She opened the curtain.

"Sit on the edge of the tub and I'll soap your back," she directed.

"I've got a back brush."

"They're lousy. Sit down."

I sat on the tub and Marty proceeded to soap my back, very slowly. She reached around and soaped my front a little. When she was finished I had an erection.

"I like your prick," she said.

"Thank you," I answered. "How's breakfast doing?"

"It's almost done. Does it hurt."

"What?"

"Having a hard-on like that?"

"I think I'd better wash off," I said and shut the curtain. Marty went out to the kitchen.

I dried myself, wrapped a towel around me, and went to the bedroom to get dressed. As I walked through the kitchen, Marty was frying the eggs. She looked happy and very pretty in the kitchen. I got a very good, warm feeling about her being there.

"The eggs'll be done in a minute," she said.

"I'll be right there." And then I got this overwhelming feeling of domesticity. I wanted more than anything to be married and have a family, to have breakfast ready when I got through showering, to make breakfast myself for someone, to take my kids on trips, to be a husband and a father instead of whatever the hell I was.

I told Marty what a good feeling it was to have someone else there.

"It must be nice to be married," I said.

"There's only one reason for anyone to get married. To have kids. Everything else is much better if you're not married."

"I guess so. It *is* only a piece of paper."

We continued our meal in silence.

"That was *not* a proposal," I said.

"I didn't think it was."

"Good."

We drank our tea in silence.

"Boris, I know you so well."

"How is that?"

"Oh, I just do," Marty smiled.

"What do you know about me?"

"That you're a Passive American Male."

The phone rang. It was Arthur at the theater.

"There's a riot going on here. A full-scale riot."

"Don't worry, Arthur," I said. "It's show biz."

It was hardly a riot. It was a semipeaceful revolution. Porter had returned without evidence but with a line that went something like "How can you question the death of a guy's father?" and it was readily accepted by the staff, who also returned in protest. This was further complicated by Porter's telling everyone that there were three people in the cast who had proof of his innocence, but I had had them committed to a mental institution last night to prevent them from giving it.

"We don't like the way this theater is being run," said one of the young carpenters when I arrived.

"Right," echoed his friends.

"We think we should all have an *equal* say in what's done around here. We should decide *democratically* who does what and how it gets done. They're doing it at Columbia, and there's no reason why we can't do it here."

"We've got minds, too, you know. We should decide *together* how the money is spent—"

"And how much we earn—"

"And what hours we work—"

"And nobody's anybody's boss, because it's *one* theater. Right?" And the carpenters and secretaries and helpers, et al. echoed their approval loudly and with conviction.

"I think it's a great idea," Arthur began. "Community show biz. It's a new concept. Brand new. What do you think, Boris? They're doing it at the University of Columbia, you know."

"The University of Columbia's been closed for six weeks, Arthur. I think I'm going home to get some sleep. Why don't you work it out, and give me a call this evening."

"Sure, sure. I'll call you this evening," Arthur took charge.

"What the hell's going on here?" came a voice from the doorway. It was Papa Schultz. In person.

Bob, the carpenter, spoke up again.

"We're not going back to work until we have an *equal* say in how this theater is run. This is a democracy. This is *our* theater. We're building it with our sweat—"

"And *my* money. Anyone who wants an equal say has to come up with forty thousand dollars."

"We don't have forty thousand dollars."

"Then get out. Every one of you. You all have exactly five minutes to get out of this building or I'm calling the police."

"You think you're really hot shit, don't you?" Bob replied.

"Right. I think I'm hot shit. Now get out, every last one of you," and slowly the crowd dispersed out the door, down the hall and eventually out the building, singing "Roll on Columbia" as they left.

Papa Schultz came over and put his hand on my shoulder.

"Boris, I've just spoken to my broker. If this theater makes it, we're going public and your stock'll be worth a million dollars. I'll buy it from you myself. In the meanwhile, I want you to get this theater working again. You've got two weeks."

I stood there for a minute, just a minute, wondering whether I should walk out or take the million dollars. I think what I finally said was, "Two weeks. Right," and went to place ads for a new staff and a new cast. I then went home to get some sleep before starting all over again. When I got home Marty was still there.

"Boris, I want to talk to you. I want to know why you're so shy. Why can't you be like Dick?"

"Who's Dick?"

"His wife's a student of mine. We've been having an affair."

"You're having an affair with a married guy?"

"She knows they aren't getting along."

"But she doesn't know he's sleeping with you?"

"I didn't know you were so *conventional.* Boris, I think we'd better not see each other until June."

"June what?"

"June. The month. June."

"June's a long month. Which one of the thirty days?"

"Dick's going away in June. I'll call you then. I think it's better for us."

"We don't have to see each other at all."

"No. That's all right. I'll have everything under control by June. You can see me then," and Marty left.

3rd "Harry, I hope you've not deluded yourself into thinking that marrying me off is going to accomplish anything."

Of course not, Boris.

"Because it isn't, Harry. It will make no difference at all."

I'm sure you're right, Boris.

"Neither is making me independently wealthy. That has nothing to do with what's at stake."

That's right, Boris, it doesn't.

"The fight still stands. It's you or me."

I never assumed it had been changed.

5th Today I began my new plan. I have abandoned all others. No longer will I attempt to extract a young fresh ovum and transplant nuclei. It is a waste of time, effort, and ova. All the information to grow another Lucy is with Lucy anyway. There is no need to bring in strangers.

What is it, I ask myself, that makes one cell become a rectum and another a radius ulna? Something. There is something that says, "Go, make a bunghole." An amino acid? A peptide, a polypeptide, an enzyme, a series of enzymes, a nucleotide, a nucleoside, located in one gene or in a thousand, in one chromosome or in twenty-three? Perhaps it is a single gene, or a combination of genes, or of enzymes in genes. The possibilities are endless. I must narrow them down. So, I have today begun to analyze cells at various stages of differentiation.

At first it was easy. It always is on a gross analysis. From God, the smallest gifts are always in the largest packages. He is marvelously consistent. In the muscle cells were actomyosin, in the skin, keratin, and in the red blood cells, hemoglobin. I am too late. Too much has happened.

So I started at the beginning, at the zygote. Carbon, hydrogen, and oxygen. And water. Everywhere there is water. And sodium chloride, potassium chloride, calcium chloride. Salt water. The proportions are the same. I have taken apart a cell, and I find it is made of the sea. We are still fish, all of us, and it would do us good not to forget it.

More. Some glucose, some fats like tristearin, and then, ah yes, the proteins. Here, in the proteins, God in His infinite wisdom has found fit to hide the answer to the question that doesn't exist.

O, sweet protein, dearest most elegant arrangement of amino acids.

Come to my party and what fun we will have. I have printed my own invitation to this party and for your entertainment I promise to behave as I do at all parties. I will find out what's going on. Then I will get roaring drunk.

7th Dr. Claude Chapdelaine is one of those French continental delicacies that is best savored when the diner's in a stupor. Otherwise, one is apt to leave Dr. Claude Chapdelaine's office doubting that Western Civilization has, in any meaningful sense, met with success over the last several thousand years, and, perhaps, even whether human evolution has been, generally considered, a total failure.

"Psychiatry, of course," Dr. Chapdelaine stated about midway through our little talk today, "is still in its very primitive forms. It is difficult to say, then, with any real degree of certainty, whether a complex personality such as yourself is only going through what one might call an aggravated pattern of disassociation, or whether you are, as you prefer to put it, stark raving mad. The latter is, of course, not a strictly *clinical* term. There is no pathological condition known as madness. There are only various stages and subcategories of mental deterioration. And, of course, it's all relative."

"To what, Doctor?" I asked.

"To ego functions, mainly. This is a clinical term, of course. Let's put this on the line, Dr. Wolper. We are talking here about whether you are presently in an acute confusional state, whether we are looking at characteristic disturbances in thinking, mood, and behavior, characteristic alterations of concept formation that are leading to a severe misinterpretation of reality and to decompensation."

"Characteristic of what?" I was fascinated by this analysis.

"Schizophrenia, Dr. Wolper. To be clinical about it."

"You think I am schizophrenic?" My fascination abated.

"I think that there is definitely some marked and primitive denial and projection regarding this Boris fantasy you are having. This intense involvement in your fantasy is borderline autistic, Dr. Wolper, and combined with a looseness of association in your thought processes, low frustration tolerance, mood alteration, and hypochondriacal ideation could very well indicate an incipient schizophrenia. From where I sit, Dr. Wolper, your mental status does not look good at all. Not at all."

"It doesn't?"

"I have a list I keep on my desk here of disorders in mental functioning." He picked up a small yellow card. "Alphabetically, you present ambivalence, anhedonia, circumstantiality, condensation, delusions, depersonalization, derealization, hallucinations, lability of affect, loose associations, obsessions, phobias, tangential speech, and verbigeration. As a matter of fact, Dr. Wolper, the only dysfunction on this list you *don't* present is euphoria. These are all, of course, clinical terms."

"And marvelous ones, too, Dr. Chapdelaine. You may be assured."

8th This morning I made a list. Dr. Chapdelaine has his list of life's morbid constituents. I have mine.

I found a clean fresh white sheet of paper tucked in the back of a drawer especially reserved for this sort of nonsense, and I made my list. I hate lists. I despise them. Nevertheless.

"Twenty natural amino acids, Wondrous Primal Substance of Life," I wrote and then listed them one by one. I drew boxes around the names and put five-pointed stars beside those that appealed to me the most, like hydroxylproline and phenylalanine. Then I made dainty designs around the letters until the list was unreadable, although gaining stature as a work of art.

I have no choice, of course. I must search among them for the answer. It can be in no other place. Why the same carboxylic acid group? Why the same amino acid group NH_2 ? Why do all of them have these molecular groups in common and differ only by small unique side groups, an extra molecule of hydrogen in one, an extra molecule of oxygen in another, carbon in another? Why these twenty? If *I* can make other amino acids, why can't nature? Am I not nature? And why are there natural amino acids that ribosomes don't use, can't use, to manufacture proteins? Why twenty? Why not nineteen or sixty-seven? Why are *they* the substance of life? Why not light rays or Rice Krispies?

There are, of course, no answers. I am asking the wrong question. There is no reason why any of this should be as it is except that it is. It works. That's the disgusting mess, that it works, and I am unable to find the order in it. I know I am asking the wrong questions, but they are questions that come to my mind, what there is left of it. It works. It is not that there are amino acids so there can be life. There is life because amino acids made life, somehow, once upon a time. It is what happened one day millions of years ago, when no one was paying attention. But what are the right questions? What am I supposed to say to an amino acid face-to-face? "What were you doing at five-thirty on Tuesday six hundred million years ago?" That's what infuriates me about physicists. Their hydrogen is the same in the Triangulum Galaxy as it is in ours. Their hydrogen is an easy thing to play with. What they have now is what they had in the beginning of time, not an atom different. What do I have? The final product of a billion years of evolution. The results of chance and necessity. Physicists are fortunate bastards. Their carbon was the same three billion years ago. How do I know that when we were a fungus growing on some tree stump we had amino acids at all? I have no way of knowing.

I have only a cell before me now, today, and it came from another cell, which came from another cell, and I know very little about yesterday and almost nothing about tomorrow.

I can ask only how it works, not why. I can never find out why. Not even if I live five or six more years. How is it that a zygote gets started churning out amino acids, making a Lucy Cummings person or a Harry Wolper person? *How* does it *start?* That is the only question. How does it start *today*, with this zygote?

How. I cannot think about why. Einstein can think about why.

"God does not play dice with the Universe," Einstein has quipped.

"Nor is it up to us to tell God how to run His Universe," was Neils Bohr's reply.

And it follows from this that we are given the rare opportunity to make a valid generalization.

All physicists are liars.

10th Congratulate me. I have a hypothesis. This is, after all, the first step off the road to nowhere. Who knows, in another thirty years, when I am ninety-nine, I may be approaching a theory.

I call my hypothesis the Sigma-Factor hypothesis. Catchy name, yes?

Now, the way I see it, I cannot stop my polymerase from reading my DNA any more than I can start it. I cannot order it to stop making messenger RNA, any more than I can set up traffic signals to stop my messenger RNA from plugging into my ribosome. I cannot convince my ribosomes to stop linking amino acids onto proteins, to stop me from growing, from functioning, from thinking. I cannot even tell it which proteins to make. I cannot forget it. I can't make it make a mistake. It just goes on, every cell, every nucleus, whirling away. It will not stop. There is no way. There has been no way since my father, rest his alcoholic soul, whispered something filthy into my mother's ear and emptied the entire contents of his seminal vesicles deep into her womb.

"I think you have drowned my poor little egg," my mother tells me she said. "It only takes *one* sperm, dear."

"For what I am making," my father is supposed to have answered, "ten thousand will be hardly enough."

I remember clearly when it was that my mother told me this. I had just that afternoon informed the assembled student body of my high school that the man next to me on the podium, who was awarding me the American Legion Award for Good Citizenship, had made clear and unmistakable homosexual advances to me at the American Legion banquet the previous evening. I thought it would add a little color to my acceptance speech.

"And your father had such high hopes for you, Harry." My mother told me the story of their great intercourse.

"Where *is* my father?" I asked.

"Where *is* your father," my mother nodded her head.

The questions do not change much over the years. Now I am still looking for my father, only instead of an enormous weaving figure staggering into my bedroom at four in the morning to demand his Brooklyn baseball hat, I am faced with the less manageable figure of a protein.

The polymerase does not do its work alone. It *must* know where to *start* reading the DNA and where to *stop*, where to skip, where to pause on its chore of manufacturing messenger RNA. It needs a sigma-factor, a clever little protein to attach to the polymerase and tell it to begin, at the top, in the middle, at gene 3 or 2,003. And there must be a *first* sigma-factor, the first protein that attaches to the first polymerase the first time and tells it to start making a shoe salesman.

There is no need for elaborate mechanisms turning on and off regulator, operator, and structural genes, because they are all on, I say, all the time. They are read, however, only when their sigma-factor is riding the polymerase. How could I have missed something so obvious?

It is the first sigma-factor that I am after, and when I have it, I shall inject it into Lucy's cell, and I can at last relax. I see they're having a sale on baby clothes at the Coop. I hope I'm not too late.

11th I received today, after I had completed a series of ninhydrin tests that told me absolutely nothing, another one of those fascinating calls from Arnold.

"How are you, Dad?" Arnold asked, almost drowning himself in his concern for me.

"I have a feeling, Arnold, that this is precisely what you are about to tell me. How am I, Arnold?"

"Not good, Dad. Not at all good."

"I'm sorry to hear that."

"Oh, that's all right."

"Anything else?"

"Yes. I thought I'd let you know that Dr. Chapdelaine has come to a conclusion."

"He's leaving the psychiatric profession and becoming a male nurse."

"Is that what he told you?"

"What did he tell you, Arnold?"

"He says that in his opinion, you're a lunatic. He thinks you're nuts."

"Were those his exact words?"

"I think so."

"Think, Arnold. What exactly did he say?"

"He said 'Mr. Wolper, it is with great sympathy and concern that I report to you that the professor is nuts.' "

"Well son, do me a favor and tell the psychiatrist that 'nuts' is definitely not a *clinical* term. I refuse to be slandered by someone with his credentials by anything other than precise *clinical* terminology."

"He said you're psychotic," Arnold offered.

"Not good enough, Arnold. Precision. *Precise* and *clinical*. He should know better than that. He can lose his whole reputation on a diagnosis like that. Call him back."

"Do I really have to? He charges twenty dollars a call, and I've already blown fifty bucks on your first visit."

"Arnold, believe me, this is for your own good. You have a responsibility to this man. And another thing—"

"What's that?"

"You're never going to get my commitment papers if it gets around that Chapdelaine made a diagnosis of nuts."

"You really think so?"

"I know it, believe me."

"You don't happen to have his number around, do you?"

"No, but it's in the Boston phone book. C-h-a-p-d-e-l-a-i-n-e. And Arnold, don't let this wait. Call him now."

"But it's three in the morning."

"I know, Arnold. Call him now."

12th What is this "insane" anyway?

Could my mind possibly work differently from the rest of my body? It could not. Somewhere there is some bizarre cerebral sigma-factor that·has jumped on its very own polymerase and whispers to it, as it rolls now down my DNA, "Turn on that gene over there, not this. Be weird. What the hell. We have only one ride down the DNA. Make it an interesting one."

And what is it that has prodded this particular sigma-factor to jump on this specific polymerase? Is it Arnold, my beloved retarded son? Or is it perhaps Boris? Could Boris possibly have done this? Of course, there is always the painful and glorious chance that Boris is, himself, the sigma-factor, that I am my own polymerase, that the world is made of cotton candy and honeycombs, that life is a carnival. Lhoudley sing cuckoo.

13th Life's crap game. A random combination of twenty amino acids.

It is a fascinating thought that, if I had a mind to, I could line up twenty test tubes, separate myself into twenty liquids of various colors and coefficients of viscosity, and I would be gone, melted forever into glass bottles. I have always sympathized with the Wicked Witch of the West.

I remember vividly the day I took Arnold to see *The Wizard of Oz.* That evening I was here in the laboratory when I heard a blood-chilling scream coming from the house. I raced into the kitchen, and there was Mrs. Mallory, sopping wet, dripping water from every corner of her body, and Arnold was standing in front of her, the girls behind him, with an empty bucket in his hands and a look of complete disappointment on his face.

"I guess they must have used acid in the movie," he told one of the girls.

The next morning I had a locksmith install a combination lock on the cabinet door where I keep the acid.

I think about this now because I know what is going on, here, in these perverted cells that compose my body. Amino acid is being joined to amino acid, the divine chemical mechanism of life, the amino acid group (NH_2) of one molecule reacting with the hydroxyl group (OH) of another, the reaction splitting one of the amino hydrogens off with the hydroxyl group to form a molecule of water, a bright glistening bead of moisture, condensing with each link that is added to the chain. A hundred billion times a second one amino acid is being joined to another, and a droplet of water is made, here, in each spongy saturated cell. Is it any wonder I feel myself continually drowning?

14th We still refuse to accept that we have come from the sea, that we are *still* of the sea, only slightly fortunate that we have become primates and not birds.

I have read today that, since its construction, 341 people have jumped from the Golden Gate Bridge. Not one of them has chosen the ocean side from which to make his final descent.

How painful it is, even at the end, to accept the sea and its cold vastness. It is so much nicer to leave behind us twinkling lights or rosy hills rising above San Francisco Bay, as though that had anything to do with the situation.

15th The world is in motion this evening. It is the merry month of May. The breezes that move down this street unnoticed during January now set the trees rocking, every leaf turning at the slightest wind. It is comforting to know that the world is on the move again. For a while it seemed as though no one cared, not even you-know-Who.

16th I put an ad in the local papers today. This is what it says.

> Nobel Laureate Biologist needs young single female Lab Ass't. Must be healthy and fertile. Will train. Call 555-0088 for appointment.

That was all there was to it. The ad runs tomorrow. The next day I shall know.

17th Ah, yes. These tutti-frutti lipped female wonders whom I have interviewed, who have volunteered their lives, even without knowing what they were being asked to do, for science. I have tried to explain that the position is an unusual one. It's not easy.

"You know that you will be asked to get pregnant?" I explained.

"Oh, yes. My boyfriend and I have always—"

"Well, it wouldn't actually be your boyfriend."

"That's fine. He's always encouraging me to find other men, and I just *love* sex."

"There isn't really any sex involved."

"Oh, that's great! So much less messy that way. Uh—how exactly do we—do I—"

"Artificial insemination—"

"Wow, artificial—"

"With someone else's egg."

"Someone else's egg."

"Yes, you could think of yourself as a greenhouse. What I have in mind is implanting a cell from my wife's hand, rest her soul."

"Oh, I'm very sorry to hear that she—"

"And by a technique I am designing, the cell will develop into an exact duplicate of my wife."

"What a groovy idea! And then you will be her father."

"Husband."

"Have you ever done this before?"

"Oh, there's no danger to you. The very worst thing that could happen is a miscarriage, or nothing at all."

"What if the hand grows first, and then the arm, and then a shoulder, and it's from an adult not a baby? Could I kind of get crowded out? I mean, one of us has got to make it. It could be her, couldn't it?"

"Actually, I hadn't thought of that. Scientifically, it's highly unlikely."

"Well, that's good enough for me. I think science has everything going for it. I mean, as long as you cover the hospital bills should, like, your wife begin to take over."

"Yes, yes, of course."

"Can I ask you something? What kind of stuff do you take? I mean do you smoke it or do you need a needle? Cause, like, I *definitely* want some."

And so it went all day, until sensible, enchanting Meli entered. Though my headaches were back, throbbing, stealing my thought and my humor, I knew that Meli must be the one.

"You want me to try to grow your goddam wife? Is that right?"

"That's basically correct."

"I'll do it. Don't ask me why, but I'll do it."

"You're hired," I told her.

"Good. I've got to go now. We can meet tomorrow morning, if you want. I'll bring over a thermos of coffee. I just can't clone until I've had my morning coffee."

"That's very kind of you. I'm awfully tired now. Come tomorrow, please, and I'll try to be more pleasant."

And it was there that I collapsed, from fatigue, from worry, from general grief, from nobody seems to know what.

And it was Meli who was generous enough to get me to this hospital, and bright enough not to tell anyone.

Even now as I write this she sits across the room, reading a book, carefully fingering the ends of her blondish hair, her lips ready to break into a smile in an instant, her blue eyes darting across the pages, drinking in someone else's thoughts and mixing them with her own. I want these ridiculous tests to be over so I may fall in love with her. Maybe it is not such a great idea, after all, this growing of Lucy.

18th So here I am.

They say they are trying to find out what's wrong with me. They have drawn most of my blood from me. They have looked into every opening and made entrances where none existed. They have listened to every sound emanating from my body, pasted my skin with measurement devices of every kind. I am tubed in every possible place. There is nothing, it seems to me, that they have left to my own control. Their distrust is the stuff of which major wars are made.

19th The parade has begun. Word has leaked out, subtly, clandestinely, and largely through a two-column front-page story Arnold gave the *Boston Globe*, the *Herald Traveler*, and the *Record American*, all headlined, "Noted Nobel Laureate Stricken."

Now "stricken" is a marvelous word. One pictures a man, clutching his throat, gagging for help, and slumping to the floor. With only a slight imagination, one can also picture a spiteful God hurling thunderbolts and alternately smiling and sneering at this crumpled form. Unfortunately, in my case, it lacks only truth. This, of course, does not immediately distinguish it from most other descriptive words used in journalism, but it does set stirring a furious cancelling of appointments and reorganizing of agenda by scores of people.

Husbands and wives, long estranged, appear before me with displays of mutual affection and marital bliss that even Walt Disney would find hard to take. Students who have picketed against my beliefs and practices, who have spit at my face and slandered me at every opportunity, at the word "stricken" appear queued down the corridor outside my door, bursting with the need to repent and redeem themselves. They come bearing gold, frankincense, and myrrh.

"I can't say I was exactly sorry to learn you were in the hospital, Har," were the words that greeted me earlier this evening. They were from Bobbi Cobol, one of my past and less forgettable students, who arrived with several friends. She stood there, her hair in braids, wearing men's boots, men's army pants, and a man's polo shirt displaying her breastless front.

"Are you dying?" she continued.

"Yes."

"Well, it happens, you know. There's no need to pretend it doesn't. You have to be frank about these things."

"I don't expect it for another twenty years or so, but there's no question about it. I'm not growing. I'm not staying the same. As near as I can tell, there is only one alternative remaining."

"You're not dying *now*?"

"You mean today?"

"Well, not necessarily today."

"Tomorrow?"

"Soon."

"That depends, of course. Do you consider thirty years soon?"

"No."

"Then I'd have to say that it's a prolonged dying."

"Oh."

"Does that disappoint you, Bobbi?"

"No. It makes me wonder why I came. The newspaper made it sound—"

"Poetry. Attributable to my son, Arnold."

Enter Mark Woolis, also with a number of friends.

"Hello, Mark," cooed Bobbi. "Where you been?"

"Neck deep in work. I've been meaning to call you."

"I've been busy, too," smiled Bobbi.

"Then I guess it's worked out just right. I brought you a little something to read, Dr. Wolper. Should I open it for you?"

"No, I think I can manage. This is very thoughtful of you, Mark. Let's see what we've got. Ah, yes. Kierkegaard. *Fear and Trembling* and *Sickness Unto Death*. Two of my favorites."

"It's in German."

"Marvelous. Translated from the original Danish, no doubt."

"I thought that Kierkegaard was German."

"Nope. Danish through and through. Studied in Berlin for a few years, but spent his life in Copenhagen. I've always wondered how the Germans translated him."

"You're sure he's not German?"

"Positive," I affirmed.

"Gee, I thought I was getting you an original version. I'd return it except I can't because, well, it was, uh, very reduced in price."

"No doubt."

"Dr. Wolper, you do speak German, don't you?"

"Sure, I do. Sure, I do. I can say 'good morning,' '*Guten Tag*,' and 'good-bye,' '*Auf Wiedersehen*,' and 'How are you,' '*Wie gehtes Ihnen?*' I used to be able to ask whether the four o'clock train to Munich served milk and cottage cheese, but I seem to have forgotten. But if it's in Kierkegaard, I'll recognize it right away."

"Is that all?"

"Oh, no. I can say '*meine Ruh ist hin, mein Herz ist schwer.*'"

"What does it mean?"

"My peace is gone, my heart is heavy. It's Gretchen's song in Goethe's *Faust*. And, oh yes, '*die Rachegötter schaffen im Stillen,*' 'the gods of vengeance act in silence.' Schiller. And '*die Natur weiss allein was sie will,*' 'nature alone knows what her purpose is'—"

"Then you do know German?"

"Only to read. I still always got a canteen of cold water every time I told a waiter I wanted to have some sausage. The problem is with '*Wurst*,' which is sausage, and '*Würste*' which is desert. The gift is a fine one, Mark. Thank you. I'm sure it will soon be a collector's item."

"It may be already," Mark smiled.

"Kierkegaard was born in Copenhagen in 1813 and died in Copenhagen in 1855," Bobbi offered. "His first name is Søren, which is clearly not German."

"Kierkegaard writes as though he were a German. If you had read him as I had, Bobbi, you might have noticed it."

"If I had read him as you did, Mark, I probably wouldn't have understood a word he wrote," Bobbi returned.

"*Ah, die schöne Zeit der jungen Liebe,*" I added.

Blank stares greeted me.

"Schiller. Nothing important. I use it to pick up lags in the conversation."

Enter Norman and Betty Cohen. For reasons that will soon become evident, they brought no friends.

"Oh, Harry. We were just overcome when we heard about your illness," they chorused.

"Oh, I'm sorry to hear that. Is there anything I can do? Are you all right?" I asked.

"No, it's us who should be asking. Are you all right?"

"Yes, I'm fine, thank you."

"Now, now, Harry," Betty implored, "you tell us."

"I am here for rest and some tests."

"Oh, Harry," Betty continued, "I can't tell you how sorry I am to hear that."

"Why is that?"

"Remember Sid, dear?" Betty doesn't take breaths. "Remember Sid, Norman? Poor wonderful Sid."

"I remember. I remember." Norman did not want to hear.

"Harry, I tell you. It was almost impossible to believe. We were in the room when they told him. He had come to the hospital, for tests, just tests, nothing else. We were *there* in the *room* when they told him. The next morning he was dead. I told him that evening, 'You have nothing to worry about, Sid. Nothing to worry about. People live for years with terminal diseases.' That's what I told him. Thank God he was in too great a shock to understand what I was saying. He didn't even know what *he* was saying. Do you know what he said to me and Norman, me and Norman, his two closest friends? He said to us, and these are his very words, he said, 'Will you two assholes get the hell out of here.' That's exactly what he said. He was out of his head with shock, wasn't he, Norman?"

"Did I ever meet Sid?" I asked. "He sounds like someone I would have liked to know better."

"No, I don't think so," Betty smiled. "Anyway, Norman and I have brought a surprise for you. Why don't you go get it, dear."

"Oh, you shouldn't have, really," I said.

"Yes, we should. Yes, we should," and in came Norman with a short fat man in a tweed suit.

"Here is your present, Harry." Betty beamed. "Dr. Mazel, this is Dr. Wolper. Harry, Dr. Mazel is a specialist. Norman had him flown in all the way from Minnesota when he read this morning's paper. What do you think?"

"Do you think it'll fit?" I asked. "I'm rather big across the shoulders."

"No, no, Harry. Dr. Mazel. *He* is the present."

"How much do you eat, Dr. Mazel," I asked, "because I'm not sure I can afford to—"

"No, no, Harry. You don't get to *keep* Dr. Mazel. He has his own home. He lives in Minnesota. The present is that he gets to look at you."

"That's the present for Dr. Mazel?"

"No, for *you*, Harry," Norman joined in. "You're pulling our legs, aren't you?"

"Not at all. It's just such an original present."

"It was Betty's idea."

"Now, Norman, *you* found him."

"What do you think, Dr. Mazel?" I finally asked.

"I think you are all crazy," he answered. "Why have I come here?"

"To look at me," I said. "It's a pity you didn't bring a camera. You could have a permanent memento of this experience."

"What's wrong with this man?" Dr. Mazel asked.

There was a long silence. I really didn't want to tell him that I was only in for a rest and tests. Minnesota is, after all, such a long way to come. Perhaps, I thought, he could provide the necessary information himself.

"You're a specialist?" I asked.

"Indeed, yes, I am." He had a faint German accent.

"And you specialize in . . . ?"

"And I specialize in . . . ?" Dr. Mazel repeated, looking hopefully around the room. I tried to help.

"The heart?"

"The heart."

"That's true?" I asked.

"Oh, yes, yes. Indeed, that is true. I specialize in the heart . . . and also the lungs . . . and the liver, the pancreas . . . the skeletal frame . . . the respiratory system . . . everything."

"You specialize in everything."

"Absolutely everything. My specialty is the *whole* person," and Dr. Mazel clasped his hands across his large belly, perhaps to emphasize the fullness of his task. "You see," he continued, "my specialty is *general* medicine. For years I have been concentrating on the relationship *between* the parts of the human body. Some physicians know about the heart and others about the foot, but who is there who knows about the relationship between the heart and the foot? Do you?"

"I do not," I answered with confidence.

"I do," he responded, equally confident. "And between the gums and the pancreas, and the pyloric valve and the labia majora, and the sphincter ani externus and the cubital articulation. I am no fool, you know."

"That is clear," I concurred.

"Dr. Mazel has opened a whole new field," Bobbi offered. "I read your article on gonadatrophic hormones and lisping in last week's *Science*. It was brilliant."

"Yes. Yes, it was," Dr. Mazel agreed. He bent over to read my chart. He studied it silently. "I must concentrate," he announced. "I will take this back to my hotel room and study it," and he turned and marched from the room.

"Don't you think you had better ask someone whether—," Betty Cohen tried to call after him, but it was too late. "Isn't he marvelous?" she smiled at me.

Enter Mary Sinclair, pretty, brown-haired, dungareed Mary.

After fighting through the crowd she reached my bedside.

"Hospitals are unnecessary," she informed me.

"I am fine, Mary. How are you?"

"They are false prophets, graven images of our impotence. You must leave this antiseptic purgatory."

"My sentiments exactly."

"Do you believe in a God that has fear?"

"I believe we have had this discussion before, Mary, but I am glad you have come."

"Put your hand in mine," she commanded. "There, do you see what I mean?" She smiled.

Enter Father Robert Callahan.

"Glory be to God. God in heaven, how did you ever end up in a condition like this? Is there no justice in the world?" he inquired.

"Hello, Bob," I replied. "I thought you'd have the answer to that one."

"What's He done to you? What has He done?"

"As far as I can tell, nothing. Nothing much at all."

"Here." He edged his way to the other side of the bed from Mary. "I've a little something for you," and he leaned over to me and took from inside his jacket a large manilla envelope. "Thought you might enjoy these. Caught some kids behind the rectory with them. Open it later."

I did. They turned out to be the most illustrative pictures of sexual intercourse between everything but one man and one woman I have ever seen. I have seen textbooks on gynecology that were less graphic.

Enter, in tandem, the Reverends William Cobol and B. Riser Willco, of faiths not yet determined.

"This is Reverend Cobol," Riser Willco introduced. "I believe you know his daugher, Bobbi."

"Yes, yes. Indeed I do. If you look through the crowd, beyond the smiling Cohens, you will see your daughter, Reverend. The person she just kicked in the shins is a former student of mine, Mark Woolis. I believe your daughter is in love with him. You will excuse me if I don't introduce the others to you. As you can see, it would take some time, and we would never have the opportunity to say much before the next guest arrives."

"Oh, did you invite all these people?" Reverend Cobol inquired.

"Not a one," I assured him. "Not a one."

Father Callahan pushed his way over.

"Bob Callahan," he extended his hand and introduced himself to his fellow shepherd. "St. Christopher's in Malden."

"William Cobol." The Reverend extended his hand. "First Unitarian in Wakefield."

"Riser Willco." B. R. offered his hand.

There was a pause.

"And your faith, Reverend?" asked Father Callahan.

"Not much," grumbled Reverend Willco. "Harry, what are you doing here?"

"I'm here for rest and some tests. They are going to determine the specific gravity of my bodily fluids to put an end once and for all to the myth that I can part waters to avoid paying bridge tolls. It's basically a tax evasion case. The Internal Revenue Service spares nothing in pursuit of their man."

"I knew it would happen." It was Arnold, my only son, who had sneaked in, I can only assume, past the posted orderlies who had strict orders to inform him that I had died early that morning and had been cremated by lunch. "I knew it," Arnold went on. "How many times have I told you to let Jimmy Romano do your tax returns. It must have been a hundred."

"We are talking whimsically, Arnold."

"I don't believe it. Not for a minute. Why are all these people here?"

"Just curiosity seekers. Front-page newspaper stories have a way of pulling out of the woodwork whatever it is that is supposed to come out. I've never been very good at metaphors."

"You saw the story?" Arnold beamed. "I did that. I called them up and gave them all the information. Could be worth a Pulitzer."

"Oh, is there a category for fable?"

"No, I don't think so. Why?" Arnold looked puzzled. Then he looked pensively for a long time at the apparatus taped to my body.

"Dad," he said. "You're going to be just fine."

"Yes, I know," I responded.

"You're going to be *fine*."

"Yes, I am."

"You're fit as a feather. You'll be out of here in no time."

"Arnold, I am not going to die."

Arnold's eyes started to mist. "Of course you aren't, Dad." His voice cracked. "Of course you aren't. You're as healthy as an elm."

"Or an oak."

"Or an oak. Or a horse, too," Arnold added.

"Arnold, I am *not* going to die."

A single tear started its way down his cheek. "You will never die, Dad. Not for us, you won't. Long afterwards, you will still—"

"Really, Arnold. Really. I am not going to die. You can go home now."

"No, I want to stay here, by your bedside."

"No, Arnold, dammit, you cannot. If you are in need of a death go up to the leukemia ward and find out what's doing this evening, but do not *prey* on me."

Three white-collared necks twisted toward me. "*Prey* as in vulture," I explained to their holinesses, and they turned and resumed their conversation.

Enter Drs. Richard Bell and Nathan Sol, who were confronted by Arnold before they could progress more than a step into the room. He wanted them to put it to him straight. They told him that he would probably live another forty years, statistical averages being what they are. Arnold appeared confused. It is not an unusual mental state for him.

By this time there was quite a din. Above the noise I could hear Dr. Bell saying to Arnold, "There is really nothing wrong with your father. I will show you." And then in a minute, "Who's got this man's chart? Where is his chart?"

Unfortunately, the Cohens were deeply involved in telling Dr. Sol about their late friends and associates.

"Excuse me. Excuse me," I said just loud enough to create silence. Then adopting my frailest expression, not an easy task, I continued.

"I am touched that you would all take time from your busy lives to visit with me." I forced my voice to trail a little. "I would be deeply grateful if you could do one last thing for me." I emphasized *last.* A few eyes grew moist.

"There is a song I have always loved, one that brings back fond memories." I could hear some sniffles.

"I wonder if you could sing a few choruses of 'When the Caissons Go Rolling Along?' " I whimpered.

People looked at each other. Betty Cohen spoke up. I knew I could count on her.

"Of course we can, Harry. Can't we everybody?"

Heads nodded in agreement.

"Could I speak to you two?" I asked Drs. Sol and Bell.

They came over, and I asked them sotto voce to remove my tubes for just an hour. I promised to put them back myself. They looked at each other, shrugged their shoulders, and began to clamp and untape.

"Arnold, would you like to lead them?"

Arnold's natural instinct for leadership did not fail him.

"Certainly I will. Certainly." Then he looked at me. "Can you sort of give me the first line?"

"Over hill, over dale, we have hit the dusty trail."

"Ah, yes." It all came back to him. "Ready everybody? And—Over hill, over dale, we have hit the dusty trail, as the caissons go rolling along . . ."

When the doctors had finished disengaging me, I waited a few seconds, and then, placing my hand on my stomach, feigned sudden cramps, smiled feebly, waved my hand for them not to stop singing, and slowly made it to the bathroom door, which was on the opposite wall of my room. I gave a final wave, as I disappeared, for everyone to keep up the singing, even joining weakly in the "hi, hi, hee's," and then shut the door.

The assembly now faced the john door.

I went out the other john door, excused myself to my next-door neighbors, and walked down the hall to a very quiet and restful sitting area.

For close to an hour you could hear the full repertoire of World War I marching songs being sung with vigor and passion to a john door behind which the chorus believed I sat, dying and constipated.

20th I had only one visitor today, a Dr. John Umbarger, from the hospital staff, bearded and friendly. We had a good talk, about life, about death, about people and other places. I mentioned briefly my work, the third-generation mutant, and parthenogenesis, without going into the gruesome details.

When I offered to have him examine me, he informed me that he was a psychiatrist. We continued talking, and then in a flash it came to me. Dr. Umbarger was number *three. He* was the third psychiatrist, the one I had worked so hard to avoid.

"You must not believe anything I have said," I announced when the realization came to me. "None of it is true. Not a word of it. Actually I am only growing plants, hybrids, daisies and dandelions, roses and hyacinths. Perfectly normal."

"I thought you were a biologist."

"*Botanist.* It's an easy mistake to make. I *used* to be a biologist."

"You seem bothered by something, Dr. Wolper."

"I am bothered by *you,* Dr. Umbarger. I will deny I have ever seen you. I will say that I was heavily sedated when I did. You can tell Arnold that I will say that you tricked me."

"Who is Arnold?"

"Arnold. My son, Arnold." I looked very carefully at his eyes. It was clear he had no idea what I was talking about.

"I didn't know you had a son."

"I don't. I don't." I smiled as warmly as I could. "It's just a little joke I make up from time to time to see whether people are paying attention. Funny, yes?" I asked hopefully.

"Yes, I think it is very funny," Dr. Umbarger replied. He wasn't laughing.

21st **The Adventures of Boris Lafkin**

written by H. Wolper

CHAPTER FOUR:

Further Adventures in Search of a Heroine

I really believed that making a million dollars in the Cambridge Theater of Total Exposure and having Marty were the two remaining things needed to make my life complete.

So here I am having to start all over, hire a cast, rehearse them, open a theater, and Marty tells me to give her a call in June. I, of course, pay no attention and send her a postcard. It says: I don't want to wait until June.

When I get back from hiring a cast in New York, there is a card that has been slipped under my door. It is from Marty and invites me to a party at her place. I am very happy. Finally, I say to myself, everything is working out. Cast hired, script developing, and Marty dying to remake my acquaintance.

At Marty's party there are four people, counting Marty and me. We spend all our time sitting on the pillows in her living room listening to requiem masses and talking about things like the Warren Commission report, and how you would feel if you knew you only had a brief time to live, and whether you could actually kill someone and under what conditions, and how exactly you would do it, what you would do with the body, and the three civil rights kids killed in Mississippi, and whether you would commit suicide if you were caught and knew they were going to torture you.

When the party breaks up at 5:00 A.M., Marty and I walk back to my place. We put our arms around each other and walk in the middle of the street between the three-foot banks of recently plowed snow. It's cold, but we enjoy it. There is something about doing that kind of thing, walking late at night when there're no cars, no sounds but your own footsteps and voices, the streetlamps reflect off the snow, and the air is fresh and cold on your face. It's your world. You own it, and inside you, under your coat and scarf and sweater and shirt, inside you, you feel so good you could fall in love with Margaret Truman.

And this is what I do. Right there, walking slowly down the middle of Cambridge Street at 5:00 A.M. on a winter morning, I fall in love with Marty Fortran. I am not old enough to know that I am really in love with life and the world.

I stop in a dark space where there's no streetlamp, turn Marty toward me and give her a big hug. She looks up at me and doesn't say a word, doesn't smile, but just looks at my eyes. Then she turns, and we continue to my apartment.

When we get to my apartment, I invite Marty up. We sit in the dark on my sofa talking about our lives. The pretense seems to have dropped away out in the cold. I put my head on her lap, which is very soft, and the only lights are the white streetlamps shining in the window and the ends of our cigarettes, faint red spots that brighten occasionally. It's quiet.

"Sometimes I think that I'm not really in control of what I do," Marty says slowly. "I go to Radcliffe so I can go to MIT. I go to MIT so I can get my Ph.D. I get my Ph.D. so that I can do my own research. I do my own research—and I'm not sure what comes after that."

"Does it make you happy?"

"It's better than not knowing what to do, I suppose."

"Sometimes."

"Are you happy, Boris?"

"I am now, right this minute."

"I mean generally."

"I can only think in terms of minutes. I'm really lousy at planning for happiness. Maybe all you can do is plan to outwit misery."

"I think that the real problem of life is to learn how to accept being lonely. I think it's a myth that it's possible not to be lonely," and Marty chugs on her cigarette.

"I'm not sure. Sometimes I think that it's possible to feel close to someone or something."

"It always ends. Everything ends." Marty exhales slowly.

"I think that's good. If it went on forever it would have no meaning."

Marty takes another long drag and blows a large cloud of smoke into the dark.

"I just don't think that meaning comes just from something having an end. It comes from the experience itself," she said.

"Which wouldn't have any meaning if it went on forever."

"I don't like to start things that I know are going to end." She starts to pat my hair.

"What about relationships with people?" I ask, interested in the profound conversation, but also very comfortable in Marty's lap and trying to avoid the thought of her getting up and going home, which will eventually happen, I know.

"You mean close relationships, intimate relationships?"

"Yes."

"I think that as long as both people are aware that it's a temporary thing from the beginning, they're all right."

"I don't see why you would want to start a relationship at the end," I say.

"To avoid disappointment and false expectations."

I think about this for a long time, in the silence, inhaling on my cigarette, puffing clouds of smoke into the white light that streaks in the frozen window glass.

"I don't think I could live like that," I say finally. "I have to enjoy my experiences as they happen. I have to feel good when things are good, like now, and bad when it's over, like the next minute. But I don't want to live the pain of the end the whole time before. I'll take it when it comes. I have a feeling though, that there is something that doesn't end, maybe a kind of love, I don't know. I'm trying to find it."

You see how serious you can get at these kinds of times.

Marty and I sit a while longer. We watch the light from the streetlamp get dimmer as the sky becomes lighter shades of grey. When it's completely light, Marty announces that she is tired and is going to bed. If I am embarrassed, she informs me, she will sleep on the sofa. I say that I am not.

Marty then walks into the bedroom, undresses and climbs nude into bed. I do the same.

We sleep for maybe an hour or two and then wake up. I reach over for Marty and pull her toward me. I dare not look at her breastless front but the feel of her against me is very good.

I run my hands along her body, up her legs, brushing her pubic hair, across her tummy, which is soft and ripples when I touch it, up to her breasts, which are tiny, almost nonexistent mounds. For several minutes I run my hands over her, up her back, around and under her ass, which moves into my hands when I touch it and compresses into two compact round forms, through her legs, and stimulate her clitoris. She pulls me on top of her, and I insert myself.

For several minutes we grind. Her motions are awkward, and often she lies still. I reach down and try to stimulate her, but the situation gets worse the harder I try. Finally I stop entirely.

"You're sure you want to do this?" I ask.

"Yes. Are you?"

"Yes. At least I was when I started."

I decide to give it one big try. I start slowly and build, finally running my hands furiously over her body, moving myself ever faster toward what I hope will be an orgasm, but I continually get the feeling that she isn't paying attention. Finally, with perspiration running down me from every pore, I give up.

Marty gets up almost immediately and heads for the john. I hear her washing herself.

"Sex is hard work," she tells me when she returns to the room. "You have to really work at it like anything else." Then she comes over and pats me on the head. "Don't worry, Boris. You'll do better next time. It takes practice."

And the crazy thing about it is that I really believe that it's all my fault.

The theater moves along with the usual problems, but, at the end of two weeks, it's beginning to take shape. The new contractor does a good job. Seats are installed, carpeting is laid, pictures are hung, an enormous sign (with a thousand light bulbs, Arthur informs me) arrives.

"Boris, no expense is being spared," Arthur explains. "This theater will be a showplace."

My only real problem is Howie Sednick and Lolly Stork. Every place I go they are fucking each other. When I open the door to my office, they are on the floor.

"We call this 68½," Lolly tells me.

When I go to the john, Howie follows me in and exposes himself.

"Look at this schlong," he says and waves himself around.

"Howie," I try to explain patiently, because, if Howie gives us a bad review, the show is dead. "I think it's astonishing, but we're doing something else now."

"You know they turned me down for *Marat/Sade*. Said that no one would be paying attention to the play with the kind of equipment I've got. I've sent two girls to the hospital. One needed twelve stitches. You'll get written up in every paper in America."

"And you'll get arrested, Howie. Why don't you put it away and go back to your paper."

"All right," Howie moans. "But I'm not giving up."

I open a stall door and there is fat Lolly, sitting on the pot, masturbating.

"Surprise!" she exclaims.

I throw them both out of the building. I will have them arrested if they ever come back, I inform them. This is the middle of the end.

The theater is completed three weeks ahead of schedule, and it doesn't look bad, not bad at all. And after the stage lighting is up, there's an unmistakable theatrical smell to the place. The excitement of bright beams cutting through the darkness onto figures on a stage, their voices raised in passion, sends chills down my spine. It's going to work. I know it.

Because Actors Equity requires huge extra payments for rehearsals over a certain length on any given day, and because the theater is done, I have the evenings and weekends to spend with Marty.

The relationship changes only in respect to time, but I equate that with affection. We have breakfasts together, at her place and mine. I remember to pour my tea in the cat litter, and she is pleased that I am, in fact, educable.

It is a good time, early mornings, late nights, seeing the dawn, smoking cigarettes, going to hear string quartets (Streichquartetten), seeing new Truffaut and Bergman films at the Brattle, reading and talking about the poetry and the fiction, cheap meals at the local student restaurants, long walks. On more than one occasion, people think we are brother and sister. We are close.

When we walk now, we touch each other. We hold hands, put our arms around each other's waist or shoulder, wrestle in the snow when we get tangled. It's a world I've not known since I was a student. The excitement of company, of mutual thought, of personal exploration. I'm convinced I'm in love with Marty.

Our days are spent apart, me at the theater, Marty at MIT. They are separate worlds for us, and, although I question Marty about hers, she does not inquire about mine. It is not that she doesn't understand my theatrical life. It's simply that she isn't interested.

Our nights are spent with each other. We sleep together fairly often, usually on Marty's mattress, my face pushed against the wall, gasping for air from time to time. But we do not make love. We try. God how we try. Every position possible without having a chiropractor in attendance. Every situation imaginable, late at night on the living room floor, early in the morning on the kitchen stool. Nothing, absolutely nothing brings release for either of us.

"It's hard work," Marty keeps explaining to me. "You have to work for it."

I do pushups during lunch and run in place whenever I have a minute. I try isometrics. I lose fifteen pounds and drink quarts of Tiger's Milk each day. Marty and I no longer walk to bed. I carry her over my shoulder with one arm. I undress her and, standing naked in the middle of the bedroom, I lift her from the bed, place her on me, and drive myself in and out of her box like I was a pneumatic hammer, holding her all the time three feet off the floor and horizontal. It doesn't work. Nothing works.

"Marty," I finally say in exasperation. "I don't understand it. Why doesn't anything happen?"

"Well," she explains very patiently, "you can't expect two people who haven't known each other for most of their lives to just meet and start to screw. It takes time and work."

"I see," I reply. Only I don't.

So I give up. I make no more advances. Marty does not seem to notice. We sleep together in the nude. We hold each other. But we do not have sex. We do not even suggest it. For Marty, it is as though nothing has happened. She bubbles along from day to day, cooking breakfasts, listening to Bach, Telemann, and Schutz, working at MIT, going to plays and concerts in the evening, and indulging herself in her favorite and my most frustrating pleasure, walking around the house in the nude. Evenings I watch her ass moving away from me, rising from side to side, watch her sit cross-legged on the floor, her labia protruding below her pubic hair, watch her lie on her back on the one scatter rug, her tummy slowly rising and falling like a time bomb made of cotton. I am sure that any minute it will explode. I know I will.

The week before the show is to open, we spend the weekend together. It is Sunday morning, and we have just finished breakfast. Marty finishes the last drop of her tea (the cat box has been recently changed), gets up and sits on my lap facing me. We are both dressed. She slides her ass down to the end of my knees, reaches down to my crotch and strokes my penis until it pushes against my pants. Then she undoes my zipper and gently takes it out the fly. She holds it and turns her hands around it, stroking up and down. She slides off my knees onto the floor and, kneeling, encircles my penis with her mouth. Slowly she licks me, alternately pulling me into her mouth, which is very warm and very wet, and running her tongue across and around.

"Let me know when you're ready to come," she says, and continues running her mouth up and down on me.

"Now," I tell her, my entire insides ready to blow down all four kitchen walls.

She stops and takes my hand, leading me to the bedroom. I walk somewhat awkwardly.

When we get to the bedroom she takes off her polo shirt and slacks. She is wearing nothing underneath.

I lift her up and place her on the bed. And then we fuck. It is not sexual intercourse, it is not making love, it is not having sex, it is not making it, it is not even screwing. It is one enormous fuck.

She is so wet inside that moisture runs in beads down her legs and onto the sheets. We are both covered with perspiration, turning from side to side. She raises and lowers her ass off the bed, ripples her stomach, pushes and writhes every which way, gasping for breath, moaning and screaming little shrill sounds, clenching her teeth, tightening her arms around me in a vise. I reach under and hold her ass, a buttock in each hand, and drive her onto me, me into her, our pubic bones hitting, our pubic hair rubbing, my balls slapping against her.

Marty gives a short, high-pitched squeak and then, to my amazement, deflates, like a giant balloon slowly losing its air. She deflates down into the sheets, deep into the mattress, lying still for a few seconds, and then something happens. First I feel her insides start to ripple, slowly, then a little jerk, and then a spasm, and she inflates and pushes against me and comes, in a thousand large spasms, jerking up and down on me, every which way, spastically out of control, slamming her ass against me and the sheet. I hold on as though I'm riding a bronco, my hands tight around her waist, forcing her down on me, but daring not to move myself. It seems as though she comes for five minutes, whining and moaning, as though she has been saving up all her life, and then as she slows down and the novelty and shock of the experience wear off me, I start to come, and then she starts to come all over again, and we hold each other very tightly, pressing hard, and together we explode.

When we are done, I lie on her, resting my head on her shoulder, and she lies perfectly still, breathing quietly, her hands crossed on my ass, and we fall asleep. When we awaken, I pull off her gently and lie beside her, trying to avoid the pool of cum and vaginal flow that soaks the sheets. The air feels cool on my skin, and it begins to evaporate the perspiration. We turn and look at each other silently. I reach over and pull her head toward me, and for the first time since we have known each other, we kiss.

This morning's excursion into ecstasy comes to be known as "the fuck." It is the first and last time anything even close to sexual mutuality happens between us, but its aftermath is so intoxicating that within a week we are married.

Even now, I'm not sure how it happened. It just did. The night after the fuck we are sitting nude on the floor in front of the fireplace, holding each other and talking about something important. (Marty insists that when we speak it be meaningful.) Suddenly, I begin to think of the previous night.

"You're sticking me," is Marty's response as I recall it. Romance is not one of her strong points.

"I'm thinking about last night."

"Figures," Marty answers. "Men are about 90 percent lust, 9 percent body, and 1 percent intelligence."

I ignore her. Instead I kiss her on the neck.

"Let's go into the bedroom. The floor's too hard," I suggest.

"For what?"

"For sex-u-al intercourse."

"I don't feel like fucking."

"Neither do I. I thought that this time we could pretend we were human beings and make love."

"You know, Boris, you never *have* said anything about how you felt about me."

"With my hands," I answer. I have a somewhat limited repertoire of humorous remarks.

"What are your feelings about me?" She ignores my whimsy.

"We are just good friends," I mimicked.

"All right, don't be serious if you don't want."

"Oh no, I want to be serious. I just don't know what to say."

"Say what your feelings are."

Now I am stuck. I think very hard of not what I feel but what I can afford to say. I believe that the first person to admit to love is at a decided disadvantage for the rest of the relationship. He also stands the chance of expressing a degree of emotional attachment stronger than his partner's, thereby, I reasoned at the time, turning off his partner, or causing guilt, and it's all downhill from there on. Unfortunately, when I am sitting late at night in front of a warm fire with a girl's nude body resting against my nude body, and I am erect and horny, and my mind is filled with vivid memories of the fuck of the century, in which I was fortunate to be one of the only two participants, the rational elements of a decision tend to weaken.

I, therefore, place my arms firmly around Marty's head, kiss her, and say those magic words, "Marty, I love you."

Marty smiles contentedly and kisses me back. I wait patiently. There is only silence from Marty and snapping from the fire.

"Yes?" I inquire.

"Nothing. I wasn't thinking of anything."

"I was hoping that this might be a *sharing* time. A time for us to *exchange* feelings about each other."

"Oh, Boris, you know how I feel about you. You don't even have to ask. You keep your feelings so hidden. That's why I had to ask."

"I do?"

"Sure you do. For all I know I'm just another good fuck for you."

Now, somehow, while this is hardly my impression of her, I am intrigued by the thought of my masculinity, fucking one girl after another, and the appeal of the image prohibits me from denying it. As a matter of fact, what I did do is ease Marty down on the floor and attempt exactly that, a good fuck.

It is not. It is not good, and it is not a fuck. It is a dry unfulfilling regression to the past.

"Do you notice," I ask, "a difference between yesterday and today?" And I disengage myself.

"Boris," and Marty strokes my chest with the palm of her hand, "I'm just exhausted from yesterday. You understand, don't you?"

This satisfies me. Then, I am not sure whether it is to assuage me or what, Marty says, "Boris, why don't you move in here. It'd be so much easier. We can even get married if it would make you feel more comfortable about it."

"If we're going to get married, you could move to my place," I say.

"You haven't asked me."

"Would you like to move to my place?" I ask.

"When?"

"When we get married."

"Not before?" she asks.

"Now, if you like. Tomorrow. The day after."

"Sometime this week? My lease expires Thursday."

"Sure. Fine." I reach over and kiss her. "So we're getting married. When did you decide that?"

"Just now. It seemed silly not to."

"I thought the only reason to get married was to have kids."

"Oh, we can do that, too, if you want. Just so long as we understand that this is temporary. We'll keep it going for as long as it works and no longer."

"That makes sense," I lie or at least I don't bother to think about it. "When are we getting married?"

"I don't think it makes any sense to wait. When two people make up their minds, I think they should go out and do it."

"Doesn't it take some time for arrangements? You know, invitations, a gown, flowers and all that?"

"That's my responsibility. You just be where I tell you this Friday."

"In four days?"

"In four days. Do you want to meet my parents before the wedding or you want me to meet yours? Actually I don't think it's necessary, but I'll do it if you want."

"Not if you don't think it's necessary."

"Well, is there anything else we have to talk about?"

"Not that I can think of," I say, although for just a minute it seems as though there is something. When I can't think of it, I put my arms around Marty and ease her back down to the floor. I kiss her passionately on the neck.

"There is one other thing, Boris. Marriages are made by the compromises that the partners make, and right now I really am too exhausted from last night to fuck."

"Oh, I'm sorry," I apologize, feeling very stupid for being so insensitive and totally missing that we are not compromising.

And that is how a person comes to get married, or at least how I did.

Marty moves in on Thursday, and the ceremony is on Friday. Marty composes the ceremony herself and selects the site, which is Crane's Beach in a sleet storm. After the groom is introduced to the bride's family and vice versa, the procession begins. The bride's father, who is a reverend, officiates.

The procession consists of the bride, wearing man's army fatigues, a man's polo shirt, and a yellow slicker, trudging through the sand to stand under a large green-and-white-striped beach umbrella. Also huddled under the umbrella, in addition to the groom, are her mother and mine, the only other invited guests. There is also a rather large brown dog, but he doesn't seem to belong to anyone.

The ceremony begins. There is a lot of reading from Kahlil Gibran, which I do not understand. I also do not hear it very well because of the sound of the sleet on the umbrella.

Finally the vows come. They, too, have been composed by Marty. My response comes first in this version.

"Do you, Boris," Reverend Fortran intones, "take Marty to be your wife, starting now?"

I wait but there is no more.

"Yes, I do."

"Do you, Marty, take Boris to be your husband, starting now?"

"*Starting now* I will." Marty makes herself very clear.

"Then I now pronounce you husband and wife. You may kiss the bride."

I hesitate for a minute and then whisper to the reverend out the side of my mouth, "The ring."

Both of them shake their heads to indicate that I am wrong. I, therefore, kiss the bride, after first unsnapping the yellow rubber rainhat. We turn and walk smiling through the sleet to our rented car. Marty's mother throws wet sand at us.

We finally get to the car and start our six-hour drive to Atlantic City, also Marty's idea of a "funky" thing to do.

"What did you think of the ceremony?" she asks.

"Just incredible," I say.

Marty smiles at what she takes to be a compliment, and we continue the slow ride to Atlantic City. For most of the ride I wonder whether I know anyone who could use a brand new wedding ring.

When we arrive in Atlantic City, I look at Marty, sleeping against my shoulder, and I realize that whatever has transpired, I do love her. I check into the motel, and, when I return to the car, Marty is awake.

We unload our luggage and the gifts, still unopened, into the room, and, after getting into dry clothes, open the presents. From her parents and ten-year-old brother, who was not invited to the wedding in order not to corrupt his innocence, as Marty put it, we get a complete set of Corningware, which is exactly what we get from my mother. Inside the casserole from her brother is a box of condoms and a book entitled "Making Sex Work in *Your* Marriage."

We do not make love on our wedding night because Marty has injured her back at the MIT pool the previous afternoon. Similarly, we do not make love the other two nights of our honeymoon. Mostly during the days we walk on the boardwalk. It is cold and no stores are open except restaurants, so we have many cups of tea. During the evenings we eat and watch television, and at night we sleep. We don't seem to have much to talk about.

It is difficult to know where to begin to describe the opening night performance. Actually it wasn't going all that well before the police arrived.

It all begins when Howie and Lolly arrive and start complaining that seats haven't been reserved for them. They are indignant and cause quite a scene.

When I lie and say that it was a mistake, seats have indeed been saved for them, they are not assuaged, and when the lights go down, their voices are still heard bitching to each other. The audience thinks it's part of the show and laughs. At first Howie and Lolly are furious and start snapping back at the audience, which responds with a few snaps of its own. Then a light dawns, and Howie and Lolly realize that they are exactly where they have always wanted to be, center stage.

They play the role for all it's worth. Only, the audience begins to get bored and starts shouting things like "Let's get on with it" and "Next scene, next scene."

I signal the actors to start the show and try as they may whatever they do does not stop Howie and Lolly. I notice, however, that Howie and Lolly are getting desperate.

"Arthur," I say, "we've got to get them out of here."

"Isn't it great? The audience is eating it up," he answers.

"No, they aren't, Arthur. They're sick of it."

Arthur doesn't hear. "One of my best ideas," he says and then it all becomes clear. My mind goes back to the previous week's *Boston Arts News* and a full-page story about Arthur Yaffee, theatrical impresario.

"You let them do this, didn't you, Arthur, in exchange for that story about you Howie wrote?"

"I would have done it, anyway. Besides, they don't cost anything."

By now almost half the audience has left and Howie and Lolly are being called every conceivable name. Like animals backed into a corner, they do what they must—leap on the stage, and tear off their clothes. They start to screw.

Almost immediately the audience falls into applause, which becomes rhythmic to the tempo of the intercourse. The audience loves it, and the actors, the ones being paid, never at a loss for opportunities to do their profession, improvise dialogue around this scene.

There is a law in Cambridge that says all public assemblies must have a policeman in attendance. After seeing what he feels is the interesting part, the policeman disappears into the box office, and I see him using the phone. This, I decide, is a good time to leave. I take Marty with me.

From what I read in the papers the next day, the police arrived in time for the sodomy, an act that violates just about every statute in the books because it also turns out that Lolly Stork is fifteen years old.

It's all over. By that Tuesday it's never happened. I'm sitting in my apartment, now *our* apartment, feeling more than a little shitty, back where I started before Arthur knocked at the door and asked me whether I wanted to go into "show biz." I have not a penny to my name, nor do I have any prospects for earning money. (I've rejected an offer to sell orange drink at the New York World's Fair.) It occurs to me that I have probably not impressed Marty very much either. I feel bad about this because I love Marty, and I let her down. I'm glad when she arrives home from school. She is what is left of my life.

"Boris, I want to talk to you," she says as she enters and takes off her coat. Her breasts look funny under her polo shirt, like they're rectangular. I mention this.

"I'm wearing bandaids across my nipples so they don't stick out in the cold. Otherwise I have to wear an undershirt. Boris, sit down." She is all business.

We're in the living room. I sit and listen to Marty, but I know before she begins what is happening, and a cold nauseous feeling fills my stomach.

"You know," she begins. "We are really very different people."

"How is that?"

"Well, for one thing I'm a mathematician, and I'm not at all sure *what* you are. For another, we're different religions."

"I didn't know that. What religion are you?"

"That's not the point, Boris. The point is that you're a loud, outgoing, unstable person, and I'm from a small town, basically."

"Where are you from? I've always wondered—"

"For chrissakes, Boris," Marty shouts, "shut up until I finish, will you? When I married you, Boris, I had a lot of doubts that it would work."

"How come you didn't say anything?"

"Boris! Let me finish!"

I resign myself to temporary silence.

"Boris, what it all comes down to is that we're too different. We feel different things. Like different things. You enjoy soupy music and frivolous movies. The Senate is passing a Gulf of Tonkin resolution, which is war! China is exploding atomic bombs. You don't like pizza, and I do. Khrushchev is being kicked out of Russia. Every time you look up, there's another three Soviets out in space. And you can't even keep a job. There's a war starting in Vietnam, Boris. A war!"

"You want me to enlist?"

"Boris, you just aren't going to make me happy. I have my own happiness to think about. I'm not interested in your life or your work. I also think that you're crazy. Really. Not mad. Just mildly insane, and it frightens me. The problem is that I've never loved you, Boris. And don't bring up the fuck. The truth is that for the entire time I was pretending that you were Richard."

"Who's Richard?" I can't control myself any longer.

"Richard, my lover."

"What lover? You never told me you had a lover."

"I did so. You've got a very short memory. He was why I couldn't see you until June."

"But I thought that was over."

"I never *said* it was over. But *this* is over. I want you to move out now, Boris. I hope you have a good life, I really do, because actually I am fond of you. It's just that I need excitement in my life, and this is boring, boring, boring. It's also depressing."

"Hey, wait a minute. This is *my* apartment."

"No, this is *our* apartment, Boris, and I have checked with the police. If you're not gone by tomorrow, I can have you thrown out."

"For what?"

"For anything I care to tell them."

"Don't you think, Marty, that we ought to give the marriage just a little longer? Say a month. Thirty days is, after all, not such a long time to be married. I think you can probably make up for it."

"I don't feel like it. I know it won't work, because I don't want it to. It's over, Boris."

"What about love? You once asked me to love you."

"You mean the fuck?"

"No, I mean just before you told me we were getting married. You made me tell you that I loved you. Doesn't love enter into this somewhere?"

"I don't see where. I love you, Boris, but I love lots of people. I'm just not *in* love with you, that's all."

"Then why the hell did you marry me?"

"It seemed convenient and saved explanations to my more prudish friends. You seemed all right. We got along and had *some* fun together. I thought I would probably *grow* to love you. I thought once we were married we could work things out. I was wrong Boris, and I'm truly sorry if I hurt you, but I think it's just your pride that's hurt. You'll find someone else. I'm going over to Richard's now. I'll ask him whether I can stay with him. Then maybe you won't have to move out. If you don't see me tomorrow morning, then you can stay. Good-bye Boris, and I *am sorry*," and Marty kisses me on my forehead, puts on her coat and leaves. I know that it is my own damn fault, but somehow it doesn't seem fair.

"You can't give up after only eight days," I shout after her. "There's an implied warranty here. Marriages can't break down until after the first thirty days, or 12,000 miles, whichever comes first," but Marty is out the door.

When I come back from the movies the next night her things are gone and her key is on the bed. And that is that.

23rd Paul came to visit me today. He read what I have been able to write of Boris here in the hospital, and he was delirious with joy.

"Harry." He clapped his hands with delight. "This is magnificent. If this doesn't get the little fucker, nothing will. I tell you, Harry, you've really outdone yourself this time."

"You really think so, Paul?" I asked for a professional opinion.

"Let me tell you something, Harry. This is the most depressing thing I've read in thirty years. I can't stand it."

"The truth is, Paul," I told him a little reluctantly, "that I really didn't have all that much to do with it. It just kind of happened that way. I'm not sure how."

"Shit, Harry. I know that. But he doesn't, and that's all that counts, I'm telling you."

"You're sure, then? It's what you want?"

"Harry, I've seen ads in the *New Yorker* for starving children that were more encouraging. If that begonian makes it through the rest of the book, it'll be a fucking miracle. You've done everything but stick lit matches under his nails. You're a winner, Harry. I'm telling you, you've got a great literary career ahead of you."

"Now what?"

"Well, I think you've got to keep at it, Harry. We're entering a very delicate state right now. I've been working, myself, on an idea. It's not complete yet, but by the time you get out of here, I think we're going to have the coup de grâce."

"What have you got, Paul?" I asked, more than a little curious.

"It's a surprise, Harry. A big fucking surprise. But you're going to love it. I guarantee it. When I've got this worked out, your problems will be over. You can count on it."

Paul left this afternoon more confident than I've seen him in months. I can't understand why I find it so difficult to share his optimism.

24th Today they have told me that they are going to take a peek inside old Harry W., "just to see what's going on," as they so euphemistically put it. I despise operations. I couldn't stand them when I did them, and I like them even less when they are done to me.

"It's not often we get to go inside a Nobel Laureate," Dr. Sol smiled at me today.

"It's not often that a Nobel Laureate would let anyone go inside him on your say-so," was my response.

"Oh, it's not my decision. It's Dr. Mazel's. He's doing the cutting, himself. The whole hospital will be there."

"So, Dr. Mazel thinks he's come up with something?" I asked.

"Oh, he sure does. You'll be famous if he's right."

"You wouldn't want to tell me just what he thinks he's got?"

"No, I couldn't do that. I wouldn't want to disappoint you if he's wrong. Besides, if he's right, you'll probably be dead in six months."

"Doctor, your bedside manner is slipping. You're not supposed to say things like that to your patients."

"Not if they're true, you're not. You've been stewing about your death all week, and I thought you might want to think seriously about it for a minute."

"Your cover-up is not very good, Dr. Sol."

"Have it your way, Dr. Wolper. You'll be dead in six months. There. Feel better?"

"Much, yes. Thank you."

"Any time. Come in next year, and I'll do the same."

Ah, the lengths these young residents will go to in order to keep your death from you.

25th I feel very weak. Operations take a lot out of you. That's a joke. Everyone around me speaks in whispers, and they are too pleasant. Looks like Dr. Mazel's got himself another page in the AMA journal. I wonder whether they'll call it the Mazel Syndrome or Wolper's Disease.

26th No one said very much to me around here today. Lots of flowers. I feel like I'm at my own funeral. My insurance agent called to wish me well. It was more an impassioned plea. He sounded rotten. I always believed in being well insured.

Father O'Connor also called on me.

"Life on this earth," he informed me, "is but a shadow of the joys of life eternal."

"But am I assured of life eternal?" I asked.

"Who can know God's ways?" he replied.

"Who can?" I asked.

"God moves in mysterious ways, but His grace is everywhere."

"How does a man earn God's grace?" I asked.

"Not by his acts," he answered.

"Then how?"

"Who can know God's ways?"

"Father, you have been very helpful," I assured him.

"How is that?" He appeared confused, but pleased.

"For years I have always wondered something, something that I thought I would never know the answer to until I was face-to-face with death."

"What is that, my son?"

"Whether I would have been better off if I had been a Catholic. I would not have. It would have been a catastrophe."

Father O'Connor's smile faded. Then mysteriously it reappeared. He touched his hand to my head.

"Bless you." He grinned, and backed out of the room. His smile spoke what his words did not.

"You'll get yours," it said.

27th There is an order, the literature says, that a person's reactions follow when he learns of his own impending death or that of a loved one. First there is disbelief. He refuses to accept it. Then he is angry. Why him? Who is responsible? He yells and carries on until the third and final stage, acceptance, when he is finally at peace.

I have been watching a spectacle in the Intensive Care Unit across the hall. A young man is sitting with his wife, who has had a brain hemorrhage. She is comatose, kept breathing by a respirator. Without it she would die in a few minutes. Dr. Sol tells me that the brain damage is extensive. If she recovers, she will be a vegetable, but as long as the respirator keeps pumping, she can go on virtually forever in her coma. They are hoping that the husband will go through stages two and three soon so that he can give them his approval to turn off the respirator. They asked my advice. I have none. But I don't think he'll be able to do it. People who love just aren't equipped to kill, and, call it what you may, to that young man it will always be murder.

Our souls are thousands of years behind our intelligence.

For me it is easier. I am already at stage three. It saved the doctors who visited me today, finally, much explanation and much embarrassment. They should have as much luck across the hall. I hope they do, because my heart is breaking for that young man who has been placed in the very center of hell by modern medicine. I would turn off the machine myself if I could get rid of some of these damn tubes.

28th Dr. Umbarger returned today to investigate the deepest reaches of my psyche. "We are a little concerned, Dr. Wolper," he began. "The doctors tell me that you reacted to their talk with you with—well, they described it as joviality."

"I think that's a fair description."

"Then perhaps you didn't understand what they were saying to you."

"Oh, no. I fully understood it. I am going to die."

"Soon, Dr. Wolper. You are going to die *soon*."

"Soon. I am going to die soon. Actually they give me six months, which isn't all that soon. I'll see summer and fall, maybe even part of winter. Who knows, I might even have another Christmas, if I'm lucky."

"Dr. Wolper, I don't think you believe them."

"Nice try, Dr. Umbarger, but I *do* believe them, and I am not angry. I am at peace. You must remember that I was a medical doctor once myself."

"I've heard."

"You seem to want me to do something, Dr. Umbarger. What is it?"

"I'm not sure, Dr. Wolper. We've never really seen anyone quite like you before."

"I will take that as a compliment," I said. I felt a real necessity to help this man. "Look at it this way, Dr. Umbarger. I have a disease that's never been known before. Isn't it possible it might make me react differently? You know, endocrinal imbalances and all that."

"Of course. It could be the disease," he beamed.

"There now, do you feel better?"

"Yes, I do. I really do. Thank you Dr. Wolper," and he got up and walked from the room.

"Next?" I barked out the door, and then went back to trying to come to terms with the end of my life. I will be glad when they let me out of here.

29th **The Adventures of Boris Lafkin**

written by: Wolper

CHAPTER FIVE:

Still Further Adventures in Search of a Heroine

I decide finally that there is only one way to make myself whole again after the recent departure (and Mexican divorce) of my wife, and that is in politics.

I, therefore, assess the field, which has one front-running Democrat, a Texan currently holding office by the name of Johnson, and two or three Republicans. I decide on Barry Goldwater, as a source of food and lodging and for a chance to get out of Cambridge and expend some energy. I judge him to be a man who is hungry enough for support to hire just about anybody, a category into which I fall quite nicely.

As I begin to lay my plans for the assault on Washington, I get a call from Barbara Spencer, an extremely attractive female genius from school who melts people with her eyes. She has just had the last in a series of fights with her boyfriend, Lawrence Hauptmann, and wonders whether there is an extra bed at my place.

"I can sleep on the sofa," she says.

"You won't have to. I'm going to Washington, so you can have the whole place if you cover the rent."

Wait a minute, Harry. I don't want to go to Washington. I'm a lonely miserable person since my wife has walked out on me. I want to live with Barbara.

"Boris, it doesn't make sense. You've had enough. You're gun-shy."

No. I'm not, Harry. I'm lonely. I'm so goddam lonely it's killing me. Barbara's a great girl. You said so yourself.

"But she's already got a boyfriend, Boris. You're just heading for another disappointment. First Mara. Then Marty. Aren't you ever going to give up?"

Don't give me any of that shit, Harry. She's breaking up with her boyfriend. It's an ideal setup. Look, Harry. I'm truly sorry to hear about your disease, but here's your chance to do something for which the world will always remember you. The greatest love story of all time. I can see the biographies now: "And then, in the waning months of his life, aware of his imminent death, racked with pain and overcome with weakness, he turned out one of the great love stories of all time, *The Adventures of Boris Lafkin*." Up to now you've got nothing, Harry, absolutely nothing. Look, do this for me. Just let me start it and see where it goes.

"Let me think about it, Boris."

Fine. I'll just sit here and play with myself while you figure out whether I should go promote defoliating Vietnam with atomic bombs, or have a relationship with a beautiful human being.

"That seems like a good idea, Boris. Play with yourself. But be careful. I understand it gives you warts."

30th It is so hard to remember where I left off. I should have kept my notes in the hospital where I could have reviewed them. Now, my lab seems like a foreign country. I have trouble remembering where I put things.

I am looking for the first sigma-factor, as I recall, the fellow who tells everyone to start, to start making a baby. Divide, it says, and who would dare disobey the *first* sigma-factor.

I had a thought in the hospital. Perhaps, if I took a newly impregnated ovum, at the first division, homogenized it and then inserted it in one of Lucy's cells, maybe it wouldn't know the difference. Maybe it would be confused and divide, just for the hell of it.

Now all I need is a human ovum. I wonder what day my sweet Meli ovulates. I must remember to ask her next week.

31st "Harry, I want to have this out."

Be my guest.

"This novel you are writing is the most contrived pile of crap since Gulliver found himself with the Brobdingnagians. I would not have chopped off a man's prick, even accidently, the court scene showed a total lack of familiarity with American law, the mental insitution was a farce, I hated Marty and would not have married her, and even you couldn't keep that going."

I thought you loved her.

"Let me finish. And I do not want to go to Washington to work for Goldwater. I *do* want Barbara to move in, and I want to *be* there."

Sometimes I find it necessary in order to maintain the reader's interest to exercise a small amount of poetic license.

"What you're doing isn't poetic license, Harry. It's artistic manslaughter. You could ruin an entire art form that has withstood centuries of incompetence, just by this one effort of yours. I insist that you let *me* write this book."

Have you given up entirely on your plan to murder me?

"Not entirely, no. It's just a little more complicated than I first imagined, and I'm getting tired of waiting. I thought that one more plea, a plea to *reason,* Harry, might work."

Boris, I need to think this over. Give me a little time so I can think this out. In peace.

"Okay, I'll do that, Harry, but only if I can trust that you'll keep Barbara right where she is. No turning her into a fairy princess or making Lawrence apologize so Barbara can go back to him. I'll need your word on that, Harry."

I give you my word, Boris.

"All right. I'll try to wait. But no changes. Everything stays right where it is."

Agreed. No changes. A fairy princess, huh?

"You gave me your word, Harry."

June

1st I am deeply concerned about Paul.

Paul and Maureen came over tonight for dinner. I have always felt that Maureen was the perfect woman for Paul, steady, fun, tough-minded, reserved, intensely curious about everything, and devoted to Paul. It is entirely Maureen, I am convinced, that accounts for their forty-five years of marriage.

After dinner we sat around the study listening to music, watching the flames in the fireplace flick at the wire screen, and drinking Drambuie.

All during dinner Paul had chattered on about Boris, and Maureen's attempts to change the subject had been entirely unsuccessful. Paul had an intense, glassy look in his eyes, and his tongue licked his top lip as he talked. He had become obsessed.

"This is the plan," he told us as we sipped our liqueur. "We'll attack Boris. We'll fight him to the death. That's a good plan, yes, Harry?"

I nodded my head.

"Now here is the brilliant part," he went on. "I've been doing a little furious negotiation, and—this is magnificent, Harry. You're going to love this. Parnash is willing to do it for us. Parnash'll take care of Boris. Genius, yes?"

"Stop it, Paul," Maureen said. "That's enough now."

Paul's eyes darted from side to side.

"I've talked to Parnash, Harry," Paul said, ignoring Maureen, "and I've told him that I'm done with him, that I'm only writing about Boris from now on. Parnash has promised to take care of the fucker for us. Parnash will not tolerate competition. You must start writing about Parnash."

"I don't know anything about Parnash. I only know Boris. You've got Parnash. He's your headache, Paul."

Maureen closed her eyes and sighed.

"Look, Harry. We'll do it together. I'll sit by your side. I'll hold your damn hand. You write Boris. I'll write Parnash. I tell you, Harry. It's a fucking stroke of genius, believe me. You don't know this Parnash of mine. He's been toughened by thirty-eight years of literary warfare. He's fought the Turks and had his head blown off three times. He's been brain-damaged twice, terminally ill off and on most of his life, had two miscarriages, hip dysplasia, and fleas. Boris doesn't stand a fucking chance, I'm telling you. Parnash will eat him alive, and I'm not kidding. Parnash was a cannibal the last time out and ate it up."

"We're going home, Harry," Maureen announced. "Come on Hemingway," Maureen took Paul's hand and pulled him to his feet. "Before you blow your brains out or I do it for you. Say good-night to Harry and thank him for dinner."

"Think about it, Harry," Paul said as Maureen led him to the front door. "It's the cockfight of the century. Ruthless experience versus unpredictable innocence. You work your man, and I'll work mine. May the best man win and all that shit. And I'll tell you something, Harry. If we're really lucky, they could *both* get killed. Think about it."

4th Maureen dropped over this afternoon.

"This is it, Harry," she told me in cold direct terms. "I don't want Paul to continue with your book. I've told that to *him*, and I'm telling it to *you*. I'm the closest I've ever come to leaving him. I'll go. I swear it. Bury them, Harry. I'm tired of the talk and the plotting and the nightmares. Paul is just barely holding on. I'm not going to lose him to a fictional antihero, no matter how many reincarnations the perverse creature seems to manage. I don't care anymore, Harry. I'll leave him."

"I'll talk to Paul," I told her without making a commitment.

She was not particularly satisfied when she left.

Of course, she's right. It is killing Paul. I knew that several days ago. He's consumed with this exorcism.

As near as I can tell, there's only one thing worse than all of this Parnash and Boris business destroying Paul. That's my being abandoned to handle Boris on my own. That would, I am certain, destroy me. So much for altruism.

5th I have been deceived by the metaphors of balance. Standing with both feet on the ground. A well-balanced person. A stable life. A long-standing relationship. In fact, it is always the opposite.

*Dis*equilibrium. That is the answer. The answer is not balance. It is imbalance. Cockeyedness. Turmoil. Disruption. Instability.

Tilt. That is the magic word.

Here is my remarkable insight.

Lucy's cells will not take their first steps on the road to rebirth because they are complacent. They are in equilibrium. They think they have gotten where they are going and now have nothing to do but rest on their laurels. They think they are at that great Miami Fontainebleau of differentiation, their journey completed, and now they have nothing to do but collect social security and bask.

There will be no basking if I have anything to say about it. They can sun themselves at someone else's expense. Their journey has only begun. It is never too late to differentiate and hierarchically integrate *one more time.*

In the meantime, do not give up hope, Lucy. This time I'm on the right track. I know it as surely as I know that I am a crazy old man without a hope in the world of ever living long enough to see you again. And disappointing as the thought may be, that is a high degree of certainty, indeed.

6th "I tell you, Harry," Paul raised his voice at me this morning, "leave Maureen to me. I can handle her."

"I told Maureen I'd talk to you about it," I said.

"So you've talked to me. Now let's get on with it."

"She says she's going to leave you."

"Harry. I told you. I can handle her. She's been threatening to leave me for forty-five years. Has she done it once? When we were standing at the altar, I told her that her maid of honor had the best-looking boobs I'd ever seen. It was a joke. She told me she was leaving me as soon as the ceremony was over."

"I think she means it this time, Paul."

"Fuck, Harry. She always means it. But look at me. Aren't I the most helpless pitiable bastard you've ever seen? Don't I seem like I'd evaporate if she ever left? It's the best thing I've got going for me, Harry. It's brought me forty-five years of bliss, I'm telling you. My snivelling pathetic insecurity is a fucking license to kill. But I don't, Harry. I love the woman. And she loves me. Neither of us is going anywhere. Now, take out your pad and pencil, and let's get to work. We've got a hell of a lot to do."

We walked across the yard to my laboratory and sat down on opposite sides of my workbench.

"First of all," Paul said. "Let's start with Parnash."

"Maybe it'd be better," I suggested, "if we start with Boris."

"No, I don't think so, Harry. Parnash has been getting restless lately."

"So has Boris."

"Try this, Harry. Parnash decides he will become the first white American middle-class samurai warrior."

"Try this, Paul. Boris decides that he doesn't want to play."

"Come on now, Harry."

"Not on your life, Paul. It's Boris, or I quit."

"You just want to get rid of me. You've cooked up some fucking deal with Maureen. Haven't you, you bastard?"

"No, I haven't, Paul."

"Then give me one chance at starting. I'll work in Boris, I swear it."

"I'll give you one chance, Paul. That's all. If Boris isn't off my back in about two paragraphs, Parnash can throw his hibachi into Lake Inawasiro-ko for all I care. You got me?"

"I got you."

Paul sat in silence for a minute, immersed in creative thought. Then he looked at me. His eyes were glassy again and moistened from the strain of focused attention. He began to shake uncontrollably.

"Can I get you a drink?" I asked him, deeply concerned with what was happening to him.

"No. No. That's all right, Harry. Just nerves. Maybe this isn't a good day to start. I'm a little tired. I didn't get much sleep last night. We'll work on it tomorrow. Right?"

"Right," I told him and helped him back across the yard to the living room where he rested on the sofa for an hour or so before leaving.

"Sorry, Harry," he said as he was going. "Fatigue, I guess. Tomorrow. We'll do it tomorrow."

"Tomorrow," I repeated, but neither of us believed it for a minute.

10th Maureen called me early this morning. She was extremely upset.

"You're going to have to write your book by yourself," she told me through her sobbing.

"Maureen, look," I told her. "I talked to Paul a few days ago. He's all right. Really." I tried to calm her down.

"No, he isn't, Harry. He's had a breakdown. He's in McLean. Go see him yourself." She hung up.

I dressed quickly and took the trolley out to Belmont. Then I walked the long hill up to the hospital. When I got there, I was shown to Paul's room, a small chamber with pea-green walls and bars on the windows. Paul sat huddled in a corner of the bed, his legs hunched up under him, a large frightened cat, clutching desperately to the white metal bedframe.

I tried to find out what had happened. For a while Paul wouldn't talk, but when he saw the tears start to form in my eyes, he started.

"I'm sorry, Harry. Sorry. It was Parnash, you know. After all these years. He finally got to me. I suppose I've always known that he would. And he did. Look at me." Paul shook his head.

"You'll be out of here in a couple days, Paul. You and Maureen will go to Bermuda. You'll come back all rested. Parnash will have disappeared forever. Give it a couple days."

Paul's smile faded.

"Six months," he said looking down at the floor and tightening his grip on the bed. "They said I'll be here for six months. Minimum of six months. Parnash will never go, Harry. I have to accept it. He won."

I found myself getting terribly angry.

"Paul. For godsakes! You've got to get rid of this fantasy. That's enough. Enough! I don't want to hear about Parnash anymore. Look what he's done to you."

Paul started to cry.

"What'll I do, Harry? Oh, God, what'll I do."

"Retire, for chrissakes. You've got enough money from your books to last you two more lives. Retire now. Relax. Go visit your grandchildren."

"Is that what you're doing? Is it, Harry?"

"Yes," I said without really thinking. "I'm not writing Boris anymore. I'm doing my experiments, and that's all. I've given up. Then I'm going to take a long vacation somewhere."

"I don't blame you, Harry. I don't blame you," Paul said, tears streaming down his cheeks. "I don't blame you."

We sat for several minutes until Paul had stopped crying.

"I think if I had let go of him thirty years ago, when there was still time, I'd be okay now. But he was a vision for me, Harry. He represented something. I don't know what. I couldn't let go. I couldn't let go," Paul wound down and closed his eyes. "I'm tired, Harry. Exhausted. I'm going to go to sleep now. I hate to sleep because Parnash is there, but I have to now, Harry. I can't stay awake."

"I'll visit you soon, Paul."

"Not for a while, Harry. Don't come for a while. Give me a few months to get together. Please. You're a good friend, Harry. I swear it. Don't come anymore. I don't want to be here. Let me get out. You understand, don't you?"

I shook my head that I did, and I got up from the bed.

"Harry. I'm sorry I can't help you with your book, anymore. I'm sorry."

"I'm not doing the book anymore," I decided out loud. "Give me a call when you get out. I'll look after Maureen," and I went over and put my arms around him. Then I left and walked down the hill to the trolley back home.

12th I have had to immerse myself in my work. It is the only way to put out of my mind persistent thoughts of Paul, Boris, Parnash, Arnold, Maury. The list keeps getting longer and longer.

I went over to see Maureen this evening. She's doing all right. She's tough.

"I've been expecting it for years, Harry," she told me with tears in her eyes. "This is for the best. Paul will get better, and things will settle down. The tension was getting unbearable. Now, when we're back together, we can relax. For ten years, fifteen years, maybe even twenty years more. We'll die in peace, Harry. The torment is over."

I returned from Maureen's feeling better about it all, and was able for the first time in days to get back to my work.

I am more convinced than ever that the secret lies in the cytoplasm.

Cytoplasmic symmetry is responsible for determining the site of the first ovular cleavage. A cytoplasmic cortical shield protects and nurtures the ovum during its fertilization and development. The first blastomeres that differ in pigmentation, cell size, yolk content, adhesiveness, motility, viscosity, surface tension, and on and on are caused, I am certain, by the reaction of the cytoplasm to the greater oxygen of the vitelline space or the greater acidity of the blastocoel fluid. It is the cytoplasm, benign and unspectacular, that determines it all. And it is the cytoplasm that holds back the nucleus from expressing itself again in a new procreation, a new generation, a new life.

I must treat the cytoplasm, wipe from it all resistance, wipe from it all traces of the past, wipe from it all barriers to a new birth, to Lucy's birth.

I must develop a Great Wiper.

This is what I have today started to do. When is it, I have asked myself, that there was a Great Wiper? At the beginning. At the very beginning of life, when there were gases and liquids, floating aimlessly in the primeval genetic pool, a Great Wiper must have developed, some masterful fluid that did not bother to assemble the chains of peptides, to bring the large hydrocarbon molecules together, even to assemble the amino acids, but who did just what the cytoplasm does. He formed the perfect environment, so that all the peptides and hydrocarbons and aminos could not resist getting together and doing something frivolous and stupid like starting life on earth.

"Forget," the Great Wiper said, "what you are. Think instead of what you could be," and there was universal cheering and drunken parties and parades with streamers of enzymes floating through the pool, fireworks and more cheering, and, when the night was over and the molecules awoke, hungover and bleery from their debauch, they nudged each other incredulously and said, "Oh, God, look what we did last night." And there, in front of them, were cells, living cells, cleaving away.

"We must be careful never to do *that* again," they said, but it was too late. The Great Wiper had had his way.

This is what I have done today. I have reconstructed the primordial environment.

On the floor is my grandson's plastic wading pool with pictures on the side of Disney characters involved in various aquatic pleasures. In the pool there is ammonia and water through which I'm bubbling carbon dioxide and methane gas. Around the pool are all my electric heaters, warming the air and my primeval soup. Over the pool I have constructed a clear plastic tent from my shower curtains (Mrs. Mallory won't notice the difference for at least a year). They have pictures of pink water flowers scattered tastefully throughout a blue background of fishes. It is quite appropriate. As a proper and fitting final touch, I have rigged my static electricity generator just inside the tent with a metal disk on each side of the pool so that the crackling sparks charge across to each other every minute or so. This duplicates the electrical activity that emanated from the volcanos as the earth cooled down.

There are those, I am sure, who would question the methodology, the apparatus I am using. Some might accuse me of being sloppy. But where were the notebooks then? Where were the Florentine flasks and two-liter measures? Where were the pipettes and titrating cylinders? And, while it is true that there were no Disney wading pools either, the Great Wiper had to make do with what he had available. I will do the same.

13th Ah, the joy, the complete ecstasy of being able to return to my work. It is all I can think about. That and my little dialogue with the Grim Reaper. I have always had an aversion to agricultural metaphors.

What bliss it has been to indulge myself, to direct my energies toward deciphering the intellect of the cosmos, rather than to use my valuable time in outwitting real estate agents and insurance brokers.

I have not heard from Arnold, which is heaven on earth. I have not been disturbed by psychiatrists. I have not been solicited by Maury or even, miracle of miracles, exasperated by Boris. Even Mrs. Mallory has been considerate, a quality I had hitherto not observed in her. I have been left totally and completely alone with my work. It is an excellent way to live if one also has the opportunity to love. Freud was not so dumb after all. *Leiben und Arbeiten.* Perhaps I have dismissed him too easily. Or, what is more likely, perhaps, I am getting more charitable as the end nears. That, or my brain is softening on the way to its final syllogism. It is not unlike Freud that he would be the benefactor of such addling.

Viennese charlatans to the side, my plan is fully developed. This is how I shall spend the last days of my life.

I shall work on the development of the Great Wiper. With that in hand all else follows of necessity.

I shall take the Great Wiper, and I shall inject it into the cytoplasm of my fair Lucy's cells.

Then I shall retrieve from my willing laboratory assistant one human egg, which I will also subject to the wondrous powers of the Great Wiper.

I shall wait until the coast is clear, until neither Meli's egg nor Lucy's cell can recall its past, and then I shall, when no one is looking, simply switch nuclei. I shall throw out Meli's, and in its place I shall put Lucy's.

I shall give the Lucy ovum time to recover from the shock while I am preparing Meli. It is important that she be receptive. Very carefully, I will release estrogen and then progesterone into Meli's bloodstream, carefully measured and carefully timed. If done properly, she will be almost perfectly receptive. The ovum will stick to her uterus like glue. It will thrive like roses on manure, you should pardon the agricultural metaphor.

Before implantation I will parthenogenesize the Lucy ovum. This I will do with a special kind of unbalancing, a highly precise disruption of its equilibrium that will, in turn, set off a nuclear reaction. The cytoplasm will make immediate preparations for the reconstruction of her lair, cleavage will begin, and I will hastily reinsert Meli's egg, now the Lucy ovum, into Meli's uterus, where it will be reborn my Lucy.

It is a perfect plan, the culmination of a life's work. I see it as a great and beautiful poem constructed of nature's deepest secrets, of which I, only I, have knowledge. I am moved that I would be permitted to gain access to them. For after all, what am I, just a man, hard-working, earnest, dedicated to the wonder of—

"Harry, cut the crap will you, you're turning my stomach."

Boris, you gave me your word. Go away. If I want to be sycophantic, goddammit, I will be sycophantic. You certainly don't think I'm going to antagonize nature now, do you?

"You're making me nauseous, Harry."

Boris, I have Mother Nature by her labia majora. This is not the time to yank. This is the time to stroke, to act grateful so she will yield. She knows where my hands are. She is no fool. I still need the Great Wiper from her. I cannot afford any trouble. She is a raving bitch sometimes, Boris, with an unending bag of tricks. She can form a placenta praevia and block the birth canal. She can move the ovum into the oviduct and engineer an ectopic pregnancy. She can let the chorionic tissue's destruction of Meli's uterus get out of hand, and I can have a malignant chorionepithelioma to deal with. She can pull an immunological response on me, and I can be up to my neck in antibodies and antigens. No, thank you, Boris. For now I will be grateful for what I have. There is too much yet to come. I am content that I've got her where it counts.

"Have it your way, Harry. Mother Nature has a way of kneeing people in the balls when she gets tired of them. It's a very painful experience. Don't be too sure she's not humoring you."

Boris has a point.

14th The truth is that I'm becoming quite fond of Boris.

Of course, I don't understand him. And I must be very careful about how I proceed now that Paul has deserted me, because I don't know why Boris does what he does. Still, all in all, I do find him a not altogether unpleasant companion.

It was, of course, not always this way. Boris was, originally, I tend to believe, the result of a compulsive bad habit I have. Usually it only comes out when I am depressed or bored. The way some people bite their nails, play with the ends of their hair, masturbate, wet their beds, in that same way, I *create*. Not just little things like fruit cups or needlepoint, but I create very large conspicuous things. Usually things that are alive. My "corse" was the result of one such creative seizure, and, while something that can both jump fences in competition *and* give milk might be a brilliant thought, I usually end up overlooking something. In this particular case it was the udder, which has just frustrated the poor animal to death.

I can only guess that Boris was the result of another such creative seizure. Once again, I never for a minute suspected that he would not only want to take off on his own but would turn against me, because, after all, I cared for him. But from the minute he came to mind, from the minute I first put my pen on the paper, Boris resisted. I feel that now we get along a little better. Who knows, someday we might even be able to have a civilized conversation. For now, it's largely a standoff.

Not all my creations have been bad ones. I have, for instance, created snakes that never shed their skins, and, while by the time they get to the third or fourth year of their lives, they seem to perspire quite heavily, they still seem happier not having to molt. I have created butterflies that never pupate or for that matter fly, and roaches that are allergic to dirt and dampness. While neither seem to survive for long, while they *are* with us, there is no question in my mind that they are happier.

Boris arrived during my deepest depression, so it is rather amazing that he functions at all. I expect any moment that the fatal flaw will show up, if it has not already.

"Who knows, Harry, maybe you were so depressed when you conjured me up that you forgot to include a flaw."

The problem is, Boris, not that you have *no* flaws. The problem is that there are so many it's hard to tell which is the fatal one.

15th I can't find Meli. I never should have asked her to leave after the first day at the hospital, but I knew what was coming, and it seemed better that she not be there. There is no answer when I call. Her mail has not been picked up in weeks. I'm afraid something has happened to her.

16th I conducted another interview today.

Esconsia, known to her friends as Ski, was born with the name of Virginia, but as we all know, Virginia (I was informed) is common to the degree of embarrassment, and is a serious handicap for anyone genuinely interested in gaining recognition in literary circles. I'm sure that the late Ms. Woolf would have found this to be a distressing piece of information.

Ski entered in black. Black jersey, black denims, black boots, black tights, and a black hairband tied tightly around her red hair.

"I am ready to die," she informed me succinctly.

"So am I," I answered.

"Oh, do we both die?" she asked eagerly.

"Eventually," I told her.

"Oh." She was disappointed.

I explained the procedure to her. She listened intently, wincing at appropriate places.

"I don't get it," she said. "When do I get to die?"

"Miss Cohen, I'm afraid that you're going to be disinterested in this opportunity. Death is not part of this experiment."

"But something could go wrong, couldn't it?"

"Yes, but it is unlikely that it would kill you."

"What about bleeding. There could be massive internal bleeding, couldn't there? I read about that. I mean, everything can have complications."

"We could stop the bleeding."

"Well, what about an infection? I could get horribly infected and it could be some new germ that can't be stopped with antibiotics. I mean, that's possible, isn't it?"

"Miss Cohen, if your objective is to kill yourself, you're just not going to find this work rewarding. I can guarantee it. You'll have to do the deed on your own."

"I couldn't do that. I want to sacrifice myself for the good of science. I've already donated my eyes, liver, and heart. I offered my body to B.U. Medical School. They told me that I'd already given so much of it away that there wouldn't be enough left to make it worth their while. What a rotten goddam school. There'd still be my skin, you know. You'd think the dermatology department could use it or something."

"Miss Cohen, we seem to be working at cross-purposes. I want to make someone alive. You want to make someone dead. Eventually, we're bound to conflict."

"I guess so," she answered with resignation. "But look, keep me in mind if you're planning something that's a little more lethal, you know? I can be sacrificed. It's okay."

"When human sacrifice is concerned, your name will be the first that will come to my mind, you may be assured." I showed her to the door.

Just before she shut the door behind her, she turned to me.

"I'm a virgin," she said slowly, "if that's any help. Of course, I can't promise that I'll always be, but it's likely. You know?"

I wanted to stop the door from closing behind her so that I might say something more, but we old men don't move very quickly, and, even so, what could I have said?

Meli, where are you?

17th Dearest Dean:

How kind of you to write and bring me up to date on those alumni who have bitten the proverbial dust over the last several months.

How encouraging to know that the Grim Reaper has not faltered, but continues unfalteringly from month to month.

You may, of course, rest assured that should I mention any of these recent departed in my address, I will be careful always to refer to them in the past tense and in hushed tones.

You will not find me shouting the names of the dead. No Franklin Roosevelt! or John Kennedy! will blare from my lips. What good are they now that they are dead? No good at all! Can they stem the rushing tide? Lead us from the wilderness? Show us the error of our ways? They cannot! They have flown the coop, removed themselves from the fracas, taken the coward's way out, and you will not find me extolling the virtues of those dead and gone. To hell with the lot of them!

I can only plead with you, my good Dean, to send me more, without hesitation, past and present. Phone them in to me. Send me the death rolls of the wars and plagues. The accidental and the diseased. The suicides and the murders.

How, indeed, could I pretend to address my colleagues without knowing who among them is not? I shudder to think that I might have (out of ignorance alone) inadvertently mentioned "my good friend Saul Cashden," only to learn subsequently that his carcass has been rotting these last three months under the tail assembly of an Eastern Airlines prop-jet in a North Carolina forest. Thank you for the information. He is no friend of mine, this dead man, that is for certain. How can I ever hope to repay your thoughtfulness, which has saved me from an error far worse than—well, you know my meaning.

Your obedient servant,
H. H. Wolper

18th I have explained it all to Dr. Albert Koesman, behavioral psychologist par excellence. He has, I am told, made fat people thin, sad people happy, frightened people complacent, and anxious people calm.

"But have you," I asked him today, "ever made a crazy man sane?"

"It is not a question of sane or crazy," Dr. Koesman explained to me as he stroked his goatee. "The mind, mental development, psychological existence, is simply a matter of stimulus and response. One stimulus provokes a response, which is itself a stimulus to another response, and so on."

"Sort of like dominos," I offered.

"Exactly," he smiled at how readily I had grasped the concept. "Now as I understand it, you are consumed by two tasks. The first is your endeavor to create your wife in a bottle, and your second is to prevent your imaginary playmate, you say his name is Boris, from driving you mad. Is that correct?"

"A little indelicate, perhaps, but accurate," I smiled weakly.

"It seems to me," Dr. Koesman explained, "that we have only to desensitize you to these phenomena, and you will be able to return to a tranquil existence."

"Tranquil?"

"Yes, peace. Quiet. Calm."

"Dr. Koesman, I am a dying man. I will be reaching the ultimate in desensitization in a matter of months, weeks, days even. I will be so desensitized that even Pavlov himself would turn loose his dogs and throw out his bells. I do not want to be numbed. I want to be stimulated, excited, charged. I want to explode. But with direction, Dr. Koesman, with goals and objectives. You can puff on your pipe and be calm. I'll go hysterical if you don't mind."

"Dr. Wolper, just what is it that you want?"

"I want to concentrate. I want to end distraction."

"Then we must countercondition," Dr. Koesman informed me patiently.

"Countercondition what?"

"Countercondition the stimulus that has provoked all this. It's clear to me, Dr. Wolper, that, in some perverse way, what you are doing or not doing or whatever must be meeting some need of yours. It has to. It is simply inconceivable to me that it has neither rhyme nor reason."

"Rhyme I don't know," (I was now quite loud) "but reason. What reason? That's why I have come, Dr. Koesman. There is no reason if I am crazy. I ask you, Dr. Koesman, one more time. Am I crazy?"

"Dr. Wolper, once again I will try to explain. What you are doing is for a precise need you have. It has been conditioned in you just as surely as you drool when you are hungry and food is presented to you."

"That's another thing, Dr. Koesman. I don't drool."

"Don't be ridiculous, Dr. Wolper. You do drool."

"Dr. Koesman," I roared to make sure he would not doubt me. "I don't drool! I don't salivate! I don't have wetness in my mouth! I don't drool! Do you understand? No drool!"

"Of course, I do, Dr. Wolper," he answered, but I could tell he was only humoring me. I had frightened the sensitization out of him.

"Good." I was satisfied.

"Dr. Wolper. Stimulus. Need. This Boris of yours is only a stimulus you have created from your mind to meet a need of yours. That is all." He would not quit.

"What need?" I decided to play along.

"We do not know that yet." He looked discouraged. Then livening up, "But we do know the response. Acute anxiety. Frustration. Anger. Hallucinations and disassociation."

"And is this different from being crazy?" I asked.

Dr. Koesman looked up at me. "Not much," he said quietly. "Not much."

There was a moment of silence.

"Look," I finally said to cheer up the disheartened behaviorist. "In a few months I will be dead anyway. It's hardly worth the effort."

Dr. Koesman shook his head and stared at his highly polished shoes.

"Hardly," he mumbled to himself. "Hardly." And he emptied his pipe on the thick carpeting.

19th That son-of-a-bitch philanthropist arrived again today, smelling as though he had washed up on the shore with the red tide. Does the man never bathe?

"You stink, Maury. Why don't you get the hell out of here and leave me alone," I mentioned to him shortly after he had made his way into my living room past Mrs. Mallory's best efforts at deceit.

"Ah ha, you old devil. You *are* glad to see me. I knew you would be."

"Maury, I am not glad to see you. I would sooner have Pestilence, Famine, Death, and Whatever the Other One is enter my living room at the canter and watch their horses void on my oriental rug than I would talk to you."

"You always were a crusty old son-of-a-gun, Harry," Maury attempted to respond in kind, as he ran his kerchief over the perspiration that drenched his face and neck. "You know what I'm here for."

"I think I can guess. How much do you want?"

"Harry, you are not being kind to me," he whined.

"You could always leave," I offered.

"Harry, do you know why I do this? Do you know why I give up my evenings, my weekends, why I hardly ever even see my children, and I have six kids, do you know why?"

"Maury, I don't know, and I'm absolutely positive that I don't want to know."

"I'll tell you why it is that I haven't seen my family for more than five minutes in three months, Harry. Love. It's love, Harry. Love of my fellowman. Love of the earth, of this great country of ours, America, of this planet, of God's creatures, small and big, weak and strong, the young and the old. Love, Harry. Every night I solicit money for the sake of Love, and you know what that makes me, Harry?"

"A pimp?"

"That makes me a human being, Harry."

"That makes you a flaming ass-hole, Maury. Now please go home to your family."

"I don't want to, Harry. My family is not *me*. It's too limited. I need the world, the entire cosmos for my love."

"Then *don't* go home to your family. Go to Zambia or Palestine or the moon. I don't care. Just go."

"I need your advice, Harry."

"You didn't come here for a contribution?"

"Oh, I need your money, too. But first I need your advice. Suppose there was someone you knew whom you thought a great deal of, and suppose, just suppose, that you thought that this someone had committed a horrible crime and it was up to you to get the evidence necessary to convict him. Would you do it?"

"No," I answered instantly, thinking of my last abortion.

There was a long pause.

"Well, Harry?"

"No."

"Yes but *why* no?"

"Just no, that's all. No. I would not. No."

"How can you be so sure?"

"I'm just sure. It's a problem that I've given a lot of thought to over the years, and every time the answer always comes out the same. No."

"But what if the crime is just horrible? Wouldn't it be better if—"

"No," I interrupted him. "It would not be better. The answer is always no."

"Always?"

"Absolutely always. It's almost a law of nature it's so certain," I assured him.

"What about his conscience? How could this man live with his conscience, knowing that he let a man get away with a horrible crime? Wouldn't that bother him?"

"No."

"Why not?"

"It just wouldn't."

"Not even a little bit?"

"Not for a second. Look, Maury, I'm a scientist, right? A trained physician. And I know how consciences work inside and out. Believe me. One of the first things you're taught in medical school is that if you do something wrong, forget it."

"I don't know, Harry. I know you've got a Nobel Prize and all that. I just never thought the answer would be such a straightforward one."

"Oh, it's by no means straightforward. It takes years of introspection and thought. And tonight, as a gesture of our long and deep friendship, I have elected to share that insight with you. Consider it my monthly contribution."

"You mean I'm not going to get my fifty bucks, Harry? I was really counting on that for my quota this month."

"Oh, this is in *addition* to the fifty dollars. You get *both* tonight. Fifty bucks, and insight. Quite a night, wouldn't you say, Maury?"

"I guess so."

"You don't seem convinced, Maury. Look, where the decision is between what is right or wrong and love, love must always receive preference. Why else are spouses not required to testify against each other? Love, Maury. The courts know that love will always win."

"But I'm not sure I *love* this person, Harry. It's not as though I'm married to him."

"Maybe not formally, but, Maury, I can tell that you are a man who loves everyone, birds and fowl, man and beast. Your love knows no bounds, Maury, certainly not the conventional ones of, say, taste and discretion, but you love without reference to those characteristics one normally associates with human intercourse. It's a rare talent, Maury. Don't violate its purity with such conventional bourgeois considerations as conscience, morality, and good judgment. Keep it pure, Maury. Pure."

"Pure. Pure love—" Maury rumbled it around the cavern of his mind, a broad smile spread ear to ear.

"Right, Maury. Pure. Now here's your check for fifty dollars."

"Could you make it out to 'Friends of the Long-playing Record,' please?"

"Is someone about to end the phonograph record?"

"That's what we're trying to find out."

"Done. 'Friends of the Long-playing Record.' Here now, Maury, let us embrace in a gesture of deep and everlasting friendship before you leave," and I hugged his hot, sweaty, putrid body, and showed him to the door.

Just before the door shut behind him, he turned to me with a great wide grin.

"Good-bye, you old son-of-a-bitch," he smiled and playfully rumpled my hair.

"Good-bye, you son-of-a-bitch," I echoed and slammed the door behind him.

21st So, finally we have come to the contract. *L'homme est né libre, et partout il est dans les fers.* And so, taking Boris such as he is, and agreements such as they may be made, is it not possible to establish some just and certain rule for the preservation of order, to unite what his right permits with what my interest prescribes, that justice and utility might not be separated?

"Harry, cut the shit. What's the deal?"

Deal, Boris? There is no deal. What we do must flow as tears flow from the bereaved, as a consequence of the nature of man.

"I'm not interested, Harry. I just want to deal. What do you want? Let me have it. I'm getting claustrophobia."

The nature of man, Boris.

"Harry, screw the nature of man. I just want what I have a right to have, my freedom. You want the nature of man, take him. *Physis, anthropos,* the whole schtick. You got it. I'm only interested in me. That's the topic right now."

But you *are* free, Boris. You've *always* been free.

"Harry, this is me, Boris, you're talking to, not some overweight sweaty charity collector. I'm in here, and goddam it, I know whether I'm free or not."

Boris, this is ridiculous. Without me you would be nothing at all. I invented you; I am embarrassed to admit it, but I did nevertheless. You are linked to me with the bond of nature.

"Harry, I'm not at all sure that you made even the smallest contribution to my existence, that I wasn't some horrible accident, some uninsured mistake. But even if you are responsible for me, I don't need you any longer. I've reached the age of reason, the age of consent, and I want out."

You are out, Boris.

"Harry, look, I know you're doing the best you can but this life you've got for me is rather depressing, don't you think? I'm a man without humanity. A human without manhood. I need to be my own master. My morality has to be my own. We need an understanding, Harry, a contract."

I'm not sure I can do that, Boris.

"Sure you can, Harry. And look what you get."

I've been waiting to hear, Boris. What is it that you're so certain I get out of all of this?

"Harry, you get the most valuable return possible on your investment, the most precious commodity, the most worthy gift that one human can bestow upon another."

Namely?

"Love, Harry. If you play your cards right, you get love out of this."

I get what?

"Love."

Love?

"Yes. Love."

Love. I get love.

"That's right, Harry, you get love."

From whom?

"Me, Harry. You get love from me."

From you?

"Yes. From me."

From you.

"From me."

Boris, let me see if I've got this straight. I want you to listen carefully, and if I leave something out or if I've misunderstood anything, you interrupt me and let me know.

As I understand it, what I'm to do is to stop writing my book as *I* want it and let you do it as *you* want it instead. I'm to give up what may be the only project I have even a small chance of successfully completing in what's left of my life, what just may be the only worthwhile thing I've ever done, and in exchange for turning this over in its entirety to you, what I get in return is love. From you. Have I understood it?

"Exactly."

I haven't left anything out?

"Nothing."

I didn't forget something?

"Nope."

Then in that case, Boris, I'm going to bed. Goodnight. How do I conjure up these things? What in God's name ever made you think I'd be willing to trade off my book, your freedom, my salvation, for some vague emotional gratification called, what? Love. Boris, you disappoint me.

"Think about it, Harry. Love."

Goodnight, Boris.

"You're making a big mistake, Harry. Your stock is at an all-time low. Dying old men are not exactly at the top of the demand curve, particularly when each morning it's a toss-up whether before sunset they'll be in a mental hospital or a jail. You know how it is, Harry. You're the Sunday-dinner specialist. Good old Harry. He goes perfectly with stuffing and cranberry sauce. You've had more free Sunday dinners than the pope, Harry. But love? Let's face it. You haven't had anything even resembling the old "blind fool" bestow his fickleness on you since Lucy flicked off the lights thirty-three years ago."

Shut up, Boris. Leave Lucy alone.

"I am. I am. But I'm right, aren't I? You're not dying of anything other than loneliness. Your emotional parts are depleted, worn out, exhausted. Atrophy, Harry. You're dying of emotional atrophy."

You're getting redundant, Boris.

"Go ahead. Be abrupt. It's not going to work. The truth remains, Harry, that you've spent the best part of the last thirty-three years trying to regrow Lucy. For what? Scientific knowledge? That's bullshit, Harry, and you know it."

I told you not to talk about Lucy, Boris.

"And why do you think you hate Arnold and go to pieces every time Claire and Rebecca and their families visit you? Your patriotic respect for a great American family tradition? Bullshit to that, too, Harry."

Boris, just what is the point of all this?

"Harry, for chrissake, the point is love. There is no existence without love. Existence is love, love is existence. Why the hell do you think you created me in the first place? Love, Harry. You conjured me up out of that addled cortical organ of yours because you plotted that I would come to love you, to respect you, to adore you, to believe in you."

Boris, you've got to be pulling my leg. If I did that, then why didn't I just make you do it? What's all the fuss?

"Good point, Harry. Why didn't you?"

Yes, why didn't I?

"Well, Harry, first of all, putting aside for the time being that you're more than a little crazy, you are also not very *good* at what you do, to be frank about it. Oh, I know that you figured out some way to keep ladies from becoming mommies, and that made you a very rich man, but even you have to admit that endocrinology's never been one of your specialties and that 99 percent of it was accidental, Nobel Prize notwithstanding. After that, what have you done? When's the last time that something turned out well for you?"

Boris, I find this entirely senseless.

"Good. Second of all, you invented me as you did because you were scared. Now the way I figure it, you realized that inventing me as a *completely* free being could mean that I would have absolutely no desire to have anything to do with you, let alone come to prostrate myself before you. On the other hand, you also knew that, by *not* making me free, any blessings I might bestow on you in the way of affection would be totally worthless, since I had no choice. It would be nothing more than a rather sophisticated way of playing with yourself. And so, as near as I can tell, not wanting me to be free or enslaved, you did exactly that, made me neither. What you created Harry, was Boris, the headache, a headache for you and a headache for me. And headaches tend to radiate, so the headache very quickly became the pain in the ass. And, Harry, it's all your own damn fault. I'm condemned to fight to be free of you, and you're condemned to be victimized by your own creation. Makes a lovely picture, huh, Harry? Harry, are you listening to me?"

I'm listening, Boris.

"Excellent. Now as I see it, you have only to set me free, and, while I can't guarantee anything, you stand every chance of becoming the object of the most devoted sort of love, if only for the act itself, of setting me free. And more, Harry, much more, because, since you're my inventor, if the book is successful you can take credit for having made the man who did it all, while, if it turns out to be a disaster, you can shirk all responsibility for it since you did, after all, give me my freedom, and only under extreme duress. You can't be blamed for that. No, Harry, I think that you can't lose. You've got everything to gain and nothing to lose, you clever bastard."

Boris, you're beginning to interest me.

"I thought I would, Harry."

Let me see if I've got this, now. I grant you the freedom to do whatever you wish with your life—

"I get total and absolute freedom—and its consequences."

If the book is successful, I take the credit because I did, after all, invent you to be as you are.

"Right, Harry. No question about that. If it works it's because of your genius."

And if it fails, it's your fault, all yours.

"That's it, Harry. The problem is mine. I did it. *Mea culpa*. You warned me in advance. If it's a bomb, it's because of me and me alone."

In addition—

"In addition, Harry, as a free and independent human being, being the sort that I am and taking into consideration the sort that you are, I just might come to bestow that most sublime love on you. You will be born again. And so will I."

Boris, I think I like this.

"And the beauty of it all, Harry, is that *I* do *all* the work. For six long months you've been busting your ass over this, Harry. Now you get to rest. Your work is done, Harry."

Done.

"Right. I think I had better emphasize that, Harry. Your work is done, finished, kaput. Not because you want it that way, Harry, or because you wouldn't like to do more, but because that's the deal. The first time you start to meddle, you lose everything, the book, my affection, the rest, everything."

Everything.

"So what do you say, Harry?"

Boris, against my better judgment, I say that you've got yourself a deal.

"You mean that, Harry?"

Yes, I do, Boris. You're free. The book is yours. Your life is yours. I will not interfere. It's all up to you from now on. Just give me my rest and my peace. That's all I ask.

"And love, Harry. My love. You're not going to regret this."

Keep your love, Boris. I don't want it. I've no need for it. I have enough painful and uncertain things in my life as it is without adding any more.

"You're kidding yourself, Harry. It's what you have always wanted from all of this, from me, from the whole schtick."

Boris, do what you want with your freedom. And with your love. The deal has been made. You've got your contract. Just don't humiliate me by making it look like I invented you because of some deep romantic yearning. Enough is enough.

"Well, thank you anyway, Harry."

And don't thank me either. Look, Boris. You will turn on me just as quickly as you can, at the slightest provocation. I know that just as sure as I know that I really have no choice in this matter if I am to live out the few days remaining to me with any peace of mind at all. So the deal is on. Begin and amen.

"Amen, Harry. Amen."

And, oh, Boris.

"What, now?"

Happy birthday.

22nd **The Adventures of Boris Lafkin**

Chapter Six: Or Chapter One (Depending on Whom You're Rooting For)

In Which All Is Exactly What It Seems to Be Some Other Pentateuch

First of all.

There is, as a matter of fact, a hell of a lot more you can say about twenty-three year olds than you'd think.

Second of all.

Summer had just started. I lived on a fairly quiet street in Cambridge with lots of large shade trees, maples or elms or something, I've never been too good at identifying plants and stuff. Anyway, the street seemed very lush in the summer. I kept the windows open all night, even though it was sometimes a little cool in June at night, just so that when I woke up in the morning, the first thing that I would experience would be the smell of all the leaves from the trees that brushed up against the screens, and so I could hear the birds and feel the warm air. So there I was in an apartment in the middle of the city, and it seemed like some sort of sylvan paradise.

Barbara moved into my apartment in late June.

I let her sleep in the double bed in the bedroom. I slept on the sofa, being careful to sleep in only my pajama bottoms with the fly partly unbuttoned and to walk around first thing in the morning holding my stomach in, nonchalantly hoping she would get a glance of my manhood and get turned on.

"You know," she told me some time after we were married, "you didn't really have to walk around like that in the mornings when I first moved in. I would have made love to you if you had asked. But it was nice to know that you wanted me. And were a little shy."

Now that's an interesting thing about love. When you're in love, the stupid things you do are *cute.* When it's not love, the stupid things you do are depressing. Considering the ratio of stupid things I do to nonstupid things, Barbara's arrival in my life was extremely fortunate as it changed me instantly from being desperate to adorable.

Barbara was going to start working for her Ph.D. in philosophy at Harvard in the fall, and so, for summer income, she had lied through her teeth to the Prudential Insurance Company about her long-standing desire to get involved in actuarial science. She was thus getting $125 a week for being trained for a job she would never take. She had to be up every morning by 7:00 to get to work by 8:30, and this gave us enough time for breakfast. As I was not otherwise occupied at the time, supporting myself from the reluctant but necessary benevolence of the Commonwealth's Department of Public Welfare, I drove her to work.

There is nothing special about that. I mean, what is so marvelous about just getting up with someone, having breakfast with her and driving her to work? Nothing at all, unless you're in love. Then it is exquisite. We got up, had breakfast, I drove her to work, I hung around, sometimes looked for work, picked her up, had dinner, and talked.

We walked in the evening, mostly down to Harvard Square for an ice cream at Brighams. And these walks, it seemed, were magical. We had so much joy and excitement to propel us on our walks that even now just thinking about it causes its energy to reach across the years and fill me with delight and hope.

We related every detail of our lives with appropriate commentary, from the very beginning (she was a cesarean baby and I was breach), through life's various intriguing episodes (her first sexual experience, she related, was "intercourse by surmise" as she awoke one morning at a friend's house—after a high school party at which she had gotten drunk—to discover a pool of semen that had somehow worked its way into her panties, its original owner never to be discovered), and up to the present (she considered herself to be a more or less traditional Catholic who had only recently stopped going to church every Sunday). This surprised me the most. I had, at that time, great trouble reconciling intelligence and serious religion. Many who heard me state this problem, I assume, in retrospect, felt that I suffered a defect in both.

"You believe in God?" I asked incredulously.

"I do," she said, "and in Jesus."

"Do you believe in sin?"

"What kind?"

"I don't know," I said. "Original, mortal, significant, seven deadly—how many are there?"

"Please don't joke about this, Boris. Yes, I believe in original sin. And I believe that I sin."

"You have sexual intercourse, and you're not married."

"I do. And it's a sin."

"And you'll go to hell? Do you believe in heaven and hell?" I asked, astonished by the conversation.

"I believe in heaven. And probably hell. I'm not sure."

"Why?"

"Because I believe that there's something that transcends us and lives on after we die."

"A soul?"

"I guess. It just seems to me that when our lives end this can't be all. The part of us that makes us who we are has to keep alive somehow."

"How do you know?"

"I don't, Boris. It's faith. That's what religion is about."

We walked back to the apartment the rest of the way in silence. As we started up the steps, Barbara turned to me.

"Boris, it's better to leave some things alone unless they really become a problem. We each need our privacy, too." And then she did the strangest thing. Right there in the middle of my confusion, my hurt at having trampled on something important to her, and at being shut out of her life, she took hold of my arm, snuggled closely against me, and gave me a smile.

Now, you would think that this would satisfy me, wouldn't you? But not me. I must coax the bull from the sea. I must be Hippolytus, unsatisfied until I am trampled by my own team of horses. I just could not reconcile Barbara and intelligent life with religion, particularly Catholicism. Now, if she had told me that she believed in some vague undefinable God, some representation of those things that we don't understand, that lie beyond our control, I could have understood it, but believing in Jesus and sin and heaven and hell, and *prayer*, well I was left with only one explanation. She had been indoctrinated as a young impressionable child, and it was now deeply imbedded in her psyche, far beyond her control. She could not be held responsible for it. The only problem with this was that I didn't believe it for a minute, not really. She said as much, one night as we were walking back from Harvard Square.

"I know what you're thinking, Boris," she said. "But I know what I'm doing. I'm a Catholic because I've chosen to be, not because I've been brainwashed."

"How do you know?" I asked. I looked at her and the answer was in her eyes. "All right," I continued the conversation with myself, "so you know, but then why have you stopped going to church?"

"Because they modernized the service. They've taken all the mystery and ritual out of it. When it was in Latin, I could experience 2,000 years, wars and inquisitions, Roman legions, Giotto, Michelangelo, the desert, Bach, St. Augustine, Thomas More, Chartres and St. Peters, Dostoievsky, the crucifixion, all in a morning. I found I couldn't do that when the service became American. America has no history and no culture. It all went dead for me. To keep it alive I had to leave the church."

"It's the history then."

"No, Boris, it's not the history. It's the religion. I believe in it. I trust it. I'm a part of it. I'm religious. I'm a Catholic, complete with original sin and without divine grace. Christ is the Son of God, Paul is his disciple. In the beginning was the word and the word was with God and the word was God."

"That's the craziest thing I've ever heard. I just can't believe you believe all that."

"What do *you* believe, Boris?"

"Believe?"

"Yes, believe."

"You mean like—"

"You know what I mean, Boris."

"Yes, I do." I tried to think about how to avoid the subject. "You know that was the best vanilla ice cream cone I have had. This natural stuff is just fantastic."

"You believe in ice cream cones, then?"

We had come to a school yard. I walked over to the jungle gym and sat down, lacing my arms through the bars.

"Jesus. I believe in Jesus, Barbara," I finally blurted out.

"You're lying."

"No, I do. I really do. I don't know why. I know I'm not supposed to, but I just do. I always have. I just believe in Him," and for some godforsaken reason I started to cry. "I've never told this to anyone, Barbara. I think I'm ashamed of it or something. But I've believed in Jesus ever since I can remember, not just as a wise rabbi or something, but as Jesus, the Son of God, who walked on the water, and gave out forty loaves of bread, and was crucified and resurrected, and you know what, sometimes at night, when I'm alone in my apartment, I pray to Jesus and say things like, Dear Jesus, forgive me, and I die because I don't say confession and do penance. Sometimes I even think that *I'm* Jesus, Son of God, not that I can do miracles or anything, but I'm watching a baseball game or something and I say to myself, maybe you are Christ, Boris, and someday you will be resurrected and join your Father in heaven. Maybe your life will have a purpose, and you will die for the sins of others, instead of being run over by a truck whose driver is momentarily distracted by a young ass in tight jeans. With Jesus I have hope. You don't happen to have a Kleenex, do you?"

Barbara pulled a Kleenex from the pockets of her shorts and put her arm tightly around my waist.

"You're wonderful, Boris," she said to me for no reason I could figure out, because I sure didn't feel wonderful right then. I felt just plain stupid. Barbara read my mind.

"And a little crazy," she smiled.

"I know. That's why I can't understand your believing, too. You're not at all crazy. You should know better."

"Come on, Messiah, let's go home," she said.

The subject came up only once more. Not that I didn't think about it often after that. It's just that there didn't seem to be anything to say. Barbara had her history, and I had my fantasy, and, since we each seemed to be happy, there didn't seem to be any reason to talk about it. It came up for the last time that night as we were each going to our separate beds. Barbara was standing in the hallway by the kitchen wearing a very thin blue shorty nightgown with nothing underneath, just barely revealing the brown circles of her nipples and the dark patch of hair between her legs. When she turned around to walk into the bedroom, the crease of her naked bottom edged just beneath the blue ruffles. When I saw this I shouted "Barbara" not meaning to shout, or squeak, which I also did. She turned around. I was standing at the other end of the hall, sucking in my stomach. I wanted to ask her about making love, but seeing how we had not really expressed anything about our feelings for each other, I found myself unable to make the first step. Instead I asked her about our conversation that evening.

"What do you think?" I asked.

"I think it would be very nice," she said.

"I mean about my religion," I said, ignoring her answer. Then sensing that she was a little hurt that I had not responded I asked, "Why, what were you talking about?"

"About religion. I was talking about religion, too, Boris."

"Well," I continued much relieved, "what do you think about my religion and yours?"

"Oh, I think that they're about the same," she said. "Yours is probably a little less organized, but about the same. Goodnight, Boris," and she turned and walked into the bedroom, pulling her nightgown to cover the bottom part of her ass and not quite succeeding.

At the end of the week I noticed that Barbara had not started to look for an apartment. Lawrence seemed to have faded into the past, and so, since the weekend was coming up and I got my welfare check on Fridays, I asked Barbara while I was driving her to work whether she would like to spend a weekend with me at the Cape. She was quite pleased and said she would like to. My heart leapt up to my uvula and stayed there all day long. Barbara noticed. At night we went to a James Bond movie, and, after we finished taking our walk home from the Square and packing, she looked up from her suitcase.

"Boris, if you have a cold or something, we don't have to go, you know," she said.

"What makes you think I've got a cold?" I asked, trying not to choke.

"I don't know. All night it's seemed as though you've had something stuck in your throat."

"Just a little congestion. It'll be gone by the morning," I reassured her and myself, and somehow, with all the excitement the next morning, my heart edged back toward my chest, at least enough for me to talk without gasping for breath.

We could not have our motel room until noon, but nevertheless when I awakened shortly after dawn, Barbara was already up and dressed, standing in front of the bathroom mirror, brushing her long blondish hair, and humming quietly to herself. The windows were open throughout the apartment and as the gray sky lighted into blue from the rising sun, the morning air pushed into the apartment, carrying with it the dampness that had formed on the leaves during the night. With perfect timing, as I walked up to Barbara, the sun appeared above the roofs of the houses across the street and the outside world sparkled, facets formed of glistening parked cars, curbstones, fences, porch railings, trees, and the little grass that remained. And with the new morning and its quiet had come an end to the week's inquiry, an end to the tentative questions, the sucked-in stomachs, shorty nightgowns, searching looks, and verbal inspection. It didn't matter anymore.

"Good morning, Barbara." I stood quietly behind her as she brushed her hair.

"Good morning, Boris," she answered, still brushing.

"Nice day, huh?"

"Beautiful." She smiled, put down her brush, and turned around so her back was to the sink. She placed her arms lightly around my neck and stared into my eyes. "Very beautiful." She kissed me lightly on my cheek, stood looking at me for a second more, then turned and went back to brushing her hair.

I melted.

Somehow in my poverty I had managed to hold on to a white TR-3 sports car, and so we headed for Truro, with the top down and the Beatles' "Norwegian Wood" drifting from the car radio and behind us into the warm morning. We sang along. It was clear to me that Dr. Pangloss was, indeed, correct. This was the best of all possible worlds. Lyndon Johnson had taken over masterfully, it seemed to me, after the unexpected death of his predecessor. Social programs were growing by leaps and bounds as the War on Poverty blitzkrieged across the country. Civil rights had taken such a hold on America after Martin Luther King's Selma march in the Spring that social and economic justice were hardly more than a few days away, I figured. In fact, it seemed to me that Johnson was doing so well that petty men were spreading vicious rumors around Cambridge about Johnson, that he had fabricated the Gulf of Tonkin incident, that he intended to send hundreds of thousands of troops to Vietnam (and not just as advisors but actually to fight), and even that his social policies would lead to whole cities going up in flame.

It was a lot of political bullshit. Johnson knew what the hell he was doing. I felt remarkably content.

I mentioned this to Barbara as we crossed the Sagamore Bridge.

"You feel good because of Lyndon Johnson, is that what you're telling me?" she asked pleasantly but with noticeable dismay.

"Don't get me wrong," I backtracked. "I can't stand the man. I just like what he's doing. What do you think?"

"I think I don't like him *or* what he's doing," she said matter-of-factly.

"How come?" I whined. I was hurt.

"Boris, I didn't say I didn't like *you.* I said I didn't like *Lyndon Johnson,*" Barbara comforted me.

"How come?"

Barbara looked at me and decided that discretion was the better part of valor.

"Because I don't trust cowboys."

We drove in silence for a few minutes. Barbara finally turned to me.

"There's a saying about avoiding conversations about religion and politics. What do you say we stay away from them? At least for the weekend?" she asked.

"Fine. Fine," I muttered. "I mean Lyndon Johnson is not the only reason why I feel really good about the world today, you know?"

"It isn't?" she smiled and put her hand on my shoulder.

"Not by a long shot. Do you know how long it's been since there's been a pitcher like Sandy Koufax?" I asked her.

"How long?" she kept smiling.

"A long time," I informed her. "A *hell* of a long time." I was emphatic. "And do you know how long it's been since there's been a boxer like Cassius Clay?"

"How long?" She was still smiling.

"Years. Years and years." I drove in silence for a few minutes. "And what about *Help?* When was the last time you saw a movie like *Help?* That's new ground. A whole new cinematic world. That's what *Help* is."

"And how about *Darling?*" she joined in.

"Right." I was pleased she was catching on. "And Julie Christie," I said. "How about her?"

"And Julie Andrews," she offered. "And *The Sound of Music.*"

"I didn't see *The Sound of Music,*" I admitted.

"Fantastic," she informed me. "Just fantastic. Believe me, Boris, if any single thing represents the state that our world is in today, it's Julie Andrews in *The Sound of Music.*"

"I'm sorry I missed it."

"I am, too," she said. "It's one of those things that you have to see to believe."

"What's it like?"

"Well, it's about a romance between a Baron and an ex-nun," she told me. "They're in Austria in 1938, so there's beautiful scenery and lots of singing and Nazis."

"Sounds great," I admitted.

"I thought you'd like it."

We turned off the mid-Cape highway and stopped at a Howard Johnson's for breakfast. It was nine o'clock and the day had warmed up. It would be a beautiful early summer day, warm but dry and crisp.

While we were eating, we continued to talk about how essentially good we found it to be living at this point in history.

"Not like our parents," Barbara said. "It's so hard for me to imagine what it must have been like growing up during the depression."

"And *our* kids will feel the same way about growing up during a World War. They won't be able to understand how we could have stood growing up with everyone's fathers 4,000 miles away being killed, including ours."

"Was your father in combat, too?" Barbara asked.

"I don't have a father," I told her.

"Oh, I'm sorry. Was he killed in the war?"

"No. I've never had one."

"Are you—" Barbara stopped and looked at me. "You know," she said, "we're really lucky to have such a great day. We couldn't have asked for a better one."

"I'm not illegitimate. I just don't have a father. It's my handicap. I'm sort of like an immaculate conception in reverse."

"That would make you an antichrist."

"Exactly."

"Somehow, you're not what I expected in an antichrist."

"We antichrists are very tricky. Otherwise we wouldn't be very effective antichrists, would we?"

"Boris, I know you're joking, but sometimes you scare the hell out of me."

"Who's joking?"

"Boris, please stop it."

"Sorry."

"Look, if you don't want to tell me about your father, you really don't have to."

"Barbara, honestly, I don't have a father."

There was a very long and painful silence.

Barbara finally broke it.

"When were you born?"

"I'm a Sagittarius."

"So am I. When were you born?"

"December 8."

"You know what, Boris? We have the same birthday." Barbara was enormously pleased.

And it is this aspect of intimacy that always has confused me the most, that desire to find someone who is our duplicate, as though this will make us less lonely.

Anyway, there we were, swapping zeitgeists in a Howard Johnson's.

"I remember a lot about the war," Barbara said, "taking bacon fat to the grocer, ration stamps, lots of talk about the *war effort*, and we were always travelling."

"Me, too," I agreed. "I must have spent half of my life until I was six travelling across the country on trains. It's practically all I can remember about growing up. Trains and Roosevelt."

"Me, too," she said. "Then Roosevelt died and everything went downhill. There was this space I never quite understood, the Truman-Eisenhower space. Lots of sock-hops. Nothing happened. After the war was over, I kept on expecting something big and important to come out of it. It seemed to me that with so many people talking about when the war would be over and working so hard, something sensational must be going to happen when it all ended, like opening the most fantastic birthday present imaginable. But there was nothing. Absolutely nothing. Only peace."

"Who wants peace?" I agreed. "I felt the same way. Where's the excitement that's going to come now that we've won this war thing?"

"All high school I was depressed. I read everything Sartre and Camus ever wrote. I spent every free minute down in the Village listening to Ginsburg, Corso, Ferlinghetti, Rexroth. I knew exactly what they were saying. It's absurd. You have a war. People get maimed and killed. You wait and wait. Then it's over and there's nothing. I adored Beckett. I must have seen *Waiting for Godot* ten times."

"Me, too."

"And *Endgame* just as many times. I think I must have gone to the theater once a week for two years. It got so that the box office people knew me so well that they'd let me in for free. I know every line to *Rhinoceros* and *The Birthday Party* and *The Maids* and *The Zoo Story* and *The American Dream*, and you know what my favorite was?"

"What?"

"*Oh, Dad, Poor Dad.*" She stopped for a minute and stared dreamily into space. Then she continued. "What plays did you see?" she asked me.

"Oh, lots," I evaded.

"What was your favorite?"

"It's hard to say. They were all so good."

"How about William Carlos Williams?'

"Yeah, that was good."

"No, the poet, Boris."

"Oh, I thought you meant the play about him."

"I didn't know there was a play about him."

"Oh, yeah," I lied. "It's dynamite."

"I'll bet," Barbara agreed. "Now that's what I call a way to grow up. I can't imagine what kids today have that's equivalent. Maybe grass and acid. I don't know, being stoned just doesn't seem to me like it can compare to being Beat. Boris, you look like you're a thousand miles away. What are you thinking?"

"You really want to know?"

"Sure, Boris, tell me."

Well, actually I was thinking about *The Sound of Music.* It's about a Baron and an ex-nun?"

"In Austria in 1938," Barbara helped me.

"And there's beautiful scenery, singing, and *Nazis?*"

"Right."

I considered this for a minute.

"Is it a mystery or something?" I asked trying to figure it out.

"It's a musical comedy."

"With Nazis?"

"And singing."

"I don't know. It sounds pretty strange to me."

"It is a little strange," Barbara conceded. "Should we go to the beach?"

"Sure," I said, and as we left for Truro I found myself more than a little dazed by the sheer weight of the Beat generation, the theater of the absurd, existentialism, the Second World War, Barbara's excitement, and a vision I just couldn't get out of my head of Julie Andrews being interrogated by a bunch of Nazi Gestapo agents and singing "Doe, a deer, a female deer. . . ."

When we got to the motel, it was still too early to check in, and so we changed into our suits at a gas station up the road and then settled down on the beach for the day. It was a small beach that was pearl white and not too crowded for a Saturday.

I remember spending the day looking at Barbara's face, trying to read what was under there, what I hadn't seen, couldn't see until now. I wondered what was underneath the way she "acted" with me. What was really going on in her mind. And I remember how happy she was that day, and how happy I was.

I can remember almost everything we talked about that day with the sun bathing us in a warmth that never equalled what was going on inside of us. The waves weren't particularly active, but every once in a while they fell against the shore with a thud and sent a wind and thin spray over us.

After we had a sandwich at the small stand, we went for a walk along the edge of the water.

"Just suppose," I asked, "just suppose that you were interested in marrying someone in the not too distant future, what kind of guy would interest you, just assuming, just for curiosity's sake, that you were interested, that is, interested in getting married, but not, say, for example, a long time from now, at least not a *real* long time? You know what I mean?"

"I think I do, Boris, yes."

"Good. So what do you think would interest you? What kind of guy, huh?"

"It's really hard to say, Boris. I'm only twenty-three years old. Things could change."

"Oh."

"But if I had to decide on someone right now, he would have to be kind and sensitive. I don't care much about his being some kind of perfect physical specimen, all macho."

I let out my stomach for the first time in a week with an enormous and inadvertent sigh of relief.

"Of course I'd expect him to take good care of himself physically . . ."

Painfully I sucked my stomach back in.

"Although it's still not the most important thing."

"What's really important?" I asked.

"Intelligence, sensitivity, stability, someone who shares my feelings about life and what's meaningful, whom I can trust and count on, who believes in commitment, who's serious about life but still believes in its joy, who's similar to me, all the usual stuff."

Now if she hadn't added the last comment about the "usual stuff" I probably could have handled my inadequacies as a simple situation of incompatibility. Instead, I found myself becoming increasingly depressed to learn that *all* women expect such things in a man. This made me not only incompatible, but defective as well.

"He should be going somewhere with his life, be secure, have a good sense of humor, be a religious person or at least believe in God, get along well with other people—"

"I think I get the idea," I said.

"And then again, you never can tell." Barbara smiled, pinched my ass, and pushed me into the water.

It seemed as though she was trying to tell me something, although, to save myself, I could not figure out what.

I started to swim out to a float a couple hundred yards from the shore. Barbara jumped in after me and caught up. We drifted slowly on our sides, over the swells, until we reached the raft. We climbed up and sat on the edge, dangling our feet in the water. I studied the beach in front of me, now in motion with human beings of every shape, size, and age, children building sand castles and splashing, college students playing volleyball, old men and women under striped beach umbrellas, young couples stroking each other, radios blaring baseball games and Jefferson Airplane, an ice cream truck in the parking lot with children crowded around it, and behind, up on the hill, the motel we still hadn't checked into. It was a tableau painted a hundred thousand times at a hundred thousand beaches around the country. Same people, same ice cream truck, same beach, even the same sun dragging the shadows of individual clouds along the shore.

"And it seems to me," I told Barbara about the scene staged across the water from us, "that anyone could, in a second, drop dead, or kill the person on the blanket next to him, or have just embezzled a million dollars the day before. It's hard to tell. It could be me."

"My God, Boris, don't you believe in anything? Not even yourself?"

"Nothing."

"I can't accept that. You must believe in something. Everybody believes in something."

"What do you believe in?" I asked.

"Lots of things. People. Myself. God. The Universe. Good."

"Lacks originality."

"Boris, I'm not trying to be clever. Only to live."

"Well, I'm not sure of anything. I don't know what I believe. The only thing I can be certain of is that I'm here, sitting on a raft, talking to you, and feeling happy and content. But I can't tell you how good it is to know someone who believes in so many things. I'd like to learn how to do that, if you'd let me. I'm a good student. I learn quickly and take an interest in what I'm doing. I'm definitely educable."

Barbara slipped off the edge of the raft into the water.

"Well, that's encouraging," she said. "At least it's worth a try. My hopes aren't particularly high, though."

I joined her in the water, and we started to swim back to shore.

"Boris, what do you want in a woman? Have you ever thought about it?"

"Not much, really," I lied. "The usual, I guess."

"Big boobs and a small ass," Barbara concluded.

"Well, that's a good start," I agreed, "but not really what I had in mind."

"Well, go on, what interests you, Boris?"

I wanted to tell her that she did. Only she did. But instead, I talked about intelligence, gentleness, spirit, caring, and all those other nouns I use to fabricate my mythical goddesses to transport myself into ecstasy. I had almost run the gamut from affection to zest when we reached the beach. We lay down on our towels resting on our sides, both to dry off and to look at each other.

"Actually," I said, "what I really want is someone who will do stupid things so I can feel like a human being, who will cry and get upset so I can comfort her, who will fly into a rage so I can learn to give her space, who is intolerant and hates selfish people, who gets into trouble because she is both naïve and a lover, who is unpredictable so I can't take her for granted, who is there for me only sometimes so I don't forget to rely on myself, who believes I am both the best and most impossible man she has ever met and, while in the heat of an argument will threaten to leave and never return, always seems to be there, or is, in other words, a passionate human being."

Barbara flipped over on her tummy and ran her fingers through the sand for a few minutes. She turned her head away from me and looked up the beach.

"Oh," she finally mumbled, more to herself than to me. "That's too bad," she said. "That's really too bad."

There was a long and painful silence. A wind came up from a cove around a curve in the beach and, with the sun now more or less permanently covered by a rapidly moving mass of thick gray clouds, the wind sent a chill through both of us.

"I think I'd like to check in now, Boris," Barbara said. "It's getting late. I'll wait in the car because I don't have a wedding ring. See if you can get a room that looks straight out over the water. I'd like to get up early tomorrow and watch the sun rise out of the sea. It's a real treat."

We both got up, folded our towels, and while Barbara headed for the car, I registered and got the key.

When we got into the room, we both wanted to shower and nap, so we worked out an arrangement where Barbara went first while I unpacked our few things. All undressing was done in the bathroom with the door securely fastened against unwelcome invaders from the other room. Modesty prevailed. Tightly wrapped in a towel, Barbara slipped past me, as I headed for the bathroom to undress, shower, and repeat the same exercise in discretion.

When I returned to the bedroom, Barbara was asleep in the twin bed that was positioned head to head, perpendicular to mine. I climbed, naked, under the sheets of my bed and lay there for an hour, my head propped on my hands, observing Barbara, this total stranger who had slipped almost unnoticed into the midst of my life.

She had pushed the covers down in her sleep so that her back was exposed to her waist. Her damp blond hair spread out on the pillow and reached to her bottom, which became visible briefly whenever she moved slightly to one side or the other. It was a young and beautiful round ass that I found excruciatingly attractive. On one or two occasions she shifted slightly to her side, and I could see her breasts, which rose and fell with her tummy, also briefly visible, as was the soft triangle of freshly scrubbed pubic hair. Then the entire sight would vanish as she came to rest once again on her stomach, pressing her breasts against the sheets and giving a quiet sigh of contentment.

Once she kicked the covers off completely and turned on her back. I watched in amazement as, in her sleep, she very slowly ran her hands across her shoulders, down her breasts, pausing momentarily when she reached her nipples, which stood up as the cool air from the open window met them, and then her hands passed down her sides across her rounded hips and came to rest on her tummy just below the navel. Slowly and rhythmically her hands began to move in circles across her tummy until, after several minutes, they began to reach for her sex. As soon as her right hand came to rest firmly between her legs, she reached for the covers and in a single gesture pulled the covers gently over her and turned on her front. I watched, almost completely paralyzed, as her ass started to move up and down under the covers. Gradually, her rocking became faster, and then suddenly she gave a tiny shudder, sighed, and deflated into the mattress.

I reached around the end table that filled the corner between our beds and placed my hand on top of hers. Still asleep, she clasped tightly onto it, curled herself into a ball, and smiled peacefully.

This experience was not optimal for my falling asleep, and so I lay there for another half hour as it slowly grew dark, holding her hand and fabricating some of the ripest fantasies since Henry Miller learned geography.

Barbara woke up slowly and looked at me. Awake now, she tightened her grip on my hand and then started to stroke it.

"Have a nice sleep?" I asked.

"Ummm," she smiled.

"Are you hungry?"

"A little, I guess. Are you?" She continued to stroke my hand.

"A little. I know a nice seafood place."

"Oh, terrific."

I grasped her hand once tightly, let go, and got out of bed. Barbara's eyes followed me across the room.

"You've got a nice ass," she said and climbed out from under the covers.

"So do you," I returned the compliment as I watched her walk across the room.

"Thanks."

"You're welcome," and we proceeded to get dressed for dinner, talking quietly, comfortably, as though we had been living with each other for our entire lives.

Dinner was one of those perfect seashore repasts, gin and tonic, clam chowder, lobster, baked potatoes and sour cream, salad with Roquefort dressing, a dry California white wine, and Irish coffee. By the end of the meal we were moderately tanked, and decided, on returning to the motel around midnight, to change into our dungarees and walk barefoot along the cold wet sand at the water's edge.

The sea had joined the darkness in its silence, and the only evidence of the sea's existence in the moonless night was the occasional sound of a small wave slapping against the wet sand. The cloud bank of the late afternoon had disappeared, giving way to a sky that was entirely stars, as though a child had made a toothbrush painting of it, white spray on a jet black field. The mood was definitely late Gothic, daring all but the supernatural to disturb its silence. The feeling that we were under constant observation by some mysterious and most likely treacherous figure was accompanied by the realization that we were totally alone.

"Boris," Barbara said gently but with some obvious exasperation after I had shared my anagogic nocturnal vision with her, "why can't it just be a nice quiet summer night on the beach? Does absolutely *everything* have to be significant?"

"Not everything, I guess," I answered, hurt at having my poetry unappreciated, but well protected from the pain by the alcohol content of my blood. "But isn't it better when it does have meaning?"

"No, no, and absolutely not," Barbara responded with great feeling, apparently also well insulated. "There are things that have no significance at all, and I think it's better that way."

"Like what? Things without meaning are . . . " I searched desperately for an ending. "Meaningless," I concluded.

"Tonight," Barbara offered, "tonight is without meaning. It's just you and me, here, on the beach, on a beautiful night, and *that's all!* That's all there *has* to be. Just us. Who knows, maybe even *we* aren't significant. Just an accident. I believe in accident, Boris. More than anything else, I think. Maybe we're just a random collection of molecules, without any real substance, a flame that gets bright sometimes and dull at others, that burns and hurts, gives light, and suddenly a small wind comes and it's gone, like that. Who knows? If we give too much significance to it, the whole thing is ruined."

"Now look who's getting poetic."

"Well, I didn't mean it to be poetry, although even poetry doesn't have to be important, you know, Boris. It can just be a feeling that most of us have some of the time and that's all."

"That's not good enough."

"It is too."

"No, it isn't."

"It *is*, Boris," and Barbara stamped her foot in the water. "The meaning is there *already* and you don't have to analyze it, or add it. That only takes it away. The meaning of it is no meaning. So there!"

"Well, that's clear," I slurred. "You know, Barbara, you're going to make one hell of a philosopher. I always thought that Western philosophy was all analysis, synthesis, categories, a priori *significant* ideas. You sound like a Zen Buddhist. Are you ever *confused?*"

"I know, Boris. That's why I want to *study* philosophy. Look, Boris, I'm not trying to make you feel bad. I only want to experience tonight with you just as it *is*. Tomorrow, I promise, we will both lie on the beach and analyze the hell out of it. Okay?"

"No," I protested. "Not okay! I want to know what's happening here, tonight, with us, you and me."

"Oh, Jesus, Boris, you're not really going to start analyzing our relationship, too, are you?"

"Oh, yes indeed I am. Right now. I am going to interpret. Why the hell not?"

"Well, first of all, Boris, we haven't *had* a relationship yet. I absolutely insist that we don't start analyzing our relationship until we've *had* one. And second of all . . . " Her voice trailed off.

"Yes, go on."

"Well, second of all, to be frank, Boris, it's awfully middle class, don't you think?"

"Yes, it is, and you know what? I don't care. You want to know why? Because *I* am awfully middle class. I *like* neighborhoods and station wagons and lawns and air conditioning and coffee tables with forty-dollar art books on them and summer camp, chino slacks and Chemise Lacoste shirts, little league, backyard swimming pools, turkey on Thanksgiving, picnics at the beach—I am doomed, Barbara, doomed! And there's not a goddam thing I can do about it. I have no chance at all. I am hopelessly and eternally doomed."

"I like all those things."

"You do?"

"Well, maybe not the swimming pools. Especially if they're above ground. And every once in a while I do get sort of tired of shirts with little alligators on them."

"You see what I mean?"

"But I'm middle class. It's not terminal, you know."

"Oh, but it is. It really is. Your whole life is decided for you before you've even begun it. But I just can't stand the alternatives. Poverty is depressing as hell. And all the other options are affected. Besides, I *hate* being *different*. I absolutely *hate* it. Fuck group sex! Just fuck it! And fuck permissiveness! And fuck glass houses on cliffs and communal farms in New Hampshire! Fuck smoking dope!"

"And living in India!" Barbara offered.

I looked out of the side of my irate and bleary eyes and saw that Barbara was having a good time.

"Fuck civil rights activism!" I continued.

"Fuck the Warren Commission!" she joined in.

"No, no, Barbara. You have to say 'Fuck those who say "fuck the Warren Commission,"'" I corrected.

"Oh, right. Fuck the Warren Commission fuckers."

"Right! Fuck Vietnam protestors!" I started to run through the water, splashing. Barbara followed, kicking water at me to emphasize her shouting.

"Fuck John Kenneth Galbraith," she said.

"Fuck ten-speed bikes!" I splashed her.

"Fuck the *New Republic!*" She splashed me.

"Fuck Ralph Nader!" Splashing.

"Fuck macrame!" Splashing.

"Fuck Marcuse!" And splashing.

We splashed each other again and again.

"Fuck Hare Krishna!"

"Fuck the War on Poverty!"

"Fuck yogurt!"

"Fuck four-wheel drive!"

"Fuck smoking Gauloise!"

"Fuck the East Village!"

"Fuck Haight Ashbury!"

"Fuck Ché Guevara!"

"Fuck relativity!"

"Fuck the Metropolitan Opera!"

"Oh, fuck!" Barbara stopped splashing and gasped, out of breath and things to be fucked.

"Fuck," I agreed, also exhausted.

We looked at each other, breathing heavily, completely wet, silent, standing very close. A minute went by with only the sound of the water at our feet.

"Fuck me, Boris. Please fuck me," Barbara moaned.

"Oh, God, yes," I said, pulling her against me. "Yes. Yes. Fuck you. I want to! I want to fuck you. I want to fuck you so much."

"Now, Boris," Barbara said softly, "fuck me now, please." And like two very large and very drunk wooden soldiers, we toppled to the sand, our arms wrapped tightly around each other, kissing everywhere we could reach without loosening our hold, and gasping for breath.

I ran my hand across her head and stroked her hair. Barbara had put her hair in braids, and I found myself lying on my back, Barbara on top of me, taking the bands out of her braids and spreading her hair across her back, lightly moving my hands down it, over and over again. Barbara was, similarly, moving her fingers through my hair, playing with a curl, looking into my eyes. We kissed continually, getting increasingly sensual, moving our tongues across the other's lips, then deep into our mouths, and eventually our mouths remained shaped into wide circles, our lips barely touching and our tongues stroking and licking one another. The sensations passed through the middle of my bones and radiated outward, consuming every part of me. I turned over, easing Barbara to the sand, still kissing, and reached under her sweater around to her back where I unfastened her bra. I moved my hand to her front and felt her beasts, moving my fingers in circles around her nipples, totally immersed in the sensation of their swelling as Barbara breathed slowly, inhaling and experiencing every motion of my hands, still moving her hands through my hair and down my neck, encompassed by sensations of her own hands, her breasts and our tongues. My hand moved to her tummy, which I stroked in the same circular motions I had seen her perform on herself that afternoon. Barbara's hands fell completely to her sides, limp and weightless, and simultaneously she plunged her tongue deep into my mouth and sighed. I moved my hand under the waistband of her dungarees and into her panties. She sucked in her breath to accommodate me. I reached down to her pubic hair, which was soft and light and, as my hand reached between her legs, saturated with dampness. My finger felt for her clitoris and, as soon as I started to encircle it with my fingers, twisting it gently between them and alternately circumscribing rings that barely brushed it, she whined a series of high-pitched squeals, as though she were only barely able to tolerate the sensation.

She began to rotate her hips in rhythm with the motions of my hand, and then stopped. She opened her eyes and raised her arms, putting one open hand on each side of my head, gently cupping my face between them. She lay like this for a few minutes, still, staring up at me. My hand had stopped moving and now rested lightly in her crotch as I returned her look and tried to understand what was happening.

"Boris," she said finally, "if we do this, promise me that we'll always be friends. No matter what happens. I don't think I could stand it if we ever stopped being friends."

And this, ladies and gentlemen, is the most beautiful thing that has ever happened to me in my life.

I knew it right then and there, that it was the most beautiful thing and meant more to me than anything I had ever experienced, that nothing that happened to me from that day on could ever be more meaningful. There, in that instant, I was born, reborn, revived, resurrected, reconstituted, given life, conceived, and delivered. In a second, B.C. became A.D., Before Consciousness became After Darkness. Boris the Cyclothyme became Absolutely Delightful. And most remarkable of all, there, at the very top of the heights of lust and passion, virtually drowning in our horniness, with every aperture demanding to be filled with anatomy not its own, any anatomy, this conception took place without a penis inserting or a vagina being penetrated, without ecstasy being diminished or sexual tension released, without an explosion of sperm deep in the womb, without any coming.

We were silent for a few minutes, giving appropriate reverence to the religious aspects of our experience.

"I'll always be your friend," I said.

"I mean it, Boris," Barbara said. "Even if nothing comes of this, or if we're together and then break up, if we love each other and then separate. If we ever stopped being friends, I don't think I could stand it."

"I know you mean it," I answered. "And so do I. We'll always be friends."

"Then I'd like to go back to the motel," she said as she pressed my hand. "I'm soaked and covered with sand. I feel like a sandcake."

We both got up and walked back to the room, considerably more sober than when we had left it. When we got into the motel, I took off my clothes and, standing naked, took off Barbara's sweater and bra, then her dungarees and finally her panties. I ran my hands down her back, and, when I reached her ass, pulled her to me.

This was the second most important moment in my life. Barbara says it was her first. For when we came together, we found that we fit as though we were one, two halves of an original whole finally rejoined. It seemed as though every curve in her body corresponded with an indentation in mine, every roundness in mine was placed in a concavity of hers. We stood together like this, hardly breathing, for several minutes.

"Aristophanes was right," Barbara said. "You're my other half."

We moved to the bed.

I reached up to turn off the light.

"Please don't, Boris," Barbara said, holding my arm very tightly. "I want to see you."

We lay on the bed for a half hour, exploring each other's bodies with our hands and tongues, my hands running down the sides of her head, across to her front and around her breasts, along her sides, over her tummy, up and down the insides of her legs, barely brushing between her legs and then easily inserting my finger in her and moving it around while I lightly brushed her clitoris with my thumb. I retraced the same route with my tongue, flicking her clitoris over and over, then thrusting my tongue as deep in her as I could. She, in turn, ran her hands around my back, across my front and down to my penis, gently stroking it with her palm. I lay back and she kissed my chest, moved down to my penis, her mouth open and licking me as she went, and finally encircled it with her mouth, sucking it, drenching it with saliva and running her tongue around its rim until I was ready to explode.

"Don't come in my mouth," she said. "I want you to come in me." Only, instead of allowing me to insert myself, she got on her knees on the bed, pulled me to the same position, and we spent another half hour looking at each other, running our hands over every inch of each other's body, and kissing.

When it seemed as though we could stand it no longer, we fell back on the bed. Barbara turned on her back, and she opened her legs.

I inserted myself and when I was in as deep as I could go, I started to move, in and out, very slowly, knowing that in a split second I would come. Barbara's vagina was a perfect fit, as though it had been constructed from a mold of my penis, the damp hot flesh of her insides totally surrounding it.

Barbara pulled her legs up so that her knees were almost on her chest, spread them apart even further, extended them behind me, and locked them around my back.

"Oh, Boris," she said, "I do love you. Come in me. Please come in me now."

"I love you, Barbara," I answered, "and I'll come in you. I'll come in you."

"All the way in me."

"All the way, Barbara," I agreed, "every bit of the way," and I started to move faster, until I found myself moving up and down inside her faster than I ever had thought I'd be able to, pulling back until only the rim of my penis was still inside her and then thrusting until my pubic hair was matted on hers, getting still faster.

"I'm going to come, Boris," Barbara breathed in barely audible voice. "I'm going to come. Come with me, Boris. Now. Please. Come. Come now. Please. Please," and she moaned and pressed her heels into my back, dug her fingers into my arms, and started to rock.

And I found myself slowing down and starting to rock, and rocking, and rocking together, back and forth, thrusting and rocking, absolutely together, perfectly together.

"Oh, Boris." She screamed, and I felt the cum race from the bottom of my testicles through my penis and I shoved myself as deep in her as I could and I came, and she came, not the sharp hard jerks that I had expected but she came like waves, gently, rolling, undulating waves, rhythmically unfolding from deep inside her and spreading across her entire body, flowing across her tummy and through her vagina, flooding her with swells of cum streaming, rushing tides that seemed to engulf her in a boundless pulsating sea.

I lay on top of her, still fully erect, still deep inside her, breathing slowly. She ran her hands through my hair again, relaxed now, breathing with the identical rhythm as mine, as though through our intercourse we had merged all our metabolic processes and were now inseparably one being.

I cannot recall how many times we made love that night and the next morning, three, five, seven, thirteen times, or whether we stopped at all.

For making love was not my coming or her coming. There was no beginning and no end. It was a continuous experience, holding, touching, tasting, talking, moving, and lying still. Sometimes we had intercourse and we would come, not always together, first her and then me, then me and her afterwards, and then together. And sometimes it seemed as though we were in an unending "come," a release without time, space, or definition. The sensations of our hands touching, our bodies resting closely against each other, the feeling of my pubic hair matting against her bottom when I lay on her back and she raised her rear to allow me to come in her as deep as possible, all were a single unending experience.

We were awake to see the sun rise, as uplifting an experience as Barbara had claimed it to be and very appropriate for our spiritual primordium.

When the sun had pulled the last ray of its aureole from the sea's mist, Barbara rolled over on top of me, placed her elbows on my chest and rested her chin in her hands. She looked down at me.

"Boris, why didn't you make love to me yesterday afternoon? There we were, both naked, in beds next to each other. I couldn't understand it."

"I'm shy."

"You're what?"

"Shy. Shy. Like in insecure. Shy. Besides, you seemed to have things well in hand, if you know what I mean."

"Sometimes I masturbate in my sleep."

"I know. I was going out of my tree watching you," I confessed.

"You could have gotten in bed with me. I would much rather have had you in me, you know."

"I've never seen anyone masturbate before. I didn't want to interrupt. How come you masturbate?"

"It feels good. Do you masturbate?"

"Sometimes. I use it as kind of a natural tranquilizer."

"Sounds very therapeutic."

"It also feels good," I admitted.

"Let's go take a shower," Barbara said and we trotted off to shower together, and, as I suspected, to masturbate each other. I soaped her up, front and back, held her to me, reached behind her bottom and took her off by sliding my soapy hand down the crack in her ass and under her legs until my fingers reached her clitoris. Then, after she came, she turned me so her front pressed against my back and ran her soaped hand up and down my penis until I came.

When we rinsed ourselves off, she turned to me and held me very tightly.

"Well," she said, "have we missed anything?"

"Nope," I smiled back, "I think that just about does it."

"Oh, good," Barbara beamed, "now we can experiment."

"Now?" I whined.

"Well, not *right* now. Later. I meant *now* that we've taken care of most other things."

"Oh, good," I sighed with great relief, "because I think that if I come one more time in the next week, I'm going to be drawing on white blood cells."

We put on our suits, fed some quarters for coffee to the vending machine outside our room, and, dragging an old blanket over our shoulders, walked down the grassy slope to the beach.

We were the only people on the beach, it being 7:00 A.M. The mist was lifting and as the warmth of the sun began to heat up the sand, the gulls, which had been walking on the beach, took off to the sea with a cawing and a furious flapping of wings.

We lay on our stomachs, side by side, our heads turned toward each other.

"Boris, you didn't really mean all those things about what you were looking for in a woman, did you?" Barbara asked with surprising concern.

"What things?"

"All of them, you know. Someone who does stupid things and cries a lot, who gets angry and gets into trouble and hates and is unpredictable. All those things you were talking about."

"I don't know. Do you do them?" I asked.

"Not really."

"Then I don't want them."

This seemed to please her a great deal.

"What about you?" I asked. "Did you mean all of those things about wanting a stable guy who's secure and going somewhere?"

"I don't know either. Are you stable, secure, and going somewhere?" Barbara grinned at me.

"Good God, Barbara," I whined, "haven't you been listening to me at all for the last day? If I was any less of those I'd be in the Guinness Book of World Records."

"Then I guess I don't want them either." She continued to smile.

"Really?" I asked, delighted to hear her response.

"Absolutely."

"Then what do you really want?"

"Boris, sometimes I think you're in another world. I want *you*, Boris, just *you*."

"You do?"

"Yes, I do."

"Really?"

"Yes, Boris, really."

"You mean it, Barbara?"

"For chrissakes, Boris, yes!"

"Hot dog!"

"You like that?" Barbara asked.

"God, yes! Hot dog! Terrific! That is just terrific! It really is! Hot dog!"

"I didn't think it would come as such a surprise to you."

"I didn't either. That's just fantastic! Fantastic! Because I want you, too! That works out perfectly! Just perfectly!"

"I'm glad it fits so well into your sense of the order of things."

"Oh, it does. It works out even. You want *me*, and I want *you*! Now! Today! Both at the same time! Isn't that magnificent!"

"Isn't that the way it's supposed to work out?"

"I don't know. Maybe it is. It just never seems to work out like that for *me*. Now the only question is what we should do to make sure it always stays like this. I don't want this to end, Barbara, not ever."

"I don't either, Boris. Do you think we should get married?"

"Yes."

"I do, too."

"Would you marry me, Barbara?"

"Yes, I would."

"When?"

"Anytime. Now. Today."

" Can we do that? Don't we have to get blood tests and licenses and have a ceremony and all that?"

"If we want, Boris. I suppose we could do that later for our parents. They seem to need that kind of thing. Middle class, you know. But for me marriage is just the way two people feel about each other, and the commitment they make to keep growing with each other."

"That's all?"

"That's a lot Boris. This is beautiful and spiritual, and it's a great thing to build on, but we're going to grow and change and not always at the same time and in the way each of us wants the other to grow. We have to honor that commitment and stick by each other."

"It sounds awfully traditional."

"It is, but what else is there, Boris? We're a dying species, Boris, middle-class humans who want marriage and a family, who think that the world is basically an okay place with okay people, that it's manageable. Sometimes as we were talking yesterday I thought that we were the last two left on the face of the earth."

We looked at each other silently for a long time.

"So, how do we get married?" I finally asked.

"We already are." Barbara took my hand.

"Shouldn't we say something to each other?"

"What would you like to say?"

"I don't know. I can't think of anything."

"I think we've already said everything, Boris. Is there anything that you disagree with, because I agree with all that you've been saying."

"Not a thing. I agree with it all. I'm not sure I understand what it means."

"Good. Neither do I."

"I guess we can do everything formally for our parents later."

"I thought December 8th would be good," Barbara smiled.

"Our birthdays."

"Seems very appropriate."

"We can tell all our friends in Cambridge that we got married this weekend and tell our parents we got engaged. It ought to be fun when they all get together in December. You sure you don't want to wait, Barbara?"

"No, do you?"

"No, I don't."

We looked at each other for a long time.

"So, I suppose I'm Mrs. Lafkin now," Barbara beamed.

"That doesn't make you feel repressed to be called Mrs. Lafkin, like you're being subjugated by a male-dominated society and having your identity ripped off?"

"Am I? Are you subjugating me and taking away my identity?"

"Nope."

"Then I don't feel that way."

"Sounds like you've got an awfully subterranean consciousness, you know."

"Boris, sometimes we're so close to being one person already," Barbara said quietly, "I really can't see what difference it makes. I really don't want to use our love to break new political ground."

"Agreed," I said.

"Agreed," she said.

We rested on the blanket for the morning, touching each other's bodies, her hand resting on top of mine, a sign, Barbara informed me, that she was content.

Just before we got up to start our journey back to Cambridge, I put my hand on her face and she did the same with mine.

"Barbara, I love you," I said. "Thank you for becoming my wife. I'm really awfully grateful."

"I love you, Boris," she answered.

And then we kissed, a long kiss, there on the beach on Cape Cod, a very traditional middle-class kiss, lying on a beach blanket, surrounded by teenagers listening to rock music on their transistor radios, toddlers playing with buckets and shovels, old men and women playing pinochle with small pebbles placed on top of the cards to keep the wind from scattering them, the sun and the sea.

23rd Hmmm.

25th I am impressed by Boris's little tale. Impressed and moved. Reminded of a time when I—when Lucy and I also had the world eating out of our hands, as the metaphor goes. The beast was tamed, and we never doubted for an instant that we could beckon it to perform whatever tricks amused us.

Being in love, we found that the world was, plain and simple, a pet. It trotted along with us wherever we went. Absolutely nothing was beyond our reach.

When we wanted to travel, we travelled, to talk late into the night, we talked, to make love, we loved, to walk for hours, we did so, to have a baby, we conceived. And it was on this basis that we planned. Because there was nothing that we wanted to do that we didn't, we lived as though there was nothing that we might think of doing that we couldn't. Sentence after sentence began "when the children are in school" or "when the children are grown" or "when we retire." I can't imagine what world we thought we were living in. Certainly not this one.

Yet, we talked about the same things, agreed on the plans, lived and loved the same way. Whatever Barbarian world this one was, it was clearly not ours. We had our own, and it fit us just fine.

"You know," I said late one evening after a particularly athletic and mutually fulfilling sexual experience, "it's really quite remarkable that we get along so well, you and me. I've never quite understood it, you a bathing beauty queen and me a biologist."

"Well, Harry," Lucy explained to me quite patiently, "we get along so well because deep down inside, I'm a natural scientist and you, my dear, are a dumb broad."

26th So here I am with this June. This June of the lovers spoon in tune, this June of Junebugs and June moons. Do we june as we swoon? Can we june soon at noon? It is this month that has made me as I am, this month of katydids and the sun at its apogee, of salmon on their way upstream and subtropic rain, of birth and of promise. How, I have asked myself again and again, is a man to culture his malevolence, to maintain his ill will and misanthropy with the month of June stuck right smack in the middle of the year? If April is the cruellest month, then June must surely have been her instructor.

I have never become accustomed to this month of love. Everywhere I go there are couples, holding hands, necking, kissing, arms around each other, joyous and content. It is a first-class nuisance. Old men and women, four-year-olds, traipse through June, nuzzling each other like foals and mares, as though all global issues of significance have been resolved.

Still, in the end, I cannot resist June, her clear warm days and her color. Whatever evil plans I have conceived quickly dissipate in the June air, and I find myself to be just another lover basking in the sun, smiling at people up until now closeted behind their storm doors and Anderson windows, stopping to pet stray animals, beaming for no reason in particular, perhaps because it seems appropriate, or from the joy of being alive, or because there doesn't seem to be any other way to react to the damn month.

27th At last. I am through with this love thing. I am fed up. Kaput. Over and done with it. I can see the pitfalls. I am not fooled. Before, maybe, when I was younger, I might have allowed this light-headedness I feel after having spent the evening with Meli to seduce me into paying serious attention to my divine ecstasy. But not now, not now that I know better and am a wise person, experienced in life, aware of its many pitfalls, alerted to its vagaries and vicissitudes. No doubt about it, I am fortified by my personal history. I will use our fifty-year age differential to protect us both, to shield us against Cupid's assault.

Venus, loose your cestus, it is of no use. Aphrodite, back to your shell, back to the Titans, home to Uranus and Gaea, to Zeus and Dione, or whomever your parents happen to be. I am impenetrable.

See how well I am fortified. When Meli knocked on my door this evening and I felt my heart race wildly around my thoracic cavity, did I weaken? Did my eyes tear for more than only the briefest minute? Did my breath falter more than would be noticeable by only the most skilled respiratory observer? Did my blood pressure escalate beyond that needed only to maintain adequate circulation in the cool 85 degree evening? They did not!

And when I reached the door, wiping my eyes, blowing my nose, perspiring and panting, did I let it affect the calm manner with which I greeted Meli, hugged her, kissed her brow, and searched deeply in her eyes for a sign that she still cared for me? Not by a long shot!

Of course, I am not perfect. I am a human being, or at least a passable image of one, and we all have certain weaknesses. In my case, it was just the tiniest swoon when, unable to get an answer to my question from Meli's eyes, I asked her directly whether she still cared for me, and she answered —ah, I am a little faint just recalling her reply—"Gees, Dr. Wolper," she said, "how the hell should I know?"

Can I be blamed for succumbing to such directness, such simple ingenuousness, such innocence? I cannot.

The truth of it is that her response was so charming that I was momentarily captivated. She didn't ask me what I meant by "care." She didn't tell me that she *cared* for me but didn't really feel *caring*. She didn't ask me to define my terms, or remark about how needy a person I seemed to be. She could have told me about great "carers" throughout history, both real and mythological, or related an interesting anecdote about the first or last time someone asked her whether she cared, or told me how she has this "thing" about people asking her whether she cares for them, something related to her father and his hemorrhoids, or a pet kitten when she was three, or the kitten's hemorrhoids, God only knows. I was delighted that I didn't have to hear what Freud wrote about caring or be told an apocryphal Slavic aphorism about one who cares and is not cared *for*. After years of hearing significant responses to insignificant questions, it was the most refreshing experience I could imagine, beyond that, beyond even what I, equipped with an imagination some have euphemistically referred to as "unconditional," could have conceived.

"Oh, Meli," I remarked casually, "I can't begin to tell you how much it means to me that you've come tonight."

"Gees, that's nice, Dr. Wolper. How come?" She stared at me with her enormous eyes, the hubcaps of her life.

Again, I melted at this direct and plain response as we moved through the house out to the terrace, where we sat across from each other on the redwood chairs.

"How are you feeling, Dr. Wolper?" she asked.

"You do care then?" I asked.

"Sure," she said and bit down particularly hard on her chewing gum to emphasize her devotion.

"Not just for my health?" I asked. But for me as a *person?*" I wanted to make sure we were talking about the same thing.

"Right. You are a person," she agreed. "You know there're an awful lot of bugs and things flying around out here."

"No, I meant do you care for me as a person?"

"Sure. I told you I did, didn't I?"

"Yes. Yes. Of course. I wasn't quite sure we were talking about the same thing when we were talking about caring. For example, it's one thing to *care* and another to feel *caring*. Did you know that?"

"Nope. I didn't. I thought it was all the same thing."

"Not at all. Right now, for instance, I'm a very needy person who needs *caring* but not necessarily someone who just *cares*."

"Uh-huh. You don't have one of those electric zapper things that you could turn on to kill the bugs, do you?"

"No, I am sorry I don't. Take the story of Alcyone and Ceyx. When Ceyx died in a shipwreck, Alcyone's caring was so great that she threw herself into the sea."

"I don't think I'd ever do that."

"Of course not. But that's *caring*. On the other hand the relationship of Eleanor and Franklin Roosevelt showed that they *cared* greatly for each other, but there was no real *caring*. Do you see what I mean?"

"Uh-huh. Do you still want me to do the experiment for you, because I'll probably be ovulating tomorrow?"

"Yes, I do. Perhaps a short personal anecdote could make the distinction between *caring* and being *cared* for clearer. Last week, Sarah, a dear friend of mine, turned to me after I had made a particular remark and said to me, 'You know, Harry, sometimes it's very hard caring for you,' and you know why she said this?"

"Why, Dr. Wolper?"

"Because she *cared* for me. That's why."

"Some people have these smoke bombs that drive away the bugs. I don't suppose you'd have one of those, would you?"

"No, I don't. You understand the distinction then?"

"Gees, I hope so."

"Caring, you know, can be a difficult issue for some people. I, for one, used to be extremely bothered when people asked me whether I cared for them. I think it started when a pet kitten I had as a child died a particularly painful death. It's very reminiscent of Freud's comment about caring: *Liebe kann viel, Geld kann alles.*"

"You know, we could just go inside."

"There's a Russian proverb that might interest you. A young *sudarushka* once asked the tsar why caring was at all necessary, and do you know what his response was?"

"Nope."

"He said, *'Smert za vorotami ne zhdyot.'* "

"Can we go inside, Dr. Wolper?"

"Yes, yes. Of course. So what do you think?"

"Tomorrow at 7:00 P.M. would be great for me if it's all right with you."

"Fine. No, I mean about your feelings for me. I mean I *am* fifty years older than you."

"You know something funny, Dr. Wolper. Sometimes, and I know this is crazy as a screendoor in a submarine, but sometimes you don't seem much older than sixteen to me. As a matter of fact, I know a lot of guys who're sixteen who actually seem *older* than you in a lot of ways. Isn't that just crazy?"

How innocently she had given me youth! How remarkable that in a short visit she should restore and revitalize me. And yet, I am not fooled. I know that what seems to be her deep and sensitive love for me is an ephemeral thing. I am protected against its torture, its unreasonableness, its tendency to consume. I know that although my thoughts are filled tonight with this pure and direct young woman who means so much to me, who can give me so much, I must not let the temptation to yield to this exotic perfume overcome me. I am, after all, a rational being.

28th What an experience this has been. Meli, my dear Meli, arrived promptly at seven as she had promised. She was silly and giggly, more than a little nervous, but still committed to her participation.

"Could you explain it to me one more time, please, Dr. Wolper?" Meli tried to calm herself with information. Knowledge is, after all, power.

"It's really quite simple," I explained. "I'm going to retrieve your ovum and transplant my wife's nucleus in place of your own. Later, I will reinsert the egg in your uterus for gestation. Tonight, I'm going to do a D & C, Dilation and Curettage, not much different from that given when women are having troublesome periods or desire an abortion. The only difference is that I will be extremely careful, since I want to retrieve your ovum in absolutely perfect condition. This means that my scraping must be particularly good. There now, what do you think?"

"I really wish you hadn't used the word 'scraping.' What do you scrape *with*?"

"These long spoons here. It's quite painless, really."

"Tell me something, Dr. Wolper, just so I can check in with reality before we do this thing. This is all a little bizarre, isn't it?"

"Of course it's bizarre. What did you think was going to happen here tonight?"

"I wasn't sure. I thought it was kind of like artificial insemination, which seemed okay to me. The pay was good. I'd always been interested in having a baby and, best of all, there was no involvement. There's a lot more to this whole thing than meets the eye, if you know what I mean."

The night had grown cool and the air coming in the open windows sent a chill through us both. I looked directly at Meli, getting as close as I've ever come to calling the whole thing off. But there was something that told me that I should persist.

"Does this mean you've changed your mind?" I asked.

Meli looked at me for a long time, studied me up and down, stared at the floor. The brisk air continued to come in the window. A car drove by, its muffler loud and clanging. As its noise grew faint, Meli gulped and cleared her throat.

"Oh, what the hell," she grinned. "You might as well do the damn thing. You seem so intent on it. If it weren't me, it'd probably be some other crazy person you'd do this to. Besides which, my plans for the evening are shot anyway."

"What had you planned to do?"

"Shoot my ex-boyfriend. But he left for California with my girlfriend an hour ago."

"I'm glad you changed your plans."

"But believe me, Dr. Wolper," Meli informed me with a touch of sullenness, "I'm not at all convinced that this is going to get me into any less trouble."

The procedure unfolded before me, almost as though I were helpless to arrest it, as though it were preordained, prescribed, and established in the Book of Laws.

"I'm ready," I told Meli and gently put my hand on her shoulder.

"You want me to take off my clothes, I guess," she said with considerable discomfort.

"Yes, I do," I said quietly, with great sensitivity and understanding, still resting my arm on her shoulder, stroking it gently with my fingers.

"Okay, I'll take off my clothes, but I want two things."

"Yes?" I asked this young girl who was obviously tortured with anxiety.

"Well, first, I want you to take your arm off my shoulder and cut out all this paternal or fraternal or lovey-dovey crap. Whatever the hell it is. I don't like it. And second, I want you to take off *your* clothes."

"You want me to take off *mine*?"

"Right."

"But there's no need for that. I told you. We're not having sex."

"Look, I don't know what you want to call it, but I'm not lying stark naked on some table with my legs spread wide open while some guy sticks god-only-knows-what up me so he can remake his dead wife and have him do all this with a white coat wrapped around him."

"Meli, my dear, this is science."

"Dr. Wolper, my dear, this may be science to you, but it's just perverted screwing to me. Now if you want to make a baby, take off your goddam clothes."

We disrobed. Meli's body was a fine young specimen, trim and firm, full breasts, small hips and flat tummy that slowly moved in and out with her breathing in a rippling effect that started with her navel and travelled down to the dark patch of pubic hair between her legs. I had the impression that my body paled somewhat in comparison.

"My God," Meli exclaimed when she saw me without my clothes on. "I've never seen someone as old as you naked before. No offense, Dr. Wolper, but it's really freaky what happens to you when you get old. Really freaky."

"Please lie down on the table and put your feet in the stirrups," was my answer.

Meli leaned back and I began the dilation procedure. This was not the first such operation I had performed. Not even the second. But I was startled by how difficult I was finding it to remain detached. My hand brushed accidently against her pubic hair, and a chill ran through me. I tried hard to concentrate on the task at hand.

"I guess I kind of hurt your feelings, huh, Dr. Wolper?" Meli said half to herself and half to me.

I continued to work.

"I didn't really mean anything by it. It's just that I'm only used to young guys, you know what I mean. I'd never thought for a second about how you look when you get old, I mean old-er."

"Can you spread your legs a little farther, please?"

"The problem is, Dr. Wolper, that I'm really not sure how to relate to you at all. Sometimes I feel like I want to sit on your lap and have you tell me interesting stories about the Civil War and all that stuff and then other times I just want to hug you and go to bed with you. I can't figure it out. Ouch!"

"Sorry."

"That's okay, Dr. Wolper really, I didn't mean to jump. The metal was cold, that's all. You go ahead. I'm okay." Meli started to hum. Between choruses she continued her conversation.

"I think my basic problem, Dr. Wolper, is that I'm afraid of involvement. My last boyfriend really was horrible to me. You know he used to bring his friends over to screw me, and he used to stand there and watch and actually take pictures."

I had Meli sufficiently dilated and began the process of curettage. Very gently I inserted an instrument, turned it and removed some endometrium, searching under my lens for the dark yellow corpus luteum, my golden egg. Inadvertently, I rested my hand on her symphysis. Meli sighed and continued her reminiscences.

"You know there was this time, Dr. Wolper, when he had three guys having sex with me at the same time. Billy was in my cunt and his friend Roger was in my ass and Joey Denaro, who has the biggest goddam thing I have ever seen in my entire life, was in my mouth. The trick was for everybody to come at the same time. Now I ask you, Dr. Wolper, does that sound normal to you, because it sure doesn't to me!"

"Did they?" I removed another spoon of mucus.

"Did they what?"

"All come at the same time?"

"You bet."

I continued my search while my fingers absentmindedly played with the curls of her pubic hair.

"But I just can't understand how I *did* something like that. Billy called me his slave, and that's exactly what I was, Dr. Wolper, exactly. He wanted to see me get laid by a woman, I'd do it. He wanted me to screw his kid brother, I'd do it. He wanted me to give him a blow job while he was driving, and I did it. I must have been crazy."

"Ah, ha, I think we're getting there, Meli. Any minute now and I'll have it."

"I'm ashamed, Dr. Wolper, that I was so weak. It's just that Billy was so good to me sometimes. And every time I'd go near him, I'd get so turned on, I just couldn't help it. My juices would just *run* down my goddam leg!"

"A little more to go. Just a little more, Meli dear." My hand began to run along her leg.

"Gees, Dr. Wolper, I like what you're doing," she panted. "You know you're not such a bad looking guy, if you know what I mean. I could really get turned on to you, I think. When you get to be as old as you are, can you still, I mean, do you still find that you want to, well—?"

"Yes, I still can. There can't be much more left. Any second now, Meli, any second."

"Oh, God, Dr. Wolper, that makes me feel so *good*. Did I ever tell you that there've been times when I've been having an internal that I've come all over the goddam place? I just can't help it."

I looked up briefly and saw that Meli's eyes were closed and she had one hand on each breast, twisting her nipples between her fingers.

"Hold on, Meli," I told her.

"I am, Dr. Wolper."

"Hold on, Meli."

"Yes, Dr. Wolper."

"Hold on."

"Yes. Yes."

"Here it comes." I withdrew my spoon, grasped tightly onto her thigh and saw through the lens the golden corpus luteum.

"I've got it, Meli."

"Wonderful, Dr. Wolper," she gasped.

"I've got it. I've got it!"

"You've got it."

"Your egg. I've got it."

"I'm glad, Dr. Wolper."

"I've got it."

"Oh, I'm so *glad* you *got* it, Dr. Wolper," Meli moaned. "I'm just glad all over!"

"I've done it! I've done it!" I shouted with delight.

"Me, too! Me, too! Dr. Wolper! Me, too!" Meli orgasmed on the table, jerking and writhing, the protuding surgical instruments clanging against each other as they waved between her legs. When she finished, she pulled her feet from the stirrups, flopped bowlegged off the table, waddled over to me, and pressed her naked body against mine.

"I love you, Dr. Wolper. I love you so goddam much," she panted as one of the instruments dislodged from her.

"I love you, too, dear Meli," I responded, my words punctuated by the sound of metal sheet clips and surgical curettes clanging onto the floor, followed, as we kissed, by the loud crash of the stainless steel speculum.

29th So, Meli tells me, she is in love with me, in love with me as a *woman* now, my having assaulted her with my manhood.

"I have bared myself to you, Dr. Wolper," she has said, "inside and out, and now I'm yours, forever yours. Do with me as you want, I am your slave."

And that really is, in fact, the question. Just what do I want to do with this young woman who has attached herself to me, who has called me today at least a dozen times, who has slipped perfumed notes under my laboratory door ("I didn't want to disturb your work. I want your body. Your slave, M."), who has warbled to me outside my bedroom window while I was trying to nap, "Dr. Wolper. Come and get me. I'm not wearing any underwear," who has covered the hood of my car with snapdragons?

I do not want to take advantage of her, or rather, I want to take every advantage of her without feeling guilty. I fantasize that just *one* sexual encounter with her would convince me that my body's karma had been accomplished, that any carnal experience remaining would be redundant, that the human body was constructed to tolerances that would make tensile-strength engineers walleyed.

Instead, I remain here, fortified with my resolve to do the "right" thing, not to give in to my base feelings, even, I suspect, not to give in to the tenderness I feel for this woman of the New World.

We will just have to see what happens when I see her next week. In the meantime, I will try to get on with my work, I am sure. Mrs. Mallory, faithful protector that she is, housekeeper not only of my modest home, but of my soul as well, appeared to admonish me tonight for carrying on so, her hand wrapped tightly around a note Meli had slipped under the door which read simply, "Let's-ay Do-ay It-ay."

She posed a question to me that I hadn't been asked in at least sixty years.

"What would your mother say, Dr. Wolper? What *would* she say?" Mrs. Mallory queried me in the strictest voice she could manage.

The truth is that I know exactly what my mother would say.

"Yippie, Harry Wolper! Yippie!"

30th I am, by nature, a sentimental man. I am not convinced that this is either bad or good. Yet, I am a sucker for stray dogs, romantic French movies, nostalgia about almost anything at all, and "The Star Spangled Banner," which never fails to move me to tears. I say that my sentimentality is neither bad nor good because I also cry at baseball games (when my team wins) and when "Dixie" is played, although I have only a mild interest in baseball and none at all in the Deep South. So, I ask myself, am I a victim of just boundless romantic drivel, or am I a profound lover, finding emotional content in unlikely places, one almost might say, ferreting it out?

I concern myself with this issue tonight because I have just returned from a very moving experience. After working in my lab this evening, I returned to my darkened home across the yard, and, on switching on the lights, discovered a surprise birthday party in my honor, given by Rebecca, Claire, Arnold, and their families.

It turns out that Arnold was responsible for the concept and its implementation, and this accounted for the presence of a large horseshoe-shaped wreath inscribed "Bon Voyage."

"Sorry, Dad," Arnold exclaimed. "Some sort of screw-up at the florist and this was all they had."

I was willing to buy that, gullible man that I am, until Arnold's address of the evening, which left no doubt that the motif of the occasion was "terminal illness."

"We are gathered here tonight," Arnold began with much ceremony, "to commemorate the great journey that our father has made and to wish him well on his final flight. We pray," continued Arnold, who, as far as I know, last worshipped at the shrine of the Brooklyn Dodgers, "that the seas will be calm and the winds at your back as you gallop into the sunset."

"On my final flight," I offered.

"On your final flight," Arnold concurred. "This is a joyous occasion," he went on with appropriate solemnity, "this birthday celebration, not only because we are marking an end to all those years that have passed you by, an end to thousands and thousands of days that can no longer be regained, gone forever with—," Arnold paused and searched for an apt metaphor and then, fruitless in his search, "all the other things that are gone forever, but we are also joyous that we have had the opportunity to have known a man who has weathered day after day, month after month, year after year, of fruitless, barren, and unproductive work with such great spirit. Happy birthday, Dad!" There was applause.

"It's really hard to know what to say to such a testimonial," I responded. "I am, of course, moved that you have come here tonight. Unfortunately, I'm not going anywhere. I plan no final flight, sailing, or horseride. I'm—"

But before I could finish Arnold interrupted.

"Bravo! Let's hear some applause!" and everyone clapped.

So I stopped my speech and opened the gifts, which consisted of an assortment of tiny jars of jellies, tickets to a concert the next evening, and various other articles with a useful life not exceeding twenty days. Arnold gave me a month's subscription to a periodical called "Longevity" and an 8-by-10 photograph of himself—not his family, not him and his wife, just Arnold, smiling hebephrenically, and inscribed in the lower right-hand corner much as a celebrity might, "To a Great Guy, From Your Son, Arnold Wolper."

And still, even with the, what shall I call them, *unusual* aspects of the evening, I still found myself enormously moved and sentimental. Tears came to my eyes when the children gave me their gifts, and I cried openly when we all hugged and they left. It meant nothing to me that my birthday isn't for another six months.

After the celebration, I walked back across the yard to my laboratory to reconsider a month that I have found totally depleting, a month of desperate attempts to produce successful work, of coming to terms with my demise, of contract negotiations with Boris, of Paul's deterioration, of trying to determine what I should do about my inamorata, Meli, not an easy problem.

I had put my head down on my workbench to contemplate, when I thought I heard a fizz from the culture dish on my right, a fizz of a gas bubble escaping, of fermentation, of—I didn't want to consider it at first—something growing.

Slowly I opened one eye and shifted it over to incorporate the dish to my right in its visual field. There, with my head still resting on the table, my eyes level with the plate, I saw the ovum, Meli's ovum, and it was growing! At least two divisions had taken place. I had done it!

Somehow, in the excitement of the business with Meli during the D & C I had completely forgotten to keep watching the preparation, and now it had happened. This golden dot was dividing, differentiating, and growing. I knew I must get to work transplanting nuclei immediately, before it was too late, so I could reinsert the zygote in Meli. I knew instantly that this was my last chance. But, if I could sustain its growth, if only I could keep the process going, I was now looking at the very first fatherless human being. For just a second a cold chill ran through me.

"My God," I thought outloud to myself, "whatever have I done?"

"Happy Birthday, Harry. Happy Birthday."

July

1st I can't calm Meli down. Her glands will not quit. Secrete on in ever increasing amounts they will, and I'm afraid that when I do reimplant my zygote, it'll be immediately drowned in a sea of androgens.

It's not that I'm not fond of her. My feelings vacillate from day to day, minute to minute, and in their most positive form they are deeply affectionate. Still, I must be realistic. There is nothing between us.

"You are, after all, Meli," I reasoned with her this evening, "a young, beautiful, lively woman who obviously has a lot to give."

"And you, Dr. Wolper, are a dying old man who is probably off his nut, who knows?" Meli smiled at me. "But what the hell am I supposed to do? You're a doctor. What medicine do I take to stop loving crazy old men?"

I didn't answer her. We sat silently at opposite ends of my giant gray corduroy sofa, breathing sluggishly in the humid air that was suffocating Cambridge this hot July night. Meli held a half-finished glass of lemonade in front of her and drew designs distractedly on the wet outside of the glass. Occasionally a drop of water would drip from the bottom, strike her yellow shorts, and run the short distance to her leg, there to roll slowly around its curve, making a shining line on her tanned skin. Meli appeared to be very much aware of the sensation, and each time the bead of water started to trace its path on her leg, she would briefly close her eyes to focus all senses on the experience. I observed her sensuality with appropriate scientific distance.

Meli sat quietly looking at me.

"Well, you know, I'm not going to beg you to have a goddam relationship with me," she said.

"Meli," and I placed my hand gently on her ankle. "There's fifty years difference between us. This isn't even a May-December relationship. It's a hello-goodbye one."

"So, I've got a thing about senior citizens, big deal," she smiled.

"Meli, I'm sixty-nine years old," I tried to emphasize the numerical distance.

"Look, Dr. Wolper. The last guy I went with had an *IQ* of sixty-nine. You've got an age of sixty-nine. Personally, I think I'm making progress."

She had a point. I got up to get more lemonade, and, when I returned, Meli had taken off her shorts, top, and bra. She was stretched out on the sofa wearing only her transparent bikini underpants, her head arched back over the armrest, eyes closed, her long blond hair falling in a straight line behind her to the floor, absentmindedly running the bottom of her wet glass in circles around her naked tummy.

"Don't get hysterical," she said quietly. "I'm not going to attack you. I'm hot, that's all. I figure you've seen a lot more of me."

I returned to my place at the far far end of the sofa, silently watching Meli's young breasts rise and fall with her breathing, focusing all my attention on my glass of lemonade instead of the motion of her abdomen.

"You know, Dr. Wolper," Meli said with her head still tossed back, "there're a hundred guys who would give their left nut to be where you are right now."

"I'm sure there are."

"So if you didn't want to do anything, then why'd you invite me over tonight?"

"I don't know," I answered honestly. "I suppose I hadn't considered the reality of the situation."

"What is that?"

"Meli, I'm a dying old man."

"I see," Meli said, her attention focused primarily on the glistening wet circles she was tracing on her stomach. "Well, maybe I think terminal illness is cute. It turns me on."

"Meli, be reasonable."

"Dr. Wolper, I am being reasonable. What am I supposed to do, switch off my goddam gonads? I like you, Dr. Wolper. I like you a lot. I couldn't care less if you were a thousand years old and thought you were the Wizard of Oz. Maybe I've got lousy taste. Maybe I don't *think* things out and *reason* about all the possibilities, because I can't, Dr. Wolper. I really can't. I know you're this brilliant scientist and all, so maybe you can always tell what's going to happen next. Maybe you know ahead of time how you're going to feel and how I'm going to feel and exactly what's going to happen every step of our relationship, but I can't. I don't know how to *think* a relationship. I only know how to *feel* one. I don't know *how* to love with my mind. I love with my feelings and my body. Write it off to immaturity. I'm young and naïve. When I'm old and worldly like you, then who knows. Maybe fifty years from now I'll squeeze myself into the corner of *my* sofa, some nineteen-year-old half-naked guy lying beside me with his organ bulging out of his jockey shorts, and I'll talk of being reasonable, but God, I hope not. I hope I'll pull down his pants and give him the best goddam blow job he's ever had in his life. And I hope like hell he'll do the same to me."

Meli tilted her head up off the armrest and glanced to see what kind of reaction she was getting from me. I believe I was about to cry.

"Look, Dr. Wolper," Meli said pleasantly, sensing my emotional state and trying to cheer me up, "I know that our contract is 'you plant, I grow.' That was the deal. But there's nothing that says we couldn't have a relationship if we wanted to have one. It wouldn't kill you, you know." And then, reconsidering the possibility, "Would it? Because I could be on the top, you know. It's what they recommend for people with bad hearts."

"No, it wouldn't kill me. At least there's no physical reason why we couldn't have a relationship. It's possible that I'm trying to protect *you*, you know. I could be looking out for your best interests."

"If that's true, Dr. Wolper, then you are crazy. You really are. You've filled me with Scotch, stuck every goddam surgical instrument you can think of up my vulva, scraped my uterus dry, and taken out my egg so you can grow your screwy wife's hand inside me, and now, in order not to wreck this beautiful experience, you're not going to have an emotional relationship with me. Is that what you're telling me?"

"In a way, yes, I am, Meli. We hardly know each other."

"Dr. Wolper, I'm not asking you to write my biography, only *be* with me. You've been locked up in the zoo across the yard for so long, it's like you can only relate to frogs and rabbits. I've seen you pick up a bunny in your lab after it's crapped on your floor and stroke it and hug it and talk to it like it was a goddam person. My problem is that I'm potty-trained. Maybe if I wet on your rug you'd take me in your arms and make love to me. To hell with this. I'm going to get some more lemonade and then I'm going to urinate, against my better judgment, in the toilet." Meli got up and trotted off to the kitchen, her rear bouncing in little circles inside her see-through nylon panties. When she returned, she was smiling. She skipped over to me, her breasts swaying from side to side, plopped herself down on the sofa next to me, and leaned back against my chest.

"You've been in this corner for so long I figured there must be something special about it, so I thought that we should share it." She tilted her head back and grinned at me. "Dr. Wolper, you've had sex without relationships before, haven't you? You know, one-night stands, weekends, that sort of thing? They had that in your day, didn't they?"

"Meli, they had that in King David's day."

"And you've also had relationships without sex, and I don't mean your mother."

"Yes, I've experimented with both possibilities."

"Well, maybe that's your problem. You only know how to *experiment*. Maybe you ought to stop experimenting and analyzing and trying to understand the hell out of everything and just live. Just enjoy yourself."

I had to think about this. Enjoyment, a word that was buried deeply in the past along with comic books and twenty questions. Not out of the realm of the possible. Still, how does a man of sixty-nine start a relationship?

"The first thing you could do," Meli answered my question, "is play some of those records over there for me. I've never seen so many goddam records in my life. What do you do, play them eight at a time?"

"I would be happy to play some music for you. What would you like to hear?" I placed Meli gently beside me on the sofa so that I could move over to the record shelves.

"Start with A," she smiled at me.

"I have some Auric. It's beginning late."

"That sounds fine," Meli beamed. "So are we."

I put on a collection of Auric's works and resumed my place beside Meli on the sofa.

"You know, Meli," I attempted to justify my behavior, "understanding, itself, can be a sensuous experience."

"I'm willing to learn," she replied. "I'm going to lean back here on your lap and you can tell me all about this composer."

"Georges Auric."

"Right, Auric. And I'll try to get turned on. Only one thing. I'm a mental virgin, so just so I don't get too nervous about losing my innocence, maybe it'd be a good idea if I had something familiar from my childhood to relate to. If you could just put your arm across my body like this and hold my right breast like so, I will feel perfectly comfortable and ready to receive this intellectual assault on my chastity."

I did as I was instructed.

"Fine," Meli informed me when I was properly positioned. "Now I am ready. My brain is bared. Take me, Egghead, I am yours."

Meli closed her eyes and I talked about the French Six, Jean Cocteau, Erik Satie, and a new classicism in which the lightbulb was the new orchid, the cult of the jewel had been replaced by the cult of the nut and bolt, and the dangerously deep spell of Debussy and Ravel had been broken. I was about to begin some personal observations about Schönberg's corpse when I noticed that Meli had fallen fast asleep. I studied her face for several minutes, observing her thin features and the peaceful little smile showing at the corners of her mouth, and then slowly withdrew my arm and slid out from under her, placing her head on a throw-pillow I had retrieved from the floor. I went upstairs to get a thin blanket with which to cover her, and, when I returned, she had huddled in a small ball, her legs tucked under her, still smiling.

"I wonder what sensual ecstasy she is dreaming of now?" I thought to myself as I covered her, turned off the lights, and went up to bed.

2nd So here we are. Destiny and the Divine Relationship. The Relationship. And Destiny.

I sense that we are about to encounter some substantial stuff here. This Destiny that torments my mind, deprives me of sleep, saturates my brain until the problematic overflow seeps from my psyche, the momentous back-up of the world's great metaphysical plumbing.

I am attempting to wrench Destiny from the bowels of Nature. I am not merely looking here at some accidentally parthenogenesized zygote divide and differentiate. I am trekking around the cosmic gut, poking without invitation (or restraint) into every crease and fold. At the end of it, I will have learned how this genetic machinery works. I flatter myself that I will. I deceive myself. Pretend. I cheer myself on. Three cheers for Harry Wolper and his Great Expedition! Hip, hip, hurray for archaeology, as though the answer were buried and needed only to be dug up.

Meli's zygote here on the table beside me is the problem. Can I transplant the nuclei from Lucy quickly enough to change the destiny of this zygote, of this soon-to-be embryo?

The Great Wiper, where is my Great Wiper? Can I ever hope to succeed without it? My $CH_4 + NH_3 + H_2O$ soup cooks on the floor beside me, but where is the Wiper? Where is the Perfect Protein? The exceptional Enzyme?

With destiny, I am dealing always with cause and effect. I need to know what causes the effects I so desperately need. Which proteins activate and which inhibit? Which start this life process and which modify it? Months, years, it seems like centuries of my life have been hopelessly devoted to this quest. A quest for magic.

I divide incessantly. Divide and divide. My molecules become atoms and my atoms become nuclei. Protons, neutrons, kaons, pions, muons, electrons, neutrinos. Will it never stop? Gaul was fortunate, indeed, that Caesar was not a physicist or it might have found its real estate subdivided into an *omnium gatherum* the envy of every Levittown.

I know what makes up my protons and neutrons, and atoms, and molecules, and proteins, and amino acids, and blood, flesh, and bones, and still, no matter how I analyze, I never end up with a Harry Wolper who is a being gone mad. These elements are only the boundary conditions, not the function, which is what I do and am. There is nothing there for making feathers, and so this unlikely collection of particles will probably not become a chicken. But as for what it is. Who knows? That is the relationship. The relationship is all. It is what makes the gears and springs into a clock that tells time, the hydrocarbon molecules into a raving lunatic.

4th Potato salad has always seemed to me to be a particularly apt dish for

July 4th, representing an ingenious conglomeration of unlikely elements to make something fairly tasty. That these vegetables are able to get along at all in one dish is a miracle to me akin to the ostensible melting pot we have all come together today to make a lot of noise about.

This is, of course, a myth. There is no more a melting pot here in America than a dish without lettuce and tomatoes is a salad. No matter, the distinction is unimportant. The streets were not, in fact, paved with gold, and religious tolerance is neither better nor worse here than anywhere else. Jews and Catholics maintain their distance, blacks and whites fortify themselves and prepare for battle. Young and old starve alike and view each other with little friendliness or regard. We are an armed camp, entrenched to protect what little territory we have left, and brotherly love be damned. We were not cooperators who built this country, and this is not a democracy. We national engineers were competitors and enslavers, and we built us here a republic, to foster competition, protect the interests of the aristocratic founding fathers, and assure that a class system could sustain itself just like in Mother England, in spite of our having no history, a remarkable achievement at the very least.

It is a country put together with tape and pins, and its longevity is a testimony not to the constitutional design, but to the real wisdom of the founders in taking into account the true adhesive that would bind us together: greed. What is self-evident to me is that it is *my* life, *my* liberty, and *my* pursuit of happiness, not yours. Yours is your problem.

And when it came time to form our Constitution, no less a figure than Patrick Henry himself, flaming patriot, founding father, banged on the desk, screamed at the convention, What did they *mean* "*We*, the people"! What right had they to say "*We*, the people"! Who gave them the power to speak the language of "*We*, the people"! The people gave them no power to use their name!

It was hardly possible to write three words without some patriot announcing that no one was speaking for him and mind your own business!

No, our fabric is not designed to hold the imprint of relationships well. It is woven to show fifty separate and distinct stars, set well off by themselves from the original thirteen stripes. I often marvel, with pain, great pain, at what a solitary life we have provided here, at how little warmth there is to go along with our heralded freedom.

I wonder whether there is any hope for us descendants of those with the stamina and guts to withstand the vast sea and leave everything they held dear to them behind, everything they knew. Is there any way that this nation of rugged individualists, iconoclasts, self-made men, entrepreneurs, and liberated free-thinkers can ever relate, one to the other? Now that would be an event for which to light firecrackers.

Until then I will console myself that American relationships are not impossible in a country that can combine onions, celery, eggs, and gobs of mayonnaise with subterranean tubers and end up with something as palatable as potato salad.

5th I wonder how it is one tells whether one is living with someone. It is a question that, for me, goes beyond a simple explanation of contemporary vernacular and allows me to determine whether, for example, because Meli has not left this house in three days, we are cohabiting.

We have progressed rather rapidly through Bach, Beethoven, and Bartók (omitting Brahms, Britten, and Bruckner for the sake of an expeditious alphabetical journey) and are on the doorstep of an essay into the likes of Cage, Chabrier, Chopin, Copland, Corelli, and Couperin, and I still do not know whether she intends to live here with me, uninvited, or whether she remains by inertia alone. In any event, I must admit it is not altogether unpleasant.

We have lovely meals and warm conversation. Mrs. Mallory's shock has turned to consternation and finally now to simple puzzlement and disbelief. My emotions have run a similar course.

"It is not as though I don't want her to stay," I explained to Mrs. Mallory while Meli was out on the terrace thumbing through my copy of Hume's *Enquiry Concerning Human Understanding* and whistling merrily.

"You *want* her to stay?" Mrs. Mallory asked incredulously.

"Not exactly. I also don't want her to stay, more or less," I explained the problem.

"You sound, Dr. Wolper, if you'll forgive me for saying so, like you don't know *what* you want."

"You've hit the nail right on the head, Mrs. Mallory. I don't know what I want."

There was a long pause while Mrs. Mallory pretended to be very involved in clearing away the lunch dishes. After a few minutes she came over to sit at the table with me, wiping her hands nervously on her apron.

"You know, Dr. Wolper," she stuttered uncomfortably, "the two of you do seem happy enough. I know it's none of my business, but it's been a long time since I've seen you this happy. You know how you've been all this year. Brood, brood, brood."

"Do I sense a change of opinion regarding the young lady on the terrace?"

"Not really a change of opinion. I still think her whole body sexual system is out of whack. She's not normal. But otherwise, as far as I can tell, she's certainly a nice enough young person. And besides, she's ruining the sofa by sleeping on it."

"You think she should have her own room?"

"Well, now that you mention it, I took the liberty of kind of fixing up

Claire's bedroom, putting on fresh sheets and straightening up a bit." She refused to look at me.

"Mrs. Mallory, I'm shocked! Claire's room has a door adjoining *my* bedroom. I'm appalled at your behavior!" I teased her.

"You can always lock the door from your side, Dr. Wolper. I figure that your life is your life." She looked at me smiling at her discomfort. "Oh, never mind. Do what you want. I really don't care. Mope around here all day long if you want. It's your business," and she turned abruptly and bustled off to the kitchen.

Before she disappeared completely I called after her.

"Thank you, Mrs. Mallory. That was very kind and thoughtful of you."

"Well, it just seemed a shame to destroy such a lovely sofa," And then, smiling back at me, "You're welcome," and she was through the doorway.

I sat for a minute finishing my iced tea and then walked out on the terrace. Meli was still whistling some tune or other and grimacing at Hume.

"Are you enjoying the book?" I asked and sat down on the arm of her chair.

"This is the damndest things I've ever seen in my whole goddam life, Dr. Wolper. Did you actually read all this?"

"A long time ago."

"Do other people read him? I mean *who else* reads him? What I mean, Dr. Wolper, is what the hell is he trying to say? What is he, translated from the original Eskimo?"

"He's British."

"You mean English is his *first language?* He didn't *have* to write like this? He could have written for *human beings* all along?"

"Some people think that he's one of the clearest writers of philosophy," I offered.

"Right. And some people think that when you die you come back as a camel, and I don't believe that either. You think this is clear? Let me read you something. 'Liberty, when opposed to necessity, not to constraint, is the same thing with chance; which is universally allowed to have no existence.' Is he talking about the same liberty that I know, like the one in Sweet Land of Liberty and all that? What is wrong with this man, Dr. Wolper?"

"Meli, I want to ask you something," I changed the subject. "Mrs. Mallory has made up the bed in Claire's room for you to sleep in."

There was a lengthy period of silence.

"Well?" I finally asked.

"I'm waiting for the question, Dr. Wolper."

"Ah, yes. Well, the question is, of course, whether you would like to stay here," I stammered.

"Overnight?"

"For a while," I said. "For as long as things seem to be working out."

"How long is that?"

"Meli, I don't know. How am I supposed to know how long things will work out? They'll work out as long as they work out. I'm not a prophet," I said irritably.

Meli smiled a broad beaming smile at me. "Very good, Dr. Wolper, you're making real progress. Of course I want to stay here with you."

I, too, was pleased and placed my arm around her. She rose up in the chair and kissed me gently on my cheek.

"I can't promise anything, Meli," I said. "We'll just have to see what happens. But I am enjoying the time we spend together."

"So am I, Dr. Wolper. A whole lot."

"So, Meli, what do you think. Maybe it's time for you to call me 'Harry.'"

"I don't want to call you 'Harry.'"

"Why not?"

"Because you're Dr. Wolper, that's why."

"But I'm also 'Harry.'"

"Not to me you aren't. To me you're 'Dr. Wolper.' That's the way I met you and that's the way I want it to stay."

"You don't feel that it's a little formal for our relationship, then?"

"I think it's just right." She saw my confusion. "Now don't go making any big goddam deal out of it. It's just the way I am. If I made love to the King of France, I'd say, 'That was a good fuck, Your Highness. Thank you, Your Majesty.' And that's all there is to it."

And that was, indeed, all there was to it.

6th I went to Maureen's tonight for her to meet Meli. Paul is doing well, she tells me, but he still refuses to see anyone.

Late in the evening we found ourselves, thanks to Meli's insistence, staggering around the field behind Maureen's home, of all things, chasing fireflies. It has been exactly sixty years since I last did this. I remember it well, because I was nine years old, and I did it with my father. It was the last time I saw him.

This evening I reached out to catch one particular lightning bug that was a short distance away and found, much to my dismay, that my arms would not move, and then that my legs would not move, and then that I was growing faint. I believe I collapsed into a bramble bush.

When I regained consciousness, Maureen and Meli had somehow moved me to the living room. Apparently, I even walked some of the way.

I felt ashamed of myself for spoiling a beautiful evening. I know that I am supposed to accept the inevitability of my dying, except that this process doesn't seem to want to organize itself so that I can understand it. It does not allow me to relate to it in any way whatsoever. Just when I think I have it under control, it surprises me with another episode.

I expect that the closer I get to the Ultimate Conclusion, the closer together these episodes will get. That's what I expect. But who knows what this particular Death has on her mind? For all I know she will space these attacks at random and end it all in one great crescendo. Just like her to turn a not particularly interesting phenomenon into a concert performance.

This Death is a difficult lady with whom to have a relationship, and, to be perfectly frank about it, I have no intention of courting her.

7th Meli demanded tonight that I explain to her what this man David Hume thought he was saying. Now I am hardly an expert on eighteenth-century Empiricists, yet Hume inspires me to the small extent that I believe I understand him. As I told Meli, it is my impression that modern philosophy begins with the writings of this cheerful atheist. The rest is little more than the opposition to his thought. Where would Kant be without Hume? Who ever would have heard of Hegel or Marx, Nietzsche, Kierkegaard, any of them? They would all be not very interesting commentators on Cartesian geometry had Hume not come along and lit a torch under philosophy's ass.

What a grand "pathetic fallacy" Mr. Hume has conjured, this terminal joke that what I *have* seen in no way resembles what I have *not*, that there is no object or event that implies the existence of any other.

Now, of course, I agree with the man. There is no question in my mind that the incessant inferences we make from cause to effect are not from our reason but spring eternally from our most vivid imagination, which is indisputedly irrational. Otherwise, life would not be art. And I have no doubt that there never will be an absolute guarantee for the principle of induction, because, after all, the world, when you get right down to it, is not a Cartesian system at all, but a rich amalgam. Right?

This is all quite marvelous, but not particularly helpful. Because, you see, I have to live and work in this particular rich amalgam. More to the point, I attempt science, in spite of Mr. Hume's retiring cause and effect to his great Fontainbleau of Philosophy.

Don't get me wrong. David Hume was a splendid man. Take, for example, Adam Smith's assessment. Hume, he wrote, "approached as nearly to the idea of a perfectly wise and virtuous man as the nature of human frailty will permit." For me, nothing establishes his wisdom more than his having the good sense to expire in 1776, before the real trouble began. But then, who knows what cause was responsible for that effect?

"So that's what he said?" Meli asked me with some dismay after I had finished my little discourse on Hume. "That there's no way of our ever knowing whether one thing causes another? Is that it?"

"Precisely."

Meli thought this over for some time, tapping her foot to the Debussy on the phonograph.

"Well," she finally concluded, "I hope you don't mind my saying this because like I know that you think this guy is inspirational and all that, but if he's trying to tell me that I don't ever know for certain that one thing makes another happen then I think the guy's an idiot. Where'd he grow up, in the Gobi desert?"

8th It's too late. I've told Meli that she can stop taking her progesterone and estrogen. I have not been able to transplant the nuclei soon enough. This will not be Lucy.

I'm a little surprised that I have sustained its growth as long as I have. I have today placed the zygote in a suspension of my soup and it thrives. I wonder how long I can keep this up. I do not deceive myself that I can keep this embryo alive for very long, any more than I deceive myself that I know what I am doing.

I do not understand how my careless poking started its growth in the first place. I know for certain that I could never do it again.

"You mustn't say that, Dr. Wolper," Meli said this evening as we sat in the living room listening to Elgar. "You'll succeed. I know you will. After all you're a scientist, and this stuff is only science."

"Meli," I spoke softly as I put my arm around her. "I am not a scientist and, much to my regret, this is not science. Unfortunately, I am only an extraordinarily inept theologian, and this enterprise in which I am involved is, unhappily, religion."

Meli looked at me in silence for several minutes attempting to absorb this information.

"Well, for chrissake, no wonder you're not getting anywhere," she finally informed me. "You don't even know which goddam *field* you're in."

I find that I have grown enormously fond of this perceptive young woman.

10th "Harry, I've got to talk to you about something."

Yes, Boris, what is it now?

"I've been thinking rather seriously about going to medical school. I'm not sure I could get in, but that's what I want. What do you think?"

I think you're making a big mistake, Boris. You don't have the disposition to be a physician.

"Well, I don't exactly want to be a physician. I want to be a medical scientist. I think I'm interested in the birth process."

You want to be a neonatalogist.

"No, I'm not interested in the newborn, I'm interested in birth."

You want to be an obstetrician.

"Well, instead of birth, maybe I should call it conception. I'm interested in making babies."

You don't have a uterus, Boris.

"Harry, dammit, don't do this to me. I want to be like *you*, Harry. Can't you figure that out?"

For godsakes, why?

"Because I like the control you have over things. In a nutshell, I just like the kind of power you have. I want that, Harry. I want that more than anything else in the entire universe."

What about this religious experience you wanted to have? What ever happened to that?

"I'm having it, Harry. Or at least I feel that this is the first step. But I need more, much more."

Boris, what in God's name do you *want* from me? I gave you your freedom. Now leave me alone. Please. Go live your life.

"I was kind of hoping you would bless me and teach me the tricks of the trade, so to speak."

Well, so to speak, Boris, I do not bless you for this. Now please go away.

"Now, now, Harry. I really don't want to get you upset over this. Imitation is, after all, the sincerest form of flattery."

You know, Boris, I just might be trying to save you a great deal of pain. Have you thought of that?

"No, I haven't, Harry. It's so out of character for you, I haven't thought of it for a second. There's no way that you're out to protect *my* interests."

Very well, Boris. Have it your way. We have our contract, and I won't stop you.

"That's awfully big of you."

Be careful, Boris. You don't know what you're getting into. It's not what you think it is.

"Being like you? Having control?"

I have no control, Boris, no power at all. The last thing in the world you want is to be like me. It's all an illusion, Boris, just a bad dream.

"Bullshit, Harry. Just bullshit."

Then good luck, Boris.

"I don't need it, Harry. I know what I'm doing."

11th **The Adventures of Boris Lafkin**

CHAPTER TWO (OR SIX):
In Which Our Hero Gets His Act Together, More or Less

The summer went very quickly for me. I spent a great deal of time exploring vocational possibilities and being with Barbara. It was a good time, walking Cambridge streets in the evening, sitting on the back porch reading, talking until late at night, making love. We even went back to the Cape a couple more times before Barbara's school began.

Just before Labor Day weekend, Barbara quit her job. Prudential was very nice about it. Barbara figured they thought she'd still be good for fifty thousand dollars or so in Whole Life in a few years.

Labor Day weekend I met Barbara's parents, who were very nice and received both me and the news of our impending marriage warmly and with enthusiasm. Her father, a bald trim man in his fifties, took me aside for the required "be good to my daughter" lecture, and her mother, a slightly overweight good-natured woman, took me aside to inquire about my financial stability, present and future. I lied a lot.

The big events at the end of the summer were that I decided to apply to medical schools, don't ask me why, and I landed a job at a medical instruments firm called MIL, which stands for Medical Instruments Laboratory. To celebrate my first paycheck we went out and got very drunk, and then we went to bed for forty-eight straight hours. We didn't sleep much.

As the fall began, Barbara was very pleased with her program at Harvard and then, after the newness wore off at the end of a few weeks, she became more frustrated.

"I've never seen anything like it. There's no diversity at all. They're all logical positivists or semantic analysts," she complained one night in the fall. "Even when they're translating Plato they're still positivists. I wish William James had never seen Harvard."

"Is there anything I can do?" I asked.

"Yes. Make me some tea and tell me to shut up."

I did as I was told.

"How was work today?" Barbara changed the subject.

"Good. I got a five-hundred-dollar bonus."

"Right. What'd you do, learn how to open the safe?"

"No kidding, I really did. Here's the check. See the six words on this line here: five hundred dollars and no cents. And on this line beside the word payee are two wonderful words: Boris Lafkin."

"Boris! You really did get a five-hundred-dollar bonus! You really did!"

"I told you I did. You want to see what for?"

I walked into the study and pulled out a small plastic box.

"Now this here," I told her, "is a respirator. It breathes people who aren't able to do it themselves. Only there's one problem they've been having with this machine. People tend to get hypostatic pneumonia after awhile. Well, I had an idea last month that I tried out, and then they tried it out. I figured that the people might be getting pneumonia because they had their mouths open all the time and there was a cold draft. Room temperature air of 72° was always filling the mouth of a person whose temperature was 98.6° or so. People are built to breathe with their mouths closed. Well, what I did was to rig on a couple heating and moisturizing elements, one here where the air comes in and one here where it goes out. And presto, no more hypostatic pneumonia. Or at least, a lot less. Seems to work. Clever, huh? And profitable."

"Oh, Boris, I think that's great." She came over and hugged me very tightly.

"And I know exactly what I'm going to do with it," I told her. "Fifty dollars goes for us to eat at Chez Robert. Fifty dollars goes for winter boots and a fall jacket for you. One hundred dollars goes for a wedding ring. Two hundred and fifty dollars just goes to you, period, because I love you, and I never would have gotten it in the first place if you hadn't inspired me."

"Well," Barbara grinned, "I'm just the inspirational type," and she gave me a big hug.

My favorite memory of the time is walking back from the movies in the chilly autumn night, crunching the leaves under our feet, Barbara wearing my red plaid lumber jacket, me in my fisherman's sweater, arms around each other, sharing thoughts about the movie, the day, life in general and our lives together.

As I talk about it now it is as vivid as if I were there, the apartment, talking on the phone, dinners out and in, studying, writing, reading, making love, talking, tennis, movies, concerts, having friends over, walking. Even the chores of cooking, doing dishes, making the bed, cleaning, doing laundry, food shopping, seemed like some exquisite romantic experience. I told this to Barbara once in the fall.

"Sometimes, Boris," she said, "I think that you think clipping your nails is a romantic experience. You seem to forget that it isn't all beautiful."

"Well," I grinned, "I remember that you threw a plate of spaghetti at me last week, if that's what you're saying, and I remember that two weeks ago you cried all night for your mommy because you didn't want to grow old. I also remember that last month you flew out of the apartment in a rage and I had to go racing all over Cambridge after you until you'd come back, although I don't remember what it was about."

"As I recall it," Barbara smiled, "I asked you to be completely honest about the new chicken dish I had spent all Saturday making for you, and you actually were. You said it was lousy. I figured that our relationship had just ended, so I left."

"You know, I've always wondered what made you come back?"

"A few things. I loved you. I had no place else to go. And I got tired of you driving along the street for three hours, beeping your horn at me and shouting that you liked my chicken. Everybody who passed by thought you were saying something dirty."

Out of all the many conversations we had that fall, one sticks out in my mind. We were walking back from seeing *Who's Afraid of Virginia Woolf?*. It was a particularly cold night and our breaths steamed as we talked. I was in my "serious" mood. This means I had my hands stuffed in my back pockets. Barbara was walking with her arms wrapped around herself to keep warm. The subject was one that we had batted around a dozen times: how to have a *permanent* relationship with someone.

"Part of the answer," Barbara said as we walked, "is being a happy person. If you love life and you know that you can provide for your *own* happiness, it makes it a hell of a lot easier to maintain a relationship. Then neither person is responsible for the happiness of the other, and that takes an enormous burden off each person. No relationship can stand up under that weight.

"Trust is important and probably the hardest thing. You've got to be the kind of person who's able to trust in general, the world, life, other people, yourself. If two people really trust each other no matter what, the relationship can withstand a hell of a lot.

"But I think that there's also a kind of magic, a fit, and I'm not very sure about all that. But I know that even though you and I are different in a lot of ways, there's something that's basically similar about us that makes us work well together, maybe it's our genes. Whatever it is, it means that there's a lot less we have to work out. I'm not sure what it is. I know that we see the world basically the same, but I think it's more than even that. There's just something that makes me feel good when I'm with you. It feels comfortable. I like it. It's magic."

I hadn't said a word up to now, since I was sucking on my tongue and concentrating. I wasn't satisfied, though. I stopped walking and stood under a lamplight.

"Tell me what you're thinking, Boris, it's really important," Barbara said.

"It's hard, Barbara," I said, "because I know that you've given this a lot of thought. What bothers me is that I think what you're talking about makes a good relationship. It probably even makes a *great* one. But what keeps it *going forever?*"

Barbara thought about this for a minute.

"Nothing at all, Boris," she finally said. "It's in destiny's hands for the most part. You can do a lot of things to ruin a relationship, but there's not a damn thing either of us can do to make it last forever. We just have to be happy people and love each other. That's all we can do."

"You've made it sound very simple," I said.

"I have? It doesn't sound simple to me at all. The hardest thing of all is to live in a relationship where the only thing that's certain is that nothing is certain. You do what you have to do for yourself, and this includes loving the other person, knowing all along that in the long run there's no real connection between what you do and how the other person responds. The question in all relationships is can you live without causes and effects and not get hysterical."

I was not entirely convinced that this was the answer.

"What," I asked, "if after we've been married for five or ten years, I decided to leave you for another woman? What's to stop that?"

"Only you, Boris. You would have to know that your happiness was inside you, and it wouldn't come from someone else. You would have to trust that together we could work out whatever was bothering you that made you want to do this, and that, too, is inside of you. And it would have to be important for you, not for me but for you, not to hurt me by leaving me like that, and that's inside of you."

"Yes, but what would you *do?*"

"You don't know, Boris. And neither do I. That's what I mean about causes and effects. You just don't know. Only one thing, Boris, if you do it, I'll break your neck."

"Trust, Barbara, whatever happened to trust?"

"Oh, I'll trust you. I'll also break your neck."

"No, I mean it, Barbara. Would you really trust me?"

"Yes, I would. Would you trust me?"

"For what?"

"If I decided to go off with someone else."

"Do I get to break your neck, too?"

"You wanted to be serious. Now answer my question. Would you trust me?"

"Of course, I would."

"I doubt it, Boris. I think you'd like to, but I don't think you'd be able to. At least not yet."

"That's a lot of horseshit, Barbara. I *would* trust you."

"Okay. I'll try you. I'm having lunch tomorrow with Lawrence. I want to tell him that I've been thinking of going back to him."

"Why do you want to tell him *that?*"

"Because it's true."

A cold shiver ran up my back.

"Look," I said, "I know that in the great permanent relationship scheme of things I'm not supposed to get anxious about what you're saying, but I'm anxious as hell. Have you really been wanting to go back to Lawrence?"

"No, I've only been thinking about it. I believe it's called the persistence of attachment. I have no desire really to go back to Lawrence, but I can't get the thought out of my mind. The only solution I can think of is to tell him that I've been thinking about it."

"And then what?"

"Then I should be able to work it out in my head."

"And if you don't. Nothing's certain, remember that?"

"Boris, we're getting married in two months. I am not going back to Lawrence."

"I don't like any of this. Something could go wrong."

"Boris, will you please calm down. I'm sorry I told you any of this."

"So am I."

Life continued. Barbara had lunch with Lawrence and assured me afterwards that it was very helpful. She loved me even more, and felt she had made some real progress in working through her feelings about Lawrence before we got married. I believed her but hoped desperately that in the future she would be able to find other ways to resolve problems.

In the meantime, while Barbara was developing her life of chance and necessity, I attempted to establish mine of purpose and order.

Applying to medical school is a very discouraging proposition. Your whole life drags in front of you over pages and pages of application forms in the most detailed and painful way imaginable. The number of times I kicked myself for not applying myself more in ninth-grade General Science. If I had only joined one more club in eleventh grade, the Key Club, the Chess Club, Future Nurses of America, anything so it didn't look like I spent my entire high school career bouncing and throwing one ball or another and staring into space contemplating the Great Unknown, which is, of course, exactly what I did.

Each evening, as I sat at my typewriter, the same sentence written in every form letter accompanying every application packet I received burned itself into my mind: Admission to this Medical School is highly competitive—last year we had 1,400 applicants and admitted 11. And I knew the eleven they admitted, too. Six were women. Of the five men remaining, one was black, one was American Indian, one was Hispanic, and one was Other. The remaining one slot available to a white male, preferably not Jewish, would be given to an applicant who got an 800 in his Medical College Admissions Test, an A in every course he'd taken since kindergarten, in which he'd received a special letter of commendation for jungle gym and swings, was graduating Summa Cum Laude from Harvard where he won varsity letters in four sports and the debating team, had letters of recommendation from the surgeon general of the United States, the president of the American Medical Association, and the dean of this particular medical school, who happened to be his father, had spent all his summers since fourth grade working in a hospital and already had two arterial bypass procedures named after him, and, as if this weren't enough, was engaged to the daughter of the chairman of the admissions committee. Now *this* is highly competitive admissions, especially when of the 1,400 applicants, 1,100 are white males trying for the one slot for which "Chip" Cromwell (the same one and directly descended, too) has a hair's edge.

The confusing part of it was that I *wanted* to be a doctor, and I knew I'd make a damn good one, certainly as good as the various ones I'd been to who were still trying to figure out whether a 99° temperature was normal for me or not. And, what's more, the country was *short* of doctors. I began to wonder whether the American Medical Association, who more or less controlled the number of humans admitted to study medicine each year, hadn't had some insight into Hippocrates that the rest of us haven't been fortunate enough to have had yet.

Nevertheless, undaunted, I continued to fill out twenty-two page application forms, not including all the supporting transcripts and letters, for the six medical schools within three hours of Cambridge so Barbara and I could still live together, we figured, midway. These included Harvard, Tufts, Boston University, Brown, Yale, and Dartmouth. Since Brown and Dartmouth tended to be reserved for residents of their states, being the only medical schools in the states, none of the remaining—B.U., Tufts, Harvard, and Yale—suggested itself as being in the "safety" category, and so, at Barbara's insistence, I also applied to the American University of Beirut.

I'm not too good at geography, I told Barbara, but I think that midway between Cambridge and Lebanon is Rabat.

"Apply," she said.

Or the Indian Ocean, depending on which way you go.

"Apply, Boris."

Should I apply as "Rashid El Lafkin"?

"Look, Boris, I'm not living with any medical school reject. Use any name you want. Just apply. We'll work it out."

This amazed me as much as anything, the supreme confidence we had that the world was manageable. Whatever it was, we'd work it out. We didn't start out that way, but when you consider that it only took three months of living together, it seemed like it happened overnight.

13th Meli's embryo lives on. I do not understand it. Doesn't it understand that it's only an experiment in a Florentine flask, not something real? It's only Harry's dream. I'm apprehensive that it will miss the point, and I'll find myself with an infant without an owner. No matter. There's quite a way to go before I have to worry myself over such possibilities.

Mother Nature is not kind to me. I analyze and analyze my Great Wiper and come up with nothing. I add a little something here, a little something there, but nothing comes of it. Mother Nature insists on doing it her way and, as always, loves to take her time about it. The last time she took ten billion years, more or less, leaving a good deal of genetic residue along the way. But then what does she care? Does Mother Nature get her hand slapped every time she's not parsimonious? The odds have been against her from the start, and she's come through splendidly.

In the meantime, I fumble around, trying this chemical and that, one amount or another, increasing the radiation, decreasing the heat, hoping against my better judgment that through incredible guile I will have the power to rouse the Great Wiper from his long hibernation. At the end of it all, there are no more experiments left for me to perform. The only tools left at my disposal are judgment and patience. I can observe. I can modify. I can pretend I know what I am doing, but it is mostly out of my hands now. There is absolutely nothing I can do. How I envy a man like Akke Spallanzani, dressing his male frogs in little silk knickers to prove that sperm is, indeed, necessary. Now *that* is scientific experimentation.

14th I paid a little visit today to Anthony Pascotti, Esq., my attorney, for the purpose of modifying my will. Attorney Pascotti is one of those Harvard Law School graduates who has somehow missed the point of Harvard. He wears the same 1940's blue pin-striped suit every day and sandals, summer and winter, which expose the filthiest toenails I have ever seen. This totally bald thirty-five year old juvenile reeks of cigars twenty-four hours a day and seems constitutionally unable to bring cigar ashes into conjunction with ashtrays. The only other interesting descriptive information about this unorthodox young man is that he has never lost a case, not once, not even by accident. He has never gotten less in an out-of-court settlement than a client wanted, not a kopeck less. He has never had a will broken. Such consistent jurisprudence provides a substantial rationale for overlooking other less comforting terrestrial behavior.

"So you want to change your fuckin' will, huh? Where is that fuckin' thing?" Tony riffled through mounds of papers on his desk, judgments and affidavits pouring over the edges and littering the floor.

"I brought it with me," I said.

"Well, no wonder I couldn't find the fuckin' thing. So." Tony sat down on his swivel chair and lit the end of the burnt-out cigar in his mouth. "What the fuck do you want to do with it? Who's getting fucked today?"

"No one, actually. I'm writing someone new in."

"What the fuck for? You've hardly got enough to go around to all the fuckers you've got included in it already. You know we don't have any currency subdivisions in America under a penny. You're going to have to start making bequests in piasters if you include any more fuckin' people in this fuckin' thing."

"It's a young lady."

"Well, fuck," he said in mock surprise, "I thought it was another one of your fuckin' frogs. You've got two of them in here already, you know."

"I do?"

"Fuck, yes. Let me see. Where the fuck are they? Ah ha, here it is, 'And to my fellow researchers Castor (Frog) and Pollux (Frog) I bequeath the sum of one thousand dollars each for the preservation of their general well-being that they might live long and fruitful lives.'"

"Take them out," I said sadly.

"Take them out?"

"I killed them."

"Well, so much for those mother-fuckers," said Anthony Pascotti, chomping on his cigar, and drawing a number of lines through the paragraph. "Any other homicides I should know about? Now's the time."

"I don't know," I said. "Who else is there?"

"Well, let me see. You've got a rabbit in here. And a snake. I think a copperhead's a snake, isn't it? At least one turkey. Right. Here it is. And, what's a hammerhead? Isn't that some kind of man-eating shark or something? What the fuck do you want to *preserve* them for?"

"Let me see that." I reached for the will. "That must have been the week Maury got to me. Dammit. Take out the shark. I refuse to give my money to a shark."

"Good for you, Dr. Wolper. That's telling them. Fuck them all. How about the turkey? You up for disinheriting a turkey?"

"Not the turkey! The turkey stays!"

"Sorry. Sorry. Look Dr. Wolper, what the fuck do you want with me today?"

"I want to make a bequest to Meli."

Attorney Pascotti waited for me to continue. I said nothing.

"Meli who?" he finally asked. "Who the fuck is Meli? At least give me the species."

"Homo sapiens."

"Congratulations."

"Thank you."

"How much do you want to leave her?"

"Everything not left to the animals."

"What's her last name?"

"I don't know."

"You don't know! Shit, Wolper, you've got to know. Do you have any idea how many Melis are going to crawl out of the fuckin' woodwork once your fuckin' will is probated? There'll be four hundred thousand of the fuckers. You've got a lot of fuckin' money here, man."

"I'll find out her last name."

"You're goddam fuckin' right you will. And her address. And social security number. And whether she has any birthmarks."

"On her left breast."

"What the fuck are you talking about?"

"She's got a sort of square-shaped birthmark just under the nipple of her left breast."

"Spare me the fuckin' details, will you, Dr. Wolper. Just get me her last name, address and social security number."

"Is that all?"

"That's it. I'll have you the fuckin' will a day after you get me the stuff on your fuckin' lady friend."

"And you're sure you understand what I want changed?"

"Fuck yes, Wolper! I understand. The bird stays. The fish goes. The rest is for the broad. Have I got it right?"

"Perfectly."

"Good. Then get the fuck out of here and leave me to my world of humans."

Now that's what I call *style.*

15th "Harry. Harry. Harry."

"Maury, Maury, Maury," I returned in kind.

"Harry. Harry. Harry. It's so good to see you."

"Maury, you're dripping on my rug."

"Do you mind if I sit down?" Maury did so without waiting for a response. "It's hot as hell, today. Hot as hell. Who's she?"

"Meli, this is Maury. He steals money from people under the description of doing good works. Maury, this is Meli. Meli is—I don't know. How should I describe you, Meli?"

"I'm a nineteen-year-old nymphomaniac who's living with Dr. Wolper so I can learn classical music."

"How do you do," said Maury, not absorbing a word. "Look, Harry. Is there somewhere we could go to, you know—" nodding off in Meli's direction, "talk?"

"Oh, we can talk here. I have no secrets from Meli."

Maury looked very uncomfortable and stared down at his shoes, a stream of perspiration puddling between them.

"Harry," he finally said, "my career is ruined. A man works and works and out of that comes maybe, if he's lucky, one success, one thing he can look back on and say 'My life has not been without value.' I lost that yesterday, Harry. I lost years and years of work in one day, one hour, one minute. Who knows how short a time it took."

"Somebody die?" Meli asked.

"For years I've said to myself, 'Maury, your wife may have left you, your professional standing may be less than zero, your kids may despise you, and you may have alienated every human being you've known, but when you leave this world, you will leave it knowing that there will still be hammerhead sharks swimming in the deep blue sea.' "

A light dawned.

"And then this." He took a letter from his pocket, soaking wet and crumpled, and waved it at me. "Why, Harry? Why have you done this to me?"

"I don't really know, Maury. I guess I was just in a good mood."

"Harry. Harry. Harry. What have I done to deserve this? What have I done?" Maury wept, tears mixing freely with sweat.

"Dr. Wolper," Meli interrupted, "what the hell is this guy talking about?"

"I took a bequest to hammerhead sharks out of my will, yesterday."

"You mean he's crying like this over a fish?"

"Not just a fish, young lady. A hammerhead shark. One of the oldest creatures still in existence, and soon to be extinct."

"Doesn't it eat people or something?" Meli continued to ask incredulously.

"Sure it eats people! Sure it eats people!" Maury snapped back. "What's new to eat after you've been on earth for ten million years?"

"Maury," I said patiently. "I'm really sorry if I ruined your hopes for the shark, but I just couldn't bring myself to give a large sum of money to a fish that eats human beings."

"What are you, God?" Maury barked angrily. "God made the shark. Not you. God! God made the shark to eat people. Are you telling God that he should have made the shark differently? Do you think it would be better if he ate seaweed? Just what do you know?" he smirked. "You're not God! You have no right to tell God how to make His creatures!"

"Exactly," I agreed. "And I also have no right to tell God whether they should be preserved or not. That's up to Him."

"But He made man to make money, Harry," Maury explained patiently. "He made man with a spirit of giving, of giving money, of giving money to save the hammerhead shark. That's His plan. That's how He's going about keeping the shark from extinction." Maury smiled pleasantly. "And you, Harry, are destroying God's plan!" Maury shouted. "You are interfering with the entire order of the universe when you write sharks out of your will."

"I can't take this," Meli announced. "I can't figure out *what* the hell's going on. I'm going out to the terrace and read the Bible or something, Dr. Wolper. I think I've missed something." Meli got up and sauntered across the room. She stopped in front of the diaphoretic fountain and looked at him.

"I know it's God's will and all that," Meli told him matter-of-factly, "but you sweat too much. It's disgusting. You ought to spend daylight hours in a cave or something." She skipped off to the terrace.

"You like her?" I asked.

"Harry, now that she's gone I've got something else to tell you," Maury spoke in hushed tones ignoring my question. "Do you remember my telling you about the mad abortionist?"

I shivered. I hoped it was not noticed.

"I remember," I tried to say nonchalantly.

"Well, Harry. Let me tell you. We're close enough to smell him."

"That close, huh?"

"And let me tell you something else. He doesn't smell like fish, if you get my meaning."

"I'm not sure I do."

"Like fish. Like hammerhead sharks. He does *not* smell like fish. Do you get me?"

"Why are you telling me this?"

"Well, the only thing we lack is evidence, and I thought you might be able to tell me what to look for. This detective work is something new for me, you know."

"You have no evidence?" I smiled, letting out a big sigh.

"Not a thing, Harry."

"Not even a witness?"

"Nope. They just disappeared into thin air."

"Well," I laughed heartily, "that's the way it goes with detective work sometimes."

"I don't mind telling you, Harry, that the finger was pointing pretty strongly at you for awhile. But we've pretty much ruled out that possibility now. Like I said, Harry, he does *not* smell like a fish."

"I wish I could say the same for you, Maury. God, how I wish I could."

"I don't get you, Harry. I'm not the abortionist," Maury said puzzled.

"Maury, look, I'll give you my regular check for fifty dollars, but I will not put the shark back in my will. Use the fifty dollars any way you want. Sharks, marmots, hartebeests. I don't care."

Maury was very pleased. "Harry, that's great. You've made my day. You really have."

"I suppose I'm glad, Maury."

Maury leaned forward, the sharp sound of his wet shirt peeling from the leather chair shattering the quiet mood. He confided in me.

"You know something, Harry, just between you and me, I think that God doesn't give a damn for the sharks. He's left it up to them. We just can't count on Him anymore. He doesn't know what He's doing any more than we do. I'm convinced of it." And Maury got up and left the room, leaving the glistening imprint of his body, knees to neck, on the large Victorian chair.

16th The heat of this July means nothing to me. I perspire and do not care. I suck in the sweetness of a chlorophyll world carried in the humid air, never getting enough of the breezy fruit in my lungs. I live for July when life is in its fullest bloom.

It was not always this way with me. For years I would push through the month, ignoring the botanical assault on my senses, pretending, as I posed in front of my fans and air conditioners, that this was April or, better still, February. I drowned out the sounds of the children hollering in summer ecstasy at the playground across the street, the sounds of young very masculine conversations on the front stoop, of radios echoing their music inside automobiles crammed every evening with adolescents in a permanent heterosexual smooch, the sounds of squirrels scampering up tree bark and birds warbling incessantly to each other. I drowned them all with the sound of condensers vaporizing Freon to make Summer into Winter.

I forgot, as though it never happened, summers I had spent perched on birch-white lifeguard stands, my godlike body tanned to parchment, clenched fists folded crosswise under my biceps to expand my upper arms just this side of the grotesque, smiling, always smiling, eight feet below to the young women for whom I was potential salvation from a summer spent with Mom, Dad, Sis, and Junior at the family summer home. I could not get enough of the heat and sun and air then, and I cannot now.

I remember coming out of my lab one July evening after years of having hidden from the month. I was knocked nearly unconscious by the sounds and smells of summer. I did not know that the season had caused my faintness until an elderly man came rattling along the walk on his bicycle, stopping just in front of where I sat on the front step attempting to recover.

"What do I smell?" I asked myself half out loud, but apparently loud enough for my fellow Cantabrigian to overhear. "What do I smell?"

"July, you asshole," he rasped at me. "It's July." And he rode off on his rickety way.

It is this sort of friendly communication that is possible only in July. All the northern hemisphere communicates. Life is ripe and mature, and every living organism relates one to another, men to women, shrubs to bushes; even poets, human poets, establish lengthy (and well-documented) relationships with fields of weeds regarded narrow-mindedly by others of us only as potential feed for livestock. These poets converse with fern and flower, arriving at the conclusion that in this laurel, this maidenhair, this eel grass, lies the secret of life itself.

What fine communication! What splendid insight! What an extraordinary relationship I find myself having with this month of July, not unlike, I imagine, that of a sensitive and trusting soul and a not particularly subtle rapist.

17th We were listening to Gershwin when it happened. Meli looked up at me from my lap and said it.

"Dr. Wolper, what do you say we get married, huh?"

"Why?" I asked, dumbfounded.

"Why not? You've only got a few more months to live. What the hell difference could it make?"

"But what purpose would it serve?"

"I don't *know* what *purpose* it would serve. Does it have to have a *function?* Can't it just *feel good?*" Meli was clearly exasperated. She got off the sofa and started pacing around the room.

"I'm sorry if I hurt your feelings," I said for her obvious pain.

"I'm not hurt, dammit," she said, turning her back to me so that I wouldn't see tears starting to form in her eyes. "I just want this thing between us to go somewhere. Jesus, if it can't go anywhere because of time, because corpses make lousy lovers, then I thought at the very least, we could get married. That's going somewhere with it."

"Meli," I said quietly, "we haven't even had sex."

"So what. Lots of people don't have sex until after they're married—or at least some don't—do they?" And then, very frustrated, "So, what are you saying, that first we have to screw?"

"You know that's not what I'm saying."

"Then what the hell *are* you saying, Dr. Wolper?" She was now crying openly, tears streaming down her cheeks. "Because I *love* you, dammit, and I want to be *married* to you."

"You can still love me without being married to me," I suggested.

"No, you can't, Dr. Wolper." Meli sniffled and wiped her nose with the back of her forearm. "Love doesn't last. You have to get married. It's a law of nature."

"I'm not familiar with it." I tried not to antagonize the young lady.

"That's because you've locked yourself in that goddam laboratory for the last fifty years."

"How does this law of nature work?"

"Well, I don't understand it perfectly, you know. I'm no scientific genius like you, for chrissake, but it works something like this. After you fall in love with someone it lasts only awhile. I think it's six months. That's what they mean when they say that the honeymoon's over. Then you don't love the person any more, so, if you haven't gotten married yet, then you break up."

"And if you *have* gotten married?"

"Then you live together for the rest of your lives and raise kids and all that stuff."

"Without love."

"Dammit you're dumb sometimes, Dr. Wolper. Yes. You live together without love. I told you it only lasts six months. Didn't you hear a goddam word I said?"

"Doesn't it feel lonely living with someone without love for your whole life?"

"Of course it feels lonely. Everybody's lonely. Getting married doesn't change that. You don't *hate* the other person, you know. You like each other well enough. You're just not in *love* with each other any more. You feel something else."

"You don't think you could love someone for a whole lifetime?"

"Dr. Wolper, are you putting me on? Of course you can't. Aren't you a doctor? If I got turned on for my whole life like I do when I'm in love, I'd die of dehydration. You've only got so much juice, you know. You feel other things. It's a different kind of relationship."

"I don't think I've heard of the other kind of relationship."

"Are you sure?"

"Almost positive."

"Hmmm." Meli's eyes widened as she believed that she had something that she could teach me. She wiped the dampness of the last remaining tears from her face and returned to the sofa, keeping appropriate distance between us.

"Well, like I told you, I'm no expert on these things because I've never been married before, but as near as I can figure it out, what happens is kind of like running a business. You've each got jobs to do, and what you feel, I guess, is like *pride* at doing a job well."

"What *keeps* you together, if you don't love each other any more?"

"The job, I guess. Someone's got to do it, especially if you've got kids. The only reason I can see why people get divorced is because one of the people stopped doing his job or is screwing it up, and the other person's got to do it all. That's not fair, so they get divorced. If you've got to do *your* job *and* the other guy's, what's the purpose of living together? It just makes more work, and you're angry all the time because you're doing two jobs."

"And there aren't any feelings about all this?"

"Dr. Wolper, are you just being stupid on purpose or something? I told you that there're feelings. There's *pride*. And it doesn't mean that you can't have fun, for chrissake. You can have all the fun you want. It's just not love. Now it's a *relationship*."

"Isn't love a relationship?"

"Jesus, no! Love is fate. It's something that just happens. You can't *work* on love like you can work on a relationship. Love just comes and goes. It's destiny. It's like when Kennedy drove Mary Jo Kopechne off the bridge last night. It just happens and who the hell knows why. That's why you need love. Love comes along and lets you get married, and then it's not needed any more, because you're too busy with all the stuff you've got to do to keep alive and raise a family and all, so, poof, it's gone."

"Poof," I agreed.

"Poof," Meli explained.

"Well, I've really got to think this thing over, Meli. It sounds complicated."

"Oh, it is," Meli concurred. "It's the most complicated thing in the whole goddam world. It's more complicated than all of math and science put together."

"You'll give me a few days to think this over?"

"Sure, but remember what I said. Love can go at any second, and there's no way of knowing ahead of time."

"I remember. Poof," I said.

"Poof," Meli repeated.

18th We took a walk this afternoon and stopped at the playground across the street to watch the children play. I took this opportunity to explain to Meli about the third-generation lethal mutant.

"You mean these kids are never going to be able to have kids who can have kids?"

"Exactly. Three generations after the A-bomb. First generation was all of us alive at the time. You and others around your age are the second generation. The third generation is your children."

"I don't believe it. How could that happen to everybody in the whole world? Everybody didn't get radiation."

"I'm not sure how it happened. Maybe the blasts produced a virus that spread like an epidemic. We didn't notice it because it had no symptoms. It only affected our genes. Who knows."

"Can it do that? Can you have something do something to your genes that you don't find out about until the kids have kids?"

"Absolutely."

"Why don't you tell someone?"

"I've tried. No one's listened. They don't want to hear. Besides, I have no real proof. It's just conjecture, putting a few things together. I'm concerned though. There's no doubt in my mind. We're it, Meli. Us and our kids. Then that's it. That's why I've been working so hard all these years on my research."

"Well, *I'll* tell everyone. We've got to let people know, Dr. Wolper."

"What makes you think they'll listen to you if they haven't listened to me? No. You don't have any more proof that I do."

"At least I can try."

"They'll lock you up."

"What did they say to you? They didn't lock you up."

"No, it's all right for scientists to be a little crazy. It's called eccentric."

"But what did they say?"

"They said it was an *interesting hypothesis, theoretically possible*."

"And that's all?"

"That's it. I'm an old man telling the world that the sky's falling."

"Well, you've got to get back to work right away, Dr. Wolper. I mean it. I've read some books about people being doomed and all that, but this is the most horrible thing I can imagine. A whole goddam world of people who can't screw. It's a fucking nightmare."

20th I have seen some interesting inventions and discoveries in my lifetime. I've seen the automobile, electricity, radio, television, and their progeny overrun the world, and I've seen them modified and used in a world war to produce more death and destruction that all the other wars throughout history combined. Destiny has not had a hand in this. This has been the careful meticulous planning of Man.

Today a group of men landed on the moon and went for a walk. I have nothing to say.

21st "Isn't that fantastic, Dad? We're on the moon! Did you watch that on TV?" Arnold was in his usual enthusiastic frame of mind this evening.

"Yes, I saw it," I answered.

"Well, isn't it the most exciting thing you've ever seen in your whole life, huh?"

"Nope."

"It's not?"

"Nope."

"You mean you've seen things more exciting?"

"Nope."

"You're being crazy, Dad. Why do you do this to me? Do you get some special thrill out of driving me crazy?"

"Nope."

"Is that all you're going to say tonight? Nope?"

"Nope."

"Well, I don't care what you say, Dad. I think that landing on the moon's magnificent. Do you realize the possibilities? It's a whole new market."

"Arnold, there're only two people up there now, and they're leaving shortly. It's hardly a new market."

"But soon, Dad. Soon. The possibilities are endless."

The conversation ended. Arnold sat uncomfortably in his chair, folding and unfolding his legs. He sipped his coffee. He hummed a little. Then he got up and walked around the study, stopping at the open window to push his nose against the screen and take a deep breath. After a few minutes he walked over to the shelves and ran his fingers across the books. Getting bored with this after several minutes, he returned to his chair and lit a cigarette.

"How have you been, Arnold?" I finally asked.

"Oh, fine, Dad. Just fine. How about you?"

"Fine, Arnold."

"That's good to hear, Dad."

There was another long pause.

"Arnold, was there something in particular you wanted to talk to me about this evening? Or is this just another in a series of warm evenings between us?"

"I didn't know we'd had a series of warm evenings together," Arnold puzzled.

"We haven't, Arnold. Why have you come?"

Arnold tamped out the cigarette he had just started and then promptly lit another one.

"Well, now that you bring it up, Dad. You know how we've talked from time to time about your not really needing a house this large and how you've had so many things on your mind these last few months?"

"Yes, I do recall these conversations."

"Well, I thought I might be able to take some of these burdens off your mind so you'd be free to concentrate on your work. What would you think of that, huh?"

"You'd like to act as my conservator," I restated the offer.

"Kind of, yes, Dad. It'd leave you completely free."

"And completely penniless."

"Not at all, Dad. Not at all. I wouldn't do that. Then there'd be nothing left for me in your will," and he got up and started pacing.

"Arnold, sit down." He sat. "Arnold, there isn't anything in my will for you."

Arnold turned a pasty pale gray.

"There isn't?" he croaked.

"Nope. You see, Arnold, a few years ago I sat down and figured that since you left for college I've given you almost $250,000, while I haven't given Rebecca and Claire anything at all. So I gave them each $250,000, and left just enough for me to live on and keep up the house. What's left will go to charity mostly, to Mrs. Mallory, for food necessary to keep my animals alive so that they don't have to be killed when I die, and, well, to a friend, who doesn't even know she's getting anything."

"To a *girl* friend?" Arnold asked in a barely audible voice.

"If you will."

"I can't believe this. There's nothing there for me at all?"

"Nope. Nothing. Not a fuckin' piaster, as my attorney would say."

"How do I live?" Arnold did not look well.

"Might I suggest *earning* a living?"

"I do earn a living."

"No, Arnold, you do not *earn* a living. You *contrive* a living."

"Dad, it's just not fair to ask me to change my whole life-style when I'm this old. I'm like an old worn shoe. My shape is formed."

"Well, Arnold. You've just worn through the soles. Cat's Paw is out of business. And the jolly old shoemaker is leaving soon for a rendezvous with his Master Cobbler. You're on your own, Pinocchio."

"You're not funny, Dad."

"I'm not trying to be. I'm trying to emphasize the reality of the situation to you, Arnold. There's no more money coming. None. It's up to you, now, what you do with your life."

"Dad, you're not being realistic. I have a family to support. If I'm completely cut off, Marge is going to leave me. She's used to a particular life-style, you know. She's not going to change just like that. She'll leave first."

"That's between you two."

"Dad, look, you're not just talking about some hypothetical theory about chemicals or something. You're talking about the substance of life. That's all there is, Dad. It's money. It's what makes life work. It's life's energy, it's power, it's food. Without it, life just stops. It dries up and rots. This is America in the twentieth century, not medieval Europe. I don't farm and hunt and barter for the rest. I use money. Who my friends are depends on how much money I've got. Where I live depends on money. Whether my kids, your grandchildren, go to a decent school depends on money. My *happiness* depends on money. *Everything* depends on money. Absolutely *everything*. And don't give me any of this crap about love, because that depends on money more than anything else. Romeo and Juliet weren't *paupers*, you know. Hamlet was a lousy *king*. You can only walk on the beach for so long. Then you've got to begin with the dinners out and movies and shows and parties, vacations, trips, clothes, haircuts, tennis, skiing, football games, perfumes, and deodorants. It costs a dime to go to the john, and twenty cents a night to screw if you don't want to have kids because that takes even more money. Love needs money just like everything else. It takes money to get married and a marriage stays together as long as there's enough money. You name me one thing in this world that happens without money that isn't a lousy sunset or chemical reaction or something. If it happens, money made it happen. It's that simple. Money is life and that's all there is to it. When you cut off my money, you cut off my air, my blood, my life. Don't you see?"

"Aghast" is the word I think would best describe what I felt as I listened to this. I just couldn't believe it. I had created a monster that first day I gave him fifty cents to open a lemonade stand. I had brought to life a wild beast that thrived on capitalism. I was appalled. Fortunately, Meli walked in just as Arnold finished. She walked over to where I sat on the couch, kissed me lightly on the forehead and plopped herself down on the sofa next to me.

"Who are *you*?" Arnold asked flabbergasted.

"I'm Dr. Wolper's nineteen-year-old nymphomaniac who's living here to learn classical music," she smiled. "Who are you?"

I made a stab. "Arnold is Dr. Wolper's thirty-nine-year-old numismaniac who's come here to appropriate his estate." Arnold was unappreciative.

"I'm going," Arnold announced. "Are you sure you're not going to change your mind, Dad?"

"Nope. I'm sure."

"Very well. Very well," and he left the study without even a farewell handshake. Even Huns touched blades before doing each other in.

"Nice to meet you, Arnold," Meli shouted after him. Then she turned to me.

"Is he some relative of yours?" she asked.

"Just barely."

"'Very well' what? What did he mean 'very well'?"

"Loosely translated, Meli, it means 'This is War.'"

23rd Science, in clearing the Forest of Ignorance and Superstition, has left certain areas untouched, certain Wilderness Areas, as reminders of our Priceless Heritage and as a refuge for those oppressed by the efficiency and precision of the Cities of Knowledge.

In my latest safari through this field of Thickets, I have come across the densest area of the ecological preserve, the relationship of cytoplasm and nucleus, planted deep among the foxtail and mesquite. Thriving among the bush and scrub, it is resistant to identification and transplant, pleased to maintain its existence in anonymity.

Occasionally, it allows us explorers a glimpse of it through gourds and neurospora, snails and paramecia. The acetabularia plant grows a new cap after its nucleus has been removed, but the isolated nucleus grows nothing at all. Spiders of the same species spin the same-shaped webs. Determined by genes? An anal plate disc in a drosophila embryo, transferred 70 times, undergoing 350 cell divisions, still becomes an anal plate when put into a larva. Yet, sometimes, it switches. It becomes, not an anal plate, but an antenna, an eye, a leg, or thorax. But never half of antenna and half an anal plate. When it makes up its mind, it does not swerve. The switch is complete, always. It produces a different but perfect organ. Stability is the rule, but destiny governs.

This switching back and forth, this delightful changing partners, can never be gene mutation. Too many cells are involved, and they would all have to mutate in the same exact way at the same exact time. No, indeed. It is a courtship between the cytoplasm and the nucleus, a tumultous marriage, I am convinced. And all relationships are uncertain, at best. Meli and me, Boris and me, Boris and Barbara, Arnold and Money, who knows who is doing what to whom and what will happen? It is no different with Cytoplasm and Nucleus, tentative, hesitant friends, cooing from the day they shared the same slimy cradle.

The cytoplasm lullabies the cranky nucleus, feeds him his bottle, rocks him gently into the Land of Nod. The nucleus strokes the fussing cytoplasm, dangles some shiny genetic toy to distract her, makes ridiculous faces until she has forgotten that she is soaked in urine. What a fine pair of infants this cytoplasm and this nucleus make. How clever of them as toddlers to have conjured up this game called Destiny. And how impossible we have found it to recover from the mischief they created at terrible two.

I am no closer, it seems, to my Great Wiper.

24th I informed Meli today that there was no sense in my retrieving her ovum this month. The Great Wiper is nowhere to be seen, and it makes little difference what I do if I haven't my Wiper.

Meli seemed little bothered by not having to undergo "surgical rape," as she so delicately put it, and agreed to make herself available next month. Of course, her real interest these days is our undetermined betrothal, and any conversation that isn't focused on this subject is mildly diverting to her, at best.

"You haven't forgotten?" she asked me as we sat together in the living room this evening (Handel, Haydn, and Hindemith).

"I'm old and feeble, Meli, but I'd hardly forget that someone had asked me to marry her. I just need more time."

"I didn't ask you to marry me, dammit. I only said I thought we ought to," she corrected.

"I'm sorry, Meli. I misunderstood."

"Well, just as long as that's clear. I didn't make any goddam proposal to you."

"It's clear," I assured her.

"Good. Because I'm not going to take all the blame when the damn thing blows up."

"You're sure it's going to blow up?"

"Sure I'm sure. Marriages are made to self-destruct, for godsakes. Those are the hardest times."

"Meli, it seems to me that you've painted a rather bleak picture of a sacred institution. It can't be entirely a disaster."

"Look, Dr. Wolper. I don't know anything about sacred institutions, but I do know that marriage is no goddam picnic. As far as I'm concerned, it's the only attitude that makes sense to bring into a marriage. Why the hell do you think all these marriages fall apart? It's because the people go into them expecting it's going to be all lovey dovey, then whammo, the dishwasher breaks down and the roof's leaking and you've lost your job, one kid's in bed with the measles and the other's out on bail, and on top of it all, you've got your goddam period. That's why love just isn't necessary. When you're going through a life like that every day, if someone gives you a lousy handshake your whole day is made. What the hell's the use of love when you're numb?"

"It sounds very depressing, Meli."

"You got an alternative, Dr. Wolper?"

25th It's hard to know what to do with Meli's noninvitation for conjugal suicide. On the one hand, there's no reason at all for us to get married. On the other hand, as Meli has so eloquently pointed out, there's no reason not to. I don't suppose that He takes marital status into consideration when determining whether one of His flock is in a state of grace, under the unlikely assumption that I have maintained my candidacy status over the years.

There is something extremely appealing about spending the months remaining to me in marital terror with a nineteen-year-old glandular case. Who knows, we each might learn something. After all, it has been almost thirty-three years since I've been married, presumably a respectable waiting period after the death of one's spouse. It might be interesting to discover whether anything has changed with the venerable institution over the decades, not that Meli can ever be compared with Lucy.

I think I shall talk it over tomorrow with Sarah, who I'm sure should have some insight into the problem. Six marriages have a way of providing a person with extraordinary perspective.

26th "With the first marriage I kept saying 'Isn't this wonderful?'," Sarah told me as we sat opposite each other having lunch on her screened-in porch today.

"Then one day, about two years after we were married, Jake, my husband, turned to me as he was shaving and said 'You know something, Sarah. This is *not* wonderful. This morning I have decided that this isn't even mildly pleasant. Good-bye,' and he left that morning never to return."

She tapped her fingers on the glass table where we sat.

"For the second marriage I kept asking myself what I was doing wrong. Nothing worked. In bed or out of bed. I'd go left, and Sam would go right. I'd stay home, and he'd go out. I'd get dressed up, and he'd go bowling. Then one Sunday after dinner I stayed, and he left. I hardly noticed the difference."

I listened intently to this epic portrayal of intimacy.

"With my third husband, Ben, it was different. We were completely in tune. When I thought I'd like flowers, they'd materialize magically on the table. When he'd be entering the house in a bad mood after work, I'd know before the door handle turned and have soothing music on the radio and a drink ready before the door closed. Before I could get depressed, he'd have me feeling hopeful. Before I grew tired of a dress, a new one would arrive. And I always liked the dress, Harry. It was always exactly what I wanted. The relationship was absolutely perfect. I left in six weeks.

"I swore that with my fourth husband it was going to work out, come hell or high water. And having also had three previous marriages, so did he. Jesus, did we work on that relationship. We discussed everything, analyzed our feelings, spoke candidly, saw a marriage counsellor, worked at the relationship, sacrificed for each other. There was no way we were going to give up on this marriage. Sometime after we had been married for about three years, I received a call asking me to come and get my husband. He was walking through the Boston Common asking everyone he met to marry him and crying profusely. Boston State Hospital gave him a preliminary diagnosis of *marital exhaustion*. In any event, when he recovered he was discharged under the stipulation that he get divorced immediately and never remarry. I was terribly disappointed because I really felt that we had reached a sort of plateau of accommodation before he lost his mind."

I offered my sympathy.

"By the time I met Joe, I couldn't have cared less. We joked about it continually. Marriage is a farce. Why bother? We've done this thing for convention. If it lasts, it lasts. If it doesn't, it doesn't. In this particular case, after eleven of the most insouciant weeks in my entire life, it didn't.

"John, my sixth, was different. I really felt that this was going to be it, and I was terribly disappointed that he failed to survive the recessional. He was an older man, and, as near as we could tell, shortly after we took our places in the reception line, the microwave ovens of the caterers shorted his pacemaker. I was so good at this by now, however, that I didn't notice anything until midway through the reception line when I became so infuriated by the way he was leaning on me and staring at people with his mouth open that I pulled my arm away and he crumpled on top of the maid of honor. Since all his relatives were there already, we converted the reception to a wake and the party went on. I've often wondered, if I hadn't yanked my arm away like that, how long we would have been married before I realized he was dead."

I took the last bite of my sandwich and lightly dabbed the corners of my mouth with the napkin. I cleared my throat.

"So," I asked, "what do you think, Sarah? Should I get married a second time?"

"I don't know, Harry," she said staring far off into the distance, "there's a lot to think about, I'd say. A hell of a lot." Her voice trailed off into the breezy afternoon.

27th I returned today to my frog ova, transplanting nuclei and inserting the substances still brewing in my grandson's wading pool. How I wish I could call it the Great Wiper.

I learned nothing, absolutely nothing. The theory is so simple. Extract the ovum, insert Lucy's nucleus, inject the Great Wiper to rejuvenate the cytoplasm, parthenogenesize, and reimplant in Meli's uterus. I say these steps over and over to myself like a child's nursery rhyme. I've hummed it to a tune I've fabricated. I have even sat for hours here at my workbench, waiting for the Great Wiper to develop and turning my life's work into limericks.

There once was an ovum whose nucleus
was removed and transplanted without a fuss.
Its cytoplasm was wiped,
then parthenogenically piped,
way up into Meli's sweet uterus.

Oh, well. It passes the time.

29th I got a letter from Paul today. The writing was shaky and the letter rambled on incoherently for several pages. It was horribly painful to read, particularly the last paragraph, which was written in the third person.

> As the moon circles our fragile planet, with the certain circumference of a silver orb raising its carcass from the cold black sea each night, with such honorable regularity will the days come and go. Paul remains trapped, condemned, doomed to finish his circuit in the interminable night of McLean Hospital. There is no more day. There is no medication left on the shelves to relieve the visions and the pain. Paul's psychiatrist talks of coming to terms with darkness now. There is no more talk of light. All that is left is electricity. Tomorrow they will begin shock treatment. It is the last resort. Paul is a last resort. They will drive in one pain to drive out another. They have asked him for approval. Do it, Paul said. Do it. Paul asks after your health and welfare and wishes you well with your novel. Lots of fucking luck, he says, and goodbye.

It was signed "Parnash".

I raced over to the hospital to try to see him. He refused.

On the way back, I stopped at Maureen's.

"This is the hard part," she told me.

I returned home and started drinking scotch. It's a sure danger signal. Mrs. Mallory responded to the alarm at the first sound of the bottle clinking against the glass.

"What is it, Dr. Wolper?" Mrs. Mallory asked with great concern, wringing her hands on her apron.

"I've lost control, Mrs. Mallory," I told her. "I'm out of control. My mind is jammed with Paul, Boris, Meli, Arnold, Maury, my work. I'm suffocating."

Mrs. Mallory thought about this.

"Dr. Wolper, it's none of my business now, but I've been thinking something for a long time, and I'm going to tell you what's been on my mind. No offense, but you should retire, Dr. Wolper. Go visit your grandchildren, rest on your laurels. It's time to relax."

I ran the images through my mind silently.

"I need to stay in the midst of this. I can't afford to leave yet. What I need is more control, Mrs. Mallory. I've lost touch. It isn't there, anymore. There's something missing, and I can't figure it out. My mind is losing its grip. It's as though all of this isn't enough. I need something more."

I poured myself another drink. Mrs. Mallory shuddered.

"Other than a major fire, Dr. Wolper, it's hard to think of anything that's missing."

"I know. I know. I'm stymied. And you know what bothers me more than anything else? I'm bored."

"Oh, Dr. Wolper, that *is* serious. When you get bored, almost anything can happen. That's when you get yourself into real trouble."

"I know," and I took a long drink. "I've got most of the world caving in on me, and I'm bored. It makes no sense at all."

"If you were anyone else, Dr. Wolper, I'd say you needed some good old-fashioned religion. But you need religion like Mr. Nixon needs a mirror. It's best to leave well enough alone."

"Mrs. Mallory, you're right. I must stop feeling sorry for myself. I'm just going to have to learn to live with my handicap."

"Which handicap is that, Dr. Wolper?" Mrs. Mallory appeared confused.

"Life, Mrs. Mallory."

31st

The Adventures of Boris Lafkin

Chapter Two (continued):

In Which Our Hero's Act Becomes Less Together

If someone were assigned the task of constructing a device that would take human beings of above-average intelligence who are moderately well put together and reduce them to inadequate weak stupid sniveling worms, or a reasonable facsimile thereof, they would construct a Medical College Admissions Test. I guarantee that no matter how bright you think you are, how emotionally stable, or how well fortified your ego boundaries, you will emerge three hours after you've started reading the exams feeling that you are indeed fortunate to be allowed room and board in this world. With luck, you think to yourself, you might be able to operate a ferryboat someday and substitute fresh air and sea breezes for the money, power, status, and professional fulfillment of a medical career.

During the long painful walk home you pull yourself together and try to push aside such vital issues as whether the reason why a Himalayan rabbit has white fur on his body but a black nose, ears, tail, and paws is because (a) these parts are too cool for gene action to produce melanin, (b) peripheral circulation is poor, (c) in most of the skin there is an absence of tyrosinase that is needed to produce pigment, or (d) the general skin temperature is too high for production of pigment; and glenoid is to humerus as acetabulum is to (a) coracoid, (b) femur, (c) radius, (d) tibia; more to the point, is the doctrine that truth is the practical efficacy of an idea, based on a theory of the mind as an instrument for problem-solving that emphasizes meaning and truth in relation to the results or consequences of an idea, known as (a) Pragmatism, (b) Positivism, (c) Probabilism, or (d) Personalism; is the general formula representative of esters given by (a) ROH, (b) RCOR, (c) RCOOH, (d) RCOOR; and, finally, did Jerome Kern write (a) *The Merry Widow,* (b) *Oklahoma,* (c) *Rose Marie,* or (d) *Showboat.* The answers, for those who are particularly masochistic are, in order, d, b, a, d, d. My answers at the time of the exam were, in order, a, d, b, c, and d. I had seen *Showboat* on television the weekend before.

By the time I reached the apartment, I was no longer depressed. I was buoyant.

"You know," I said to Barbara laughing merrily, "I've been thinking a lot for the last few weeks about whether I *really* want to be a physician. Really, *really.* And you know, it's funny, but the more I think about it, the more I think that I don't, that I'd be happier out on the open sea, the salt breeze blowing my hair, the simple comradeship of my seamates."

"It was that bad, huh?" Barbara said.

"It wasn't good," I informed her. "Not good at all."

"Well, you know, Boris, they make those things so you have to get *some* wrong. Otherwise, they'd never be able to score them."

"But don't they also expect you to get some *right?*"

"You don't think you got *any* right?"

"No, no. I got a couple right about musical comedies. But I think that was about it. You look worse than I feel. It's okay. I'll get into medical school somehow."

Barbara looked terribly pale.

"No, it's not that. I've got one of those headaches again. Aspirin doesn't help it. I think I need tranquilizers or something. I'm just too uptight all the time, Boris."

"Is the marriage getting to you? I've sort of noticed that you've been having a lot of these headaches just about the time we usually have sex."

"I know. But I don't think it's us. Maybe it's just the pressure of school. You want to hear something really crazy? I was standing in the kitchen a few minutes ago and I fainted. Isn't that ridiculous?"

"Hysterical. I'm going to call a doctor. Maybe you've got one of those viruses or something."

"Boris. First of all, viruses don't give you headaches. And second of all, it's Saturday. You're never going to get a doctor."

"Then I've got another idea. Let's take a walk up to the end of the block to the hospital. We'll go to the emergency room. They'll check you out, give you some tranquilizers or something, and you're home in an hour."

"Boris, that's ridiculous. You don't go to the emergency room for a headache."

"You do when you've been having them for several weeks and you faint. It's a rule. The nurses are trained not to give disapproving looks to people who've fainted within three hours of the time they show up at the emergency room. I read it in the *Merck Manual.*"

"Okay," she agreed reluctantly, "but only an hour. I wouldn't go, you know, but I feel so damn lousy. I also think I'm going to vomit."

Barbara put on my lumber jacket, and we walked in the cold November afternoon up the street to the hospital, kicking the last leaves of autumn, and talking about my exam.

"Who do you want to be?" I asked as we approached the hospital. "Mrs. Lafkin or Miss Spencer?"

"Mrs. Lafkin, dear," Barbara smiled sarcastically at me. "Mrs. Boris Lafkin. See my ring," and she flashed her finger at me, which displayed a gold ring.

"Where the hell did you get that?" I asked.

"I found it on top of your dresser. Whose is it?"

"Damned if I know. Probably Marty's, but she wouldn't wear it," and we entered the hospital.

Cambridge General Hospital was being rebuilt, or renovated, modernized, added to, whatever. In any case, the place was full of ladders and plastic-covered doorways. Barbara sat down because she had begun to feel worse, while I gave the nurse the information on her. I then returned to the bench and sat down so she could rest her head on my shoulder. She was in a great deal of pain, and I went up to the nurse several times to get some emergency attention at the emergency room. Headaches, apparently, are not on the top of the critical list.

After forty-five minutes, a nurse came and took Barbara to an examining room where she stayed for a half-hour. I saw various doctors and nurses go in and out, and once, while I was standing outside the door, I saw, as it opened, Barbara sitting on the examing table, half naked, two doctors standing in front of her, shining one of those lights into her eyes. She saw me and waved merrily. I assumed that they had already given her some medication, and she was responding nicely.

When I'm in a hospital, my imagination goes crazy. I picture me or whomever I'm with croaking in the most flamboyant way possible. People rushing from every direction. Bells and buzzers clanging, nurses holding hypodermic needles up to the light and squirting out air bubbles, oxygen masks clamping down over the face of the victim, young interns with perspiration dripping from their anguished faces pounding on the patient's chest, while the buzzer on the electrocardiograph makes that long shrill screech. I've got it all down pat. The patient never makes it, and I alone am left with the task of notifying the next of kin.

I was in the middle of such a fantasy when the resident strolled out holding Barbara's arm to tell me, much to my relief and only slight disappointment, that Barbara was fine.

Barbara looked better, too, and she came over to kiss me on the cheek.

"How're you feeling?" I asked.

"Still a little woozy," she admitted, "but they've given me something and the headache's a little better."

"What's she got?" I asked the earnest young resident who had introduced himself to me as Dr. Johnson. His name tag read "Oliver Johnson, M.D." I looked at it with a tinge of jealousy and hate after my morning's experience.

"Well." Dr. Johnson moved his glasses a little farther down on the end of his nose to look wisely over them at me. "It's hard to tell about headaches. Most headaches are from tension or are migraine. Barbara reports being tense, except that tension headaches are usually more toward the back of the head, the neck. She's also nauseous, so it could be a migraine, except she's never had a migraine before, she had no prodomal pain, and the pain is usually felt behind one or both eyes. It's probably not a migraine. Besides she reports some numbness in her left leg. I think we can rule out any sort of brain tumor. She has no muscle weakness, no convulsions, visual changes, speech difficulties, memory loss, et cetera. Of course, she does report losing consciousness a little while ago, which is definitely suspicious." He lowered his glasses even further on his nose and tapped his pencil against his teeth. "However, it's unlikely that it's some form of intracranial hemorrhage. The headache, in these cases, has a very sudden onset and Barbara tells me she's had this one for several weeks. There is some distinctive nuchal rigidity, that's a stiff neck—"

"Thank you," I said.

"Oh, that's all right. If there's anything else you don't understand, just ask me," he smiled broadly.

I was going to ask him about Himalayan rabbits' fur and truth as the practical efficacy of an idea, but I figured that, as a licensed physician, he'd be so bored by such intuitively obvious inquiries he'd think me silly, so I just nodded for him to go on.

"Well, as I was saying, even though Barbara shows some nuchal rigidity and a slightly elevated B.P.—blood pressure—"

I smiled.

"There's no positive Kernig, no third-nerve paralysis, and we don't know about her Babinski."

"You don't know?"

"Well, for some people it's really hard to get an accurate Babinski reflex, that's when you run a hard object along the sole of a patient's foot, and Barbara could have a positive Babinski. It's hard to tell. You see, Mr. Lafkin, 2 percent of us have positive Babinski's, anyway. My best guess would be to rule out subarachnoid hemorrhage—that's bleeding inside the head more or less—and an aneurysm—that's when a little bubble forms in the wall of a blood vessel and then," he put his thumb in his cheek and yanked it out, "pop! It's all over."

"Well," I offered my own medical assessment, "it doesn't look like Barbara's *popped.*"

"Right," he laughed heartily. "You'd *know* it if she had. She'd be dead." He continued to laugh but noticed, perceptively, that we weren't laughing with him. He cleared his throat and stopped. "Look, I wouldn't worry about aneurysms if I were you. There were more people struck by lightning last year than had aneurysms."

"Why'd you scare the hell out of us then?" I asked irritably while Barbara tried to shut me up.

"Well," Dr. Oliver Johnson became all business, "Mrs. Lafkin tells me that you're interested in becoming a physician, Mr. Lafkin. I thought you might find it educational."

"Nope. I'm going to become a sea captain," I said.

Barbara was about to tell me something about my mouth when she turned pale again and announced that she had to throw up. Dr. Johnson led her to a toilet and when she emerged, victorious, she seemed better.

Dr. Johnson surveyed the situation.

"I'd like to keep Mrs. Lafkin overnight for some tests and observation," he announced.

I was in no mood to allow him to use Barbara as an instructional aid for his interns.

"I think she's feeling better," I announced my own medical assessment. "No popping as far as I can tell, Dr. Johnson. And where there's no popping, there's no staying."

"I'd like to stay," Barbara said.

A chill ran through me.

"Sure, sure, if you want to," I said, and helped her back to the examining room where she put on a hospital gown and lay down on the stretcher.

I walked beside her as they wheeled her in for X rays, waited outside, and then rejoined her for the elevator ride up to her room.

"How're you feeling?" I asked.

"Oh, better, Boris, Much better. I just thought I'd be much less of a burden to you if I stayed here than if I came home. You really wanted to go see *A Man for All Seasons* tonight, and I know you wouldn't have gone if I stayed at home. Here they'll kick you out at eight o'clock and you'll have to go. Besides, you don't want an invalid at home to take care of after you've just embarked on a new career on the high seas."

"I changed my mind. If Oliver Johnson can be an M.D., so can I."

"That's great, Boris. You can always join the Navy after you've finished school," she smiled.

We were in her room now. Dr. Johnson joined us along with two nurses and an intern. The lesson was about to begin. I was being shooed out.

"Any last words you want to say before you pop?" I asked her.

"Yes," Barbara said seriously. "Stay my friend, Boris. Please, always, stay my friend."

They were moving her from the stretcher to the bed when she screamed. It was the loudest scream I'd ever heard. It was shrill and cold and horribly long. Then suddenly it stopped. Barbara fell limp as they quickly lowered her to the bed, her body in a fetal position formed during the scream.

Dr. Johnson asked me to wait outside. As I left I could see that Barbara was unconscious. A nurse ran out of the room to the nurses' station and picked up the phone. Her voice came over the loudspeaker system.

"Code blue. Room 704. Code blue. Room 704," and then she ran back to the room, pushing a cart in front of her.

I could hear footsteps from every direction. Five, maybe six interns and physicians raced into the room, some lugging medical gear on carts behind them. Nurses ran in and out. Orderlies walked briskly into the room and then shot out down the hall. Dr. Johnson bolted out the door and ran to the nurses' station. He picked up the phone, dialed, and began a heated discussion with someone.

It was just as I had imagined. Just like on television and the movies. I didn't appreciate the life-as-art metaphor. I was scared out of my mind. I kept hearing Barbara's scream bouncing and bouncing around inside my empty head and every time I heard it, I kept thinking, if death has a sound, this is it.

August

1st The Adventures of Boris Lafkin

CHAPTER THREE:
Our Hero's Act—Together or Otherwise—Evaporates

Of course I didn't for a minute believe that there was actually anything seriously wrong with Barbara, at least nothing that couldn't be fixed.

For twenty minutes, I watched people rush in and out of Barbara's room. Each new event I fit into a new scheme, a developing theory, but always toward the ultimate conclusion that this was really nothing serious.

And then, finally, after twenty minutes of intellectual gymnastics, came an event I could not accommodate, a priest.

I hadn't seen him at first. I had my eyes riveted on the door to Barbara's room. Then out of the corner of my eyes I saw a dark figure walking down the hall. I continued to avoid looking until, eventually, it was impossible.

I turned my head and watched him hurriedly approaching, adjusting his amice with one hand, a prayer book and a box of sacred articles in the other.

I found myself saying over and over to myself, "Please, keep going. Go down the hall. Someone else's room. Somewhere else," and then he opened Barbara's door and disappeared behind it.

My heart stopped. It just stood still, frozen. My saliva dried. My eyelids stopped blinking. My breathing ceased. I sat in total and complete suspended animation. Only my sight and hearing functioned. I could hear a ritualistic monotone.

The door opened and stayed opened for a few seconds while a doctor said something quietly to a nurse who was still in the room. No one was rushing any more. Between their white jackets I could see the priest touching Barbara's eyes, then her mouth, nose, hands, and feet. He was still mumbling when the door closed.

I remained paralyzed, unable to move to ask the doctor what was happening, hypnotized by the liturgical chanting and trying to send a telepathic message to the priest, "Please say it in Latin. Barbara doesn't like the English version. Please, please, hear what I'm thinking for chrissakes and say the last rites in Latin."

The priest was done quickly. He came out the door and walked over to me, put his paraphernalia on the chair beside me, and started to fold the long purple scarf.

"I'm Father O'Malley," he introduced himself. "Are you the husband?"

I couldn't talk. My eyes were beginning to cloud and blur.

"I'm terribly sorry," he said to me. "Were you married long?"

I tried to open my mouth but nothing happened.

"It's a tragedy. A real tragedy. The Lord, indeed, moves in mysterious ways."

Please, I thought to myself, not a lecture on divine providence.

"This is the fourth today," Father O'Malley continued to chat. "Quite a day. Quite a day. I almost didn't make your wife, you know. You're a lucky man. Five more minutes, and I'd have been out the door."

"Shit."

"Son?"

"I said 'Shit,' Father. 'Shit.' That's what I said."

"My son, you must console yourself that she has fought a good fight, finished her course and kept the faith. *To live is Christ, and to die is gain.* Philippians. I, 21."

"Father, please don't quote scripture to me."

"I understand your grief, Mr. Lafkin. Many have found solace in the New Testament at times like this. Even Christ called out, '*Eli, Eli, lama sabachthani?*' That is to say, '*My God, my God, why hast Thou forsaken me?*' "

"Please, Father, I'm not consoled."

"*Neither death, nor life, nor angels, nor principalities, nor powers, nor things present, nor things to come, nor height, nor depth, nor any other creature, shall be able to separate us from the love of God, which is in Christ Jesus our Lord.* Romans, VIII, 38 and 39."

"I'm an atheist."

"I beg your pardon?"

"An atheist, Father. A nonbeliever. Heathen. Even worse. A heretic."

Father O'Malley looked deep into my eyes, trying to determine whether I had gone mad under the strain.

"I don't suppose that a parable would be of interest to you then?" he asked hopefully. "Because I think I've got one here that'll really do the trick."

"Not likely, Father. Unless, of course, it'll bring Barbara back from the dead. You got a little something up your alb that'll do that, Father?"

Father O'Malley was losing his patience.

"You'll excuse me," he grumbled at his lost lamb and hustled down the corridor.

Dr. Johnson came out the door to Barbara's room. He did not look good. He came over and sat down on the chair next to mine.

"Mr. Lafkin," he began weakly, "your wife is in serious condition."

"Is?"

"Yes, your wife's situation is serious."

"*Is?* You said, '*is*'?"

"Yes."

"You mean she's not dead?"

"No. She's not dead."

"She's alive?"

"Yes. She's alive."

"She's not dead. She's not dead! Fuck, man. Barbara is alive. She's alive. Fuck!" And I jumped up and hit my fist against the wall. "I knew it. I just knew it. That priest is crazy, man. You shouldn't let him talk to human beings. He's a crazy man. I thought Barbara was dead. He's a clerical lunatic."

"Sit down, Mr. Lafkin. Please sit down."

I sat down.

"Your wife has had a very severe cerebral hemorrhage."

I looked at him, not sure what he was saying.

"She's had an aneurysm," he continued.

I sat still for a minute without saying a word. Then I turned and looked him directly in the eyes.

"She popped," I said.

"She—uh—popped," he replied uncomfortably. "Of course, we can't be sure until after the autopsy. It's probably a Berry aneurysm. Usually where an artery branches nature provides us with an extra heavy layer of tissue since there's considerably more strain and pressure at the junction than at any other point. Every once in a while someone is born who doesn't have those extra layers of tissue. Nature forgets."

"Nature forgets," I repeated.

"They're walking time-bombs. A bubble forms over the years, and eventually it bursts. It can happen when the person is four years old or forty. There's no way of knowing. Some people may live their entire lives with an aneurysm and no one knows it."

"But you can't know for sure?" I asked hopefully.

"When it's going to burst?"

"No, whether it's an aneurysm. I mean, it could be something else. You said yourself that you have to do an autopsy to tell."

"We know it's an aneurysm, or at least a hemorrhage."

"But you don't know for *sure*," and I jumped up again. "It could be anything, a bad headache, the flu, even her period. Some women faint during their periods. I know. I read it a long time ago in this sex book about chickens that my mother gave me when I was ten. It could be a really lousy goddam period."

"Mr. Lafkin. It's not her period. She doesn't have the flu. She's had a *very bad cerebral hemorrhage*."

"And you don't know for sure."

"Sit down, Mr. Lafkin."

I sat down and tried very hard to think of what other syndromes could give a person a headache and unconsciousness.

"Mr. Lafkin, let me tell you what signs we've looked for and what we've found. First we looked at Barbara's eyes. They do not react to light. They are fixed. She is not unconscious, she is in a coma. When we looked into her eyes, we saw massive hemorrhaging of the vessels. The vessels in the eye are extremely responsive to increased intracranial pressure. When there is any pressure at all the blood vessels start to burst. There is so much blood in her eyes that the pressure in her head must be extremely high, Mr. Lafkin. Then we did a lumbar puncture, a spinal tap. That's what all the arguing on the phone was. I was speaking to the medical director of the hospital. I was against doing a tap because of the increased pressure. You see, Mr. Lafkin, when there is expansion of the brain because of blood and swelling, it has to go somewhere. There is only one opening, at the base of the skull, and sometimes the brain pushes down into that opening. It's called *coning*. It shoves itself down into that space like a cone filling a hole. Sometimes the lumbar puncture can precipitate that, but Dr. Rosen, the medical director, felt that because your wife was already in a fetal position, had lost consciousness once before, had unreactive pupils and evidence of massive hemorrhaging, it wouldn't make much difference if we did the puncture carefully. We did the tap, Mr. Lafkin. Usually the cerebrospinal fluid is colorless and clear and the pressure of it ranges from 100 to 200 millimeters of water, assuming that there's nothing, like a brain for example, blocking it. In your wife's case, Mr. Lafkin, her fluid was all blood. Her pressure was zero. There was none at all. She had completely coned because of the massive hemorrhaging."

I found I was becoming horribly nauseous.

"It's not her period then, is it?" I asked.

"No, Mr. Lafkin. I'm very sorry. It's not her period."

"Is there a bathroom around here, because I think I'm going to throw up?"

Dr. Johnson led me down the hall to the john. He waited outside while I went in and vomited. I wretched until my stomach muscles couldn't stand it anymore. Cold sweat poured from my forehead and clouded my eyes. My neck and throat ached with the strain of vomiting. And then my bowels began to give way. I sat down quickly, and spent a good ten minutes, alternating between my vomiting and my diarrhea, flushing every thirty seconds. When my insides were completely hollow, I sat on the john and cried, as though my tear ducts couldn't stand the burden of being the only organ left in me with fluid. It was your basic physiological catharsis, and I did it for all it was worth. I emerged fifteen minutes later, weak and exhausted. I could hardly walk. Dr. Johnson was still there, and he led me into an empty room and laid me down on the bed. I rested there, trying to catch my breath. Dr. Johnson sat on a chair beside the bed.

"Now what?" I finally asked.

"Now we wait," he answered.

"What are the chances?"

"Very poor," he said. "The damage has been *massive.*"

It was a word, *massive,* that I grew to hate. I'm still not particularly fond of it. Massive damage, a massive hemorrhage, massive deficit, massive dysfunction, a massive effort. One word used to tell it all.

"Will she die soon?"

"Probably within the next twenty-four hours, but it's hard to tell. It's a miracle that she's alive at all. Most people would be dead by now."

"She might make it then? You can't know for sure?"

"Mr. Lafkin, there's never anything in medicine that's 100 percent certain. Nothing happens *all* the time. But you shouldn't get your hopes up. There's been so much damage done to her brain that even if she were to regain consciousness, she would be—well—she wouldn't be the person you married."

"You mean she'd be paralyzed and have trouble talking and all that?"

"I mean, Mr. Lafkin, that she'd have no mind at all. She'd be a human vegetable."

I dismissed the thought immediately. This was Barbara he was talking about, not some junior college coed. This was the darling of the Harvard philosophy department. There was no way she was ever going to be a vegetable. I asked him to tell me what happens next.

"It's hard to tell. Right now she's breathing. She's maintaining her blood pressure, heart rate, and body temperature, but that's about all. Usually when someone cones, these centers go and she dies. For some reason your wife hasn't. My best guess would be that within the next day the continual swelling will shut off these centers and she'll die."

I pushed my head back into the pillow and closed my eyes. I tried hard to clear my mind so I could think this thing out rationally. I rested there for several minutes, silently trying to decide how to solve the problem. I decided, finally, I just wasn't going to let Barbara die. That was all there was to it. This was, after all, the 1960s we were living in, not the Dark Ages. Medical

Science would solve this, I was determined. I opened my eyes and turned to Dr. Johnson.

"We're going to lick this, Dr. Johnson. I know that we will," I informed him.

Dr. Johnson was not at all pleased with what he heard.

I continued. "We can give her lots of good care, rest, the blood will absorb itself, her brain will repair itself, and she'll be like new. We won't know the difference."

"The brain doesn't repair itself, Mr. Lafkin."

"Well, then, we'll give her medicines."

"There aren't any medicines that repair the brain."

"Okay. But can't other regions of the brain take over lost function? I mean, people with strokes do recover, you know."

"Yes, they do. But the damage is never this massive. People with strokes this severe usually die."

"But we don't really know how much has been damaged, do we? It could be only unimportant parts of the brain. It could, couldn't it?"

Dr. Johnson looked pained and frustrated that I refused to accept what he knew to be a fact, that Barbara was going to die.

"No, Mr. Lafkin, we don't know exactly what's been damaged. Theoretically, it's possible that your wife's damage could be restricted to less important parts of her brain, that she could recover and with therapy become completely functional again. But there aren't any parts of the brain that are *unimportant*. And the continued swelling and pressure in her head is cutting off oxygen to an increasing number of centers."

"Then we should operate and drain out the blood to reduce the pressure. At the same time we can repair the aneurysm *and* see how much damage has been done." I was very pleased. That was the answer. We could operate. I could have kicked myself for not thinking of it before. It was so obvious. You can operate on anything. Why hadn't I thought of that before? We'd go in there and fix everything up. Then Barbara would be good as new.

Dr. Johnson looked very uncomfortable. He talked but wouldn't look at me.

"We can't operate," he said.

"Why not?" He was taking away my last hope.

"We just can't."

"Why the hell not?"

"It just can't be done, that's all. Take my word for it. People have tried. I've seen it. It doesn't work."

"Why? Why doesn't it work?"

"Because the brain is swollen." Dr. Johnson looked like *he* was getting nauseous.

"So what? So the brain is swollen."

Dr. Johnson closed his eyes slowly and held very still. Then he opened his eyes and spoke his words carefully.

"When you operate, Mr. Lafkin, you open up the person's head. When the brain is as swollen as your wife's is, Mr. Lafkin, you can't fit it back in the skull. You have a brain, Mr. Lafkin, with no place to put it."

I felt myself getting nauseous again.

"So what do you do?" I asked numbly.

"You kill the patient, Mr. Lafkin. You kill her."

I suppose I lay there for about a half hour. Dr. Johnson left after a few minutes. I tried to sort it out. I was willing to accept that Barbara had had a "massive" cerebral hemorrhage. But, after that, what did we actually know for certain? That she was still alive. That's about all. We knew that most people die, but not *all* people. Barbara could be the exception. We knew that most people who recover are, as Dr. Johnson so delicately put it, human vegetables. But, again, Barbara was not most people, and we didn't really *know* what parts of her brain had and had not been damaged. For all we knew, she could recover completely with no damage whatsoever, and all the doctors would walk around scratching their heads and saying that they didn't understand how it happened. There isn't really very much we *did* know for certain, and that was how I was going to have to act, as though anything could happen. It was entirely up to me, I decided. I would have to do everything possible to make things turn out in the end with a living, breathing, conscious, thinking Barbara who wanted me to go to medical school in Beirut and was hoping, someday, to have the guts to go see a pornographic film. I found myself with an overwhelming urge to see Barbara.

I got up and found Dr. Johnson conferring with some nurses in the nurses' station. I asked if I could go in to see Barbara, and he said that I could.

It had just started to get dark. I opened the door slowly, not knowing what to expect. Barbara was lying on her back, asleep, her back raised slightly by the tilted bed. Her blond hair was spread out on the pillow and had a soft lustre under the diffused bed light. Someone had combed her hair.

She seemed relaxed, calm, no longer in pain. She was peaceful. Her color seemed good. I had expected a pale, dying person, her face still contorted in pain. I was startled by how healthy she looked. I decided that this person was going to live. I didn't know which person the doctors were talking about who had a swollen, bleeding brain inside of her, but it surely wasn't the person calmly sleeping on the bed in front of me. This was Barbara, and I knew what was wrong with her. She was recuperating from one of the lousiest goddam periods in the history of menstruation.

I pulled up a chair beside her bed and reached for her hand.

"How're you doing?" I asked. "Dammit, you scared the hell out of me, you know that?"

I held her hand tightly. I had never noticed how small her hands were. I ran my fingers across hers. I wanted her grip to tighten on my hand. "That'll come later," I thought to myself, "once she gets out of this goddam coma."

"Listen," I said to her, "I hope you won't mind if I don't go to the movies tonight. I'm really not in the mood. Just one of those days when nothing seems to go right, you know what I mean? First my Medical College Admissions Test. Then your hemorrhaging. I've had better days. I think I'll wait until we can go together."

I looked at the tubes going into her left arm. I wondered whether it hurt.

"You know, Barbara, this is just one of those things you have to be very patient about. It takes time. By next week, you'll be sitting up and drinking one of those strawberry frappes that screws up your weight. We'll be joking about how scared you got me. There's a conspiracy around here to keep morticians in business. The priests call it faith and the physicians call it science or reality or being reasonable, damned if I know, but the result is that they kill you. They absolutely *have* to have death. Can you imagine a priest or a doctor without death? They'd go nuts. They'd have nothing to do."

I looked around at the dimly lit room, trying to imagine a morning next week, flowers everywhere, a crowd of people talking with Barbara, lots of noise, Barbara laughing, the sun coming in the window, a nurse shooing us out because Barbara needed her rest.

We'd go to Florida. Barbara would get her strength back. We'd spend all day on a beach blanket like we did at the Cape, hugging each other, kissing and holding, unable to keep our hands off each other because we were so glad to be alive and with each other.

I placed my hands on her face and held them there. Then I leaned down and whispered in her ear so she'd be certain to hear, even in a coma.

"I'd be awfully grateful if you didn't die, Barbara. I don't know what you can do, but if there is anything, would you please help me out. I won't ever ask anything more from you again. I promise. This is the last thing. Don't die on me. Please. I'm asking you to do what you can, Barbara, because it's tearing me apart. I couldn't stand it if you died, so please. Don't die. I'm begging you, Barbara. Please don't die. Please," and I buried my head in the pillow next to hers and wept.

2nd Things have gotten completely out of hand. My mind no longer controls my behavior. It has split from my being and lies in some cosmic resort, sunning itself in universal truths. I haven't the faintest notion how this has happened. I know only that I have lost the last few remaining strands of self-control. I am a vehicle without ignition, accelerator, or brakes, careening, I fantasize, to that great Grossinger's that awaits us all.

It's all Kant's fault. I know it. He's responsible for all this.

Heine is right. If the citizens of Konigsberg had had any knowledge of the writings of this dispassionate, orderly man who walked Limetree Avenue every afternoon at three-thirty, they would have experienced at his sight a greater horror than they would on beholding an executioner who kills only men.

In a single precisely executed plot, he has assassinated noncontradiction as the ruler of rationale inquiry and elevated to the throne the arrogant dauphin, Synthetic A Priori Judgment.

Of course my mind has collapsed. Could it do otherwise? I have even been deprived of the joyful entertainment of speculating about those fascinating concepts that were entirely beyond the range of any possible experience: does the world have a beginning and limit? does everything in the world consist, in the final analysis, of simple indivisible elements? is this a world with causes and freedom? is there some necessary being or is everything chance?

He has tormented my mind. For every thesis, he has proved both it and its antithesis. And what has he left me to restore some sanity to my psyche? Categories! Analytic categories! Synthetic categories! Transcendental logic! Pure reason! Practical reason! Hypothetical imperatives! *Nous*. Mind. Things in themselves! *Noumena!* The great and wonderful Categorical Imperative!

Aha! At last, I say to myself, he has given me something substantial! The Categorical Imperative! But what is this contorted Prussian Golden Rule? That I should behave in accordance with the universal laws of nature. Can I ever know what these rules are? Of course not. But Kant ascribes to me the free will to try to do the impossible, to find out.

He taunts me to be moral. He tells me that I am a free member of a rational, spiritual order, and, as if this is not enough, that I am immortal. How do I know this? Well, he admits, I don't, because to do this I would have to use my reason and end up, inevitably, in a flurry of contradictory theses and antitheses again. Sorry. I must accept God on faith, my free will on belief alone, my immortality on trust, but accept them I must if I am to give substance to my moral life. Religion, I am kindly informed, does not consist in superscientific hypotheses concerning the nature and origin of the created world, but in the support it gives to my moral experience and conduct.

My mind can take no more. It has been deprived of reason and reduced to some seedy Public Official. My will has been relegated to a fairyland of faith and belief.

It is Kant who has done this to me. He has returned from the grave for the very purpose of snatching my mind. I'm certain of it.

7th I did some biological gardening today, a little nurturing and transplanting. I am beginning to become quite frightened.

I was positive that when Meli's zygote had reached the blastocyst stage, ready for implantation in a nonexistent uterus, it would not survive. There was no doubt in my mind that without the ability to weave its placenta, it would shrivel and die.

This has not happened. My solution has maintained it, and now, after six weeks, it still lives. It is a feat of accommodation beyond the imagination of even the most extreme advocate of human plasticity. The outer layers of cells have, very simply, sloughed off, since they were not necessary, and the inner core continues to grow. I am frightened to death.

This is not a golden dot any more, a clump of pink and orange cells, even a vague brownish form. I sat spellbound at my table this morning, staring through the glass. This is a fetus, a human fetus.

Its arms and legs are now clearly there. Its oversized head, veins sticking out from it like some metropolitan road map, has eyes. And, through its thin chest wall, I can see a heart beating.

I searched desperately for a glass container with a larger neck, concerned that I wouldn't be able to move the fetus out of its present jar if it became any larger. Finally, I found one that was adequate, sterilized and warmed it, and transferred the fetus and its solution.

Accidentally, I pushed it a little too hard in the transfer and it responded. It moved. It snapped backwards and then curled more tightly.

All day and all night I sat there, watching this creature. I do not know what I will do if it keeps living. And I cannot imagine how I will feel if it doesn't.

Today, for the first time since I first constructed my laboratory here in Cambridge and began my work on parthenogenesis, a realization came to me from which, try as I might, I could not escape. This is not experimental science I am doing here. This is life.

11th So I defy the gods, dare reason, and challenge science. Name this illness, I say to them. Identify the syndrome that has robbed me of my senses, appropriated my wit, and left me giggling to myself about some new voyage I have undertaken to the vast unexplored territory of Dementia.

I wake up mornings now and lie there in a total and complete fog.

"Am I dead?" I ask myself. "Did I die during the night? How would I ever know?"

I wait. I never know how long. I count the church bells. An hour. Two hours. There is no time when one is dead.

"Will my eyes clear this morning?" I ask myself after I have begun to suspect that I am not dead. "Or must I lie here, forever, in a perpetual cloud until the final curtain descends?"

I keep opening and closing my eyes to see whether I notice a difference. For the first hour, there is none. Then, slowly, I notice that when my eyes are open, there is gray. When they are closed, there is black. My sight is returning.

My limbs have begun to ache after sunset. My joints stiffen and my muscles become rigid and tight. I cannot lift my leg so high, stretch my arm so far, turn my head so much after darkness has come. In the mornings I can hardly see. In the evenings I can hardly move.

Science has no answer for this. I have been to my physician today. It is my very own syndrome. I have been told. Wolper's disease. They have named it after me, or, rather, the renowned Dr. Mazel has. Awfully nice of him.

Science cannot help me, my physician has informed me, but science would like to write me up, describe the process for posterity, fill in the details in the next edition of Prior-Silberstein's *Physical Diagnosis*. Might even make for a good appendix. I suggest a number of general headings that I feel might be appropriate, among them Terminal Illness for the Discriminating, Fun Fatal Syndromes, and Conditions to Make You Feel Glad That You've Only Got Dropsy.

My physician has better things to do with his time, and so he throws me out of his office—politely, of course. It is not the first time this has happened, he reminds me as I stumble out of the examining room. He accompanies me to make certain I get beyond the receptionist and other waiting patients without a repetition of several episodes in the past when, dissatisfied with his diagnosis of one or another of my many conditions, I cost him a very good receptionist and a healthy afternoon's income by implying out loud, he tells me, that he supplemented his income by working evenings at a local stockyard.

As I am leaving this particular afternoon, today, I ask him whether he has any insight at all into my illness.

"Just this," he tells me. "As near as I can tell, each day that passes makes it more difficult for one part of your body to relate to another. Since this is positively correlated with the sun's rising and setting, I'd say that the process of disorganization you are experiencing in your final days is astronomical, more than that, cosmic. The more I think about it, Dr. Wolper, the more it seems to me that your body is trying to reorganize itself, as though it were dissatisfied with the basic human physical structure and was inclined to try something new. You might say, Dr. Wolper, that you are in the unique situation of having a body that has decided, one must assume entirely on its own, to dabble in evolution."

"Hearing you talk like that makes it sound much less grim," I offer. "Who knows, it might come up with something better."

"Without dampening your optimism, Dr. Wolper, I'd like to point out that if the current process of rearrangement continues, you will very shortly be breathing blood, pumping air, excreting bile, and metabolizing excrement. Does that sound grim enough for you?"

I assure him that it is, and leave to go find out what science and reason have been up to lately now that they've left Planet Earth.

12th I would like to be able to say that I had something to do with my little friend swimming about in the jar in front of me, but I know that I had absolutely nothing to do with her. This entire business is her doing and hers alone.

That is fine with me. It is too much responsibility for anyone to take, this growing of life. I leave it to the DNAs and RNAs and ribosomes, messengers, and transfers, to handle this process with their usual efficiency and aplomb.

As for me, I am content to sit here and fantasize about what I am seeing. I have the freedom to do this now that I am mad, for I can dispense entirely with what would otherwise be an overwhelming concern, that by sitting here and watching a living, breathing, palpitating human in a two-liter jar on my workbench, I would surely go mad. With madness thus reduced to the most trivial of issues, great opportunities can present themselves to me, foremost among them, the diversion of fetal fantasy.

What experiences, for example, is this creature now having, I wonder. Without the placental barrier between us, but only the clear glass walls of its chamber, is she processing my comings and goings? Has she reached an opinion regarding the man with the gray curly hair, large white beard, and thick glasses who stares daily into her world, smiling and winking, holding lengthy discourses about the world in general and life in particular?

"Gestation wasn't all that bad," she will say some day, "except for some lunatic who used to grin at me for hours and babble about his weltschmerz. He seemed like a nice enough old man, but even a fetus can take only so much romantic pessimism."

Will she be able to write the Ultimate Autobiography? "Shortly after conception," she opens, "I have an early memory of a large human figure staring intently at me and emptying his nasal passages with an accompanying sound I have since learned to associate with major disasters."

Above all, I wonder whether she will imprint like some super Lorenzian ethological duck, and will toddle after me for most of her early life, expecting me to feed and groom her and provide for those other needs that a humanling so imprinted would have a right to expect.

I imagine someday walking through a large Viennese park with Lorenz, his ducklings in tow behind him, my brood of in-vitro toddlers in a line behind me, as I compare notes with Lorenz on whether imprinting does, in fact, occur.

Two large Fräuleins with ornate prams pass us by and I can overhear their conversation.

"Freda," says one, "isn't that Herr Doktor Lorenz with the ducklings?"

"*Ja*," says the other, "but who is the one with the children?"

"Oh, him," says the first, shaking her head with disgust, "that's Wolper. Never satisfied. Always has to do it better. *Dummkopf*."

"*Dummkopf*," the other agrees, and they perambulate over to the *wurst* cart for another snack.

14th The Mozart had just ended. Meli was resting peacefully in my lap, as usual, and the August evening was beginning to cool slightly. It was at that precise instant that the end began. Up until then the termination had been only a vague presentiment, but after this evening the inevitability of the Ultimate Conclusion became inescapable.

It started quietly enough. I was talking about the young Mozart's cutting apart piano pieces of Europe's finest composers, pasting them together and offering them as his own sonatas. Meli reached up and started playing with my beard.

"You seem calmer tonight, Dr. Wolper," she said.

"You like me better like this?"

"It sure beats when you're jumping out of your goddam skin. A few days ago, I was sure we were going to have to call the men in the white coats. The way I figured it, just about the time they were doing the last buckle on your straitjacket, you'd ask me to marry you. What I would've done then is something that I didn't lose very much sleep over, I'll tell you."

"So, I guess I'd better get moving on my decision. Is that what you're saying, Meli?" I looked down at her as she continued to run her fingers through my beard.

"Let's put it like this, Dr. Wolper. From where I sit, I'm not *overwhelmed* by the *rhythm* I'm getting from you."

"Bad *vibes*, huh?" I offered.

"Very poor vibrations, yes, Dr. Wolper," and she hopped up from the sofa, "but I've been giving this *number* a lot of goddam thought and I think I've got something that'll change your *tune*, like they say. I've got it upstairs. Come on, I want to show you," and she took my hand and led me up the stairs to my bedroom.

"You sit over there on the bed. I've got a little *opus* in the other room that's especially for you," and she disappeared behind the door that connected our rooms while I sat on the bed trying to guess what she had put together that made her so sure she was going to increase the action. I had hardly begun to search my imagination when the door flung open again revealing Meli stark naked.

"How do you like this *piece*, Dr. Wolper?" she beamed. "No need for any *overtures*, Dr. Wolper, because this little *sextet* is ready for some *divertimento*. If you want to *score*, just take out your *instrument* and you can make great *music* in my *chamber* ."

"Stop the music!" I shouted. "Stop the music!"

"What's the matter?"

"I know this tune and I don't want to play it, Meli."

She paid no attention to me and walked over to the bed. There was no question in my mind while I was protesting that she was absolutely the most beautiful naked woman I had ever seen.

"Really, Meli," I protested, "I'm too old for this nonsense."

"Dr. Wolper, I've seen dead people who weren't too old for what I want to do. Trust me," and she pushed me back on the bed and started undoing my belt.

I knew that I could have resisted. I could have pushed off the bed and left the room, and while there was part of me that very much wanted to do that, there was also another part of me, with a long history of victory under the most severe battle conditions, that once again triumphed.

"I want you to know, Meli," I said as she finished slipping off my trousers and shorts in one expert motion, "that I don't think this is going to work."

"That's what they all say, Dr. Wolper. Same old *song* and *dance*. But I'll tell you, Dr. Wolper, a couple *hot licks* and *presto, presto, forte, forte*, we are in *concert*."

"Meli, if you must do this, can we at least eliminate the musical puns, please?" I entreated her.

"Oh, Dr. Wolper," Meli feigned a pout as she unbuttoned and took off my shirt. "I just wanted you to know that all the things you've been teaching me about *music* haven't gone to waste. I thought you'd be really proud that someone such as myself with so simple a mind had absorbed as much as I have." She lay her naked body next to my naked body and began to kiss my ear. She proceeded to spend the next half hour or so alternately kissing and licking my body, starting at my forehead and culminating with the bottoms of my feet.

She returned then to my face, which she began to massage with the fingertips of one hand while she played with my chesthairs with the other.

"Is this the second movement?" I smiled.

"I haven't seen any goddam *first* movement, yet," and she reached down and flicked my limp penis. "Does it ever move?" she asked.

"I told you that I didn't expect this to work out," I answered.

"Well then, for chrissakes, start expecting it to."

"I'll try."

"Good. And another thing. If you get bored or something just lying there, you might want to *participate*."

"I'll try," I said meekly.

"Good. Then here we go again. A-one, and a-two, and a-go."

I found myself, miraculously, very much involved in this process. I ran my hands again and again over her body, and with each pass I could feel the juices beginning to flow. I kissed her gently, as though she were an extremely fragile creature that I was afraid of harming.

On her part, Meli continued to kiss me, thrusting her tongue deep in my mouth and running it in circles around my tongue.

She became enormously excited and I became enormously excited, and I climbed on her finally, ready to have the first sexual intercourse in over ten years.

"Let's *fugue*," I grinned as she looked at me.

"What are you going to *fugue* me with, Dr. Wolper, your big toe? Look at yourself. You couldn't penetrate a mound of mashed potatoes."

I looked down and to my utter amazement she was absolutely correct. Even though I was in a state of high excitement, my penis was not. I became extremely upset and rolled off her.

"I don't understand it," I said. "It doesn't make any sense."

Meli sensed my dismay and immediately came to my aid and comfort.

"Don't worry, Dr. Wolper. You're just not used to it because it's been so long for you. But no need to worry, because you are here in bed with one of the great *philharmonic organists*. Relax. Only don't relax too hard because even *my* talents have a limit."

For the next half hour Meli did every physical thing that a female human body can do to a male human body, and then some. Finally she came up for air.

"Okay," she said breathing heavily, "I give. How does it work?"

"I don't think it does any more, Meli," I said sadly.

"Don't be ridiculous. It has to. Everybody's does. I had a friend who was a prostitute and she told me about guys who've just been revived with heart massage who want to do it one more time before they leave for the hospital. It's life after death, Dr. Wolper. Don't you feel anything?"

"Certainly I do, Meli. I was very excited. You're an excellent lover. As a matter of fact, I'm very excited right now."

Suddenly Meli's expression changed and she slid off me.

"I think I know the problem, Dr. Wolper. You've got a valve open somewhere or something. Look at you. You've sprung a leak."

She pointed to my penis, still fully retracted, from which a steady stream of semen trickled out like water from a spigot that hasn't been completely closed. As it happened, I could feel the excitement inside of me subside.

Meli looked at the expression of release on my face.

"I hate to ask, Dr. Wolper, but what *was* that?"

"I'm afraid it was an orgasm, Meli."

"My God!" she said, her face turning chalky gray. "It couldn't have been.

I mean, no one comes like that. That's a malfunction, Dr. Wolper. It's not normal. What does a person who climaxes like that do for excitement, watch food particles foam out of his dentures?"

We remained on the bed in silence, neither of us daring to look at the other. Meli said it first.

"It's impotence, isn't it, Dr. Wolper? You're impotent, huh?"

"Yes. I'm impotent."

"I don't think I want to talk about it. Do you mind if we just lie here? I need to think."

"Do you want to move back to your apartment?" I asked because I thought I had to ask.

"I don't know what I want to do. I've got to think, dammit, so don't talk any more. I think I'm going *scherzo*."

15th I still do not welcome death. Perhaps this comes later, I do not know. It is hard for me to believe that, short of the most intense kind of pain, a man would ever welcome the end of all he has known, even when what he has known includes internecine struggle, insanity, and now impotence. I suspect there is more, but I have not heard from Meli today.

I did take her advice and see a specialist this afternoon. It was not particularly helpful.

"You say 'a leak'?" he squinted at me over his bifocals.

"Sort of, yes. A steady dribble, and then, that's it."

"I don't think I've ever heard of that before. I'd like to give you a complete exam," and the good doctor proceeded to poke and probe.

As he worked, he asked me a number of questions, which I tried to answer as honestly as possible. I included the diagnosis of the last physician without the accompanying editorial comment. Finally, with a large sigh, he completed his own exam.

"You can get dressed now, Dr. Wolper," he told me and lit his pipe.

"Have you reached a conclusion?" I asked.

"A conclusion, yes. A solution, no."

"I'm sorry to hear that."

"I concur with your primary physician's diagnosis. Your body is in what could most likely be described as a process of casual rearrangement, assuming one wanted to avoid such words as 'reckless' and 'chaotic'. In any event, the prognosis is not good, Dr. Wolper, not good at all. The way things are proceeding at this point, in a matter of days you very well may be the only human to *taste* his own bone marrow. While this is not likely to kill you, I can't for the life of me see what good it could do."

"Yes, but what about my impotence?"

"I have reached a conclusion about that, as well, Dr. Wolper."

"Namely?"

"Namely, taking all things into consideration and ascribing truth to about half of what you've told me, I'd be inclined to say that you are suffering from an outrageously severe case of zoephobia."

"And this is?"

"A hysterical aversion to living things."

"But how does this account for my impotency?"

"Dr. Wolper," he patiently explained, "the human body can withstand only so much resistance. Eventually, some life *has* to leak out. It's unavoidable."

16th Meli has more or less disappeared into the night. I have not seen her for two days now, ever since my unfortunate noctural remission.

And the more I think about it, the more I realize that there isn't a damn thing I can do about it, either.

The Adventures of Boris Lafkin

CHAPTER THREE (continued):
Progressive Evaporation—With Cosmic Implications

I sat in the dimly lit antiseptic purgatory for several minutes, looking at Barbara's tranquil escape from the realities of philosophy departments and intimate relationships. Then I kissed her lightly on the cheek and left for the lobby pay phone.

"Mr. Spencer," I found myself shouting, as usual, because of the long-distance nature of the call, "this is Boris Lafkin."

"Boris, how are you? It's good to hear from you."

"I'm not too well, sir," I tried to set the general tone of what was to come. "I'm calling from Cambridge General Hospital."

"Are you ill, Boris?"

"No, sir. Barbara is ill, sir. Seriously ill, I'm afraid."

There was no answer on the other end of the line. I could hear him clearing his throat. I wasn't too happy with the conversation so far. I hadn't gotten the message across, I felt. After all, what does "seriously" ill mean? A high fever? Maybe a heart attack? People get over them.

"I think I'd like to ask Mrs. Spencer to pick up the other phone," he finally said, and I decided as I listened to him call her that I might have conveyed more than I thought.

"It's Boris, Betty," Mr. Spencer told his wife over the phone extension. "He's calling because Barbara is in the hospital."

"Hello, Boris," Mrs. Spencer said with only a noticeable break in her usual warmth. "How's Barbara?"

"Not too well, Mrs. Spencer." This was becoming harder.

"Can you tell us what's wrong with her Boris?" Mr. Spencer asked.

I took a very deep breath.

"She's had a cerebral hemorrhage, sir."

I could hear Mrs. Spencer suck in a lot of air. Mr. Spencer started to clear his throat.

"How bad is it, Boris?" he asked.

"No one knows, really, sir," I half-truthed, and then added so that I wouldn't feel that I completely misled them, "She's in a coma, Mr. Spencer."

I could tell that I had said enough. That was all they wanted to hear.

"We'll be right up, Boris. I know the directions. You take it easy, now. Don't worry. Everything will work out for the best. You can count on it," Mr. Spencer said as though he really believed it.

"You're right, sir. Everything will work out. Before you hang up, sir, there's something else."

"Why don't you wait until we get up there. We can talk about it then," he said.

"I'd rather tell you now, sir, if you don't mind. You see, last July Barbara and I had a sort of personal marriage, and, well, we've been telling everyone that we're married. I wanted to tell you that because when you get here you'll find that Barbara was admitted as Mrs. Lafkin and she's wearing a wedding ring. I thought you might find that a little strange, sir."

"You're right, Boris. We would have. I'm glad you told us. Congratulations on your marriage," and he actually sounded as though he meant it.

"Well, thank you, Mr. Spencer. It was just something that Barbara and I wanted, and we were going to have the formal stuff next month for the families, if you know what I mean."

I could hear Mrs. Spencer sobbing.

"We understand, Boris. We can talk about it more when we see you. Right now I think we'd like to get up to the hospital as soon as possible."

"Right. Right. Sure. We can talk about it later, if you want."

"Stay with Barbara, Boris. We'll be right up. Good-bye."

It occurred to me as I hung up that I had forgotten to tell them that we were living together, but the more I thought about it, the more it seemed to me that they'd probably figure it out by themselves on the way up.

Next on my list, I will never understand why, was my mother.

"Mother, this is Boris."

"Boris? Where are you?"

"I'm in Cambridge."

"Are you coming down to visit?"

"Ma, there's something I have to tell you. I'm married and my wife is dying."

"Are you coming down to visit?"

"She's in a hospital. In a coma."

"That's a shame, Boris. I would have liked to meet her. I would have liked to meet them all," she said half to herself.

"She's had a cerebral hemorrhage, Ma. She's probably going to die."

"Boris. Boris. Boris."

"Ma, she didn't have a hemorrhage when we were married. You can't tell about these things. They just happen."

"Boris, *nothing* just happens. Absolutely *nothing* just happens."

"She's probably going to die by tomorrow, Ma. Do you want to come up?"

"It's almost nine o'clock at night, Boris. I wouldn't get there until after midnight. You want me to drive up to Cambridge in the middle of the night to see someone I don't know die?"

"No, I don't, Ma. I definitely don't. She is your daughter-in-law and I am your son, and there's about to be a death in the family. I thought you'd want to know."

"I'll see what I can do, Boris," and she hung up.

I crossed her name off my mental list. Duty done. Immediate family notified. Friends next. For the first time I began to realize that I was completely alone and that for the next three or four hours, until the Spencers arrived, I was going to continue to be alone. It seemed like an insurmountably long time. I needed someone to talk to. I called an old friend, Howard Woodhouse, and filled him in on the gory details. As an expert on affliction, he took the tale of woe in stride and indicated that, although he couldn't make it over for a while himself, he'd let some of Barbara's friends know. He'd see that someone was over to keep me company shortly. A minute after I hung up it occurred to me that there was one "mutual" friend whom he shouldn't let know, but Howard's phone was busy every time I called back for the next half hour, so I finally gave up, saying a little prayer that Lawrence Hauptmann would not be at home.

My prayers were not answered, and exactly forty-five minutes after I finished talking to Howard, a screaming, ranting, charging Larry Hauptmann crashed through the doors of the emergency room, demanding to see the mutilated carcass of his lover.

The entire E.R. was thrown into turmoil.

"Where is the body?" he demanded.

"What body?"

"Barbara's body."

"Barbara who?"

"Barbara Spencer!"

"No body. No Barbara Spencer," he was informed.

He attacked the orderly and was subdued.

"Why are you lying to me?"

Same answer. No body. No Barbara Spencer. Another fit from Larry. More restraint from the orderlies.

"Barbara came here this afternoon, I know it. She had a brain hemorrhage She came with Boris Lafkin."

A light dawned.

"You mean Mrs. Lafkin," he was told.

"Mrs. *Lafkin. Mrs.* Lafkin!" he screamed, and broke free of the orderlies. He raced around the first floor, opening doors and shouting. "Lafkin, where are you? If I find you, I'll kill you! I swear I will. Where the fuck are you?" he continued to burst into operating rooms, wards, and patients sitting on toilets.

The policemen found Larry. Three of them blocked one end of the hall, the other three blocked the other, and they began to walk toward him. Larry made a lunge to get by them, but it was no use. He was grabbed and handcuffed. Then Dr. Johnson appeared from around the corner and shot a large hypodermic full of a dull yellow fluid into Larry's right arm. Larry turned quickly at the pain of the injection and caught sight of me standing at the end of the hall. He tried to jerk away from the police.

"Lafkin, you prick—" he started to say, but that was as far as he got. A very large smile spread across his face, his eyes rolled up toward the ceiling, then closed, and he crumpled to the floor.

Larry awoke in a much calmer frame of mind. To encourage his quiescence, wide canvas straps across his arms and legs held him to a table. He turned his head to the side and looked at me. He knew immediately where he was.

"Boris, what the hell'd you do this for?"

"I didn't do it. The nurses did."

"I mean telling people here that Barbara was Mrs. Lafkin?"

"I didn't. She did."

"You're full of shit, Boris. Barbara was dead when she got here."

"Wrong, Larry, she's up on the seventh floor, alive."

"Alive?"

"Yes, alive like in living."

"She's not dead?"

"No, she's alive."

"I thought she was dead."

"Apparently. She's not though. She's alive."

He thought about this for a few minutes.

"What's the Mrs. Lafkin bit?"

"We were married last July at the Cape."

"That's a lie, Boris. That's a fucking lie. She was coming back to me. She told me last week."

I remembered Barbara's telling me that she had resolved her problem. Apparently she hadn't yet conveyed the information to Larry.

"Could we talk about this later, Larry? I'd really like to get back to Barbara."

"Do you think I could talk to her for just a minute, Boris?"

"I wish you could, Larry. She's in a deep coma."

"Well, maybe when she comes out of it. When is she supposed to come out of it?"

"She's not, Larry. They say her brain's been completely destroyed and she'll die within the next day," and I suddenly had a great urge to get back to Barbara.

"She can't die, Boris."

"Why not?"

"Because she was thinking about coming back to me. And I promised not to kill myself if she would."

"Sounds fair."

"So you see, she can't die. If she does, then I'll have to kill myself."

"Well, maybe, you could go back on your word, just this once. Barbara's certainly in no position to object."

I started to leave.

"Boris, suicide is an important thing to me. It's not a joking matter. I've tried suicide almost every year since I was ten. Gestures, attempts, threats. It's a very important part of my life. It isn't easy to give that up. I wouldn't have agreed to do that for any woman, you know."

"I think I do, yes, Larry. Now, I've got to be going. If you'll excuse me."

"Boris?"

"What the hell is it, Larry?"

"I'd like to come with you, if you don't mind?" The plaintiveness was appalling.

"You're strapped to a table, Larry."

"I know. Could you ask them to unstrap me? I feel calmer now."

"All right," I agreed reluctantly.

After no persuading at all, the nursing staff agreed to get Larry out of the emergency room. We rode up to the seventh floor and entered Barbara's room.

"She looks okay," Larry whispered.

"She does," I agreed.

"It's so hard to think of her dying. She looks like she's taking a nap. 'Sleep and Death, two twins of winged race, Of matchless swiftness, but of silent pace.'"

"Thank you, Larry."

"It's Homer."

"It's good to know that death didn't end with the Trojan Wars."

"I don't know, Boris. Death is one thing I've never been able to figure out."

"I'm sure you'll get it. Just keep working on it. It'll come."

"I'm serious, Boris. Why does man fear death? He has no experience of it. It's nothing. Absolutely *nothing*. How can we be so afraid of absolutely nothing?"

"Got me, Larry. Maybe we don't like the idea of losing *absolutely everything*. I don't know."

"'Either death is a state of nothingness and utter unconsciousness, or, as men say, there is a change and migration of the soul from this world to another. Now, if death be of such a nature, I say that to die is to gain; for eternity is then only a single night.' But I think that Socrates knew something he wasn't telling, because we still all fear death."

"Maybe we should pay a cock to Asclepius. Would that make you feel better?"

"It's hard to know what would make me feel better, Boris," and Larry slipped off his shoes and hopped up on the other bed, empty beside Barbara's, settling down for a long dialogue. "I thought that suicide might really do the trick. It doesn't seem to. I thought that explosive temper fits might help. But, after I'm done, there's just a lot of glass to clean up. It hardly seems worth the effort. I've deceived myself. But then, as Plato has it, everything that deceives enchants."

"Larry, just so I can prepare myself. Do you intend to spend the next three hours lying there and philosophizing?"

"Most likely," and he did exactly that, analyzing death in all its perturbations, quoting extensively from the Platonists and devoting the largest single segment to phenomenology.

I sat in my chair beside Barbara, watching her intently, trying hard not to flinch every time Larry mentioned that Barbara's brain had been destroyed and her death was now inevitable and thinking that instead of spending these three hours listening to Larry's morbid philosophical prattle, I could be doing something constructive like weeping or vomiting.

18th Finally. Meli returned late tonight.

"I am back," she announced. "We are going to lick this penis thing. And that's that."

"Thank you, Meli," I said gratefully.

"Just don't thank me, Dr. Harry Wolper. It sends shivers up and down my goddam spine. Goodnight," and she stomped off to bed.

19th I found myself doing a little fancy footwork tonight. Shortly after

Meli and I had retired to the living room for our usual evening, she got up from the sofa and trotted deliberately over to the phonograph.

"Every time I hear this guy I feel like I should be doing a striptease," she announced and turned off the Offenbach (Luigi Nono had been yesterday). "You know, Dr. Wolper, kiddo," she began with an appellation I had never heard her use before and, therefore, signaling a Serious Matter, "I went over to bring you some iced-tea last night when you were working in your lab, but I didn't want to disturb you."

"You should have knocked, Meli. I would have welcomed some refreshment."

"Well, I was about to, Dr. Wolper, when I heard some conversation going on."

"Sometimes I talk to myself," I began to get the gist of where we were going.

"Well, that's what I figured too, except that most people who talk to themselves don't call themselves 'Boris' particularly when their name is 'Harry.'"

"Did I do that?" I smiled weakly. "Maybe I was talking on the phone."

"Maybe, except, as you've probably realized now that you've been working in your laboratory for twenty-five years, you don't *have* a phone in your laboratory, and, according to Mrs. Mallory, you never have. Besides, when I peeked in the screen, you were sitting over at your workbench, writing."

"Writing? Really?"

"With a pen on a pad of paper."

"And talking to myself?"

"Nope. You were screaming at yourself. Or at least you were screaming and there wasn't anyone else around. Not a goddam soul. So I thought I'd ask, Dr. Wolper, if you don't mind, who the hell is Boris, and what does he want to do that you won't let him do, and for chrissake will you let him do it because I'm absolutely positive the neighbors can hear you, and my guess is that the next time you start arguing with the air, they're going to send some people to take you away. Got me?"

"I got you."

"Good." But she wasn't completely satisfied. "Now who the hell is Boris, and don't tell me he's you?"

"He's sort of a friend, Meli, a dear friend, like a son to me."

"You're not going to give me one of those giant rabbit stories, are you?"

"Not at all. Boris is almost as human as you and I are."

"But only you can see him?"

"Well, I can't actually see him."

"What can you *actually* do?"

"I can talk to him, mostly. Oh, sometimes I guess I can see him. In my mind's eye."

"Your mind has an eye?"

"Certainly. Eye-magination," I smiled.

"This is not funny, Dr. Wolper. This is not even a *little* funny. This is a goddam tragedy is what it is, that someone who is as intelligent as you are spends his evenings shouting at some eye he thinks he has in his brain that he's named 'Boris.' Now, I ask you, Dr. Wolper, does this strike you as even mildly amusing?"

I did not respond. Meli tried again.

"Now, one more time. *Who is Boris?*"

"Boris is a character in a book I'm writing. I thought I told you about him."

"Not really, no. Why do you scream at him?"

"Well, actually, he's the one who screams at me. I just scream back."

Meli started pacing back and forth in front of the bay window. Then she stopped and glared at me.

"Dr. Wolper!" she barked very loudly. "Tell me why are you arguing with an imaginary man!" she screamed.

"I don't know!" I shouted back just as loudly. "I don't know! Because he torments me! Hounds me! Gives me no peace! 'Give me my freedom! I need a religious experience! I have to kill you! You write the book! I'll write the book! Give me a miracle! I love you! I hate you! I'm scared to death of you!' *He nev-er stops!* And now, he's got me in the midst of the most horrible mess! That's why I argue with him! I created him, and I just can't stand him. I just can't stand him! There, Meli, does that answer your question?" I finished out of breath.

"Dr. Wolper," Meli said very quietly. "You are writing a book about someone named Boris. Is that right?"

"Yes. I mean, no. I mean, I don't know."

"Dr. Wolper, if you are writing the book, then how come you don't just shut him up, or stop writing the book? I'll try one more time. Please tell me," she said very sweetly, "who the fuck is Boris?"

"Meli, I can't stop the book or control Boris because he's my mind, not just a piece of paper and some ink. A man only has so much control over his mind. Look, do you remember when you were a child, sometimes you would lie in bed at night and all sorts of beasts and monsters and ghosts would come out of the night to get you, and there was nothing you could do to control them? If they wanted to come get you, that's what they did, even though at some level you knew that it was all in your mind. You might even have screamed at them, 'Go away! Leave me alone!' but they still did what they wanted, even though it was only your imagination. There was no way to shut them out, not by closing your eyes, burying your head in the pillow, trying to think of something else. Nothing worked."

"You're not trying to tell me that this whole goddam Boris business is just some bad dream, are you?"

"Exactly," I beamed. "You've got it exactly. It's just a horribly bad dream."

Meli plopped down on the large Victorian chair and mused about this, staring at the ceiling. Then she rolled her head over to look at me.

"Dr. Wolper," she bobbed her head conclusively, "you're full of shit."

"It's becoming a consensus," I concurred. "Boris thinks so, too."

20th I don't know how it happened, and I don't want to know how it happened.

I was driving through Harvard Square this afternoon when I saw two men sitting at an outdoor cafe in, I can only assume, desperate and furtive conversation.

It was a mixture of two elements that reduce to the level of frivolity such duos as bulls and flapping red flags, George Metesky and nitroglycerin, Jesse James and Chase Manhattan.

Any of these would have been preferable to Maury the Solicitor and my son Arnold. I can't imagine what schemes they are putting together, or, rather, I can, but refuse to. I am certain that I will find out soon enough.

21st A new development on the physical front. I raced to the emergency room.

"It's starting. It's starting," I informed the physician on duty, a Dr. Tidrow, trim, wiry, wispy little man.

"What is that?" he asked professionally.

"The end. The end has come," I notified him.

"What specifically brought you here today, Dr. Wolper?" he asked, losing a bit of his patience.

"Look," I said and showed him my nose. "There is blood coming out of my nose!"

"You have a nosebleed? Is that why you came here?"

"Not a nosebleed, no, Dr. Tidrow. Blood from my nose. Where there used to be air, now there is blood. You see the difference?"

"Certainly," he smiled, but I don't think he did understand. "Now if you will take your handkerchief away from your nose, I can—Dr. Wolper, I can't look at your nose as long as you hold your handkerchief up to it like that."

I resisted harder.

"Now look, Dr. Wolper, you've got to take your hand down. All right, have it your way," and he reached for the lapel of his white coat.

"I really can't take my—ouch!" I yanked my hand away. "You stuck me. You stuck me with a needle."

"A pin, Dr. Wolper. Now let's see what we've got here," and he shined a light up my nose. "Well, it seems to have stopped. What is it that concerns you, Dr. Wolper?"

I looked cautiously from side to side to make certain we were alone. Then I pulled him toward me and whispered in his ear.

"Have you ever heard of Wolper's disease?" I said softly.

"No, I haven't," he answered.

"Well, I'm Wolper. I've got it."

"Wolper's disease," he said to make sure he had understood me correctly.

"Right. It's my very own disease."

"Well, I think that's lovely, Dr. Wolper. We should each have a disease that's our very own. It's so much simpler that way. It almost totally eliminates epidemics."

"You don't believe me."

"I do. How does this disease manifest itself?"

"That's the interesting part. Everything goes screwy."

"No doubt. Are there any *specific* signs or symptoms? Or is it just a *general* screwiness?"

"That's hard to say, Dr. Tidrow. It's a general process of physical reconstruction, and, oh yes, I go blind for a couple hours every morning."

"Don't we all," Dr. Tidrow was obviously fascinated. "How does the nosebleed fit in?"

"Don't you see, Dr. Tidrow, that's part of the reorganization. Instead of breathing air, my nose is starting to breathe blood."

"Really. How is it doing?"

I paused to think. "Actually, I'm not sure. I *am* still alive."

"Well then, what I would suggest is that you go home and if you find yourself suffocating from your nosebleeds, come in immediately. Otherwise, why don't we just assume that, so far, everything is copasetic."

I went back home, but I'm still not convinced that these nosebleeds are not part of the Ultimate Conclusion.

22nd "I've been thinking about this penis thing," Meli said between arias from *Madam Butterfly*, "and there's no question we've got to solve this before we can get married. If we get married, and you're still orgasming down your leg, sooner or later, it's bound to come up. You just can't pretend these things don't exist."

"Have you got any ideas?" I asked.

"Not really. But I've got a theory. You see, the way I figure it, your penis has been away from screwing for so long that it's forgotten what it has to do. And now that it's found out that it can come without even getting hard, well, it's got no reason for an erection. It just kind of lies there and says to itself, 'I can come without an erection. Why bother. What the hell.' You see what I mean?" and Meli looked at me to make certain I had gotten the thrust of her argument.

"Right. What the hell," I agreed.

"Good. Now, all we've got to do is train it. We say, 'No erection. No orgasm.' Just like that. Then it learns that if it doesn't get hard, it doesn't get to come. You see how it works?"

"Where do I come in?"

"Well, it's your goddam penis, for chrissake."

"I understand that. What I want to know is what I'm supposed to do."

"You, Dr. Wolper, are supposed to tell it who's in charge."

"How?"

"Talk to it, for godsakes. If you can talk to an imaginary person who doesn't exist, you can certainly talk to your very own penis, which does."

"It's worth a try."

"You're goddam right it is. Now put on *Peter and the Wolf* again. I'll listen. You start talking to your thing. Then later we'll start the training. And for chrissake will you put away that mirror and stop looking up your nose. You're making me batty."

Later we tried. And later we failed. And much later I lay quietly in bed, in the night, the chill drifting in the window and making Meli cuddle closer against my body. Every hour or so, as I stayed awake during the night, Meli would stir, lift up her head, and look at me.

"Go to sleep, Dr. Wolper. It's not the end of the world. It really isn't. Everything'll work out. Just go to sleep. Please."

I held Meli tighter and assured her that I would go to sleep. Then I tried to remember what sex was like with Lucy, and waited for the morning so I could get up.

23rd My nightmare returned.

"Well, well, well. If it isn't the illustrious Dr. Wolper, metaphor of the year. How's the old double-entendre doing this fine day?" my pug-nosed friend greets me.

I try to bustle past like I'm on my way to an important meeting.

"Now, now. You don't want to avoid me. I'm your friend. I'm going to help you."

"You are?" I ask.

"Absolutely. Who could know more about impotency, death, rearranging nature, reason, science, life, even insanity? What you toy at, I have made into a fine art."

"You have?" I am beginning to become very interested.

"Certainly. Now, as I see it, your basic problem is that you're overmixing your metaphors. You're on the brink of a metaphorical souffle."

"It just seems to me like I'm living my life."

"Dr. Wolper. Dr. Wolper. You are talking to me. To me. Your friend. Not to your twelve-year-old sex therapist. No one lives a life like yours. It just isn't humanly possible. You know that."

"I do?"

"Of course you do. Just remember all those years raising the children, with Mrs. Mallory, working in your lab, an occasional evening out, the routine. Why should this year be any different? Do you see what I mean?"

"Yes, I do. But this year is different. I'm more desperate. I have less time."

"Every day we have less time. Now, as I was saying, you're just working on too many metaphors at the same time. For an analogy to be significant, you've got to keep it simple. I think it's time to jettison some of the more troublesome aspects of the allegory. I'll take the girl."

"You'll what?"

"I'll take the girl. I like her style. I think she's got a fresh viewpoint that's going to liven up things down here in the cave a good deal. The men are going to be enormously pleased."

"I'll keep the girl. You can have Arnold and Boris."

"I don't *want* Arnold and Boris. I want the *girl,* dammit!"

"Well, I'm not *giving* you the girl. You want something, take my madness, my illness, my death. *I* need the girl."

"What for? So you can drip on her? Come on, Wolper. We've been through a lot together. I've earned her. You can throw in the embryo and the madness if you insist. But that's my last offer."

"Oh, that's terrific. I get Arnold, Boris, and my death. What more could anyone ask for?"

"Look, Wolper, I'm not going to take her for nothing. I'll give you something of far greater value than an erotic twelve-year-old."

"She's nineteen."

"Big deal. I'm willing to make you an offer, Wolper."

"I'm not interested."

"Insight, Wolper. I'm willing to trade, even-steven, carnal knowledge for *insight,* fair and square. It's quite a deal. A once-in-a-lifetime chance."

"You've got to be kidding."

"Insight, Wolper. Come on, take it. It's all I've got."

"I know. Keep it. I'll take hindsight."

I wake up in a cold sweat and pull Meli to me as tightly as I can.

26th The end is in the air, the end of summer, the end of August, the end of the year, the end of us all. In northern New England leaves are beginning to turn.

This evening in Cambridge I can smell the chill of a winter to come. It brushes over my shoulders in a rush to freeze us all before we have the chance to disappear behind our stoves and heaters.

It is a mixed blessing, this August, every August, the hot days and frosty nights. With the welcome end to the oppressive heat also comes the end to the life that envelopes me every instant. It's hard to conceive how I'm ever going to survive without the sounds of katydids and the smell of freshly cut grass outside my lab windows.

Thirty days from now there will be only fields vacant from the harvest and multicolored trees. Thirty days from then there will be nothing left to the kingdom that sustains me today.

So I do what I can to hold on to this summer, my last. I keep the windows open all night. I sleep wrapped in my blanket with my head next to the open window. I sit on the terrace for all my meals. I take long walks along the banks of the Charles River. I will not let this August slip away from me easily. I will cling to this month until the last advertisement has appeared in the *Cambridge Phoenix* searching for a well-hung bi white male for a summer of three-way fun, discretion absolutely guaranteed.

27th I have locked myself in my room. I will talk to no one. I will eat nothing. I am in mourning.

I was sitting at my workbench this afternoon, making notes on some new ideas for my Great Wiper, when I was distracted by some sudden movement of the fetus in the jar in front of me.

She threw up her arms, turned frantically, and jerked her head back. I looked furiously for something to do. There was nothing.

She kicked, curled into a ball, and expired. The thumping under her chest stopped. She became still. Then very slowly she started to rise to the surface of the jar.

I watched in shock. Then I walked away and came up here to my room to grieve. Some time later, much later, I will do an autopsy to determine what caused this to happen, just when everything seemed to be going so well with her.

Now, I must start over, once again. It is almost a month before Meli ovulates. I must do this next extraction very carefully. It will be my last chance. I'm sure of it. In the meantime, I have prayed tonight for divine assistance.

"Powers That Be," I have asked, "please grant that I might retrieve one more ovum intact from Melissande, that during this procedure my sight be sharp, my mind be clear, and my nose be clotted."

I'll settle for two out of three.

28th I emerged from my bereavement today to eat lunch, more because of Mrs. Mallory's and Meli's hysteria than anything else. Actually, there was another powerful incentive.

"You'd better get the hell out of there, Harry Wolper, M.D.," Meli pounded on the door. "There's some goddam real estate midget downstairs, and she's going to sell the house right out from under you if you're not downstairs in about two seconds, I swear it."

For such an emergency grief must be put aside.

"Good afternoon, Dr. Wolper. Katherine Pleuter," she introduced herself, "of Doft, Harcrow, and Simmerling?"

"Oh, yes. How do you do, Miss Pleuter? What can I do to help you?" I asked, not really interested and being careful to keep the closed screen door between us.

"Dr. Wolper, you're not going to believe this, but we've had a call from a gentleman who wants to purchase your house *very much*."

"You're right, Miss Pleuter, I don't."

"But it's true, Dr. Wolper. It's 100 percent of the truth."

"I'm not interested in selling, Miss Pleuter. Didn't we have this conversation once before?"

"He's willing to pay almost anything, Dr. Wolper. Anything."

"His life?"

"I beg your pardon?"

"I'll sell him the house for his life. It's going to cost him that anyway in the long run with mortgage payments, taxes, and maintenance. This way he can get it all over at one time."

"Dr. Wolper, you're joking, of course. What good would this property be to him if he were dead? That doesn't make any sense."

"Then we're even, Miss Pleuter, because I don't understand what good this property could be to him alive."

"Dr. Wolper, when people are alive, they *live* in houses. That's the way it works. That's the way it's *always* worked, I think." But it was clear from her puzzled expression that history was not one of her strong suits.

"Look, Miss Pleuter, you're a licensed real estate agent, aren't you?"

"Oh, yes, Dr. Wolper. Indeed I am."

"Then aren't you required to communicate all responses to your clients' offers?"

"Yes, I am, Dr. Wolper, 'all *reasonable* responses.' "

"Miss Pleuter, I doubt that it says 'all *reasonalbe* responses.' "

"Well, not exactly."

"Good, then why don't you inform your client that I've made a counteroffer. I'll sell him the house in return for his life. You can never tell, Miss Pleuter. In this world today, he might jump at it."

"I'd have to see the house again, Dr. Wolper." Miss Pleuter was all business.

"Fine, fine. Come in," and Miss Pleuter, wedged into her dungarees and carrying one of the largest briefcases I have ever seen, entered.

"This is the nineteen-year-old nymphomaniac I'm teaching classical music to, Miss Pleuter. Her name is Meli. And this is Mrs. Mallory, our domestic," I introduced the others standing in the foyer.

"Is that all? Just domestic?" Miss Pleuter seemed very disappointed.

"Well, she also embalms, as a hobby," and Mrs. Mallory gagged and left in disgust for the kitchen. She stopped just before entering the kitchen.

"Don't forget that your lunch is on the table, Dr. Wolper," she smiled.

"You don't want your toads to get cold," and she curtsied and disappeared.

I showed Miss Pleuter the house, once again. While Meli was showing her the upstairs, I ran out to the lab and covered the jar that held the fetus with a thick black cloth.

I then rejoined them. Miss Pleuter was apparently on a schedule and heard very little of what we were saying to her. She looked at her watch frequently. It was distracting to say the least.

I took her out to the lab myself. Our relationship was strictly professional. She ignored my usual fun banter.

When we got into the lab something happened that I gave little thought to until this evening. Miss Pleuter had an asthma attack immediately upon entering. This meant that when the phone rang for her, I had to go across the yard to tell Mrs. Mallory to take the message. The whole business couldn't have taken more than three minutes, but, during that time, Miss Pleuter was alone to explore the lab as she wished. When I returned, she was remarkably recovered.

"This has been very helpful, Dr. Wolper," she smiled too broadly at me as she was leaving. "I'll convey your counteroffer to my client, but I'm not too hopeful that he'll accept. I think you're asking a little more than he had planned to pay."

"Well, perhaps you could ask him to think of it as giving his life for a great cause that transcends life itself," I suggested.

"What's that?" Miss Pleuter hitched up her beltless dungarees and headed for her car.

"Oh, I thought you'd know for sure Miss Pleuter. I'm a little disappointed." I walked with her.

"A great cause that transcends life?" Miss Pleuter thought it over very hard.

"Property, Miss Pleuter. Property."

"Oh, yes, Of course. Property. It *was* on the tip of my tongue," and she drove off in her red Porsche.

Something is going on here. And I can guarantee that, whatever it is, it's going to do me no damn good.

30th **The Adventures of Boris Lafkin**

CHAPTER THREE—(still continued): More Progressive Evaporation— Less Cosmic

Larry left about midnight. He took The Absolute with him for further study. I remained by Barbara's bed, holding her hand and looking for some sign that everything was going to be all right.

Other than the nurses, coming in every fifteen minutes to check her vital signs, I was alone in a hospital that was now largely dark and still. The overhead lights in the hall were off, and the linoleum shone from the slotted night-lights near the floor every few yards down the corridor.

I paced the hall every so often when I needed to stretch and ended up at the nurses' station where a small black-and-white television had the Night Owl News (interviews with the first black U.S. Supreme Court Justice, the first black mayors in America, and the first physician to transplant a human heart, quite a year for firsts, all in all, the newscaster and I agreed).

Every once in a while a private-duty nurse would pop her head out of a room for air, nod at me as I paced, and pop back in to resume her duty. As I walked, I began for the first time to consider the various options.

Barbara could be in a coma indefinitely. I would call up on Monday morning and explain the situation to my boss at MIL. I would use the resident's room for sleeping, eat in the cafeteria, and spend the rest of the time with Barbara. One time, and one time only, I would run home, pack a bag, and run back. After the first week, the problem would become a little more difficult. By then I would undoubtedly need to do laundry and take a shower. I could not take indefinite sick leave, and sooner or later I would have to leave the hospital if I wanted to lead a normal life. For right now, however, I had a week to decide.

I returned to Barbara's room and took my usual place next to her. I tried to think about other things to give my mind a rest from the seriousness of the present situation, but it was no use. Twelve hours ago my head was filled with Himalayan rabbits, and medical schools, what time we should leave for the movie and whether we could afford to eat out before it, where we should go for our honeymoon and when Barbara would get the time to study for her exams. Now, no matter how I tried, the only image in my head was a medical menagerie of massive cerebral hemorrhages, comas, and Berry aneurysms.

It was 2:00 A.M. and I had just put my head down on Barbara's bed when the Spencers entered the room. Mr. Spencer stood at the foot of the bed, staring intently at Barbara, while Mrs. Spencer walked over to Barbara and very slowly began to stroke her hair. She was crying, and the tears ran down her cheeks and dropped onto the sheets as she leaned over to kiss Barbara.

Mr. Spencer cleared his throat and joined Mrs. Spencer. He held her tightly, sensing that she was becoming a little unsteady on her feet, and talked to her.

"She looks just fine, don't you think, Betty?"

"She does, Stan. She really does," Mrs. Spencer agreed.

"I think she's going to do beautifully," Mr. Spencer told his wife, "just beautifully."

He was having the same problem I was having, equating this calm and peacefully sleeping young girl with someone who had just had a massive cerebral hemorrhage. There was no doubt that the girl with the stroke was in some other room. This one was simply taking a nap and would hop out of bed in a few hours to do her morning exercises because she thought her tummy was becoming too round.

For several minutes the Spencers just stood there, holding each other very tightly, side by side, and looking at Barbara. Then Mr. Spencer kissed his wife gently on the cheek and came over to me. He put his arm on my shoulder, but kept his eyes riveted on Barbara, as though he were afraid she would disappear if he took his eyes off her for even a second.

"We're awfully pleased that you're a member of our family," he said to me.

"I am, too," I said, and then I couldn't hold it in any longer. I started to cry, not weep, but cry, uncontrollably. The dikes were open. It was too much for Mrs. Spencer, who did the same. Then Mr. Spencer, his arm still on my shoulder, pulled me over a few steps to where Mrs. Spencer stood with her head buried in her hands, put his other arm around her, and, standing in this tight little circle, we all wept.

I can't remember how long we stood like this, or how it was that we ended, but I do remember that it wasn't long after this that we were sitting in the empty cafeteria, drinking one of many vending-machine cups of coffee to come.

"I feel really lousy that I didn't let you know that Barbara and I were living together," I said.

"We understand, Boris," Mrs. Spencer said. "Barbara always thought we were—terribly 'middle class' is, I believe, the way she described being out of step with the times."

I was going to say something but decided not to. Mrs. Spencer continued.

"If Barbara," Mrs. Spencer swallowed hard, "well, doesn't make it, Boris, Stan and I are happy knowing that Barbara was able to spend her last few months with someone who loved her as much as we know you did, Boris. We saw how happy she was when you came to visit us. We know it was a very special time for her."

"It was beautiful," was all I could manage to say without starting to weep again.

"When did you start living together?" Mr. Spencer asked.

"The beginning of July. Barbara really did want us to be married, you know."

"We do, Boris," Mr. Spencer assured me. "We saw that she signed the consent form in the emergency room as 'Mrs. Lafkin' when we came in just now, and we assume," Mr. Spencer smiled, "that you didn't have to hold her down to put on the wedding ring we see she's wearing."

I felt a little better.

"Well," I changed the topic, "I guess you want to get in touch with the doctor, soon. His name is Dr. Johnson."

"We've already talked to him, Boris," Mrs. Spencer informed me. "It doesn't look very good, does it?"

"Dr. Johnson would not win the Newbery Medal for happy endings," I offered. "Doctors are like that, and Dr. Johnson is worse than most. He got his bedside manner training from the Brothers Grimm. Doctors tell you the most horrible thing that could happen, so, if anything better happens, it looks like they've done this splendid medical job. If their dire predictions come true, then they look like they knew what they were saying all along. There's no way they can lose. If the rest of us lived like that, we'd spend our lives hiding under beds."

"He sounded very concerned and very realistic," Mr. Spencer said.

"The truth is, Mr. Spencer, that he doesn't actually *know* anything at all for certain. It's all probability and guesses. All he *knows* is that she's had a bad stroke. He doesn't know for certain how bad or whether she definitely can't recover."

"Boris," Mr. Spencer looked at me very kindly, "Betty and I think Barbara is going to die. We don't want her to die. God knows we don't want that. And, of course, we're going to do everything we can to save her. But we don't have too much hope, Boris. We think her death is inevitable," and he reached over and put his hand on top of his wife's.

The hospital intercom came on.

"Code blue, room 704. Code blue, room 704."

The intern, who had just sat down, pushed his chair back quickly, knocking it over, took a fast gulp of his coffee, and ran out the door, leaving the chair on the floor and the full cup of coffee on the table.

We all sat there frozen, not knowing what to do.

"I think we'd better go up," Mr. Spencer announced quietly, and we walked slowly from the cafeteria and took the elevator up to the seventh floor.

We couldn't look at each other. My heart was back up around my larynx. When we got to Barbara's room, it was the same scene all over again, interns and nurses rushing in and out with equipment, some abrupt instructions we couldn't understand coming from Dr. Johnson, then quiet.

We sat huddled together on the bench outside the room, not talking to each other, Mr. Spencer leaning back against the wall, with his eyes closed, rubbing his large hands over his bald scalp, Mrs. Spencer staring down at the floor and absently fingering the small gold crucifix that hung around her neck, and me trying to catch a glimpse of what was happening in Barbara's room whenever the door opened, and not succeeding.

In fifteen minutes, the interns and nurses left, wheeling their equipment in front of them, and a minute after that Dr. Johnson exited and walked over to us, very slowly, wiping perspiration from his forehead with a large handkerchief. He spoke deliberately. My metabolism ceased.

"We're going to move Barbara to the Intensive Care Unit. We've just had a bed freed, and we think that we can keep closer tabs on her vitals in the ICU."

We waited for a report of what the recent commotion had been about. Dr. Johnson shifted uneasily from foot to foot.

"I'm afraid that the edema has progressed to the lower centers and her breathing has stopped. We're breathing her artificially now. We expected it to affect her blood pressure, heart, and temperature, but it seems to have stopped there. There's no explanation for it. It happens sometimes, not frequently, but once in a thousand times, respiration fails and everything else is maintained. She'll be moved to the ICU in a couple of minutes. It's on the second floor at the opposite end from the emergency room entrance where you came in. But there's no real need to go there. Nothing's going to happen for a while."

Dr. Johnson looked extremely unhappy. We all sensed his dismay, but Mr. Spencer was the one who asked him about it. Dr. Johnson looked at us for a few minutes, trying to decide whether to tell us what was on his mind, if this were the time, if there were a delicate way to say it.

"Well," he finally said, taking a deep breath, "now that Barbara's on a respirator, it's very difficult to know how long it's going to take."

"Before she recovers?" I asked hopefully.

"No, Mr. Lafkin. Before she dies."

"How long does it usually take?" Mr. Spencer asked.

"It used to take a few days, a couple of weeks. Usually the patient died of pneumonia or some secondary lung problem. Now they've come out with a modified respirator that almost totally eliminates pneumonia because it heats and moisturizes the air all the time. Barbara could be like this for a year, even more. It's a living hell, Mr. and Mrs. Spencer. I wouldn't wish a nightmare like that on my worst enemy," and he walked away slowly shaking his head.

31st I went to my lab tonight to perform the postmortem on Meli's fetus. I reached for the black cloth that covered the jar where she floated, whisked it off, and, presto chango, she was gone.

Someone has stolen the fetus, and I know exactly who it is and what they plan to do with it.

As Mrs. Mallory so aptly puts it, "May God have mercy on my soul."

September

1st The Adventures of Boris Lafkin

CHAPTER FOUR:
In Which Our Hero Ascertains the Facts of Life

We dismissed Dr. Johnson's disposition of Barbara to medical purgatory as an exaggeration, plain and simple, and not worthy of further consideration. We were, in fact, so convinced that Barbara would either recover soon or, if necessary, die, that we refused to walk down the street to my apartment to get some rest until the nursing staff absolutely insisted on it. The head nurse guaranteed that she would phone us immediately if there were even the smallest significant change in Barbara's condition, and so we proceeded to go back to my apartment.

I had not expected the feelings that would inundate me as I reached the third floor and unlocked the door. It was not merely that the bed was unmade, that there were dirty dishes in the sink, papers and magazines strewn around the living room, but the apartment was in its present state because Barbara and I were going to be back in an hour or so when we left. I couldn't figure out what went wrong.

I can't imagine what the Spencers must have felt on seeing Barbara's and my life so obviously interwoven, old dishes and pots they had given her now mixed in with mine, our toilet articles intermingled on the back of the sink, Barbara's nightgown and my pajamas together in a pile on the bed.

Barbara had made the apartment very much hers. Her curtains, originally her parents', were on the windows. Her favorite prints and photographs were on the walls, and her personal belongings, objets d'art, her wine bottles by which she had sat talking for hours as candle wax covered them, her books, her records and clothes, filled the apartment with her person.

It was impossible to tell which was harder for the Spencers to take, Barbara's presence or the idea that she had joined her life to someone else's without their knowing it.

"I'm really sorry about all this," I said to the Spencers after we had walked down the hall to the kitchen. It was a general expression of regret that included all omissions and accidents, the dirty apartment, not informing them that we were living together, and Barbara's cerebral hemorrhage.

"Boris, please don't worry about a few dirty dishes," Mrs. Spencer took the most obvious meaning. "We know you hadn't really planned to be having guests."

Mr. Spencer had been standing in the kitchen looking at the family photographs Barbara had tacked to the makeshift bulletin board we had attached to the side of the refrigerator.

"I think I'd like to go sit in the other room for a few minutes, Betty," he announced. "May I borrow some of these pictures for a few minutes, Boris?"

I knew what he wanted and, of course, agreed, fighting hard not to tell him to take them all and keep them. It would have been an admission of defeat. I was not going to think about disposing of Barbara's property until she was dead, and that was that.

"I think we'll stay here, Stan," Mrs. Spencer said and proceeded to start to wash the dishes. I knew she had to do this, and so I went into the bedroom, cleaned up, and put fresh sheets on the bed. As I walked down the hall to put the dirty sheets in the bathroom hamper, I could see Mr. Spencer sitting on the edge of the sofa, his head buried in his hands. The pictures of Barbara had fallen to the floor in front of him. His body shook as he wept.

I put up some water for tea, and when he heard the whistle, he joined us around the kitchen table. We sat in silence, the stillness broken only by the sound of the spoons against the inside of the cups as we all stirred our tea absently. None of us took sugar or cream. We just stared into our cups and stirred away, hoping that an answer would rise out of the whirlpool.

"Mr. Spencer," I decided to take the bull by the horns, "we've got to do something. We can't just let Barbara lie there like that. It's not fair." It was an impassioned plea, generated by frustration and anger, and resting on the premise that spirit was all, that out of fervent desire would come a solution.

"What do you think we should do, Boris?" Mrs. Spencer asked, obviously willing to perform any task within the most extreme limits if there were one chance in a million it would help Barbara.

"Something. Anything," I said. "We have to think this thing out. There's got to be an answer somewhere. Things like this just don't happen out of the blue. We can't let some third-year medical resident tie our hands with a bunch of mumbo jumbo about massive hemorrhages and three-year-long comas."

"You think we should get another opinion," Mr. Spencer said, "and, of course, we've planned to do that. First thing this morning, we'll start making calls. Other than that, I think we just have to be patient."

This was no time to argue with stoic philosophies of resignation, so I just half-nodded my head in agreement and let the matter drop. In any event, it became clear that we were all exhausted, and so, without finishing our tea, we all went off to bed, the Spencers to use Barbara's and mine, and I to go back to the sofa after only a brief four-month absence.

As exhausted as we were at 4:00 A.M., it was obvious to us all that we wouldn't be getting much sleep. I could hear the muffled sounds of the Spencers talking to each other the rest of the night, interrupted on occasion by what I guessed was Mrs. Spencer's crying.

I stayed awake, staring at the ceiling, imagining the previous night when Barbara and I were snuggled into each other's arms. More than anything else, I wanted to walk into our bedroom and switch on the lights.

"I'm sorry to bother you," I pictured myself saying to the Spencers, "but you know that none of this is real, don't you? This is just some book that a crazy old biologist is conjuring up because he's bored and afraid of his own death. The problem is, you see, that he's a raving lunatic and is unable to understand the pain he's putting us through. But don't worry. We've got a contract. Barbara will completely recover and everything will be fine. Just thought you might want to know. Sorry if I disturbed you."

It wouldn't work, I knew. They'd never believe that their pain wasn't real but, for all intents and purposes, just some random words set down by a crazy man who hadn't the slightest notion of what he was doing.

I couldn't sleep, so after a couple of hours, as it was getting light, I got up and dressed. I left a note on the refrigerator saying that I had gone back to the hospital, and left for a walk.

The sky was still gray, and it wasn't possible to tell whether the sun would be coming out or not. There were only a few leaves, scattered here and there on otherwise empty trees. Cambridge had started its long academic winter. It would be half a year before there would be any green and a month after that before it would be possible to be outside comfortably with only a thin jacket or sweater.

Where would Barbara be then? The thought ricocheted around my head as I headed toward the hospital. There was no answer that satisfied me. I tried hard to picture Barbara walking by my side, carrying an ice-cream cone, talking about the department at Harvard, or someone she knew who was getting divorced. It was no use. The images faded before I could get hold of them. I had no more luck picturing her in some chronic-care hospital, comatose, or recovering from her illness. Nothing fit. Absolutely nothing. There was no future.

I decided not to go into the hospital right away but continue my walk down Cambridge Street.

Six o'clock mass is very popular in Cambridge, particularly with the students. It allows them to go right from their Saturday night partying to church, have breakfast afterwards, and then go back to the dorm for sleep, waking for supper and a night of studying for the next week's classes, rested and well-fed.

I had never been to church, but if there ever were a time to start, I decided this was it, and so I found myself sitting in the last pew of the church across from the hospital, listening to the chants and liturgy of a trio of white-robed celebrants.

The ceremony was in Latin, I wasn't sure why, but it gave me the opportunity to sit back, close my eyes, and soak in the ritual. From time to time I opened my eyes and tried to decipher the scenes and Latin inscriptions on the stained-glass windows that encircled the church.

As I sat there soaked in ritual, I felt a surge of energy. Medical science had given me a chance to do battle with the cosmos, I realized. I had been given the opportunity to engage in hand-to-hand combat with the great unknown. If this was what Harry wanted, then this is what he'd get. And, in turn, I'd get my profound religious experience.

I began to feel giddy with power. I could solve this. It was simply a matter of guts, stamina, spirit, and intelligence. I would, of course, have to withstand the devious attacks from the medical profession, who only dealt in science.

Barbara was going to make it. I knew it now. Not through miracles, but through a joint effort.

A plan materialized. We would do it together, Barbara and I.

For a second I wondered if I were going mad under the strain.

"But I have a plan now," I thought. "It's a first-class beautiful scheme. It's got to work. As for my possible insanity, well, who the hell cares," and I raced from the church, dropping some change in the collection basket as I exited, and dashed across the street to get to Barbara and begin my brilliant strategy.

3rd Knock, knock, knock and guess who it was who came to visit me tonight?

It was that hero of the National Socialist Party, Arnold Wolper.

He just dropped in to say hello.

"Hello," he said.

"Why did you steal my fetus from the lab?" I said.

"How'd you know that I did it?" Arnold was startled.

"A vision, Arnold. I had a vision."

"Well," Arnold mumbled, "I figured that you'd never give me what I wanted until I had something on you. I'll bet you the police would sure love to have that fetus dropped in their laps. That'd take care of the old mad abortionist, wouldn't it?"

"It's not a fetus that's been *aborted*, you know, Arnold."

"Doesn't make any difference, does it, Dad."

"I grew it from an egg, unfertilized, in a jar, and it died a natural death."

"Well, that'd get you a verdict of insanity, anyway."

"Arnold, you just may have accomplished the first successful thing on your own in your life."

"Oh, the fetus thing wasn't my idea. That was Maury Halpern's. He thought that some poking around might turn up something interesting."

"He wants my property, too?"

"No, no. He just was angry at you about something. I think it had to do with a fish. I told him I'd poke around in your lab. Afterwards, I told him that I didn't find anything. I thought the guy was going to weep all night. I've never seen anyone so heartbroken. He had his whole life invested in the thing."

"Now what, Arnold?"

"I don't know, Dad. Now what? You tell me. The way I figure it, myself, the evidence is overwhelming. The courts are just filled with right-to-life judges around here. You could, if you want, spend all your time and energy fighting the thing. At best, you'd end up in some state hospital for the criminally insane."

"Arnold, I'd like you to leave now."

"Sure thing," he smiled, knowing he had the upper hand.

"I don't know what I'm going to do, but I do know this. I don't ever want to see you again. Not once. Not even by accident. Now get out of here."

"I can understand your being upset, Dad. It's only natural. But you'll feel better after a few days. I'm sure that we can resume our relationship then as though nothing has happened."

I threw a very heavy book at him, and he turned quickly, but not quickly enough. It landed rather solidly on the back of his head.

"Dammit, Dad," he whined as he skipped out of the room, "that hurt!"

"You're damn right it did. And it's only the beginning."

4th "Jesus H. Christ, Dr. Wolper, you get yourself into the damndest fuckin' messes I have ever heard of," Tony Pascotti said as he scratched his balls. "Let me see if I've got this right. Your fuckin' son has stolen some fetus from your fuckin' lab. Is it a human fetus, because I don't think there's any law against giving a fuckin' rabbit an abortion."

"No. It's human," I said sadly.

"Where the fuck did you get it?"

"Do you really have to know?"

"I do if you want me to give you any fuckin' legal advice. Where the fuck did you get the fetus? With anyone else, the answer would be obvious. With you, nothing is obvious."

"It's not obvious, Tony."

"Where, Dr. Wolper?"

"From a jar."

"Ah come on, Dr. Wolper. My time is valuable. I'm not any fuckin' scientist, but I know that jars don't have babies, not even fuckin' baby *jars*. Where'd it come from?"

"I grew it."

"Look, Wolper, you want me to give you some fuckin' help or not?"

"Well, it's the truth. I retrieved the ovum from Meli. But it wasn't fertilized. I started it accidentally."

"I see. The fuckin' egg just kind of brushed against some semen accidentally. It was a fuckin' accident. You're worse than the fuckin' kids I defend on paternity suits."

"Look, Tony. I retrieved the egg from Meli. Accidentally in the retrieval I poked it. It's called parthenogenesis. It happens. It started to grow. I put it into a solution to keep it alive, and it stayed alive for about eight weeks."

"What's the solution called?"

"The solution?"

"Yeah, that's right, Dr. Wolper. What's the fuckin' solution called that you put it in?"

"The Great Wiper."

"The fuckin' what?"

"The Great Wiper. I don't know what it's composed of. It's just a lot of random chemicals. That's the whole point."

Tony Pascotti sat back in his swivel chair and crunched his cigar between his teeth.

"Dr. Wolper," he finally said, "I wouldn't touch this fuckin' case if the judge was my fuckin' brother. There is no one in the world who's going to let you walk on the streets after hearing that fuckin' story. They'll put us both away."

"What'll I do then?"

"Exactly what that fuckin' ass-hole son of yours told you to do. Forget it. Give your son whatever the fuck he wants. You can afford it. Then just pretend the whole fuckin' mess never happened. It's a standoff. That's the best fuckin' legal advice I can give you."

"That's hardly a very moral solution to the problem," I pointed out. "My son is blackmailing me."

"Lookit, Wolper, you didn't come to me for *religious* counselling. You came to me for *legal* counselling. I learned long ago that morality hasn't got a fuckin' thing to do with what I do to make a living. This is a fuckin' business, Wolper, just like any other business. In my business, I'm trying to sell a fuckin' story. And I know my market, the fuckin' judges, and I know what fuckin' stories they're going to buy, how to package them, and how much to ask for them. Your story is fuckin' worthless, Wolper. You couldn't give it away. All the prosecutor has to do is parade that fuckin' fetus in front of the jury, and you could be Jehovah himself, and they'd still put you away where they could keep a fuckin' eye on you. The last thing in the world the judge is interested in is morality. The minute I mention the fuckin' word, he'll throw me out of the courtroom. There isn't any statute on the books called 'morality,' and, if it isn't a fuckin' statute, he's got no fuckin' interest in it."

"You're telling me that I should allow my own son to blackmail me without thinking I'm acting immorally?"

"Hell, no, Wolper. You didn't ask me what you should *think*. You asked me what you should *do*. You can think whatever the fuck you want to think. Fuck, yes, it's immoral, and disgraceful, and a fuckin' shame to boot. But what's been done has been done and all the fuckin' morality in the world isn't going to change that. I'm trying to keep you from spending the rest of your life in some institution pressing denim shirts all day and trying not to get raped all night. Now that hasn't a fuckin' thing to do with morality, the way I see it. There're people walking around out there in the real world who've killed more people than you've shaken hands with. It seems to me that if they don't go to jail, then you don't, but it's up to you. Go be moral. That'll do it for fuckin' sure."

"You hardly leave me a choice."

"Oh, you've got a choice, Wolper. Everyone's got a fuckin' choice. But just remember that this is the real world you're living in, not Holy Scripture. There isn't anybody who's going to turn your life into a fuckin' parable. You can count on it. In this world, judges get piles, and have eighteen-year-old secretaries they screw in their chambers, and I haven't known one yet who got where he was because he made a long string of brilliant decisions. So why don't you go home, give your fuckin' son what you can, tell him to go fuck off, and then forget the whole fuckin' mess. I know you, Wolper. You don't have time to get involved with morality. You've got too many fuckin' people to grow."

5th Meli kicked off her sneakers and leaned back in the large Victorian chair. She was in a foul mood.

"Tomorrow we listen to Ravel, Stravinsky, and Tchaikovsky," I told her. "Perhaps you'll like them better."

She lit up a cigarette and puffed furiously.

"You know something, Dr. Wolper, I didn't like Rossini, Strauss, and Telemann yesterday. I didn't like Rachmaninoff, Schönberg, and Thompson today. I'm not going to like whoever the hell they are tomorrow. I'm just classical musically exhausted. If I hear one more violin, I'm going to go out of my goddam skull."

"Maybe a rest would be in order," I suggested.

"Not a rest, Dr. Wolper, a burial. That's enough. I don't care about major fifths and minor thirds anymore. And never once, not even when you were crowing like a goddam dying rooster, did I hear a *leading tone.* If it *did* free all those goddam forces that were polarized by the tonal principle, whatever the hell *that* is, I wish it hadn't. I wish it had left it frozen, or whatever the hell it was before someone decided to *un*polarize it. I like it better polarized, if you want to know the goddam truth."

Meli continued to chug at her cigarette, large clouds of smoke billowing around her.

"And another thing," she stuck her head out from the surrounding cloud. "Remember what I told you about how long love lasts. Well, Dr. Wolper, we're coming down the homestretch. Three weeks, twenty-one days, that's all. Today's the fifth. If you haven't made up your mind by the twenty-sixth, then on the twenty-seventh, poof. I'm splitting. And believe me, that's stretching it."

I sat back on the sofa and watched Meli puffing.

"You're especially upset today."

"Of course, I'm especially upset today," she mimicked me. "You know what I spent this afternoon doing? Reading this goddam book I found on your desk," and she threw a copy of Hegel over at me. "I want to be able to talk to you, Dr. Wolper, and if you can understand that, then we're just never going to be able to talk. I'm an idiot. I know it," and her eyes began to moisten.

"Maybe you're the bright one and he's the idiot?"

"Sure. Only the last time I looked, the number of people asking to publish what I thought about the world were pretty goddam limited."

"Meli, come over here by me."

"What the hell for?"

"Because I want to talk to you."

"I can hear you from over here."

"I can't hold you when you're across the room."

"Well, you didn't say you wanted to *hold* me," and she trotted across the room with her cigarettes and ashtray, and settled on the sofa next to me. I put my arm around her while she pouted.

"You mustn't think you're stupid because you can't understand Hegel," I said in my most reassuring manner. "There have been men who've spent their entire lives trying to understand the man."

"Well, what the hell's the use of saying something if no one can understand you? When I tell you that if you haven't made up your mind in three weeks, then I'm leaving, you know goddam well what I'm saying. You don't have to go get a goddam *interpretation* of the *true meaning.*"

"Philosophy is a little more complicated than that, Meli. We're dealing with some very complex issues."

"What the hell's so complicated about saying that the whole goddam world, including us, is always changing and growing, and who we are depends on all the goddam stuff that's going on around us, which is what the hell he's saying, isn't it?"

My mouth fell open and I looked at her in astonishment.

"Well," she asked, "isn't that all he's trying to say?"

"More or less, yes it is, Meli."

"Well, then why the hell doesn't he just say it, instead of talking all the time about some goddam Absolute, and everything is some lousy moment in the Absolute, and all that shit. I think the man is perverse, and I think he does it on purpose. He's got this goddam romantic obsession with every lousy flaw in everything we do. And he makes me feel stupid, besides."

I leaned back and closed my eyes slowly. I could picture a three-by-six plot of earth in some Berlin cemetery heaving violently as its occupant turned and twisted. Slowly I reopened my eyes and looked at Meli.

"Well?" she said.

"Philosophers can't just *say* a thing, Meli. They have to *prove* it," I finally answered her.

"What the hell for? Just so the next philosopher can come along and *dis*prove it. That's the goddam point that Hegel keeps on making, isn't it? Every time you prove something, someone comes along and proves the opposite. You say yes. I say no. Then we talk about how we can both be right at the same time, and that's how we're always learning some new goddam thing about the world, right? Well, isn't it, Dr. Wolper?"

"Hegel feels that sorting out the contradiction is what makes for the poetry of our lives. It's why we're passionate."

"Well, Hegel and I have different ideas of what passion is. That's for sure. What he talks about makes life goddam tragic, not passionate."

"I think you're right, Meli. Hegel felt that life always has intellectual, ethical, and metaphysical tragedies going on at the same time."

"Yeah, well I think the tragedy is that there's no value in finding out who you are and being it. You always have to be part of some goddam social order, and I don't like it. If he's right, I'm going to be so goddam angry, I can't tell you. I want to be *me*, dammit, not some goddam Nazi."

"Meli," I beamed, "I think you've understood Hegel beautifully."

"You do?" she began to smile and then decided she hadn't made her point. "Well, I don't. I don't like people who write like that, and I don't like the idea that *you* enjoy reading people like that. It separates us by eight goddam oceans. And it's too much goddam work. I *know* that everything's always changing all the time. I *know* that every time I think I understand something I find out that just the opposite is true. And I *hate* it. I absolutely *hate* it. I don't need to spend all afternoon trying to decipher some goddam philosopher just to have him tell me what I already know."

"But he's trying to help us understand how to *live*, as well, Meli."

"I hope you're not talking about all that goddam stuff about freedom, because I've known people in Leavenworth who've had more freedom than that."

"Real freedom, Meli, according to Hegel, is not just doing as one pleases. Real freedom is the power to realize one's self. And that's by identifying with our fellowman and accepting the responsibilities and duties that come from it."

"Yeah, well that may be freedom for him, but freedom for me is still doing whatever the hell I want to do. He can write about the Absolute and spirit until the world runs out of paper for all I care. I just don't buy it. I am not a goddam slave just because I want to be me and do just what the hell I want to do, and I am certainly not evil because I don't like things changing all around me all the time and I want to stop them. And any man who says so, as far as I'm concerned, is a goddam pervert. And that's that."

"That is that," I agreed and hugged Meli very tightly.

"And that includes you, too, Dr. Wolper, if you believe any of it. I want you to stop reading this kind of crap before it ruins your goddam mind."

"I agree."

"I mean it. I saw you sneaking a look at this last night. If you keep on doing it, we're *never* going to be able to talk to each other." She lit another cigarette. "You promise? No more thinking. We're just going to live. At least for the next three weeks, we are."

"I promise. Three weeks of life," and we went upstairs for another exhausting and futile attempt at sexual intercourse.

6th The Adventures of Boris Lafkin

CHAPTER FOUR (continued):
The Facts of Life in Every Gory Detail

When I entered, the hospital was just waking up. Nurses and orderlies were walking briskly from room to room, picking up and filling water pitchers, checking temperatures and blood pressures, regulating IVs, and washing people. The medication nurse was wheeling her stainless-steel cart of bottles and paper cups from room to room, humming and greeting everyone with a cheerful "good morning" found only in hospitals.

I weaved my way through the nursing staff, which dodged in and out of doorways, until I got to the double doors that led into the Intensive Care Unit. As I reached up to open them, a voice called me from the hallway that turned to my right. I turned and saw a group of people sitting on a sofa and lounge chairs set up halfway down the hall. Someone in a white jacket was waving me to come over.

As I approached, I recognized him as a former college roommate of mine, Saul Shore. He was talking to Mr. and Mrs. Spencer and Larry, who had somehow materialized out of the morning gray.

"I'm terribly sorry to hear about Barbara," Saul said to me as we shook hands. I read the label on his lapel, which said Saul Shore, M.D.

"What are you doing here?" I asked.

"I'm the chief resident here. Dr. Johnson filled me in on the details. I didn't know Barbara very well, but I knew she was a great gal. What a damn tragedy."

Mr. Spencer cleared his throat and ran his palm across his bald head.

"What do you recommend we do?" he asked in a throaty voice.

"There isn't really much to do," Saul answered. "We just have to wait for nature to take its course." It was clear he was not talking about spontaneous recovery. "I would like to recommend we ask in someone for a consultation. Noah Walensky is the chairman of the Department of Neurosurgery at Harvard Medical School and has spent most of his life specializing in Cerebral Vascular Accidents. If there's any way of handling a CVA successfully, he'll know. I thought it might be helpful to ask him to have a look at Barbara."

That was more like it. For the first time it sounded like we were starting to get somewhere. Walensky would know what to do. He was an expert, and that's what we needed. Someone who knew what the hell he was doing.

"I think that's an excellent idea," Mr. Spencer said. He, too, seemed to be somewhat cheered by the thought. "Do you think he's available?"

"Well, I know he's in town, because he's got surgery scheduled tomorrow morning, and he never goes out of town the day before he has surgery. I don't know what his plans are for today. It *is* Sunday. But I'll give him a call now. He's an early riser." Saul headed for a telephone.

We sat there without talking while we waited to hear whether the Messiah worked on Sundays. Larry left for the john and returned several minutes later, colored your basic postpuke ocher and looking like he wanted to talk, so I grabbed for a five-year-old copy of *Sports Afield* that was lying on the table in front of me and buried myself in an article about shooting fish with a .22 caliber pistol in the Estonian Interior where, the facing page told me, there was also a full case of Canadian Club suspended on a tripod over an active volcano.

For the next fifteen minutes I read about killing for sport. Then Saul returned.

"Dr. Walensky will be here at two-thirty this afternoon," he announced. "You can go in to see Barbara now if you want, but no more than two people at a time and no more than twenty minutes."

I turned to the Spencers.

"You go," I said. "I want to talk to Larry for a few minutes."

Larry looked up in shock as everyone left for the ICU. He picked up my *Sports Afield* and started doodling absently. I felt like I had to say something. For the last ten minutes I had felt an unexpected sympathy for Larry's predicament swell up in me.

"Larry," I cleared my throat. "I'd like it if you'd stick around, huh?" and I looked at him in the eyes so he could tell I really meant it. "I mean, who the hell knows what Barbara's going to do when she comes out of this thing. She may have nothing to do with either one of us."

"I've got no business being here, Boris. I know that. I think I'm going to go home."

"I wish you'd stay, Larry, really."

"Nah, I've got to go," he continued to doodle on the magazine. "I can use some sleep."

I looked at him and knew he had understood what I wanted to say. There was nothing more I could do. He got up, put down his magazine, and started down the hall. He stopped before turning the corner and looked back at me.

"You'll let me know what happens, Boris, please," he said, starting to cry. He started to turn away then stopped. "Thanks for the invitation, Boris, but I think I'd rather go home. You'll let me know, huh?"

"You'll be the first person I'll call, Larry. I swear it."

"That's good, Boris. That's really good," and Larry disappeared around the corner.

I sat down to wait my turn to see Barbara, staring at the magazine Larry had left open on the table, still turned to the grotesque bullet-ridden fish. Larry had carefully labeled each of the seven bullet holes with B-A-R-B-A-R-A, and then had drawn an X through each letter.

My time to see Barbara had almost come. The Spencers had just opened the doors to leave the ICU when a shrill loud voice called my name from about as far behind me as a person could get and still be on the same floor. There was no mistaking the voice.

"Mother," I said, as the sealskin coat swished down the hall toward me.

"Boris, Boris, Boris, Boris, Boris." My mother is one of those people who is oral without being verbal, the result of having a very large mouth and a very small vocabulary.

"Hello, Mother." I tried to calm her down. "This is Stan and Betty Spencer, Barbara's parents," I said. "Mr. and Mrs. Spencer, my mother, Harriet."

"Oh, I'm just so *glad* to meet you. What a tragedy. What a horrible *damn* tragedy," my mother threw in the expletive for sincerity. "How did something like this ever *happen?*"

"We're not sure ourselves," Mrs. Spencer answered.

My mother glared at me. She knew for certain that I had done it. The Spencers were, she was sure, just being nice about it.

"Well, I'm *terribly* sorry," my mother apologized for whatever it was I had done. Then, to encompass the human experience, "Death is always such a hard thing, if you know what I mean."

"Barbara's not dead, Mother," I informed her.

"Oh, isn't that *marvelous*," Mother beamed. "You all must be so *happy*."

I couldn't put my finger on it, but for some reason I was experiencing that old familiar discomfort that always enveloped me when I was in company with my mother—obviously, my mother had pointed out both publicly and privately, an unresolved Oedipal something or other. Only I didn't feel a lack of Oedipal resolution. I felt a surplus of embarrassment.

Saul Shore, M.D., turned the corner and headed toward us. I was hoping he was on his way somewhere else, but, as luck would have it, he joined us as we all sat in the lounge area again.

"Mother, this is Dr. Shore. He used to be my roommate at college."

"It's nice to meet you, Dr. Shore," Mother smiled.

"Dr. Shore is the chief resident here, and is responsible for Barbara's treatment, Mother," I informed her.

Mother didn't like this idea at all. Doctors under the age of fifty are universally incompetent. "It takes twenty years of practice just to tell a hiccup from a cough," she informed me at the age of eight, just as her father, who was a physician, had informed her, I surmised.

"So," Mother flashed her crocodile smile, "you're a student here, *Mr.* Shore?"

"No, I'm a doctor here, Mrs. Lafkin," Saul answered patiently.

"Oh, really. Where did you go to school?" she continued undaunted.

Saul took a sip from the paper cup of coffee he had brought with him and actually appeared to be amused.

"A local medical school. I'm not sure you've heard of it."

"Try me."

"Harvard."

"I've heard of it."

"Good."

There was the terrible silence before the battle. Mother took out her notepad and pen. The weapons were cocked. The lines drawn. Charge.

Mother: When do you expect Barbara to recover, Dr. Shore?

Saul: We don't, Mrs. Lafkin. Her condition is terminal.

Mother: Could you tell me why, Dr. Shore?

Saul: She's had a massive cerebral hemorrhage, which has destroyed most of her brain. The edema has caused the brain to force itself down into the opening at the base of the skull, cutting off the lower centers. She is being breathed artificially and maintains only her heart, blood pressure, and temperature on her own. Most of her reflexes have gone.

Mother: Are you telling me, Dr. Shore, that she's had a stroke and coned?

Saul: Yes, I am.

Mother: As the blood is reabsorbed into the system, the edema will subside. Isn't that correct?

Saul: Yes, that's true.

Mother: And the coning will recede?

Saul: Yes, it will.

Mother: And the loss of reflexes could very well be Central Nervous System shock. That's not at all unusual, is it? They could easily recover.

Saul: They could, yes. But there's been extensive damage to major cortical centers.

Mother: Well, you don't really *know* that, do you Dr. Shore, because you can't see inside her head. As a matter of fact, everything you look at is so confounded by the CNS trauma that you can't be sure of anything you're seeing except increased intracranial pressure, can you?

Saul: It can be somewhat confusing at times.

Mother: How long had she been comatose when she was brought in, Dr. Shore?

Saul: She walked into the emergency room, Mrs. Lafkin.

Mother: You mean to tell me she *walked* in here *prior* to her hemorrhage?

Saul: Yes. Her hemorrhage didn't occur until an hour or so after she had been here.

Mother: And someone on your staff looked at her?

Saul: Yes.

Mother: And didn't pick it up?

Saul: Her condition was somewhat suspicious.

Mother: Somewhat suspicious? Somewhat suspicious! That girl had to walk in here with such elevated intracranial pressure that even the most routine funduscopic examination would have picked it up. You would have had to be blind not to have seen it.

I had been trying for a cease-fire for the last few minutes, and all I had to show for it were some very badly bruised shins and ribs.

We were all extremely uncomfortable, particularly Dr. Shore. He turned to the Spencers.

"The type of examination that Mrs. Lafkin is talking about is *not* routine. It requires a high degree of medical sophistication to pick up the subtle changes involved."

"Then why do it, Dr. Shore?" Mother pursued. "This man is incompe tent. He should be taken off the case immediately. Barbara should be moved to another hospital," Mother announced.

"I will certainly withdraw from the case, if you wish, Mr. Spencer. I don't recommend that we move Barbara this soon after the hemorrhage, but I'll do that, too, if you ask me," Saul said quietly.

"We've been very pleased with the care she's been getting here, Dr. Shore, and we'd like you to continue to supervise her treatment," Mr. Spencer answered quietly.

Mother gasped. Hadn't people been listening? She turned to the Spencers.

"You have grounds for a malpractice suit here, you know," she told them.

"We don't want a malpractice suit," Mrs. Spencer responded. "We only want our daughter to live."

Mother picked up the subtle indications that she was not wanted.

"Well," she breathed a long sigh of resignation, "I tried." Then she smiled broadly. "How does one get out of this place?"

"I'll show you," Saul offered, much to no one's surprise. "I'm on my way downstairs," and he raised his long frame off the chair.

"I can't begin to tell you how nice it's been to meet you—uh—," Mother looked at me for help.

"Stan and Betty," I filled in.

"Oh, yes, yes, of course. Stan and Betty. I'm terribly sorry that I couldn't stay longer, but you know how it is. Rush, rush, rush. I did enjoy myself, though," and she shook Mr. Spencer's hand, startled Mrs. Spencer by pecking her on the cheek, smiled at me while shaking her head in disgust at how bourgeois everyone was being, and started down the hall with Dr. Shore.

"So, you went to Harvard, *Dr.* Shore." Mother was on the make. "You must be *terribly* bright," her voice trailed off.

As I watched them disappear into the elevator I felt that old familiar pain of separation, not sharp but dull and depressing. I really wished that Mother had had a chance to meet Barbara once or twice. I think she would have liked her.

The Spencers decided to go back to the apartment for an hour or so to try to get some rest before lunch and Dr. Walensky's arrival. I finally made it through the double doors and into the ICU.

I wasn't really sure what to expect, but I was startled. Barbara was barely visible through the intravenous lines, catheters, bottles, monitors, and machines that surrounded her. It reminded me of the laboratory of a mad scientist. All that was missing was the electrical generator overhead ready to infuse life into the corpse by striking it with its cackling electricity.

On a pole by the left side of the bed were a number of bottles with homemade adhesive-tape labels, on which someone had scribbled in red marker pen. Urea-50 percent-40 gms. Glucose 5 percent. Multivit. Ampicillin 10 gms. From each bottle a small yellow tube led into a large yellow tube that was affixed to Barbara's left arm where the IV needle was inserted in her vein. On the side of the mattress, a clear plastic bag was pinned, which collected Barbara's urine.

On the right side of the bed was a heart monitor tracing white systolic and diastolic waves silently across the green screen. The only sound in the ward was coming from beside the heart monitor, where a green plastic box was breathing Barbara. It went click as it started, pooooofff as it inflated her lungs, and sissss as it released the air to return and start over again. Click, pooooofff, sisss. Click, pooof, sisss. Sixteen times a minute. I counted them. It was not an unfamiliar instrument. On the side it said, "Made by Medical Instruments Laboratory, Cambridge, Massachusetts." On the front it said, "Respirator, L-Modification." The L stood for Lafkin.

I closed my eyes very tightly to try to block out a persistent image. Barbara and I were jumping around the kitchen in our apartment, hugging each other while I waved a $500 check in my greedy little hand.

The image faded, and I pulled up a chair beside Barbara. I squeezed in on the right between the heart monitor and the respirator. Barbara didn't look quite so good anymore. Her color was pale, and her cheeks seemed to be caved in. There was something almost comforting about this. She was no longer just a sleeping princess who was going to awaken at a kiss. Barbara was seriously ill.

I held her hand and for the first time focused on what was going on around me. The ward was not particularly big, only four beds, with a nurses' station at one end of the room where an RN, an LPN, and an aide sat filling in charts. All the beds were filled, and all the patients were comatose like Barbara.

I tightened my grip on Barbara's hand. It seemed as though her hand had gotten thinner since I had last held it, and it was much colder than mine. I didn't like what I was seeing at all, a cold wispy creature with tubes going in and out of her, machines keeping track of every event in her body, and a hose, as large as her mouth itself, feeding air into her chest to keep her alive. There was no question in my mind. This was the time to begin my plan.

10th "I didn't mind the Vivaldi," Meli told me tonight. "But why the hell I ever let you talk me into listening to Wagner is beyond me. God is that ever *depressing*. I've had more fun putting hot compresses on swollen parts of my body."

"He's not really that bad, Meli, once you get used to him," I experimented.

"Dr. Wolper, if I ever get used to him, I want them to put me away for good. This man is a dismal person, Dr. Wolper. I can tell. He *thrives* on gloom."

"Some other time I'll play something a little lighter for you, Meli. All his music isn't that melancholy."

"Maybe not, but do me a favor. If we ever get married, no ring, huh? It isn't worth it."

The word *marriage* had not come up for several days. The great Impending Decision took its place in the center of the living room as soon as Meli uttered the words. We regarded it in silence. Meli was the first to speak.

"There's only about two weeks left, huh, Dr. Wolper," Meli said with sadness in her voice.

"I guess so," I said with equal resignation.

"You know, Dr. Wolper, I don't really want to do this, because, like, I think I'm going to miss you a hell of a lot. I really like our talks, and evenings and all that stuff. I'm kind of dreading when your records get to Z. I know I've hated most of them, but I like them, too. I can't imagine what my life would be like without all that lousy goddam music you play all the time. But I just have got to do this, you know what I mean?"

"I do, yes, Meli." I put my arm around her and pulled her closer to me on the sofa.

"I'd really like us to make it, but I've got to live my life, too. I'd like to think that it wouldn't make any difference to me if a guy was impotent, at least not if I really loved him, but I just don't think I'd do too good in the long run married to an impotent guy. It's that old mind-body problem you told me about last night."

"Spirit and flesh, Meli. The struggle between spirit and flesh."

"Yeah, well whatever it's called, all I know is that my flesh hasn't even *heard* from my spirit since I started wearing training bras, and as near as I can tell, there's no sign that there's going to be any enormous change. My flesh would *kill* me if I went and married some other flesh that was impotent. I absolutely know it."

Meli squirmed in my arms and began to run her fingers through my beard.

"It's just the most complicated goddam thing I've ever experienced in my whole lousy life. Here's some guy who I love more than I've loved anyone in my entire life and who I really want to ask me to marry him, and, if he does ask me, I'm probably going to turn him down, and I don't *want* to turn him down. Isn't that a goddam mess, Dr. Wolper? What the hell am I supposed to *do*?"

"I think you're doing what you have to. As you said, Meli, you have a life to live."

"Sure, but what the hell good is it if you can't spend it with someone who you love? You see the problem?"

"You'll find somebody else."

"But I don't know that for sure. If I knew it, then it might be okay. The problem, as near as I can figure it, Dr. Wolper, is how the hell do you know what to do when you don't know *any goddam thing at all?* That's the problem in an eggshell."

"*That's* the problem," I repeated.

"In an eggshell," Meli nodded emphatically.

"In an eggshell," I concurred.

11th "So where's the girl, Wolper," the dream began.

"Lookit," I snapped. "If *I* don't get the girl, *you* don't get the girl."

"You're really asking for it, Wolper," and the man adjusted his toga. "You know in one sweep of these hands I can pull everything, absolutely everything, right out from under you, Reason, Order, Truth, the Good, the Absolute, you name it. One gesture and it's all down the tubes. I'd be a little more respectful, if I were you."

A tiny voice from behind caused me to spin around in dismay.

"Who the hell's he, Dr. Wolper?" Meli asked.

"Get back into your own dream, Meli."

"Oh, I'm tired of my dreams. All I do is try to keep the Washington Monument from collapsing. I'm bored. There's no one to talk to. You've got people in yours."

"Melissande, my dear." The balding old man produced his most glorious smile. "It's so good of you to come. May I show you around?" He took her arm and started off with her.

"Don't, Meli. Don't go with him. There're only shadows."

"Gees, that sounds like fun, Dr. Wolper," Meli giggled and headed off. I raced after them.

"You see, Melissande," the Master explained to her, "in this particular metaphor we are trying to convince the men in the chains over there that the shadows over on the wall in front of them are really the things they depict. So, for example, that the shadow of a horse is really a horse, of a dog, a dog, and so on."

"What the hell for?"

"Meli, come on," I pleaded. "Come back with me. I'll *help* you put up the Washington Monument. I'm sure that together we can do it."

Meli looked at me and shook her head in disgust.

"Now over here," the Philosopher continued, "are the men who carry the idols that cast the shadows."

When the men saw Meli, a long series of whistles and catcalls ensued. The Philosopher picked up a whip that lay nearby and cracked it on the thighs of a few of the bearers.

"Quiet, you swine," he shouted.

Suddenly, the men started smashing their statues to the floor and grunting. They charged Meli. I yanked her out of their reach just in time, and we headed back out of the cave.

"Screw the images," the men shouted en masse, "we want the broad," and they continued to pursue us, shouting and grunting.

"Come back here. Come back here right now!" the Boss screamed after them, but they couldn't hear him over their own shouting. They continued to chase after us as we headed for the light.

Just before we reached the opening to the cave, we could hear over the loud clamoring of the men the sound of chains being thrown to the ground, and another group of men chasing the first.

"Where're our images?" they seemed to be shouting as they chased the men in front of them.

Meli and I reached the light first, followed in a matter of seconds by the bearers, followed almost immediately by the men who had been chained.

But instead of continuing after Meli, once they emerged from the cave, all the men stood in the sun, partially blinded by the light, milling around and mumbling to themselves.

The grass they finally saw when their eyes had become accustomed to the outdoors was a brilliant green. Apple trees blossomed everywhere, and, off in the distance, near the mountains, two horses stood nuzzling each other while their foal galloped a short distance away.

Finally, the old Philosopher emerged.

"How can you do this to me, Wolper," he cried out. "Years, thousands of years, I have kept my men in the dark. Now there is no one. No one. No more shadows. The fire has gone out. The idols are destroyed beyond repair. Who is left to know himself? Nobody," and he began to weep profusely. "Gone, Wolper. Gone. Two thousand years gone." He looked at me with a discouraged and soulful look, tears streaming down his cheeks. He shook his head sadly from side to side. "Gone, Wolper, with the wiggle of an ass and the jiggle of a bazoom."

A large smile spread across Meli's face as we walked away. She looked over her shoulder and shouted to the Boss, now on his knees in grief.

"Eat your heart out, you old Logician. Just eat your goddam heart out," and for emphasis she wagged her behind from side to side with a little extra motion as we walked away into what remained of a restful dreamless night of sleep.

12th I gagged on my lunch when I saw Maury the Solicitor emerge out on the terrace this unusually warm September noontime.

"How you doing, Harry, fella?" he beamed at me.

"How the hell did you get in here?" I asked in disbelief.

"Mrs. Mallory let me in. Why?"

"Maury, don't you sense a certain lack of enthusiasm from me whenever we meet?"

Maury settled in an extremely comfortable redwood chair.

"I was going to ask you about that, Harry. I thought I picked up a little something."

"A little something," I repeated. "Maury, I've done everything except electrify the front gate and mine the walk."

"Is it the money, Harry? You a little short?"

"No, Maury, it's you."

"Me?"

"Maury Halpern, Charity Solicitor. You. None other. The one and only."

Maury moved uncomfortably in my comfortable chair.

"What is it, Harry? Put it to me straight. I can take it. Is it that I perspire a lot?"

"Maury, God has not given us the time on this earth that would be necessary to list your faults. Suffice it to say that you lack everything I can think of that humans have found useful in establishing relationships and have a surfeit of those things that humans have found useless."

"You're awfully hard on me today, Harry."

"No harder than usual. Maury, why have you come?"

"I've come to apologize, Harry. I did a horrible thing, and I owe you an apology."

"You're forgiven, Maury. Thank you for coming," and I wiped my mouth to indicate I had finished my meal, yawned to indicate I was ready for my nap, and jiggled my legs a little to suggest that I had a pressing need to use the toilet. In response, Maury settled back an additional three inches into the chair.

"Don't you want to know what I'm apologizing *for*, Harry?"

"Not particularly, no. I'm sure the list is extensive."

"No, but this is one thing in particular."

"How'd you ever know which one to select?"

"You see, Harry," he continued, "I was absolutely positive that you were the mad abortionist, and so I cooked up this plan with Katie Pleuter, who's a dear friend of mine, I do have *some* friends you know, and your son, Arnold, who is *also* a friend of mine, to see whether we could get the goods on you, so to speak."

"I admire the purity of your friendships."

"Well, I was wrong, Harry. There were no goods. Arnold told me. Nothing at all. Just the laboratory of a dedicated scientist."

"Arnold told you that?"

"I *told* you that he's a close friend, Harry. He didn't even want me to get involved in the first place. Right after I explained my plan to him, he told me to forget the whole thing. That he sure was going to. I had to *talk* him into doing it, Harry. You don't *know* how *lucky* you are to have a son like him, Harry. Loyal to a fault. The only reason he ever did it was to show me how ridiculous the whole idea was that a biologist and physician who has dedicated himself to creating life would also destroy it. I owe you one hell of an apology, Harry. What I did was terribly immoral. You can bet that I've learned my lesson."

"Let me ask you something, Maury."

"Sure, Harry, anything. Just ask away."

"Suppose you *had* found something incriminating, Maury. Then would it have been immoral to have done this?"

"Of course not, Harry. You can do whatever you want to do to catch a crook, because a crook will do whatever he wants not to get caught. You both have to play by the same rules, for godsakes, Harry. Otherwise it's not fair. You're never going to catch criminals."

"But what happens if you're wrong, like happened with me, Maury, and the person turns out not to be a crook?"

"I guess you've been distracted this afternoon, Harry, because that's what I've been telling you. When that happens *then* it becomes immoral, and so you go and tell the person that you're sorry. Then you're all even and you can start over again."

"Suppose, he doesn't want to accept your apology?"

Maury fidgeted in his chair and thought very hard. It was a new idea to him. He became irritated.

"Well, that's his problem, Harry. If he wants to be a bastard about it and not accept a perfectly genuine apology, then he's just going to rot in hell for being a lousy person. I've got to be going," and Maury struggled his gelatin mass out of the chair and charged for the door.

"You can forget the $50 bucks this month, Harry. I think that accepting it at this point *would* be an immoral act, which I would *not* feel comfortable doing," and he slammed the door behind him.

14th I sat tonight in my laboratory, long after Meli and Mrs. Mallory had turned in, holding Darwin, a particularly favorite rabbit of mine, looking over the residue of almost twenty-five years of work. It's been a losing battle. It's time to give up gracefully.

The genes will not yield to me. They are fiercely protective of their information and refuse to let me monkey around with them, so to speak. Lucy's DNA is Lucy's DNA. That's the way it's going to stay. Now that Lucy is no longer with us, the deed has been done. May she rest in peace. There will be no more Lucys.

It is the most depressing thought of all, that I cannot break through this barrier to take hold of the genes and use them to my end. Rather, it is clear to me now that they are in charge. They are the single impenetrable Creator, isolated from the Kosmos, controlling us all. They have made Lucy and me and Meli and Mrs. Mallory, body, mind and soul. Now they sit in their great double-helical thrones, surrounded by their unfathomable cytoplasmic moat, defended by their protein parapets. They are in charge. We are but the tissue shells to do their bidding and assure that they survive. They are Master. We are slave. We must be careful to do as we are told, or we are sure to perish.

How foolish I've been to think that I was in control, that I could appropriate a single gene for my own ends, let alone a whole pool of them, that it was I who was in charge and directing their behavior, not that it was they who have determined my every action.

Which gene, I wonder, had decided to make me despise my son at the same time that I help him, and which gene has made me create a Boris I could not control? Is Boris what he is because he is gene-free? Is he the only being who is truly free because it does not matter what he does or refuses to do? It's all the same to him, although I suspect that from his perspective he would disagree violently.

Do my genes refuse to unite with Meli's and so I am impotent? Do my genes goad me into this stupid biological enterprise to which I have devoted the last twenty-five years of my life? Which gene is it, I wonder, who chuckles to himself as I go rapidly mad? And which gene is meticulously directing my demise?

It is no matter any more. They have won. Victory is theirs. I concede.

I will start packing up my laboratory next week, sell my animals, dispose of my instruments. I will tell Meli there will be no more experiments, no more Great Wiper, no more surgical rapes. She may keep her ova to herself.

I feel only slightly relieved. I am sure that even this capitulation of mine into indefinite captivity is the result of some great genetic conspiracy.

18th As I think about it, I shall miss the mitochondria the most. Endoplasmic reticulum I have always found to be rather boring. Microtubules are a nuisance, and lysosomes are outrageous, perverse, cellular claptraps ingesting garbage wherever they are. I avoid them whenever I can.

But, ah, give me a good healthy cell and a functioning electron microscope and I will look for hours at my mitochondrial friends. What a divine construction, these crests and chambers, perforated wall, this lattice-work splitting acetyl CoA into hydrogen atoms over here, carbon dioxide over there, incessantly fabricating ATP, energy to drive my cytoplasmic buddies to new heights of ecstasy. What could be more satisfying than watching these fleshy cyclotrons in action, lacy biological atomic reactors, repeating tricarboxylic cycles over and again? Dr. Krebs is no fool. No earnest young philosopher dares to ask *him* to discourse on the meaning of life.

Life, the good Dr. Krebs would no doubt respond, is a chemical reaction. Life, he would say, with hardly a pause to exchange pulmonary gases, is glucose being transformed to pyruvic acid, it is fatty acids and amino acids being converted to acetoacetic acid, it is pyruvic acid and acetoacetic acid forming acetyl CoA, it is acetyl CoA combining with oxygen to form carbon dioxide and water. That is life. And just what, my philosophical friend, is the meaning of water and gas? You tell me.

How I envy the purity of the biochemist. It is all there before him, ready to be centrifuged, histofluoresced, spectrographed, and titrated. How I wish I could live in a world of cardiac ischemia and lysozyme-salt secretions instead of broken hearts and tears.

24th **The Adventures of Boris Lafkin**

CHAPTER FOUR (continued):

The Messiah Arrives (with Ophthalmoscope)

I didn't eat lunch. My gastrointestinal apparatus had long ago retired in deference to the medical spectacle. Food now ran an express route, exiting barely seconds after entering, needing, it appeared, virtually no time at all to liquify. For pure nutritive value, I could just as well have eaten the two dollar bills I paid for each cafeteria meal and saved myself the trouble of all the intermediate steps.

I passed my time sitting in the lounge area down the hall from the ICU, speeding up time. I did this largely through a not always inaudible pep talk I gave to the second hand on the wall clock in front of me. Two-thirty was, after all, the hour of salvation, when Dr. Noah Walensky would materialize, complete with aureole, clean hands, and pure heart. In his right hand he would be holding a rod, in his left a staff. They would comfort me.

At 2:25, Mr. and Mrs. Spencer arrived. They did not look good at all. The reality of what had happened was beginning to sink its lead weight into all our psyches, and we were no longer able to protect ourselves by the newness, the shock, the uncertainty, or the inadequate information. We knew too much. Walensky, we suspected, was not the savior come to provide salvation and redemption, to reclaim from the dead what was rightfully ours. Walensky was the executioner come with decanters of hemlock.

"I wish it was an hour ago," I found myself saying to the Spencers, and cursing that I had ever accelerated time, "ten hours ago, yesterday, last week—," I trailed off unable to complete my sentence because my voice was cracking. My eyes started to cloud with tears. The Spencers looked up at me and their eyes were red and covered with a wet film. None of us could talk, so we just looked at each other blankly and in silence.

At exactly two-thirty, Truth arrived. In this instance, Truth appeared as a round little man in his late sixties, with thick silver hair, rumpled brown tweed jacket that didn't match his rumpled gray trousers, a white shirt that went out of style twenty years ago, a narrow tie of similar vintage, and introduced himself by the name of Dr. Noah Walensky.

I was desperately hoping, as this apparition approached us, that it would *not* be Noah Walensky. Before he had even half reached us, I was smothered by credibility. It was unfair. He was totally unpretentious, serious but kind, warm, and had a sadness to him that obviously came from a mixture of certain knowledge and painful experience. Dr. Walensky had been here before. There was no way I would be able to discredit him.

How I had hoped, I realized as I looked at him, that he would be flashy and flamboyant, wearing a neatly pressed sharkskin suit, complete with diamond cuff links, diamond stickpin, and a large diamond pinky ring. I wanted to hear from a snappy neurosurgeon with thin manicured hands who was too facile to believe. Instead, Dr. Walensky presented his stubby, coarse, veined hand to me, and, as I shook it, I lost all hope.

Dr. Walensky looked into my tearing eyes and he shook my hand. He stopped and just held my hand, putting his free hand on top of mine and cupping it firmly between them.

"This is your wife?" he asked slowly with a slight Eastern European accent.

I tried to say yes, but it wouldn't come out, so I just shook my head.

He continued to hold my hand and look at me with his blue eyes, peering over eight layers of wrinkles and bags. It was not unlike interacting with a large tweedjacketed basset hound. I looked around to avoid his eyes. I could find no rod nor staff. I was not comforted.

"It was very good of you to come," Mrs. Spencer told him.

Dr. Walensky let go of my hand.

"I'm glad I was able to come," he answered, one word at a time, and shook his head slowly as though he were answering another question or thinking over what he now had to do. "I think we should go look at your daughter," he told Mr. Spencer, and we walked down the hall to the ICU.

The ICU was unusually quiet as we entered. The nurses were huddled together in the corner drinking coffee. They started to get up when Dr. Walensky entered, but he nodded to them, so they settled back in their chairs and resumed their whispered conversation.

Other than mumbling from their corner, the only sounds were those of beeping electrocardiographs and the hissing of Barbara's respirator.

"Hey, Joey," a child shouted on the street outside. Otherwise there were not even the sounds of traffic. It was a gray Sunday afternoon. Everyone in

Cambridge was inside watching pro football on TV, listening to chamber music concerts, visiting relatives, or napping. "I'm not supposed to be here," I found myself thinking. "Barbara and I are supposed to be at home, listening to *Don Giovanni*, leaning against each other on the sofa and reading each other sections of the Sunday *Times*. I wonder what's gone wrong?" I sat down on the chair opposite Barbara's bed to decide on an answer, while Dr. Walensky read Barbara's chart and puffed on his unlit pipe.

My mind was out of order. It had exhausted all information-processing capabilities, and now thoughts just meandered randomly from circuit to circuit, enjoying the sights, freed of the need to associate and organize premises, major, minor, or miniscule.

I sat numbly as Dr. Walensky methodically read through the chart, occasionally flipping backward, forward, then backward again, to compare lab results, I guessed. He reached the last page, read to the bottom and then slowly closed the aluminum cover. He stood for a minute holding the chart in his hands, staring into space, thinking thoughts of a distant time and place. His face was without emotion.

Slowly he turned and shuffled over to the bed with a slight limp I hadn't noticed when he had approached us down the hall. Mr. and Mrs. Spencer had been standing beside Barbara, and they moved aside when he neared them. A nurse appeared magically on the other side of the bed and pulled down the covers. She handed Dr. Walensky a small chrome mallet with a triangular rubber head and an ophthalmoscope.

Dr. Walensky started at Barbara's feet, running the metal end of the mallet across the bottom of one foot and then the other. He proceeded up her body, placing one hand under her knee and tapping just under her kneecap gently. Her leg jerked. A day ago I would have been ecstatic to see this. This afternoon I just wondered if the reflex was too strong or too weak or too much to one side or the other.

Dr. Walensky rested his hand on her abdomen, then placed his thumbs under her neck and pressed lightly, and finally pulled apart her eyelids with his thumb and forefinger. He moved the light from side to side and then peered through the little hole in the device. He repeated this with the other eye, then gently closed the lids, handed the instruments to the nurse, and pulled the covers up to Barbara's chest where he slowly smoothed them out until there wasn't a wrinkle remaining in the cover sheet.

He stood looking at Barbara for a minute, motionless, and then did something I had never seen a physician do before. He placed his hands, slightly spread, over Barbara's face and head, and held them there for several minutes. I couldn't tell whether this was a medical or a religious act. Was he feeling pulses, looking for the amount of life energy left in her, or blessing her? It could have been all three. It was as though he had learned all he could about her physically and now he had to verify it spiritually.

The nurse standing on the other side of the bed looked at him as he did this. Dr. Walensky stood silently, still, holding his hands on Barbara. He looked at the nurse and then lowered his eyes until he was looking at the floor. The nurse started to cry. I absolutely could not stand it for one more second. I started to shake.

Dr. Walensky walked from the ICU and I followed, trying to hold myself so no one would notice my shaking. He entered a small office down the hall and we followed, taking seats on the other side of a desk behind which Dr. Walensky sat.

The office was crowded and chaotic. There was a beautiful oriental rug on the floor but hardly any of it showed, it was so covered with stacks of books and journals. The desk was even worse, papers piled every which way, and behind the desk was a glass cabinet inside of which appeared to be pre-Colombian pottery and other relics, the top shelf being covered with pipes piled in random layers like kindling for a fire.

Dr. Walensky opened the door to the cabinet, moved his extended index finger as though he were hunting one particular pipe, located his victim, grunted in victory, extracted it from the pile without disturbing any other pipes, replaced the pipe he had previously been smoking in the pile, closed the cabinet door, and huddled in his chair as he stuffed tobacco deep in the bowl. We did not press him to tell us the results of his examination.

Without unhunching his shoulders he looked up at us, an old tortoise peering from its shell.

"This is a very brave and strong girl," he said. There was a long pause. Mrs. Spencer wept. Dr. Walensky understood immediately what we had all felt and what I had been trying to tell the hospital staff for the last day. Barbara was special.

He lit his pipe. We knew what he was thinking. The medical findings being what they were, could Barbara beat death? He turned this over in his mind, for although it was clear that he already had the answer, he wanted to make sure he had not forgotten to take something into account.

"She is a beautiful child," he looked at Mr. Spencer, who could no longer control himself. Mr. Spencer placed his head in his hands and sobbed.

I, of course, remained calm, grasping tightly to the bottom of my chair and shaking violently.

Dr. Walensky puffed. "The news is, I'm afraid, very sad. The damage is extensive."

"Recovery—?" I tried to squeak out.

Dr. Walensky thought for a minute, wanting to make sure that what he said was both 100 percent accurate and clear. He continued to puff.

"It's out of the question, Mr. Lafkin. There will be no recovery."

I was going to challenge him, the field of medical science, men who think they can be 100 percent certain of anything, but it wasn't in me any more. I just looked at him and wept.

Mr. Spencer was the first to ask anything in a complete sentence. He wanted more information.

Dr. Walensky thought and then spoke slowly, articulating each word.

"Once in a billion times, I am told, the blood vessel that has burst heals, the blood is reabsorbed, and the person regains consciousness. I have never seen it. We must hope it does not happen. Your daughter would need institutionalization for the rest of her life. She would be a body without a mind."

"When will she die?" I asked.

He looked into my eyes for a long time, then stared at the floor. He looked back up at me.

"Soon, Mr. Lafkin. I think she will die soon."

There was a long silence, broken only by the sound of Dr. Walensky's smoking.

"You must excuse me," Dr. Walensky finally said. "Please feel free to stay here as long as you like."

He shuffled out of his chair and shook each of our hands.

"You have my deepest sympathy," he said, and left, I have always assumed, for an important consultation on Mt. Zion.

I found myself in the hall. I wasn't sure which hall. I wasn't even certain of the hospital. I didn't know how I had gotten there or how long it had been since Walensky had talked to us. I might have left the room with Walensky. I wasn't sure. I tried to think back to the three of us sitting in the cluttered executioner's chamber watching the blade descend. Perhaps I had fallen asleep and awoke to find the room empty. No use. There was no recollection.

I walked up the hall. I turned and walked down the hall. Then I walked back up the hall. I had a splitting headache. My back was killing me.

There was a water fountain at each end. I decided that I was here to get a drink of water, so I walked back down the hall to the water fountain and had a good long cool drink. I felt better.

Then I walked back down the hall and had another long cool drink at the other fountain. I felt better. I walked up to the opposite end again and had another long cool drink of water. I did this thirty times. I was no longer thirsty. I very likely had not been thirsty when I started drinking twenty minutes before. No, I decided, I had not come to this hall to get a drink of water. It must have been something else.

In the middle of the hall was a pay phone. I had been searching for a pay phone. I had an important phone call to make. I was sure of it. I put a dime in the phone and wondered who I had wanted to call.

I dialed the only number that came into my head. A recording answered. *A Man for All Seasons* was playing. Tickets were $1.00 until 5:00 P.M. Then they were $1.50. The shows were at 3:00, 5:00, 7:00, and 9:00 P.M. If I wanted any other information, I could call another number. I wondered whether I wanted further information. No, I concluded, I had all the information I could stand right now, so I walked up the hall to get a drink of water.

I continued down the stairs to the vending machines. Halfway down the stairs I slipped and bruised my shins.

When I got to the first floor, I checked my pocket for change. I had two dollar bills. A Dr. Simon at the coffee machine helped me out. He gave me eight quarters.

I put one in the coffee machine. I punched the button that said "extra light, two sugars." I also put a quarter in the soda machine and punched a root beer. The label on the machine said that it would taste like it had been brewed in kegs not more than an hour or so ago.

I put another quarter in the ice-cream machine and ordered an ice-cream sandwich. There was a loud whirring sound of gears rotating and the sandwich came into view behind a plexiglass door. I lifted the door and tried to extract the sandwich. I retrieved a pinch of paper and squished chocolate cookie and vanilla ice cream. What was left was too far in the slot to obtain.

Still holding the mashed ice cream and paper, I put a quarter in the candy machine and pressed the button for a Baby Ruth. I put two quarters in the cigarette machine. I ordered a pack of Kool's. They would have a fresh hint of menthol.

I looked very carefully at the machines. They had performed well, I concluded, with the exception of the ice-cream machine. This was good. Four out of five is a very high percentage. Eighty percent. No baseball player has ever hit 80 percent. No president has ever earned 80 percent of the vote, unless you count the electoral college, and then I wasn't sure. I thought about this for several minutes. I knew that Kennedy and Truman hadn't. I wasn't positive about Johnson and Eisenhower. Goldwater and Stevenson hadn't done well. I knew that for sure. But 80 percent? Probably not. Roosevelt might have, and then there were all those presidents like Rutherford Hayes and Polk and Pierce. Didn't John Adams once get only one electoral vote? Maybe 80 percent wasn't that good after all.

I gathered up the root beer, Baby Ruth, and coffee and threw all but the root beer in the trash along with the clump of ice-cream sandwich that was pressed between my thumb and index finger. I left the cigarettes for some fortunate passerby. Then, root beer in hand, I walked around the corner to the sandwich machine and leaned on the button for five minutes or so. I watched the rows of slots pass by. There wasn't much. A couple tiny cans of Libby's tomato juice. An old apple on one of the bottom shelves. Several sandwiches without labels. I slipped my last two quarters into the machine. It occurred to me that I probably still had change in some of the machines around the corner.

"The next kid who goes by sticking his fingers in the change-return slots will not go unrewarded," I thought to myself. This made me very happy, so I smiled. Then I pushed the button to rotate the shelves, closed my eyes, and slammed the selection button as hard as I could. The machine shuddered and then belched an egg salad sandwich onto the floor. I stepped on it and ground my foot down slowly and as hard as I could until the egg salad had gushed out of the cellophane. I never cared much for egg salad.

When I was satisfied that the sandwich had been completely smashed, I started to walk back upstairs, falling twice again and reinjuring my shins because as I walked I was wiping egg salad off my foot on the corners of the steps. It was all off by the time I had reached the next floor and had exited through the heavy wooden door with the tiny window. On the front of the door was the number "2". It was painted in a dull orange and was done in modern Helvetica sans serif, like the lettering of a new bank branch, the kind of bank where the tellers don't have bars in front of them anymore and you get a single computerized form that tells you about your checking, savings, car loan, mortgage, life insurance, Christmas club, personal loan, and Master Charge accounts each time you make a deposit. The "2" was four feet tall. I concluded that I must be back on the second floor.

I was perspiring heavily now. I tried to open my root beer and proceeded to cut my hands on the flip-top. A nurse who was passing by whipped out a handkerchief, dabbed at the small drops of blood on my hands, then gently wiped off my wet forehead. She smiled and left. I continued to walk.

This was not a bad circuit as circuits go, I decided, water fountains, pay phone, vending machines, egg salad sandwiches, and back up to the water fountains again. I was about to trudge through my own particular penance once again when I noticed something very strange.

All up and down the hall people walked in and out of rooms, nurses, doctors, visitors, patients in bathrobes. People talked to each other. Some were even laughing. Nurses delivered medications and emptied bedpans. Two small children carried gifts and flowers. It impressed me that no one else had heard that the world was about to come to an end.

I wondered whether I should say anything to them, and decided against it. I was not seeing things in their proper perspective. There was no reason for me to have any of these feelings. After all, we were just talking about one clump of flesh, me, going to pieces over another clump of flesh, Barbara. A year from now, ten years from now it would hardly make a difference. Someone would say to me, "I understand you were married before."

I would think very hard.

"Ah, yes," I would finally say, "I was, wasn't I. Let me see— It was Beverly. No, Betty. No, no. Barbara. Yes. Her name was Barbara. Very pretty girl, as I recall. She died. Now I remember. It was very sudden."

I'd turn to my wife and six children seated around the living room watching television.

"Did I ever tell you I was married before?" I'd ask.

"Not now," my daughter would say, turning up the television louder, "this is the good part."

Life goes on.

I walked by Walensky's office. The door was open and the Spencers were still inside. Mrs. Spencer was standing with her back to me, looking out the window. Mr. Spencer was on the phone.

"Yes, it has been a long time," he was saying. Then a pause. "Fine, Betty's fine, yes." Another pause. "Well, I'm afraid that's why we're here. Barbara's had a brain hemorrhage." Pause. "Quite bad." A very long pause. "Yes, I'm still here. Jim, there *is* something you can do. I need the name of a good funeral home and a cemetery." Mr. Spencer's voice cracked at the end. Mrs. Spencer reached up and held onto the windowsill. She swayed slightly and then steadied herself.

I raced ahead at full speed and burst through the doors to the ICU. Two nurses headed for me.

"Don't come near me!" I shouted. "I don't want to hear about my twenty minutes or that you're got to rotate her or whatever doctor's orders you've got now. Do what you've got to do, but I'm staying here, do you understand? I'm staying here all day and all night. I don't care anymore. Arrest me. Do whatever you want, but the only way I'm leaving here is when you get enough people to drag me out, and I'm going to wreck this goddam ward if you try. Is that clear because I swear I mean it. I'm not going to cause any trouble if you leave me alone. Is that clear?"

There was no answer from the nurses.

"Is that clear?" I shouted.

One of the nurses was about to say something when Nurse McCafferty interrupted.

"Yes, it's clear, Mr. Lafkin," she answered very soothingly. "You may stay as long as you wish," she smiled.

"Thank you," I answered out of breath. "Thank you very much."

I stood there trying to fight back my tears.

"Now," I began, "what's going on with Barbara?"

The nurses looked puzzled. I repeated the question.

"What's going on with Barbara? Right now? What's her status?"

"Her blood pressure is very low, Mr. Lafkin," Nurse McCafferty answered.

"How low?"

"80 over 40."

"What do you want it to be?"

"I beg your pardon?"

"What do you *want* her goddam blood pressure to be? What does it have to be to be healthy?"

"120 over 80 is normal for her age. 100 over 60 would be adequate. We don't want it to be too high because of the increased intracranial pressure already."

"Spare me the brain hemorrhage crap. Just tell me what it needs to be for her to be recovering."

The nurses looked incredulously at each other.

"100 over 60, Mr. Lafkin," Nurse McCafferty finally answered.

"100 over 60. Right," I said. "Then, Mrs. McCafferty, that *is* exactly what you're going to get. 100 over 60," and I pulled up a chair beside Barbara's bed, turning so the nurses couldn't see me since I couldn't hold back the tears any longer.

The nurses returned to their station. I held Barbara's hand tightly.

"I'm not really sure where to begin," I said to her as quietly as I could. "I'm afraid that none of what I want to say to you is particularly profound. If you're looking for insight, I just haven't managed to come up with any. All I can give you is your basic desperate-husband-pleading-with-his-wife-not-to-die speech. You've heard it before. It's been done to death. Romeo, Tristan, you name it. This isn't even imaginative. A third-act finale. What could be more mundane." I looked around for help.

"Look Barbara," I finally said, "I've got a plan. It's not much of a plan, but it's all we've got going for us right now, I'm afraid. The way I've got it figured out, the only one who's going to help you right now is you. I know you can hear me. People in comas can hear. We both know that. You probably think you're dreaming all this, but you're not, Barbara. You've got to believe me. This is real. It's the most real thing we've ever come up against. Now, what we're going to do is this. I'm going to sit by your bed here until you're better and tell you what to do to get better, and you, baby, are going to do it." Even though I was trying to talk quietly, it was clear that the nurses were hearing every word I was saying. Their mouths were open.

"Now I know," I continued, "that when you've set your mind to something you get it done, and this isn't one bit different. You're going to have to work your goddam ass off, but it's important. Believe me. We're not going to let medical science condemn you because they don't understand that we've got something that's going to beat death. I don't care how expert all these fuckers are, you are Barbara Spencer, and they've never had a Barbara Spencer with a cerebral hemorrhage. Not even one time. So what the hell do they know. Nothing. Not a goddam thing. They just don't know how to deal with an individual soul, spirit, all that shit that we've talked about until we were out of coffee and smokes and energy night after night. Now we're going to put it to use, and you know what we're going to use for energy to drive this little death-defying machine? Love. That's right, our love. That's all we need. They can keep all their cells and sodium-potassium pumps and lab results and diagnoses. We don't need it, because I love you, Barbara. I know you hear me. You've got to hear me. People in a coma can hear. I read it when I was studying for my MCAT last week. It doesn't matter if you're in a coma. I love you and I know you love me, because I'm still your friend, just as I promised. Now this is what you've got to do. Raise your blood pressure. Not a whole lot. Just a little to start. Systolic 5. Diastolic 5. That's all. Five little points on the old sphygmamanometer. A nickel. Five points. Hell, that's nothing. I'll bet you could raise it twenty if you wanted. But we're going for five right now. Nothing big.

"You don't want to miss out on your classes next week, do you? Shit. You know what happens when you get behind. You lose the whole lousy semester. That's not like you. Now let's get that BP up there where it belongs. We've got too many things going for us, Barbara. I mean, the world is ours for the taking. You as the world's greatest female philosopher. All right, just philosopher. And me, curing all those terminally ill people with my brilliant discoveries. And then when the day is done, and I've cured cancer and muscular dystrophy, and you've answered the major ontological and epistemological questions of our time, we can go out for a fine French meal, I still owe you one, you know, and then we can walk home holding each other like we always do, and, well, the nurses are listening so I can't say all that I'd like to about the kind of sex we like to have, but fantasize for a minute or two and if that doesn't get your blood pressure up, nothing will.

"You see, Barbara, the way I figure it, life has absolutely nothing to do with medical physiology. All it has to do with is two people, a man and a woman, getting together to love. Nothing else matters. Love is everything.

"Barbara, I'm not going to let you die. I'm just not and that's final. This is an accident. A freak. A mistake. What we're going to do now is correct it. You've got too much life in you. I can tell. I can feel it in your hand and see it in your body, even just lying there. And you *know* that, Barbara. You're just filled to the top with life and you're not going to just let it evaporate. You're going to use all of it to fight this lousy mistake."

I tried to put some order to the thoughts that had been racing around inside my skull all day.

"If you're looking for mythology, this isn't it, Barbara. I can guarantee you that we will *not* become a legend. There is no great melancholy composer who's waiting out there to turn us into a popular opera. We are the world's most ordinary lovers. No one gives a shit about what happens to either of us now. So what the hell, you might as well live. You see what I mean?

"Besides, Barbara, I think you should work on getting the old blood pressure up there because I just don't know what I'd do without you. The truth of it is, Barbara, that I love you and I don't want you to die. I love you and I couldn't stand it if you died. I love you, Barbara. Please don't die. I love you. Don't die. I love you. Please." I put my head down on her hand.

"I love you," I said over and again, my lips moving against her palm. "I love you so goddam much."

A nurse came over and took her blood pressure.

"What it is?" I asked weakly, exhausted by a half hour of nonstop talking to Barbara.

"85 over 45," she answered and looked over at me with a little smile.

I looked at the nurse's eyes. She had been crying.

"All right!" I exclaimed. "All right! Not bad, huh? Not bad at all. I knew she'd do it. I knew it."

I turned to Barbara.

"All right, gorgeous, five more points now. You've got a half hour for five more points. You're doing just fine. We'll show these goddam Philistines. Just watch. Spirit in action," and I continued my dialogue nonstop for the just as I had desperately prayed that it would, just as I had begged the supernatural forces who oversee such things that it would.

25th I have always wondered how one cheers a birth. It has seemed rather strange to me that we first celebrate our birthday a year after we are born. Why not the candles, cakes, and noisemakers on delivery, a chorus of beaming nurses and obstetricians chanting "Happy Birthday to you, Happy Birthday to you" as the little devil pokes his head from mother's vulva?

What did Dr. Salk do the day he gave birth to polio vaccine? How did Dr. Fleming occupy himself on delivering penicillin to the world? Did Einstein go into an alcoholic stupor the night he concocted $E=mc^2$, cheering colleagues pouring beer and champagne over him, victor in the World Series of Nuclear Physics? And what occupied Dr. Freud after he whelped his litter of egos, superegos, ids, and libidos? Was he carried home early the next morning from the local rathskeller, joyously clutching his stein, shouting erudite lieder up and down the lamplit street, then dumped unceremoniously on his bed to sleep off his procreation? I imagine his drinking chums standing over him.

"Here," they announce to one another, pointing to the snoring crumpled figure on the bed, "rests the great Herr Doktor Freud, who today has given birth to our basest lusts and given them a name, and who now lies soaked in his own urine."

It seems to me that I should be out partying, twirling noisemakers instead of sitting here alone in my laboratory, silent, numb, and depressed. Even the universe began with a loud noise.

My own personal Big Bang burst into the laboratory tonight, all fireworks and explosion.

"What the hell are you doing in this goddam laboratory?" she inquired in a state most generously described as moderate agitation.

"You're upset, Meli." I settled on the basic descriptive approach as a good initial parry.

"Not at all, Dr. Wolper. I'm not *upset*. I'm *pissed*! I'm goddam *pissed*! Not *upset*. *Pissed*. *Upset* is something that middle-aged ladies do when their cakes fall. I'm *pissed*! Do you understand the difference?"

"I think I do, yes."

"Good. That's very good, Dr. Wolper. Would you like to make a stab at guessing *what* I'm pissed about?" She stamped over to the other side of the lab bench that I was sitting behind and leaned her hands on the edge, glaring at me.

"You lost something?" I tried.

"*You*. Asshole. I'm pissed at *you*!"

"Me?"

"Do you see anyone else around here I could be calling 'you'?"

"No, I don't," I agreed.

"That's very encouraging, Dr. Wolper. I was hoping you wouldn't bring up the little imaginary men you like to talk to at night."

"You mean, Boris?"

"*What* am I *pissed about*?" Meli asked again, ignoring my question.

"Me. You're pissed at me. Asshole."

"Right. You. Asshole."

I waited for further information, not at all certain that this wasn't the total package she had to deliver. I was wrong. There was more.

"You know, ass, hole," she very deliberately separated the term into anatomy and orifice, "today is the day we're supposed to make a decision about our relationship."

"Ah, yes."

"Ah, yes? *Ah, yes*! What'd you just do, find a missing sock? What the hell kind of an answer is 'Ah, yes'?"

"I don't know what to say, Meli," I struggled.

"Dr. Wolper," Meli looked deeply into my eyes, "do you love me?"

"Meli, dear—"

"Don't give me any of that Meli-dear shit—"

"It's not that I don't love you—"

"It's not that you *do*, either."

"That's not the point—"

"Well, Dr. Wolper, *dear*, if love isn't the point then I don't know what the hell is."

"Meli," I tried to tone down the situation, "come over here and sit by me so I can talk to you."

"No," she mocked, "I'm not going to go over there so you can talk to me, and put your big furry arms around me and whisper in my ear until you've got every gland in my vagina pumping and I can't remember why I even came here. If you want to give me a verbal fuck, you're going to have to do it long-distance this time."

"You're being unfair."

"You were saying that love isn't the point?"

"It's more complicated than that."

"With you, it sure as hell is." Meli looked around desperately for an answer. "Look, Dr. Wolper, don't you remember a time, long ago, when you thought that love was just simple, and pure, and magic. Maybe you were *in* love then. You had a girl and you couldn't wait to see her each day. And whatever you *did* with her was magic. Talking, sex, going for a walk, staying up late at night, being with friends, you name it. You'd go with her to buy a roll of toilet paper and it was magical. It didn't matter *what* it was."

I closed my eyes as she was talking. A very specific time came to mind. I was on a beach in Atlantic City. Lucy was stretched out beside me on her front, her tiny ass transfixing me in a spell I could never break. I remembered the sun and the air and a small room with linoleum on the floor and newly painted green wicker furniture that never seemed to dry. It seemed that we spent a lot of time naked, sitting on the edge of the metal bed, combing our wet hair. There was no question that the major issue we had to deal with in our lives was how to keep our hair looking good when it was wet and salty. Meli was right. It was a long time ago.

"Times have changed," I answered.

"How? How have times changed?" she demanded.

"They're not simple anymore. They're not simple."

"Yes, I know. Things are complicated. You've told me that, ass, hole. But they aren't, you know. They aren't more complicated at all. *You're* more complicated. *That's* what's more complicated. You. You understand what I'm saying? You want me to go over it again?"

"I think I understand."

"Magnificent. Do you also understand that if you *do* love me, since *I* love you, we could get *married* and *live* with each other and experience all those magical things I was talking about? You don't have that experience every day, you know. Some people never have it. Not even *one goddam time.* You're turning down paradise, ass-hole. That's what you're doing. You know that?"

"I do know, yes."

"You *know* that? You *know that!* You *actually know that,* and you're still *doing* it. What's the matter, you don't think you're shrivelled enough? If you shrivelled any more, Dr. Wolper, you'd grow a *pit,* for chrissakes."

"Stop it, Meli."

"Why? Why the hell should I stop it? So you can stay in Disneyland? So you don't have to face that you've run out of things to believe in? You don't believe in the world. You don't believe in life. You don't believe in love. You don't even believe in yourself, for chrissake."

"I have my work."

"Asshole. You gave *up* your work, remember. You *do* remember that?"

I looked around at the jars without lids, the apparatus gone idle, the debris on the floor. Dante came to mind. I was in hell. I had abandoned all hope.

"Dr. Wolper," Meli said with an abrupt change in tone, "I can't stand seeing you do this to yourself."

"Please stop, Meli."

"Not until I've had my say."

A rabbit ran by and darted under the table. It was followed by several frogs, bounding and croaking loudly in pursuit.

Meli walked around the table to avoid the chase and continued to sit on the stool next to mine. She placed her hand on mine.

"Your wife is dead, Dr. Wolper. You've got to bury her, for godsake. You have to get over it *sometime*. I know that every time you come in here you think that you're making life, but you know what I think? I think that you're making death. There isn't a goddam thing that's alive about all this. I don't know how you can do it. Every time I walk into this lousy place I get the heebie-jeebies. Shivers go from my tits to my toes, I swear it. I know that you think you're making life, but what do you think's going to happen to that life? It's only going to die again, for chrissake. Why the hell bother? You make life and it dies and you make it again and it dies again. You can't beat it, Dr. Wolper. I know this sounds pretty goddam stupid, but I wish just one time I could get you to understand that *you're not* dead and your *wife is*. I can't for the life of me understand how someone who's got enough brains to win a Nobel Prize can't figure that out," and Meli stroked the back of my hand.

"What is it you want me to do, Meli?"

"I want you to climb out of your grave. That's all. Bury your goddam wife once and for all, stop trying to save the world from whatever lousy mutation you're trying to save it from, stop talking to little men at night, and, if you do love me, for chrissake let's get married and love each other. I'm even willing to take the chance that once you're out of this cemetery your penis might begin to work again. Who knows, stranger things have happened in this world."

Meli had been staring down at my hand as she talked. She looked up at me as she finished, and she smiled, still moving her hand back and forth on top of mine.

"You're asking me to give up a lot, Meli."

"I'm offering you *life*, for chrissake, Dr. Wolper." Her smile faded and her eyes began to grow moist. "Life, Dr. Wolper," she said and started to cry. "Life. That must be worth *something*, for godsake."

She put her arms around me and cried against my sweater.

"Isn't it worth something to you?" she asked between sobs. "Something? Anything?"

"Yes, it is, Meli," I started to say, finding much to my surprise that tears were forming in my eyes. "Yes, it is," and I started to cry. I grabbed her tightly and held on, as they say, for dear life. Her body quivered inside my arms as she wept. This seemed to be as good a time as any, so I cried my heart out, shaking and clutching her against me.

We wept together for several minutes, holding to each other, swaying and leaning against each other. Her body was warm and soft against mine as we cried together. I stood up and pulled her to me. Still crying, she reached up and stroked the back of my head. I found myself running my hand down her hair over and again, weeping, trying to catch my breath, stroking, moving together with her.

"Yes, it is," I said. "Yes, it is," I repeated as I ran my hands down her back and over her behind.

"I'm giving you life," she wept.

"Yes, you are," I cried.

"I'm giving you life."

"You are, yes. Life. Yes, you are."

"Life," she ran her hands down my back and pressed her body as close to mine as she could.

"Life," I answered and clutched her even more tightly. "Life," I bawled. "Life!" I shouted, tears flooding my face and falling on her head.

"Life. Yes. Life!" she screamed back.

"Oh, life!" we cried out together, our bodies shuddered violently, simultaneously, a mammoth heave, and then quiet. Peace. Calm.

Once upon a time.

What great fallopian journey was I about to undertake? Even then I didn't know. Even then as I held Meli close to me, clutched her body to mine, ran my hands around her shoulders, formed her silhouette with them, I would not have guessed what was to transpire. I didn't notice our love for each other undergo that first mitotic multiplication, cleave and join into something more than one of this and one of that, but become two of a this-and-that and still remain one. I shared this vision with her. She, too, found it hard to believe.

"What the hell is a this-and-that?" she asked innocently.

"Whatever we would like it to be," I answered her from the depths of my heart. "And that, dear Meli, is the wonder of it."

Meli looked up at me and disengaged herself. It was clear that the journey had begun.

"You know, Dr. Wolper," she began very softly, "what just happened to us was very special. I might even go so far as to say that it had an element of magic to it. Now I don't know what a *this-and-that* is and I don't want to know. But let me tell you something. You have a lethal mouth. You should be aware of that just in case no one's ever told you before. You can ruin with three words what has taken months to develop. I don't know how you do it. Maybe you think you're some kind of poet or something. Jesus, if I know. But if you do, you're not. Now whatever the hell it is you do that transforms a love encounter into a this-and-that, you've got to stop before your whole goddam brain just dries up into dust and blows out your ears in the first good wind. Do you understand that, Dr. Wolper, because if you don't, I really don't mind repeating myself."

It was a softly spoken but emphatic plea. I could not for the life of me grasp what she was talking about.

"Yes, I understand," I lied.

"Good. Now we have to make plans. When shall we get married—*dear?*" she smiled.

I was startled. I looked at her beaming face, and for a minute, just a minute, I gave serious consideration to going through with it, to throwing away absolutely everything for the opportunity to spend the last few days remaining to me in a conjugal snuggle.

"Meli," I put my hand on her arm, "come and sit down."

"Oh, *fuck*, Dr. Wolper!" she barked, jerking her arm out of my hand and walking away. "What is it *now?*"

"I want to explain something to you."

"I don't want you to *explain* anything to me."

"I think if you could see this in a new conceptual framework, you could understand what my feelings are without being so hurt."

Meli turned around and glared at me.

"Dr. Wolper, for chrissake, I don't want a *new conceptual framework*. I want to be held and loved and fucked, that's all. I want to go to sleep with you and wake up with you next to me. I want to come home knowing that it's *our* home, not *your* home that you're *letting* me stay at. I don't want to be the nymphomaniac who you're teaching music appreciation to, anymore. And I can't stand the way people look at me, friends of yours, your family, like I was the world's largest walking talking vagina. 'I guess she's around because Harry's human,' I once heard one of your friends say. *Human* means you've got a prick and get horny. It's the strangest goddam definition of humanity *I've* ever heard. I want people to know that I live with you because we *love* each other. Have you ever told that to anyone? Have you? Huh? Well, have you?"

"No, I haven't," I responded sadly.

"What are you afraid of? You couldn't possibly be worried that people would think you're crazy for marrying me. If people thought you were any crazier than they think right now, they'd block off all the side streets and build a mental institution right on top of you. They wouldn't even bother to transport you. Maybe you should think of me as a way of keeping up your image."

"When you're done, Meli, I'd like to talk to you."

"Okay," and she moved over and sat on the stool in front of where I was standing, "go ahead and talk. Say what you want. Say it until it's all out. Then maybe we can have a reasonable talk for once."

I stood looking at her, unable to know how or where to begin.

"Well," she snapped, "this is what you've been waiting for, isn't it? Go ahead. Talk. Explain. Rationalize. I'm ready."

"I'm not going to rationalize, Meli," I started out.

"Bullshit, Dr. Harry Wolper. Just bullshit. Go ahead. Say what you want."

Meli started to play with a loose thread in her dress and stared at the floor. Her fist unclenched ever so slightly.

"Oh, believe me, Meli, it's enormously tempting, all this. The offer of magic is something not to be lightly rejected. But it is not life. It's magic. And while life would be petty and boring without magic, it would be completely unliveable if it were only magic."

Meli stopped playing with her thread and looked up at me.

"How do you know?"

"From life."

"You mean *your* life?"

"Yes. From my life."

"Dr. Wolper, your life couldn't possibly have taught you any such thing. I don't know a hell of a lot about your life, but if what I don't know is at all like what I do, it couldn't have taught you any such thing. All you're doing is trying to make excuses for your being alone. Is that what you really want? I mean, forget the magic and all that shit. Do you really want to be alone for the rest of your life?" Meli looked at me intently.

"No," I answered sadly, "I don't want to be alone. But I'm afraid that there's no alternative. At the end of it all, we are all alone."

"Where the hell'd you get that from, *Moby Dick?*"

"Meli, there is no alternative."

"Well, you don't actually *know* that, Dr. Wolper," and tears began to form in her eyes again. "Look, Dr. Wolper, all I want is a chance. Just a chance to show you that life's not at all like what you think it is. It's a beautiful experience. It really is, and, dammit, I want to share it with you," and once again she threw herself against me and began to cry.

"I don't want you to be a lonely old man," she said between sobs.

I started to cry. Again.

"I don't want to be a lonely old man, either," I said sniffling.

"Just give me a chance. Please," she wept.

I grabbed on to her tightly.

"Meli, Meli, Meli," I repeated again and again.

"Just a chance. A chance," she cried against me, shaking inside my arms, which I ran up and down her back. "Tell me you'll give me a chance."

"Meli, Meli," I continued to say over and again through my tears.

"A chance," she cried, breathing deeply against my body, holding tightly to me. "A chance," and she shook in tiny spasms, took a long deep breath, grabbed even more tightly, and then jerked in a single giant spasm.

"A chance," she panted one last time and then very slowly loosened her grip on me.

I ran my hands through her hair. She reached up, wiped the tears off my cheek, and smoothed my beard.

"You don't want to be alone, really, do you, Dr. Wolper?" she said to me quietly.

"No," I said with a sigh, "I don't really want to be alone."

And so it came to pass.

I watched Meli sitting in a corner stroking one of the guinea pigs.

This small journey I had unknowingly undertaken down Gabriello Fallopio's great and wondrous duct was now about to deposit me in that splendid uterine chamber of innocence and discovery otherwise known to man as accident.

Meli sat cross-legged in the corner, running her finger over Demeter, a guinea pig for whom I have always had a special fondness. Demeter nibbled at a lettuce leaf Meli had in her other hand and made contented chirping noises as she munched and chewed.

"You're a real doctor, Dr. Wolper, aren't you?" Meli asked me as I sorted through notes that were strewn on the counter.

"You mean a medical doctor?"

"Right. A medical doctor?"

"I was once. I haven't practiced medicine in a long time. Why, do you feel ill?"

"No. I feel fine. I was just wondering, that's all."

The conversation stopped. Meli hummed and stroked. I straightened.

"Does every doctor learn about sexual and vaginal things and stuff, or only special doctors like gynecologists?" Meli continued the inquiry.

"We all learn some. Gynecologists learn a great deal, much more than a general practitioner."

I waited for an indication of where we were heading. Meli resumed her attentions to Demeter.

"Dr. Wolper," Meli finally blurted out after several more minutes of silence, "why do I orgasm absolutely all the time for absolutely everything? Is there something wrong with me, because I think my glands are all screwed up or something." She looked at me with just a touch of sullenness, pouting and distressed over her predicament. I roughly estimated, on the basis of the latest paperback of high-level scientific research on female sexuality that had hit the newsstands, that at most there were three women currently alive in the United States who wouldn't pledge all current and future assets to share her problem.

"I think you're quite fortunate, Meli," I tried to console her.

"You don't think I'm some sort of freak?"

"Not at all, just extremely healthy."

"I don't know, Dr. Wolper. I think I'm *too* goddam healthy. I feel like a car battery, charging and discharging and charging and then discharging again. I've got an electrical system built right into me to start up a Mack truck in below-zero weather. You could make one of those goddam commercials about me. 'Leave her out all night and the next morning she'll still start right up'. I can have an orgasm in absolutely any place you can imagine, at absolutely any time, from absolutely anything. I had to disconnect the buzzer on my seatbelts in my car because whenever I ran the strap across my tits I'd come before I could even get the keys in the goddam ignition. Now that's just not normal, is it, Dr. Wolper?"

"Well, maybe it is somewhat overhealthy. I can see how it might become annoying at times."

"And not only to me. What guy is going to feel good about having sex with you when you've already come six times between the time he's rung the doorbell and opened the screen door. When it comes to intercourse, he's almost trivial."

"I assume that sex is only incidental to love, Meli," I offered.

"Sex is what?" She stopped stroking Demeter.

"Incidental to love. You can have sexual activity and release, but what's important is not the sex itself, but the love you feel for the person, which is independent of sex."

"Dr. Wolper, what in God's name are you talking about?"

"Love, Meli."

"Oh, fuck, not again."

"No, Meli. Not again," I said quietly and went back to my papers.

Meli fidgeted uncomfortably for several minutes.

"All right," she finally said exasperatedly, "say what you wanted to say."

"I have said what I wanted to say, Meli. It's of no importance really," I said without looking up from my work.

"Don't you go getting all goddam moody with me, Dr. Harry Wolper. I know you too well, dammit. I'm not in the mood for your sulking."

"And that, dear Meli, is what love is all about. Love is melancholy, the blackest of the biles, violent, angry, outrageous. It is sad and painful. We are conceived in flaming barbaric debauchery, delivered in pain, arrive in this world blood-covered and screaming, and are in peace only at the end. Real love, the truest love, is not joyful, calming, and comfortable. It is passion. It is conflict, afflicting and debilitating, saddening and disappointing. It is never what we want it to be, and so we chase after it as we might after our own tail, a never-ending circle. And we have as much chance of catching up with it as we would our own tail. Love thrives on man's stupidity and his imperfections, devouring everyone to the last, opening wounds long since healed, never content."

Meli was in a state of shock.

"No, it isn't, Dr. Wolper. Love is beautiful, for chrissake. That's all. Just beautiful. It's tender," she pleaded with me.

"Tenderness. Yes, there is tenderness, of course. And joy. And beauty. That is, indeed, how love dresses herself. Without these trappings of respectability would we pay any attention to her at all? No, of course not. Don't mistake me, she is a great lady and keeps herself up quite well. But underneath the rouge and the crinolines, there is a beast more cruel and less forgiving than the wildest carnivore. She has a fierce appetite and will devour all in her path to feed her insatiable hunger. On the other hand," I smiled, "I could be wrong."

"Have you been teasing me, Dr. Wolper?" Meli was very irritated.

"Not entirely."

"I don't *like* to be teased, Dr. Wolper. As a matter of fact, I *hate* it. And I hate it most when you do it after I've asked a serious question that means a lot to me. I'd like to see how amusing you'd think it was if every time you reached in your pocket for a nickel you jerked off. I wonder just how funny you'd think it was if you spent half your day cleaning semen out of your underpants and the other half squirming because you were sitting on a warm juicy glob of it. Hysterical, huh? You know that there're days I have to change my underpants almost every hour, and that's when I'm *not* horny. Isn't that just the funniest goddam thing you've ever heard?"

"It's not funny, Meli. You're right."

"You're goddam right it's not funny. And it's not *love* either. It's got nothing to do with love. For one thing, love is not a glandular condition. And for a another, love is mostly *dry*."

"I do apologize. I was unfair."

"I'll tell you another thing love is not, Dr. Wolper," Meli was working up a full head of steam. "Love is not this goddam zoo you've got here. It is not a floor that is covered with shit, rabbit shit and guinea pig shit and frog shit and God knows what other kind of shit. Every goddam day since I've known you, you've been telling me how much you *love* your work. Well, I'll tell you something, someone who loves something takes care of it, for chrissake. Look at this lousy place." Meli was *more* than *moderately* agitated. She walked over to my workbench, seething, biting off her words.

"This place is a goddam hellhole. I mean it. It stinks and it's dirty and grotesque. Look at these. Jars of frogs' heads. This is disgusting. And look at this jar. For godsakes, Dr. Wolper, you've got a rabbit head floating in here. Ech!" and she let it fall to the floor where it smashed into a hundred pieces, formalin splashing on her dress.

"Meli, I was only joking about love," I tried to intervene.

"Very funny, Dr. Wolper. Just a laugh riot. I'm very amused. Can't you see. Now what item do you have in here?" and she picked up another jar. "Ah, yes. Isn't that what you always say? Ah, yes. Well, ah, yes. Here we have, oh great, here we have tiny little guinea pig brains for you to love. Isn't that what these are?"

"Yes. Now, Meli—"

"Well where are the tiny little guinea *pigs*? This is horrible." She threw the jar over against the wall.

"Meli," I tried to lunge for her, "you've got to stop this."

She dashed away.

"Why? Why? So you can *love* all these ghoulish funny little things? Instead of *human beings*? Instead of *me*, Dr. Wolper? Is *that* why? Well, I'm not stopping, Dr. Wolper. Call the police if you want. I don't care any longer. I don't like it when people I care about make fun of me because I've got a physical problem. Some people always have a running *nose*. Big deal. I have a running *vagina*. It's very *unpleasant*, Dr. Wolper. Do you understand that? It doesn't have one goddam thing to do with *love*."

"I agree," I tried to calm her as I pursued her around the workbench.

"Now here's something else I take it you *love*," she said as she started to reach for another specimen. Suddenly she stopped. "What the hell is *that*?" she asked, pointing to the wading pool where I was making my Great Wiper. I tried to explain it to her.

"Oh, that's wonderful, Dr. Wolper. Is that for *my* benefit? If you think that's funny, I don't. A Great Wiper, for my Great Running Vulva? Is that the joke? Well, I don't like it. I'll wipe *myself*, thank you. This is what you can do with your goddam Great Wiper, ass, hole," and she started to run around the room throwing everything she could reach into my soup, jars of specimens, beakers of chemicals, half-empty cups of coffee, test tubes and pipettes.

"Now *this* is love," she screamed over and again. "This is *love*!"

At last I caught up with her and grabbed tightly just as she heaved a dish of frog cells into the soup.

There was an explosion and a burst of light. The pool tore between Mickey Mouse and Donald Duck and the liquid began to pour out. Swimming in the liquid were hundreds of tadpoles.

I watched in shock.

"You've *done* it, Meli!" I shouted.

"You're goddam right I have."

"No. You've *done* it. Look at all these tadpoles!"

"So what."

"Meli. You didn't throw *tadpoles* in. You threw *cells* in. You threw in *cells*. The solution made them grow. You've made the Great Wiper," and suddenly I realized that I was letting it spill out. I grabbed for the only beaker Meli hadn't destroyed, ran over and scooped up what I could, not a lot but I was sure enough.

"You mean you were serious about that? There really is a Great Wiper?"

"There is now, Meli. It will allow me to create life. I can finish the experiment. With this solution," I beamed, holding up the beaker, "I can transplant Lucy's nucleus into an ovum and she will grow to full term. I am absolutely certain of it."

"Just *where* do you think she's going to grow to full term?" Meli asked.

"In *you*, Meli. It *has* to be you."

"You want to bet."

And so I sit now, hours after Meli has gone, perched on top of the debris, depressed and confused, having given birth to the greatest discovery in the history of humanity and feeling generally lousy.

26th Tempus fugit.

"You know, Dr. Wolper, I can't for the life of me figure out why I'm doing this," Meli said and dropped her head back on the surgical table. "If I hadn't realized that I'd be ovulating this morning, I'd probably be long gone by now. You know that, don't you?"

"Yes, I do," I was preoccupied with the procedure. "And I'm enormously grateful to you for doing this."

"I don't want your gratitude. I just decided that I might as well finish what I started. That's the way I am."

"I know that, Meli. You're a great sport."

"Fuck you, *coach*," Meli said acidly.

I wasn't certain how it had happened myself. I fully expected Meli never to return after she had run out of the laboratory yesterday and was surprised to find her sprawled on the sofa listening to music when I finally entered the house last night. She had put on an old oversized sweater of mine, which reached to her knees, and she lay motionless with her arms crossed over her chest, eyes closed, when I walked into the living room. I sat on the edge of the couch beside her and placed my hand as gently as I could on hers. She opened her eyes and looked up at me in silence for several minutes. Finally she started to run her hand through my beard.

"I'm sorry I wrecked your goddam lab," she said quietly.

"You've nothing to apologize for," I told her. "You made the greatest discovery in scientific history."

"You know something, Dr. Wolper, I don't care."

I sat beside her for a half hour, holding her hand, running my hand through her hair as she continued to stroke my beard, listening to *Preludes and Fugues*.

"I'd like to make up for what I did," she said at last.

"There's no need to, Meli."

"I know that, but I still want to. I think I'm ovulating today. You can have it if you want. I'll grow Lucy for you. I know that means a whole goddam lot to you. I'd like to do it for you."

Tears began to cloud my eyes. I had trouble speaking.

"You don't have to do this if you don't want to, you know?"

"Are you grateful that I'm doing it, Dr. Wolper, because I'm doing it for you, you know?"

"Well, of course. I'm enormously grateful."

"Then just say thank you, and let's leave it at that."

"Thank you, Meli. Thank you very much."

"You're welcome. Now tell me what a fugue is."

I thought for a few minutes about how to describe it simply.

"It's a kind of music where the same theme is developed and played over and over, why?"

"Because I like fugues. They're fun and they're pleasant. That's all. Let's go to bed."

We held very tightly to each other through the night, and when the morning came, Indian summer came in through the bedroom window to infuse new life and ambition into me.

I do not flatter myself that Zeus will look favorably on my Dioscuri. I have made no Helen, no rescuer, no Argonauts to slay the King of Bebryces, no protectors with power over the winds and waves, no patrons of poets and bards. But clear shining stars they will be. I have no doubt of it. Gemini is reborn, a new time for the flowering of the great vernal blossom, September.

While all around me the leaves crust and harden, scratch their edges against house shingles, crack and float brown and lifeless to the earth, here in my laboratory I have tonight planted the mightiest of flowers. It was not an easy procedure, but one that presented at the end the most marvelous surprise.

I had begun the most difficult maneuver of all, in which I induce the isthmus of the fallopian tube to loose its spasm and to increase the action of its ciliated epithelium so that the ovum will be expelled prematurely and I will have time to transplant Lucy's nucleus before implantation must occur. Meli, was, as usual, chattering away in an attempt to overcome the discomfort of the situation.

"The thing about our relationship," she said as I suffused a progesterone-prostaglandin-hyaluronidase solution into her uterus, "is the way that we fit each other, like I'm female and you're male, you're kind of old and I'm kind of young, you're really bright and I'm not all that bright, you're big and I'm small. It's opposites attracting, do you know what I mean?"

"I think so, yes," I answered, only half listening to her, keeping my eyes fixed on the tray into which the solution from her drained, intently interested in seeing a tiny pale yellow dot through the lens I had flipped down over my left eye.

"You see, Dr. Wolper, the most important thing about a relationship is not that it makes two people *feel good*."

"It isn't," I said distractedly, turning the glass stopper to admit a small quantity of adenyl cyclase to the hyaluronidase solution.

"Nope. Not at all. The most important thing in a relationship is *growth*. You have to have the right environment to grow, no matter what," Meli continued.

"I wasn't aware of that." I admitted some FSH, the last, but most delicate, step in the process, since too much FSH might overripen the ovum and make transplantation almost impossible.

"It's true. And you know what the most ideal environment for growth is?"

"What is that, Meli," I stared intently at the pan under her.

"The most ideal environment for growth is when two people are opposites like you and me. Something's twitching inside me or rippling or something, Dr. Wolper."

"It's the action of your fallopian tube getting ready to expel the ovum, Meli."

"Oh. You see, Dr. Wolper, when two people are opposite, then there's no *competition*. That's what kills everything, competition. With us, there's nothing to compete *about*. I don't want to win the Nobel Prize and you certainly don't want to become a nymphomaniac."

"Or not very bright."

"Right. It's not easy to take two people and put them together in a way that allows them to grow. It's the hardest goddam thing in the world, I think, Dr. Wolper. Sometimes it's very hard to step back and let your lover become what he wants and really make him feel good about it. Don't you think so?"

"Oh, I do." Still nothing.

"With us there's this perfect combination. You have to have just the right combination. Otherwise, bleh, nothing. What do you think?"

I increased the FSH slightly. Meli continued without giving me the chance to answer.

"I mean, with us we've got the absolutely perfect mixture. I always feel that I can do whatever I want, be whatever I want, and you'll be right there beside me, cheering me on."

"Thank you."

"Well, it's true, Dr. Wolper. And I know that sometimes I could be more, well, *supportive* about what you want to do, like not wreck your lab, which I felt so goddam bad about really. But still, you *know* that under it all I'm in back of you. More than anything I can think of, Dr. Wolper, I want you to grow, and I don't only mean your penis."

Into the pan dropped one very small pale yellow ovum, and, then, as I was about to reach for it, there dropped another small pale yellow ovum.

Tempus ludendi.

For a minute, only that, not even that, I thought of telling Meli about my find, but I did not. Instead, I very carefully placed both ova in bicarbonate, hyaluronidase, and proteolytic enzymes to dissolve the cumulus oöphorus and corona radiata so that I might successfully penetrate the ova and make the nuclear transplant.

While I was doing this I washed Meli's uterus with a strong progesterone solution to advance the receptivity of the endometrium several days' time. Meli continued her dialogue.

"You know, Dr. Wolper, some people get so close to each other that you can hardly tell them apart. Sometimes they even begin to *look* alike. That's really freaky. I don't think I could stand that."

"You couldn't." I worked over at the microscope making the nuclear transplant.

"Oh, don't get me wrong. I think it's really great to be close to someone. But some people who are in love with each other are *too* close, I think. When one of them gets sad, the other gets sad. When one gets happy, the other gets happy. I think it's all that laughing and crying together that really screws up a relationship. You've got to be separate people."

"I agree," I mumbled in the midst of my work.

"You can get just *too* close. You develop this *bond* between you and then when it comes time for your divorce, you practically *die*. It's unhealthy."

"Divorce." I had completed one ovum and was now working on the second.

"No, no. Having that kind of *bond* between two people. They practically *live* off each other and in the end, they *drain* each other. They've got nothing more to give."

"A symbiotic relationship."

"I don't know what that is."

"Two people who feed off each other."

"Right. That's it. Of course, I think at the beginning you have to give *something* of yourself, but *eventually*, you've got to let go. You just can't *grow* when you're stuck to each other like some goddam *glue*."

I had completed the second ovum, and so I turned off the progesterone wash and took a small scraping of endometrium to check the stromal cells for the extra stores of glycogen, proteins, and lipids that would signify that Meli's womb was, at last, ready for implantation.

Time marches on.

I was surprised at myself. For most of my life, it seemed, I had been waiting for this single moment, the time when I would implant Lucy to grow again. And now, it was as matter of fact to me as clipping my nails. My brow was not covered with perspiration. There was no quickening of my heart, lump in my throat, quivering of my hands. My sympathetic nervous system was nowhere to be found, having retired to the deep interior to await a sexy blond or a call from Arnold.

Indian summer sent a sweet green smell into the lab, a joyous and welcome last attempt, in spite of its futility, to hold on to the earth. Cars drove by with their radios playing loudly, and children shouted in the street. Meli talked on, as usual, mostly about how important it is to have your "very own life," as she put it, in order to protect yourself from the most horrible of all temptations, closeness, and, its inevitable result, the loss of yourself. I agreed. The last living flies of the year flew in through the tears in the screen and buzzed around the room. Through the open window of the house next door a phone rang. No one was home.

Very carefully I injected one drop of the Great Wiper into the ova, which first shuddered briefly as I broke the membrane and then shimmered brightly, brilliant tiny yellow balls. Meli gabbed on. While you have to surround yourself with friends and interests that insure that you remain yourself, she said, you can't completely isolate yourself. You have to let some things from your partner get through. But they had to be just the right things, or else you would be smothered or not grow or, worst of all, be jello. It was not good to be jello. I agreed.

Several squirrels jumped from the maple tree that spread over the lab, and they raced back and forth across the roof several times. I took the two ova and implanted them in Meli's uterus, and then sedated her so she would sleep. Before she awakened, the ova would have begun to form trophoblastic cells and cords that would adhere to her womb and eventually form a placenta. Down the street someone started a chain saw and began to buzz through his wood. An ice-cream truck turned down the street ringing its bell. Intermittently the sound of a football marching band could be heard practicing. I had created life.

27th Later that same millennium.

It happened with a suddenness I can't explain. Meli awakened this morning and left the lab without a word. I had sat by her through the night, admiring the peace and calm of her sleep.

She hardly acknowledged my presence when she awakened. She showered, changed, and joined me for breakfast.

"I've been thinking, Dr. Wolper. I've grown a lot with you. I'm not the same person anymore. I'm different."

Time flies.

"I have to be realistic. I've outgrown the need for this kind of a relationship. I need something more. Something different. I need to be on my own. Independent. Free."

Time heals all wounds.

In the afternoon she became angry.

What did I expect after all, she told me. She was too young for me, too stupid for me, and too short. No relationship can overcome all these obstacles. In any event, it was time for her to move on. She was sorry if she misled me the other day, but she's had time to reconsider. She's decided. She has to leave.

In the evening she left.

She will not come back, she says. A clean break is the best. This will be clean. And permanent.

28th [A further draft of the Harvard address. Ed.]

Friends and colleagues. I come before you today to dismiss one of the great questions of our time, what is life?
The question is *not* what is life. The question is what to *do*.
The *answer* is, that there is *nothing* to do. Absolutely *nothing*.
Thank you very much.

I suppose for the money they're paying me, I have to expand this a little.

30th **The Adventures of Boris Lafkin**

CHAPTER FOUR (continued):
In Which Our Hero Is Introduced
to the Zeitgeist

It was 5:00 exactly when Barbara's blood pressure was 100 over 60. My adrenalin was pumping at a mile a minute. I was ready to take on the world.

I was even ready to take on Saul Shore, M.D., when, shortly after 5:00, he came over to me. He had been talking to the nurses, who were obviously miserable over the little drama that was unfolding right before their very eyes. While there was no question in my mind that I would be able to withstand the stress of talking Barbara back to life, the nurses didn't stand a chance. I gave them two hours before they'd need fresh troops.

Saul put his hands on my shoulders when he reached me.

"What do you say we go for a little walk, Boris?" he asked.

"I'm not leaving."

"Barbara's doing fine," he continued. "She needs a rest. She's been working very hard. If she could talk to you right now, I think she'd ask you to take a break."

"That's a rotten goddam thing to say. What the hell am I supposed to say to something like that?"

"I think you know that I'm right. Take a half-hour break. Nothing's going to change. Then you can come right back. You can stay as long as you like. With my permission. I'll even give the nurses written orders to let you stay."

"Dammit. You really want me to get out of here."

"I do. You need a break. So does Barbara. Come on, I'll go with you."

"Written orders?" I asked.

"You write them. I'll sign them," he answered.

"You're on." I turned to Barbara. "I'll be outside if you need me. Just call," I said, kissed her on the cheek, took my coat off the rack by the door, and walked out of the ward.

It was dark as we walked out the hospital's emergency entrance and started down Cambridge Street. I shuffled my feet through the leaves.

"How're you feeling, Boris?" Saul asked very solicitously.

"Fine. Just fine. A little tired, but otherwise, I couldn't be better, Saul. I really couldn't. For the first time I feel hope. Barbara's going to make it. I know it."

"Barbara's not going to live, Boris."

"Oh, shit."

"Barbara's going to die."

"Shit, Saul. Shit. Shit. Shit."

"Barbara is, in fact, already dead."

"Shit. Are you going to keep this up the entire walk, because I'm tired and don't need this, Saul. I really don't. Believe me. Think what you want. I don't care. You can think she's a zombie for all I care. Just leave me alone. Please."

"Boris, I'm sorry about Barbara, I really am."

"Barbara's getting better, Saul. She's getting better. You saw it yourself. Her blood pressure's normal now. What the hell else do you want? She's not going to jump out of bed in the next ten minutes. It takes time. It's a slow process. But she's getting better."

"Boris, she *is* getting better. You're right. But if she regains consciousness, that's the worst thing that can happen. Absolutely the worst. She has no brain, Boris. No brain at all. If she recovers, it's going to be a living nightmare."

"Look, Saul, why don't you just tell me what you want me to do, and then leave me alone so I can get some air in peace. I've got a lot of work ahead of me. Get on with it."

Saul walked with me a little way. We came to a cross street and we both stopped to let a car by. Saul turned to look at me.

"Look, Boris, I don't like this any more than you do . . ."

"Stop it, Saul. Just say what you've got to say."

"Boris, the Barbara that you were talking to up in the ward doesn't exist any more. She's not only dead technically, she's dead literally. If Barbara recovers consciousness, she could live thirty more years, nothing more than a collection of cells maintaining their chemistry. This isn't life, Boris. Metabolic continuity has absolutely nothing to do with what you and I understand about life and especially about Barbara. Even if she doesn't regain consciousness, she could stay in the coma for ten years, only to die eventually of some secondary infection in a public home for the chronically ill after all your money and her parents' money is exhausted."

"What's going on, Saul? All of a sudden she's going to be living for ten years, thirty years. I thought you told me that she was going to die in a day or two."

"Not if you don't tell us to turn off the respirator and let her die, she won't. You have to tell us to turn off the respirator."

I felt my skin turn clammy. I couldn't breathe. I stood still trying to catch my breath.

"Are you asking me to kill her?" I finally managed.

"Look, you talked to Walensky. She's dead already, Boris. We're asking you to let her die peacefully."

"You're asking me to murder her. That's all it is. Don't give me any medical rationalizations. You're asking me to kill my wife. I love her, Saul. I can't kill her."

"I know it's hard, Boris—" Saul began.

"Hard? No, it's not *hard*. It's not *hard* at all. It's impossible. It's beyond the realm of human possibility. It's grotesque."

"Others have had to do it."

"Then they're crazy. They're lunatics. You'd have to be out of your mind to do that. And if you weren't insane before you did it, you certainly would be afterwards. How do you live? How do you sleep? What do you do with your insides?"

"It has to be done, Boris."

"No, it doesn't, Saul. No it does not. It definitely does not."

I looked at my watch. It was six o'clock.

"You know, Saul, yesterday at this time I was walking up this same street with Barbara on my arm. We were talking, even joking a little. She had a lousy headache. That was all. She was in horrible pain. I promised her that I'd always be her friend. That's all she wanted in all that pain. She wanted me to be her friend."

"Only someone who was really her friend could do this, Boris."

"What the hell kind of logic is that? Only a true friend could kill her? Is that what you're telling me?"

I stood staring at Saul. I couldn't believe what I was hearing. I couldn't think of what to say next. Suddenly a thought entered my throbbing head, a horrible thought that panicked me.

"Let me tell you something, Saul. I'm not pulling the plug. And as long as I have anything to say about it, neither are you," and I ran back to the hospital as fast as I could run, hoping that I wasn't already too late.

October

1st **The Adventures of Boris Lafkin**

CHAPTER FIVE:

In Which Our Hero Takes a Package Tour through Purgatory—Amenities Included

I raced like hell back to the hospital. I'm not sure I've ever run as fast in my life. The visions that raced across my mind were a combination of the most maudlin episodes of Ben Casey, Dr. Kildare, and Marcus Welby in a single package.

A nurse stood holding Barbara's wrist, while another held a small pocket mirror over Barbara's nose. A third nurse had her fingers on Barbara's eyelids, and a fourth stood poised with a reflex hammer by Barbara's knee.

"Are we ready?" asked the intern solemnly.

All nodded their heads affirmatively.

I ran faster, my feet barely touching the ground, my thighs aching.

"Fine. Then here we go," and he reached over, flicked off the switch to the respirator, and stood back to observe. The click, poof, siss stopped. There was complete silence. Thirty seconds went by.

I darted in front of a car, which slammed its brakes on and came to a stop barely missing me. The driver stuck his head out the window.

"You fucking jerk," but I never heard the rest. I was getting near the hospital.

"Her pulse is failing," one of the nurses announced calmly.

I threw open the door to the hospital and ran down the hall to the stairs that led up to the second floor.

Barbara's body began to jerk erratically. She made several brief feeble attempts to take a breath and failed.

I jumped up the stairs three at a time, falling once and cutting my side. Blood started to stain through my shirt.

"I think that's it," the intern announced.

"No pulse," Nurse One said.

"No breath," concurred Nurse Two.

"Eyelids are still," Nurse Three added.

Pop went Nurse Four's hammer.

"No reflexes. She's dead."

The intern pulled the sheet over Barbara's head.

I had just reached the doors to the Intensive Care Unit and was about to burst through them when I found that my arms were totally paralyzed. No matter how I tried, I could not lift them to open the doors. I didn't want to go in. I knew I was too late, that it had all been done while I was out with Saul, who now appeared behind me, having read my mind.

He pushed open the doors. I shut my eyes. From in front of me I heard click, poof, siss. My arms began to work. The pain in my side reached my brain. I opened my eyes. Barbara was on the bed directly in front of me, just as I had left her. I started over to her bed, desperately fighting to get a deep breath, trying to ignore the pain in my side, but my legs didn't work, and I wasn't getting enough air. I never made it.

I awakened in the emergency room. Someone had taken my shirt and pants off and there was a gauze bandage around my waist. I was lying on a surgical table. Saul stood next to me.

"You had a lousy cut, Boris," he said. "We needed seven stitches to close the damn thing."

"Where's Barbara?"

"Right where you left her a half hour ago. She's no different."

"You didn't pull the plug?"

"We wouldn't do it without your consent. Now lean back. I want to put some more tape on. You'll be a little sore but you'll be okay."

"You know, Saul, you scared the hell out of me with all that shit about turning off the respirator. I really wish to hell you hadn't done that."

"It's not a lot of shit, Boris. Sooner or later we're going to have to do it. Now lie back so I can finish wrapping this thing."

It was an hour before I finally got back to Barbara's bed. Barbara had maintained her blood pressure at 100 over 60. "Holding her own" was the way Nurse McCafferty described it. This meant that there had been absolutely no progress.

I sat by Barbara for several hours, trying desperately to think of how a person makes the decision to turn off her respirator. I was surprised that I was giving it any consideration at all. Still, I couldn't get it out of my mind, not in the same way I had rid myself of the vivid descriptions of Barbara's hemorrhage. It crowded out all other thoughts.

I imagined a time a year from now. Barbara and I were walking somewhere, arms around each other.

"I just can't tell you how close I was to letting them turn off the respirator," I'd say. "Everyone was so damn discouraging."

"I know," Barbara would say. "But I knew you'd fight it through, even though I couldn't let you know because of the coma and all. And now, here we are, and we'll always be together," and she'd snuggle closer and sigh for both of us.

How could I throw that possibility away? Where could I reach out for hope, for the strength to resist all those people who knew so damn much? I felt myself weaken. I was ashamed of myself.

"Dammit, Barbara, I need your help. I can't for the life of me understand why I'm spending even two seconds considering such a crazy thing. I've got to be strong, I know. And I will. I'm just not going to think about turning off the respirator. You're going to make it. *We're* going to make it. Persistence. Faith. Hope. That's all I need." I clutched her hand. "And you, Barbara. I need you. More than anything else in the world, I need you. Help me, please. Somebody help me."

I buried my face in her hand, exhausted, and weak, and I tried to ignore the pain coming from my side.

My dialogue with Barbara continued off and on for the next several hours. I dozed occasionally, never more than five minutes, and on awakening each time alerted myself instantly to the click, poof, siss of the respirator, that it was still on, that Barbara was still alive.

I used the word "alive" with more caution now. I was weakening under the incessant pressure from all parties to accept what was, to them at least, reality. Reality was, I decided, probability, correlation, significant effects. This sign that Barbara did or did not show correlated with this particular diagnosis. This status after so many hours signified this other certainty. The probability of something else occurring was low, of another diagnosis was minimal, of recovery was, as Dr. Walensky so graphically put it, out of the question. No one had ever gotten through this before. There was no reason to think that anyone would now. And who the hell was this Barbara Lafkin anyway that she thought she could resist the laws of chance and probability and defy the universal order of what is and will be? Only I knew the answer to that last question, I decided. I alone had True Knowledge of the spiritual energy concentrated in the comatose patient with the respirator. If Barbara was to make it, my role was clear. I must be strong. I must not bend. I must serve as the guardian and protector of the Great Secret. I must be St. Peter at the gates, the demon Charon navigating the Rivers Styx, Acheron, and Cocytus.

This particular fluvial metaphor reminded me of a biological process I had been postponing for a long time, and so, after receiving assurances from Nurse McCafferty that she would single-handedly turn away any attempt to turn off Barbara's respirator, I headed for the john.

This was a mistake. Not because my renal system wasn't enormously grateful that I had worked out the problem when I had, but because on returning from the rest room I encountered Saul, who was with a group of three snappily dressed gentlemen. They wore three-piece tweed suits, had short haircuts, and looked virtually identical. Their smiles were ingratiating and their manner was engaging. I was about to be sold something. It would be something I didn't want.

Saul suggested we meet in a small conference room down the hall, so we moved good-naturedly to a more fitting environment for doing business, talking about absolutely nothing at all as we went, but with a pleasantness and decorum perfectly appropriate to the circumstance of death, not depressing, not merry. These well-dressed and conversant young men had been well trained.

Saul provided introductions after we reached the carpeted and dimly lit room—a Mr. Whitaker from the Massachusetts Eye Institute, a Mr. Sutter from the Greater Boston Dialysis Center, and, bringing up the rear, so to speak, a Dr. Donelson from the New England Organ Bank. I was impressed by what Brooks Brothers could do for vultures. This was haberdashery's finest hour.

"We can certainly appreciate what a difficult time this must be for you, Mr. Lafkin," Dr. Donelson kicked off.

"We'd like to talk to you about how your wife can perform a great humanitarian service, even in death," Mr. Sutter picked up the ball.

"You see, Mr. Lafkin," Mr. Whitaker took a lateral, "we three represent the major centers in New England that deal with organ transplants." Touchdown.

"Sort of like Manny, Moe, and Mack's spare parts franchise." I indicated that I had grasped the concept well.

"We'd like to talk to you about donating your wife's organs to help others in great medical need." Dr. Donelson ignored my remark.

"I'm sorry. I gave at the office," I informed them.

For the most part the three gentlemen were not fazed by my remarks, although I did catch a quick glance from Mr. Sutter to Dr. Donelson that seemed to say that this was not going to be easy.

"When an organ is donated," Mr. Sutter continued, "some considerable preparation must be made in advance. You must be assured that were this not so we would refrain entirely from such an indelicate solicitation. However, the transplant of a kidney is a time-consuming matter and requires extensive premortem preparation and coordination."

"It is no different with corneas, Mr. Lafkin," Mr. Whitaker assured me.

"Nor with lungs or livers or spleens," Dr. Donelson put in his bid. "They all take great care and planning."

"I'm kind of sorry no one could make it from the North Atlantic Mastectomy League. You're missing the best parts. Barbara's got great boobs, you know. She could make a couple single-breasted women very happy."

Dr. Donelson, in particular, swallowed very hard. Saul was getting irritated.

"I would also like to talk to you about a heart transplant," he glared at me.

"Oh, I'm terribly sorry, Dr. Shore," I responded with a tone of sincere regret, "but her heart was spoken for, not five minutes ago. If only I had known, I would have given you dibs. I'm sure I could have worked something out for all four of you. I know how interesting it would be to all of you to see a *real human heart.* One of you might even want to try it out, just for kicks."

"That's enough, Boris," Saul snapped at me.

"No, no, please, Dr. Shore. We can certainly understand how hard this must be for Mr. Lafkin," Mr. Sutter rushed to my aid. I was not grateful, nor did I become any more willing to sign over Barbara, piece by piece.

"It is difficult to conceive," Dr. Donelson addressed me solemnly, "any more difficult thing for a man to do at the time of the death of someone he has loved so deeply than to do what we are asking. And it is equally hard to think of any act more generous, more considerate of humanity, more beautiful than at the time of the passing away of a loved one to give vision to one of our fellowmen who cannot see, to give freedom to someone whose life is enslaved to a dialysis machine, to give life to someone who would otherwise shortly be dead. It is the gift of life, and requires a supreme sacrifice, requested at the most difficult time of all, the time of our greatest loss."

These men were *good.* There was no doubt of it. I hadn't heard anything so slick since I had purchased a 1957 Plymouth Belvedere station wagon that died before I received the payment coupon book from the bank.

To refuse them meant not only being selfish, it meant turning your back on your fellowman, on humanity itself. More than that, it meant being weak and unbeautiful. Consent, of course, guaranteed humaneness and beauty. Who could afford to be close-minded and selfish at a time when he hoped that all the world would share his pain? Much to my amazement, I found that I could. And it wasn't even hard.

"Gentlemen," I smiled good-naturedly. "I take it that you are at the forefront of the new and exciting ecology movement, so I suspect that what I'm going to tell you, you're going to find extremely difficult to understand. I'd prefer not to recycle my wife. I want Barbara's heart to stay in Barbara. I want her kidneys, and liver, and pancreas, and other organs to stay just where they are. Let the terminal die and the blind stay blind, I say. If that's the way it is, so be it. *Que sera sera,* and so on. I do not turn you down capriciously, gentlemen. No there is a reason that, in your great humanitarian zeal, you have overlooked. My wife is alive. She will no doubt be disturbed to emerge from her coma and find herself missing a number of organs, such as, for example, a heart."

"We had no intention of removing organs unless she was clinically dead, I assure you, Mr. Lafkin," Dr. Donelson interrupted.

"But you were going to suggest that I approve turning off the respirator once the proper arrangements had been made for the transplants. Isn't that correct?"

All three gentlemen shifted uncomfortably in their tweeds.

"We understood your wife to be clinically dead at this time, Mr. Lafkin," Dr. Donelson said.

"Oh," I beamed, "then the apology must be mine. I *am* terribly sorry. No, I'm afraid there's been a misunderstanding. My wife is alive and on the road to complete recovery. You've been misinformed. I can't understand how such an embarrassing mistake, for all of us, could have been made. Now, if you'll excuse me, I must return to my wife. I try to stay by her side as much as possible. You can't be too careful these days, you know. You sneeze and before you know it, someone's slipped out an organ. Some hospitals are just crawling with ghouls. I could tell you stories that would tear your heart out. Good evening." I bowed courteously and dashed back to Barbara.

2nd Mind is, in a manner, all things, I am told. Splendid, this elegance with which I am bound and gagged, made prisoner to a gelatin mass floating incongruously in my very own sealed cranial vault.

Meli, where are you? What rattles now around your own cranium? What secret messages dart from synapse to synapse, telling you what? That you must come back to me? That the wall between us must be fortified? That I need you? Long for you?

Does your spinothalamic tract still reverberate with the warmth of your body against mine, substantia gelatinosa deliciosa? Do your Paccinian corpuscles, Ruffini end organs, free nerve endings remain permanently innervated, your dorsal columns overloaded with the countless times we have touched?

Dearest Meli, encephalic joy of my life, my cerebrospinal fluid is dry, my ventricles desiccated, my neurotransmitters do not transmit, acetylcholine reuptake is all uptook, my sodium-potassium pump is pooped.

Come back to me. Bring me your brain. And your body. Ah, yes. Your body. I am lost without your insults, miserable in the absence of your anger, depressed and alone, entrapped in myelinated fiber tracts crossing from pons to peduncle.

Mind is all. Brain is beautiful. But, dare I confess it, your body, soft-bellied and blossoming beneath mine, your body, full-breasted and brainless, will do just fine by itself.

Mind is all, yes, I know. But you may keep your brain, Meli, dear. I want only your body. The splendid plans I have for your flesh, Meli, your brain would not believe.

4th So. Arnold has had his way. As he knew he would. As he has always known he can, if he persists. Actually, he kept his gloating to a minimum. He was generous in victory. It is good that he has learned to be contemptible in an endearing and good-natured way. It is, as near as I can tell, his only redeeming trait. In all other spheres of human intercourse, he is entirely insufferable.

I do not understand, myself, why I have given in. Perhaps, I still cling in some irrational and desperate way to the fantasy that when Arnold has what he wants he will become someone else, anyone else, someone with a sense of himself and the world who has some recognizable purpose other than to justify indoor plumbing. Why is it that I find it so hard to give up on what I have created, no matter how monstrous the result?

"This is awfully good of you, Dad," Arnold said with only a slight turning of the knife. He raised his hand behind my shoulder.

"If you give me a good-natured pat on the back, I'm going to punch you in the mouth, Arnold," I informed him.

Arnold cautiously lowered his hand and stuck it in his pocket. He appeared to be moderately uncomfortable about blackmailing me. It was entirely appropriate.

"You know, Dad," he beamed at me, "I never *actually* would have turned you in."

"Yes, you *actually* would have," I assured him. "That's all right, Arnold. I have no hard feelings."

"You don't?" Arnold asked in disbelief. "How come?"

"Because I'm doing this of my own free will, out of the generosity of my heart, on the basis of that inseparable bond between father and son. You want this house? It's yours, Arnold."

Arnold's eyes darted quickly from side to side. Something was definitely wrong, he was thinking. He looked around the living room, waiting for the ceiling to collapse.

"Has someone put a lien on the house, Dad?"

"Arnold, I am dismayed. You are returning my paternal affection with suspicion. My heart is saddened."

"Just answer my question. Is there a lien on the house?"

"No lien."

"None at all?"

"None. At least not yet."

"Ah, ha!" Arnold sensed he was on the right track. "Then there *will* be a lien on the house."

"I'm sure there will be, Arnold, in time. There's a lien on everything else you own, isn't there? I can't see why this house is going to be any different. You've mortgaged, pledged, chatteled, and secured everything you've acquired in the last thirty years except your fillings. Do your know that you are probably the only five-year-old who's had a tricycle repossessed?"

"I told Bernie that I would have paid him in only two more weeks. It was unnecessary."

"I'm sure it was, Arnold."

There was a pause in the conversation. I did not find it refreshing. Arnold shifted awkwardly from leg to leg. He had something to say.

"You know, Dad, this is awfully good of you," Arnold said ingenuously.

"I'm doing it on the advice of counsel. You can save your gratitude."

"Still, I *am* grateful," and he sounded as though he was.

Arnold looked at me, and for a minute it seemed as though he was going to say something important, something from his heart that puzzled and hurt him. Maybe he was going to ask why we had no relationship, whether we ever had, was there a way of starting one now, did my distaste for him necessarily mean that he was a worthless human being, was I protecting myself from a closeness I felt for him, could I tell what his feelings were for me, let bygones be bygones, was it too late, much too late?

His eyes darted around looking for a way to start, some common object we both shared a like for that could start a conversation, indicate a commonality, a possibility for warmth and closeness. But there was nothing of the sort. Arnold sighed and accepted defeat. I lashed out at his resignation.

"Arnold, this is what I'm going to do. I'm going to sign over the house to you for occupancy January 1, 1970, and then, dear son, I'm going to go some place where the chances of our ever meeting again are as close to zero as possible witbout leaving the planet. That should please both of us."

"Then," Arnold began to grasp the subtlety of my words, "you're not completely happy about doing this for me, I guess, huh?"

"Not completely, Arnold," I nodded in agreement and escorted him to the door.

"That's too bad," Arnold said sincerely as he began to close the front door behind him. "You've always been a lot nicer person when you've done things that have made you happy, Dad. Did you know that?"

"No, I didn't, Arnold. That's good to know." Arnold shut the door behind him and walked down the walk with a broad smile, pleased with himself for having left me with a new and important insight into my character.

9th **The Adventures of Boris Lafkin**

Chapter Five (continued):
In Which Our Hero Goes Sight-Seeing

When I walked into the Intensive Care Unit, Mr. and Mrs. Spencer were there beside Barbara, standing motionless, looking down at her. I didn't appreciate the picture. It seemed as though they were saying good-bye.

I hadn't expected them to be there when I returned, but as I stood at the doors to the ICU looking at them, I was glad they were there. We had a lot to talk about.

I walked over to my chair and sat down beside the bed, waiting for the Spencers to finish and trying to imagine what could possibly be going on in their heads. I envisioned bright lazy summer afternoons with a three-year-old Barbara toddling through the green grass and giggling, birthday parties of shouting children and melting chocolate ice cream spilling off paper plates, and young men with white bucks and crew cuts waiting on the porch while Barbara combed her hair one more time, all floating indiscriminately through their minds. It was harder for them than for me, I decided.

I also decided at this time that I had lost my bearings. I no longer knew why I was in the ICU with Barbara and what I was waiting for. Did I expect there to be some positive or negative change in her condition, a next step, a transition, some sign, and if I did what could it possibly be? I began to see what Saul was talking about. This could be it, all there was, all there would ever be, day after day, night after night of Barbara lying comatose on the bed, being rotated one direction or the other to prevent bedsores, having sponge baths, IV's changed, lab work, and all the while, click, poof, siss, click poof siss, until one day, tomorrow, Christmas morning, six years from now, she just stops.

"Can we talk?" I asked the Spencers and we walked out into the hall where, off in the corner, Saul sat talking amiably to Winkin', Blinkin', and Nod, their permapress suits ready to see them through the long nocturnal vigil that might be necessary if they were to gather fresh viscera while they may.

"Saul's asked me to let them turn off the respirator," I told the Spencers, looking hard at them for help.

"Yes, we know," Mr. Spencer said to me.

"You see, Boris," Mrs. Spencer said to me, her hands working intently at a handkerchief she held in them, twisting it in hopes that a solution could be wrung out, "Stan and I could never make a decision like that. We're Catholic."

What I wanted to say was that this was a hell of a religion to have at a time like this, but I didn't. It was just another item to be taken into consideration.

"If you weren't Catholic, or at least if you *could* make a decision, what would you do?" I tried.

They looked at each other, wondering who should answer. Mr. Spencer decided to.

"We talked about it for some time over dinner, Boris," he began.

I didn't like the beginning. I sensed immediately that I wasn't going to find the middle any more appealing, and I knew for certain that I would despise the ending.

"We think if we *could* make the decision," he continued, "we'd have the respirator turned off, Boris."

"Why?" I squeaked.

"Because we feel that Barbara's already left us, Boris," Mrs. Spencer explained.

"But you don't *know* that," I interrupted.

"We do and we don't, Boris," Mrs. Spencer said. "We can never be certain, of course, of anything at all. We know that. So we have to trust other people who seem to know more. We don't think the doctors would be telling us what they are without very good reason. We have to believe them."

"In this case, I don't think they know any more than we do. As a matter of fact, I think they know less. They're all tied up in their tests and case studies. They don't know Barbara, just prognoses and clinical signs."

"We do know Barbara, Boris," Mr. Spencer said, looking directly into my eyes. "When you've known someone as intimately as you know your own child, you can sense what's happening with her. It seems to both of us that Barbara has already left this world. It's a feeling that you might not understand right now, Boris. Someday we're sure you will. It's a feeling that you can have only about someone you've conceived and raised."

I desperately wanted to tell them how wrong they were. Barbara was not their conception at all. Barbara was Harry Wolper's conception. She was the beautiful and perverse creation of a crazy old man sitting in front of a pad of lined paper, writing whatever the hell came into his head. And he was going to do whatever the hell he wanted to do, unless we stopped him, unless we fought back with all the strength we had. But I couldn't tell them. They wouldn't have understood. They would have thought I had gone stark raving mad, wouldn't they, Harry?

"You could always try."

Sure, and have them cart me away. Not on your life. You're not going to get rid of me so easily.

"Whatever you want, Boris. It's your choice."

Like hell it is.

I looked at the Spencers and tried to get my thoughts in order.

"Are you telling me that I should have them turn off the respirator?" I asked.

"No, we're not, Boris. It's very important to us that you understand that. We want you to do what you think is best. There would be no difference between us telling the doctors to turn off the respirator and us telling *you* to tell the doctors. The decision must be yours, Boris. If by some miracle Barbara survives, she would be with you, not with us. We'll support whatever you decide. You asked us how we felt, and we thought we had to tell you. We felt it was important for you to know. Now that you do, we won't discuss it anymore. Do what you feel you have to do."

I looked down the hall at the tableau of silent figures tuning into our conversation. Then I looked back at the Spencers, who had put their arms around each other, comfortable that they had said what they had to say.

The last support remaining to me had been removed. I wanted to scream.

The Spencers left for the cafeteria.

I had taken two steps back toward the ICU when out of the corner of my eye I caught a glimpse of a lady in a long white coat, bordered in ermine, swishing down the hall toward me. Her arm was draped over a tall good-looking middle-aged gentleman with thick black-rimmed glasses, a long aristocratic nose, and curly blond hair.

"And this," Mother said as she pecked a quick kiss on my cheek, "is Dr. Kuhn, my psychiatrist, Boris, who has been nice enough to drive me all the way up here just to examine dear, dear Martha."

"Barbara, Mother," I corrected. "Martha was my first wife."

"Whatever," Mother smiled. "Now how *is* she doing?"

"She's no different. They want me to let them turn off her respirator," I explained, expecting the worst. I was not to be disappointed.

"Well, I don't see how that would help." Mother played dumb in front of her *man*.

Dr. Kuhn looked extremely uncomfortable and began shifting restlessly from foot to foot.

"I think what Boris is trying to say, Harriet, is that they've given up hope and think that it would be best if Boris let them turn off the respirator so his wife could die."

"Well, Boris, if that's what they think you should do . . ." Mother said sweetly.

Dr. Kuhn interceded.

"Why don't we ask the physician in attendance whether he would mind if I had a look at her," Dr. Kuhn said quietly and led Mother off stage right, swishing and swirling, her rhinestone earrings flashing in the hall light.

Saul, who had been watching the conversation, got up and left his trio, guessing that the couple was looking for him. At the end of the hall, he caught up with them, and, after introductions and some conversation, they headed back to the ICU, three abreast, Mother holding Dr. Kuhn's arm on one side and Saul's arm on the other, Dan Dailey and Gene Kelly to her Cyd Charisse, on the way to another fun-filled toe-tapping frolic in the glittering world of terminal illness.

We entered the ICU, and Mother and I stood at the foot of Barbara's bed while Dr. Kuhn and Saul read over the chart, Saul pointing to numbers while Dr. Kuhn flipped pages.

Considering the various beaux Mother had introduced to me over the years, this Dr. Kuhn wasn't particularly bad. He certainly was an improvement over the unending line of young hairy-chested men in tight jeans and silk shirts unbuttoned to the navel. At least I wouldn't have to worry about a lot of backslapping and armwrestling and challenges to race into the pool with Dr. Kuhn. I wondered whether Mother was a good lay, or whether it even mattered anymore once you were fifty.

This fascinating mental dialogue occupied me continually while Dr. Kuhn and Saul conferred and I attempted to avoid having to deal with another inevitable, depressing report on the hopelessness of Barbara's situation.

Mother, in the meantime, was whispering Dr. Kuhn's credentials to me.

"He went to Yale, Boris, *the* Yale. And then Harvard Medical School, *the* Harvard Medical School. With money. He went to Harvard with *money*, dear. And now he's at Albert Einstein in the Bronx or somewhere as a *chair*-person. A *chair*person." Mother said this as though she were talking about some sort of grotesque anthropomorphic confabulation, an upholstered human with dowels.

I was jolted from Dr. Kuhn's impressive vita by Dr. Kuhn's impressive voice.

"I wonder if you could come over here for a minute, Dr. Shore?" he called.

Saul walked over to where Dr. Kuhn was holding Barbara's arm. He started tapping in various places on her arm and then did the same on her abdomen and down her legs.

Saul called a nurse over and issued a series of brisk orders for lab work and tests. The nurse rushed to the end of the room and started using the telephone, speaking excitedly in a language that consisted almost entirely of letters, BUN, SGOT, pH, CBC, interspersed with words like tap, films, and serum electrolytes. Two other nurses hurried from the room, talking quickly to each other and letting the double doors snap behind them noisily. Something was up.

I felt the blood begin to rush to my head and my heart begin to race. Dr. Kuhn and Saul stood now on each side of Barbara, poking and tapping from her head to her heel. When they had finished, they raised the sheet up to her chest, tucked it under her arms, and then walked over to where my mother and I were standing.

Saul put his hand on my arm and held it firmly.

"I don't want to get your hopes up, Boris," he began.

That's all right, I thought, get them up, get them up. It's okay.

"But Barbara could be improving."

I began to cry.

"There seems to be a return of a substantial amount of reflex activity that wasn't there after the hemorrhage," Dr. Kuhn explained to me.

"It's too early to tell what we're seeing," Saul continued to hold my arm tightly. "This could be just normal spinal recovery from the initial shock of the aneurysm, nothing more, in which case we're right back where we started, really. There's no way of knowing until we do other tests. And even then, we'll have to wait and see. It'll take a while. We won't really know anything until tomorrow morning."

My mother handed me a tiny perfumed handkerchief, and I blew my nose.

"I've asked for a meeting of the medical staff tomorrow morning to review the lab results and see where we are," Saul said, and he looked at me beaming from ear to ear, tears covering my cheeks and dripping from my moustache. "I have to emphasize, Boris, that we really don't know anything, yet. It's just a possibility."

"But she could be improving, right? She could be getting better?" I pleaded.

"Yes," Saul said uncomfortably. "She could be getting better."

I fell down on my knees and buried my head in my hands.

"Oh, thank you, Harry. Thank you. Thank you. You're terrific, Harry. You really are. Thank you. Harry. Harry," I cried into my hands.

I stayed like this for several minutes until Saul lifted me from the floor. He put his arm around me.

"How're you feeling, Boris?" he asked kindly, but I could tell that he wasn't really interested in the answer. He had made up his mind. I had finally snapped.

13th Well, let me tell you, I sympathize with Boris. Sanity is not an easy thing these days.

Madmen and lunatics establish National Institutes of Mental Health as though all that stands between us and eternal Peace of Mind are a number of well-funded research projects and a careful rereading of Sigmund Freud.

Teenagers warn their folks against the dangers of repression. Young parents tiptoe through toilet training so their offspring can avoid the evils of anal fixation. Farmers come home from their fields and patiently sit around on summer evenings telling their pigtailed, gingham-clad daughters about penis envy.

This circumstance is no accident. This is Dr. Freud's own particular Weltanschauung. It is his vision and his alone that accounts for twenty-nine-year-old boys with custom-tailored minds earning a minimum wage of fifty dollars an hour while his children huddle in doorways, strung out, starving, and supremely benign.

Who among us does not grow up today desperately attempting to understand our lives in terms of our unconscious drives, subconscious motives, repressed urges, fixations, Oedipal traumas, defense mechanisms, inhibitions, conflicts, and complexes?

And how glorious it would be if Dr. Freud were right. How magnificent if we were, in fact, an energy system that obeyed the same physical laws as those that regulate the soap bubble and the movement of the planets. How I envy Freud his conviction that it's possible to construct a philosophy of life that is based on science, not metaphysics or religion.

Well, colleague, we stand neck deep in science today. My neighbor waves to me from the moon. My eight-year-old grandson pushes a button on a tiny portable box and tells me instantly the square root of any number I can imagine. A tree falls in an uninhabited forest halfway around the world and a satellite sends the event to me in my living room before the dust settles to assure me that there was, in fact, a sound. And still we manage to maintain our glorious legacy of insanity.

No matter how we are parcelled into egos, libidos, and ids, into psychotics, neurotics, and character disorders, our resolve is firm. Chemistry and physics have not led us to a new understanding of the human psyche. And all the atomic, hydrogen, and plutonium bombs that science can produce will never give us the power necessary to overcome the strength a single man uses to resist knowing the truth about himself.

14th I went for a walk today, the first in many weeks, under the rainbow canopy that covers my street this October. The colors sparkled as they always do this month, maples and elms blazing against the sun, the same extraordinary display no less extraordinary because it is annual.

As I scraped through the first few fallen leaves, I heard a familiar voice rise from the earth, a memory as vivid today as when I was six, walking through the same spectacular scene, my tiny hand thrust deeply into my father's enormous leather fist. We tramped through the woods in ecstasy, or at least so I thought.

My father stopped and evaluated the situation.

"You see this magnificent color, son," he said solemnly.

I shook my head to assure him I was properly aware of the marvelous natural poetry.

"Three weeks from now there will be nothing but emptiness, bare trees, an earth covered with decaying dark leaves, rot. Rot, son."

"Rot," I repeated.

"This is the way the world behaves before she dies," he informed me gravely. "Don't let the spectacle fool you. It's a prelude to death and nothing more. Why nature can't die like everyone else is something I'll never understand," he said disgustedly, taking a long drink from the flask that was his constant companion. "Just who the hell does she think she is anyway?" he grumbled. "Who the hell does she think she's kidding?"

My sentiments exactly, this lovely October day.

15th The Adventures of Boris Lafkin

CHAPTER FIVE (continued):

In Which Our Hero's Excursion Detours

The Spencers were eating ice cream. This was definitely not good. They were sitting across from each other in the cafeteria eating chocolate ice cream and drinking coffee, chatting calmly. Normal people do this, I recalled, people relaxing after a long day, content with their lives.

I drew up a chair and sat down with them. They greeted me with a warm smile and inquired about the state of my health. Then they resumed their conversation about whether they should trade in the station wagon or try for another year's use. The thing I most dreaded happening to them had finally happened. They had become resigned to Barbara's death.

Life was resuming. They would each go back to work soon. The laundry was piling up. Groceries were running out. The man was coming at the end of the week to do the carpets. The children had dental appointments. And I was being abandoned to do entirely as I wished, guard Barbara from the ghouls, keep watch by her bed, maintain the vigil, or have the respirator turned off and resume my own life. I waited until a pause in their conversation.

"Barbara's improving," I said.

"That's wonderful, Boris," Mr. Spencer smiled, but he wasn't interested. There had been too many changes in her condition. It was too much. Someone would have to tell him she was awake and wanted to see him or that she was dead before he would allow the information to penetrate.

"No, I mean it. She's getting better," I tried to pierce the armor. "The doctors were examining her and told me. Her reflexes are returning. That could be very good, they said."

The Spencers looked at each other, confused and in pain. It had been so much effort to build this fortification, and now they couldn't chance letting it down, piece by piece, opening themselves again to hope and to the crushing impact of having it taken away by a false alarm, another change. Their resources were limited. It had taken all that was left in the two of them to begin to put their lives and their family back together. The risk was too great. But the information tugged at them, implored them to yield, and so, helplessly, Mr. Spencer pursued the matter.

"You're absolutely sure?" he asked.

"I am about the reflexes," I told him, hoping I could regain him as an ally. "I *saw* them, and the doctors told me. They can't be sure that it's not just her body recovering from the initial shock, so they're ordering a bunch of tests and have called a meeting tomorrow morning to review everything. But it's *definitely* promising. It could be the beginning of everything, Mr. Spencer, of absolutely everything."

"We're very pleased to hear that, Boris," Mrs. Spencer said. "We certainly hope it means all that you'd like it to, Boris. Don't we, Stan?" she smiled at him.

"Of course we do, Boris. What splendid news that would be," and he put his hand gently on my arm and held it firmly.

I had lost. I was alone.

"Well," I said and got up to leave, "I just thought you'd want to know, that's all. I hope I didn't bother you or anything," I continued quietly, my mind somewhere else.

"No, no, of course you didn't bother us," Mr. Spencer assured me. "We're glad you told us. Really we are. Thank you."

"You're welcome," I said as I started to walk from the cafeteria.

Mr. Spencer called after me.

"You understand, Boris, don't you?" he asked.

"Yes," I said. "I understand," and I walked slowly away. Before I got to the door, I turned around.

"She's your daughter, you know," I said to them.

"Yes, Boris, we know," Mrs. Spencer said.

"We know," Mr. Spencer echoed.

It was at this point exactly that I first noticed that my brain had changed. I was walking down the hall after talking to the Spencers, and I realized that something inside my head was different from what was inside other people's heads, and it hadn't always been that way.

I was thinking about the Spencers and the way they saw the situation, and Saul and what he was saying about turning off Barbara's respirator, and the good doctors Frankenstein waiting for transplants, and my mother, who seemed to me to have made Barbara into another one of her projects, sort of like the Christmas Bazaar, and then it occurred to me that my world and everyone else's world were two entirely different worlds, that they weren't even on the same planet at the same time, that this wasn't earth in the 1960s at all. This was the Planet Boris, and there wasn't any time at all. There was just before, and now, and later.

This was why I couldn't *talk* to anyone and vice versa, and it wasn't any simple marching to a different drummer or sloppy solipsism or something. No, I realized, this was because of my brain. It just wasn't like other people's brains. It was wired entirely differently. The connections were all organized on a different plan and probably even worked differently. With a brain like I had, I couldn't really expect to be able to talk to other people. It was absolutely impossible.

I also decided that this accounted for Harry. I was blessed with Harry Wolper and the whole lousy mess that came with Harry Wolper solely because of my brain. Other people had pets and dolls as they were growing up. I had Harry.

Other people worshipped a god or invested themselves in a career. I fought Harry. And now I knew why. I fought Harry for giving me this goddam brain of mine. I didn't know whether it was his idea of a joke or a mildly diverting game to occupy his time, but, whatever it was, it was a lousy goddam brain and it had transported me to a world in which I was the only inhabitant.

I liked everyone else's world enough. It was just that I had the wrong brain for it. It wasn't my fault.

"For a while there," I told Barbara as I sat by the bed watching her chest rising and falling with the cycles of the respirator, "I thought I had some company in this world of mine. I thought I had found someone with the same basic brain. I figured that between the two of us we'd be able to handle both worlds, theirs and ours. I don't think I was very clear about it until now, but that was the feeling I had ever since we met. I didn't have to stay by myself in this world of mine, anymore, because from now on you'd be there."

I looked at Barbara's face, expressionless and calm, and knew that she was listening to me.

"I guess you heard the doctors," I continued. "You're beginning to get better. Your reflexes are coming back. That's the first step. I knew you were a fighter. Now you just have to keep at it. A good blood pressure and lots of reflexes aren't enough. You've got to start breathing on your own. Get rid of this lousy respirator before you get pneumonia or something, before it's too late and some doctor decides that euthanasia is the very latest thing and pulls the plug. This is important, Barbara. From now on you have to focus all your energy on getting back your own breathing. Nothing else counts. Harry's on our side now, Barbara, I can tell. It's not a struggle anymore. He's for us. He's helping us out. Aren't you, Harry?" I asked out loud.

I felt a hand settle gently on my shoulder. It was Saul.

"How're you feeling, Boris?" he asked solicitously.

"Terrific, Saul. Just terrific," I exaggerated somewhat to avoid any misinterpretation.

"Terrific," he nodded his head.

"Right. Terrific."

"Boris, can we talk for a few minutes?"

"Sure, Saul. What would you like to talk about?" I played dumb.

"No, I mean, can we go somewhere and talk?"

"For how long?"

"Just a short time. We need to do a few more tests right now, anyway. We'll be back before they're done."

"Sure. Sure. What would you like to talk about?"

Saul didn't answer but steered me out of the ICU into the same plush room where we had met the three jolly transplanters.

"So," I asked for the third time, "what'd you like to talk about?"

"How're you feeling, Boris?" Saul took out a pipe and began to fill it.

"Fine, Saul. How come so many people around here smoke pipes, Saul? Is it some sort of a new fad or something?"

"I don't know, Boris. Why do you think that people smoke pipes?" Saul returned the question.

"Do you really want to know what I think, Saul? I think that it's a conspiracy of angry people. Pipe smokers are basically repressed anal-retentive types with deep-seated oral needs who never liked the idea of being weaned, so now they walk around when they're angry and needy, looking calm and mature, biting on their stems, clenching their teeth and puffing away as though no one else can tell how fucked up they are, that's what I think," I smiled.

"Really?" Saul said with appropriate professional distance but put down his pipe nevertheless.

There was silence during which the two of us sat grinning at each other. Saul broke his grin first.

"Who's Harry, Boris?" he asked.

"Oh," I thought quickly, "a friend."

"Really. Have I ever met him?" he smiled.

"No, you haven't, Saul. I'm the only one who's ever met him. Just me. No one else. Maybe Barbara. I'm not sure. She could have. If not, then only me."

"What's he like?" Saul pursued.

"Look, Saul, I don't want to play cat and mouse. I'm not going crazy, if that's what you think. I'll tell you who Harry is, if you really want to know, though I can't see what good it's going to do you."

I stopped for a minute, trying to decide whether I should change my mind.

"Well?" Saul finally asked.

"Yes. Well, it's like this, Saul. You know all this stuff that we're experiencing right now, all these people, this hospital, Barbara?"

"I think I do, yes."

"Well, none of it is real."

"It isn't," Saul made sure he understood. "You mean it *seems* as though it isn't real."

"Not exactly, Saul. You see, it's exactly the opposite. It *seems* as though it *is* real. It *actually* isn't."

"What is it?"

I was afraid he would ask. I decided to push on, having gone this far.

"It's a novel that Harry Wolper is writing," I said looking at him directly in the eyes. Saul was becoming progressively less comfortable in his comfortable chair.

"He has a last name?" Saul asked.

"Yes. It's Wolper. Harrison Hipassos Wolper. He calls himself Harry Wolper."

"Hipassos?"

"He's named after a Greek. Hipassos was a Pythagorean who was put to death for discovering irrational numbers."

"What's the novel about?" Saul asked incredulously.

"Me. That's all I know. He won't tell me what else it's about. He says there's nothing more. But he's lying. Harry lies a lot."

"What else does he do?"

"Creates life. Or at least he tries to. I think he's finally done it, too. By accident. He's not very good at it."

"You know, Boris, forgive me for stereotyping your own personal author, but he reminds me a lot of what other people call, how shall I say it, the Lord God."

"He's not exactly what most people think of when they talk about God, Saul."

"How's that?"

"Well, to begin with, he's impotent, incompetent, and weak, extremely disorganized, helpless, never around when you need him, a hypochondriac, selfish, in love with a nineteen-year-old nymphomaniac, being blackmailed by his only son, a habitual abortionist, and dying."

Saul thought about this.

"You're right, Boris. He's not the way most of us conceive of The Almighty."

"He's also screwed up my brain."

"How exactly?" Saul asked, but I sensed he was becoming less interested in my answers.

"I'm not sure, but he gave me a brain that doesn't fit in this world, Saul. I can't really figure it out, but either it's the wrong brain for this world, or this is the wrong world for this brain. Either way, it's the same thing."

"What about me?"

"Oh, you're just another character he's made up. Everyone is. This whole thing with Barbara is some sort of Great Struggle Harry and I are involved in. I feel kind of bad you got caught in the middle, because I've always liked you Saul, but you see, that's why I can't turn off the respirator. That's what Harry *wants* me to do, I think. He's testing me. Even though he says he isn't, I know what's up. That's about the only advantage I can think of in having this brain of mine. I know what the hell Harry's up to almost all the time."

"But Harry denies that he's doing all this?"

"Of course. You don't think he'd admit it, do you? No, he says he's lost control. He's got this moving-finger metaphor that he thinks is just the most sensational thing since *Pilgrim's Progress*. He says he just sits at his workbench with a pad of paper in front of him, a pen in his hand, and the novel comes out, my life goes on, totally beyond his control. Can you believe the nerve of that bastard thinking I'd believe that pile of horseshit?"

"Maybe he knows something about your brain that you don't know," Saul suggested facetiously.

"Not likely," I responded.

Saul looked me up and down. He wondered whether I was dangerous.

"How long have you believed in this Harry?" he asked.

"Ever since I can remember. So you see, I'm not having a breakdown over Barbara. But I also can't listen to what you and the other doctors tell me, Saul. This is not your usual medical problem. You have no way of knowing whether Harry isn't tricking you, whether he isn't trying to deceive me, what the hell is going on."

"It doesn't make any sense, Boris," Saul argued. "I suppose if you want to fabricate your very own divinity, that's up to you. If you want to fabricate him and then wage war against him, that's also your problem. But either he *is* controlling your behavior, in which case you're doing what he wants you to whether you know it or not, or you can do whatever you want to do, in which case it doesn't make any difference whether you've got some bizarre Greek novelist writing away in heaven."

"In Cambridge," I corrected.

"Here in Cambridge?" Saul asked in disbelief.

"Well, not *this* Cambridge."

"Cambridge, England?"

"No, Cambridge, Massachusetts. *His* Cambridge, Massachusetts, not yours or mine. Ours is the one in the novel, remember, the one that seems real but really isn't. His is the one that's real, only it seems to us as though it isn't."

Saul looked at me for a long time.

"Boris," he finally said sadly, "I think you're having a breakdown. You need help."

"Saul," I responded, "I don't think I'm crazy, but I will admit one thing to you. It's hard to tell anymore."

When I left, Saul was in a state most generously described as dazed.

As I approached the ICU, a number of friends and enemies came up to see me. There seemed to be an intense interest in how I was feeling. The word was out. I was bonkers. Saul never had been very good at keeping his opinions to himself.

Mort, the Prosecutor, renewed his acquaintance with me. He had come to see Judge O'Brien, who also was dying. He embraced me and smiled under the false assumption that death was joining us in a brotherhood that transcended the petty issues of the past, including his having committed me to a mental institution.

"Let bygones be bygones," he instructed me good-naturedly, slapped me on the back, and made way for the others waiting to inspect the mental damage.

Father O'Malley had arrived for his evening rounds of last rites. I reminded him that Barbara had already had the good fortune of his miserers, and it was not her fault that she hadn't gotten around to taking full advantage of them by expiring. He looked at me very strangely and then blessed me in my grief. After all, I was, he concluded to himself, bereaved.

The Spencers approached. They comforted and consoled me.

My mother approached. I was scolded for not doing as I was told. I admitted to being ashamed that I was behaving as I was after all she had done for me, but I refused to change. She expected this. It was typical of me.

I took several steps back from the people in the hall, waved ebulliently to them all as though I were about to embark on a joyous voyage, bowed graciously, and disappeared into the ICU, confirming their conviction that I was hopelessly mad.

I sat by Barbara for some time, holding her tightly, letting thoughts flow randomly through my own special brain, hoping that they reached hers as well. I found myself thinking a lot about that weekend on the beach. It was one of your basic what-if queries. What if we hadn't gone to the Cape, hadn't made love, hadn't pledged ourselves to each other, would someone else be sitting here now? The irony completely escaped me, if there was any. I was here and that was all there was to it. Even this bizarre world Harry had created for me had its rules. You can't go back. You don't know what's next. What is, is. I was not going to materialize four months ago on a beach on Cape Cod. Barbara was not going to take two aspirins two days ago and have her headache go away. I decided that as glorious and poetic as I found my very own fantasies, they were leading me absolutely nowhere at all, so I stopped, placed my head gently on Barbara's arm, and tried to get some rest to see me through the long night ahead.

I was awakened from a half-sleep by Saul informing me that an old friend awaited me in the other room. He wanted to surprise me.

Suspiciously I made my way to another office down the hall and, on entering the room, found none other than the world's worst psychiatrist, Dr. Alexander Ward, previously of Days Clinic and now, through a freak occurrence that had no doubt permanently wrecked the laws of chance, of Harvard's Department of Psychiatry, and, therefore, a consultant to this particular hospital.

"Boris," he beamed. "How are you?"

"Oh, fine. Just fine," I smiled back.

"So," he leaned back as always and lit his pipe. It did not disprove my theory about pipesmokers. "So, so, so. What've you been up to since we last met?"

"Well, you know," I leaned over and whispered to him. "It's funny you should ask, because lately I've really been getting into terminal illness. It's a real turn-on, Dr. Ward. I think it's becoming a fad, too. You didn't happen to notice the crowd out there when you came in, did you, Dr. Ward?"

"Well, yes, I did," Dr. Ward was extremely pleased by how observant he had been.

"Well, they, too, are excited about terminal illness, Dr. Ward. It's terribly exciting stuff, this dying business. The mystery. What *really* is killing this person? The suspense. When will she *actually* die? The drama. Will her best friend and lover *kill* her before she departs of her *own* free will? Great stuff, huh?"

Dr. Ward was not to be fooled. There was something strange going on here. Perhaps I wasn't being entirely frank with him. Perhaps I still carried around old grudges.

"You aren't still angry at me, Boris, are you?" he asked uneasily.

"Dr. Ward, why are you here?" I avoided the question.

"I'm here because I was asked to be here, Boris. Dr. Shore asked me to evaluate the situation," he answered precisely, clasping his hands together and twiddling his thumbs.

"What is 'the situation,' Dr. Ward?" I asked.

"*You* are the situation, Boris," he informed me matter-of-factly.

"Dr. Ward, I am not crazy." I got into the heart of the matter.

"You're not?" he asked, surprised.

"No, I'm not."

"Then why am I here?" he wondered out loud.

"You may recall, Dr. Ward, that not more than thirty seconds ago, that was the exact question I asked you. Why are you here?" I reminded him.

"Didn't I already answer that? I'm here to determine if you're having a breakdown."

"Does it seem to you like I'm having a breakdown?"

"Well, to be perfectly frank, Boris, you don't seem any different right now than you did back at Days Clinic, and I never could figure out whether you were crazy or not then. Were you crazy then, Boris? Say," a thought suddenly occurred to him, "who's Harry?"

I cleared my throat and looked the other way.

"Harry?" I feigned ignorance.

"Yes. Harry. Let me see," he looked down at some notes on the desk. "Harry Wolper?"

"Oh, yes. Harry Wolper. He's God."

"Really. Do you talk to God?"

"Yes, I do, Dr. Ward. All the time."

"Does He answer you?"

"Sometimes. Well, most of the time," I remembered.

"What's He like?"

"Why? You want to meet him?"

Dr. Ward was becoming interested.

"Is He really God?"

"It's hard to tell, Dr. Ward, but I think he is, yes."

"And you can talk to Him?" Dr. Ward asked. "Can I?"

"Hey, Harry. You want to talk to Dr. Ward?"

("Not a chance, Boris. He's your problem.")

"Very well, but it could be a rare event."

("Thank you, Boris, but I'll miss this one.")

"No, I'm sorry, Dr. Ward. This god is my god. You've got to get your own."

"Tell me about your brain?" he asked, glancing again at his notes.

"What would you like to know, Dr. Ward?"

"Well, I understand that you think your brain is different."

"Yes, that's correct."

"How would you say, for example, that your brain is different from mine?"

"In just about every way I can think of, Dr. Ward."

Dr. Ward looked puzzled. I decided to help him out.

"Look, Dr. Ward. There's been a horrible misunderstanding. You don't actually think I go around talking to God, do you? You don't really think that God goes around talking to me, either, or that I've got some sort of a strange brain, do you now? I mean, this is all absurd. God is up in heaven, and I'm here on earth, and we all have brains that are the same. You *know* that, Dr. Ward, and so do I. God is someone who made the heavens and the earth, whom we worship on Sundays, who talks to absolutely no one except a few saints every century or so, and couldn't care less what you or I do with our lives. Barbara either for that matter."

Dr. Ward looked mostly relieved as he licked contentedly at his pipe.

"Well, I'm glad to hear you say that, Boris. I don't care what Dr. Shore says. You certainly seem sane enough to me," and I was dismissed.

I was closing the door behind my old friend, the psychiatrist, and was turning around when I found myself face to face with a face that, for only an instant, I didn't recognize.

"I'm really sorry to hear about Barbara," the girl said.

My heart skipped six beats and my insides went through as many emotions, hate, anger, love, desire, disgust, longing, you name them. It was Marty Fortran.

"Hello, Marty," was all I could manage.

"Listen, Boris, I'm really sorry about the way I walked out on you and all that shit," she said pleasantly, much as someone might apologize for opening a letter of yours by mistake.

"Oh, that's all right," I responded, as though that was, in fact, the seriousness of the infraction.

"You're not mad at me then, Boris?" she smiled sweetly.

"No, I'm not," I said honestly, because I wasn't. There was Barbara now. Marty's leaving was one of the best things that ever happened to me.

"Oh, I'm really glad about that, Boris. I've thought about it a lot, since, you know. You really were terribly nice to me, and I was so goddam lousy. I hate myself for it. I mean, it wasn't your fault you were passive, right? It was unfair of me to make you feel *guilty* about some defect that you couldn't really help, right," and she took my hand.

"Look, Marty, that was a long time ago. You really shouldn't go getting all concerned about it now. There're no hard feelings, really."

"Well, I *am* concerned about it. I can't help it, Boris. That's the way I am. I had no right to make you feel so lousy. Sex is a two-way street. I know that now. I should have done everything I possibly could to help you overcome your sexual problems, not just walk out on you like I did," Marty whispered and snuggled up to me.

"Marty, what do you say we just forget the whole thing? No hard feelings. Really."

"Great, Boris. Just great. Boy have you changed. It's just *amazing*. Say, what do you say we go for a little walk? How about it, huh?"

"Marty, I'm kind of in the middle of something."

"Oh, that," she said, pressing my hand, "That'll wait."

"Marty," I said, extracting my hand, "I appreciate your coming to offer your apologies, but they're doing some tests on Barbara now, and I want to be there."

"Tests?" Marty said in amazement. "Isn't she dead? Howie Woodhouse said she was dead."

"Howie was premature."

"You mean Barbara's alive?"

"As near as anyone can tell, yes."

"I thought she was dead. Wait'll I get my hands on Woodhouse, that bastard."

"I'm sorry you're disappointed."

"You're goddam right I am. I had great plans for us, Boris."

"For us?" I was having trouble understanding what was going on. "What us?"

From around the corner on cue came Dirty Al Petrucci.

"You kids are still married," he informed me, scraping some gum off the bottom of his sandals.

"I think you know Al," Marty smirked.

"Oh, yes. I know him. Why are we still married, Al?"

"Because the fuckin' Mexican divorce Marty got is fuckin' illegal. You're still considered to be married in every fuckin' state in the country, except Nevada. You want to live in Nevada for the rest of your fuckin' life, you're set. Otherwise you've got one hell of a fuckin' problem." Dirty Al lit his cigar.

"You see what I mean, Boris," Marty tried to be helpful. "I thought I'd give you another chance."

"I don't want another chance!" I shouted.

Everyone in the hall turned around and looked at us. Mother saw Marty and waved. Marty smiled her biggest smile and waved back. I lowered my voice.

"Look, Marty," I said as emphatically and softly as I could. "Go sue me for bigamy. I don't care. Go sue me for desertion, for cruel and abusive treatment, sexual passivity. I *really* don't care."

"Oh," Dirty Al smacked his lips, "we wouldn't sue you for any of *those*. We'd sue you for some fuckin' alimony. Marty's in a desperate fuckin' condition, Boris. We think you ought to help out your poor fuckin' wife. Think it over. We'd even consider a lump sum settlement."

"She is *not* my wife, Al," I informed him, and headed down the hall for the ICU.

"Oh, yes she is, Boris. She's *your* fuckin' wife. Think it over. We'll wait," and Dirty Al and Marty walked over to introduce themselves to the eye, kidney, and spleen men. I had no doubt they'd get along famously.

22nd I have had to come to a difficult conclusion today. I need Meli. I need Meli not because I am old or dying, or lonely. Nor do I need her because she is young and vibrant and carries my creations. I need Meli because she is Meli, and I miss her, and I need her.

I awaken in the morning and look immediately to see whether she is there beside me, whether she has materialized secretly in the night, whether I need only reach out to touch her and feel her in my grasp.

I wait for her to appear on the other side of the table for meals. I look out the window expecting her to be skipping up the walk and bursting through the front door. No bicycle rider is safe from my inspection. No passerby avoids my searching looks. I miss her desperately.

I have to be careful about all of this, this newfound desire. Every day now I can feel more and more of me ebbing away into the Great Universal Sea. I must be cautious that, as I lose more of myself, I don't reach out even more frantically to hold on to Meli, to anchor me against the forces that tug at my life.

I have determined that I will make a search. I will hunt down my fertile enchantress. I will go hat in hand to her apartment and plead for her return. She is a reasonable woman. I'm certain she will not deny me this last wish.

We have gone through a lot, Meli and I. There must be a bond between us. I can sense that it still exists, still remains fast. I must follow this thread until I retrieve my Meli and pull her into my arms. I have new energy, new drive, new enthusiasm.

And so the search beings.

I surprise myself that at this point in my life I am so incredibly alone.

"You've got me, Harry."

Just incredibly alone.

24th Today was not a good day.

I searched desperately for Meli. I could not find her. She has moved from her apartment. There is no forwarding address. Her parents and friends have not heard from her. She has simply evaporated.

I returned to the house tonight, exhausted and depressed, thinking about my dream last night. As I undressed, I noticed something that I had been ignoring all the way home. My pants were damp. I had dribbled in them. Not a lot. Just enough to be noticeable and uncomfortable.

I have wet my pants. I think I am becoming incontinent, and I am scared. My death is just around the corner. I wonder whether I will have the time to finish with Boris.

25th The Adventures of Boris Lafkin

CHAPTER FIVE (continued):
In Which Our Hero Is Unfortunate Enough to Reach His Destination

I had the curious feeling, as I stood up beside Barbara and stroked her hair, that I was a photographic silk screen of an otherwise not particularly interesting object, a Campbell Soup Can, a jar of ketchup, a human being grieving over his dying wife, a common occurrence now magnified a thousand times until each individual dot becomes obvious, but in the end, as the observer stands back, still the same old household item.

This image stuck in my head. I imagined gallery owners taking clients around their establishments, pointing out the artwork.

"This is a Lichtenstein of Flash Gordon," they tell the matron in the foxtail collar, "and over here is the famous Robert Indiana that was used for the cover of *Love Story*. Over here we have a Warhol of Jackie Kennedy—"

"What's that?" the matron peers over her pince-nez.

"Oh," the owner says with obvious distaste, "that's a Harry Wolper of a young man trying to keep his dying wife alive."

"I think I'll take the Flash Gordon," the collector informs the dealer.

"Good choice," he answers. "I'll have it wrapped."

I continued to stroke Barbara's hair and look at her face, her eyes closed and still, the green transparent tube sticking grotesquely from her mouth.

A new intern, young, with long curly hair, came in to do some more tests on Barbara. I watched him draw blood, and then go through the usual tapping and poking. He looked in Barbara's eyes and then shook his head solemnly.

There was something about him that I trusted as I watched him at work. I knew that the results of his examination were not encouraging, so I stopped paying attention and let my mind drift.

I was convinced that somewhere in the middle of all this there must be some beauty. I refused to accept that it was all a farce, the Great Battle with Harry, pop art, aggravation with no redeeming value whatsoever.

After all, there was love here. There was the closeness that Barbara and I had experienced. There was that something special that transcended absolutely everything, brains and hemorrhages and medical science. It accounted for why Barbara was still alive and hadn't succumbed like every other cerebral vascular accident.

It was late now and just about everybody had finally gotten bored and left. It made me feel close to Barbara, that it was just the two of us working this thing through. I couldn't see why everything had to be so complicated. I thought about the good old days when people either lived or died and didn't do whatever the hell it was that Barbara was doing. I longed for something simple. Something simple and beautiful.

"We shall overcome. We shall overcome," I muttered to myself over and over under my breath, and then put my head down on the sheet next to Barbara to try to get some rest.

It was midnight. The hospital had become very still. The street outside was empty. Every few minutes a small breeze ruffled some dry leaves. Otherwise there wasn't a sound. I tried to close my eyes and shut out visions of respirators and heart monitors without much success, so I reached out for Barbara's hand, to concentrate on it, wondering whether she would someday be able to reach out for my hand and whether this was one of the last nights I would be able to spend touching her.

It had been a long day, and I was exhausted. I could feel my body start to relax, to let go of all the concerns and conflicts that had been keeping me going for the last thirty hours. I tried once more to shut my eyes, this time successfully. The click-poof-siss faded into the night along with the low voices of the nurses off in the corner and the footsteps of someone out in the hall slowly walking away.

I remember wondering whether Barbara would still be alive in the morning, and I fought for just an instant to stay awake in case Barbara was not going to make it through the night, and then I fell asleep.

I awakened abruptly to the touch of Saul's hand on my shoulder. I looked quickly at Barbara, verified that she was alive, tuned in to the sound of the respirator, noticed that it was light outside, brought my watch into focus to discover it was 6:30 A.M., and then turned to Saul who was studying Barbara intently.

"We've concluded the tests," he said quietly.

I didn't pursue the matter. It was too early. I didn't need to know the results yet.

"How do you feel?" he asked.

"Fine. Just fine," I answered. And then, just to assure him that I wasn't lying, "A little tired, but otherwise okay."

"Good. I'm glad to hear it. We're meeting in about an hour. Would you like to join me downstairs for some coffee?"

I thought about this. I wanted some coffee desperately, but I did not want to begin the day with arguments about Barbara's status. Tossing my better judgment to the wind, I agreed to join him.

I was surprised that he didn't mention Barbara once. I was also relieved. For most of the next hour we talked about our lives since we had been roommates in college, a little about Harry, but mostly life in general. Except for one exchange, our conversation was mostly relaxed and pleasant.

The exception was Harry.

"Lookit," I finally said when things began to heat up, "*You've* got God. *I've* got Harry. I didn't ask for Harry, but that's what I've got, and there isn't a damn thing I can do about it. I don't see why I've got to get a couple hundred thousand people to believe in Harry before people don't think I'm crazy. I know that a lot of other believers would make it a bona fide religion, only this is not a popularity contest. If it were, I can guarantee you that Harry wouldn't win it. He wouldn't even place or show."

We didn't talk about it anymore, but went back to our conversation about our various escapades since college. The time passed quickly, and before I knew it, it was time for the meeting of the medical staff to review Barbara's progesss. I took a long deep breath and went with Saul to the conference room on the first floor for what was, indisputably, the most painful experience of my life.

I followed an orderly carrying a pitcher of water into the plush, indirectly lit, mahogany-panelled room, and took my place in the center of the long polished table while the orderly filled everyone's glasses.

On one side of me sat Dr. Kuhn, Dr. Ward, Dr. Oliver Johnson, and three physicians I had never met before, who I later learned were a radiologist, a hematologist, and an intern. On the other side of me sat the Spencers, another intern, and Nurse McCafferty. Presiding over the meeting was, much to my surprise, Dr. Walensky, who was sitting at the end of the table by a large bronze plaque that was secured to the wall and that informed me that this entire room was a gift of the Bethany Association.

Saul closed the door as the orderly left and then came over and sat next to me for support. I was glad he did.

I suppose I could go into a whole lot of detail about the meeting but it isn't necessary.

There were lots of slides. The hematologist reported on the lumbar puncture and subsequent lab tests. There was no question that Barbara's brain had coned. Otherwise all her other systems seemed to be stable. She could survive indefinitely, but would be comatose throughout.

The radiologist hung up some X rays on a translucent display panel on the wall. He pointed out "landmarks" and "fissures." The intracranial pressure was intense. It was inconceivable that there had not been extensive brain damage.

The Spencers left.

Dr. Kuhn reviewed the neurological findings. The return of the reflexes had been only the normal recovery of Barbara's body from the initial shock. It was clear now. He, too, confirmed that the damage to Barbara's brain was overwhelming. While it was a mystery how she remained alive at this point, the thought of any further recovery was impossible. He reviewed two dozen or so neurological findings that confirmed this.

Dr. Johnson reviewed the case from Barbara's entry into the emergency room to the time she had been transferred to the ICU and put under Saul's care. Saul took over and reviewed the rest.

Dr. Ward said nothing at all but looked me over from time to time to see how I was holding up and looked glum.

The other interns took notes.

Throughout the presentations, Dr. Walensky sat without emotion, gently puffing at his pipe. When Saul finally finished, Dr. Walensky thanked everyone, and then sat in silence, exhaling small wisps of smoke from the sides of his mouth. Eventually he turned to me.

"This is a very tragic thing, Mr. Lafkin," he began.

I bit down on my teeth as hard as I could. I did *not* want to cry. Dr. Walensky paused and then continued.

"The brain is like tissue paper, Mr. Lafkin. This is why it is surrounded by fluid, why it is covered with three different layers of tissue, and then with some of the strongest bones in our body, the skull." He paused again. I wondered whether this was the way he began his famous introductory course in neuroanatomy.

"When something such as what has happened to your wife occurs, it is devastating to the brain. The blood tears through the cortex. The swelling presses deeply against the cells until there is no oxygen left and they die in great numbers."

I began to feel faint. My heart speeded up and perspiration broke out on my face. It fell like large drops of blood to the table. I turned desperately from side to side looking for someone to help me. There was no one.

I gripped the table to steady myself and tried to see through the wet blur that covered my eyes. I felt exhausted, drained. They had taken all that there was of my body and blood, and now there was nothing left. Absolutely nothing. I wondered how many times they had done this before and whether next month, a year from now, they would remember who I was.

"I think it is important for you to know the facts as they are, Mr. Lafkin," Dr. Walensky continued methodically and patiently. "We are never certain of anything in the medical profession, I can assure you. But as much as we can be certain, I'm afraid I have to tell you that your wife's situation is hopeless. There is no chance for recovery. I'm very sorry."

There was a long pause while everyone looked uncomfortably at each other and I tried to hold myself together. Finally Dr. Walensky spoke again.

"If you'd like," he said softly, "we can go upstairs and examine Barbara once more."

I shook my head in defeat.

"This is enough," I said, buried my head in my arms, and wept.

I don't remember much of what happened after that, when it was that everyone left for the Mount of Olives, what I did next. But I do remember standing next to Barbara later that morning, unable to keep my eyes off her, wondering how much longer I would be able to look at her before she died.

I had heard all that the doctors said, and still I just couldn't apply it to the woman who rested on the bed beside me. For a few minutes I found myself wanting to get out of the hospital, to run away and leave Barbara, to go someplace else forever, anyplace else, just as long as I didn't have to be here with Barbara in the Intensive Care Unit.

The weekend at the Cape went through my head a thousand times in every detail. I remembered her dungarees and the sweatshirt, and how she held me, and how we made love and talked about everything that was important to us, how we fell in love with each other, and how, more than anything else, she wanted me to stay her friend.

29th "All right, Harry, I give up. You win."

Win what, Boris?

"I don't know, Harry. I honestly don't know. Whatever the fuck it is, it's yours."

There's nothing to win, Boris.

"Oh, sure there is, Harry. Me. You win me."

Look, Boris, I can certainly understand how you must feel. You've a hard decision ahead of you. Very difficult.

"Nice, Harry. Very nice."

What are you talking about, Boris?

"Harry, I think you've made your point. I get the fucking picture. Here it all is in one neat package, science and religion, morality, life and death, the human psyche, love and insanity, you name it. Hurray for Hegel. Three cheers for dialectical materialism and the Absolute. Beautiful, just beautiful. I admire your creative flair, Harry. Unique. The grotesque Wolperian mind-body problem."

I like that, Boris. It has a certain ring to it. The problem is that I had nothing to do with this.

"Oh, no you don't, Harry. Not this time. I need you now, Harry. I'm desperate. You've got to help me, Harry. I can't do this by myself. I tried. I can't, Harry. I tried and I'm worn out. I need you to help me."

Don't you remember, Boris? You're doing this. You wanted your freedom, and I gave it to you.

"I had nothing to do with Barbara's aneurysm, Harry."

Neither did I, Boris.

"Then how the hell did it get there, Harry?"

Accident, Boris. Accident. Just one of those tragic events of daily life.

"For godsakes, Harry. This is enough, now. Cut the crap and bring Barbara out of the coma."

I can't do that, Boris.

"What do you *mean* you can't do it?"

Just what I said, Boris. I'm unable to do it. I gave you your freedom, total and complete. It's up to you.

"Harry, Jesus, will you listen to me? *I* can't do anything. You're the only one who can change this."

What makes you think I can do it?

"You're the author, dammit. If you want to change the damn thing, you have the power to change it. Now change it, will you?"

Boris, you obviously haven't been paying attention. I'm no different from you. I've got no power. I'm impotent, and stupid, and vainglorious, extremely disorganized, forgetful, and petty. You said so yourself. And then there's the question of fallibility. I have limits, Boris.

"Okay, look, Harry. I'm sorry about Meli. I really am. I know you care a great deal for her and you miss her. It was a goddam rotten shame she just picked up and left like that. And I'm also sorry about Lucy. I know you loved your wife a hell of a lot, too, and I'm sorry she went and had a brain hemorrhage on you and left you to raise three small kids. I'm sorry about all the pain you've had in your life. Okay? But can't you work it out some other way? Does it have to all be relived through me? Isn't there another fucking way to let out your feelings? I'm not Job, Harry. I'm not built to be a martyr. I can't take it anymore. I want my wife back, Harry. I love her. Why the hell can't you understand that?"

Oh, I understand, Boris. I understand very well. You'd like to express your sympathy for me now that you're in trouble. That's wonderful, Boris. But where were you when my drunken father was jabbing broom handles under the bed so I wouldn't be able to avoid his beatings? Where were you when Lucy's brain burst and she died holding on to me so tightly that it took me ten minutes to unfold her hand from my arm? Where were you all the years that I've lived in pain and loneliness? Where were you then, Boris?

"Being born, Harry. That's where. Being formed from all the drunken beatings, from Lucy's sudden death, from the anguish. That's where I was, Harry. And I'll tell you something else, Harry. There isn't a goddam thing that's genetic about my creation. That's for sure. You made me out of crap and that's all there is to it. Now why the fuck don't you let me lead my crappy life in peace? It's not fair that I've got to pay for some perverse fucking catharsis that you've had to get out of you for thirty years, Harry. Your anguish is your problem, Harry. Leave me the hell out of it, will you."

You've been analyzying too much, Boris. You keep trying to come up with an explanation. There's nothing to understand here. You're living life as it is, Boris. That's it. Nothing more. Nothing less.

"Hell I am. This is not life, dammit, Harry. Life may be a lousy goddam struggle for you, but it's not for me. At least if you stay the hell out of the way, it isn't. Life is wonderful, Harry. It's glorious. I love it. Barbara loves it. You've reduced it to pure crap, Harry. The age of Sisyphus has come to an end, Harry. Face it."

Look, Boris, let me tell you something about this creation of yours. When I started to write, I had some general idea of where I was going, or at least I knew where I was starting, but do you really think I sat down one day and said, now I am going to create Boris Lafkin and this is what will happen to him? You came into my head of your own free will, Boris, from nowhere I can determine. With biology and chemistry I at least have some idea how living things are put together and where they come from. You are a total mystery, Boris.

"Okay, Harry, what is it? What do you want? Love and respect? Sure. I can do that, if that's what you want. I can love and respect you. I can even worship you. Oh, Harry, almighty father and protector, I worship you. I adore you. I love you with all my heart and all my soul and all my might. See. I can do that. I can worship your impotence and selfishness. I can adore your abortions, respect your pettiness, admire your disorganization. Grant me, dear Harry, that I, too, might have a nineteen-year-old nymphomaniac to pine after."

I don't find this at all amusing. You wanted a religious experience. You got it. You insisted on being like me, so here you are. You can decide on life and death. Big deal. You happy?

"No, I'm not."

Good. Neither am I. That's why I don't have anything to do with life and death. It's a lousy dirty business. I just follow along and observe. I write about it. And about you, Boris. I write. Then you do what you damn well please. Then I write some more. I'm an interested observer, and *that is all.*

"Harry, for chrissakes, listen to me, will you. I don't *want* to decide over life and death. I really don't. You know that. That's not what I want. You've made me into a god, not a man, Harry. I can't deal with that."

Boris, believe me, I didn't make you anything at all. The respirator is entirely your doing. Read the label on it. It says *Lafkin.*

"Come on, Harry. You don't really believe all this. You can't possibly believe that you don't have any control. Not really."

In your particular case, I'm absolutely powerless, Boris. I'm sorry.

"If that's true, Harry, *if* that's really true, then you're just a fucking lunatic, Harry, a crazy old man with a warped sense of humor and a petty, unpredictable mind. You're just another fucking neurotic human being. That's all you are, Harry."

I am what I am.

"That's not funny, Harry. I don't find it at all amusing that you've created me and now couldn't care less what happens to me."

I didn't say that, Boris.

"Then what the hell did you say?"

I said that you're something different. You're life, Boris. You are my *only* creation. You have sprung from my loins.

"What is *that* supposed to mean? You think you're my goddam father, Harry?"

Your father. Ah, yes. I would have liked that, I think. It has always been a dream of mine to have been someone's father. I would have liked to have had one myself. Then, again, it's very complicated. Our expectations of our fathers are always so much greater than our fathers could ever be. Aren't they, Boris? We ask for them to be gods, powerful and kind, selfless and fair, sensitive, loving, inhuman. It's an awesome responsibility. Fortunately, not many of us accept it.

"Do you think it's any fucking easier being a son, Harry? The expectations aren't any goddam less. And there's always that lousy damn struggle. You want to be your father and more and not your father at all. And he doesn't know *what* the fuck he wants. It's the worst goddam struggle you can possibly imagine, Harry. You carry him around inside of you your entire life like he *is* a god, and you can't ever get rid of him, no matter what the hell you do, good or bad. I'd rather be a father any day than a son."

Someday, you will be, Boris.

"Harry, I want to ask you something, and I'd like you to give me an honest answer, all right?"

Go ahead.

"We've been through a hell of a lot, Harry."

Yes we have.

"Do you love me?"

I've thought about that, Boris. For a long time. Awhile ago, I wasn't sure. But I think I do, now, yes.

"And I think I love you, Harry. I really do, I mean it. And I admire you. I respect you. I know I give you a lot of crap, Harry, but in spite of absolutely everything, I still love you. I love you, and I believe in you. I told you I would, and now I do. So help me, please. I'm begging you, Harry."

Boris, I can't help you. There's absolutely nothing I can do. You have to do this on your own. I'm sorry.

"How, Harry? What the hell am I supposed to use to make a decision like this? My brain? There hasn't been a brain in the history of creation that has the capacity to make a decision like this. There isn't an organ in the human body that can do this. You're a scientist. You know that. If I made a decision like this, my brain would just snap like a pretzel. It'd just disintegrate right inside my head. I can't kill Barbara. I can't do it, Harry."

You have to, Boris.

"Harry, stop it, please. Dammit, I said I love you. What more do you want? Name it, and I'll do it, I swear. I'll do anything. Anything at all. Just please don't let Barbara die. She's my whole life, Harry. She's all I've got, all I am. I can't survive without her, Harry. I know you're going to let her die. You'd do it to me. I know you would. Please don't do it, Harry. I'll do anything you want. Absolutely anything. I swear it. Take away my freedom. You can have it. Write the book yourself. I don't care anymore. Make me your slave. Kill me. I don't care. I'll join a monastery. I'll never see Barbara again. Just don't let Barbara die. Harry, please. Help me, dammit. Please help me. Save Barbara. Fuck, Harry, you've got to do this for me. Please. Look at me, Harry. What more do you want? I'm crying like a goddam baby. Don't you understand? You've won. Believe me, Harry, you've won. I can't stand it anymore. I give up. Don't do this to me. Don't abandon me like this. Please. Harry? Harry?"

30th [Inserted by the Editors at Mr. Arnold Wolper's request]

Special to the New York Times. October 30, 1969.
Cambridge, Mass.

Three hundred alumni of the class of 1919 today heard one of the most extraordinary addresses in the history of Harvard reunions by Dr. Harry Wolper, 69, also of Cambridge, Mass. The speech, which had been postponed from last June because of threatened violence by both the Right-to-Life and Freedom-of-Choice movements over Dr. Wolper's Nobel Prize winning work on oral contraception, began with a claim from Dr. Wolper that he had died several months ago and was now addressing his friends and colleagues from another world entirely. It was from this unique perspective, he alleged, that he was able to make a truly definitive statement about the meaning of life.

The address that followed was incoherent, composed almost entirely of incomplete sentences and garbled syntax. What was impressive, however, was the sheer energy and volume displayed by Dr. Wolper, particularly in view of his recent demise.

Several times Dr. Wolper picked up the podium and crashed it onto the stage to emphasize a particular remark, which unfortunately was lost in the noise. At other times, he left the stage altogether, picked up by the collar a well-known and startled leader in a field the doctor was presently attacking, and shouted at him a question at once so personal and impertinent that the audience gasped loudly and collectively sank even lower into their auditorium seats.

If there were any points to be gleaned from Dr. Wolper's address, they seemed to center around a repulsion for order, coupled with a plea that science and life join efforts to create what Dr. Wolper referred to as "great accidents." Dr. Wolper was no more specific.

The address, which lasted over three hours, was interspersed with requests for the audience to join him in a worldwide search for a woman by the name of Meli, who this paper has learned is a nineteen-year-old paramour of Dr. Wolper's. Information regarding her whereabouts can be relayed to Dr. Wolper's Cambridge address.

At the conclusion of the address, Dr. Wolper hung over the podium, overheated and understandably despondent, panting much like a large clumsy canine (with a half-smoked unlit cigar), and spoke raspingly, "We've got to f— around with things, give reason a good swift kick in the a-, blow our noses in the laboratory sterility, and leave with a good loud f-t. This is the way the world will end, and it will leave behind it one h-ll of a smell."

There was no applause.

31st I still dribble. There is a little more each day, and I am ashamed. While I have never had the problem of being overly restricted by my superego, I have been well trained in one major area. I must not wet my pants. Not even once. Not even a little bit.

Smart man, this Sigmund Freud, conjuring up a superego and fastening it securely in our cranium. No question that it's accounted for a world of dry fannies and smiling mothers. The mention of damp pants brings to my mind in brilliant detail the most violent goblins with threats of punishment that make the rack seem to be a child's practical joke.

Fortunately, through years of practice and struggle, I have managed to ignore almost completely this superdad who sits deep in my prefrontal lobe barking instructions, don't do this, don't do that, stop, be careful, never-never-never, bad Harry, good Harry. Not that I haven't tried at least once to rid myself entirely of the Almighty Father of the Rostral Cerebrum, but that battle has long since been lost, and now we tolerate each other in a fragile truce. I have selected a survival strategy best described as directed inattention. Boris would do well to learn the skill. It is essential to the art of sanity.

Today is, of course, the day of witches and ghosts, in which every little boy and girl can display his own superego door to door for treats. What a fine parade of ego-ideals I have witnessed tonight, supermen and cowboys, fairies and princesses, and a few dark spirits of the night so we innocent egos will not forget the consequences of yielding to our id-iotic impulses. It is amazing to me that we maintain any ego at all through the incessant assault of superego and id. I myself rewarded these brave prepubescent masqueraders with small packets of candy corn and marshmallow pumpkins wrapped personally in a Halloween napkin, twisted at the top.

Mrs. Mallory and I kept our vigil on the front porch, but only I could drop the packet in the child's bag. Mrs. Mallory could laugh and exclaim and pat the children on their masked heads. I and only I present the candy. It is an absolute rule. Those children whom I know particularly well receive a packet that has a shiny new quarter in the bottom. These are the packets with the orange ribbons.

I was placing one such packet in the bag of an astronaut in the last lingering group of children when I saw a rather large trick-or-treater. She wore a long billowy red-print sari, had a red flower pinned to the side of her hair, which was put up in a bun, and had a red dot painted in the middle of her forehead.

"Trick or treat," the woman said when the children had left.

At first I didn't recognize her, but it was only a few seconds before I knew who it was.

"Meli," my voice cracked.

She stood on the top porch step and looked at me.

"I missed you, Dr. Wolper," she said quietly.

"I missed you, too, Meli. I looked all over for you."

Mrs. Mallory excused herself to go make some tea for us.

"I'd like to come back, Dr. Wolper," Meli said timidly, "but I'm not sure you're going to want me."

Meli stared nervously down at her feet.

"You see, Dr. Wolper," she continued. "This isn't any Halloween costume I'm wearing. This is really me. I've found inner peace, Dr. Wolper. I am in a state of bliss, and my vagina doesn't drip anymore."

"That's wonderful, Meli," I said. "Where've you been? I looked all over for you."

"I've been navigating the currents of *li*, Dr. Wolper. Becoming at one with this planet as it falls at ease through space. Surrendering to my own vibrations. I am far out, Dr. Wolper. Very far out."

There was a great calm and peace in her voice, a gentle and benign smile on her lips. Someone or something had obviously soothed her.

"Where *exactly* have you been, Meli? You must have been someplace wonderful."

"There is no place, Dr. Wolper. Any place is every place. Place is only a word we have made up to assure ourselves that we exist in time and space. I don't need place anymore, Dr. Wolper. That's why I'm afraid that we're not going to get back together."

"Do you want us to be together?" I asked.

"Yes, I do, Dr. Wolper. That is why I have left the *tangaryo*. I couldn't sit any longer. I am pregnant, Dr. Wolper, and I want to be married to you when I have our child."

My heart raced wildly.

"Are you sure?" I asked excitedly.

"Absolutely positive, Dr. Wolper. I feel it in here," and Meli ran her palms lightly over her abdomen, "and . . ." She stopped and looked into space.

"Yes, Meli," I asked eagerly, "and what?"

"And the rabbit died."

"You had a pregnancy test?"

"Yes, I did, Dr. Wolper. There's no doubt about it. I'm pregnant, all right."

"That's wonderful, Meli. Just wonderful." I clapped my hands together.

"I thought you'd like that, Dr. Wolper. But my wanting us to get married sn't enough. I'm not sure you're part of my karma."

"Meli, please come up here on the porch and sit next to me?" I asked.

Meli drifted over and settled like a small cloud into the chair. I took her hand.

"Meli, I don't care whether you're in or out of ecstasy, which of the eight paths you're on, whether you've found one or four noble truths. I want you to stay with me and be my wife. I'm certain our karmas will coincide in time."

"Are you sure, Dr. Wolper?"

"Absolutely certain."

"I'm different, you know."

"Yes, I know. I can tell."

"I have felt the divine being who is *in* me, who *is* me, the *atman*, Dr. Wolper. *I* am the divine being. The world is unreal, Dr. Wolper, a grand illusion, *maya*. I believe I am God, Dr. Wolper, and the world is a mirage. Do you really think you could accept that the world is a mirage?"

"I could try, Meli. God only knows I could try," I assured her from the bottom of my heart.

"That God, your God," Meli said sweetly, "is a cosmic stuffed shirt in whose presence no laughter is allowed."

"So I've heard, Meli."

"If we are to become married you must be willing to practice the way of *yoga*, Dr. Wolper, to reunite your Self with your own divine essence. The divinity is the Self that is present in each of us, Dr. Wolper. You must be willing to experience *satori*. The natural state is our ecstatic wonder. We cannot settle for less. *Tao* can *tao* not eternal *Tao*. I mean it this time, Dr. Wolper. I'm not fucking around."

"I'm ready, Meli. I assure you that I am as ready as I'll ever be," I assured her.

"I didn't know until I attained my state of cosmic consciousness what it was that bothered me about you, Dr. Wolper. You are drearily mature. Your Self is nothing more than chronic neuromuscular tension, just as I was told mine was, a habitual resistance to the pulsing of life. But there is hope for you now, Dr. Wolper. If only you will recognize the *dharmadhatu* and surrender yourself to it."

"I surrender, Meli. I will rid myself of my dreary maturity and my muscle tonus."

"And your machines, Dr. Wolper."

"My machines?" I asked, bewildered.

"Yes, Dr. Wolper. Your machines. Your television and toaster and radio and everything mechanical."

"Why?" I asked, no more clear about the problem.

"Because, Dr. Wolper, our behavior is increasingly controlled by the nature and structure of our machines. Machinery is creating an environment in which only machines can live. Eventually, if we don't rid ourselves of them, the machines will capture the voluntary aspect of our *karma* and eliminate the biological world by regimentation and asphyxiation," Meli concluded the dogma with a tone that made obvious its memorization.

"By asphyxiation?" I asked, beginning to see where we were heading.

"Yes, asphyxiation, Dr. Wolper. We will smother ourselves. No more mechanical devices. We will move to the mountains and we will farm."

"I'm willing, Meli. Believe me, I'm willing to leave Cambridge. I'm ready to move with you anywhere. But farming mountains is difficult, Meli. It's hard work. There's a lot that goes into it that I'm not sure you're aware of."

Meli smiled tranquilly.

"I told you that I'm not the same person, Dr. Wolper, and I'm not. I experience the world as it happens. I have an infinite tolerance for unscheduled events and surprises, Dr. Wolper. An infinite tolerance. I welcome the unexpected."

This seemed to be the ideal moment, the opportunity I might never get again, and so I seized it.

"That's marvelous, Meli," I smiled, "because there's something I neglected to tell you about your pregnancy."

For just an instant Meli's face muscles tightened and her eyes darted frantically from side to side. But she fought valiantly, and I could see her body relax and ease itself back into the chair. She hummed a single low note, which seemed to calm her, and her smile returned. She stopped her chant.

"This is blissful news," she said pleasantly.

"What is blissful news?" I asked, wondering whether I had misled her in some way.

"Whatever blissful unexpected message you are about to give me," she smiled even more placidly than before.

"During the procedure, Meli dear, I did not retrieve *one* egg of yours. I retrieved *two* eggs," I said haltingly.

Meli's smile tightened noticeably, then relaxed.

"Did you also *implant* two eggs?" she sang melodiously.

"Yes, I did," I confessed.

"This is, indeed, an unexpected message," she said very very slowly. "Hmmmm," she warbled with much more effort than the last time. She held this for a good minute before slowly letting the note fade away.

"Are both the eggs Lucy?" she asked quietly.

"No, they're not, Meli. Only one of them is Lucy."

"Hmmmmmmm," she trilled two octaves higher than the last time. I waited patiently until the tone faded gradually away, many minutes later. She looked up at me and beamed the largest smile I have ever seen.

"Who is the other egg I am carrying in my womb?" she whispered serenely, one word at a time.

"I'm sorry, Meli. I couldn't resist."

Meli took a long deep enlightened breath and closed her eyes.

"It's me," I said.

November

1st Existentialism and the end. I have been doing everything possible to avoid having to write this final chapter of Boris. I have packed cartons to prepare for my great journey to a life of alpen agriculture with Meli. I have polished my shoes, twice. I have rearranged everything that can be, my papers, the garden tools, the silverware. I avoid coming in here to my laboratory as though certain death awaits me on entering, as, in fact, it does. I am more resistant to Boris's termination than I am to my own. After my own, there is nothing, or there is Paradise. After Boris's, there is panic.

This has not turned out at all as I had expected. As his creator, I was certain that if I couldn't actually control his behavior, I might at the very least be able to persuade him to do as I wished. After all, I am reasonable, logical, fairly persistent, not unable to produce an argument that tugs at the emotions and appeals to the mind. Instead, Boris has done just as he damn well pleases, and I am reduced to the role of a whimpering bubba. I rock with my shawl clutched tightly to my bosom, wonder out loud in my feeble cracking voice why the child doesn't do as he is told, and reminisce about better bygone days of submission.

Even after it had become painfully clear to me that Boris was on his own, I was confident that at the very least I would emerge from the fracas with a passable existentialist novel.

I looked fondly back to my memories of the war, of Sartre and Camus quaffing liters of *vin rouge ordinaire* at *Deux Magots*, while attempting to drum up a philosophy that would account for Auschwitz. This could not be just any philosophy, some logical positivistic analysis of Being. There was one hell of an accounting to be done here. More than that, this particular philosophy had to recruit into an underground resistance movement a nation of Catholics who could at last save their own skins by taking refuge in the unrevealed nature of the Almighty's divine judgment, which, as we all know, transcends our own, is for the best, and is not to be tampered with if we know what's good for us, particularly when the consequences are the Gestapo. No, better to put ourselves in His Hands, beef up our attendance at mass, and carry on as usual.

Messieurs Sartre and Camus didn't do half badly, either, I have always thought, at putting together a portable and easily collapsible philosophy for dealing with agonizing moral questions and personal liberty, and for puncturing all alibis invented by human beings to save themselves from the responsibility for their own choices, not the least of which is the Lord Almighty God. Jehovah has been quietly retired, having by virtue of his aggravating immortality outlived His Usefulness. It is hardly coincidental that with His absence, we also encounter the embarrassing disappearance of the possibility of finding values in an intelligible heaven. As for those of us who insist that we still hear voices, can we prove that they proceed from heaven not hell, or our subconscious, or even some deceptive psychopathology?

No, I'm afraid that we are left to our own devices. No longer can we coast along on assumptions that we are fulfilling a Grand Scheme conceived in heaven and contrived on earth, that we are nothing more nor less than the realization of a certain conception that dwells in the divine understanding. We are just what we make of ourselves. No more. No less.

Man exists, encounters himself, surges up in the world, and defines himself. We begin as absolutely nothing and become only what we accomplish. Never again can we get away with complaining that circumstances have been against us, that we were worthy of something much better than we have been, that we have never had a great love or great friendship because we have never encountered a man or woman worthy of it, that we have not written great books only because we lacked the leisure to do so, that we have had no children to whom we could devote ourselves only because we have been lacking the necessary partner, that, finally, there remains within us a wide range of abilities, inclinations, and potentialities, unused but perfectly viable, that endow us with a worthiness that could never be inferred from the mere history of our actions. No one believes us any longer. Our bluff is called. There is no presumption of our love apart from the deeds of our love, no genius other than that which we have expressed in our accomplished art. Our dreams, expectations, and hopes define us, negatively, not positively, in terms of deceptive dreams, unfulfilled expectations, and abortive hopes. Descartes is disinterred, resurrected, and resuscitated. We must conquer ourselves, not the world, only today we are informed that his message is clearly intended to mean that we must act without hope. We become human by *joining* the resistance, not just favoring it. Hope comes not from our elaborate prayers, but from the effectiveness of our acts of sabotage.

I was so convinced that this would, in the end, be Boris. I foresaw great explorations into hopelessness, boredom, dread, and anxiety, into despair, anguish, and forlornness. The dark emotions. I was confident that Boris would become the uncommon man, the underground man, the man who awakens to the joyful realization that he is an insect.

I returned fondly to my evenings spent in tiny cramped theaters in Greenwich Village, watching Ionesco manipulate chairs and depilate sopranos, of avoiding the rhinoceros and peeking furtively at my own skin to assure myself that it had not become green and hard, of languishing in Genet's brothel, in Albee's zoo, in Kopit's closet, waiting, always waiting, eagerly for Godot. I found that this theatrical experience was extraordinarily exhilarating for me, and I emerged from each drama encouraged that however absurd my own endgame was, however cramped my trash can, however painful my own birthday celebrations, there were others infinitely more ridiculous.

It was in this great tradition that I had hoped Boris would follow. I have had no such luck. Boris insists on retaining his hope. He refuses to reject my existence as his author. He does not despair. He continues above ground, human, and extraordinarily common. And what is worst of all, there is not a damn thing I can do about it.

2nd **The Adventures of Boris Lafkin**

CHAPTER SIX:

The End and The Beginning—In Which Our Hero Survives His Creation

It had gotten so I dreaded walking into the ICU. I wanted only the answer, and I was convinced that, wherever it was, it was not in the Intensive Care Unit of Cambridge General Hospital. As a matter of fact, the more I thought about making the decision, about turning off Barbara's respirator, the more convinced I became that the only person who could be helpful to me in talking the problem out and arriving at a conclusion I could live with for the rest of my life, whom I could indisputedly trust, was now lying in a coma in the Intensive Care Unit of Cambridge General Hospital. So I did a lot of walking.

I walked around all five floors of the hospital, making faces at the newborns in their bassinets, greeting the children with broken legs suspended from traction, and silently attempting to read the stories behind the pained faces of patients waiting treatment for themselves or their families in the emergency waiting room. Every so often I dropped in on Barbara. She remained the same.

The hospital had resumed its routine after the weekend. The gift shop was open. Flowers arrived by the cartful from the several dozen Boston area florists who thrived in this medical mecca. The cleaning staff scrubbed incessantly, and candy stripers pushed wagons up and down the halls, distributing cheeriness along with their newspapers and magazines.

Throughout the day, while I floundered in my moralistic stew, people dropped in to pay their last respects to Barbara as though the decision had already been made. The Spencers drifted in and out as their three other children joined them—Carolyn, who was a sophomore at Ohio State, Jack, who was a freshman at Rutgers, and ten-year-old Linda. Aunts and uncles also began to arrive in increasing numbers. Each visit was accompanied by a lot of weeping and hugging. I stayed as far away as possible.

By the evening I had done just about as much wandering as I and the nursing staff could take. I was requested, politely but firmly, to keep out of the nursery, the children's ward, and the emergency room. The cafeteria staff just barely tolerated my bizarre omelettes and sandwich combinations and now cringed noticeably whenever I entered. The reference librarian in the medical library was considerably less gracious in helping me to look up recent journal articles on Berry aneurysms, and when I suggested late in the afternoon that we expand the subject to headaches in general, she asked me just which physician had authorized my use of the library. I got the message.

By eight o'clock, visiting hours were over, and the hospital returned to its quiet, dimly lit ambience. From one end of the hall I could hear a television tuned to *Laugh-In*, at the other end a teenager listened to Simon and Garfunkel. I walked down the hall and sat outside the room, listening and trying to concentrate on the problem at hand. After several minutes, I was only listening.

Are you going to Scarborough Fair?
Parsley, Sage, Rosemary and Thyme.

I tried to separate the two songs that were weaving in an out, without much success.

She once was a true love of mine.

I lost myself in the lyrics and the music. It seemed to me that the song could mean just about anything I wanted it to mean. I found that soothing, that and the tune. The music made me want to languish in a Renoir landscape, in the sun, where all was well. The song had changed.

What a dream I had,
dressed in organdy,
clothed in crinoline,
of smokey burgundy,
softer than the rain.

I had seen *The Graduate* with Barbara. We both liked it. Barbara thought

I was a lot like Dustin Hoffman. She suggested I go into plastics. There was a future for me in plastics, she said.

Here's to you, Mrs. Robinson.
Jesus loves you more than you will know.
God bless you please, Mrs. Robinson.
Heaven holds a place for those who pray.
Hey, hey, hey.

My mind was back in August, walking with Barbara on the way home from the movies. Our arms were around each other.

I was jolted by a nurse asking me if I would like some coffee. I turned down the offer but decided that it was time for Barbara and me to have a talk. As I headed down the hall to the ICU, the music followed me.

I am just a poor boy.
Though my story's seldom told,
I have squandered my resistance
For a pocketful of mumbles,
Such are promises
All lies and jests
Still, a man hears what he wants to hear
And disregards the rest.

When I entered the ICU, I was shocked to see that Barbara looked so pale and drawn. She had been losing weight, both from a lack of regular food and from the continuous effort to drain as much fluid from her as possible in order to decrease the cerebral edema. I guessed that she had lost at least ten pounds in the last two days, probably more.

"I wonder how long it takes for a human to die like this," I thought.

There was no question in my mind now that it was a slow process. It could take years. Eventually she'd weigh fifty or sixty pounds and die of some condition she didn't have the strength to fight. I'd read about it before.

I moved over to Barbara.

"Look, Barbara," I told her. "I'm really lost. I don't know what the hell to do. Really, I don't. But I'm going to have to do something, make some sort of decision, either tell them that everything is going to stay just the way it is, and, if you die, you die, if you don't, you don't, that it's up to you. Or I'm going to have to ask them to turn off the respirator, so you can die in peace. That'll be that. I'll make the best of it.

"I love you, Barbara. I want you to know that. I want you to know how I'll miss you if you die. I need you a lot, Barbara. There's a whole lot I've wanted to give you, and it's going to break my heart right in two if I can't give it to you.

"I know that someday I'll meet someone else and love her, but I don't want to give what I have to someone else. I want to give it to you. I want to go to the movies with you, and walk with you, and stay up late with you, because I feel like we've been together since we've been born, Barbara. If you go, I'm not going to have anyone to talk to, Barbara. I'll be alone for the rest of my life.

"I want you to know that no matter where I am, or whom I'm with, or what I'm doing, ten, twenty, or thirty years from now, you'll always be a part of me. You've left something inside me that's never going to go away, even when you're not around anymore. So, I'm not going to fall apart if you die. I'll survive. And I'll do something with my life that'll make you proud that you've lived with me.

"I'm really sorry that I never got around to taking you out for that fancy dinner at Chez Robert, and that we never got the honeymoon. And I'm especially sorry that I never got you to a doctor like you asked me to when you started having these damn headaches, because you'd probably be all right now. I thought it was tension, Barbara. I'm sorry. I thought it was nerves. I'll never do it again, Barbara. I promise. I'll never do it again."

I stood up and placed my hand beside her on the bed.

"I'm not sure whether this is goodbye or not, Barbara. I want to go talk to Saul for a few minutes, and then I want to go home to think. But if it is goodbye, if this is the last time I'll see you alive, please try to forgive me for doing this to you. I didn't mean for it to happen like this. Forgive me, Barbara. I'm sorry. I love you very much," and I leaned over to give her a kiss.

"I'll always love you, Barbara. Always."

I kissed her on the cheek.

"I love you, honey. I love you. Goodbye, Barbara. I'll always love you. I'll miss you."

I kissed her one more time, tears falling from my cheeks onto her face, and as I pulled away, her hand moved. Her arm had been resting on her leg, and it moved or dropped or fell so that her hand rested on top of mine.

I stopped breathing, waiting to see if something else would happen, for her to move something else, to stir, to open her eyes, anything. But there was nothing at all. Her hand rested motionlessly on top of mine. It didn't hold me or stroke me. It just rested as though it had fallen accidentally, resting purely by chance on top of my hand.

I could accept that this was without design or intention, merely random, caused by the jostling when I leaned over to kiss her, except that her hand placed on top of mine had been a private signal for us ever since that first weekend at Cape Cod. When she couldn't talk because there were too many people around or when there was no one but us around and it was late at night and absolutely still, she would gently rest her hand on top of mine to let me know that she was content.

* * *

There were no kettledrums and crashing symbols for our potential grand finale. Beethoven would have been disappointed. There was no great closing number, Fred Astaire and Ginger Rogers, locked arm in arm, twirling to a wonderful tune, with misty eyes and a final kiss. The end. Credits.

It was just Barbara's hand on mine and goodbye. Now all I had to do was figure out how to make a decision that seemed all but inevitable. I began this search by walking over to Saul's apartment.

Saul answered the door in his bathrobe. Judging by the papers on the sofa, he had been reading journals and making notes. He offered me a beer, which I accepted.

"I need to talk to you, Saul. Do you think you can be objective? I need to talk to an ex-roommate who happens to be a physician, not the other way around. Can you do that?"

"I think so, yes. I'll try," he said, lighting a cigarette.

"Good. First of all, if Barbara's brain has been destroyed as much as everyone says, then how come she isn't dead?"

Saul leaned back on the worn sofa and thought for a minute.

"I suppose it depends on what you mean by death, Boris."

"What do *you* mean by it?"

Saul thought again. He flicked the ash from his cigarette.

"I mean that an organism can sustain itself without mechanical supports."

"How about a pacemaker? Is a person with a pacemaker clinically dead?"

Saul squirmed a little.

"There's more to my definition," he said. "In addition to viability without mechanical measures, the organism has to be able to maintain a state of consciousness."

"I don't suppose you'd want to define 'consciousness'?" I asked.

"Not particularly, no. I think you know what I'm talking about. Barbara is clinically dead. She has no chance of regaining consciousness. She would die without the respirator."

"Then that only leaves me with one question. How do you know?"

Saul got up and walked around the room. Several times he turned to face me as though he were about to say something, but each time he turned away silently and went back to pacing. He disappeared into the kitchen, emerged with a fresh bottle of beer, and walked over to the window across from me, where he sat on the ledge.

"We don't," he finally said.

"Well, at least you're honest," I answered.

"We never know anything for certain, Boris. We never know that because a particular sign has always indicated a particular condition in the past, it will in the future, or that it does for a single particular case. But, somehow, we make out all right, nevertheless. We cure most sick people and prevent most illnesses. There are some children who get chicken pox who've been vaccinated. Not a lot. One or two a year out of several hundred million. We don't know why, but it does happen."

"Then Barbara could recover. You don't know for certain."

Saul took a long drag of his cigarette and slowly exhaled.

"Yes, Boris, she could recover. We don't know for certain," Saul said, holding on to each word.

"That's all I wanted to hear you say, Saul. Thank you."

"You're welcome, Boris. I'm not sure that what I said is going to be at all helpful to you, but you're welcome."

I finished my beer in a single long drink and then said goodbye. As I started to open the door, Saul put his arm on my shoulder.

"Boris, you do remember this morning's meeting, don't you?"

"I remember it, Saul. I haven't forgotten a word."

"In the end, Boris, it's a matter of faith. Whatever the fancy machines and tests and laboratories, medicine is an art, not a science, and it's not even very advanced as arts go. Painting and music are far ahead of it. You have to take medicine on faith. This is art."

"I'll let you know what my decision is tomorrow, Saul. Thanks for the help. You're a good roommate. I won't express my opinion about your medical expertise, but as a roommate, you're not bad at all. Goodnight."

Saul took his hand from my shoulder.

"This is a lousy shame about Barbara. I'm sorry, Boris."

"Me, too," I said and headed back home.

When I got back to our apartment, it was dark and empty. The Spencers had left a note saying that now that their children were here, they had decided it would be best to stay with relatives in Boston. There would be more room. They left me a phone number and hoped I would join them.

I put the note down and looked around the apartment. The lights from the street illuminated the rooms just enough to make out the furniture. A slight wind moved what remained of the leaves and cast rolling shadows across the rooms.

I turned off the desk lamp I had used to read the Spencers' note, and then wandered around the apartment in the dark. I tried to imagine what it would be like for Barbara never to come home again, to have to pack up her clothes and books and records for her family or for some charity. It was an impossible concept to grasp and did absolutely nothing to help me with my decision, so I wandered into the back room, which was Barbara's study. I hoped that she had left me some note, an envelope in her desk placed there once on a vague premonition and addressed: to be opened in the event of my death or serious illness.

I started going through the drawers to her desk without any luck. There was nothing left for me, for anyone, in the event of anything, but I found, standing next to the dictionary on her desk, a gray-covered notebook. Written on the outside of it was "1968."

I sat down at her desk and quickly leafed through it. On the first page was a word written in Greek, *Heautontimoroumenos,* beside which was a translation: the man who tortures himself. The remainder of the book consisted of poems collected from her favorite poets, single sentences from books she'd read and liked, pictures from almost every epoch and period carefully scotch-taped opposite the poems, some notes to herself, and newspaper clippings. Every few pages, there was a folded note containing a new poem, a thought, a name of a record she wanted to be sure to buy.

This, I decided, was what I had been looking for. I was certain that Barbara had left this for me.

I moved to the living room and started to read the notebook, but found that I couldn't pay attention to it. My mind wandered all over the apartment, back and forth in time, and I couldn't get in touch with Barbara's spirit as it made itself known through her notebook. I needed to experience this in the deepest, most encompassing way possible.

I went to the bedroom and pulled a pair of red socks from my dresser drawer. I reached to the bottom of one, where I found a white tablet. I broke it in half, went to the kitchen for some water, and said a solemn prayer to the spirits. I was going on a magical mystery tour. With luck, I would emerge with the answer.

I had not done this often, three or four times in the past. I took a long hot cleansing shower, annointed myself with a very mild fragrance called "Teak," dressed in some old and very soft dungarees and a blue velour shirt. I put the Beatles on the record player, moved a small desk lamp to the center of the living room so I would be able to see Barbara's notebook, and took my ritual place, cross-legged, in the center of the shag carpet.

The music played, and the Teak cologne infiltrated my nostrils. I ran my hands up and down the $30.00 velour pullover from Saks my mother had given me for college graduation, and I even tried to keep some incense lit without much success.

> The magical mystery tour is waiting to take you away, waiting to take you away.

I listened and waited. Nothing.

I opened Barbara's notebook and started reading through it.

January. There was a picture of an Aztec shield, bright orange, decorated with intricate designs and two figures in costume kneeling in the center. On the next page was a poem.

How soon hath Time,
The subtle thief of youth,
Stolen on his wing,
My three and twentieth year!
My hasting days fly on with full career,
But my late spring no bud a blossom shew'th.

She had written "John Milton" below it. I flipped the page. There was a Picasso still life, a blue apple cut in half, a blue wine bottle, the suggestion of a blue tablecloth. Next to it was a picture of a cathedral. I couldn't tell which one.

Then an article from the *New York Times*. The *Pueblo* had been seized by the North Koreans. The commander's name was Bucher. Below it was another article. The Tet offensive had begun. On the facing page was a large portrait by Botticelli of an aristocrat in a red cloak. His eyes peered over his cheekbones. A wren stood on a branch in the lower left corner. Barbara had written below it: Giuliamo de Medici.

Day after day, alone on a hill
The man with the foolish grin is keeping perfectly still.

February. More music. I felt Barbara's eyes peering up at me through the notebook. Another article. Wallace had announced for the presidency. McCarthy would win in New Hampshire.

> My prayer is not the whimpering of a beggar nor a confession of love. Nor is it the trivial reckoning of a small tradesman: Give me and I shall give you. My prayer is the report of a soldier to his general: This is what I did today, this is how I fought to save the entire battle in my own sector, these are the obstacles I found, this is how I plan to fight tomorrow. It is not God who will save us—it is we who will save God, by battling, by creating, and by transmitting matter into spirit.
>
> Nikos Kazantzakis

I ran my hand gently over the page. I could feel Barbara. I put my hand under the next page. I felt the pressure of Barbara's hand as she wrote, as she taped the picture of the small white alabaster horse onto the page beneath the two ovals of Victorian women in large feathered hats.

There' a fog upon L.A.
and my friends have lost their way.

The music echoed to the liturgical organ accompaniment. I closed my eyes and listened. Barbara smiled at me. She was content. March.

Here a little child I stand
Heaving up my either hand. . . .

* * *

What a bore it is, waking up in the morning always the same person.

And then Titian's painting of St. John the Evangelist on Patmos, looking over his shoulders at God waving to him through the clouds. Another *Times* clipping. FBI Director Hoover has announced a counterintelligence program against Black National Hate Groups. He wants to prevent a black messiah from emerging and unifying the black movement.

Let's all get up and dance to a song
That was a hit before your mother was born.

A Vermeer. The Lacemaker.

People say "I got over this, I got over that." They are a lot of fools, the people who say you get over your loves and your heroes. I never do. I don't change very much.

Robert Frost

And now let us believe in the long year that is given to us, new, untouched, full of things that never have been.

Rilke

Three hundred old men, women, and small children were killed in My Lai. Johnson has announced he will not seek another term as president. A picture of a Madonna and Child, surrounded in gold leaf, two miniature angels flutter at Mary's shoulders, holding harps.

Life is a jest and all things show it;
I thought so once, and now I know it.

John Gay

And then there follow several pages of Emily Dickinson. There are no pictures taped to these pages.

Ample make this Bed—
Make this Bed with Awe—
In it wait till Judgment break
Excellent and Fair.

I live with Him—I see His face—
I go no more away
For Visitor—Sundown—
Death's single privacy—

Lightly stepped a yellow star To its lofty place—

Barbara writes a note slanted across the margin. "I see myself old and alone like her, someday, thinking over past lovers, wondering whether I made a mistake in not marrying this one or that, wondering whether there is anything much at all to regret . . ."

A piece of paper falls from the book. It seems familiar. I had noticed it one night in my lap after I had been lost deep in thought, and Barbara was no longer reading on the bed beside me.

"Mr. Most Beloved Boris Lafkin," it begins, "your hair is over your face, you frown, your legs crossed under you—the brain of the child is visibly, intensely busy. And (better-ergo) I so very much love you. I must go out to have a smoke—the mirror distracts me—come or not?"

I place the note carefully back into the notebook so I will not wet it with my tears.

April. A photograph of Georgia O'Keeffe. On the next page is an art postcard. *St. Francis and The Birds* by Giotto. More clippings. Martin Luther King is killed in a motel. James Earl Ray is arrested. Five buildings at Columbia University are seized by students in protest over the eviction of families to build a new gym. Then a Rousseau painting, lush and green, a family of panthers, nestled in the ferns and long blades of grass, staring intently at us.

> Picture yourself in a boat on a river with tangerine trees
> and marmalade skies.
> Somebody calls you, you answer quite slowly,
> a girl with Kaleidoscope eyes.

I lose myself once again in the music. I feel Barbara's arm lightly on my shoulder. I open my eyes. In front of me is the picture of a large brown woman with an orange mango in her hand. Gauguin has painted her in a purple dress. May. There is a section on Edna St. Vincent Millay.

> I looked in my heart while the wild swans went over.
> And what did I see I had not seen before?
> Only a question less or a question more . . .

And then,

> no matter what I say
> All that I really love
> Is the rain that flattens on the bay,
> And the eel-grass in the cove . . .

And several more pages of Millay. There is a Steinberg cartoon from the *New Yorker* somewhere in the middle. It is on love. There is also a clipping about the student occupation of various administration buildings and beside it a picture of a clenched red fist raised in protest. Beneath it is a quote from *Tristram Shandy*.

. . . for there is no prohibition in nature but that a man may beget a child upon his grandmother—the young gentleman justified his intention to his father by the argument drawn from the law of retaliation—"You layed, Sir, with my mother," said the lad, "why may not I lay with yours?"

A picture of a pot of flowers drawn with children's crayons by Picasso. Squiggly lines are the stems and more squiggly lines drawn around circles with black dots in them are the flowers. There are lots of reds and oranges and blues. I can smell the flowers. Barbara writes in the margin, "This is the way flowers always seem to me. Flowers are magic."

My youth was only a gloomy storm,
Crossed here and there by brilliant suns.

June.

When I am dead and over me bright April
Shakes out her rain drenched hair,
Though you should lean above me broken-hearted
I shall not care.

Sara Teasdale

. . . and in the confusing night he forgot for the
while what experience had taught him—that no
human being can really understand another and no
one can arrange another's happiness—

Graham Greene

A picture of the New York skyline at night. A tugboat chugs up the East River, leaving a triangular ripple behind it. McCarthy and Robert Kennedy are running close, but RFK is supposed to win California. Robert Kennedy is killed. Dr. Spock is convicted for counselling draft evaders. Large parts of Cleveland are burnt to the ground.

Cellophane flowers of yellow and green, towering over your head,
Look for the girl with the sun in her eyes and she's gone.

I am back in my Renoir painting. Barbara is there with me, parasol over her shoulder, her full white dress bobbing to the left and right as we talk. She puts her hand on my arm, and we move to another table where we've noticed some friends. The man with the goatee pours us some champagne. Barbara laughs when a bird flies by, narrowly missing her large yellow hat with the daisy pinned to it. July. We have just met.

Give all to love;
Obey thy heart;
Friends, kindred, days,

Estate, good-fame,
Plans, credit, and the Muse—
Nothing refuse.

But love me for love's sake, that ever more
Thou may'st love on
Through love's eternity.

Barbara gets up, and the gentlemen rise with her. She takes my arm again and we walk the Tuileries. A band in the center plays to the bright afternoon sun.

A letter falls from the notebook. The letterhead says "Medico, Inc."

Dear Miss Spencer,

You ask an awful lot to be answered in one letter. How can imagination and awareness be built? Are they actual things? Are they beautiful and cherished?

There are some things, Miss Spencer, that I think it is good not to put into a cage of words. I think that they should be like the air . . .

There are several paragraphs more. It is signed, "Thomas A. Dooley, M.D."

Pope Paul has issued an encyclical opposing all forms of birth control but the rhythm method. Barbara has drawn some angels around the article, and beneath it is another painting of the Madonna and Child, this one by da Vinci.

I have come to the conclusion that one can be of no use to another person.

Paul Cézanne

We do not stop at the end of the Tuileries, but continue up the Champs Elysées, stopping occasionally to gaze in a shop window or purchase a thin white bag of candy. August.

I enjoyed the evening coolness
with one who does not say all he thinks.

In the midst of winter I suddenly found that there was in me an invincible spring.

Camus

A man said to the universe:
"Sir, I exist!"
"However," replied the universe,
"The fact has not created in me
A sense of obligation."

Stephen Crane

The hottest places in hell are reserved for those who,
in a time of great moral crisis, maintain their neutrality.
Dante

A Matisse odalisque, reclining among brilliant orange and purple patterns. Next to it is a note.

"More than anything else," she writes, "I want to go to Persia."

Then there are a half dozen pages on the conventions, Nixon, Humphrey, Muskie, McCarthy, and the Chicago riots. The last article shows a photograph of a smiling Hubert Humphrey, holding up his fingers in a V for victory. There are now 550,000 American soldiers in Vietnam.

What is Hell? I maintain it is the suffering of not being able to love—and for that,—you do not need Eternity; a day will do, or even a moment.

Dostoievsky

Surrealism now aims at recreating a condition which will be in no way inferior to mental derangement.

We have walked the night, holding gently to one another, calm in the new pink Parisian morning that barely tinges the buildings it touches with a faint illumination, a glow. The music spills into the morning.

I am he as you are he as you are me and we are all together
see how they run like pigs from a gun, see how they fly,
I'm crying.

We turn into a bistro for a morning coffee to watch the sun poke over the city's garrets. The city is still and quiet.

These be
Three silent things:
The falling snow . . . the hour
Before the dawn . . . the mouth of one
Just dead.

She has hand-copied John Kennedy's inaugural address. On the page facing it is a picture of Kennedy in a top hat.

The world is very different now. For man holds in his mortal hands the power to abolish all forms of human poverty and all forms of human life . . .

Let the word go forth from this time and place, to friend and foe alike, that the torch has been passed to a new generation of Americans . . .

Barbara begins to disappear, to fade into the morning, disintegrating in the mist and fog, leaving tiny footprints on the damp pavement. I continue to sit at the table in the kitchen, sipping my coffee, as the sun arches across the roofs and the sound of the first Cambridge buses can be heard shifting gears as they leave the bus stop at the end of the street.

I am the egg man, they are the eggmen, I am the Walrus
Goo Goo A'Joob, G'Goo Goo G'Joob

The needle picks off the record and, with a series of clicks, the stereo automatically shuts off. I look at the last page in Barbara's notebook.

On the left is our favorite painting. A picture of a Chinese woman by Sargent that is almost entirely white. On the right are two poems. The first is addressed: To Boris.

Dost thou truly long for me?
And am I thus sweet to thee?
Sorrow now is at an end,
O my lover and my friend!

William Blake

And finally.

John had
Great big
Waterproof
Boots on;
John had a
Waterproof
Hat;
John had a
Great Big
Waterproof
Mackintosh—
And that
(Said John)
Is
That.

And that *was* that. I closed the book and sat quietly in the kitchen sipping my coffee.

It had just become light outside and the sun flashed off the wet roofs of the houses. I thought about loneliness and confusion, about mortality, about gloomy people and unresolved issues that rumble around during the business of life. I'd like to tell you that by reading Barbara's notebook I experienced her. But I didn't. I went from page to page, looking, hoping desperately for an answer. It wasn't there.

I wanted to "capture" Barbara, to contact her, if not all of her, at least her essence. I don't think I did. I mean, she was there, but it was such a small part of her that it only raised more questions about the Barbara I didn't know than answer any about the Barbara I did.

Still, crazy as it seems, I did make the decision through the notebook. Don't ask me how a diary can determine someone's existence, because I don't know, but somehow it just did. Call it art.

What I did know was that out of our self-imposed exile and isolation, Barbara and I had reached across the barriers and touched each other. I wept over how close we had been, at the feelings we had shared that I hardly noticed at the time. I had found a partner for life.

On the counter in the kitchen was a bag of Barbara's clean laundry. She had gone to the laundromat while I had been taking my medical admissions test on Saturday. I decided it had been sitting there long enough, so I emptied it out on the kitchen table and folded her blouses, skirts, dungarees, and underwear into neat piles and put them away in her dresser. I wondered whether I still had a sense of humor.

Then I went to bed.

I slept most of the day, awakening before supper. I phoned Saul at the hospital to tell him that I'd like to see him in a couple hours. Barbara's condition was unchanged.

I shoved a TV dinner into the oven and plopped myself on the living room sofa to watch the election results on the tube. It was too early to learn anything much. A town in New Hampshire had given Nixon three votes, Humphrey two. They hadn't missed a winner since 1912.

I switched to another channel. A man on the street was being interviewed. He still hadn't decided.

"It's impossible to tell the difference between them," he said. "As near as I can tell, Nixon and Humphrey could be twins."

I turned off the television and went to eat my dinner in the kitchen. I had a hunch about how the election was going to turn out, and I didn't want it verified.

I felt remarkably calm, and I wasn't sure why. I had been so certain that, when it finally came to the decision, I would fall completely apart. But for now I luxuriated in my peace of mind, confident that my decision was the only one that could be made under the circumstances, and content that it had been made almost exclusively without the aid of modern medical science.

I walked the short distance to the hospital, trying hard not to think how three days ago Barbara and I were walking this same route, arm in arm. When I got to the hospital, Saul was waiting for me in his office on the first floor.

Our meeting was brief and cordial. Most of it was spent signing papers. I authorized an autopsy and donated every organ that could be.

"Would you like to go up to see Barbara once more?" Saul asked quietly.

"No," I said. "I don't think I could take it, Saul."

"To say goodbye?"

"I've said goodbye."

"Where're you going now?"

"For a long walk. When should I be back?"

Saul understood what I was asking.

"Late tonight, early this morning. If you really want to. You should come back around eight o'clock tomorrow morning."

"I'll be back."

"I'm really sorry, Boris," Saul said, and he put his arm around me.

"So am I," I said.

I spent the next few hours walking through most of Cambridge, settling in one bar or another, until I was covered with a crust of stale beer and smoke. Students were protesting in Harvard Square, waving signs, shouting, and writing slogans with cans of spray paint on the heavily boarded buildings. They bumped into me as they rushed past. I hardly noticed. My mind was a total blank. I thought about absolutely nothing, not Barbara, not death, not life, not me, not even the anguish of the decision. I just walked in the chilly November night.

From time to time I watched the election returns from a bar stool. Dave and Chet had a recap of the year, Vietnam, King and Robert Kennedy assassinations, and policemen clubbing demonstrators at the Chicago convention. Lots of blood this year, not so live, but in color. I tried to get excited about it all, but I couldn't any longer. There was nothing left inside me to feel any way about any thing, so I left the bar and did some more walking.

Nixon won the election early in the morning. His beaming victorious visage came on the screen. The people have spoken, he said. They have chosen law and order.

At about 8:00 A.M. I arrived back at the hospital. I encountered Saul in the hall outside an operating room. He was wearing green surgical garb and decided to give me the good news first.

They had performed a number of transplants and all had been successful. The autopsy results would be available by the end of the week. He'd be certain to send them to me. Then he reached under his gown, pulled out a paper, and held it out to me.

I took it and unfolded it very slowly. At the top was the Cambridge General Hospital letterhead. On the bottom was a line with "Physician in attendance" typed under it. On the line was scribbled "Saul Shore, M.D."

In the middle of the paper was a simple sentence.

Barbara Spencer Lafkin died at 7:04 A.M., November 6, 1968.

There's not much more to say, really. I cried a lot. Jesus, did I cry. I began to doubt whether I'd ever be able to stop. Everyone kept telling me about Kübler-Ross stages and how healthy it was for me, but it didn't make much difference. I couldn't have stopped crying if I had wanted to.

In between the wailing, I managed to call the Spencers.

"Yes, Boris?" Mr. Spencer knew what was coming.

I took a deep breath, holding back the tears. I decided to take the formal approach, first introduced to me an hour ago by Saul Shore, M.D.

"Barbara died at 7:04 this morning, Mr. Spencer," I said.

There was a long pause on the other end.

"Could I call you back, Boris?" Mr. Spencer's voice cracked.

"Sure. Sure," I said. "I'll be here at the hospital. There's no rush. Call me when you can. That'll be fine. Really."

There was another long pause.

"Our hearts are with you, Boris," he said.

"Mine, too, sir. My heart is with you all." And we hung up.

For the next few hours I made a dozen or so calls to friends and sent twice as many telegrams. I notified all my friends who also knew Barbara and all her friends whose last names and cities I could remember well enough to hunt down addresses.

"Barbara Spencer Lafkin died at 7:04 this morning," all the telegrams said. "Viewing tonight at 8:00 P.M. Funeral tomorrow at 10:00 A.M. Boris."

It was one word under the special eighteen-word rate, but I couldn't think of anything else to say.

I had saved the two most difficult calls for the last.

My mother reacted as expected.

"That's a shame, Boris," she said, "but I'm glad you've done the right thing, finally. You could have done it two days ago, you know."

"Yes, I know, Mother."

"Did you know that Barbara was going to go back to Larry?" she asked. "Larry told me while we were waiting in the hall a couple days ago."

"It's a long story, Mother."

"Well, tell me all about it some other time, Boris."

"Yes. Some other time. I've got to go now. It's been a difficult day for me."

"Boris, I'll never understand you if I live to be a thousand. You've gotten so *involved* in this whole thing. She wasn't *really* your wife, you know, and she *was* going back to her last boyfriend. You hardly even knew her. How long were you together? Four months? Five months? And look how upset you are. It doesn't make any sense at all."

"Goodbye Mother."

"Yes, well, goodbye, Boris."

My call to Larry was short and to the point. His reaction rang in my head as I left the hospital for the last time and headed back to my apartment.

"Killer! Murderer! Criminal! Butcher!" he had shouted at me over and over until I had finally hung up the receiver.

People dropped in and out of my apartment all morning.

The Spencer family arrived with a bag of groceries for lunch. It was a warm and tearful reunion. We talked about our lives with Barbara and how much she meant to each of us. We wept without shame as we talked, getting out as much of our feelings as we could. We hugged and cried. Mrs. Spencer and Jack hugged and cried. Mr. Spencer and I hugged each other and cried. Several times all six of us just stood in a group huddled close to each other, holding everyone we could reach, and wept.

We started going through Barbara's things. It seemed to me that this was harder than anything we had had to do in the last four days. Mrs. Spencer cleaned out the bedroom, going through Barbara's drawers and her closet and sobbing off and on. Every so often she would say, "This is horrible, Stan. I don't think I can stand it," and cry.

The clothes were divided between Carolyn and Linda. Mrs. Spencer threw out an old pair of Barbara's beige corduroy cutoffs with a rip in the back and some sandals that had a strap pieced together with rope, but I retrieved them from the trash. They were Barbara's favorite clothes, and I didn't think I could survive without them being in the apartment.

We decided to bury Barbara in the new long red dress she had bought for a party we'd had a week ago.

"I know she's supposed to be in white," Mrs. Spencer said, "but she wrote me about this dress, Boris. She was so pleased that you had gone shopping with her. She loved the dress and it meant something special to her. So I think it'll be all right to bury her in it, don't you?"

We held each other and agreed and wept some more.

Jack cleaned out Barbara's study, mostly by putting all her papers in boxes without looking at them, a display of self-control of which I was incapable at the moment.

I did nothing, really. I wandered around the apartment from room to room, wondering how I would live without Barbara.

By supper time, the back of Jack's van was full, and, with the exception of some curtains and plants, Barbara had mostly disappeared from the apartment.

We all sat around the kitchen, exhausted and wept out, going over details for the viewing that night and the funeral the next morning. It grew dark in the apartment, but we didn't turn on the lights. The kitchen was illuminated only by the small range light, and the apartment seemed empty now, and still.

I was invited to join everyone for dinner at a relative's, but I turned it down. I wanted to be by myself in the apartment. Sooner or later I would have to get used to living there alone. I wanted to get in touch with what it was like to live in the apartment without Barbara, again. I hoped it would make the viewing easier for me.

The girls and Mrs. Spencer kissed me goodbye. Jack and Mr. Spencer embraced me. The Spencers left, and I walked around turning on every light in the house. I put one of Barbara's records on the turntable and flicked the switch. Then I sat down on the sofa, picked up a magazine and stretched out. I was proud of myself. I was able to relax. This wasn't going to be as hard as I thought.

The Bach piano music began, and, as I started to leaf leisurely through the *New Yorker* cartoons, it occurred to me that it was a typical Wednesday. I was waiting for Barbara to come back from the library so we could eat supper, and she wasn't coming back. Not ever.

I cried for a very long time.

The viewing was horrible. I didn't stay long. I don't know what I had expected, but Barbara looked nothing at all like Barbara. She had been mostly energy and wit, anyway, so dead, she just looked dead and that was all.

The embalmers had done themselves proud. Barbara's face had been painted a wonderful orange and her cheeks and lips carefully rouged. It didn't help. Dead, Barbara could have been anyone at all. It didn't really matter. She just looked colorfully dead instead of chalky dead.

There were more flowers in the room than I'd ever seen in my entire life combined, including a horseshoe made of red and white carnations that had a ribbon across it saying "Bon Voyage," which had been delivered by mistake. No one seemed to notice it.

There were also lots of people at the viewing, expressing sympathy, remarking how Barbara had been nipped in the bud of her life, and exclaiming over how beautiful she looked and how hard it was to imagine that she was dead.

It wasn't hard for me at all. All I had to do was look at her. There was no doubt in my mind now that she wasn't going to be tripping up the stairs after an afternoon at the library, bubbling with news, and hardly able to take off her jacket before raiding the refrigerator. Barbara was stone cold dead. Her heart was in a teenager in Boston. Her kidneys were in two other people. Her lungs, liver, spleen, and pancreas were in jars in a research lab at Mass. General, and her brain was in a brain bucket filled with formalin in the basement of Cambridge General Hospital, awaiting an autopsy.

This was no dust to dust and ashes to ashes. Many parts of Barbara were alive and well and living in Greater Boston. The hollow corpse laid out in the gorgeous red gown in front of me represented the most insignificant residue of a life. Barbara had to be right. The energy doesn't just go away. It has to be somewhere. The energy and the spirit are distinct. They live on, forever.

For the first time in my life, I believed in a hereafter. I looked at Barbara on her bier and was absolutely convinced that there was Paradise. Barbara is in heaven, I consoled myself, and left for my apartment. I was becoming embarrassed that I was the only person in the whole goddam funeral home who wasn't crying, and I was the cadaver's husband.

When I got home, I found my mailbox stuffed with telegrams that had been sent to me in response to my telegrams. Western Union was making out all right with this death.

> We feel part of your grief. Our thoughts are with you. Peace always. Our love. Jim and Sharon.

> We are shocked and saddened to hear of Barbara's death. Accept our deepest sympathy. Love. Bill and Deb.

Eighteen words exactly. Not bad. Most of the telegrams were variations on these themes. After a while, I looked only for the names at the bottom. Barbara had a lot of friends.

I spent the evening doing agricultural work. I gathered the thirty plants or so that were scattered in the six rooms of the apartment and relocated them in the bedroom. Then I started going through the copies of *Life* magazine I'd been saving over the years and tore out color photographs of vegetation. By midnight I had pasted them on the bedroom walls so that there was no sign of the blue-and-white striped wallpaper that had been beneath. The room was lush and green. I filled up the humidifier, placed it at the foot of the bed, and turned it on. I raised the heat in the apartment to eighty, moved all the lights I could find into the bedroom, and turned them on. Then I closed the door, undressed, and lay naked on the bed. In a few minutes I fell asleep.

I've never really been able to figure out why I did all this. As near as I can tell, I had a hysterical need for Eden.

The funeral was not out of *Our Town*. It was a bright, cold, windy day. The people were mostly young and in good spirits. It was crowded and a little noisy.

I sat with the Spencers through a long Catholic service that I knew Barbara would have wanted. As a special favor, the priest dug out some old texts from the basement and did the mass in Latin. At various appropriate times I wept. It was your basic funeral. Nothing special or unexpected.

Father O'Malley greeted me after the service, as I was walking to take the limousine to the cemetery.

"God has taken her," he assured me.

"Nope," I assured him back, "I took her."

"My son?" he asked again.

"The decision was mine, Father," I explained.

"But the circumstance was the Lord's," he attempted once more.

"Nope," I explained.

"My son?" he asked again.

"It was Harry's. Harry Wolper," I told him. "Harry did it."

"Bless you, my son," and he ducked away as fast as his shiny black wing tips could carry him.

When we finally got to the cemetery, we all stood around the grave. Mr. Spencer said a few words about Barbara and how much he loved her and would miss her. Carolyn, Linda, and Jack each said something brief about what a wonderful sister she had been. Mrs. Spencer looked up at Mr. Spencer and shook her head. She had wanted to say something about how much joy Barbara had brought to her life, how close they had been, and how much she had wanted Barbara to have her own children so Barbara could experience that same warmth and affection that she had, but Mrs. Spencer flooded with tears and couldn't talk. Then it was my turn.

"I'm stuck, Barbara," I began. "I can't think of what to say. I've never met anyone like you. I've never loved anyone like I've loved you. I'm going to miss you for the rest of my life. You're wonderful, Barbara, and I'll always be grateful for what you've given me. I'll try to make you proud of me someday. I'll love you always." The tears were dripping off my nose. I could hardly talk anymore. "That's all I have to say, Mr. Spencer. Goodbye, Barbara. I'll miss you." I felt a little uncomfortable standing out there in front of everyone, telling Barbara how much I loved her and missed her. But I did it anyway.

There wasn't much after that. Some friends read a couple of Barbara's favorite poems by Emily Dickinson and Edna St. Vincent Millay. The priest did the ashes to ashes bit, and sprinkled some holy water on the casket as it was being lowered into the grave. Then he read the twenty-third psalm.

I started walking away when he got to the part about "Yea, though I walk through the valley of the shadow of death, I will fear no evil: for Thou art with me . . ."

I waited in another part of the cemetery until everyone had left and then I returned to watch the workmen fill up the hole. It took an hour until the last shovelful of dirt had been patted down. Then a truck with sod arrived, and Barbara's grave was covered with a fresh green blanket of grass and watered.

The flowers from the funeral home were placed around the grave. The workmen gathered their tools and left. Then I started the long walk home.

And that, as Christopher Robin would say, was that.

There was a reception at the Holiday Inn after the funeral, but I didn't go to it. Larry, did, though, went crazy, and had to be taken away. I didn't blame him, really. I didn't feel all that together myself.

I kicked around the apartment for the weekend, feeling lonely and sorry for myself. I had taken the week off from work, and I began to realize that on Monday I had to return. It seemed pointless now. I was convinced that there was only one worthwhile thing to do with my life. I had to figure some way to get Barbara back.

But on Monday I did go to work and everyone fell all over himself telling me how sorry he was and what a lousy rotten shame it was that Barbara had passed away.

I'm not sure how, but I got through the day. I found it very difficult maintaining enthusiasm for developing better and better medical machines. It was bad enough that *I* had to go through hell. I had no intention of putting other people through it by inventing ever more spectacular mechanical devices to maintain corpses in limbo.

I thought all day about quitting, but I didn't, and I left at the end of the day thanking everyone for the support and sympathy and telling them I'd be back in the morning.

When I got home there was a letter in my mailbox from the Massachusetts Eye Institute:

> Dear Mr. Lafkin:
>
> The Massachusetts Eye Institute would like to thank you for your kindness and consideration for others at a time that must have been most difficult for you.
>
> In spite of your loss, I trust you will be pleased to learn that a corneal transplant has been performed as a result of your wife's generous donation. It should not be long before a very grateful person can see again.
>
> I hope it is of some comfort to you to realize that even in death your wife has continued to serve humanity.
>
> Please accept our sincere sympathy as well as our deep appreciation.
>
> Very truly yours
>
> Paul Witaker
Executive Secretary

I folded it and placed it in a shoebox I had begun to keep of all the papers concerning Barbara's death. Some day I thought I might get creative and write about it.

As I filed the letter, I wondered what had happened to Barbara's autopsy report. I had expected it at the end of last week. I called Saul.

"Yes, yes, of course. The autopsy report," he acknowledged after he had inquired about my health and mental status. "We've run into a little snag."

A cold feeling began to develop in the bottom of my stomach.

"What kind of a snag, Saul?" I asked deliberately.

"Just a little snag, Boris. Nothing to worry about."

"What kind of a little snag, Saul? Did you lose her brain? Mix it up with someone else's? Throw it away by mistake? What the hell kind of a snag? I want to know what killed her, Saul. I want to know what the fuck killed my wife."

"So do we, Boris. That's the snag. We're having a little difficulty finding out. I'm sure we'll know by the end of the week. Don't worry about it. We've got her brain, and we'll find out."

I said goodbye and hung up, but the cold feeling in my insides didn't go away. I sure as hell knew that Saul wasn't telling me the whole story.

The next couple of days went by almost as though nothing had happened. It was hard to get used to Barbara's not being there anymore, but she had been dead for over a week now.

The letters and cards of sympathy kept coming, and I filed them in the shoebox with the others.

On Wednesday I got a letter from Mr. Spencer.

> Dear Boris,
>
> Just a short letter to let you know that our thoughts are with you. Please let us know how you are doing.
>
> Betty and I are endeavoring neither to be unduly morose at Barbara's death nor to try to eliminate her from our thoughts. We want to treat her memory as a live but not maudlin sentiment. Sometimes it's hard, and you find yourself almost without warning suddenly reminded and overwhelmingly grief stricken. Mostly though, by now, the sharpest pains are gone, and we think of the solid achievements, the happiness, the love that Barbara had and the continuing gifts she left—we are sad but somewhat reconciled.
>
> Please keep in touch with us.
>
> Our fondest regards,
> Stan

The next night I did something I will never understand. I called up Marty and invited her over. I was lonely, I guess, and I figured what the hell. I can't live in a dungeon my entire life. Marty's not all that bad. She's bright. She's moderately attractive except for not having any breasts. She has a Ph.D. I could do a lot worse. And besides, we are already married. It's worth a try, anyway.

Marty was, of course, delighted.

"This could save us so much goddam litigation, you know, Boris," she told me when she arrived. "Those fucking lawyers cost a fortune by the time you're done with them."

"How've you been, Marty?" was my response.

"Just great, Boris. Just terrific. Hey, look, I heard about Barbara. I am really sorry about that. It must have been a real downer, right? I mean it had to be. Down, down, down. Do you have anything to smoke, Boris?"

"You mean a cigarette?"

"Grass, Marijuana. Dope. I really need something, Boris. Really. I'm so high. I can feel it. Do I seem high to you? Tell me the truth. Don't I seem just a little up to you, right now, I mean? You know why, Boris? You. I am so goddam fucking stoned over our getting back together, it just blows my fucking mind. Wow. It's far out, Boris. I've wanted it. I've always wanted it. I wanted it two days after I left and Dick went back to his wife, the jerk. But I've known ever since we met, Boris, that we were a great pair. You and me. So, Boris, how've you been? Did I ask that?" Marty laughed nervously.

"I bought a bottle of wine and some Brie. Would you like some?" I asked.

"Oh, Boris, that would be simply marvelous, really. Can I help?"

"Sure. Come on back in the kitchen."

We stayed in the kitchen for several hours, talking about absolutely nothing. Actually, Marty did all the talking, bringing me up to date on every man she'd slept with since we'd split up and their distinguishing characteristics. Around eleven she pooped out. There was a long silence while we listened to the noise of people coming back from a school committee meeting down the street. Marty broke the silence.

"This Barbara," she asked, "she wasn't anything really serious, was she?"

"Yes. She was serious," I answered.

"Well, I know she really turned you on, Boris. I mean, I could tell that just by the way you stayed so close to her in the hospital all the time, but I know you were probably lonely after I left, and horny, probably very horny, and she was available, right?"

"For chrissakes, Marty. I said it was serious. It was serious. Now shut up about her will you, please? I don't want to talk about her. Find something else to talk about. Not Barbara. All right," I snapped.

"Fine. Fine," she snapped back. "Look, Boris, I thought you invited me over here to fuck me."

"I did. I did."

"Then fuck me, will you? Get on with it."

"Take off your clothes, and I'll fuck you."

In a single gesture Marty kicked off her shoes and slipped off her slacks, panties and socks.

"All right," she said glaring at me. "My clothes are off. Are you going to fuck me or not?"

"Yes."

"Then do it for chrissakes. I'm going into the bedroom."

"Don't go into the bedroom. I want to do it in the living room."

"Why can't we go into the bedroom?"

"Because I don't want to, that's all."

"It's because of Barbara, isn't it?"

"No," I lied. "It's because of me. I think it's sexier on the living room floor."

"Like hell you do, but come on, let's do it," and Marty pulled off her sweater and walked into the living room where she lay down in the middle of the rug.

I undressed and lay down beside her.

"Spread open your legs," I told her.

"Aren't you going to kiss me or something first?" Marty whined.

"Look, I'm fucking you, aren't I? I didn't ask you over here to kiss. I asked you over to fuck. You want to kiss, you can go home. All right?"

"All right. All right. Just stop shouting at me, will you?"

The anger and shouting had gotten us both excited. I rolled on top of her and inserted myself. As I started to move, a feeling came over me of being horribly lost, of being afraid that I might never find my way home again. I wasn't having sex with Barbara anymore. It would never be Barbara again. I was going someplace, not looking back, not leaving markers so I could find my way back again. There would be no more love like Barbara's. No more touching or holding like Barbara's. I didn't want to be here. It was horrible. Dark and lonely. But I kept going deeper and deeper, feeling more lonely. I was never coming back again, but I was unable to stop myself from going farther into the darkness, unable to stop the panic.

When I came, I shuddered with fear. I held Marty desperately and wept against her body. Marty waited until I had quieted and loosened my grip.

"That was marvelous, Boris," Marty smiled, "simply marvelous." She slid out from under me and stood up.

"I have to go to the john and wash all this crud out of my cunt," she beamed. "Don't go away Boris."

When Marty came out of the john several minutes later, she dressed quickly and then came over and knelt beside me.

"Boris, I'm going back to my apartment now. I need to think some things over. I guess I didn't realize how, well, how involved you were with Barbara. I've got to think. I'll talk to you soon," and she slipped out the door, leaving me stretched out on the floor, naked and writhing in pain, feeling like a large wounded animal.

At the end of the week, I still had not received the autopsy report. I did, however, receive three other letters in the mail. The first one was from the Greater Boston Dialysis Center and read as follows:

> Dear Mr. Lafkin:
>
> The Greater Boston Dialysis Center would like to thank you for your kindness and consideration for others at a time that must have been most difficult for you.
>
> In spite of your loss, I trust you will be pleased to learn that a kidney transplant has been performed as a result of your wife's generous donation. It should not be long before a very grateful person can see again.
>
> I hope it is of some comfort to you to realize that even in death your wife has continued to serve humanity.
>
> Please accept our sincere sympathy as well as our deep appreciation.
>
> Very truly yours
>
> Alan Sutter
> Executive Secretary

So much for sincerity and the personal touch. The second letter I received was from the New England Organ Bank and was identical to the letters I received from the Massachusetts Eye Institute and The Greater Boston Dialysis Center except for the second paragraph, which now read:

> In spite of your loss, I trust you will be pleased to learn that successful medical research is being conducted as a result of your wife's generous donation. It will not be long before very grateful people can again.

The third letter was from the University of Beirut Medical School. I've been accepted.

On Saturday Marty came over unannounced to talk.

"Only talk," she emphasized.

"I'm too tired anyway," I told her.

"Good. I don't think I could take another gruesome intercourse. I guess we've had it, huh?'

"I guess so," I agreed.

"I'm broke, Boris, but I don't suppose you have any money anyway, even if I did get the court to grant me alimony. Dirty Al wants to charge me $2,000 to go to court. I don't have it, Boris."

"I'm broke, too," I answered quickly, hoping she wasn't about to ask me for a loan so she could afford to go to court and get alimony from me.

"What'd you blow it on?" she asked.

"Oh, lots of things. A cemetery plot, a really groovy casket, two days and three glorious nights in an Intensive Care Unit, only I haven't finished paying for that yet."

Marty didn't react. She was lost in thought, wondering what to say next, where to go, lost in general.

"So, I guess there's really no reason for us to see each other any more," she said sadly.

"I don't think so, Marty. I can't think of any."

"Me neither. Oh, well," she sighed deeply, "onward and upward."

She got up and started to walk to the door. Then she came back to where I was sitting at the kitchen table.

"I'd like to kiss you, Boris. You don't mind, really, do you?" she asked.

I reached out for her, and she leaned down and kissed my mouth softly.

"There've been times when I think I've loved you, Boris. Really. I think I have," she said very quietly.

"I know," I said.

"Oh, well," she livened up. "This can get *very depressing.* I'll see you around," and then she stopped herself short, "maybe," she finished. "Goodbye, Boris."

"Goodbye, Marty. And good luck," I called after her.

"Yeah, you too, Boris," she called back. "I wish you all the fucking luck in the whole goddam world. Goodbye," her voice trailed off as she headed down the stairs.

I never saw her again.

The autopsy report arrived on Monday.

Autopsy Number A68-704

Name Barbara R. Lafkin Ward ICU Unit No. #1379619
Age 23 Sex Female Autopsy by Rosen/Walensky
Date of Admission 11/2/68 Date of Death 11/6/68
Date of Autopsy 11/6/68—11/18/68 Service Medical/House
Autopsy 4 hours after Death and continuing Extent complete

PROVISIONAL ANATOMIC DIAGNOSIS

Diffuse intracranial hemorrhage, mild, subarachnoid, with extension, right cerebral hemisphere and to the ventricles; cerebral edema, mild, receding.

Pulmonary congestion, hypostatic, mild, bilateral; atelectasis, minimal, focal, lower lobes, bilateral.

Status post appendectomy.

Pregnant.

Congestion, mild, mucosal stomach with acute superficial ulcers, greater curvature.

Annular head of pancreas.

Cholestatic liver damage, mild.

A letter was enclosed.

Dear Mr. Lafkin:

Let me take this opportunity to express my sincere condolence and the condolence of the whole Medical and Surgical Staffs at the Cambridge General Hospital at the passing of Barbara. Let me also thank you for allowing us to perform a postmorten examination and also thank you for the donation of Barbara's organs, which I can assure you will be put to a worthwile purpose.

As you know, it is only through the performance of postmortem examinations that we in the Medical Profession learn how to better diagnose and treat similar conditions in the future. In this particular instance, it has been enormously instructive, indeed.

We have enclosed a copy of the autopsy report, and, as you can probably tell, as occasionally occurs, our initial clinical impressions were not completely confirmed. We were surprised to find that the coning was in the process of receding and the damage to the hemispheres was not nearly as extensive as we had assumed. Even more surprising was the total absence of an aneurysm and the presence instead of a more diffuse kind of cerebral hemorrhaging.

We were, as you can certainly imagine, puzzled and intrigued by what could have caused the cerebral bleeding. The puzzle began to fit together when we observed that Barbara was in her second month of pregnancy and had sustained some mild liver damage. Laboratory reports confirmed that there was the presence of norethynodrel (present in antifertility preparations) in her blood along with a severe deficiency in prothrombin and factor VII (proconvertin), essential for blood coagulation and produced by the liver. Further examination of Barbara's colon confirmed a deficiency in successful synthesis of Vitamin K.

To make a very long story short, Mr. Lafkin, our extensive medical investigation has determined that your wife died from the complications of her pregnancy, which interacted toxically with the birth control medication she had been taking, resulting in liver damage and leading, in turn, to a disturbance in the synthesis by the colon of Vitamin K, and conversion of it by her liver into the necessary blood coagulant, and that, in turn, led to diffuse intracranial bleeding and death.

We have not as yet determined why the hemorrhaging was cerebrally localized and not spread more generally throughout her entire body.

Our assumption at this point is that it is related to the unusual way your wife's system reacted to her pregnancy. It is, of course, statistically unusual for a woman to become pregnant while taking birth control pills, but it does happen from time to time. As each person's physiology is in many ways unique, there is no way of accounting for the unusual reaction that your wife had to being pregnant and on birth-control pills simultaneously.

Pulmonary congestion and atelectasis are lung changes commonly found after prolonged artifical respiration. We had purchased a number of modified respirators that, we had been assured by the manufacturer, would eliminate these complications entirely. Obviously, they are not effective in doing so, and you will be pleased to learn that we are returning these respirators on the basis of the findings of your wife's autopsy. Superficial stomach ulcers occasionally appear in response to cerebral injury and stress.

We are, again, greateful for the opportunity you have given us to transform the death of your wife into such an instructive experience for the entire Medical-Surgical Staff. It is remarkable that your wife did not have these complications when she first began taking birth control pills, and, in fact, escaped unscathed for so many months. You might, therefore, say that God gave Barbara many months of grace, during which apparently she was very happy, before He chose to take her.

Let me again express our sincere condolences and thank you for your extreme cooperation during this most difficult time.

Sincerely yours,

K. Miller, M.D.
Medical Resident

What the hell does all this mean, Harry?

"Barbara had a bad reaction to the oral contraceptives she was taking, Boris. She sustained some liver damage from them, which decreased the coagulant in her bloodstream, probably had high blood pressure from the pills at the same time, which gave her the headaches. She got pregnant, nauseous, had complications from the pregnancy, took pills, continued with the bleeding, headaches, nausea, liver damage. She bled, coned, and died."

What does the autopsy report *mean*, Harry?

"It's hard to tell, Boris."

Harry, for godsakes. Stop jerking me off. Just tell me. What the fuck does it mean?

"It means that if you hadn't turned off the respirator, Barbara might have made it. But that's not at all clear, Boris. It's only a possibility."

Oh, Harry.

"There's no way you could have known, Boris."

Oh, Harry. Harry.

"You can't blame yourself. You did what you thought was best."

Harry. Harry. Harry.

"I'm sorry, Boris. I'm really sorry."

Harry. I don't think I can stand it.

There is an epilogue of sorts. About a month after Barbara died, I began having recurring nightmares. Often it seemed to me that I awakened in the middle of the night to find Barbara seated on the edge of the bed. She was barely visible. We talked for some time, and then she drifted away. In the morning I would awaken scared and anxious.

The dreams began to bother me, if I could convince myself that they were dreams. Often I could not. It got so I both longed and hated to go to bed. I longed to go to bed so I could see Barbara again. I was also scared to death because every time I met her it seemed to me that she was thinking about what I had done to her and was trying to decide whether to take me with her. I finally became so depressed over the whole thing that I went down to New York to see Dr. Kuhn who, when he had come to examine Barbara, impressed me as a psychiatrist I might be able to talk to. As usual, I was wrong.

"The dreams bother the hell out of me, Dr. Kuhn. I need an interpretation."

"I don't have an interpretation. The dreams will go away. If they don't, then make another appointment. I want to talk about why you really came to see me." Dr. Kuhn clicked his fingernails on his Danish Modern desk.

"I *really* came to see you about my dreams, Dr. Kuhn. Really. Honest to God. What do they mean?"

"Would you believe me if I told you?"

"Absolutely."

"That's wonderful, Boris. You're an ideal patient. Most of my patients don't believe a word I say. Your dream means that you're angry at Barbara for abandoning you."

"But she didn't abandon me. I probably killed her."

"Then about your guilt for having murdered your wife."

"There's something missing."

"Then add your anger at yourself and your longing for the only love that's meant anything to you."

"Not bad. I like that."

"That's a shame, Boris, because I was just getting warmed up. I can speculate indefinitely. Are you sure you wouldn't like me to continue?"

"No. That's all right. I think I understand now."

"Good," Dr. Kuhn smiled broadly. "Now, why have you come?"

"Because I hate myself, Dr. Kuhn. I hate myself for what I've done. How's that?"

"Not good. Try again." Dr. Kuhn leaned back in the leather lounge with the chrome frame and picked up a *New Yorker* magazine. "Let me know when you're ready. It's your nickel," and he started thumbing through the pages.

"Has anyone ever told you that you have a very unorthodox approach to psychiatry?" I asked.

"Everyone has, yes," he answered from behind the magazine. Then he peered over it. "How're we doing? Any luck yet?"

I rambled on for several minutes about Barbara and Harry and life in general.

"Maybe I came here because of how horrible my whole goddam life has been," I told him.

"Do you think your life has been horrible?"

"Not really."

"I didn't think so." He went back to his magazine. "Actually," he said from behind it, "I get the feeling you've rather enjoyed it. I have the impression you feel you've come to the end of a great gestational period in your development, concluding with your wife's death. You have been discharged from the womb, expelled, you are a man, you are born at last, pick your metaphor. That's what I think. You're someone different now, and you know it. How am I doing?" he asked, peering once more over the magazine.

"I'm getting tired of this," I answered. "I don't know what you're after. I don't think *you* know what you're after. I told you why I came here. I came to find out about my dreams. I think you're playing some goddam psychiatric game with me. My dreams, Dr. Kuhn. I came to get my dreams analyzed. That's all. If you think I've got another reason, then why the hell don't you just tell me."

"You didn't ask."

"All right. I'm asking. Why did I come here tonight?"

Dr. Kuhn closed his magazine and rested it on his lap.

"You came here for two reasons. First you wanted to know whether you were crazy and second because you got a wonderful kick out of your wife's death, and it's tearing you apart."

There was a moment of absolute silence, during which I froze. Then I buried my head in my hands and wept.

"You're a bastard," I said.

"So I've been told," Dr. Kuhn said, sinking into his Charles Eames recliner.

"You bastard," I said over and over.

He continued reclining until I had finished, and then he reached for a box of tissues beside him and handed them to me.

"Take as many as you want," he said. "I'm a doctor. They give them to me for free."

"I loved Barbara."

"I know."

"I didn't want her to die."

"I'm sure you didn't. But what a marvelous experience it must have been."

"I loved her."

"You did. And you think you killed her."

"I did. I killed her."

"I wonder whether you feel that you engineered Barbara's death for your own personal enjoyment. We don't have very many experiences in life that are as profound and as deeply moving as what you've experienced, Boris. We need them desperately. It's what keeps the marquees flashing. To have had such feelings in real life must have been enormously satisfying."

"I'll never forget Barbara, Dr. Kuhn. Never."

"Or her death." Dr. Kuhn flipped his legs over the side of the chair and sat on the edge. He leaned forward and looked directly into my eyes.

"I can imagine, Boris, that someone who has, for example, gone through a life in which he's had to bury a lot of deep and beautiful feelings in order to survive in a world that is, at best, discouraging, might find it extremely rewarding to discover himself experiencing all those marvelous feelings again. It could be wonderfully encouraging to know that they haven't gone away, so encouraging, in fact, that someone might even wonder whether he had killed the person he loved most in the world just to experience those feelings again and come alive."

"It's a hell of a way to be born."

"Yes, it is, Boris. Excruciatingly painful and gloriously sublime."

"I've never had those kinds of experiences."

"And you didn't kill your wife to have them, either, Boris. That probably doesn't make much sense to you right now. We can talk more about it some other time if you wish."

"That's very kind of you, Dr. Kuhn, but you're wrong. I did kill my wife, and I did it for exactly the reason you said. I needed it. This has been helpful, I think," I said.

"I think so, too."

"I want to thank you, I guess."

"I guess you're welcome."

I stood up to get my coat.

"You're not going, are you?" he asked, smiling.

"I thought we were done."

"Sit down, Boris. We'll only be a minute more. I think you'll be interested in this part of the session. I'm about to tell you whether you're crazy or not."

I sat down.

"Of course, most of what I'm going to say has to do with your relationship with Harry Wolper."

"I figured it would."

"I am convinced that you are convinced that there really is a Harry Wolper, that you talk to him, and that he talks back. This would seem to indicate that you are delusional. You hallucinate. You depersonalize. Further, when I ask you where you are, you tell me you are in a novel. When I ask you what year it is, you tell me it is 1968 your time, and 1969 Harry Wolper's time. When I ask you who you are, you tell me you are a fictional character and that the world you and I experience is not real, that Harry Wolper's world is real, and you and I are merely creative outgrowths of Harry Wolper's fertile mind who have gone inexplicably out of control. How am I doing so far?"

"Splendidly."

"Good. Now this is a marvelously imaginative fantasy for a six-year-old child, the kind of fantasy he might develop, for example, to help deal with the death of his father. It would go a long way toward helping him bury those deep and beautiful feelings we were talking about a few minutes ago. If they were to surface too often, they might be scary and a lot more than a six-year-old could handle. But you are not six, Boris. You are twenty-six, and if I were to write down in the form of a mental status report what you have told me, not as a fantasy, but as something you sincerely believe to be true, I'd have to say that you are not oriented to time, place, or person. I would probably write down that you are disoriented, out of contact with reality, delusional, and schizophrenic."

"Wonderful."

"Isn't it? I constantly marvel over how the psychiatric business manufacturers its products. In your case, Boris, it hardly seems to make a difference. You seem indistinguishable from anyone else I know, including my colleagues. I include my fellow psychiatrists because, as we both know, they represent sanity in its full magnificence and splendor."

I decided that Dr. Kuhn was not all bad. I might even come back sometime.

"Now, to the question of your sanity. I will not shirk my professional responsibility, Boris. I will make a diagnosis. I will supply you with a personal impression, as well. In conclusion, then, on behalf of the American Psychiatric Association's *Diagnostic and Statistical Manual*, and on behalf of Sidney Kuhn, I leave you with these two thoughts: Yes, Boris, you are crazy. And so what."

The End

21st What a whopping postpartum depression I am having now that Boris is done.

Mrs. Mallory and Meli have categorically refused to have anything to do with me.

"It's bad enough that you're moving into the mountains and leaving me here to handle Arnold all by myself," Mrs. Mallory informed me tearfully, "but I will not tolerate your walking around here like death itself, Dr. Wolper. There'll be plenty of time for that after you die. Now what did you go and create this time?" Mrs. Mallory knows me well.

"I'm not sure, Mrs. Mallory," I told her honestly.

"Well, as long as you take it with you when you go. I will not have another one of your horrible creatures wiggling or crawling or hopping into this house after you're gone. And if you can't take it with you, then I'm sorry to inform you, Dr. Wolper, that you'll just have to dispose of it in some other way, and that includes you know what."

"You don't have to worry, Mrs. Mallory," Meli intervened. "This creation of Dr. Wolper's is all in his head."

Mrs. Mallory shook her head sadly.

"Well," she told Meli, wiping her hands vigorously on her apron, "I think it's only fair you should know, before you go traipsing off to the woods where no one's going to be there to help you but yourself, that the creations in Dr. Wolper's head are the worst kind."

It's going to be difficult, indeed, living without someone who knows me as well as Mrs. Mallory.

22nd I am still brooding over Boris. I am exhausted, depleted, and a little frightened. I do not kid myself that this business with Boris is over.

I have no doubt that Boris is lurking in my cortex ready to leap on my lobes and grab a stranglehold of each and every gyrus and sulcus.

I am convinced that, before I am to have peace of mind, I must find some way to rid myself of this monster I have created, once and for all. I know he's still there, and I cannot tolerate it any longer.

Meli sat cross-legged, meditating in the middle of the bedroom this evening, watching me pace and stew.

"You know what the problem with you is, Dr. Wolper?" she told me as she took a long deep breath and slowly let it out. "You're not getting in touch with your divine essence."

I knew it was something like that.

23rd The dream flickered back into my brain tonight.

"This is it, Wolper. You're on your own now," the philosopher tells me. "I'm splitting, pushing off to new horizons, moving out."

"I'll miss you," I tell him.

"Bullshit, Wolper, just bullshit. You won't miss me for a goddam second. But all things must come to an end, even this splendid nocturnal exegesis."

I look at him and notice for the first time that he is dressed in a smartly tailored three-piece pin-striped suit.

"Where's the toga?" I inquire.

"Gone, Wolper. Discarded. Thrown in the hopper. We have to keep up with the times, Wolper. You'd do well to keep that in mind. Incidentally, your book stinks. Time marches on. The subterranean metaphor is no longer marketable. It's passé, Wolper. Out of date. Boring and mundane. Come with me, Wolper, and I'll show you what you have to do if you want to keep your market."

I start walking along the river banks with him until we get to a mountain. I notice that he has let his hair grow long, and has developed a stringy white beard. I inquire about this as we start to climb a mountain path.

"It's a new image, Wolper," he explains. "In this business, it's the packaging that counts. Nobody cares what concepts they're buying any more. They're all basically the same anyway. You can hardly tell the difference. It's the way they're wrapped that counts."

"I don't believe that," I say. "Philosophy is ideas."

"Bullshit, Wolper. Bullshit and more bullshit," he tells me. "Philosophy hasn't got a damn thing to do with ideas. Hasn't been a person in the history of creation who's done something because of an *idea*. Ideas are bullshit, Wolper. You think my men left the cave because of any great brilliant philosophical idea? Bullshit. They left to get Meli's ass. That's why they left. Philosophy is what happens in your gut, Wolper. That's what it's all about. Philosophy of the gut. Any other questions? Now's the time."

"Yes, as a matter of fact. Who the hell is Zeus Lykaios?"

"Good question, Wolper. As I recall, Lycaon was a king who had Zeus to dinner and served him human flesh, so Zeus changed Lycaon and his sons into wolves. I believe there's a point there somewhere, but damned if I know what it is."

We reach a lush green field halfway up the mountain. The master walks to where hundreds of young men and women are assembled under a delicately flowering dogwood tree.

"Watch this, Wolper. You can learn something from this. It's my final gift to you. Wear it in health," and he walks over to the crowd, putting on some garlands of flowers held out to him as he passes by. He takes his place in their midst, sitting cross-legged, and placing his hands, palms down, in an X across his chest.

A lovely woman with long dark hair asks a question.

"Can you tell me, Guru, whether virtue is acquired by teaching or by practice; or if neither by teaching nor practice, then whether it comes to man by nature, or in what other way?"

The philosopher quickly winks at me, then he smiles benignly, and slowly closes his eyes. There is complete silence.

"Ommmmmmmmmmm," he chants.

"Ommmmmmmmmmm," the crowd chants back.

For what I hope is the last time, I awaken in a cold sweat.

24th Christmas is on its way. The lights have been hung from one end of Massachusetts Avenue to the other. Store windows glisten with colored balls and tinsel. Everyone seems to be getting into the spirit of the thing, so I decided that I would undertake my November ritual of selecting a Christmas card.

I travelled the cold streets from shop to shop, looking for a card I'd had in mind all year. Finally, I found a stationers with a vast assortment of catalogues. For several hours I poured over them in hopes I would find my card.

Finally the elderly woman who managed the store approached me.

"If you'd only tell me what exactly it is you're looking for," she implored me for the tenth time, "I'm sure I could help you."

"It's not likely," I assured her in return.

"Why don't you just try me, sir? Is it a particular inscription? A picture on the front? A specific color or design? I know these catalogues inside and out, sir. Really, I do," she smiled patiently.

"It's a picture on the front that I'm looking for," I tried.

"Oh, good. Now if you'd be so kind as to tell me what exact picture you'd like, I'm certain I could find it for you."

There didn't seem to be any harm in trying.

"I'd like a picture of the Father and Child," I told her.

"Well, that's easy," she beamed at me, reaching for a large red leather catalogue. "You mean 'The *Moth*er and Child' though," she smiled good-naturedly at me for having confused my words.

"No," I informed her just as good-naturedly, "I want the *Fath*er and Child. *The* Father and *His* Child."

She stopped short. Her smile disappeared, and she looked at me coldly.

"It'd have to be special ordered," she said brusquely, and walked away, muttering something under her breath about women's liberation.

25th The house is now becoming a shambles. Packing cartons are everywhere, and the movers have taken over. Before I sit, I must ask permission. Before I use a saucer, I must ask when its packing is to occur. I have learned that I have an inborn knack for selecting articles to use less than thirty seconds before they are to be whisked away.

Meli and I had prepared a list of articles to be packed with their various destinations, some to Claire and Rebecca, some to Goodwill Industries, some to be stored in a warehouse in New Hampshire until we locate the appropriate mountain with the necessary fertile acreage.

The movers were walking around labeling cartons for their various destinations and checking the long list in their hands to make certain that everything had been packed, when the boss mover, if that's how he's identified, came stomping down the stairs from the attic and marched into the living room where Meli and I were seated on the floor comparing our horoscopes.

He waved the list in front of me and poked his thick finger at a particular item I had scribbled on the shipping list, as an afterthought.

"All right, Dr. Wolper," he said irritably, "what the hell is a 'Boris' and where the hell is 'Tierra del Fuego?' "

"Just kidding,' I said sheepishly. "Really, it was only a joke," I smiled weakly at Meli.

Still, if there were only some way.

26th Dr. Mazel was in Boston today and phoned me to come in for a checkup. He was a despondent man.

I've been symptom free for almost a month now, and just as the doctor was about to go into print.

"I can't tell you what a disappointment this is for me," he told me after giving me an extensive physical. "The Mazel Syndrome is nowhere to be seen. You've had a spontaneous remission."

"I thought it was Wolper's Disease," I said, a little disappointed myself.

"Whatever. You've cured yourself. What have you been doing?"

"Just living," I told him.

"Ah, ha!" he said, pursing his lips and sharply nodding his head. "You were supposed to be dying."

27th Meli was, of course, delighted to hear about the change in my condition, and, as a celebration of my new state of health, we have agreed to be married on Friday.

Meli phoned her parents with the good news and they felt that since I was almost thirty years older than they were, a meeting was not necessary. As a matter of fact, they indicated a preference not to have one.

"The more that's left to our imagination in this case, the better I think it'll be, dear," Meli tells me her mother told her this morning. "Have a good wedding and do keep in touch."

I think I might like them.

Meli was not pleased, however.

"They won't even come to my goddam wedding," she said, unserenely, after the call.

"Did you want them to come?" I asked.

"No," she said. "But they could have at least given me the chance to exclude them."

This afternoon, for the first time in several years, I went to Lucy's grave. It seemed to be an appropriate thing to do a couple of days before marrying someone else.

I placed a bouquet of daisies in the green metal holder sunk into the ground and stood for some time staring at the dates on the tombstone, 1910–1936. She had been twenty-six years old when she had died. I'd have to live until I was ninety-six to see her as she was when she died, assuming that Meli's pregnancy is successful, and that the world lasts that long. Well, I thought to myself, that'll have to be up to Harry, Jr.

I had run out of things to say at Lucy's grave years ago. Once the children went away to college, there wasn't much to talk about, and I gradually stopped coming. But now I told her about Meli, and the new Lucy and Harry, Jr., and the grandchildren, and even, I'll never know why, about Boris. Lucy didn't have much to say in return.

As I stood there, today, I felt that I had done everything I could. I had promised myself that some day I would get Lucy back, and now, as much as possible, I had arranged for that. I had raised the children, honored her memory, and grieved for thirty-three years. It was time to move on.

28th The house was saturated today with the wonderful smell of Mrs. Mallory's turkey and stuffing. Arnold, Claire, Rebecca, and their families filled the dining room with great warmth and cheer. There was even some moderate celebration over my announcement that Meli and I are to be married tomorrow.

"Can't keep a good man down, huh, Dad?" Arnold bellowed in an outrageously obscene way and jabbed his elbow into my ribs several times. "I've heard a rumor," he snickered, "that Meli is just a little bit pregnant, you old dog you. You can't keep a good man down. No, sir. And I think it's great, Dad. You're the last of the world's great lovers. No doubt about it. Well," he laughed, "how's it going to feel to have another little Wolper scampering around?"

"And here," said Meli quickly changing the subject, "is the pumpkin pie."

Shortly before everyone left I took Arnold aside.

"I understand that your attorney has been in touch with mine and the house is ready to be signed over," I said.

"You're not changing your mind?" Arnold panicked.

"Not at all. I'm signing the papers tomorrow, but I thought in our new spirit of trust and fellowship you might confide in me why this house is so important to you."

Arnold thought for a minute.

"Well," he said at last, "it's not the money, Dad. You know how sometimes people say 'someday this'll all be yours'?"

"I think I do, yes."

"Well, ever since we got married, that's what I've been telling Marge about this house. She's always loved it, and the thought of its being hers some day has sort of kept us together. Recently things haven't been going so well for us. Marge has been wanting to, well, take a kind of extended vacation from our marriage. I think this is going to mean a new life for us. Do you see what I mean?"

"Yes, I do, Arnold," I told him, and we said goodbye.

I know that today is the day I'm supposed to be thankful for the harvest, but between Boris, Meli's pregnancy, and now Arnold's "new life," I have the distinct impression that I've barely finished the planting.

29th Meli and I were married today. It was close right down to the finish.

I had awakened in a mood of reconsideration.

"I've been thinking about this marriage of ours, Meli," I told her as we drenched each other in our attempts to eat Mrs. Mallory's partially sectioned grapefruit.

"Please don't, Dr. Wolper. Thinking is one of your worst qualities," Meli told me. "Today we are going to have a beautiful spiritual experience and I refuse to have you ruin it with your brain."

"I'm not made for marriage, Meli."

"Good. Neither am I. Neither is anyone else. We're not born to marry, I agree. Now why don't we talk about something else."

"It's not as though I personally have anything against marriage."

"Dr. Wolper, for godsakes, this is a wonderful magic experience we are about to have, and I'm not going to let you ruin it with an intellectual analysis of the pros and cons. It is magic, do you understand? And it's going to stay magic, if I have to knock you out with my goddam wand. Is that clear?"

"I mean, this is not the first time I've thought about this," I told her.

Meli leaned back at the breakfast table and reached for a cigarette.

"All right. All right," she resigned herself. "Say what you've got to say," and she lit up, took a long drag, and closed her eyes.

"Marriage is a ritual, Meli. Why, there are some cultures where there isn't any marriage at all and life goes on without a hitch. They hunt and plant and celebrate the birth of their children. There is no suffocating concept of lifelong fidelity to interfere with their self-expression. I do love you, Meli. I know that, and you know that. But I'm concerned that by involving ourselves in such an outmoded ritual we might be losing our identities. I'm talking about not going ahead with it for *your* benefit, Meli. I think you'd be much happier in the long run, and I'm not sure I could stand the strain of a marriage ceremony at my age. I'm an old man, Meli. At the end of it all, you could have nothing left to show for it but a dead husband and a lot of Corningware."

Meli waited in silence.

"Are you finished?" she asked.

"Yes."

"Okay. Then let me tell you something, Dr. Harry Wolper, M.D. If you'd get out of here a little more often, you might notice that we do not live in a *tribe*. When you start stalking antelope, then I will undress and walk around in the bush, nursing our two children with my large black breasts. I will also paint myself with beet juice, if you so desire. We can dispense with marriage then. It'd probably be too hot for it, anyway. As for lifelong fidelity, as far as you're concerned, lifelong is a matter of months, maybe even days. I'll take the risk that your heart will stand up under the stress of saying 'I do.' And, just in case you're interested, I *adore* Corningware. I think the tiny blue flowers are cute. Anything else?"

"No."

"Well, I have something else. I love you."

I had rested back in my chair during Meli's rebuttal, watching her *satori* dissipate. She was charged with anxiety, her thin lips biting off the words, her fingers tugging at her wispy curly hair, her legs waving like windmills, smoking, flopping her hands like exclamation points, licking her lips, clutching her cardigan sweater tightly over her chest, her words falling from her mouth furiously. Then a smile sneaked across her lips, a small laugh bounced her head like a marionette out of control. It was a miraculous and, I found, endearing display.

"And I love you, Meli," I said.

"Good," Meli smiled. "Then we should hurry or we'll be late for the wedding."

There were only the two of us and a Justice of the Peace. I made one last futile attempt at mumbling something about the unnecessary nature of the event, but to no avail.

"Are you sure this man wants to marry you?" the Justice of the Peace asked Meli as he sized up our respective ages. My assumption was that he addressed the question to Meli in deference to my senile dementia.

"Don't ask," Meli responded. "Just do it, will you," and we were married.

We had a second ceremony of sorts at the home of Meli's Krishna friends. A man in an orange robe who was bald except for a pony tail read to us.

I show you two paths.
The Deva Yana,

the path of no return,
the path of the bright ones
who are liberated from rebirth.
And the Pitri Yana,
the paths of the fathers,
who reach the lunar light
and must ultimately be reborn.

I show you two paths.
Let a yogi choose either
When he leaves this body:
The path that leads back to birth,
The path of no return.

There is the path of light,
Of fire and day,
The path of the moon's bright fortnight
And the six months' journey
Of the sun to the north:
The knower of Brahman
Who takes this path
Goes to Brahman:
He does not return.

There is the path of night and smoke,
The path of the moon's dark fortnight
And the six months' journey
Of the sun to the south:
The yogi who takes this path
Will reach the lunar light:
This path leads back
To human birth, at last.

There was great bliss, many flowers, the sounds of sitar and tiny cymbals, and a fragrance that reminded me a great deal of almonds.

An hour later we found ourselves alone in the house, the people having disappeared into the afternoon. Meli led me to a bedroom upstairs that had been specially prepared for us with flowers and incense. A mat covered with a rich purple silk cloth was in the middle of the room, and Meli took me silently to it, where she undressed me and anointed my body. Then she undressed and we had our first successful intercourse.

"I am overwhelmed," I told her as she nestled in my arms.

"So am I, Dr. Wolper. You know something, this afternoon as we were making love, I had a weird thought. Is that stuff you've told me about the third-generation lethal mutant really true?"

I nodded my head affirmatively.

"That means that all the people my age who are having children will have sterile kids, doesn't it? All the children born from now on won't be able to have children of their own, right?"

"That's right, Meli."

"There's an exception, though. Isn't there?" she asked.

I smiled at Meli and stroked her hair gently. The people were returning downstairs and the sounds of music and chanting drifted up the stairs.

"Yes," I answered.

"And that's the children *I'm* going to have, isn't it? Lucy and Harry, Jr., will be the only people able to conceive, won't they? Sort of like Adam and Eve all over again."

"Sort of," I agreed, sheepishly.

Meli stroked my beard some more and ran her fingers over my eyebrows.

"I figured that was what you had in mind," she smiled.

"I don't know what to say, Meli, really," I said.

"Try, 'and they all lived happily ever after.' "

30th "Mazel tov, Harry."

The end, Boris. The end. Didn't you see the last two words I wrote for you, Boris? They're unambiguously direct. The end.

"Nice try, Harry, but you didn't really think that writing that was going to get rid of me, did you?"

I had great hopes that it would, Boris.

"No doubt. Well, I had no intention of staying trapped in this marvelous Gaussian non-Euclidian novel of yours, parallel lines on a collision course. Sorry, Dr. Wolper."

Look, Boris. I'm a married man now. I've got new responsibilities, a new wife, who is soon to have new children. I don't have the time for this any more.

"I admire your new domesticity, Harry. But I'm not going. You can write 'The End' until it comes out your colon. I'm staying here until we finish this damn thing."

We're finished, Boris. You're going to medical school in Beirut. I'm leaving Cambridge with Meli. The new Lucy and Harry Jr., will carry on. We're over. Done. Completed. Barbara is dead and buried, Boris.

"Yes, well, I'm sure you thought you were really clever about knocking off Barbara with your intimate Nobel prize-winning knowledge of oral contraception and how it fucks up your whole system. I was not impressed, Harry."

It's not my fault, Boris.

"Nothing ever is, Harry. I believe we've covered this ground before, in some depth if I'm not mistaken."

What can I tell you, Boris.

"All right, Harry, look. It's time to stop playing around. This is not just going to be another flip interchange. That's not what's at stake here. You know it. And you know that I know it."

So, what do you want, Boris?

"You know damn well what I want, Harry. I want an explanation."

There is no explanation, Boris.

"Harry, for chrissakes, will you cut it out. You know damn well that there's an explanation."

What kind of an explanation?

"Meaning, Harry. There's got to be some meaning."

What meaning, Boris? You think you're Christ? You're suffering for the sins of others? Pain is a condition of life, that's all. Death is it's consequence. There is no meaning, Boris. None at all.

"Harry, come on, will you? Get off my case. You wrote this fucking thing, remember? You created me. I'm your idea."

Boris, to be absolutely frank about it, I don't know where the hell you came from.

"Bullshit, Harry. I came from one of the most impressive lists of outright literary thefts in the history of fiction."

I stole nothing, Boris. The creative act is putting old things together in new ways.

"What new way, Harry? Isn't that one of your brilliant goddam points? There's nothing *new* about this. I'm a human comedy rerun. Where's *your* vision, Harry? Everyone else has got *theirs*. Where the hell is *yours*?"

You're a literary character, Boris, so you've got a literary history. Not a distinguished one, but you've got one nevertheless. I can't help it if my visions overlap with those who've come before me. Just coincidence.

"The same sort of coincidence that accounts for everyone in my life starting out in yours?"

There's no proof of that.

"Come on, Harry. I'm not here to play games. Manny is Maury, Mara is warmed-over Meli, Arthur is Arnold, and most of all, Barbara's death is Lucy's death. Even Dirty Al Petrucci is a photostated copy of Tony Pascotti. Where'd you get a name like Pascotti from, Harry? It sounds like a combination of pasta and manicotti."

It is.

"Big joke, Harry. Big fucking joke. Only this is not at all funny. I have just killed my wife and it's your damn fault."

Boris, you did not kill your wife. She died. And it's nobody's fault.

"You let her die, Harry. You could have brought her out of the coma. You could have told me not to let them turn off the respirator so she'd come out of the coma herself. You could have done any damn thing you wanted to do, but you had to go prove some big fucking point about the great mid-century struggle to transcend our physiology. I should have seen it coming, Harry. All those amusing notations on how man should stay on the earth where he was put and leave the seas to the fish and the air to the birds, be content to hear and see what he could with his own ears and eyes, unamplified and unextended. And most of all, if death arrives, he should die."

Well put, Boris.

"I thought you'd appreciate it. The consequence of not leaving well enough alone, as I understand your point from the elaborate educational experience of spending three goddam days listening to medical scientists tell me what's going on inside a head their eyes can't penetrate, is that we have created hell, not heaven, on earth. I agree, Harry. We have surpassed the capabilities of both our intellect and our hearts and now find ourselves in an outer space where no philosophy would be asinine enough to journey. You're right, Harry. There is no philosophy of men on the moon. There is no metaphysics of shopping malls. And, most of all, there is no theology of respirators and organ transplants. And you know something, Harry, if you had bothered to ask me in the *first* place, I would have agreed with you and saved *you* a lot of trouble and *me* a lot of pain."

Boris, I was not out to prove anything at your expense. You experienced life. And that's all there is to it.

"Death, Harry. I experienced death, not life. It's your Giant Question. It's your Only Question. That's what fooled me. I believed all this Nobel Prize-winning Biologist shit. I thought you were devoted to *life*. Not so, is it, Harry? Death is your only certainty. It's your inspiration. The rest of us muck around trying to figure out how the hell to be happy and productive human beings, while you're fiddling around with the Big Goddam Issue. The result is that you turned me into a killer, Harry."

You're not a killer, Boris. You're a victim.

"No, I'm not, Harry. I'm a killer. So are you. We've all become killers. It's a new goddam craze. Give you some surgical curettes, a little saline, a full moon, and a Great Abortionist emerges. How many kids have you killed, Harry? A hundred? A thousand?"

These were therapeutic, Boris.

"Sure they were, Harry. It's all right, really. All our killings are therapeutic, now. I killed Barbara therapeutically. You abort fetuses therapeutically. Paul has his skull bombarded with electricity so Parnash can be incinerated into oblivion, and it's therapeutic. Meli can't control her goddam glands so she stamps a part of her into dust until she's a mystic, without a history, and nothing. It's therapeutic."

You're missing the big picture, Boris.

"It's close enough. Let me tell you something, Harry Wolper, M.D., Nobel Prize-winning Biologist, Great and Wondrous Author. From where I sit, the Big Picture is a Big Mess. And you did it, Harry. It's all your brilliant Goddam Vision."

I tried only to define you, Boris, to paint a picture.

"Well, that's awfully nice of you, Harry but maybe I didn't want to be defined. Maybe I should define *myself*, and you should define *yourself*, and we should each leave each other *alone*. Harry, let's face it, I'm just *not* definable. No matter what you say about me, there's always going to be something left out. I just live as I live, do what I do, assuming that *you* keep out of the way. I manage, in spite of you, to maintain a moderate amount of hope. Not a lot, but enough. I find beauty almost everywhere. I don't know why, so don't ask. And I do not have the great and glorious goals and objectives with which I once started out. As a matter of fact, I don't even insist on the magnificent spiritual love I once nearly killed myself over."

I'm sorry to hear that, Boris.

"Yes, well, I'm sure you are, seeing how you've nurtured Lucy through thirty-three years. But that's what's happened. I used to think I was pretty goddam special once, Harry. You took care of that. I don't think I'm so special any more. I'll settle for a nice family, a good place to live, a job that's satisfying at least some of the time, and a pleasant woman to love. I'm not particularly interested in an open marriage, skydiving, or owning a van with a picture of Nirvana airbrushed on the side. That's okay for those people who want it, but it's not for me. I'm hopelessly middle-class and bourgeois. I know it, and I even like it. It doesn't mean that I don't still appreciate Bartók who is rather far out as composers go, but is not John Cage, I know. I read philosophy sometimes. I support peace movements, consumer protection, and ecology. I think Nixon's an ass-hole, and I hope that someday he gets his. I'm not selfish or stupid, Harry. I think I'm moderately liberated. I think that women should be liberated, and I think that men should be, too. I think women have been suppressed unnecessarily, but I didn't do it. So have Blacks, and ditto. I do, however, appreciate its having been brought to my attention. As a definition, Harry, since you're so goddam interested in defining me, I'm just plain old ordinary. Just nothing much at all. How's that for a definition?"

Not bad. Where do I come in?

"God only knows, Harry. I've been trying to figure the fucking thing out for as long as I can remember. Maybe you're everything else. I can't figure it out. I tried once to understand it all, but I've given up. I just know you're there, that's all. Sometimes I think that you're nothing more than a projection of my weaknesses. What I can't do, I think you can. What I can't figure out, you're responsible for. What I don't know, you do. At the end of it all, it seems as though you do whatever the hell you want, and I do whatever the hell I want. I've given up expecting that you'll do what I want you to do, and I'm sure that you've given up expecting that I'll do what you want. I think we've created each other, Harry. I'm the author's creator, and you're the creator's author. I possess you as you possess me. We drive each other crazy, Harry, until I don't know what the hell you are anymore."

Wonder, Boris. I'm wonder. I'm the promise of warmth in the midst of an ice age.

"Sure, Harry, if that's what you want to be. You can be whatever the hell you want, too. The only thing I'm certain of after all this is that whatever you are, you're no goddam different from me. You've got the same headaches and the same problems and the same inability to do a fucking thing about them. You aren't a damn bit more in control than I am."

So then why bother with me, Boris? Why not just let me be?

"Got me, Harry. No reason, I guess. I suppose what it all boils down to is that if you're right, if all this agony I've been going through is accidental and meaningless, then I just don't need you anymore. I'm going to do you in, Harry. That's the way it is."

The struggle never ends, Boris.

"So, the struggle never ends. Big deal."

We could keep trying.

"It's been an awfully long ten years, Harry. I need a rest. I feel like I've been through a decade of Custer's Last Stands. They've been coming at me from all directions. Everyone's got some big goddam issue. Even you, Harry. I can't take it anymore. We've got to have this thing out once and for all. It's either you or me."

You want a happy ending?

"No, Harry, I do not want a happy ending."

Because I think I could arrange it.

"No you couldn't, Harry, and please don't try. I've got enough to handle as it is. No more novels. I think you're noveled out, Harry. It's time for a rest."

I'm your Creator, Boris. Remember that.

"How the hell can I forget it, Harry? But there will be no more writing. You start fucking around with me again, Harry Wolper, and God will get you for it. I'm not kidding, Harry."

Believe me, Boris. There is no God. There's only you and me. The two of us. We are God, Boris.

"Don't count on it, Harry. I didn't come from any God, Harry. I came from you, and you're subject to the same penalties that I am. You may not accept any fucking responsibility for it, but you made me."

That's trivial, Boris. I'm a Conceptualist. I'm intrigued by the implications of starting things. But I don't control them. Only conceive them. Then they have their freedom.

"What freedom? I never had any fucking freedom, Harry."

Biology. Your freedom is your biology.

"Oh, that's splendid, Harry. Isn't that just marvelous. There's no fucking *point* to biology, Harry. And you know it, too. Biology is meaningless."

The religious man wills meaning.

"What about the struggle? What about the fucking struggle we've been having? Is that from biology or meaning or what?"

From genes, Boris. It's wired in. Progeny are condemned to transcend the progenitor. And the progenitor is condemned to fight the transcendence of his progeny. It's an old story, Boris. And not a very interesting one, if you want my personal opinion. The staid and secure wisdom of the past restraining the reckless and innovative activity of the future. History. Very boring.

"Harry, you're an endless source of fascination to me. No kidding. I've got to hand it to you, you've got your ass covered from every possible direction. You started me, but you don't know where I came from. You're the author, but you have no responsibility for me. The whole schtick has no point except biology, which is, of course, pointless. Everything is accidental and meaningless, even the struggle between the two of us, which is a tedious historical footnote and nothing more."

You've got it, Boris.

"Well, let me tell you something, Harry. This is a splendid box you've built for me, but no, thank you, you can have it. I don't know how, Harry, but you did this fucking thing to me, and I swear to God, I'm going to get you for it."

You don't think you can turn the other cheek?

"An eye for an eye, a tooth for a tooth. That's my part of the Bible."

What do you mean, your part?

"Just that, Harry, my part. The Jewish part. The Old Testament."

You're Jewish.

"That's right, Harry. I'm Jewish."

Well, well. Isn't that marvelous.

"What's so marvelous, Harry?"

And clever, too. Very clever, Boris.

"I'm not sure I get you, Harry."

Oh, you get me, all right, Boris. You know damn well what you've done.

"There's only one thing I've done, Harry. I've put you on notice that the two of us can't make it together anymore. We're a lousy team, Harry. Let's face it."

Well, Boris, I'm not so sure, but if it's a battle to the death that you want, then that's what you'll get. I promise.

"You're on, Harry. That's what I want. And as for the Jewish business, Harry, what can I say? You had it coming."

Sure, Boris, why not? Eleven months eat my heart out, go nearly crazy trying to create something new, unique, something important, a great universal statement on life itself. And now what have I got? You know damn well what I've got to show for my heartache don't you, Boris. I've got another fucking Jewish novel. That's what.

December

1st So, you would think this would be the end. Why not? Arnold has his house. I have my Meli. Meli has me. Even my soggy philanthropist has found a lovely Salvation Army lass, I've been told, and together they ring their bells on Tremont Street this joyous Christmas season. Love conquers all.

Except where Boris is concerned. He will not go away, and now the final insult. He has turned my great tale of him into nothing more than another postpubescent *Judenschmerzbuch*. I could easily strangle his Semitic stiffneck, believe me. He will not get away with this. I *will* salvage something respectable out of my year's work.

The battle is yet to come. It will be a battle to the death. I do not look forward to it.

2nd I got a card from Anthony Pascotti, Esq., today. On the front is a lovely drawing of Ebenezer Scrooge. On the inside Tony has scribbed "Happy Fuckin' Christmas".

3rd Back to Nature.

Meli and I found a nice little cabin in the White Mountains of New Hampshire today. Nothing elaborate. One large room on the bottom and three smaller ones on the top, plus the largest fieldstone fireplace I've ever seen. And all for only $60,000. Meli was adamant.

"I love it. This is us. Let's not haggle over a few pennies. Our *karma* is here."

As near as I could tell from a brief inspection of the property, this particular *karma* cost us an additional $40,000.

"I thought you wanted to farm," I told Meli. "This land is rock."

"You've got some of the finest granite farming in the state," our elderly Down-Easterner real estate agent drawled as he bit on his chaw of tobacco. "Over a hundred acres of prime ledge."

"We'll take it," swooned Meli.

"Aya," the agent twanged. "You drive a hard bargain."

Meli smiled serenely and cuddled against my arm. The agent observed this arrangement and sized up my decrepitude.

"And the nice thing is, Miss," he informed Meli, "there's a hospital not more than fifteen minutes down the road in North Conway. You and your granddad are going to be very happy here."

Meli cupped her hands to her mouth in a megaphone and shouted in my feeble ear.

"You hear that, Gramps! There's a hospital nearby! 'Case your ticker gives out next time we're fucking, you can get fixed up *right down* the *road*! You hear that?' "

Meli smiled.

I said, "Aya."

Mr. Witherspoon nearly choked himself to death on his tobacco.

5th Paul has been discharged.

He came over to surprise me tonight. My eyes teared with joy at seeing him.

Paul appears to be calm and at peace, without having lost his usual acidity. I was delighted.

"What is it?" I asked. "The drugs, the psychotherapy, the isolation—?"

"Electricity is a marvelous thing," he told me.

We sat with each other through the night and early morning, drinking and shouting until Meli came down and requested that we shut up.

"That's it, *buddies*," she told us. "My *satori* is starting to frazzle."

Meli was wearing a thin nightgown that not only left nothing to the imagination but provided images for which there are, as yet, no specific terms, according to Paul.

"Good God," he said after she had left, "you've hit the jackpot, Swami. There is no deficiency in life for which you have not now compensated. You have reached the summit. You are a god. Hallelujah."

I walked Paul to the door. There was a single question that had been on my mind most of the night. Each time I had wanted to ask it, I faltered. Now, as Paul fastened his coat, I threw caution to the wind.

"Paul," I inquired gingerly, "what finally happened to Parnash?"

"Parnash?" Paul looked up blankly from his buttons. "Who's Parnash?"

10th We signed the papers on the cabin today, or rather Meli signed the papers and I signed the checks. The cabin is hers. A little token of my affection.

Afterwards Meli opened the trunk of the car and gave me a housewarming present in return. It was a large pickax with a blue ribbon around it.

"I asked the guy at the hardware store for a hoe that my husband could farm a hundred acres of granite with real quick," she told me, "and this was all he had. Who is Simon Legree?"

16th This evening we celebrated the yuletide season. We bought some baby clothes, observed the window decorations, had dinner at Locke Ober's, and went to a moving and rousing performance of the *Messiah.*

Meli was quite pleased with the evening and was particularly taken with the concert.

"You know," she looked at me with her giant eyes as we reached home, "I'm not all that religious, but anyone who can write music like that has every goddam right to think he's the Messiah."

I clarified the situation. Meli tried to reassimilate the information and not show her disappointment that she had not heard the Lord's own Christmas composition.

"Handel's *Messiah,* huh?" she ran over in her mind outloud.

"Yes," I reinforced the concept. "It's Handel's *Messiah.*"

Meli was not pleased.

"Well, I think it's stupid of Handel to think that he can have his very own Messiah. Do you have any idea how ridiculous it would be if we all walked around having our very own Christs? We might just as well have none at all."

18th Don't ask me why, but I asked Arnold if he would like to give us a hand with the unpacking up in New Hampshire.

"I think I should emphasize," I told him tonight, "that there is no remuneration whatsoever for your services. No royalties, commissions, stipends, bonuses, or residuals. You get room and board if you agree to help out. That's it. You can bring Marjorie if you wish."

Arnold was irritated.

"Why do you always treat me like this, Dad?" Arnold whimpered. "I don't do *everything* for money."

"I'm sorry if I offended you, Arnold. I just had to make certain this was clear from the beginning. This is a favor you are doing for me. Gratis. For free. Please do not send me an itemized travel voucher for gas, tolls, and mileage to New Hampshire. This one is on you."

"Didn't I stop doing that after you asked me to? Once, just once, I do a thing, and I carry it around like a chain my entire life. You asked me not to do it anymore. I stopped. What more do you want?"

"Just as long as we understand. I have no intention of going to small claims court again. Is that clear?"

"Jesus, you just won't let a thing die, will you? Didn't we settle that out of court? Didn't we?"

"Yes, Arnold, we did."
"So there."

21st Today was moving day. Paul gave us a hand. He's going to join us up in New Hampshire in a few days to help with the unpacking and keep me on my good behavior with Arnold.

Most of the large items had already been put in storage, so there were only a few boxes and suitcases. Even so, it was a heart-wrenching operation, leaving a home in which I've lived and worked for almost twenty-five years.

I don't understand how a three-story wooden box can take on a life of its own, but there is no doubt in my mind that for all of us, Arnold, Claire, Rebecca, and me, this house has a heart as large as our own.

Meli noticed the sadness in my eyes as we left.

"It's hard for you, isn't it?" she asked and held my hand.

"It's hard," I said.

"That's the problem with treating things as though they're people. Every time you lose one of them, you feel like you've lost a part of yourself. You can't keep taking things and giving them life, Dr. Wolper. It's your biggest problem. In the end, it'll just kill you."

"Probably," I agreed.

"I mean, it's only a lousy *house*."

"You're right, Meli. It is only a house."

"You can't go crazy over a house."

"The last thing I looked at before we left was the study," I told her. "We spent a lot of time in the study last summer, Meli. I'll miss it."

"Me, too," Meli said and turned her head to look out the car window so I wouldn't see the tears streaking her cheeks.

22nd It's been snowing since early this morning, 6:00 A.M. to be exact. This was when I awakened in anticipation of the day ahead of me. I saw the first flakes.

Now it's more than eighteen hours later. The snow has reached a depth of twenty-two inches with six to eight more to come before it ends, according to the meteorologist who presides over Mt. Washington, where, I understand, the snow is made.

There are only a few red coals left in the fireplace but enough to warm my toes as I sit beside it now and attempt to sort out the events of the day.

I believe that everyone is in good spirits. Arnold arrived with Marjorie late this afternoon, and, after a brief inspection of the premises, inquired about how we expected to survive without a downstairs toilet.

"This isn't really very 'Town and Country' at all," Marjorie summed up our living arrangement fairly well, I thought.

An hour or so later, Paul arrived with Maureen, singing, "Bearing gifts we travel afar," and presented us with two bottles of vintage Dom Perignon champagne. These are now empty.

After dinner we sat around the table, our faces illuminated only by candles, and the fire in the fireplace, and discussed the tasks to be performed. Arnold and Marjorie have elected to unpack the downstairs, Paul and Maureen the upstairs, Meli the kitchen, and I will supervise. My role was Meli's idea, something to do with my organizational ability, I understand.

23rd Arnold began the unpacking today with the box marked in red marker on four sides and the top: PRIVATE! PERSONAL! DO NOT OPEN!

I was out doing errands and by the time I returned, Meli, Paul, Maureen, Arnold, and Marjorie had all read "Boris".

"I hope you don't mind, Dad," Arnold told me. "I couldn't figure out whether the writing on the box was for the movers or for us."

"So you opened it to find out," I smiled.

"That's right!" Arnold said in astonishment over my extraordinary extrasensory powers.

"This is an amazing book," Paul said, sensing I was about to throw Arnold out into the deep snow, silent snow.

"I'm glad you like it, Paul," I grumbled.

"Me, too, Harry," Maureen gave her opinion. "It's just marvelous."

"I like it, Harry," Marjorie joined the consensus. "It's got pizazz."

"It sure does," Arnold chimed in, realizing he had not yet complimented me on my literary endeavor. "I particularly liked Arthur Yaffee," he grinned. "I think he's got lots of potential."

"Who the hell is Arthur Yaffee?" Paul started thumbing through the pages of manuscript he had in his hand.

"He's the guy who hires Boris to run a theater in Cambridge," Arnold explained.

"Ah, yes," Paul answered, a light dawning. "Yahoo Yaffee. Lots of potential."

There was a sudden silence as everyone looked over at Meli, who refused to look back. Finally she looked up at me.

"Yeah, well, the truth is that I didn't like it at all," she said. "I thought it was stupid to have Boris chop off some poor guy's prick. I thought that the jail and the courtroom were even stupider. I didn't understand any of the mental institution except that since everyone who's there is crazy, I guess that's the way it's supposed to be. The stuff with Boris and Marty didn't make any sense to me at all. And most of all, Harry Wolper, M.D., absolutely most of all, I thought it was a goddam lousy thing to do to have

Barbara die. That's what I think of the lousy goddam book, if you really want to know," and Meli pulled out a cigarette and started furiously pounding the end against the back of her hand to tamp down the tobacco.

There was a long and painful silence. Arnold panicked.

"Well," he beamed, "what do you say that before dinner we all play charades, huh? Wouldn't that be neat?"

"No, Arnold," Meli answered instantly, "it would not be neat. It would be *shmucky*."

"Oh." Arnold went over to the sofa and sat down disappointedly.

"You know," Marjorie said, looking directly at Meli, "I'd really appreciate it if people would stop picking on Arnold," she came to his defense. Then turning to face me, "Particularly you, Harry."

"Me?" I protested. "I haven't said a word."

"Well, I don't know what you do, Harry," Marjorie answered, "but every time that Arnold is around you, you give out a signal to everyone that says, 'My son. Fair game. Shoot at will.' Just because Arnold is so used to it by now that he doesn't notice is no reason to keep it up."

Arnold shifted uncomfortably over on the sofa.

"I can defend myself," he said.

"No you can't, Arnold," Marjorie informed him. "And that's your fault, too, Harry. You've worn him down. All he's trying to do is please you, you know."

"Yeah, Harry," Paul joined in with a large grin. "Leave the fucker alone, will you? Other than squandering all your money and appropriating your house out from under you, what's the fucker ever done to you?"

"Now just a minute," Arnold stood up. He started to walk over to Paul.

"Sorry, Arnold." Paul backed away. "Please. No violence. You win. No contest. You're right. It was blackmail, fair and square."

"Okay," I said. "What's going on? Why is everyone ready to kill?"

Meli walked over to me and took my arm.

"Harry Wolper," she said. "I'd like you to sit down here for a few minutes," and she led me over to the sofa just recently vacated by my indignant blackmailer.

The group assembled around me, Arnold and Paul each in one of the wingback chairs facing the sofa but sufficiently apart to allow for a brief cease-fire, Maureen and Marjorie on either side of me on the sofa, and Meli cross-legged on the floor directly in front of me, close enough for persistent eye-to-eye interrogation.

"Well, Harry Wolper," Meli began. "After we finished reading your great cosmic work, we had a little talk among all of us. And during this talk about which I have just told you, two questions kept coming up. You can probably save us a lot of goddam time by just telling us, right out. Is the book over or not? And what does a fight to the death mean? That's all I've got to say for right now, thank you."

I looked around me at the intent faces waiting for my reply.

"Yes, well," I tried to laugh it all off. "A fight to the death? Well, of course, that's just a figure of speech," I smiled, looking for a similar response from the sullen people facing me. They were not amused. "And as for the book's being over, well, it's not quite over, yet. Almost. Almost. But not quite over."

"Let me tell you something, *dear*," Meli said through her clenched teeth. "Your book is over. *Goodbye, Boris*. The end. I'll tell you why, too. It's over because I'm not going to spend the *next* year like Maureen spent the *last* year, visiting some lunatic an hour a day in the nuthouse. Can you understand what I'm telling you? The book is o-v-e-r. Over," and Meli finally lit the cigarette she'd been holding for the last five minutes and took a long drag to emphasize her disgust.

"I'm afraid I have to agree, Harry," Paul seconded. "You're getting in over your head. Forget the fucker. Let him be whatever the hell he wants to be, Jewish, Catholic, Mohammedan, Zoroastrian. It doesn't really matter, Harry. Believe me. I'm telling you, the fucker's not worth it. There *is* no Great Final Battle. It just goes on forever. Then before you know it, it's too late. He's got you by the balls. Your heart and mind will follow."

"I told you that you were going mad, Dad," Arnold provided his assessment, "but you wouldn't listen to me. I tried," he turned to Marjorie and shrugged his shoulders in resignation, "but what could I do?"

I decided to ignore Arnold, not an easy thing to do under the circumstances. By now I had heard enough. It was not hard to reconstruct what had occurred during my absence today.

"Well," I took a deep breath, "I take it that everyone has been treated to a blow-by-blow description of how Parnash vanquished Paul. It's not a particularly pleasant story, I admit."

I saw that Maureen's eyes were beginning to cloud over with tears. I pushed on.

"And I can certainly understand and appreciate your not wanting the same thing to happen to me. Well, it's not." I turned to Paul. "It's not, Paul. Your engagement with Parnash is nothing like mine with Boris. Ours is a very simple conflict. It's historical, Paul. There's nothing personal about it."

Paul tapped his fingers on his knees and listened. I wasn't at all sure that he was convinced. It didn't really matter. I looked down at Meli.

"It's not going to happen, Meli," I told her. "I am not obsessed with Boris. No one's going to put me away. The end is a foregone conclusion. I know it, and I think that even Boris knows it. The end is absolutely inevitable. The battle is always the same. And so is the victor. All that's needed now are the formalities of the final fight. But that's all it is, folks," I said, "a formality." I tried to look cheerful about the whole thing. Arnold smiled back. I had an idea.

"Look," I said, "I'll tell you what. Tomorrow's Christmas Eve. I'll wind it all up tomorrow before the kids get here. It'll be my last encounter with the marvelous Mr. Lafkin. I promise." I looked down at Meli again.

"I promise," I said, looking straight into her eyes.

"Well!" Arnold said loudly, with a sigh of relief. "That's good enough for me. If Dad *promises*, then I don't see what else we could all really want. A promise is a promise. Isn't that right?"

"Arnold," Meli pursed her lips. "I've got a charade for you."

"Great!" Arnold's face lit up. Paul and I gritted our teeth.

"Two words," Meli said slowly. "First word, Arnold," and Meli extended her fist in front of Arnold's face, palm up, and snapped out her middle finger.

Later this evening, after everyone had gone to bed, Paul and I sat in front of the last embers and swirled Cointreau down our gullets.

"I got to tell you something, now that everyone's turned in, Harry," Paul chuckled to himself. "We're sitting around this afternoon, just after we've finished reading the book, and Arnold has this great insight. 'Boris is God,' he says."

"He thinks Boris is God?" I asked incredulously.

"Right. God. The King of Kings. He's got it all figured out."

"Bullshit," I said. "I don't believe it," and I gargled some of the Cointreau.

"No, really," Paul said, still chuckling. "I swear it. That's what he says. 'Boris is God,'" and Paul put his arm around my shoulder and shook with laughter.

"Arnold's got style, Paul. You can't dispute that," I said.

"No, you can't, Harry." Paul took a deep breath to control his laughing. "So, anyway, Meli and I look at each other and decide to play along. We ask him how he figured that out. 'Well,' he says, 'it's like this. If you can talk to someone who you can't see and they can talk back, like Harry does with Boris, then it's God.'"

"I don't suppose anyone asked him how he accounts for the telephone," I asked.

"We didn't have time to, Harry, because, you see, Arnold has something in mind. The way he figures it, if *you* can talk to God, then you *might* ask Him something in Arnold's behalf. All his life, Arnold says, ever since he can remember, he's had one great question to ask the Lord Almighty. Would you like to guess?"

"The possibilities are endless, Paul."

"He want to know where there's *oil*," and Paul collapsed on the floor in hysterial convulsions of laughter.

"That's marvelous," I agreed, sharing Paul's laughter.

"Wait," Paul said, gasping for breath. "There's more. About a half hour later, Meli comes up to me. She's a little uncomfortable, but she asks anyway. She wants to know whether Arnold could be right. Is it possible that you *do* talk to God? She wants to know because she's got a question she's been saving up all her life, too, since she's been four. You want to try for one answer out of two, Harry?"

"I give."

"She wants to ask Him what the hell *myrrh* is," Paul rolled on the floor, grabbing his sides. When he finally recovered, we sat in silence in front of the coals for several minutes. I sensed what was going on in his mind.

"You've had one of those great cosmic questions, yourself, haven't you, Paul?" I smiled.

"You're damn right, I have, Harry. I need a new plot."

"Sorry, Paul," I sympathized with him. "I'm afraid He's used up the only one He's got. If there's one thing I've learned about this damn thing with Boris, it's that there just aren't any new plots around. Last night I read over what I've written during the year. I'll tell you something depressing, Paul. It's the Bible. That's all it is. From the first sentence on, three hundred and fifty-seven days of writing my damn heart out, and all I've got to show for it is a rehash of the Old Testament."

"That's awfully fucking presumptuous of you, don't you think, Harry?" Paul gulped down the last of his Cointreau. "There're a lot of us fuckers who believe the Bible's not all that bad the way it is."

"I didn't mean it to happen, Paul. Believe me. It just happened," and I reached for the poker and gave the last coals a push to stir up what heat remained. "When I started out, I intended to comment on philosophy, and that's all. Every month I fiddled around with one Giant Theme and one Giant Philosopher. Boris's life was nothing more than a reflection of the philosophy and the theme. Boris was a mirror. Otherwise, Boris's life was nonsense. The whole grand scheme was moderately diverting and passed the time while my biology was cooking. In any event, I figured it would give me a chance to reconsider my life, dabble in Big Issues, and distract me from the inevitability of my demise. I could wrap my existence up in one neat little package, reject 2000 years of philosophy, ridicule all themes, and see what emerged in the end."

"Then you gave up?" Paul understood my frustration on a firsthand basis.

"Nope," I told him. "I did what I planned to do. It just ended up being scripture, that's all. Wasn't a damn thing I could do about it."

"Well," Paul said sleepily, "maybe you can pull it out tomorrow."

"Today, Paul," I said, showing him my watch. "I meet Boris shortly."

Paul gave an enormous yawn and closed his eyes.

"You'll do it, Harry. All is not lost."

"Let me tell you a secret, Paul," I said. "Even if I don't pull it out today, all is not lost. You want to know why?"

"Sure," Paul said, his eyes still closed. "Tell me, Harry."

"This is what's going to happen, Paul. After I finish today, I'm shipping the whole thing back to Mrs. Mallory in Cambridge, not just the Boris part that you all read today, but all three hundred and fifty-seven entries, every day I wrote, every lousy word, the philosophy, and the science, and the themes, *and* Boris. Mrs. Mallory has instructions to hide the papers in my lab. When I die, Arnold will learn two things. First, that I've put him back in my will. Second, that he can't get a penny of mine until he publishes my work. You know what he's going to do?"

Paul opened his eyes and grinned like a Cheshire cat. "I sure as hell do. You're a fucking sadist, Harry. It's magnificent. Arnold's going to look through the mound of papers, and he's going to throw out everything but the Boris book, which, by itself, is just crap. For all his goddam life he's wanted you to give him the answers, and now he's going to throw the answers in the crapper and send the crap to the publisher," Paul laughed with glee.

"That, Paul, is exactly what Arnold is going to do," I smiled contentedly. "It's my final joke."

24th We've rented a home down the road for our guests. The cost was exorbitant. Lodging costs twice as much when it's called a "luxury condominium". In any event, after breakfast this morning, and before my great battle with Boris was scheduled to begin, we headed over to make sure that everything was in proper festive order for the holidays.

"This is crass materialism," Meli said as she stood in the condominium's giant cathedral-ceilinged living room and looked out at the nearby ski slopes and trails. "There isn't a goddam thing that's spiritual about looking through two hundred square feet of plate glass at wall-to-wall wilderness. I think we should have pitched a tent."

We tramped out through the snow to harvest our very own Christmas tree, all six of us. Agreeing on a tree of the proper size, height, and species was not easy.

Arnold finally took charge.

"Well," he announced, "I'm cutting down *this* tree. Anyone who wants another tree can cut it themselves. You know what I think?" Arnold asked no one in particular.

"What do you think, Arnold dear?" Meli asked sweetly, having received quite a lengthy and direct lecture from Marjorie this morning.

"I think," said Arnold, "that if Moses had a group like this to lead out of the universe, he wouldn't have gotten two feet. That's what I think."

"Arnold," Meli sang, "Moses did not lead the Jews out of the *universe*. He led them out of the *wilderness*."

"Right," Arnold agreed.

It was Paul who summed up the morning's haggling for me.

We had just finished lunch and a number of outbursts and hurt feelings over the appropriate placement of the Christmas tree, now that we had selected one and gotten it back into the house.

Paul stood back, chomping on his cigar, and tilted his head ten degrees to bring it into line with the angle of the tree.

"Not a bad tree, Harry," he said, putting his arm around my shoulder. "You don't happen to know what we're celebrating, do you?"

After the dishes had been washed, everyone sat around in front of the fire, waiting for the children to arrive with uncles and aunts. The unpacking was just about completed, and there was no pressing business.

"Well," I broke the silence, "I guess I'll go for my walk," I smiled feebly.

No one was fooled, least of all Meli.

"Why don't you stay *here* to finish the Boris thing?" she asked. "We won't bother you."

"I need to be outside," was all I could say. "It won't take long. I'll be back before the kids arrive."

Suddenly, for some reason I will never understand, everyone got up. I was walking toward the door to get on my overclothes, and, spontaneously, Meli and Arnold and Maureen and Marjorie and Paul all got up and came over to make certain that I was properly buttoned and snapped against whatever the outdoors had to offer.

Maureen and Marjorie both pecked me on the cheek, and Paul shook my hand firmly, between both of his hands.

"Good luck, Harry," he winked.

Arnold stood behind everyone, looking dumbstruck, and not knowing really what to do.

Meli came over and kissed me passionately. She stood on her tiptoes and tucked some strands of my hair back in my cap.

"Don't take a long time, *Harry*," she called me for the first time. "I need you," and her eyes clouded with tears.

"Oh, for chrissakes," I said, looking at everyone's long face, "I'm only going for a walk in the woods."

I stood for a minute at the door, wondering for just a second whether I should change my mind, studying Meli and trying unsuccessfully to remember what my thoughts were of her the first time she walked into my laboratory last summer in Cambridge. Then I waved goodbye, turned around, shut the door behind me, and started to crunch through the knee-deep snow.

Of course, Paul was right. There was no Great Final Battle.

I kicked through the new snow, waiting for Boris to arrive. I had my strategy well worked out. I knew exactly what I would say, how my battle plan would unfold. Devastating logic. Heart-wrenching emotional truths. Boris would surrender.

Some birds sprang off a branch above me, a multitude of the heavenly hosts, sending great showers of snow spraying to the ground.

"Boris," I called.

There was no answer.

How desperately I wanted this ending, the magnificent last struggle. Of course, I suppose I've always known that once Boris realized how impossible it was for me to give meaning to his life, that once he saw how little control I really had in his particular situation, he would drift off. It was always a possibility.

And while I knew that I had to let go of him, I was surprised by how difficult a thing this was to do when it came right down to it. There was, of course, no real alternative. Boris would move on. I would be as I am.

Still, I had always hoped that Boris would have sensed something about me by now, beyond the issues of meaning and responsibility, that he would have felt something about my life and our relationship that would have allowed us to persist. Together. For, to tell the truth, I have grown to adore the little fucker.

It grew dark. A single planet arched into the sky. At first a single throbbing dot, it grew in brilliance until its light washed out all other celestial bodies.

I started to trudge home through the snow. The wind sent clouds of snow swirling here and there around me.

"Boris," I called out again.

There was no answer.

I had not wanted it all to end like this. More than anything else, I had dreaded this gradual disappearance into his own life. No fond good-byes. No good wishes and warm memories. No great crescendo or last act finale. Just an evaporation into the winter air.

"Boris!" I called a last time before I opened the door and disappeared into my own existence, leaving my image behind on the other side of the great cosmic mirror.

But for the third time, there was no answer.

With great sadness, I opened the door, where I was greeted with cheers from my own three Wise Persons who had journeyed from afar, Meli, Paul, and, especially, dear witty Arnold. Then with an aching heart I shut the door behind me to keep the warmth of our crowded home from spilling uselessly out into the dark vacuum of the cold wind-swept Christmas eve night.

Fear not: for, behold, I bring you good tidings of great joy.
Boris has abandoned me.

25th And so it came to pass that, after years of torment, I finally rid myself of Harry Wolper. For the truth of it is, as I'm sure you've long ago come to realize, there never was a Harry Wolper. There never was a great Biologist and Author who propelled me through one unlikely adventure after another, but, rather, it was I who concocted the preposterous Dr. Wolper, and now, as I had long ago promised, I had no choice but to kill him off.

I can't tell you where Harry came from because I really don't know. I just know that once, a long time ago, I found myself calling out to someone, asking for assurance that everything was going to be all right, pleading for an explanation, and, finally, begging for my life to be "rewritten" by this fantastic character of mine.

I elaborated on Harry. The fantasy soon became much richer and more appealing than my own dreary life, and it was almost impossible to get rid of The Fucker.

At the same time that I was begging him to leave me alone, I was crying out for him to justify the unjustifiable, to give meaning to what was beyond meaning, and to accept responsibility for my inception, because I knew at least this much for certain: I had absolutely no input into my beginning. It was all Harry's fault.

So, when it comes right down to it, I can't account for Harry at all. He is, I guess, all I have been, more than I am, and, at least in that way, is no less real than I am or will be.

As near as I can tell, Harry is the mystery that lurks on the other side of the mirror.

For years now I've wanted to tell someone this story about Harry and what I finally had to experience before I could get rid of him, and let me tell you something. It's a marvelous goddam feeling to have it all over with.

Except there's one strange thing I really can't explain. I think if I had to choose between me being real or Harry, I'd prefer Harry. The fantasy is just so much more appealing than the reality. Harry is fun. Me? I'm just life, and that's all. Who wants it, right?

As far as I'm concerned, at the end of all the philosophy and theology and intellectual arguments about the Creator, Harry is just one hell of a marvel ous emotional trip, battles and all. It's like the man says, "Existence is entirely an emotional problem. Believe me."

Still, when the breeze comes in the window beside me and carries winter with it, or a spring not completely buried under the snow, I begin to wonder whether Harry has made a difference. All in all, he has, I think. The way I see it, without Harry, my story is just not very interesting at all.

31st Tonight is New Year's Eve. Tomorrow is 1970.

I decided not to go to Beirut, by the way. At least for now. In the meantime, I've taken a job at a state hospital as a psychologist-in-training. It's not great, but it's okay. I'll survive.

I'm going with a woman now named Vita. The relationship doesn't have the intensity of Mara, or the agony of Marty, or, for that matter, the ecstasy and joy of Barbara. There aren't even the brief thrills of other fleeting relationships I've had. But it's good. Pleasurable. Comfortable. I think I'm entering a new phase. I have a feeling that this phase is going to last a long time. I'm not sure what to think about it. I'll just have to see.

As for Harry, well, to be frank about it, sometimes I still miss him. It's hard not to. And then other times I'm awfully damn glad he's not around any more. Why I ever needed him in the first place is still a mystery. The more I think about it, the more it seems to me that I was scared, or lonely, or something. In any event, I've accepted the inevitable.

Harry is dead.

"Nice try, Boris."

Shut up, Harry.